THE MISSISS[illegible]ER

Natur[illegible]
and Travel Sites along the
"Mighty Mississip"

Tom Weil

HIPPOCRENE BOOKS, INC.
New York

For information, address:
Hippocrene Books, Inc.
171 Madison Ave.
New York, NY 10016

ISBN 0-7818-0030-7

Printed in the United States of America.

CONTENTS

In memory of my grandfather, Maurice Weil, who a century ago left the Rhine River Valley to settle in the Mississippi River, and To Mississippi River travelers past, present and future

"...as if the place for these things were assured, the earth for all time earth, the sea level fixed for all time."

Max Frisch, *Man in the Holocene*

A WELCOME TO THE READER

At the Boston Museum of Fine Arts there hangs a Tahitian painting by Paul Gauguin with the haunting title: "Where did we come from? Where are we going? What are we?" Anyone who lives along the Mississippi for any length of time sooner or later starts to pose the same sort of questions about the river: Where does it come from, where do its waters go, what happened along the great waterway in bygone times? Born by the Mississippi and a lifelong resident along the waterway, in time I, too, became curious about the river and for years wondered about its place in the country's history and geography. Any number of books tell the Mississippi's story—its discovery, settlement, development—but there existed no up-to-date comprehensive guide for travelers along the river who wanted to explore the waterway for themselves. This volume, intended to fill that omission, is meant to serve as a practical, functional work describing the river's many remarkably varied sights on its long journey through the continent, and what occurred along its shores in the past.

The book presents a series of itineraries, arranged by state, descending the river from Minnesota to Louisiana. This seems to me the clearest and most logical way to arrange the material, although I realize that many people will "cluster" their trip and visit both sides of the river in a limited area. Those travelers who criss-cross the waterway can find the necessary information by consulting the index or simply by locating the material for the adjoining state at its logical geographical place. A look at the map will thus in effect indicate the place any particular location occupies in the text, which is arranged strictly by geography. As for the designations "Upper," "Middle" and "Lower Mississippi," these represent an arbitrary but hopefully helpful organizational device to clarify in a general way the Mississippi's geography, so directing readers and travelers to the chapters most appropriate for them.

Although the suggested itineraries for the most part follow the River Road, that 3,700 mile long highway network which borders both banks of the Mississippi from the Minnesota north woods to the Gulf of Mexico, the book does not limit itself to that route, for this is a guide not to the Road but to the river. I have therefore not slavishly restricted the narrative to the River Road, for also included are some especially worthy or unusual attractions near the Mississippi—perhaps not directly river-related but certainly part of the Mississippi Valley's culture—which travelers along the waterway would no doubt deem worth seeing. At a few points I have also suggested an alternative route more interesting than the one which follows the River Road or the highway nearest the Mississippi. In considering whether or not to include places off the river itself the question arose as to how far afield the itinerary should wander. It seemed to me logical that the greater the attraction's merit, the farther the distance allowable, but these ancillary sights receive but a brief mention, sufficient only to call a traveler's attention to them, and in no case do they lie any great distance from the Mississippi.

In order to avoid repeating certain background material of a general interest—such as information on the system of locks and dams, the levees, log rafts, the Corps of Engineers and other such broad subjects—these are covered in some depth only at the most appropriate point in the text, which can be found by consulting the index. Although the book serves as a guide to various separate areas along the long waterway, the text can also be read by armchair travelers in an integral way, for the narrative as a whole includes the story and history of the entire Mississippi. Because the book is arranged geographically, the historical dimension remains fragmented, for many events or developments initiated in one part of the river unfolded elsewhere along the waterway. Events thus do not appear as they happened but, rather, where they happened. Taken in its entirety, however, the book does present a fairly complete and integrated picture of the Mississippi both as it is and as it was.

Although the Mississippi occasionally flows east or west, and even due north, the river generally travels from north to south. As a matter of convenience I have in virtually all cases referred to the Mississippi's path as heading south, even where the waterway might in fact flow in another direction. Frequent references in the text to sights listed on the National Register of Historic Places (referred to in the book as the National Register) arises because Register listing, although not infallible, seems to me to indicate an attraction's probable merit. Criteria for Register designation include "significance in American history, architecture, archeology, engineering, and culture" of places with historic or artistic value or connected with prominent figures.

Anyone writing about the Mississippi River faces what I call "the Mark Twain problem." So eloquent, witty and delightful are Twain's writings on his beloved waterway that it is all too tempting for a latter day author to let the master's words describe any number of river-related subjects rather than including one's own impressions and comments. In *Mark Twain's Mississippi,* T.H. Watkins maintains that "any book on the Mississippi that does not rely heavily upon the work of Twain is only half a book." At the risk of producing only an "ok" rather than a complete "book," I have by design refrained from all but a very few brief quotations from Twain. His words and works on the Mississippi speak for themselves and are best read and enjoyed in their own inimitable context, without being abridged and inserted into another narrative which would inevitably suffer from comparison with Twain's eloquence.

As with my previous Hippocrene USA travel guides—*America's Heartland,* on the Middle West, and *America's South,* on the eleven Southern states—this book includes, along with the more obvious and renowned sights, many lesser known but no less interesting back road, off-the-beaten-track-type attractions. Although I have tried to direct the inquisitive and interested traveler to virtually all the places along the Mississippi of cultural, historic, and scenic interest, space limitations prevented inclusion of every attraction at each such site, so inquiries made on the spot will often yield information on additional local sights worth seeing.

For the preparation of this book I traveled the entire length of the Mississippi along both sides, from the source at Lake Itasca to Pilottown, the last inhabited settlement, near the river's mouth. Along the way I asked hundreds of river-related questions to a wide range of people who live or work along the waterway. Virtually every person I talked to responded with gracious patience. To those who gave me information and shared with me their knowledge of the river which forms part of their lives, as it does mine, I extend my sincere appreciation.

Over time, the river slowly seeps into your very being. T.S. Eliot, who grew up in St. Louis by the "strong brown god," as he called the Mississippi, once wrote: "There is something in having passed one's childhood beside the big river...[which has] made a deeper impression on me than any other part of the world." For one who has lived along the waterway for many years, travelling the Mississippi in its entirety affords a remarkable experience. This is particularly the case for a traveler who undertakes the journey intending to write about the waterway, for that project requires the observer to become intimately familiar with the river and to develop an attitude toward it.

A Welcome to the Reader

In *Where Goes the River,* Albert S. Tousley suggested that "to write about it without a feeling of possession is impossible. The river takes for its own all who associate with it; yet those same persons feel a sole ownership in the river." And so, after all the years of living along the Mississippi, and the many months of travel, reading and research, I view the waterway as a kind of companion with whom I have shared many pleasant experiences. But, of course, there are many Mississippis and no one can ever possess or even grasp all the dimensions of that phenomenon of nature which follows its own course through the land and the years, for the great river belongs only to the earth and to the long sweep of time.

THE MISSISSIPPI

All rivers flow through time as well as place. The Mississippi, as much as any river and more than most, lies embedded not only in the landscape but also in a timescape filled with events which unfolded along the waterway over the long years. "It has been the fortune of few rivers or other physical features of the globe to appear as continuously in the annals of discovery and diplomacy" as the Mississippi, wrote Frederic Austin Ogg in *The Opening of the Mississippi*. Time and place intersect on the great river, for a sense of the past imbues almost every spot along the Mississippi, while its course through the years has left many history-haunted sites. The waterway evokes ghostly images of Indians, explorers, fur trappers and traders, adventurers, missionaries, pioneers, settlers, keelboat and flatboat roustabouts, steamboat pilots, de Soto and La Salle, Lewis and Clark, Lincoln, Grant, Black Hawk, Twain and any number of other characters whose former presence lingers all up and down the river at places with worldly names—St. Paul, St. Louis, Sainte Genevieve, St. Joseph, St. Francisville, New Madrid and New Orleans, La Crosse, Genoa, Prairie du Chien, Guttenberg, Hannibal, Carthage, Cairo, Memphis, Baton Rouge, Venice—which lend the Mississippi a cosmopolitan flavor.

This rich mix typifies the waterway, for—in the center of the continent—"The Mississippi River is the great cosmopolitan which unites all people, which gives a definite purpose to their activity, and determines their abode, and which enables the life of every one, the inhabitants themselves and their products, to circulate from one end to the other of this great central valley," observed in the 1850s Swedish writer Fredrika Bremer in her *America of the*

Fifties. The river links far-flung regions with little or nothing in common, except their position along the banks of the Mississippi. The lake-checkered Minnesota north woods, plantation houses which grace Louisiana's landscapes, Iowa cornfields and the cotton fields of Mississippi, the Midwest's Twain and twang and the South's Faulkner and drawl all occupy positions in time and place by the watery ribbon which flows through disparate areas and eras, tying them together temporally and geographically. The Mississippi and the River Road which flanks it travel to a wide range of Americana—farms and factories, small towns, ancient Indian villages and modern metropolitan areas—and also to pockets of the past where hamlets lost in time seem unchanged and unchangeable.

The Mississippi presents a paradox of change and continuity. Never ceasing to change, the restless river from one day to the next revises itself, here crumbling a bank, there adding a bar, now swelling its currents and then once again resuming its slow rhythmic flow through the heart of the continent. So great have the changes in the Mississippi's channel been over just three centuries that much of the 1,300 miles floated in 1682 by La Salle, the first European to travel down the river to its mouth, now lie on dry land. Ceaseless change, over thousands of years, gradually forged the Mississippi Valley. The Upper Mississippi, bordered by bluffs and controlled by locks and dams, resulted as the river carved its way through the landscape, etching the valley. The Lower Mississippi, flanked by lowlands and controlled by levees, originated when the sea washed over the countryside. "Again and again the sea flowed back over part of its former floor," relates *The Culture of the Middle West*. "Thus, while the northern part of the basin was sculptured continually into greater relief, the southern part was smoothed and protected by successive veneerings of sediment. So the cotton belt was the gift of the sea, and the Middle West was the work of the river."

However, with all the changes over the centuries the Mississippi, once formed, also preserved a kind of invariable continuity. Men lived and died, generations came and went, but the river remained. To the early day Indians the Mississippi seemed a mystery, a force of nature which appeared from a far off land and disappeared to an equally remote corner of the earth. "No one tribe knew both its fountain and its delta, its sources and its mouth," wrote John Finley in *The French in the Heart of America.* "To those midway of the valley it came out of the mystery of the Land of Frosts and passed silently on or, in places, complainingly on, to the mystery of the Land of the Sun."

For centuries the river—ever-changing but eternal—wound its way through the years and the countryside. Over the years only scattered Indian tribes dwelled along the banks of the waterway, remote and lost in the little-touched wilderness. So remained for ages the pristine stream, that "great river, called the Missisipi, running due South to the sea, through a fine country unpossessed by any white nation," as Thomas Jefferson, with his eccentric spelling, described the waterway in his essay "The Limits and Bounds of Louisiana." The French, then the English and the Spanish, tried to possess the Mississippi Valley, which eluded their grasp. But, finally, citizens of the new United States managed to populate the old waterway, which soon saw service as a highway when steamers began to ply the river. As the *New Orleans*, the very first steamboat to travel the stream, arrived at Natchez in 1811 a black man on the wharf, watching the strange new vessel dock, threw his hat in the air and gloated, "Old Mississippi done got her master now."

Steamboats, then trains, changed the Mississippi, but no one could ever master it. Locks and dams, levees and flood walls tame the river, when it allows itself to be tamed. The Mississippi, however, possesses a mind—and perhaps even a soul—of its own. It sometimes seems an animate force, alive and willful, and it always presents a remarkably evocative and moving panorama—

of place, of time—for "the noblest river in the world" remains invariably "invested with an interest and grandeur, which will cause, that a faithful account of it can never become trite, or tedious," asserted Timothy Flint, an early nineteenth century Mississippi River Valley traveler.

And so flows on in all its infinite variety and rich past the Mississippi, sun-dappled or cloud-shadowed, storm-swept or heat-drenched, a "dark and inexorable river,...rolling like a destiny, through its realms of solitude and shade," wrote historian Francis Parkman. There is no telling what mood the changing, changeless river will reveal at any particular point in time or place—perhaps turbulent and angry in the great spring floods, or leaden and sullen under grey winter skies, mellow and misty on a crisp autumn eve, or serene and soft in the dusk of a long summer's day. Whatever its passing manner, the magnificent and mighty Mississippi continues its long meandering journey over the land and through the years, for the eternal river flows on—its rolling, roiling waters swirling down to the sea—as it has since time began and as it shall forever.

I.

THE UPPER MISSISSIPPI

1. Minnesota

2. Wisconsin

3. Iowa

1. MINNESOTA

It begins—as many great things begin—in a small way. Modest and unassuming, the Mississippi River trickles into existence as a mere rivulet in a remote corner of north-central Minnesota. "The beginnings of a river are insignificant," wrote Pliny, "and its infancy is frivolous; it plays among the flowers of a meadow, it waters a garden, or turns a little mill." And thus does the eventually mighty Mississippi spring to life there in the north woods—a straggly little creek which in no way suggests the river's downstream grandeur, its legendary personality, or its rich history.

There is something poignant about the famous waterway's humble origins. Anyone who has encountered the mighty Mississippi in its more mature phases, farther south, will be surprised to see how modestly the great river begins. And anyone familiar with its lore and legends, its fabled past and impressive presence will find the unpretentious creek there at the headwaters no different than a thousand other woodland streams which bubble into existence only to flow their way into obscurity. Far from the Mississippi's source at Lake Itasca, in mood as well as miles and years, are the river's colorful characters, its history and its culture: long-gone flat boats and keel boats, and latter-day mile-long freight barges; roustabouts and river pirates; Mark Twain, Lincoln, Marquette and Joliet, Lewis and Clark; the saintly settlements—St. Cloud, St. Paul, St. Louis, Ste. Genevieve, St. Francisville—and the devilishly devastating flood waters; plants in the North, plantations in the South; Civil War memories and Indian mounds, Indian summers and faded sounds, like the swish of a paddlewheel churning through the river, the slow call "m-a-r-k t-w-a-i-n," and the cry of a steamer's whistle, a sound which haunts the river still and ever will. The Mississippi is a river of mythic proportions—and disproportions. So much of America—its past and present, legends and life—survives in the river's folklore and resides along its long shores which begin in that far corner of Minnesota at Lake Itasca. "There are a hundred towns and cities that the Father of Waters has nourished," noted Walter Havinghurst in *Upper Mississippi: A Wilderness Saga*, "and to name any half dozen of them over—Minneapolis, La Crosse, Keokuk, Galena, Rock Island, Hannibal—is a certain American music and evokes in unexpected ways the American story."

Some half a million people a year make their way to the rather remote Itasca area to see where the famous river originates. Not far from the north entrance to Itasca State Park lies the headwaters enclave, where a visitor center contains displays on the discovery of the source, old photos and a relief map of the area which shows the waterway as it winds its way sixty miles north to Lake Bemidji, "the wildest, untouched and unpolluted segment of the Mississippi River," claims the notice. A nearby path takes you across a short wood bridge which spans the infant Mississippi, here the most tranquil and docile little creek imaginable. It's pleasant to pause a time on the mini-bridge there where you first encounter the Mississippi. Wrinkles and ripples perhaps pattern the water as a breeze skims over the brook's surface. The path leads on to a clearing in the woods at the northern edge of Lake Itasca. Before you stretches a low line of rocks across the new-born river, which at this spot trickles gently, tentatively from the lake, then slowly flows off to the right and soon disappears to the left around a bend, the first of many turnings and twistings the wandering waterway will contort itself into. So begins the great Mississippi.

Like much connected with the Mississippi, its point of origin evokes a quaint combination of fact and myth. Ever since Henry Schoolcraft, a mineralogist and adventurer, came upon the lake on the morning of July 13,1832 it has been generally accepted that Itasca—or Elk Lake, as it was then called—merits the distinction of being the Mississippi's source. Any number of other waters in the soggy maze of ponds, lakes, rivers and wetlands in the area also contribute to the river's first flow, so the Mississippi's true source is really the entire watershed of the nearby marshland. Lakes such as Morrison, Little Elk, Whipple and De Soto—ten feet higher than Itasca—feed into the main body of water. The almost too neatly done and civilized source site confected there by the lake does not preserve what Schoolcraft saw but was in the 1930s recast and reconstructed for tourism purposes. The river, indeed, starts to flow in its channel at that point, but where the very first waters which bubble forth to form the Mississippi actually materialize remains a mystery. And perhaps this is as it should be, for a force of nature such as the Mississippi should—like the seasons, the stars, and life itself—keep some secrets. In his introduction to *Huckleberry Finn,* Mississippi River native T.S. Eliot, who grew up in St. Louis, noted: "The River itself has no beginning or end. In its beginning, it is not yet the River. What we call the headwaters is only a selection from among the innumerable sources which flow together to compose it." Huck himself described how it was out on the river when "We had the sky, up there, all speckled with stars, and we used to lay on our backs and look up at them, and discuss about whether they was made, or only just happened." In a similar way, those who come to know the age-old mythic Mississippi—set in "time beginningless and endless," in Walt Whitman's phrase—wonder whether the river was made or, somehow, just happened.

At that selected point by Lake Itasca—the designated beginning of the Mississippi—the visitor experiences a certain ineffable feeling, a kind of awe that here originates one of the nation's most prominent geographical, cultural and historical features. By the rivulet that trickles out of Lake Itasca stands a much-photographed notice written on a log post stating: "Here 1475 ft. above the ocean the mighty Mississippi begins to flow on its winding way 2552 miles to the Gulf of Mexico." Steps away begins the row of rocks which span the river. Over the rocks and through the water, visitors walk or wade, here, for once, enjoying the sensation of being able to cross the fabled waterway and to enter into a kind of communion with it. It is gratifying to be able to engage the river, elsewhere so formidable and so unapproachable by boatless admirers. "If one has seen the Mississippi River, and in some way been affected by it," state Stephen Feldman and Van Gordon Sauter in *Fabled Land, Timeless River: Life Along the Mississippi*, "then one should have a knowledge of its origin; and there is something deeply satisfying about seeing the rivulet that sets in motion the great river that flows on for 2500 miles."

Upon leaving the parking lot near the source you'll see to the right the first of hundreds of Great River Road markers—the green and white steamboat pilot's wheel, an emblem adopted in 1958 to indicate the 3700 mile route which passes through ten states and 125 counties and which gives access to 1583 historic sites, 217 wildlife areas, 90 registered national landmarks, 72 state parks, 36 locks and dams, and 288 river towns. The concept for the Great River Road began in 1936 when Missouri Governor Lloyd Stark requested a recreational survey of the state. Two years later A.P. Greensfelder, a St. Louis construction executive, spearheaded the foundation of the Mississippi River Parkway Planning Commission, which included representatives from all the states bordering the river. World War II delayed the project, but between 1973 and 1978 Congress authorized $314 million for the development of the Great River Road, which extends from that first sign down to the southern tip of Louisiana (in 1956 Canadian routes in Ontario and Manitoba were added to the network). A total of $740 million in federal, state, provincial and local funds have been spent on the Road, whose last stretch was officially designated in 1985. By 1990 the Road included 2068 miles of federal routes along with 1629 miles of supplementary state highways, with Minnesota boasting the most extensive network—770 miles—followed by Illinois (629), Missouri (425), Louisiana (408), Mississippi (352), Iowa (319), Arkansas (309), Wisconsin (246), Tennessee (187) and Kentucky (51). Thus do the Great River Road and the waterway which it follows bring together disparate and distant regions of the nation located in the continent's vast central section, much as Stephen A. Douglas—Lincoln's opponent—proclaimed in an 1850 speech to the U.S. Senate when he spoke of "a power in this nation greater than the North or the South—...the great West—the Valley of the Mississippi, one and indivisible from the gulf to the great lakes." (For information on the Road and the Great River Road Association: Suite 1513, Pioneer Building, 336 Robert Street, St. Paul, MN 55101; 612-224-9903).

After you exit from the parking lot by the headwaters, a left turn takes you to the start of the Wilderness Drive auto tour, a ten mile (mostly) one-way route that circles around Lake Itasca while passing through areas of historic, scenic, and natural history interest. Soon after starting the tour you'll pass on the right Bert's Cabin, a resort established more than half a century ago by Bert Pfeiffer, a relative of one of Itasca State Park's first settlers, Johanna Wegmann, who with her husband Theodore for many years operated a general store housed in a log building, a replica of which stands at the northeast tip of the lake. Farther on lies rustic Squaw Lake Cabin, one of the park's seven housekeeping cabins, a facility so popular that places there are allocated by a drawing held in the spring. The Drive continues on past trails, a Forestry Demonstration Area, by lakes and on to two champion-sized Minnesota trees—the state's largest white pine (112 feet tall, 55 feet in diameter) and, a bit farther on, the tallest red pine (120 by 37 feet). The red pine was formerly more commonly known as the Norway pine, so called as lumberjacks who emigrated from that country thought it resembled trees back home; some say, tongue in cheek, that the name change—from Norway to red—originated with jealous Swedes. Just down the way, at Nicollet Creek—named for scientist Joseph Nicollet, who four years after Henry Schoolcraft discovered the Mississippi's source confirmed the find—archeologists excavated bones and artifacts of a campsite used some 8000 years ago when Indians gathered in the autumn for their annual bison hunt. For those with time to linger, Nicollet and De Soto Trails, two of the park's twenty-four marked walking itineraries, take you through tree-thick areas to isolated lakes deep in the woods. A mile or so from Nicollet Creek the Wilderness Drive ends and you soon reach Douglas Lodge.

Constructed in 1905 as Itasca Park's first structure for visitors, Douglas Lodge—an attractive log building perched above the lake's east arm—was patterned after places of accommodation, such as Yellowstone's Old Faithful Inn, built around the turn of the century in national parks. Nestled there among the trees with a view down onto the lake, Douglas Lodge provides an especially pleasant place to enjoy the area's north woods ambiance (for reservations: 800-765-2267; the Lodge remains open from Memorial Day weekend to the first weekend in October). The *Chester Charles*, a fifty passenger boat moored behind the Lodge, offers tours on Lake Itasca (Tu-F 2, Sat and Sun 1 and 3; for reservations: 218-266-3654), while near the landing begins Dr. Roberts Trail, a one mile walk which passes by another rustic log building, the Old Timer's Cabin, built in 1934 out of huge white pines so thick that only four logs suffice to form each of the walls.

More obscure but rather more affecting in the Douglas Lodge area is the off-the-beaten track marker which commemorates Schoolcraft's discovery of the Mississippi's headwaters. A metal plaque affixed to a boulder, reached by a path from the front door of the lodge across two foot bridges and on to a spot between cabins number six and seven, reads: "Itasca Lake Source of the Mississippi River discovered by Henry P. Schoolcraft from the summit of this hill July 13, 1832." Beyond and below, through the trees and the leaves, sparkle slivers of the lake which gives rise to the river. Schoolcraft first visited the area as a member of an 1820 expedition led by Lewis Cass, governor of Michigan, commissioned by the Secretary of War to investigate the sources of the Mississippi. This enterprise traveled up the river to within three days' journey of the headwaters, then abandoned the search. Twelve years later Schoolcraft, a mineralogist and Indian agent, returned to the area and engaged the services of Ozawindib ("Yellow Head"), an Ojibwe chief, who led the party to the spot now indicated by the marker. Schoolcraft recorded the final phases of the find in his journal:

> Every step we made in treading these sandy elevations, seemed to increase the ardor with which we were carried forward. The desire of reaching the actual source of a stream so celebrated as the Mississippi—a stream which LaSalle had reached the mouth of, a century and a half (lacking a year) before, was perhaps predominant; and we followed our guide down the sides of the last elevation, with the expectation of momentarily reaching the goal of our journey. What had been long sought, at last appeared suddenly. On turning out of a thicket, into a small weedy opening, the cheering sight of a transparent body of water

> burst upon our view. It was Itasca Lake—the source of the Mississippi.

Thus did the beginning point of the Mississippi become the river's last major feature to be discovered.

In his poem "On Reaching the Source of the Mississippi River in 1832" Schoolcraft rhapsodized:

> Ha! truant of western waters who hast
> So long concealed thy very sources—flitting shy,
> Now here, now there—through spreading mazes vast
> Thou art, at length, discovered to the eye

He concluded: "I quaff the limpid cup at the Mississippi's spring." Well might Schoolcraft drink to his discovery—named by him "Itasca" from the adjoining syllables of verITAS CAput, Latin for "truth" and "head"—for adventurers, explorers and European empire builders had for years wondered about the location of the Mississippi's headwaters, whose whereabouts remained a mystery long after other sections of the river had become well known. Schoolcraft's discovery occurred at a relatively late date in the Mississippi's history, for by the time of his find navigational guide books to much of the river had appeared and the steamboat era had already gathered steam downstream.

After early European explorers failed to find the river's beginnings the first official attempt to pinpoint the headwaters originated in August 1805 when Thomas Jefferson ordered Lieutenant Zebulon Pike to "proceed up the Mississippi with all possible diligence" and "to ascend the main branch to its source." Accompanied by twenty soldiers, Pike left St. Louis on August 9, 1805 and headed up the waterway on his 5000 mile, nine month journey in a 70-foot-long keelboat. While wintering on the west bank of the river near present-day Little Falls, Minnesota, he and a small contingent continued north, reaching a fur post at Leech

Lake (eighty miles and five lakes east of Itasca) which Pike averred was "the main source of the Mississippi." This designation, of course, proved to be incorrect, and only later did Pike gain lasting fame for his exploratory prowess when the Colorado peak he discovered in late 1806 took his name.

In 1823 Giocomo Costantino Beltrami, an Italian adventurer, traveled from the Old World to the heart of the New where he attempted to locate the Mississippi's source. Suspecting Beltrami of scheming to establish a separate Italian kingdom, authorities forced him into exile in 1821, and after wandering through Europe he set sail for America, then took a steamboat down the Ohio River and arrived at the confluence with the Mississippi in April 1823. Although intending to continue on to New Orleans, Beltrami impulsively changed his plans and decided to travel north, and at St. Louis he boarded the *Virginia*, the very first steamboat to reach Fort St. Anthony (later Fort Snelling), located where the Minnesota and Mississippi Rivers meet, in present-day Minneapolis. The Italian attached himself to an official expedition led by Major Stephen Long, assigned to map the border between the United States and Canada. The boisterous Beltrami and the militarily precise Long, a West Point graduate, disliked one another from the day the expedition set forth on July 7, so the Italian hired two Chippewa Indians and an interpreter and struck out on his own in search of the river's source. The intrepid Italian was no doubt the most colorful character, literally and figuratively, ever to undertake the search for the source: during his trip Beltrami set up in his canoe a large red silk umbrella to shelter his luggage from the rain. The Chippewa soon abandoned the enterprise but Beltrami pressed on in his quest, paddling with his red umbrella unfurled on to Red Lake, some fifty miles north of Itasca. The explorer made his way to a small lake to the south he named Julia, after a former paramour, and here, by hills which he designated "the highest land of North America," so Beltrami decided, rose the "famous Mississippi, whose course is said to be twelve hundred leagues, and which bears navies on its bosom, and steam-boats superior in size to frigates," he wrote excitedly in his account of the supposed discovery. After pausing briefly to mediate a dispute between two Chippewa warriors named Wide Mouth and Cloudy Weather, Beltrami returned to Fort St. Anthony, then left on October 3 for St. Louis. Although Beltrami wrote a book about his supposed discovery of the headwaters, his claim inspired no acclaim. But his name survives in the area in the designation Beltrami County, established by the Minnesota legislature in 1866, eleven years after the unappreciated adventurer died, to commemorate the Italian's odd odyssey to locate the Mississippi's source. On his house in far off Filottrano in northern Italy appears a stone monument bearing a bust, a globe and the inscription: "Costantino Beltrami of Bergamo, important jurist, officially honored by Napoleon I, from long journeys to foreign lands he returned having made the glorious discovery of the source of the Mississippi." But only in Filottrano, half a world away from the north woods where the Mississippi begins, is Beltrami considered the man who discovered the river's headwaters.

Following Schoolcraft's successful expedition to the source in 1832, nine years after Beltrami's attempt, another displaced European, Joseph N. Nicollet, visited the area in 1836, confirming by scientific observation that, in fact, the Mississippi indeed originated at Lake Itasca. Like Beltrami, Nicollet was forced to leave his homeland in his forties, but the Frenchman departed for economic rather than political reasons. It seems that Nicollet attempted to apply his new theory of mathematical probability to predict the stock market, an exercise which resulted in ruinous losses when the Paris Bourse crashed after the Revolution of 1830. In 1832 Nicollet left for America where he soon settled on a project for his new life in the New World— a study of the Mississippi River system. After travels through the south, Nicollet arrived at Fort Snelling (Minneapolis) in July 1836. Lawrence Taliaferro, the Indian agent at the fort, soon questioned the new arrival, asking Nicollet if "he could go to the source of the Mississippi," to which the Frenchman replied, "Yes, sir." After Nicollet responded similarly to every question, Taliaferro joked, "Suppose I say can you go to hell, you say yes." At this point the official's wife intervened to avow, "None of us will send you that route if we can prevent it," to which Nicollet countered, "Well, then, madam, change my route to the upper Mississippi." The Frenchman soon departed for his desired destination, spending three days at Itasca where he observed "the very first trickles that will form the Mississippi." Not far from the source he found that "this infant stream already shows signs of the capricious and encroaching propensities that characterize its power and course along its various stages of growth all the way down to the Gulf of Mexico." Having confirmed Schoolcraft's finding, the Frenchman left Itasca on August 30. At Otter Tail Point near Leech Lake, Chief Flat Mouth invited the white man for tea, during which Nicollet showed the Indian a snuff box bearing a full length portrait of Napoleon. Flat Mouth carefully examined the image and closely questioned Nicollet about the personage pictured, then observed, "Well, it is strange, on whatever side I turn it, the figure looks at me, and seems to say, 'thou art my brother warrior.'" Unlike Indians like Chief Flat Mouth, by then the "warrior" in far off France exerted no territorial claims over the Mississippi country, for in 1803 Napoleon had sold "Louisiana," defined as the drainage basin of the Mississippi, to the United States. On September 28 Nicollet returned to Fort Snelling, where he announced that his observations indicated that, as Schoolcraft had claimed, the Mississippi did begin at Lake Itasca.

Nicollet's conclusion settled the matter for very nearly everyone but a character named Captain Willard Glazier, who half a century later mounted an expedition which he asserted discovered a secret stream south of Itasca that "invalidated the claim of Schoolcraft." Searching the area in 1881 for "feeders" which led into the lake, Glazier finally found a creek he stated was "the Infant Mississippi." Glazier's supposed discovery created a storm of controversy, but the matter was settled when the Minnesota Historical Society commissioned Jacob V. Brower to survey the Itasca basin. After studying the area in 1888 and 1889 Brower determined definitively that Glazier's find in no way contradicted Schoolcraft's discovery, so only as recently as a century ago was the question of the Mississippi's source finally settled.

Jacob Brower's role at Itasca greatly transcended the study he undertook for the Minnesota Historical Society, a project which marked only the beginning of his efforts at the lake. Born in Michigan in 1844, Brower in his early days worked as a school teacher, fought in the cavalry against the Sioux, sailed as a seaman with the Navy, practiced law and served in the Minnesota state legislature. He later become interested in archeology, and after extensive domestic travels, published an eight volume series entitled *Memoirs of Exploration in the Basin of the Mississippi.* After the Itasca assignment, Brower drafted and singlehandedly pushed through the state legislature a bill to create a park at the headwaters, after which the governor appointed him the facility's first commissioner. Since the state failed to appropriate funds to acquire land for the park, Brower proceeded at his own expense to purchase the property which in 1891 became Minnesota's first and one of the nation's earliest state parks. Now, a century later, the nearly 33,000 acre (fifty square miles) park includes one hundred lakes and ponds, stands of two century old pine trees, more than one hundred species of birds, sixty kinds of mammals and, of course, the beginnings of the Mississippi, which from here flows on to collect the water of 100 thousands of tributaries with 15,000 miles of navigable waters, draining thirty-one states covering one and a quarter million square miles (some forty per cent of the nation's area) and 13,000 square miles of Canada, as the great river winds its course from Lake Itasca, where it modestly eases its way into existence, down to the distant Gulf of Mexico, where it finally disappears, merging with the sea.

From Itasca State Park the river, beginning its long journey, heads northeast for sixty miles, an unusual direction for the generally southwardly flowing waterway. The river's route makes its way between two nearby watershed systems which, had the lay of the land been slightly altered, might have drawn the Mississippi into different patterns of flow. Not far from the headwaters lie lakes which drain into tributaries of the Red River, whose waters pass through Lake Winnipeg and continue on to the Hudson Bay and the Arctic, while to the northeast flow streams which empty into Lake Superior, whose waters link with the St. Lawrence and eventually the Atlantic. And, finally, fewer than twenty miles west of the Mississippi source lies a rise—some two hundred and fifty feet higher than the headwaters—which comprises part of the Continental Divide, beyond which rivers flow away from the central section of the country. Escaping by relatively few miles these various possible diversions, the Mississippi remains a river of the middle part of the continent, where it fulfilled its destiny as a waterway central to the nation's development.

The Great River Road leaves the north side of Itasca Park via Highway 2, which crosses the scrawny young Mississippi a few times as the route heads north. The stream you encounter on this stretch presents an untypical appearance, for only briefly, here at the beginning, does the waterway remain so puny and, seemingly, vulnerable. At Bemidji, less than thirty miles ahead, the Mississippi flows at a rate of one hundred cubic feet a second; at Grand Rapids, a thousand cubic feet; and upon entering the Twin Cities, more than seven thousand cubic feet; then ten thousand cubic feet below the Minnesota River, fifteen thousand below the St. Croix River, and double that at the Iowa border, but the thirty thousand cubic foot flow there represents only one and a half per cent of the Mississippi's volume at the Gulf of Mexico. It is therefore worthwhile to linger a time along this first part of the River Road to observe the Mississippi—here a quiet and serene stream—in a guise which it never again reveals. Here, as Pliny said, "it plays among the flowers and meadows," while downstream Old Man River, its playful youth behind it, works its way to the Gulf.

As the green and white pilot's wheel sign indicates, county road 40, which heads east off Highway 2, connects with County 9, a rustic dirt road through the back country. Two and a half miles after the turnoff from 2 on to 40 (before it reaches 9) you'll pass Coffee Pot Landing, one of five canoe access points between Itasca and Bemidji. Of the five, Coffee Pot lies closest to the road, so here it is convenient to pause and follow the short path downhill to the wood plank bridge, lined with rusty rails, which crosses the Mississippi, perhaps ten yards wide and at this point in its development in no way a prominent or noteworthy natural feature: Here the Mississippi—undistinguished and undistinguishable from other backwaters which vein the remote Minnesota landscape—remains only a river of potential, not of accomplishment. A few boulders litter the waterway as the creek bubbles and glides along to bigger and better things which await it downstream. Highway 10 runs into 3 which soon crosses into Beltrami County—named for the red umbrella-toting Italian adventurer who sought the headwaters—and then becomes 7, the route into Bemidji via Iron Bridge Landing, where you can also see the Mississippi by walking only a short distance from the road.

Near Bemidji—geographically the first city on the Mississippi but historically the last settlement anywhere along the river's entire length, from Itasca to the Gulf—the Mississippi reaches its northernmost point. Founded about 1895 when loggers headed to the northern regions of the river country after depleting the timber on tributaries to the south, Bemidji became the area's last lumber boom town. To the new settlement swarmed a polyglot mixture of characters—Indians, French Canadians, Scots, Irish, Scandinavian, others—whose capacity for hard liquor inspired one leading local citizen to remark, "The chief ambition in life of the professional lumberjack is to keep every distillery in the United States running to its full capacity." A few blocks from where the Mississippi enters Lake Bemidji, after passing through the adjacent Lake Irving, stands a statue of the most famous lumberjack of all, Paul Bunyan, and his pet, Babe the Blue Ox.

Bunyan and his crew were truly larger than life: Sourdough Sam, the camp cook, favored an acre-sized griddle his helpers greased by sliding on the pan wearing bacon slabs on their feet, while bookkeeper Johnny Inkslinger, whose pen was linked to a barrel of ink, saved five barrels of the fluid a year by omitting to dot "i's" and cross "t's," and woodsman Jigger Jones used to prance along a felled spruce and with his bare feet kick away the knots. After Paul brought in big bees to destroy the huge mosquitos they mated and become even more pesky, but Bunyan used the mosquitos' stingers to drill holes in maple trees. He also trained giant ants, which ate nothing but the best imported Swedish snuff, to haul logs. As for Lucy the Purple Cow, Paul fitted her with green glasses to make the snow look like grass. So cold was one winter that Lucy's milk turned to ice cream before it hit the pail. Local legend has it that on one occasion when Babe—the blue-roan ox Paul's father gave the boy as a pet on his first birthday—was pulling a water wagon, it sprang a leak which created Lake Itasca and the Mississippi River. By Lake Bemidji, near the river, stand statues of Bunyan and Babe, built in late 1937, and in the same area is the local tourist office, which houses the Fireplace of States, built of rocks from every state (except Hawaii), as well as a display of oversized items which belonged to Bunyan: a huge Dr. West's Miracle-Tuft toothbrush, a horseshoe-sized belt buckle, fingernail clippings the dimensions of potato chips, a foot-long toothpick, candy bars about as big as this book, and moccasins containing sufficient material to make leggings.

A few other places to visit lie scattered around Bemidji, a low-key town with a pleasant, open feeling about it. Perched on a point by Lake Bemidji, north of downtown, nestles the park-like campus of Bemidji State University, while at the north edge of the lake lies Ruttger's Birchmont Lodge (218-751-1630), one of the most attractive of the area's sixty or so hostelries, many of them resorts. On the lodge grounds operates from mid-June to mid-August the Paul Bunyan Playhouse (218-751-7270). Back in town you'll find the Bemidji Woolen Mills factory store and, south of town, The Old Schoolhouse, whose six classrooms and two cloakrooms now serve as shops. On Turtle River Lake, north of Bemidji, the Concordia Language Village—a language school based on using a country's culture and customs as teaching aides—includes such European-type enclaves as Waldse (German), Lac duBois (French) and Skogfjorden (Norwegian) Villages. A sign on Highway 89 twelve miles north of Bemidji marking the Continental Divide states that from this point 1396 feet above sea level waters flow either north 3200 miles to the Hudson Bay or south 1800 miles into the Gulf of Mexico. Not far east of the Divide lies Lake Julia, where a bronze plaque on the southeast shore commemorates the 1823 visit by Giacomo Beltrami, who averred that at the lake originated the Mississippi. Headwaters Canoe Outfitters in Bemidji (12404 Lands End Lane SE, Bemidji, MN 56601, 218-751-2783) offers equipment for trips on the Mississippi.

East of Bemidji the Mississippi continues its lake-laced course, flowing through Cass Lake and then Winnibigoshish as the river heads east for a hundred and twenty miles. At the Ottertail Power Dam near where Highway 12, the River Road, crosses the Mississippi, the river reaches its northernmost point, just eighty-seven miles from Canada. Farther on, in the town of Cass Lake, rises the headquarters of Chippewa National Forest, installed in one of the country's largest log structures, built of red pine. The preserve now includes more than twice the 312,000 acres it contained when established in 1902 as the nation's first national forest. Cass Lake also boasts the Old Forestry Center and Museum, an old-time logging camp with antique implements and equipment. On Wednesdays the camp's cookhouse serves up a "Logger's Meal," featuring apple pie and homemade bread. The town developed in the late nineteenth century as a logging community, while in 1912 a new source of income originated when the first resort facility on Cass Lake opened. Out in the lake, through which flows the Mississippi River, perches Star Island, unusual as it contains its own lake—a lake within a lake. On the island lived Ozawindib, the Indian who in 1832 guided Henry Schoolcraft to the Mississippi headwaters at Itasca. Twenty-six years earlier Zebulon Pike, also in search of the source, arrived at Cass Lake—so named by Schoolcraft to honor Lewis Cass, leader of the 1820 expedition in the area—which Pike adjudged to be the river's origin. At Walker on Leech Lake, due south of the town of Cass Lake, Peacecliff Bed and Breakfast (218-547-2832) offers accommodations in a Tudor-style house by the water, while the more elegant Hotel Chase (218 547-1531) also provides bed and breakfast.

East of Cass Lake on U.S. Highway 2, where the River Road joins it, you'll pass a huge fish figure which marks the Big Fish Supper Club. "Help feed the fish," urges a sign requesting a fee, while another one threatens, "No donation no picture." Two and a half miles farther east, at the southern edge of Lake Winnibigoshish, known locally as Lake Winnie, lies Bena, which grew up around a general store local logger Ernest Flemming established here in 1898. In 1933 Flemming built the Bena Standard Oil Station and Motor Court, a curious relic of the old days, which still stands on U.S. Highway 2 in town. Now called

Chux's, the fanciful complex, listed on the National Register, includes a gas station with an upper level which recalls a Mississippi River steamboat pilot's house, while over the pumps stretches a structure somewhat like the entrance gate to a Chinese pavilion. South of U.S. 2 spreads the Leech Lake Indian Reservation, one of ten such enclaves in Minnesota, four occupied by Sioux in the southern part of the state and six Ojibwe reservations in the north. Until the mid-eighteenth century the Sioux (Dakota) had lived peacefully for several hundred years in the northern woodlands and lake area, but the Chippewa (Ojibwe) Indians moved down from the Lake Superior and St. Lawrence River regions and proceeded to push the Sioux out. For years the two tribes fought over the area's rich wild rice beds until the Sioux finally retreated to the south, leaving the fertile region in the north to the Chippewa, a word which means "wild rice gatherers." Starting in 1855 the Chippewa began to cede large tracts of their hard-won territory to the United States, and by now the tribe—the fourth largest in the nation—finds its terrain limited to the six reservations. On the nearly 27,000 acre Leech Lake Reservation live about 4600 Chippewa, some of them still wild rice gatherers and others employed by the Minnesota Chippewa Tribe Construction Company. On the 4th of July, and at other times during the year, the tribe holds a Pow Wow festival at the Veterans Memorial Grounds two miles northwest of Cass Lake (for information, the Leech Lake Indian Reservation number is 218-335-2206). In addition to Cass Lake and Bena, other Indian communities within the reservation on U.S. 2, the River Road, include Ball Club, next to the lake of that name, so called by the Ojibwe as its shape resembled the racquet they used to play la crosse, and Deer River, where the consolidated grade and high schools for the area were one of the few public schools in the country with dormitory facilities. South of Highway 2 lies Schoolcraft State Park, which affords good views of the Mississippi—rather wider here than upstream—as it flows through the pine woods there.

Beyond the park the river abandons its short southerly stretch and again heads east, toward Grand Rapids, named for a three and a half mile stretch of rapids which marked the uppermost point of navigation on the Mississippi. As you approach town from the west on county 76, the River Road, you'll pass the Forest History Center (May 15-Oct 15 10-5, rest of the year visitors' center only 12-4), whose displays and reconstructed turn-of-the-century logging camp recalls the lumber industry which began in the area in 1850. The Woodland Trail at the Center follows the Mississippi as the path winds through a dense pine forest. On the Mississippi west of town the Army Corps of Engineers built in 1884 the Pokegama Dam, one of six such barriers on the upper river. Until the Corps installed these dams the river's water level fell and rose erratically, according to the amount of rain and snow. Such variations resulted in flooding during wet years and in dry seasons interfered with navigation and the operation of water-powered mills. On the north bank of the Mississippi in the center of Grand Rapids stands the Blandin Paper Company factory (tours M, W, F June through Labor Day), the first industrial plant reached by the waterway. The huge installation, which produces coated magazine paper, offers a reminder that the Mississippi is a work-horse of a river, serving along its long length any number of power plants, factories, mills, and other industrial facilities, while also supporting extensive ship traffic.

A few blocks from the factory rises the National Register-listed Central School building where arts and crafts shops and a restaurant called the First Grade, its menu written on the blackboard, occupy classrooms used from 1896 to 1972. The Itasca County Historical Society Museum (M-Sat 10-5, also Sun 1-4 from Memorial Day through Labor Day), installed on the second and third floors, includes an old drug store, period rooms and a recently mounted (1990) collection of memorabilia pertaining to Judy Garland, born Frances Ethel Gumm in Grand Rapids on June 10, 1922, including the script of the "Wizard of Oz," which the "yellow brick road" just outside the building recalls. The walkway consists of yellow bricks purchased by Garland fans and personalized with sentiments such as, "Remembering Judy, Sybil and Bob G.," "No place like home? Try the Forest Lake Inn," and a quote from the "Oz" Munchkin coroner: "She is most sincerely dead." At 727 Second Avenue N.E. survives the Gumm family house, moved there from elsewhere in town, while about where the Rialto Theater and an auto parts store on Pokegama Avenue stand, a block from the Mississippi, once rose the New Grand, the theater owned by Frank Gumm, Judy's father, where "Baby" Gumm, as the family called her, gave her first stage performance—a rendition of "Jingle Bells"—at age two and a half. Show business resurfaces every summer at Grand Rapids when the *Mississippi Melodie*, a small scale version of an old-time Mississippi showboat, moored in the river west of town, presents performances (mid to late July; 800-227-1960). In early August the town celebrates its logging heritage with the annual Tall Timber Days festival, featuring log sculptures carved with chain saws, log rolling, climbing and chopping competitions, and other lumbering events.

For a look at a facility which recalls the other major natural resource produced in the area the Hill Annex Mine, a state park at Calumet, fourteen miles northeast of Grand Rapids, offers tours of a National Register-listed mining camp and mine of the type which produced almost all the nation's iron ore earlier this century. The Mesabi iron range extends northeast from Grand Rapids for 120 miles at a width of one to three miles. Since the Mesabi Iron Company began operations in 1882, miners have extracted from the range millions of tons of iron ore, shipped by train to Lake Superior for transport on to steel mills in the East. Between Grand Rapids and Calumet lie such other old mining settlements as Coleraine, a company town—with two churches listed on the National Register and the 1911 mining superintendent's residence—Bovey, Taconite and Marble, where one of the boarding houses erected by the Oliver Mining Company, a U.S. Steel subsidiary, still stands on Jessie Street, north of Alice Avenue.

For the Mississippi the Mesabi Range, a geological fold on the earth's surface, performs a crucial function, as the elevation there bends the river southward and thus prevents it from reaching an untimely end by spilling its waters into Lake Superior. In this area exists one of America's most important watersheds. Near Chisholm, about twenty miles northeast of Calumet, a Continental Divide marker indicates the location where three great waterway systems flow their separate ways: the Mississippi, which travels south to the Gulf; the Great Lakes-St.Lawrence River, whose waters end in the Atlantic Ocean to the east; and the Hudson Bay drainage to the north. Here, then, the Mississippi finally begins its southwardly flow, after initially meandering north and east.

Between Grand Rapids and the Twin Cities the river remains pleasant and pristine, largely unspoiled by industrial areas, traffic and overdevelopment. The River Road through this section takes you to some out-of-the-way rural stretches of the waterway where, as William E. Lass notes in *Minnesota: A Bicentennial History*, "the river has retained much of its natural beauty. The broad valley, the swiftly moving water and verdant islands and banks, are not so greatly changed from the time of the early explorers, and there remain places along the river where there is no sound other than that of flowing water or leaves moving in a summer breeze."

Typical of those back roads is Highway 3 south out of the Grand Rapids, a route which follows the Mississippi as it winds its way through the sparsely populated countryside. This unpaved and largely deserted road affords occasional views of the river, in these parts no different than any ordinary everyday run-of-the-mill back woods fishing stream. Soon after the road becomes County Route 10 you pass a rusty, rather forlorn railroad trestle which crosses the waterway. A few miles farther south across the Mississippi lies the village of Libby (no bridge, but accessible on Highway 65, which parallels the river on the east), a one-time important way-station on the old trade route between the Mississippi and the East. The 15,000 acre wilderness at Savanna Portage State Park, northeast of Libby, preserves a stretch of the old Portage Trail connecting the East Savanna River, which flows into Lake Superior near Duluth, and the West Savanna, which enters the Mississippi. Across this pathway—introduced in the seventeenth century by Chippewa to Daniel Greysolon, Sieur du Lhut, whose name came to designate the lake port of Duluth—passed voyagers, Indians, fur trappers and traders, adventurers and other Upper Mississippi country characters, laden with packs and carrying canoes as they struggled along the difficult portage. "Its muddy, mosquito-ridden trail was considered by the voyagers one of the more unpleasant routes," notes Thomas F. Waters in *The Streams and Rivers of Minnesota*.

Back on the remote road on the west side of the Mississippi, Route 10 leads you on to the back woods settlement of Palisade, established as a logging center a century ago. The town became a major riverboat stopping point, with such ships as the *Irene*, the *Oriole* and the *Andy Gibson*—at 130 feet, the upper river's longest—putting in at Palisade regularly. On the town's water tower appears a representation of a canoe occupied by two people, symbol of the 1984 canoe trip completed on the entire length of the Mississippi in the record time of twenty-three days, ten hours and twenty minutes by Verlen Kruger and Valerie Fons-Kruger. Just by the river nestles Berglund Park, named for an early settler who established a store to serve the loggers and the railway workers, brought to Palisade in 1910 to lay tracks for the Soo Line. Dedicated in 1981, the park provides a pleasant place to linger for a time and enjoy watching the Mississippi's gentle waters before you continue on down Highway 69, the River Road, which takes you over a rickety one lane wood bridge and then on, via 21, a dirt road, U.S. 169 and Highway 1 across the Mississippi, here just a creek, into Aitkin.

Unlike some cities along the Mississippi, Aitkin remains conscious of its river heritage. On various roads leading to town signs which bear a picture of an old time paddlewheeler proclaim Aitkin as a "Mississippi Riverboat Town." At the former Northern Pacific train depot, listed on the National Register, the Aitkin County Historical Society Museum (W and Sat 1-5, June through August) contains a riverboat history display, as well as Indian artifacts, an old schoolroom and other local items. Gold letters on a door of the 1915 depot indicate the "Women's Retiring Room." The Northern Pacific arrived in town in 1871, a half century after fur trader William A. Aitkin established a permanent settlement in the area. In 1881 opened the first large sawmill, fed by timber floated down the Mississippi, busy with steamboat traffic that brought travelers, settlers and freight to Aitkin until improved roads in the 1920's led to the demise of riverboats. But the city remembers those times with the annual Riverboat Heritage Days, held at the County Fairgrounds the third week of July, while during the first weekend in February the town commemorates a more exotic form of transportation with the Mid-Minnesota Sled Dog Race, including ninety and hundred and fifty mile races and mushers banquets (open to the public). On Minnesota Avenue, a block north of the stoplights downtown, survive two relics, the art-deco style Rialto Theater, with a neon-lit marquee, and Grandpa Butler's, a variety store—with displays of old-time wares—installed in the 1903 Opera House building, which contained an auditorium upstairs and a general store, buggy warehouse, barber shop, hardware shop and bank on the ground floor.

The River Road west of Aitkin continues on to the Cuyuna area, the southernmost of Minnesota's iron ranges and the most recently developed, with the first ore shipment taking place in 1911. The region acquired its designation by combining syllables from the names of Cuyler Adams, who in 1904 discovered ore deposits and then organized mining there, and his dog, Una. Before playing out the Cuyuna Range yielded some 100 million tons of ore, with the peak production occurring during World War II. A few of the old open mining pits, which reached depths of nearly five hundred feet, later filled with water and now comprise some of the area's hundred and fifty lakes. The Evergreen Mine Company once operated at the range one of the world's few sintering plants, which employed heat to convert ore dust into lumps so the iron could be used in blast furnaces. The Road passes through Deerwood—a statue of a well-antlered leaping deer stands by the street in the town—where Walden Woods Bed and Breakfast offers accommodations in a log house on forty wooded acres (218-692-4379), while at Crosby, the next town, Hallett House Bed and Breakfast (218-546-5433) takes guests in a handsome green-trimmed white residence built by Ernest Wilbert Hallett, one of Minnesota's richest men, who started with a hardware store in Crosby in 1911. Just down the road a sign indicates the way to Croft Mine Historical Park (10-6 Memorial Day to Labor Day) where dioramas, machinery, original buildings, a simulated descent into a mine and Cuyuna Range founder Cuyler Adams' office evoke the days nearly a century ago when he struck paydirt in the rich red ore.

At the north end of Crosby, as you leave town on Highway 6, you may want to stop in at a private house at 20 4th Street North (turn right at the power sub-station) where wild rice can be bought at a price lower than in stores. For centuries the northern Minnesota wetlands have yielded wild rice, a grain which comprises fully one quarter of the early woodland Sioux and Chippewa diet. About one-third of the state's 30,000 acres of naturally growing wild rice (of which 15,000 acres are hand-harvested) remain reserved for harvest by Minnesota's Indian tribes. Travelling in hand-propelled boats no bigger than sixteen feet long and thirty inches wide, ricers bend stalks over the boat with a thirty inch stick and tap the plants to dislodge ripe grains, all just as the ancient Indians gathered the crop. Machines are prohibited to ensure that adequate rice will remain to reseed the lakes, and to enable wildlife to share in the harvest. In recent years an increasing proportion of the wild rice supply originates in cultivated paddy-grown areas, with farmed rice comprising about eighty per cent of the crop's annual 6½ million pound yield. Although lake-grown and paddy wild rice supposedly taste the same, in 1990 Minnesota passed a law banning the use of Indian-motif graphics on packages of lake rice, so consumers won't confuse the two types.

North of Crosby Highway 11 crosses the Mississippi, here very narrow—so scrawny, in fact, that the river seems completely unlike its downstream version. But this suggests one of the waterway's alluring characteristics: its unpredictability, and its ever varied appearance in many guises and sizes, moods and demeanors. The River Road follows Highway 19, a narrow route which winds through sparsely settled farm and wooded areas. Shortly after again crossing the Mississippi just north of Brainerd you pass on Highway 25 the large Potlatch paper factory (tours 10 a.m. M-F early June to late August) and then continue on into town. Brainerd began in 1870 as a Northern Pacific Line railway camp for the construction of a bridge over the Mississippi. The railroad's president, John Gregory Smith, refused to let the early settlers call the town Smithville, so they named it for his wife, Ann Eliza Brainerd Smith, who had been commissioned a lieutenant colonel during the Civil War. After the railroad arrived, lumberjacks swarmed to the area, and for forty years, until the early twentieth century, three hundred logging camps in the area felled the white pine, spruce and tamarack and floated the logs on the Mississippi to downstream mills. After the lumber boom ended, Brainerd evolved into a resort region, and now the so-called Brainerd Lakes Area boasts a hundred and forty-five lodging establishments, including more than a hundred and twenty resorts, some of them worth visiting as tourist attractions in their own right.

National Register-listed Grand View Lodge (800-432-3788 in Minnesota) on Gull Lake includes the imposing 1919 Cedar Log Lodge, an attractive flower-garnished two story wood building, the resort's centerpiece. Madden's (800-233-2934, in Minnesota 800-642-5363), also located on Gull Lake, northwest of Brainerd, boasts the state's largest golf course as well as Lumbertown U.S.A., re-creation of an 1870s logging settlement, including thirty old buildings. Farther north, on Pelican Lake, Breezy Point Resort (800-328-2284, in Minnesota 800-432-3777), listed on the State Register of Historic Places, sports stone walls and thick-beamed ceilings, and the house where Clark Gable and Carole Lombard honeymooned. At the Driftwood Family Resort (218-568-4221) on Whitefish Lake, still farther north, you'll find the Minnesota Resort Museum, said to be the world's only display devoted to resorting, an industry which in Minnesota began with Ruttger's Bay Lake Lodge (800-328-0312, in Minnesota 800-247-0402), east of Brainerd, established in 1898 with a few cabins and a cow pasture fenced in for golf, and now the state's oldest continuously operated resort. Area bed and breakfast places include: Woods of Interlachen (218-963-7880), at the northwest side of Gull Lake; nearby, the Sherwood Forest Lodge (218-963-2516), with a huge cut-stone fireplace; Stonehouse (218-568-4255), east of the Pequot Lakes; Pelican Brook Country Inn (218-543-4520), north of Pelican Lake; and Lo-Kiand, (218-692-2714),to the far north near Lower Whitefish Lake.

As at other areas in northern Minnesota, Paul Bunyan's larger-than-life presence enlivens the town. The Paul Bunyan Amusement Center includes a huge talking image of the famous woodsman, supposedly the world's largest animated figure, while the nearly six hundred acre Paul Bunyan Arboretum offers three thousand species of plants, hiking trails and flower-filled meadows. Above the tourist office, located on the site of the first Northern Pacific depot (1871), towers the town's former water tower, a local landmark, used from 1922 until 1959, which looks like a stray section from a medieval European fortress—a castle on the Mississippi rather than the Rhine.

The River Road continues south on Highway 371 to Crow Wing State Park, located eleven miles from Brainerd at the junction of the Crow Wing and the Mississippi Rivers. The crow wing-shaped contour of the land at the confluence inspired the name of the area, an historic corner of the countryside. A remnant in the park of the once busy Red River Ox Cart Trail, which passes the remains of the formerly thriving town of Old Crow Wing, recalls the days in the mid-nineteenth century when regularly scheduled ox cart convoys carrying furs and buffalo robes would arrive from Pembina and Fort Garry (where Winnipeg, Canada now stands) on the way to St. Paul. On the return trip back north the wagon trains would haul tobacco, salt, sugar, tea and other provisions. As many as five hundred wagons per caravan—the vehicles held together with buffalo hide thongs and rolling on solid wheels sliced from logs— screeched and creaked their way along the trail as the procession forded the Mississippi. Earlier, Indians fought over that strategic crossing. During the years of incessant tribal warfare, the Chippewa established themselves in 1760 on the Mississippi's high east bank from where they ambushed a Sioux war party whose canoes the river's currents brought into range of the attackers. After the massacre by the Chippewa, the Sioux withdrew from the area to less hazardous lands and waters farther south.

By the time the Mississippi winds its way from the source at Lake Itasca to the Crow Wing—where its volume again doubles—the famous waterway has traced a huge half-circle of

375 miles, only to end up at this point a mere seventy-five miles, as the crow wings fly, from the headwaters. Here, finally, the waterway abandons its native land and rather determinedly flows south. Perhaps it could be said that the Mississippi here loses its childish innocence, for below the Crow Wing, the first significant tributary, the currents flow more briskly and swiftly, offering greater challenges to canoeists, and abandoning its backwater ways. Below the Crow Wing the previously juvenile stream exhibits the beginnings of its more mature phases, reminiscent, perhaps, of Samuel Taylor Coleridge's description, in "Kubla Khan," of a newly formed river: "And from this chasm, with ceaseless turmoil seething,/ As if this earth in fast thick pants were breathing,/ A mighty fountain momentarily was forced/... And 'mid these dancing rocks at once and ever/ It flung up momently the sacred river."

South of the Crow Wing and west of the Mississippi spreads the 53,000 acre Camp Ripley Military Reservation, the nation's largest National Guard camp, opened in 1931, which annually hosts some 50,000 troops—including 15,000 in the winter—sent there for training. Just after the turn-off to the camp, marked by a tank perched atop a mound, the road crosses the Mississippi on a bridge which affords a good view of the river, then the route continues on alongside a long, low, grey, granite wall to the post's rather forbidding prison-style entrance, flanked by octagonal stone towers. The Minnesota Military Museum (10-5 except M from Memorial Day to Labor Day) on the base houses exhibits on the state's martial history, on wars, on the development of small arms, and on the history of frontier forts, including the original Fort Ripley, established in 1849 to protect the Winnebago and to bring peace to the warring Sioux and Chippewa. The War Department closed the fort in 1857 after deciding that the Chippewa no longer presented a threat, whereupon the tribe pillaged settlers in the surrounding area, prompting the government to reactivate the post. Settlers sought shelter at the fort during the 1862 Sioux uprising, and in 1877 the government finally abandoned the facility. From the pioneer era now survive only the ruins of the powder magazine, the old encampment's sole stone structure.

The River Road south on the way to Little Falls takes you through a stretch of terrain bearing the alluring name Belle Prairie. In this area Father Francis Xavier Pierz, a missionary to the Chippewa, established central Minnesota's first Catholic parish in 1852, recalled by the attractive little Holy Family church (1880), garnished with a quartet of cross-topped towers, tucked away at the end of a tree-lined lane. The nearby Belle Prairie Ox Trail Park—with an old cemetery and stands of virgin pine—includes trails along the Mississippi.

A few miles on lies Little Falls, an attractive community which spreads out from both banks of the Mississippi. Unlike some towns, where the river remains somewhat removed from the mainstream of life, at Little Falls the waterway, which cuts right through the center of town, occupies a prominent position. Attracted by the falls, in 1848 James Green arrived at the site where the following year he built a low dam and established a sawmill, and ever since the Mississippi has played a part in the city's commercial life. The bridge across the Mississippi affords a good view of the waterway and the present cement dam, erected in 1920 by the Minnesota Power Company. Nearby stands the 1900 depot of the Northern Pacific line, whose arrival in 1877 set off the decline of Crow Wing, a competing river town (its remnants located in present-day Crow Wing State Park upstream). Listed on the National Register, the depot was designed by Cass Gilbert, a well known architect whose works include the Minnesota State Capitol, the U.S. Supreme Court and the Woolworth Building in New York City. Nearby, along the river, lie two commercial firms: to the north, the Larson Boat Works, established in 1914, and to the south of the dam stands the Hennepin Paper Company plant, Minnesota's first paper mill, founded one year before Charles A. Weyerhaeuser organized the Pine Tree Lumber Company in 1891, which operated a sawmill and planing factory on the Mississippi at Little Falls until 1919. The Weyerhaeuser Memorial Museum (Tu-Sat 10-5, also May-Oct Sun 1-5) on the river, south of town, contains exhibits relating to the company as well as other displays on the area's history and culture.

Just up the road, back towards town, stands the childhood home of Charles A. Lindbergh, as well as an Interpretive Center (May-Labor Day 10-5, Sept-April Sat 10-4, Sun 12-4 only) with displays on the famous aviator's early years in Little Falls and his later flying career. "Lindy" spent his summers from 1907 to 1917 at the grey frame house, listed on the National Register. Original family furnishing fill the residence, which backs up to the Mississippi, a river that, Lindbergh once noted, "has wound its way in and out of my life like the seasons." During his final visit to the boyhood home in 1973 to dedicate the Interpretive Center, Lindbergh reflected on the great waterway: "I think of the centuries that the river beside us carried a traffic of Indian canoes. Surely hunters with their bows and arrows killed game where we are assembled now. I can even connect the Mississippi here with aviation," Lindbergh said, recalling the time he saw a plane winging its way upriver over the house. "Of course, I wanted to fly in it, but my mother said that would be much too expensive and dangerous." The local lad recorded other memories of his early days along the river in his book *Boyhood on the Mississippi*. (Another famous author, Nobel Prize winner Sinclair Lewis, grew up at Sauk Centre, forty miles southwest of Little Falls.) Lindbergh's beloved Mississippi flows along just by the nature trail which begins near the Interpretive Center and continues on as far as the Weyerhaeuser Museum a short distance downstream.

When Lindbergh returned to Little Falls in August, 1927, after his solo overnight flight May 20-21 across the Atlantic, he stayed at the Elks Hotel, now the Pine Edge Inn, downtown on the Mississippi's east bank. In the lobby hangs a montage of Lindbergh photos, while another frame holds the program and menu for the banquet given at the hotel on August 25 to honor the hometown hero. The nearby rainbow-hued marquee of The Falls movie house and the green awnings at the First National Bank (German-American National until the "German" was omitted during World War I) lend touches of color to the downtown area, while a few blocks east stands the rather colorful 1891 Romanesque-style Morrison County Courthouse, listed on the National Register. From the same era, the 1893 Dewey-Radke House (open weekends) on the west side of town preserves a typical residence of a century ago, while another carry over from the old days is the grave of Chippewa Chief Hole-in-the-Day, buried on the Balder Bluffs above Highway 371 north of town. The name of the chief—who died in 1847 when he fell from a Red River cart near the mouth of the Platte River—refers to the eclipse of the sun which occurred in 1800 on the day of his birth.

The River Road, heading south out of Little Falls past the Lindbergh house, soon loses its pavement and becomes a dirt road which, no doubt, only locals and true Mississippi enthusiasts travel. This stretch presents views of the river in a completely rural context. At a now flooded site where the Swan River enters the Mississippi by the 1924 Blanchard Dam, seven miles south of Little Falls, Lieutenant Zebulon Pike set up his winter camp during the expedition he led to discover the source of the Mississippi. When Pike reached the area in mid-October, 1805, he encountered at the place that became Little Falls a series of rapids which proved too difficult to surmount, so the party returned to the Swan River where Pike built a cabin and two blockhouses. There, most of his men remained during the winter while he proceeded northward with a small group, reaching Cass Lake, which he deemed the Mississippi's source, on February 1.

In early April Pike arrived back at the Swan River outpost, from where the expedition returned to St. Louis, the starting point, on April 30, 1806.

The Road continues through the countryside, with occasional views of the river. At tiny Watab (the Chippewa word for jack pine roots which the Indians used as thread to sew birchbark canoes) early residents erected in 1855 the first bridge across the Mississippi above St. Anthony Falls (Minneapolis), but before completion, a strong wind threw the superstructure into the river, so ending the attempt. On the east side of the river at Sartell sprawls the huge blue-hued Champion International paper mill, successor to the Watab Pulp and Paper Company established there in 1905. The firm originally produced newsprint, then in 1915 began to manufacture book paper, and in 1980 a $350 million expansion program added a giant machine, four stories high and two football fields long, to make coated magazine paper and uncoated paper for mail order catalogs. The plant (tours June-August 8-3, 612-251-6511) now consumes four hundred cords of aspen, spruce and balsam fir logs a day to produce more than eight hundred tons of paper. The area's most famous product, however, is granite, an industry which began at St. Cloud, just to the south, in 1863 when prisoners quarried the stone to build the world's longest continuous granite wall—twenty-two feet high, four and a half feet thick—around the Minnesota State Reformatory, the state's first correctional facility. At the Friedrich Park Natural Area near the penitentiary (east of Musinger Park, which lies on the Mississippi's east bank) survive the original Dodd Quarries inmates mined for the wall, while at the Heritage Center Museum (June-Aug M-Sat 10-4, Sun 12-4, Sept-May Tu-Sat 10-4, Sun 12-4)—installed in a low grey granite building west of town not far from Crossroads Center shopping mall of Prairie Home Companion radio show fame—a life-sized granite quarry replica, designed by the group which created Disney's Epcot in Florida, recalls the industry's history and operation. The museum also houses a display of local river lore and history, including a forty foot mural which depicts life on the Mississippi, and other waterways, through the years. In the downtown area of St. Cloud—also known as a printing center, with nineteen such firms, and as one the world's leading optical lens producers, the sixteen local manufacturers turning out nearly half of the nation's lens supply—stand the 1921 granite-heavy Stearns County Courthouse, a ponderous yellow-green pile, listed on the National Register, and a stretch of 1880's-vintage commercial buildings, also Register listed, from numbers 14 to 30 Fifth Avenue South (number 18 houses the D.B. Searle's eatery, which sports a whimsical neon knife, fork and spoon sign).

Although the Mississippi seems, at least in the central section of St. Cloud, somewhat removed from the city's flow of activity, the river played an important role in the settlement's development. The town's position near what was in the mid-eighteenth century the head of upper Mississippi River traffic contributed to St. Cloud's growth as an outfitting post for the fur trade, with steamboats carrying away huge piles of pelts after delivering cargoes of provisions used to supply wilderness outposts and the more distant Hudson's Bay Company in Canada. Eight years after the railroad arrived in 1866, the last regular steamboat trip took place, although the Pirates Cove Supper Club revives the old ways with river excursions on the *Mississippi Brass Bell* and the new *Anne Bonny* paddlewheeler, inaugurated in 1990 (weekends May-Oct, 612-252-8400). At Apollo High School, 1000 44th Avenue North, a transportation mode more modern than the old riverboats adorns the front entranceway—a space capsule from one of NASA's Apollo missions. Into the Mississippi at St. Cloud one midnight in 1858 a group of slave-owning Southerners who had settled in the area threw the type and press of the *Visitor* newspaper, published by abolitionist Jane Gray Swisshelm, who later agreed never again to attack slavery in the *Visitor*. She stuck to the agreement by changing the name of the paper before resuming her criticisms the next day. Along the Mississippi south of town, but rather removed from the river, stretches the campus of St. Cloud State, founded in 1857 and now Minnesota's third largest university. Lamb's Bed and Breakfast (612-363-7924) at St. Joseph, west of St. Cloud a mile south of St. John's University, known for its abbey church designed by Marcel Breuer, offers accommodations in a New England-style saltbox house.

At Elk River—named for the herds of elk Zebulon Pike encountered during his 1805 expedition up the Mississippi—thirty-five miles south of St. Cloud lies the Oliver H. Kelley Farm (May-Oct 10-5; Visitors' Center only Nov-April, Sat 10-4, Sun 12-4), homestead of the Boston-born tailor's son—"As full of public spirit as a dog is full of fleas," so Kelley described himself—who founded the national Grange organization. In 1867 he and several associates established the Order of the Patrons of Husbandry, and within ten years farmers around the country started nearly 25,000 local Grange chapters. Kelley's nearly two hundred acre property, run since 1961 by the Minnesota Historical Society, now functions as a "living history" farm where attendants clad in period garb demonstrate nineteenth century agricultural practices. The farm, which lies along the east bank of the Mississippi, includes a nature trail by the river. Across the Mississippi southwest of Elk River lies Ostego, Minnesota's newest city, the first town in fifteen years officially to receive that designation (1990), while on the waterway's eastern bank at the confluence of the Rum River lies Anoka. Although the Dakota Indians called the stream the Moe Waken, or "spirit," the early fur trappers, who favored spirits of a different kind, named it the Rum. Through the Anoka area occasionally spin tornados, created when warm moist air which wafts up the Mississippi River Valley from the Gulf encounters colder northern breezes which spin in to replace the rising warmer winds, so creating the turbulence. In 1939 a tornado at Anoka whirled all of the water out of the Mississippi along a quarter of a mile. At the cemetery in Anoka stands the Jonathan Emerson monument, erected by the deceased a year before his death, which bears more than twenty-five hundred words of Bible verses and his philosophy of life. Because of Anoka's once thriving milling industry—based on the Mississippi and the Rum, which carried the first pine logs cut in the state—the city's citizens assumed that the settlement would become Minnesota's leading metropolis, but the advent of rail transport and electric power diminished the importance of water power and the Mississippi's transport prowess, so nearby Minneapolis developed into the state's largest and most important industrial center.

On the way in to the metropolitan area you'll pass the Coon Rapids Dam Regional Park which occupies terrain on both sides of the Mississippi, spanned by a thousand foot-long walkway affording close views of the river. The eighty mile portion of the Mississippi which twists through the Twin Cities area presents the waterway in a new light. No longer does the Mississippi quietly flow as a river of small towns and meadows, country roads and isolated stretches. Here urbanized—locked and dammed, and well bridged—it serves the metropolitan area's 2.2 million people (second, on the Mississippi, only to St. Louis) in its "up-town" city guise.

The Minneapolis half of the twin began in 1831 when soldiers from nearby Fort Snelling on the Mississippi to the south established a saw and a flour mill at St. Anthony Falls, the river's greatest cascade (sixteen feet), discovered in 1680 by Franciscan Father Louis Hennepin and named by him for St. Anthony of Padua. In 1846 settlers arrived to establish the village of St. Anthony on the east side of the Falls, and in the 1850's a new town named Minneapolis—a curious hybrid word derived from the Sioux "minne" (water) and the Greek "polis" (town) — began to develop on the west bank. Soon, nearly a hundred water wheels gathered the river's power into energy, and by 1871, twenty years after the first commercial flour milling began, the Minneapolis mills were producing more than two million barrels of flour annually. In 1881 the C.A. Pillsbury and Co. firm completed on the east bank the seven story high Pillsbury "A" mill, its four thousand barrel a day capacity later increased to enlarge the facility into the world's largest flour mill. In *Growing Up in Minnesota*, edited by Chester G. Anderson, one time *New York Times* correspondent Harrison E. Salisbury recalled the riverside industrial scene there where the Mississippi tumbles through town: "The mills stood at St. Anthony Falls in their corona of flour dust like block houses guarding the rapids of the river. The grain poured in from Montana, the Dakotas, the Red River valley. It poured into the Minneapolis mills, and the flour in its cotton sacks and its great jute cloaks filled countless red freight cars and poured out over the country and over the world."

The city's river heritage survives today in the so-called Mississippi Mile section of town, an historic stretch which borders the waterway between Plymouth Avenue and I-35W. The Mississippi still flows over the Falls (depicted on the seals of both Minnesota and Minneapolis), but now a Corps of Engineers-built concrete apron anchors the cascade, which—since Father Hennepin's time—had by erosion advanced six hundred feet upstream.

In 1956 the Corps completed at the Falls a dam and the Lower Lock, with a lift of nearly twenty-five feet, and seven years later the Engineers added the Upper Lock. These projects made it possible for boats to travel north of the Falls, so extending the Mississippi's navigable waters four and a half miles upstream to the Soo Line railroad bridge. There, 1823 miles above the Gulf of Mexico, lies the absolute head of navigation on the great river.

The observation platform which overlooks the Falls and the Upper Lock offers a splendid vantage point to observe one of the Mississippi 's most interesting and historic stretches. The Upper

Lock's nearly fifty-five foot lift, necessary to cope with St. Anthony's drop, is the greatest of the twenty-nine locks located on the Mississippi between here and St. Louis, most of them installed in the 1930s to facilitate traffic on the river. Nearby lies the site of the first hydroelectric plant of the Western Hemisphere, built in 1882 by the Minneapolis Brush Electric Company. On the opposite shore a red neon sign advertising "Pillsbury's Best Flour" perches atop the century old red brick Pillsbury "A" mill. Just off to the right stretches the splendid 1883 twenty-one arch stone bridge (two arches were removed for construction of the Upper Lock and Dam) built by James J. Hill, president of the Great Northern, to serve as the last link between the wheat fields of the great plains and the flour mills just across the Mississippi on the east bank. The line's successor, the Burlington Northern Railroad, still owns the 2100-foot-long span, second oldest on the Mississippi (St. Louis's Eads Bridge dates from 1874), last used by trains in the early 1980's. A short distance upstream the new Hennepin Avenue suspension bridge creates a modern version of the original 1855 span, the first bridge ever to cross the Mississippi. On Nicollet Island, reached by the bridge, stands the Nicollet Island Inn (612-331-1800). Another riverside hotel in the area is the Whitney (612-339-9300), while at the adjacent Boom Island Park moors the *Anson Northrup* paddlewheeler excursion boat (612-227-1100). On the east bank of the Mississippi, on cobblestoned Main Street, stand Riverplace and St. Anthony Main, two shopping centers, the latter installed in late nineteenth-century restored warehouse buildings, and the Pracna, a century-old eatery occupying an 1850's structure, with a sidewalk cafe overlooking the Mississippi. Nearby lie the 1857 Our Lady of Lourdes, the city's oldest church in continuous use, and the 1848 Greek Revival-style Ard Godfrey House (by appointment only, 612-870-8001; June-Sept F, Sat, Sun 12-3:30),built by a Maine millwright who helped construct the early dam and saw mills at St. Anthony Falls.

From the Mississippi Mile you can continue on the River Road through Minneapolis via North Washington Avenue and on Cedar for two blocks, then left on 4th Street. This leads to the West River Parkway, an attractive route first proposed a century ago when Minneapolis landscape gardener H.W.S. Cleveland wrote in an open letter to the park commissioners in 1886: "The Mississippi River is not only the grand natural feature which gives character to your city and constitutes the main spring to its prosperity, but it is the object of vital interest and the center of attraction to intelligent visitors from every quarter of the globe, who associate such ideas of grandeur with its name as no human creation can excite... It should be placed in a setting worthy of so priceless a jewel." For most of its length the parkway travels on the high ground above and removed from the glittering "jewel" below, but at its north edge the road runs alongside the river for a short distance. Off to the left, moored (off-season) by the east bank, below the University of Minnesota medical center, bobs the Centennial Showboat, which visits Minnesota river towns during the summer. Beyond the Franklin Avenue Bridge, the road climbs and leaves the Mississippi, now hidden away far below, as the parkway passes through a thickly wooded area with attractive houses on the right. Shortly after the parkway turns away from the river, you can take a side street down to Lock and Dam Number 1, tucked away below steep bluffs in a peaceful enclave where the city seems far away, while the Mississippi is now close at hand. After Congress in the 1920's directed the Corps of Engineers to create in the upper Mississippi a nine foot deep channel for river traffic, the Corps constructed a series of twenty-nine locks and dams, between Minneapolis and St. Louis, to serve as a "step ladder" for ships traveling the waterway, which falls some 420 feet in the 669 miles between the two cities.To compensate for this variance, the locks provide a series of "steps' which ships climb or descend as they travel through the "lakes" (called pools) between the locks. The dams at each lock serve to control the flow of water to maintain the nine foot channel. Below St. Louis no locks and dams are needed, as the river runs deep and free.

From the lock and dam, a road leads up to Minnehaha Falls, the highest cascade along the Mississippi at fifty-three feet (St. Anthony Falls is the highest on the river itself), described by Henry Wadsworth Longfellow in his "Song of Hiawatha". Nearby stands the mid-1870's Milwaukee Road depot, laden with Victorian era "gingerbread" trim and known affectionately as the "Princess," used until 1963 to serve visitors to Minnehaha Park. Down the road lies the Stevens House, moved there from its original site just west of St. Anthony Falls, where in the mid-nineteenth century Colonel John H. Stevens maintained a toll-free ferry for soldiers stationed at nearby Fort Snelling, perched on a bluff above the confluence of the Minnesota and the Mississippi Rivers a few miles south of Minnehaha Park.

Fort Snelling began in 1819 as one of a series of outposts established by the United States to gain control of the upper Mississippi valley and adjacent areas. Along that strategic river the federal government built Fort Armstrong, at present-day Rock Island, Illinois; Fort Crawford, at Prairie du Chien, Wisconsin; and Fort Snelling, the northwestern-most link in the chain of frontier outposts and Indian agencies which extended from Lake Michigan to the upper Missouri River. For nearly thirty years Fort Snelling remained the main enclave of civilization on the upper Mississippi. Fur companies established posts nearby, the Dakota and Ojibwe Indians frequented the fort to trade, missionaries stopped by en route to the pagan-inhabited wilderness, early settlers found shelter there, and such pioneering adventurers as Giocomo Beltrami and Henry Schoolcraft passed through on their way north to seek the Mississippi's source. Beltrami arrived in May 1823 on the *Virginia*, the first steamboat to travel up to the Mississippi that far north. The Dakota Indians, whose villages spread along both sides of the river near Fort

Snelling, found this new apparition a wonderment. As J.W. Bond described the scene in *Minnesota and Its Resources*, published in 1857:

> As the boat approached the mouth of the [Minnesota] river, they stood, in multitudes upon the shore, men, squaws, and papooses, gaping with astonishment to see the huge monster advancing against the current. They really thought it was some enormous water-god, coughing and spouting water in every direction, and puffing out his hot breath. The women and children fled for the woods, their hair streaming in the wind, while some of the warriors, retreating to a more respectful distance, stood their ground until the boat passed and landed. The boat being one of those awful high-pressure boats, which blow off steam with a noise like unbottling an earthquake, when she "blew out" shook with terror the knees of the stoutest braves, and in a twinkling, every red skin had vanished in the woods, screaming and shouting with all their might.

So began the steamboat era on the upper Mississippi.

Perhaps it could be said that the *Virginia*'s arrival marked the beginning of the end of the frontier: now, finally, the upper Mississippi was connected with more settled and civilized regions in the lower part of the river. As F. Scott Fitzgerald — who grew up a few miles from the Mississippi, in St. Paul — wrote in *The Great Gatsby*, the frontiers once upon a time seemed "a fresh green breast of the new world. Its vanished trees, the trees that made way for Gatsby's house, had once pandered in whispers to the last and greatest of all human dreams: for a transitory enchanted moment man must have held his breath in the presence of this continent." Now, there on the Mississippi at Fort Snelling in 1823, the enchanted moment had passed.

By the middle of the century the frontier had expanded north and west, and new installations — such as Fort Ripley on the Mississippi to the north — succeeded Fort Snelling, reduced to serving as a supply depot. Finally, in 1858, the government sold the property to real estate developers, an inglorious ending for the famous old fort. But during the Civil War, Snelling received a new lease on life when the facility resumed service as a training center, while later in the nineteenth century it functioned as military headquarters for the Department of Dakota, which extended from the Mississippi to the Rocky Mountains. After further service during the two World Wars the government decommissioned the fort, which in the late 1960's preservationists rallied to save following announcement of a plan to demolish the installation for a freeway. Now, splendidly restored, Fort Snelling —with its towers, barracks, sutler's store, and other yesteryear facilities—vividly evokes the old days, more than a century and a half ago, when it served as the first outpost in the vast wilderness of the upper Mississippi Valley.

Below the fort, at water level, stretches Fort Snelling State Park, with trails leading to Pike Island where the Minnesota flows into the Mississippi, doubling its volume. The River Road passes above the State Park as the route crosses the Minnesota on the way to Mendota where the 1835 Sibley and the 1837 Faribault Houses recall the pioneer era. The earlier residence, built by Henry Hastings Sibley (his middle name designates the next city south, beyond St. Paul, on the Mississippi), Minnesota's first governor (1858), also served as a state headquarters for the American Fur Company, while fur trader Jean Baptiste Faribault's home next door later contained a hotel and a warehouse. Tours through these handsome honey-colored stone structures begin in the 1854 du Puis House, up on the highway above the show homes nestled in the little valley below (May-Oct Tu-Sat 10-5, Sun 12-5). Also in Mendota stands 1853 St. Peter's church, Minnesota's oldest house of worship and one of the few established before creation of the state in 1858.

The River Road now crosses the Mississippi to enter St. Paul, established in 1839 as a port town called Pig's Eye Landing, named for Pierre Parrant, a French Canadian with defective vision but effective booze, for he prospered as a whiskey runner. From its earliest days St. Paul — so designated in 1841 for the log cabin chapel of that name — owed its existence to the river, and still today the Minnesota capital boasts a longer shoreline along the Mississippi, twenty-nine miles, than any other urban area on the waterway. Shepard Road borders the Mississippi as it passes the boxy brick Schmidt's Brewery, Unocal chemical tanks, boats moored on the opposite bank, the High Bridge (so named as horseless carriages in the early days crossed the span in high gear) and other riverside scenes until reaching downtown St. Paul. At the foot of Jackson Street lies Lambert's Landing, the original Lower Landing established there in 1840 just after the city began and renamed in 1937 to honor Colonel George C. Lambert, who led the campaign to establish the Mississippi's nine foot navigation channel. From Harriet Island, a few blocks upstream, named for Harriet Bishop, St. Paul's first school teacher, the Padelford Packet Boat Company operates the sternwheelers *Jonathan Padelford* and *Josiah Snelling* on river cruises (612-227-1100). The Minnesota Historical Society, now housed in its new (1991) building half a mile from the state Capitol, presents some river-related exhibits, while the Minneapolis Grain Exchange (tours 8:30 and 10:15, 612-338-6212), established more than a century ago and the world's largest commodity cash market, recalls the area's origin as a milling town based on the Mississippi's water power. On the heights above the Mississippi sprawls the campus of the University of Minnesota, chartered in 1851 and established in a two story wood building erected at a site the regents described as a "most eligible situation on the bluff, just above the mills, fronting Main Street and the river, and commanding one of the most beautiful prospects in the Territory." A few years later the university moved to a new site known as "Campus Knoll," its present location on the bluffs next to East River Road, which borders the Mississippi.

An alternate and remarkably rural-like route from Mendota takes you along the west (here mostly south) shore of the Mississippi, by-passing St. Paul's urban area. This route curves down from the Sibley Memorial Highway, just past the 35E bridge across the Mississippi, to Lilydale Road at water level. In a secluded spot on the river stands the Pool and Yacht Club, a boat-like building with porthole-like round windows and sporting a yellow canopy and blue trim. Farther on lies Pickarel Lake, seemingly lost in the remote countryside—as if in the north woods where the Mississippi begins—although St. Paul lurks nearby, and then Lilydale Park, a rustic river-side enclave. Lilydale Road becomes West Water Street which connects with Plato Avenue, bordered by a light industrial district, and this leads to the Highway 3 bridge which crosses the Mississippi, bordered on the east side by Warner Road, into downtown St. Paul.

Warner Road takes you along the Mississippi, away from downtown St. Paul. On the left, after crossing the train tracks, lies Indian Mounds Park, which overlooks the Mississippi. Officials established the enclave in 1887 to preserve the six burial mounds which remained of eighteen discovered in 1766 by Jonathan Carver, one of the Mississippi's earliest explorers. An adventurer from New England, Carver set out that year on his trek through the upper Mississippi country to locate the river's headwaters and to investigate the region's Indian tribes. His colorful account of the journey, *Travels Through the Interior Parts of North America*, published in 1778, contains many tall tales and short stories about the region. The terrain along Highways 61 and 10, the River Road to the south of Indian Mounds Park, once served as the homeland of Indian bands. Between the road and the river just to the west dwelled from 1838 to 1852 Sioux Chief Medicine Bottle and his braves and squaws. Nearby lay the Sioux village occupied by the Little Crow clan. Across the river, beyond Pig's Eye Lake and Island, erupted in 1842 the Battle of Kaposia, touched off when the Chippewa attacked the local Sioux.

Within a decade a new adversary appeared on the scene west of the Mississippi—the white man. An 1837 treaty with the Indians permitted pioneers to settle on land east of the Mississippi, but not until the 1851 Treaty of Mendota could the western states be settled (apart from licensed fur traders). After the treaty, four land speculators tried to capitalize on the new opportunities by acquiring a town site west of the river, where they established Hastings, so called when the paper bearing that word was drawn from a hat which held each of their names.

Early settlers at the new Mississippi River village designated Hastings included: Richard Washington, a descendant of George Washington's brother; Frances Bleeker Ellison Pringle, member of the family which gave its name to New York City's Bleeker Street; Marcus Marx, a dry goods merchant who in 1880 moved to Chicago where he helped found Hart, Schaffner and Marx; Charles W. Lowell, descendant of the well known Boston family; and Ellen Kellogg Cadwell, of the breakfast cereal family. Hastings today survives as a delightful throwback to those early days, for in the town lingers the atmosphere of a nineteenth-century steamboat-era settlement. With more than sixty structures—thirty-five commercial and twenty-eight residential—listed on the National Register, Hastings offers a treasure trove of Victorian and turn-of-the-century architecture. These relics include many old houses on West Second Street, the 1870 Dakota County Courthouse, a row of brick buildings on Sibley Street, and the business structures along wide East Second Street downtown, among them the Mississippi Belle restaurant, remodeled to resemble a steamboat, located on the site of Hastings' first construction, and a trading post and inn called The Buckhorn. The side wall of the Maco-B Bar across the street bears a colorful mural picturing the paddlewheeler *Charles M.*

Adams. On Vermillion Street south of downtown rises the Gothic Revival-style fifteen room limestone LeDuc-Simmons House, recently restored, completed in 1867 for General William G. LeDuc, a lawyer and railroad entrepreneur. To the north of town stands Lock and Dam Number 2, where a viewing platform affords a close look at the Mississippi. From the Veterans Memorial Levee downtown at the foot of Sibley, the view upstream includes the lock and dam framed by the gracefully arched blue-hued bridge. Completed in 1951, that span replaced the 1895 Spiral Bridge—successor to a rope ferry—which curled down into town so travelers would arrive in the commercial district rather than over-shooting it and thus hastening on without pausing to spend money at the stores in Hastings. Hastings recalls its river heritage with the annual mid-July Rivertown Days, featuring a flotilla parade of lit and decorated boats on the Mississippi, while on the second weekend of May the unusual Front Porch Festival—celebrating the city's many porches—takes place. Thornwood Inn in Hastings offers bed and breakfast (612-437-3297), while south of town the Alexis Bailly Vineyard and Winery, with 7000 grape vines on twelve acres, offers tours (June-Oct F, Sat, Sun 12-5).

Farther south, on the river's Prairie Island—where early French pioneers established a trading center and fort in the late seventeenth century—lives a community of Dakota Indians, who in recent times have shared the area with a nuclear power plant. A few miles downstream sits Lock and Dam Number 3, through which every year some 21,000 boats, commercial and pleasure, pass. Somewhere along this stretch of river not far south of Hastings the ultra light-draft (one foot, unloaded) packet *Chippewa Falls* ran aground on a sand bar in 1864 but managed to float free when the pilot, so he later claimed, shifted the ship's balance by moving his tobacco quid in his mouth. At Red Wing, the Mississippi becomes a somewhat different river, now spreading majestically across the cliff-lined valley. Even today, three centuries later, it takes little imagination to visualize how the great bluff-bordered waterway appeared when Father Louis Hennepin descended the river in 1680: "The young Mississippi, fresh from its northern springs, unstained as yet by unhallowed union with the riotous Missouri," wrote Francis Parkman in *La Salle and the Discovery of the Great West*, "flowed calmly on its way amid strange and unique beauties—a wilderness, clothed with velvet grass; forest-shadowed valleys; lofty heights, whose smooth slopes seemed leveled with the scythe; domes and pinnacles, ramparts and ruined towers, the work of no human hand."

Nestled among a scattering of those elevations along the Mississippi lies Red Wing, one of the river's most attractive towns. A clean, open, spacious feeling characterizes picture-perfect Red Wing, which spills across the hills along the waterway. With twenty-two National Register-listed sites and three National Register Districts, remnants from yesteryear abound in the town, established by Swiss missionaries in 1837. By the 1870s Red Wing had become the world's largest primary wheat market, with a warehouse capacity of a million bushels and shipment of 2.4 million bushels in 1874, the peak year. After the grain trade declined the town diversified into other commercial activities. The Minnesota Stoneware-Red Wing Potteries (1883) occupied the cavernous four story factory (1900), later restored and listed on the National Register, after production ended in 1967. Converted into a retail mall in 1982, the old building now houses some fifty shops. Elsewhere in town, the Red Wing Shoe Company, founded in 1904, occupies its old-fashioned looking, still operating original factory on Main Street. Here (and at the main plant in a local industrial park) the firm converts 236,000 cattle hides into 1.8 million pairs of shoes annually. Part of the leather supply originates with the S.B. Foot Tanning Company in Red Wing, a firm founded in 1873 and still the largest tannery west of the Mississippi. The public-spirited shoe company acquired the nineteenth century row of commercial structures in the 300 block of Main Street and in 1988 reopened the restored historic buildings, where old photos on the walls recall the city's early days. Similarly, in 1977 Red Wing Shoe purchased the then century-old (1875) St. James (612-388-2846), one of those splendid steamboat-era Mississippi River hotels, also restored and reopened (1979) as a delightful relic of the old days along the waterway. Model paddlewheelers and old riverboat photos decorate the Port of Red Wing restaurant downstairs, and each of the St. James' sixty rooms bears the name of a nineteenth century steamer. With its picturesque old-fashioned reading room, antiquated atmosphere and antique decor, the St. James—not to be missed—survives as a true period piece.

Opposite the hotel stands the "Uff da" Shop, which brims over with all manner of Scandinavian wares, including a glossary of what "uff da" means in Norwegian (pretty much anything and everything). Down on Levee Street the *Princess Red Wing* (excursions on the Mississippi mid-May to mid-Oct, 612-388-0800)—with its crown-like gold peaks atop black smokestacks, red trim and bright, white paint—adds color to the waterfront. Off nearby Bay Point Park, the photogenic Boathouse Village remains as one of the nation's few surviving "gin pole" river settlements—not very settled, as the sheds ride up and down on poles to adjust to the waterway's changing level. Change also dominates the Mississippi's course here, for offshore to the north, the waterway bends in what is supposedly the sharpest curve on the entire river.

Red Wing boasts a few other attractions. In the 800 and 900 blocks of West Third and West Fourth Streets stand a number of venerable houses and other structures, including the 1904 T.B. Sheldon Auditorium, home of what is believed to be the nation's first municipally owned theater. In 1990 the American Museum of Wildlife Art (M-Sat 10-5, Sun 12-4), west of town, moved to Red Wing, while in the 1960's the Goodhue County Historical Museum (Tu-Sun 1-5, Jan. and Feb. closed weekends) moved from the courthouse to its commanding position on Oak Street from where visitors can enjoy a view down onto the snug little town and out to the five mile wide Mississippi River valley. Off to the right—in a perspective not unlike that from Cardiff Hill overlooking the river at Hannibal, Missouri, downstream—rises Barn Bluff, a landmark for ship pilots for two centuries, reached by paths and stairs. From the top stretches a view Mississippi scene painter Henry Lewis adjudged "indescribably beautiful." Bed and breakfast establishments in the area include Pratt-Tabor Inn (612-388-5945), Candle Light Inn (612-388-8034) and, outside town, Hungry Point Inn (612-437-3660) and Swanson-Johnson Inn (612-388-FARM).

On the River Road south of Red Wing rises the basilica-like Minnesota Training School, a Romanesque-style brick and stone pile built in 1889 for "unfortunate and erring children." At Wacouta, now a hamlet but once a competitor of Red Wing for the county seat, the Mississippi widens to form Lake Pepin, a thirty-four mile long pool formed by silt and other debris deposited at the mouth of the Chippewa River, downstream, so as to create a natural dam. The river now begins to present a series of especially scenic scenes. In *The Amazing Mississippi* Willard Price notes that from Red Wing to and along Lake Pepin "the road hugs the Mississippi and affords views that can hardly be excelled elsewhere in America."

Ten miles beyond Red Wing lies Old Frontenac, a small enclave, dating from the 1870s, now within Frontenac State Park. In the late 1720s the French authorities, headquartered in Montreal, built Fort Beauharnois, which they abandoned in 1737 due to harassment by the Indians. All traces of the fort have vanished—no one even knows exactly where it stood—but the Old Frontenac Historic District still preserves a few mid-nineteenth century structures, many listed on the National Register, from the time when the two Garrard brothers from Cincinnati established the village. Later, in the 1870s and 1880s,

Frontenac became one of the nation's most fashionable summer resorts, with the 1859 Lakeside Hotel (originally the Frontenac Inn) catering to tourists who arrived by steamboat. Over part of the winter of 1883-4 Grant La Farge and George L. Heins, architects of St. John the Divine Cathedral in New York City, visited the area, and later they selected the rich, creamy limestone at the Frontenac quarry for the church's interior and apse. Not far north rise the Point-No-Point bluffs, so named by boatmen who found that the cliff—set back from the actual shore—seemed to disappear as they drew closer, and on a knoll to the south stands Villa Maria, a former convent school established in the late nineteenth century by Ursuline nuns, who now operate the huge structure as a retreat.

Continuing south, the River Road borders the sparkling (in fair weather) expanse of water where the river masquerades as a lake. On the lake (river) north of Lake City stands Waterman's, a restaurant overlooking the water, while in town masts of white boats stab the sky at the marina where the diminutive *Spirit of Salt Lake City* excursion boat (612-345-5432) is moored. A nine hundred foot breakwater protects the marina, home port for more than six hundred boats. At Lake City in 1922, eighteen year old Ralph W. Samuelson succeeded in water-skiing on eight-foot-long pine boards he had steamed in boiling water to curve the tips, a feat the American Water Ski Association honored in 1966 by recognizing Lake City as the birthplace of that water sport, commemorated in the annual Water Ski Days held the last full weekend in June. The Chamber of Commerce, 212 South Washington, contains a replica of those first skis, long angular boards with a simple leather strap over a rubber mat. Lake City's turn-of-the century jail, a box-like building, now houses a gift shop, and the 1899 limestone and brick campanile-topped City Hall, listed on the National Register, bears Romanesque and Queen Anne-style touches. In a grove of tall pines south of town stands the Wild Wings Gallery, a veritable still-life zoo with animal and bird motif coasters, posters, original prints and other outdoorsy items (for catalogs: 612-345-3663). Four places in the area offer bed and breakfast: Pepin House (612-345-4454), Red Gables Inn (612-345-2605), Victorian Bed and Breakfast (612-345-2167) and, in a country house on a sixty-five cow dairy farm, Evergreen Knoll Acres (612-345-2257).

The River Road, here a lake road, borders the water and affords excellent views of the Mississippi as it rolls south in its temporary incarnation as Lake Pepin. The river—in good weather—seems serene, the scene picture perfect. White wakes of pleasure craft etch patterns in the wide expanse of water. In the nineteenth century this alluring area greatly inspired poets and artists. William Cullen Bryant rhapsodized, "This place ought to be visited by every poet and every painter in America...It is a grief that Americans should wander off to the Rhine and the Danube, when in the Mississippi they have countless Rhines and Danubes." And Mississippi River panorama artist Henry Lewis noted in 1848: "City dwellers need go no farther than this if they seek romantic solitude. One cannot imagine a more lovely expanse of water than Lake Pepin in quiet, clear weather and no wilder scene than when, whipped by the storm, its waves bound against the rocky cliff."

Tiny Reads Landing on the lake now consists of just a few houses and the Wabasha County Historical Museum, installed in a cupola-topped 1890 school building. It is hard to believe that only this mini-hamlet remains where a thriving town once bustled with activity as one of the busiest ports on the Mississippi. Fur traders, lumberjacks, boatmen and other river characters flocked to Reads Landing, patronizing the twenty or so saloons and the rowdy hotels and boarding houses. Back in the late nineteenth century, the city served as a major wheat shipping point and—thanks to the Chippewa River just across the Mississippi here—as an even more important center for the lumber trade. This trade originated in the mid-nineteenth century when commercial logging began in Wisconsin and Minnesota. Unlike the Mississippi River valley at points farther south—Iowa, Illinois, Missouri and elsewhere—the upper river country was settled by men wielding the ax and saw rather than the seeder and plow. After the crosscut saw came into use in the mid-1870s the wood trade boomed. Great log rafts floated down the tributaries—mainly the St. Croix, which enters the Mississippi at Hastings, and the Chippewa—and then, in some cases, on down the main waterway to the mills. One of the most famous logging raftsmen was Stephen Hanks, a cousin of Abraham Lincoln, who for some forty years ran rafts. Until after the Civil War, the great log convoys floated down the Mississippi without power, but in 1865 steam-powered towing (or, more commonly, pushing) began, and soon hundreds of towboats employed to propel log rafts chugged up and down the river. All true rivermen soon learned the sixty line ballad consisting solely of raft boat names:

> The Fred Weyerhaeuser and the Frontenac,
> The F.C.A. Denckman and the Sandy Mac,
> The Menominee and the Louisville,
> The R.J. Wheeler and the Jessie Bill,
> The Robert Semple and the Golden Gate,
> The J.C. Caffrey and the Sucker State.

Log rafting peaked in the 1880s, and by the summer of 1915 the colorful trade ended when the *Ottumwa Belle* pushed the last log tow down the Mississippi—the end of an era.

Just south of Reads Landing lies Wabasha, where a distinct down-home, small town, old-time river atmosphere lingers. Low brick buildings line Main Street, center of the National Historic District which includes nearly sixty structures, three-quarters of them dating from the nineteenth century. Behind the 1884 Smith's Block—on which appears a metal medallion extolling Big

Jo Flour, "Best in the world"—towers a grain elevator topped by a large red "Big Jo Flour" sign. Nearby, across the street, stands the 1880 H.H. Jewell Building, which housed a hardware firm and, upstairs, the Ladies Library Association. Up the street, beyond the new brown-beamed bridge, the venerable Anderson House, Minnesota's oldest operating hotel, still takes guests (800-325-2270, in Minnesota 800-862-9702). Like the St. James at Red Wing, upriver, the Anderson House survives as one of those splendid old Mississippi River hotels dating from the steamboat era. Most of the furniture there the day the establishment opened in 1856 remains in place at the inn, run by fourth generation descendants of Grandma Ida Anderson, who bought the hotel in 1896. Many of her Pennsylvania Dutch dishes—beer and cheese soup, raisin-baked beans, sixteen varieties of bread—enhance the menu. Pampered guests get a mustard plaster to treat colds, a hot brick delivered in a quilted container to warm cold beds, and a shine for shoes left overnight outside rooms. All contain antiques, and some include whimsical touches: Cupid metal door-knockers greet arrivals to the bridal suite. The most unusual enhancement, however, originated in 1974 when a recuperating patient from the Mayo Clinic at nearby Rochester, Minnesota asked the hotel proprietor if he could borrow a cat from the owner, and ever since then guests can obtain one of the dozen or so house cats as room companions. When off-duty, the cats lodge in their own room, number 19, on the second floor. Cat motif wall paper, family pictures of the felines and a dormitory with designated cushioned cubicles—"Tom-Tom," "Tiger," "Goblin," "Pepper," "Ginger," "Morris" (once almost kidnapped) and others—provide pleasant surroundings for the lucky kitties to take their catnaps.

Back in the center of town, at the foot of Pembroke Avenue, a deck which extends out over the Mississippi affords good views of the waterway. Opposite stretches the serene green shore, completely undeveloped and seemingly little changed from the 1820's, when a trader established here on the waterway a fur post, the only non-Indian settlement between Prairie du Chien, Wisconsin, downstream, and Fort Snelling (Minneapolis). This early outpost underlies Wabasha's claim to be Minnesota's oldest city. Back in those days, the Mississippi formed a distinct line of demarcation between the settled, civilized east and the unsettling Indian-infested lands west of the river. In his diary published as *With Pen and Pencil on the Frontier in 1851* Baltimore artist Frank Blackwell Mayer noted at (probably) Wabasha how "on one side civilization had advanced & the log cabin & neat frame of the New England settler looked over the river to an Indian village where council smoke is still seen & the scalp dance still celebrated." Inside the 1930's-era post office at Wabasha a colorful mural depicts that pre-European time, showing two Indians on a bluff overlooking the Mississippi as they puff out smoke signals with a blanket. On East 3d Street stands the Gothic-style Grace Episcopal Church (1900), listed on the National Register, designed by Cass Gilbert, architect for the state Capitol, the U.S. Supreme Court and other noteworthy buildings. West of town, the Arrowhead Bluffs Exhibits (May-Dec Sun-Th 10-9, F and Sat 10-7) include wildlife, pioneer and Indian displays, as well as a collection of Winchester rifles. Great River Houseboats at Wabasha (612-565-3378) rents outboard motor-powered three cabin craft which they will train you to operate, so allowing the most grounded landlubber to become a Mississippi riverboat pilot. On Hiawatha Drive outside town stands the boxy, brick, National Register-listed Velvet Rooster restaurant, installed in a building which once formed part of the Wabasha County poor farm, established at the site in 1873, where indigents lived and performed chores.

The River Road passes through sleepy Kellogg, a once lively town eventually bypassed by the railroad, where the spires of United Methodist and St. Agnes Churches seem to vie with one another. PJ's Bed and Breakfast in Kellogg offers accommodations (507-767-2203). Continuing south, tree-filled bluffs line the Wisconsin shore across the river, along this stretch relatively pure and pollution-free due to Lake Pepin's filtering action and the fast flowing waters of the Chippewa, whose currents have formed many sandy beaches (difficult of access without a boat) in the area.

At Weaver survives the 1875 Register-listed Mercantile Building and not much else. In 1955 artist Carl E. Noble and his wife Marie moved into the two story brick Italianate-style structure, where he established his studio, residence and a gallery. Murals and paintings by Noble, originally an editorial cartoonist and then an advertising artist, decorate the store-house, now run by his widow (he died in 1973) as a bed and breakfast establishment (507-767-2244). The whimsical Safari Room includes zebra-striped sheets and walls, while on the kitchen wall appears a large mural by Noble of the Mississippi as the artist saw it in 1972 through the window before trees blocked the river from view.

Tiny Minneiska, founded in 1851, formerly thrived as a wheat shipping center, but the town declined with the arrival of the railroad, a development which took place up and down the Mississippi and provoked rivermen to spit a curse on each train track as they crossed. Beyond Minneiska rise Faith, Hope and Charity, three limestone bluffs in John Latsch State Wayside Park with trails to their tops, which afford panoramic views of the Mississippi. Just north of Minnesota City stretches Lock and Dam Number 5, the dam an impressive six hundred feet long and equipped with fully thirty-four gates, while on the Wisconsin shore above the dam runs a three mile long earth dike.

Minnesota City occupies the site of a failed communal settlement promoted by the Western Farm and Village Association, a group of New York mechanics who proposed to establish a new town called Rollingstone City there on the Mississippi. In 1852 when the first settlers reached Galena, Illinois, to board steamers headed north carrying an illustrated map of the seemingly developed settlement, they refused to believe the boatmen who insisted that no such place existed. Fortified by the map which depicted a substantial community—in fact, only the proposed town—the settlers demanded to be taken to the site, a wild and undeveloped place which attracted four hundred people before word finally reached New York that Rollingstone City existed only on paper (although a different Rollingstone, settled in 1855 by immigrants from Luxembourg, now lies up the valley to the west).

Winona, just to the south, enjoyed greater success. Captain Orrin Smith, skipper of the *Nominee*, founded the settlement in 1851 as a supply point for wood to feed the steamer's furnace. Winona may be the Mississippi's only city of any size originally established by a riverboat pilot. The town quickly became a leading lumber center, with ten sawmills and more than 2000 workers producing some 115 million board feet a year. By 1860 Winona's population (2464) nearly matched that of Minneapolis (2564). After the Civil War, Winona developed into the nation's fourth largest primary grain market, a trade which attracted boats by the hundreds—in one year nearly 8600—to the levee. In time, however, the lumber and grain trades dwindled—as elsewhere along the upper Mississippi—and the town diversified into other commercial activities which by the 1930's enabled Winona to deem itself the nation's wealthiest city of its size. Solid old structures—nearly half of the city's houses date from the nineteenth century—testify to Winona's prosperous past. In the downtown area remain such landmarks, all listed on the National Register, as the 1857 Huff-Lamverton House, an Italianate-style villa; the 1900 Renaissance Revival-style Exchange Building, which housed the Grain and Lumber exchange; the H. Choate department store, built in 1888 by "merchant prince" Hannibal Choate as successor to his original wood frame emporium, spared in an 1862 blaze as firefighters were induced to appear there by promises of whiskey for services rendered; the 1897 Public Library, an Italian-style villa of the type designed by sixteenth century architect Andrea Palladio; the splendid Prairie-style Merchants National Bank (1912), a huge brick cube with detailed terra cotta trim outside and inside stained glass windows and murals of area landscapes; and the heavy-set stone 1888 Winona County Courthouse. An earlier courthouse project helped preserve the city's Mississippi-based prosperity. When the river's currents created a new channel some distance away from the waterfront in 1857, the city's leader's hastened to eliminate the threat by announcing a plan to build a courthouse out of stone from Wisconsin. After they quarried the material at the bluffs across the river, the barge transporting the huge load of building blocks just happened to sink where the stones blocked the new channel, so forcing steamboats again to follow the old route which led to Winona.

Old and unusual architecture abounds in Winona, but perhaps the most curious building in town is the Winona National and Savings Bank, one of the nation's relatively rare Egyptian Revival-style structures. Resembling a temple from Pharoanic Egypt, the bank building seems to belong more on the banks of the Nile than there on the Mississippi. Stained glass and bronze work by the famous Tiffany Studios of New York embellish the interior, which also houses a collection of items from an African safari the founders once took and, upstairs (reached by a pair of sinuous staircases), elegant furnishings. Nearby rises another structure which mimics an archaic style, the Armory (1915), replica of a medieval fortress, originally used as a troop center and now as the county history museum (M-F 10-5, Sat and Sun 1-5). Around the corner stands The Hotel, a still functioning establishment (507-452-5460) installed in a restored (1980) century-old building constructed by the Schlitz Brewing Company, one of a handful of vintage hostelries along the river which evoke early days on the Mississippi.

Old times on the river also linger at the nearby Julius C. Wilkie Steamboat Museum (May-Oct 9-5, Nov-April by appointment only: 507-454-6880), a life-sized replica "moored" (actually emplaced) at Levee Park. In 1956, the County Historical Society purchased the steamer *Pearson* and installed the ship (renamed for a donor) at the levee where it remained until destroyed by fire in 1981. Two years later the replica opened, crammed with river-related exhibits, including early photos, models of steamers, Mississippi memorabilia, and a collection of original letters and documents written by steamboat inventor Robert Fulton. Magenta tassel-fringed drapes and chairs and other such plush touches embellish the period-decorated Grand Salon, which recalls the opulent "floating palaces" that once plied the waterway. Winona's annual Steamboat Days festival in early July celebrates the city's river heritage, also remembered with river scene murals on the concrete dike wall below the Julius C. Wilkie. The endearingly small paddlewheeler *Jollie Ollie*, moored by Levee Park, offers excursions (May-Oct, 507-454-6027) on the Mississippi, while for land-based views of the river you can drive along the levee. Beneath the nearby web-like steel girder bridge a farmer's market operates in the summer and fall (June-Oct on Saturdays 7:30-2, July-Sept also Wednesday 11:30-4). The river also dominates the scene as seen from the upstairs dining room at Zach's On the Tracks, installed in an old brick building, and at Finn & Sawyer's, a modern restaurant perched above the waterway.

Winona boasts the headquarters of one of the river's most important nature areas, the Upper Mississippi National Wildlife and Fish Refuge. This encompasses 200,000 acres of wooded islands, marshes and waters two to five miles wide and extends more than two hundred and sixty miles southward along the river bottoms past some seventy towns from Wabasha to Rock Island, Illinois. Congress established the Refuge in 1924 as a preserve for smallmouth bass. After the locks and dams built in the 1930's created marshy pools rich with aquatic plants providing food and habitat for wildlife, the emphasis shifted to migratory waterfowl. The Upper Mississippi Refuge—one of about four hundred and fifty such natural preserves, twenty-five of them along the Mississippi—contains some two hundred and seventy bird species, fifty-seven types of mammals, forty-five amphibian and reptile species and one hundred and thirteen kinds of fish. Bald eagles winter in the Refuge, and during the fall migration down the Mississippi Flyway—an important bird route—up to three-quarters of the canvasback duck population in North America arrives along the river not far south of Winona. A convenient place to get an idea of the environment found in the Refuge, visited by more than three million people a year, is Prairie Island Nature Trail, a few miles north of Winona, which includes an observation deck overlooking a Mississippi River backwater slough teeming with wildlife.

Back in town, a few other diverse local attractions lend Winona a varied ambiance. The Polish Museum (May-Oct M-F 10-3, closed Sat, Sun 1-3) occupies the former Laird Norton Lumber Company building, a firm which employed many of the immigrants who arrived from Poland in the last half of the nineteenth century. The museum contains photos, household items, religious articles and other displays reflecting the local Polish culture. The company vault, where workers collected their $1 per day wages, paid in gold, now houses the gift shop. The 1894 St. Stanislaus church, with its eclectic architecture and silvery dome perched atop a high roof, also recalls the old country. Another dome-topped structure just up Liberty Street, a rather heavy-set block-long building (1913), houses the headquarters of Watkins, Incorporated, founded in 1868 (moved to Winona in 1885) by Joseph R. Watkins, whose salesmen peddled "Dr. Ward's Liniment" from horse-drawn wagons of the sort displayed in the lobby. Watkins—the world's oldest direct-selling company—initiated what is believed to have been the first money-back guarantee for a consumer product, molding into the liniment bottles a "trial mark" line so that customers could consume up to one quarter of the potion before deciding if they wanted a refund. The huge arched ceiling of this cathedral of commerce—once supposedly the nation's largest single-firm office building—glistens with colored glass, while the dome bears blue and gold mosaic work. The retail store off the lobby sells a selection of Watkins' extracts (the vanilla variety remains the company's most famous product), spices, health and beauty aids, personal care items, and household products (for a catalog: 800-533-8018).

In 1924 Paul Watkins, the founder's nephew, constructed a thirty-nine room Tudor-style mansion, listed on the National Register, known as "the house that vanilla built," which contains a large collection of artwork (tours of the house, now a nursing home, by appointment: 507-454-4670). Another firm with local associations is Winona Knits which claims to be the country's oldest and largest sweater retailer, and whose severely modern new (1990) store stands by a pond out on highway 61 (other Winona Knits outlets along the Mississippi include shops in Minnesota at St. Paul and Red Wing, and at Galena, Illinois; for information: 800-888-2007). Near the store stands Sugar Loaf Mountain, a five hundred foot high elevation which once served as a landmark for early river pilots when the Mississippi's main channel passed through Lake Winona just below. The peak's present shape resulted from quarrying operations which left an eighty-five foot pinnacle projecting above the rock dome. Sixty-two years after the extraction of limestone and dolomite ended in 1888, the D.A.R. bought the peak and donated it to the city. Garvin Heights, a short distance to the north, gives a panorama onto the Mississippi and the surrounding countryside similar to the view seen by the Sioux in bygone years when the Indians tended signal fires atop Sugar Loaf. Carriage House Bed and Breakfast (507-452-8256) near downtown Winona puts up guests in a three story garage built in 1870 to accommodate six carriages.

At Homer, a few miles south of Winona, stands the National Register-listed Bunnell House (Memorial Day, Labor Day, M-Sat 10-5, Sun 1-5, weekend only through mid-Oct), built in the late 1850's by Indian trader Willard Bradley Bunnell, who named the settlement after his birthplace in Homer, New York. Built of Northern White Pine and never painted, the Gothic Revival antique-filled residence nestles tucked into a hillside just by the Mississippi. Another delightful relic of the nineteenth century survives at nearby Pickwick, where a restored six story limestone and timber watermill (1858) vividly evokes the old days. The facility ground up to one hundred barrels of flour a day which wagons hauled to La Moille, now the site of Lock and Dam Number 6, for shipment to the east coast or overseas. In the late nineteenth century a turbine made the waterwheel obsolete and roller mills replaced the mill stones. With those improvements the firm no longer ground flour for farmers' personal use or for bulk sale but began to produce a commercial product marketed under the brand name "Itasca". A flood on Big Trout Creek threatened the mill in 1980, two years after it ceased production, but area citizens formed a group (they call their newsletter "The Daily Grind") to preserve and restore the relic. In 1977 the Minnesota State Historical Society had adjudged it the state's best facility to indicate the history of nineteenth century flour milling.

O.L. Kipp State Park, a few miles south, offers scenic overlooks with views onto the Mississippi from high on the bluffs bordering the river. It was from an elevation very near here —perhaps at Gwinn's Bluff, three miles north of Dakota, 1176 feet above sea level and about six hundred feet above the waterway—where Stephen H. Long, a topographical engineer, paused in 1817 to enjoy the panorama while traveling upriver on an assignment to map the West: "Lay'd by a while to ascend another hill said to be the highest on the Mississippi... The view from its summit direct to the river is rendered exceedingly terrific by one of the most frightful precipices I ever beheld... The beauty, grandeur & magnificence of the scene completely baffles description."

This southeastern corner of Minnesota, typified by a rugged landscape with steep slopes, rock outcroppings and deep valleys, owes its contours, which offer "exceedingly terrific" panoramas, to having escaped the glacial action which a million years ago levelled the terrain farther north. During the Ice Age the huge ice sheets pushed southward in four advances, covering almost a third of the earth's surface under a frozen layer as much as a mile thick. The ice never covered southeastern Minnesota and northern Iowa, where the glaciers split and by-passed a stretch three hundred miles below the Chippewa River to leave an unflattened region known as the "Driftless Area". From the O.L. Kipp State Park you can see the five hundred foot Queen's Bluff, a curious relic of Ice Age action much studied by botanists. On the sunny south side the bluff contains prairie terrain, while on the north slopes grow dark conifer groves, its tree types remnants of the glacial age when the advancing ice forced into the area flora whose natural habitat lies above five thousand feet.

At Dakota you can continue south along Highway 61, the River Road, or follow the Apple Blossom Scenic Drive, which parallels the Road just to the west. The highway takes you alongside the island-clotted river to Dresbach, site of a mid-nineteenth century limestone quarry, where Lock and Dam Number 7, completed in 1935, crosses the waterway. Some 1200 commercial vessels and more than ten times as many recreational boats pass through the lock every year. Farther on lies La Crescent, the terminus of that eight mile long scenic route which runs along the ridge above the Mississippi as the road passes through the orchards—established in 1856—that make the area Minnesota's apple center, commemorated by the annual Apple-fest held in mid-September. Six orchards produce nearly twenty-five varieties of the fruit, sold at stands and shops in and around

La Crescent. You'll also find on offer at many places Mississippi Brittle, a rich and addictive pecan-laced English toffee confection made locally by Sara Weihaupt (for mail orders: 507-643-6279).

La Crescent took its name as a foil to La Crosse, its sister city across the river in Wisconsin. When the early settlers, mostly from Kentucky, platted the town the Mississippi stood at flood stage, so the surveyors supposed the new settlement sat by the river. But the town in fact stood on a backwater, forcing people to ferry out to the main waterway. In 1855 the *Wild Kate*, a toll ferry, started up to connect La Crescent and La Crosse, and later the *Honey Eye*—which built up so much steam it paused halfway across to simmer down—entered service. The National Register-listed 1871 Daniel Cameron House in La Crescent, topped by a boxy lookout, belonged to the brother of fur trader Peter Cameron, the earliest settler, who arrived in 1851.

The River Road south, Highway 26, passes through a sparsely settled rural area. In the Mississippi bob buoys to mark the channel. At Brownsville—once a lively settlement, with a bustling commercial area—survives the starkly simple wooden Church of the Holy Comforter, listed on the National Register. It was built in 1869, some twenty years after arrival of the first settlers, among them a character named "Wild Cat Jack", who accidentally shot himself in a gun fight with town founder Job Brown. Between Brownswille and Reno (near which, out of sight, lies Lock and Dam Number 8) the winding riverside road offers splendid views of the Mississippi, here quite wide. Off to the east, on the opposite shore in Wisconsin, lie wooded bluffs, and not far south a green and white sign welcoming you to Iowa indicates the end of the River Road's Minnesota itinerary. At this point the Mississippi has passed through ten of its twenty-nine locks and dams and has flowed along for more than one quarter of its 2552 mile long course from Lake Itasca to the Gulf.

MINNESOTA PRACTICAL INFORMATION

Phone numbers of tourist offices in Minnesota's principal Mississippi River cities: Aitkin: 218-927-3003; Bemidji: 800-2920-2223; Brainerd 800-432-3775 (also in Brainerd is the state's regional tourist office: 218-828-2334, in Minnesota 800-345-2537); Grand Rapids: 800-472-6366; Itasca State Park: 218-266-3654; Little Falls: 612-632-5155; Minneapolis: 612-348-4313; Red Wing: 612-388-4719; St. Cloud: 612-251-2940 (in Minnesota 800-247-1058, ext. 220); St. Paul: 800-627-6101; Wabasha: 612-565-3829; Winona: 507-452-2272.

Other useful numbers for travels along the Mississippi River include:

Minnesota Travel Information Center: 800-657-3700; Minnesota Department of Natural Resources (information on state parks and other outdoor areas): 800-652-9747; Minnesota Historical Society: 800-657-3773; Chippewa National Forest: 218-335-2226. The state of Minnesota operates highway travel information centers at Dresbach and in St. Cloud. For information on biking: 612-297-1838; for bicycle trail maps: 800-652-9747 in Minnesota. For Mississippi River canoe rentals: Headwaters Canoe Outfitters (located in Bemidji), 218-751-2783.

The U.S. Army Corps of Engineers (St. Paul): 612-220-0200. Mississippi River navigation charts are available M-F 9:30-2 at room 1033, 180 East Kellogg, St. Paul.

Special Places Inc., 612-938-3326, is a bed and breakfast booking agency, and Michel Farm Vacations, 507-886-5392, places guests in farms and cottages in southeastern Minnesota.

Organizations for people with a special interest in the Mississippi include: Mississippi River Revival, 612-871-1149, a Minnesota-based group (its motto:"She'll be clean once more") which promotes clean river causes, and the Great River Road Association, headquartered in St. Paul: 612-224-9903, which is also the number for the quasi-official Mississippi River Parkway Commission.

2. WISCONSIN

"There is no more beautiful country in the world than that which is to be seen in this vicinity", wrote artist George Catlin in 1841 about the bluff-lined upper Mississippi River which forms the 250 miles of Wisconsin's "West Coast", the state's border with Minnesota and Iowa. For much of its route in Wisconsin, the River Road winds its way between the great waterway and those craggy cliffs, striking features which present a series of splendid vistas along this stretch of the Mississippi.

At Prescott, Wisconsin's westernmost city, the 170 mile long St. Croix—a National Scenic River, and the world's only waterway protected along its entire length—pours its blue waters into the brown Mississippi, doubling its volume. In 1860 French explorer and trader Daniel Greysolon, Sieur du Lhut, whose name designates the Lake Superior port city of Duluth, discovered the river route which linked the lake with the Mississippi, via the Brule and St. Croix Rivers, and for the next century and a half trappers and traders followed this canoe connection. During the timber era in the nineteenth century woodsmen floated rafts of logs down the St. Croix to the Mississippi, which then carried them south. Prescott, founded in 1839 by Philander Prescott, a land agent for army officers at Minnesota's nearby Fort Snelling, began to develop in the 1850's when river roustabouts who ran the rafts frequented the town. The 1853 Daniel Smith House in Prescott recalls the era. Just to the south the Steamboat Inn, built to suggest an old fashioned river boat, perches on the St. Croix by the spiffy new auto bridge that seems to upstage the rusty old railway draw bridge which spans the mouth of the St. Croix. At tiny Mercord Mill Park you can see where that tributary enters the Mississippi, here 520 miles downstream from its source at Lake Itasca in north-central Minnesota. For bed and breakfast in Prescott Inn-on-the-Hill (715-262-4288) and Oak Street Inn (715-262-41100) take guests, while near River Falls to the northeast Knollwood House (715-425-1040) offers rooms in a renovated farmhouse.

The River Road, Highway 35, heads south through its most hilly stretch in Wisconsin. The route winds and climbs and dips its way to Diamond Bluff, whose name recalls that in the late nineteenth century in Pierce County diamonds were found. Scientists theorize that ages ago a glacier carried the gemstones to the area from a deposit in Canada. The glaciers, however, stopped near here, sparing the southwest corner of Wisconsin, including the section along the Mississippi. That so called "Driftless Area" remained a region untouched by the ice, which flattened much of the countryside—now gently rolling farmland—to the north, but left the bluffs, some rising 500 feet, standing along the river. In the side of one bluff a few miles east of the river and north of Bay City appears a large bow and arrow rock outline, first noticed in 1902 by Minnesota archaeologist Jacob V. Brower. Visible across a corn field from the highway, the formation remains a mystery, for no one knows its date or how the figure relates to Indian lore or traditions.

Less puzzling is another bluff called Maiden Rock just to the south which towers 400 feet above the Mississippi a little north of Stockholm. The town of Maiden Rock, located between Bay City and Stockholm lies not far from where the waterway widens into Lake Pepin, formed by sand deposited in the river by the Chippewa tributary about twenty miles downstream. Maiden Rock's name recalls an old Indian legend. One version of the tale relates how Dakota Chief Red Wing tried to force his daughter, Winona, to marry Kewanee, also a Dakota, a band of the Sioux, even though she pined for Chippewa brave White Eagle. When Kewanee lavished gifts on Winona, Red Wing ordered the wedding to take place, but the brokenhearted maiden retreated to the bluff, sang a death song and plunged to the water below. Even as late as 1851—long after most of the other tribes had buried the hatchet—the Sioux and the Chippewa continued to do battle in this area. At Maiden Rock the IGA store houses a doll collection, and the old school building now serves as an arts center. At the south end of town, above the River Road, perches the Harrisburg Inn (715-448-4500), a bed and breakfast place with views onto the Mississippi (Lake Pepin).

Thanks to the bluffs and the river's great width, the thirty mile stretch between Maiden Rock and Alma offers some of the most striking scenery found along the entire length of the Mississippi. You'll come first to Stockholm, established by Swedish immigrants in 1855. A pleasant village of just over 100 people, Stockholm contains many reminders of its Old World heritage: Swedish flags brighten the town while the Stockholm Cafe, which offers area tours and river cruise bookings (715-442-5162), sports a Swedish crown and post horn symbol, and an eatery installed in a bright white "gingerbread"-trimmed Victorian era building bears the name Jenny Lind Cafe. The post office also houses the Mississippi Pearl Jewelry Company, which sells pearls plucked from river clams. Down the street in the 1903 former general store the attractive Amish Country shop offers hand-made Amish quilts, wall hangings, furniture and other such items, all of them crafted with simplicity and taste. Next to the Stockholm Antique shop across the street stands the 1864 Merchants Hotel (715-442-2113, open April-Nov), a delightful old fashioned inn. The Stockholm Institute next door houses a one room museum of town history, including old photos and riverboat posters. Although Stockholm went into decline after World War II, the town revived in the early 1970's when artists and craftspeople began to arrive in the village, one of the most picturesque settlements on Wisconsin's River Road.

Between Stockholm and Pepin on the shore of Lake Pepin lies the site of Fort St. Antoine, built in 1686 by Nicholas Perrot, a French explorer and fur trader. Fearing increased English influence in the area, the French government decided formally to claim the territory, so in May 1689 Perrot held a ceremony at the fort to take possession in the name of Louis XIV of the entire region west of the Great Lakes "no matter how remote". Thus did the Sun King, in far off France, become the first official sovereign to rule over the unruly upper Mississippi valley. These formalities perhaps impressed a few Indians but certainly not the English, for the empty exercise recalled the realities French explorer Pierre Radisson noted in his journal while wintering in a remote north woods area in 1660: "We weare cesars being nobody to contradict us." In this region, as in much of the rest of the Mississippi Valley, the French failed to press their advantage; they established few permanent settlements. As John R. Spears observed in *A History of the Mississippi Valley*, "the French were trying to take the wild region for a vast game preserve, wherein to gather furs, while the British were trying to get it for home sites." Even nearly a century later, in the 1760's, when the French ceded this portion of their North American territory to England after the French and Indian War, France possessed no permanent settlements along the upper Mississippi.

At Pepin a small commercial area stretches along the Mississippi. At the corner of Main and First overlooking the marina stands the accurately named blue-hued Harbor View Cafe, while the Ship's Wheel restaurant at the port—filled with bright white sailboats tucked into the shore—runs the tour ship *Zephyr*, which offers cruises on the Mississippi (715-422-4900). At the south end of First the Pickle Factory, another eatery, occupies a barn-like building once home of the Pepin Pickling Company, established in 1904. It produced pickles and sauerkraut until the operation closed in 1937. Half a century later the facility was recycled into a restaurant which opened in 1988. On Second

Street, next to Dan's Cash Store grocery, which occupies a century old general store building, Tom and Kitty Latané operate a metalsmith workshop and store (F-Sun 11-5) offering the couple's hand-forged early-American and medieval-style wares. The Pepin Historical Museum (May 15-Oct 15, 10-5) stands on Third Street, the River Road (Highway 35). The rustic wood building contains old household items, antique furniture and books and memorabilia relating to author Laura Ingalls Wilder, born near Pepin in 1867. A few blocks north of the museum Wilder Memorial Park, so named in 1962 to honor the local celebrity, includes a small museum (May 15-Oct 15, 8-5) in the old Burlington Northern depot. The building was moved twice before finally settling at that site, and thus no doubt is the line's best traveled station. Near the depot stands a remnant of the trains' great rival, the once dominant steamship whose era the railroads hastened to an end—the anchor and chain from the *Phil Scheckel*, a Chippewa River craft commanded in the last half of the nineteenth century by Captain Scheckel, supposedly that waterway's most renowned pilot.

On Highway 183 seven miles east of Pepin—where Pepin Prairie Winds (715-442-2149) offers bed and breakfast—you'll find the Little House Wayside, a copy of the cabin where Laura Ingalls was born. But this rather too neatly fabricated version of the old-time homestead recalls Wilder's comment: "Now is now. It can never be a long time ago." Wilder began her writing career at age sixty-five with *Little House in the Big Woods*, set in the Pepin area. Surprised by the book's success, she commented, "I was amazed because I didn't know how to write. I went to little red school houses all over the West and I never graduated from anything."

Thirty miles long by three miles (at the widest) Lake Pepin, an enlargement of the Mississippi, owes its existence to the sandbars formed by the Chippewa River, whose mouth lies just south of Pepin. Sand and sediment washed into the Mississippi from its banks or carried into the river by tributaries eventually created obstacles hazardous to navigation. The Chippewa is considered one of the worst offenders, for the river constantly brings sediment into the Mississippi. In 1878 Congress first mandated the Army Corps of Engineers to dredge "problem areas of the river to a depth of 4 ½ feet, that vessels might pass through without mishap". Nearly thirty years later officials approved a six foot channel, but not until 1939 did the present nine foot channel open. The Corps of Engineers bears the responsibility for maintaining this channel along 860 miles of navigable waters in the upper Mississippi. The Corps' St. Louis District clears the route between Cairo, Illinois, where the Ohio River enters the Mississippi, up to near Hannibal, Missouri; the Rock Island district covers (or uncovers) the river north to Guttenberg, Iowa; and the St. Paul District handles the 242 ½ miles from there to the Twin Cities. After the annual spring flooding the Corps, using poles or by electronic means, surveys the river to check the channel. The St. Paul District employs three main dredging units, two hydraulic and one mechanical, which remove from 100,000 to 1 million cubic yards of material every year: the 47-person crew *William A. Thompson,* whose 20 inch pipeline can carry away 25,000 cubic yards a day; the *Hauser,* a mechanical dredge, manned by a crew of 38, with a bucket able to scoop up 3500 cubic yards a day; and the *Dubuque,* with 18 crewmen, outfitted with a 12 inch pipeline capable of collecting up to 5000 cubic yards daily.

Apart from the Chippewa's sand and silt which constantly vexes the Mississippi, the tributary also carried a more useful cargo. Back in the late nineteenth century timber firms floated millions of logs down the waterway and then on to mills farther south along the Mississippi. At Beef Slough, a warren of coves, backwaters and bayous at the Chippewa's mouth, lumbermen sorted the logs and identified each with a stamp punched into the end by a mall-driven disk. Workmen assembled 50 by 5000 foot log rafts, called a "brail", which the men surrounded with a frame of logs attached to one another with chains connected to plugs embedded in the ends. Four to six chained brails formed a huge raft, guided down the Mississippi by crews housed in rough cabins built on the floating felled forest. Raft pilots, who earned $5 or more a day (in 1850's) for the three week float down to St. Louis could, in a year when the water was good, complete five trips. The eight or so crewmen on a raft each received $1-2 a day. Mills and lumberyards along the Iowa and Illinois shore bought the logs, with any left over sold at St. Louis. Occasionally floods washed logs away from their winter storage areas in sloughs or piled on the banks, and scavengers would harvest the stray wood to use for construction.

In 1866 the "Beef Slough War" erupted. The conflict arose when mill owners in Chippewa Falls and Eau Claire acquired land at the mouth of the Chippewa in an attempt to block shipment of logs to competing downstream mills. Those firms organized the Beef Slough Manufacturing, Booming, Log Driving and Transportation Company to fight their Wisconsin rivals. When the Mississippi River group tried to establish improved log-handling facilities at the slough, the upstream elements threatened to prevent the addition by force of arms. The dispute ended when a ruling decreed that the Chippewa had to be kept open for navigation, and so the log rafts continued to sail down the Mississippi.

Although 70 per cent of Wisconsin's rivers drain into the Mississippi, apart from the logging trade, the waterway did not play a major role in the state's commercial life. "The Mississippi never held the importance for Wisconsin agriculture that it held for neighboring Iowa and Minnesota," stated Robert C. Nesbit in *Wisconsin: A History*. "This was partly because the rivers that flow into the Mississippi from Wisconsin were not suitable for navigation. The largest of these, the Wisconsin, was shoaled and did not develop as a carrier except for logs and lumber rafts."

South of the Chippewa River and Lake Pepin lies Nelson, founded in 1844, later a way-station for lumberjacks heading to timber camps in the Chippewa Valley. The town offers River Road travelers an opportunity to see where one of Wisconsin's most typical products is made. Inside the Nelson Cheese Factory, installed in a tin-roofed building just by the highway, gleam the plant's stainless steel equipment, while an array of cheese tempts visitors to the factory store. Milk cows first arrived in Wisconsin in the late 1830's, and the state's first cheese factory started up in 1864. The industry began to flourish in the 1870's, with cheddar and colby—an original Wisconsin type, a milder and moister version of cheddar—the most popular varieties. By the turn of the century, when 90 per cent of Wisconsin's farms owned dairy cattle—17 per cent were primarily dairy farms—the state produced more than a quarter of the nation's cheese, and within twenty years almost two-thirds. At one time, some thousand cheese factories operated in Wisconsin, whose license plates boast "America's Dairyland", but by the 1980's only about half that number survived, one of them the Nelson Cheese Factory, now run by the fifth generation of the family which owns it.

Back before the cheese era Nelson served as a ferry town. After Englishman James Nelson settled there in 1834, a ferry ran between this point, called Nelson's Landing, and Reed's Landing in Minnesota. Madison Wright, the first permanent resident on the Wisconsin side, who arrived in 1848, started to trade in Wabasha, Minnesota, across the Mississippi, where he eventually spent most of his time, seldom visiting Nelson. After he died, Wabasha sent the Nelson town board a bill for the funeral, but the Wisconsin settlement replied that since Wright had spent most of his time, and all of his money in Wabasha, they should bury him. A new (1988) bridge now connects the two towns, permitting Nelson residents to visit Wabasha and then easily return home, thus avoiding such post-mortem disputes.

Bayous and backwaters abound in this area. Two, called the Tiffany Bottoms and the Nelson Bottoms, are filled with nooks and coves and crannies where wildlife gathers. Unfortunately, buffalo—recalled by the name of the county and of the stream you cross on the way to Alma—no longer gather to graze on area grasslands, as the nearly extinct beasts did in bygone times. In an account of his 1680 expedition in the region, explorer Louis Hennepin referred to the Mississippi as "the River of Wild Bulls", a reference to the buffalo herds along the waterway. Just north of Alma stretches Beef Slough, an offshoot of the Mississippi, named because a herd of cattle drowned there. Alma, a two street town founded in 1848, lies tucked into the bluffs which tower up to 500 feet over the river. Rivermen called the rise Twelve Mile Bluff as it lies that distance from the Chippewa's mouth upstream. At one time a big boulder hung precariously at the edge of the bluff just above the village, whose inhabitants constantly feared the threatening rock, which finally fell in 1891 without causing any damage. From Buena Vista Park above Alma extends an expansive view onto the river as well as its islands, Upper and Lower Wiggle Waggle Sloughs, and the tidy little village, self-designated as "the New England of the Midwest".

Old buildings around town, a National Historic District, include three establishments which take overnight guests: 1866 Sherman House (608-685-4929), with an antique saloon; the 1864 Alma Hotel (608-685-3380); and 1863 Laue House (608-685-4923). The 1897 Queen Anne-style Ibach House perches by one of the stairways which connects Alma's upper and lower streets. The Polin and Tester Building, an 1861 balcony-bedecked structure listed on the National Register, formerly served as a general store and as a grain depot. It now houses an art gallery, gourmet food shop and a three bedroom bed and breakfast inn (608-685-4975). The granddaughter of Jacob Berg, who constructed the building, once recounted the story he told her about the time an Indian from across the Mississippi arrived at the store in search of whiskey. Told that shop did not carry any liquor, the irate brave emptied his gun into the ceiling and threatened to return with his fellow warriors to attack the village, but he never showed up again. The small Alma Museum (Sat and Sun May-Oct) contains an old-time doctor's office along with exhibits on local history, while the town Historic Society offers walking tours (608-685-4975).

Alma is one of the few places along the Mississippi where a lock and dam exists right by the city. An elevated walkway over the train tracks leads to a viewing platform. Up and downstream lie river-related facilities, including two places which rent houseboats for excursions on the Mississippi: Cruising Houseboats (608-685-3333) at the marina, just north of Lock and Dam Number 4, and Great River Harbor (608-248-2454), three miles south of Alma, home town of Dr. Arnold Gesell who founded the well known Gesell Institute of Child Development in New Haven, Connecticut. From the very beginning, the river played a role in the life of Alma, settled by Swiss immigrants who cut cordwood there to sell to steamers for fuel. The town became a logging and wheat port, serving as one of the main grain shipping points between La Crosse down-river and St. Paul. The arrival of the railroad in 1883 diminished the grain trade and even physically cut the town away from its river heritage, for the tracks separate the settlement from the waterway.

Just south of Alma's business district stand two huge smokestacks at the Dairyland Power Cooperative Plant. Farther on adjacent to Cochrane, named for the engineer on the first train through town, lies Buffalo, the state's smallest incorporated city (population: 894), whose seven public parks give it the nickname "City of Parks". Merrick State Park, to the south, takes its name from George Byron Merrick, a Mississippi pilot, who became an historian of the upper river.

Brick buildings on the north side of Fountain City—named for the many springs which emerge from the bluffs—house a

Corps of Engineers service facility, including a boat yard where the dredge *Thompson* moors. Founded in 1839 as Holmes Landing, Fountain City nestles beneath towering Indian Head Rock and 550-foot Eagle Bluff, one of the highest points on the river. Terraced gardens and hill-side houses lie on the lower sections of the steep rise. A scattering of old brick buildings lend the town a nineteenth century atmosphere, while the half-timber chalet-like bank building, embellished with seal emblems of Swiss cantons, recalls Switzerland. This Wisconsin "Swiss bank" on the Mississippi's bank does not house any secret numbered accounts or bars of bullion, but it does boast another treasure—a rare albino male deer, mounted and on display. The riverside Captain's Supper Club in Fountain City claims that "When you dine at Captain's, you're the captain and we're the crew"—a nautical slogan sure to please the most confirmed land-lubber. Just south of Lock and Dam 5A, about five miles south of Fountain City, bobs Freddie's Fishing Float, supposedly the Mississippi's only floating bar, where you can fish, sip and laze away the day watching the waterway flow by. The hamlet of Bluff Siding, not far south, took its descriptive name from the railroad siding once installed there to pull trains over when the line to Winona, just across the river in Minnesota, included only a single track.

As you head toward Trempealeau, slightly off to the east lies Galesville, which offers an old town square, listed on the National Register; antique shops; High Cliff Park, with a swinging foot-bridge to Beaver Creek's spring-fed source waters and the Register-listed Ridge Avenue Residential District, by Lake Marinuka. Nearby is the 15-room Italian-style house, also on the Register, at A.A. Arnold's Eastside Farm, established by a New England gentleman farmer, which includes inside the barn what was supposedly the nation's first up-right silo. You'll also find in town the Lloyd Scarseth Primitive Art Museum. Two places in Galesville take bed and breakfast guests: Barenthin House

(608-582-2320) and Clark House (608-582-4190). Southeast of town stands Decorah Peak, named for a one-eyed Winnebago chief who signed a treaty with federal authorities in 1825, and who in 1832 accompanied Black Hawk to Prairie du Chien when the Sauk chief surrendered after the Black Hawk War. Between Galesville and Trempealeau runs a nature trail which follows an old railroad line that once connected the two cities.

North of Trempealeau off Highway 35 stretches a nearly 6000 acre National Wildlife Refuge, mostly wetlands, with a 4 ½-mile long self-guided driving tour. Farther south lies Perrot State Park, where in 1685 French explorer and fur trader Nicholas Perrot established an outpost. Two centuries after Perrot's presence in the area a railroad work crew unearthed remnants of his fireplaces, and later excavations found other traces of the trader's post. The park includes Indian mounds, hiking trails, Perrot Ridge, and the even higher 520-foot Brady's Bluff, complete with a view of squat Mount Trempealeau, a longtime Mississippi landmark which gave its name to the nearby town, river and county. Indians called the 384-foot high peak "Soaking Mountain" and "Bluff in the Water", as the hill appears to rise directly from the water. As early as 1731 the French described the formation the same way in their language, "la montagne qui trempe à l'eau", a phrase whose last three words came to designate the area's features. Past the park and through the Refuge runs a 22 mile biking and hiking trail, opened in 1988, which cuts across the Mississippi River bottomland.

In 1886 Reverend David Van Slyke, a Galesville Methodist minister, published a pamphlet entitled "The Garden of Eden", a tract which argued that because four rivers—the Mississippi, Trempealeau, Beaver, and Black—flowed through the serpent-filled (rattlesnakes) pastoral area, the valley conformed to the Biblical description of the Garden in Genesis 2:8-14. Bluffs at the end of the valley, Van Slyke maintained, represented the gate of the Garden of Eden.

Although the town of Trempealeau does not exactly evoke the paradise where Adam and Eve dwelled, the idyllic little settlement does offer a delightful old-time Mississippi River village atmosphere. Here, as much as anywhere else along the river, lingers the ambiance of yesteryear, a time when steamers plied the river and small town life flowed along with a smooth and rather regular rhythm, like the calm currents of a country creek. Times now flood forward, Mississippi-like, but sleepy Trempealeau remains a laid back sort of place straight out of another era. Along picturesque Main Street, which rises rather steeply from the river, stand a few late nineteenth century brick buildings with period facades, while across the street stands the venerable National Register-listed Trempealeau Hotel, which sports a triangular colored glass window inscribed "1871", an old sign advertising "Complete dinner 25¢", and a red neon notice which boasts "Good food". The well-windowed dining room, decorated with old photos, affords views out onto the Mississippi, while the eight rooms at the hostelry (608-534-6898), restored and opened in 1988, contain antique furniture and period decor.

Main Street became the town's commercial artery after a fire in 1888 burned the buildings which stood along the river front. Across from the hotel at the bottom of Main stands the accurately named River View Motel (608-534-7784), while a few blocks away the National Register-listed Coman House, a boxy Italianate-style 1850's gallery-surrounded structure, now serves as an antique store (April-Dec F and Sun 12-5, Sat 9-5). Along First Street up river survive the remains of the old Melchoir Brewery, which kept its renowned lager cool in three caves in bluffs behind the factory. By the village stretches Lock and Dam Number 6, completed in 1936 for $5 million, that makes an average of twenty lockages a day, about half of them for commercial tows which every year carry a total of more than 12 million tons of cargo, mainly coal, grain, chemicals and petroleum products. Trempealeau began as Reed's Landing in 1851 when James

Allen Reed, an agent for the fur post based in Prairie du Chien, arrived in the area. Six years later, river boats began putting in at the settlement, followed in 1871 by the railroad, which carried passengers until 1922. Now only fast freights and slow ships pass through to enliven the tranquil old town.

Heading on toward La Crosse, just before you make a sharp right turn off Highway 93 onto U.S. 53 (also designated State Road 35), two miles north of Holmen, you'll pass on the left a marker noting that the stretch of highway from here across the Black River was dedicated on August 21, 1952 as the first portion of the so called Mississippi River Parkway, or River Road, in Wisconsin. During the late nineteenth century logs and lumber floated to markets farther south down the Black River and on into the Mississippi through nearby Lake Onalaska, rejuvenated in 1989 by the Army Corps of Engineers. Onalaska gained its unusual name from the practice of Thomas G. Rowe, an early tavern owner, of declaiming verses from Thomas Campbell's 1799 "The Pleasures of Hope", which included the line, "The wolf's long howl from Oonalaska's shore". The settlement took the designation (minus the extra "o") of that remote Aleutian Island fishing station, and later one-time resident William A. Carlisle, who moved on, so named towns in Texas (1904) and in Washington state (1914).

By the end of the nineteenth century, the logging industry in the area employed more than 400 workers, including raftsmen and sorters as well as mill hands, who worked in the thirty or so sawmills which operated over the years between Onalaska and nearby La Crosse. Onalaska—"Sunfish Capital of the World" —spreads over a ridge with views onto the river valley and clusters of land in Lake Onalaska, including French Island. La Crosse airport runways criss-cross the island. Just off Fisherman's Road on its east shore, you'll find the National Fishery Research Laboratory, where scientists investigate non-game fish species. In 1989 the Onalaska Historical Museum opened, installed in the new library near the high school. In the area descendants of the Blackdeers still live. The Blackdeers were an Indian family which managed to remain in Onalaska even after federal troops forcibly removed most of the Winnebago to Minnesota between 1848 and 1874.

Fun 'n the Sun (608-783-7326) in Onalaska rents houseboats for self-piloted excursions on the Mississippi. At Onalaska the 22½ mile long Great River Trail starts (or ends) and then follows the abandoned Chicago and Northwestern Railroad bed through Midway and on beyond Trempealeau, crossing eighteen bridges as the path runs along a route just east of the Mississippi.

At West Salem, not far east of Onalaska, another back country route begins, Rustic Road Number 31, one of the fifty-six byways designated by Wisconsin, starting in 1973, as offering especially alluring scenery or natural features. The 2.6 mile itinerary, designated along the way by brown and yellow markers, begins at the West Salem exit off Interstate 90, passes through town to County Highway C, continues north to State Highway 16, loops around Swarthout Lakeside Park, then returns to 16. On the way, you'll pass the National Register-listed Gullickson Octagon House, the 1859 residence (now a museum) of town founder Thomas Leonard, and the homestead of Pulitzer Prize-winning author Hamlin Garland, born in a log cabin near West Salem in 1860. In 1869 the family moved to Iowa and in 1884-89 Garland lived in the east to study at the Boston School of Oratory. After visiting the Midwest in 1887 he began to write stories about his homeland, including the series of books on the "middle border"—*A Daughter of the Middle Border* won the Pulitzer in 1921—an area he later stated "was but a vaguely defined region even in my boyhood. It was the line drawn by the plow and, broadly speaking, ran parallel to the upper Mississippi when I was a lad. It lay between the land of the hunter and the harvester." Garland and his wife Zulime, sister of Illinois sculptor Lorado Taft, spent summers in West Salem at the house he had bought in 1893 for his parents. With earnings from his writings, the native son enhanced life in his hometown by installing at the house West Salem's first indoor bathroom. After a fire damaged the residence in 1912, the author rebuilt it, and now the Hamlin Garland Homestead (Memorial Day-Labor Day 1-5; other times by appointment: 608-786-1399) serves as a museum devoted to the life of the writer, who died in 1940 and reposes in the family plot at Neshonoc cemetery in West Salem. The 500 acre Wolfway Farm (608-486-2686), homesteaded more than 130 years ago by the Wolf family, offers three bed and breakfast rooms on a working dairy farm in the countryside near West Salem.

Well-watered La Crosse stretches along the Mississippi and the Black Rivers and flanks the La Crosse River, which enters the Mississippi just by Riverside Park. Park sights and services recall the city's Mississippi heritage. A museum at the Visitor's Bureau includes river-related exhibits, among them photos of dredging and harvesting ice from the Mississippi, and also of early steamers, such as the *Cotton Blossom* showboat and a water-borne touring Methodist church. The museum also includes items removed from the *War Eagle*, burned and sunk on the Mississippi in 1870 when a cooper upset a lantern on a leaking oil barrel he was repairing, while fish tanks with river specimens include a commentary by "Catfish Charlie". By the park—in which Indian and bald eagle statues stand—moors the *La Crosse Queen*, an old-style paddlewheeler which offers river cruises from May to mid-October (608-784-8523). The *Island Girl* (608-784-0556), moored out at Barron Island on the Mississippi's west channel by the Island Inn (800-447-9676), also offers cruises. Elsewhere in La Crosse, Riverboats Inc. (608-788-4420) and Captain's Cruises (608-784-3088) rent houseboats.

Not far from Riverside Park survive some remnants of old La Crosse, so named for the Indian ball game which reminded early French traders of "la crosse", a phrase used in France, as the racquet for the sport resembled a bishop's crozier.

Across from the box-like Radisson Hotel, perched by the Mississippi, stands the 1865 former Pamperin Tobacco Company, which sports a metal front and a brick fringe along with a sign advertising "high quality cigar clippings". Another relic, the National Register-listed century old Burlington Railroad freight depot, 107 Vine, houses the Freighthouse Restaurant and the adjacent Christina Winery.

More whimsical, if less venerable, is another eatery, Piggy's, 328 S. Front, which sports a picture window view onto the Mississippi. Named National Pork Restaurant of the Year, the establishment includes a huge old bar once supposedly used in a Philadelphia bawdy house, and a menu inviting patrons to "pig out". On sale are hog decorated ties and T-shirts bearing a top hat, cane-carrying, strutting pig.

Even more whimsical than Piggy's amusing menu and motif are the "Cheddarheads" items on sale at T.J.'s, 215 Pearl—shirts, mugs, cards and other novelties decorated with cheese-headed characters created by Wisconsin cartoonist T.J.Peterslie. A wedge-shaped chunk of cheddar forms the head of figures shown in gag scenes: an executive, described as "The Big Cheese"; a barbershop customer asking for just a little slice off the top; corn-headed Iowa football players facing the Wisconsin team warn, "Watch out for that wedge formation."

For the real thing, Hill County Cheese, 728 S. 3rd, sells a selection of the Wisconsin product, including its own type made at the store Thursday, Friday and Saturday. Down the street the late nineteenth century Gantert Building, 110 S. 3rd, houses antique shops, and nearby 1876 Powell Place, 200 Main at 2nd, contains shops and offices. Mr. D's Donut Shop, east of downtown, 1146 State at West Avenue, is a local institution, featuring meals half the day—4:30 a.m. to 4 p.m.—and donuts, fresh baked at 9 p.m., all through the night as well as premium type Kona coffee from Hawaii.

La Crosse's most famous consumable—Heileman's beer—flows from the brewery located not far south of downtown. Free tours (8-4 on the hour M-Sat) take you through the 1982 plant—a sign warns, "Shhh—Heileman Beer Aging Here Slowly, Naturally"—which produces 12, 000 kegs of brew a day. At a console dotted with red and green lights sits the person who, by computer, single-handedly runs the entire brewing operation. Outside the old brew house stands a colorful statue of Gambrinus, "King of Beer", credited with inventing the beverage in the thirteenth century. Across the street rise huge storage vats painted like a six pack, containing 22,000 barrels of brew, equal to more than 7 million cans. Down an alleyway from the house, where brewmaster Gottlieb Heileman lived in the nineteenth century, spigots emerge from a wall. They tap the artesian spring water the brewery uses, a different type of source from that at St. Louis's huge Anheuser-Busch plant (Chapter 5), which takes Mississippi River water for the beer.

Another local factory turns out the nationally distributed La Crosse brand rubber footwear, sold at an outlet store, 1320 St. Andrew, called "The Garage" (M-F 10-6, Sat 9-5, Sun 12-5). The shop stands across from the block-square four story well-windowed plant which seems a relic from the early industrial era. The company began at the site in 1897 when the original factory, located there at Indian Hill (supposedly once owned by Buffalo Bill) produced rubber horseshoes used to outfit city horses. Later the firm, using crude rubber supplied from Ceylon and Brazil, made rubber-coated fabrics and rainwear, then in 1906 switched to rubber shoes and boots, now turned out at a rate of some 20,000 pairs a day. Not far from the La Crosse factory stretches Red Cloud Park, located on the site of a Winnebago village and named to honor Corporal Mitchell Red Cloud, Jr., a Congressional Medal of Honor winner killed in the Korean war. Back to the west but still north of the La Crosse River the aptly named Sweet Shop, 1133 Caledonia in the Northside District, presents a picture out of the past, with an old-time soda fountain, wooden booths, and a one-room candy kitchen, all reminiscent of the era when Cecil Allen founded the firm in 1921. The aroma of chocolate and other such sweet smells permeates the air in the shop; visitors no doubt gain weight simply by inhaling.

Less culinary and more cultural attractions at La Crosse include the National Register-listed Hixon House (Memorial Day-Labor Day 1-5), 429 N. 7th, built in 1859 by lumber barron Gideon Hixon, embellished with embossed velvet and hand-painted canvas walls and outfitted with original furnishings; the Swarthout Museum (Tu-F 10-5, Sat and Sun 1-5, closed Sun June-Aug), 9th and Main, with changing exhibits on the city's history; Smith Valley School Museum (Memorial Day-Labor Day Sun 1-4), an 1887 one-room schoolhouse at 3393 Smith Valley Road, east of town; and the imposing Romanesque-style Mary of the Angels Chapel, 715 S. 9th, and the Perpetual Adoration Chapel. This is definitely not a hyperbolic name, for there, since August 1, 1878, at least two Franciscan Sisters have without interruption been present to pray. Among the local parks are 570 foot Grandad Bluff in Hixon Forest, east of town, with a panoramic view of the Mississippi River Valley which includes parts of three states. Houska Park on Isle La Plume, boasts a three-story observation deck overlooking the river. The river-side Pettibone Park, originally in Minnesota, and traded to Wisconsin in 1917 for land near Winona, occupies Barron Island in the middle of the Mississippi. Finally, Myrick Park, 2000 La Crosse, took its name from town founder Nathan Myrick, who in 1841 built a cabin at the site of present day Pettibone Park.

La Crosse began to develop the next winter when the New York native moved to the mainland. Here in 1844 Myrick began to raft logs from Black River pineries via La Crosse to St. Louis. Sawmills and other logging facilities developed, and in time the town became a leading port, with as many as 200 steamers a month stopping there. In the 1860's, the Northwestern Union

Packet Company, which controlled the steamboat business in the upper Mississippi, maintained its office and a shipyard in town. One of the earliest strikes on the river occured when the firm's Commodore W. F. Davidson refused to raise deckhands' wages. In 1876, eighteen years after the Chicago, Milwaukee, and St. Paul line reached the city, a railroad bridge spanning the Mississippi connected the area with points west, and so began the end of the steamboat era in La Crosse.

On the south side of La Crosse—where Martindale House (608-782-4224), an Italianate-style 1850's residence, listed on the National Register, offers bed and breakfast—lies the Pleasoning Factory, 2418 South Avenue (tours: 800-328-8322, ext.696), which produces low- and no-sodium seasonings, on sale at an outlet store. Also in the area survives the New Villa Restaurant, 2132 Ward Ave., established more than sixty years ago on the site of an early day poultry farm, which suggested the eatery's former slogan: "Food and cocktails to crow about". Five miles south of town Goose Island Park, a county facility, spreads over Mississippi River islands. Six miles from La Crosse off Highway 35, the River Road, tucked into a riverside bluff lies Mt. La Crosse ski resort (800-426-3665), one of the Mississippi Valley's few such facilities. Off to the east of the River Road two bed and breakfast establishments offer rooms at Wesby, a Norwegian-like village with the National Register-listed 1909 Coon Prairie Lutheran Church, the century-old Wesby House (608-634-4112), which also houses a restaurant, and the Old Parsonage (608-452-3833), a 1912 former residence for pastors at Coon Valley, where you'll also find Norskedalen (May-Oct 9-4:30, Sun noon-4; Nov-April Sat 9:30-4, Sun. noon-4), a 350 acre nature enclave with wildlife; an arboretum; eight buildings which comprise the Bekkum Homestead, a typical 1850's Norwegian farm; and the Thrune Visitors Center with archives and exhibits on the area's natural and cultural history.

At the Coon Creek watershed area the U.S. Soil Erosion Service (later the Soil Conservation Service) selected in October, 1933, 90,000 acres for the nation's first large-scale demonstration of soil and water conservation. The Service and the University of Wisconsin trained area farm leaders to practice crop rotation, strip cropping, terrace farming, stream bank erosion control and other preservation techniques now common throughout the Middle West.

Farther south along the River Road, Highway 35—which for the most part runs within view of the Mississippi—lies Stoddard, not a river port in the old days, but a railroad town which shipped out such Mississippi products as fish and ice. Where Coon Creek meets the Mississippi just south of town, the first Norwegian settlers arrived in late1840's, then made their way up the stream toward the Wesby area. Farther south, the Old Settlers Overlook atop a 500 foot bluff offers views onto the Mississippi at one of the waterway's widest points, five miles.

Genoa began in 1854 when Joseph Monti laid out a settlement he called Bad Ax after the river of that name. In 1868 Italian settlers decided to call the small fishing community Genoa, as the area's hills and rivers reminded them of that northern Italian town. Many of the villagers supposedly spoke Italian well into the twentieth century. The town's Old World heritage and St. Charles Borromeo Church, with its bluff-side cemetery filled with gravestones bearing Italian names, makes Genoa "a bit of Mediterranean beside the Mississippi", as Albert S. Tousley described the settlement in *Where Goes the River*.

No one is likely to confuse Genoa with such north Italy Mediterranean resorts as San Remo or Positano, but the place does resemble a North Carolina farm town, for by the Mississippi stands a metal warehouse labeled "Northern Wis. Co-op Tobacco Pool". In Vernon County, and adjacent Crawford, grow some 4000 acres of tobacco, one of the river valley's more unusual crops (Mississippi area farmland also yields tobacco in Louisiana;

see chapter 8). Commercial tobacco cultivation started in Wisconsin in the 1850's and peaked in 1903 with 70 million pounds. A decade ago, 13,400 acres yielded 26 million pounds, but since then production has fallen to about a third of that amount. In early spring, white cheesecloth coverings atop seedlings dot the landscape. Farmers later transplant the strongest plants into adjacent fields, which soon glisten with tobacco's characteristic long, green leaves. Of the three methods used to cure tobacco—smoke, smoke-free hot air and fresh air—Wisconsin growers use the fresh air technique. Barns—called sheds in Wisconsin—store the leaves for curing, with vents atop the structure to allow air to circulate. The shed's length indicates the amount of tobacco inside. A vent sits atop the roof of each "bent", a 12 to 16 foot section, which holds the yield from about five acres. In the past, tobacco grown in the Mississippi River county served as binder for cigars, but the crop is now used to produce chewing tobacco.

Just beyond Lock and Dam Number 8 south of Genoa—where Houseboating Adventures (608-788-4420) rents river boats—rises the Dairyland Power Cooperative plant, built as a nuclear facility, but converted in 1987 to burn coal, a cheaper fuel. The installation consumes every year some 800, 000 tons—533 barge loads—to generate one-third of the power used by 180,000 families in four surrounding states. At the bottom of a pool of filtered and demineralized well water hide 33,300 slim cylinders, 8 ½ feet long and less than inch thick, filled with thousands of uranium pellets once used to fuel the plant. The uranium continues to fission and generate heat, so there in the netherworld by the Mississippi the lethal substance will remain as it decays over the next few thousand years.

Farther south, at the mouth of the Bad Ax River, stands the Genoa National Fish Hatchery, which raises fish to stock rivers. Although the river retains its original name—so called as Indians found the local limestone too soft for crafting a good ax—area inhabitants, fearing that "Bad Ax" would deter prospective settlers, changed the county's name to Vernon in 1863. In this area unfolded the last events of the Black Hawk War, a victory over the pesky chief recalled by the name of the hamlet Victory seven miles south of Genoa. On August 1 and 2,1832 federal forces and frontiersmen cornered Black Hawk's band on the river bottoms by the Mississippi. When the Indians tried to escape over to Minnesota, the steamer *Warrior* shelled the fleeing tribe as they struggled across the waterway. Most died, but Black Hawk escaped to the east where Winnebago braves soon captured him and then delivered the feared chief to Fort Crawford at Prairie du Chien. Asked later why he had continued to wage war against the encroaching whites, Black Hawk replied, "Rock River [in Illinois] was a beautiful country; I loved my towns, my cornfields, and the home of my people. I fought for it."

Blackhawk Park, just south of Victory, nestles in a pleasant wooded enclave, maintained by the Corps of Engineers, along the Mississippi. On the east side of Highway 35 near the turnoff to the park a small, rather obscure marker tells of a certain N. Spaudling "who in Oct. 1904 rode an unbroken colt to Victory at 2 a.m. and saved a limited train from going through a burned culvert." Farther on, De Soto, located in two counties, occupies the site of a Winnebago village headed by Chief Winneshiek, who sold furs to white traders. Originally called Winneshiek's Landing, the town was renamed by Nantucket sea captains who settled there for Spanish explorer Hernando de Soto, who in 1541 discovered the Mississippi south of present day Memphis, Tennessee. Farther on lies Ferryville, originally called Humble Bush, where in the nineteenth century a ferry connected this point with Lansing, Iowa. Ferryville claims only one street, the River Road. What the town lacks in width it makes up in length, however, for the settlement stretches along the Mississippi a good distance. According to local lore, an ordinance passed at the time of incorporation stated that only when the village covered more than a mile could liquor be sold there, so thirsty imbibers quickly staked out far-flung houses which set the pattern for the town's great length.

At the north end of town stands the brown-shuttered, yellow building which houses the Ferryville Cheese Company, where from a hallway behind the packing area you can see a welter of pipes, tubes, conveyers and machinery which jam the production area. Farther on, in the center of town, stands a pleasant looking white house, Ferryville's most attractive residence, which contains Mississippi Humble Bush Bed and Breakfast (608-734-3930). A bait shop, the Wooden Nickel Saloon, and the Swing Inn lend the town atmosphere. From the Inn's sign dangles an addendum advertising "catfish", while inside a rattler's skin on display highlights the fact that those snakes inhabit the nearby bluffs.

Off to the east of the Mississippi around Gays Mills in the Kickapoo River Valley lie apple orchards, originally planted in the early part of century. The Apple Tree Farm Market (May 1-Nov 30 9-5), east of town has been designated one of Wisconsin's twenty-two Certified Farm Markets, while the nearby Fleming Orchards (Aug 1—Thanksgiving) boasts a collection of antique wagons and carriages, many of them Amish-built. Back on the River Road, the highway continues south to Lynxville, built as a stop for Mississippi steamboats. The steamer *Lynx* brought the surveyors who laid out the original plat for the town, a leading log shipping point a century ago. On the bluff above the tiny town (population: 174) perch cut-out figures of the Biblical Wise Men.

South of town, along an especially alluring stretch of the river, stands Lock and Dam Number 9, beyond which, across the waterway, extends a 9100 foot long earth dike connected to higher ground on the Iowa shore. When a ship arrives, the lock's great steel doors, faced with wooden planks, slowly swing open as the machinery emits a pleasant hum. From the observation platform by the lock a wide ranging panorama of the Mississippi spreads before you, with the view up stream uncluttered by islands of the kind that dot the waters to the south. Here, so close to the great river, you gain a feeling of intimacy with the powerful waterway.

River views continue to enhance the drive south, as the highway threads its way between bluffs to the left and train tracks which border the Mississippi on the west side of the road. Fifteen miles south of Lynxville lies Prairie du Chien, an historic town where memorials of early days on the upper Mississippi linger. When French traders and trappers arrived in the 1750's they named the settlement after Fox chief Alion (Indian for "dog": "chien" in French), who had lived in the area with his people a century before. Prairie du Chien dates its founding from 1781 when three French Canadians made a land claim at the then remote Mississippi River outpost. At this time, less than 200 whites lived in Wisconsin, which before the nineteenth century had only one other true settlement, a fur village established at Green Bay in 1764. As exemplified by those two tiny towns in Wisconsin back then, fur furnished the motivation for the early inhabitants to venture into the wilderness. A late seventeenth century ditty versified: "Friend, once 'twas Fame that led thee forth / To brave the Tropic Heat, the Frozen North, / Late it was Gold, then Beauty was the Spur; / But now our Gallants venture but for Furs."

So it was that the fur trade inspired the growth of Prairie du Chien, for after the War of 1812 with England the U.S. government, following a policy promoted by George Washington, established at Prairie du Chien—and, later, at Green Bay—a federal fur "factory". This "factory" did not serve as a production facility but, rather, as a trading post run by a factor, a government agent charged with weaning the Indians away from the English and converting them to the American cause. "The principal object of the Government [is] to secure the Friendship of the Indians", stated a typical instruction list, which also warned against extending credit except to "Principal Chiefs of good character". When authorities assigned the army to protect routes favored by fur traders, troops arrived at Prairie du Chien in 1814 to establish a fort by the Mississippi, and by 1820 the town boasted a permanent population of more than 200 people, most of them engaged in the fur trade.

Although the army later moved that post and renamed it Fort Crawford, originally the base stood on a large Indian mound now occupied by Villa Louis, successor to the house built in 1843 by Hercules Dousman, who arrived in Prairie du Chien in 1826 as an agent for John Jacob Astor's American Fur Company, which in 1822 had persuaded Congress to eliminate the competing factory system. Wisconsin folk writer August Derleth recounts Dousman's frontier fur adventures in the historical novels *Bright Journey* and its sequel, *The House on the Mound*, that title referring to the lavishly furnished 1870 Villa Louis (May-Oct 9-5). In the same riverside lowland enclave of St. Feriole Island where "the house on the mound" stands survive other relics of Prairie du Chien's early days, including the National Register-listed Brisbois House, a stone block structure built around 1837 by a fur trader associated with Astor's American Fur Company; the white clapboard 1841 Rolette House, later a hotel; a stone and wood building which houses the Fur Museum; and the elevated visitor center, built two feet higher than the high point reached by the 1965 flood, with exhibits on Villa Louis and a painting crammed with portrayals of local personages which traces the city's history from 1673 to 1900. The Prairie du Chien Museum, just beyond Villa Louis to the north, contains dioramas on the town's past, including a scene showing the 1816 U.S. Fur Factory. Outside on the ground nearby lines mark the foundations of the first fort, moved in 1829 to higher ground on the mainland.

Afficionados of the Mississippi River and its history will enjoy lingering a time on St. Feriole Island. This quiet corner of the river, cut off from the mainstream of contemporary life, offers a pleasant place to get a feel for the old days along the waterway. Because the island suffers from occasional flooding, it remained largely undeveloped and thus—unlike most riverfront areas on the Mississippi—the enclave evokes how an unspoiled stretch of waterside land might have looked a century or more ago. The past revives every year on Father's Day weekend at the Island with the colorful Fur Trade Rendezvous, which includes participants clad in period garb, restricted to using only old-time implements. Stationed on railroad tracks south of Villa Louis stand orange-peach hued passenger cars which now house shops, the Bar Car pub, a deli and the office of Ray's River Rides (608-326-6065) where you can book excursions (late May-mid Oct) on the *Belle of Prairie du Chien*, built in 1923 as the cattle and horse and wagon ferry *Addie May* and now supposedly the oldest operating paddlewheeler on the upper Mississippi. By the nearby bridge spanning the river over to Marquette, Iowa, stands a statue of Jacques Marquette. He and Louis Joliet became the first Europeans to travel the upper Mississippi, entering the waterway in 1673 from the Wisconsin River just downstream.

In a quiet residential area to the south stand a few surviving remnants of old Fort Crawford. The reconstructed 1831 hospital houses a Medical Museum (May-Oct 10-5) which contains an 1890's pharmacy, displays on Indian herbal remedies, and a section on Dr. William Beaumont, who practiced at the fort in the 1830's. Beaumont became famous for his observations of the digestive process through an opening in the stomach of *voyageur* Alexis St. Martin, treated by the physician for a gunshot wound in 1822. In December, 1829, at Fort Crawford, Beaumont began a series of experiments with St. Martin which lasted for nearly two years. At this time Colonel Zachary Taylor, later U.S. President, served as commanding officer at Fort Crawford, where in August, 1832, chief Black Hawk surrendered and was imprisoned. While stationed there as a lieutenant, Jefferson Davis, later President of the Confederacy, met Sarah Knox

Taylor, the commandant's daughter, who the dashing young officer married—much to Colonel Taylor's chagrin—in 1835. Davis retired from the army and took his bride to his Mississippi plantation, where she died of fever a few months later. Neumann Hause (608-326-8104) in Prairie du Chien offers bed and breakfast, and J & D Livery (608-326-6475) runs horse-drawn carriage tours of town in the summer.

Just past Bridgeport, not far south of Prairie du Chien, the River Road crosses the Wisconsin River, just above where the waterway loses itself in the Mississippi. Here on June 17, 1673—a century and quarter after Spanish explorer Hernando de Soto had discovered the Mississippi in 1541—Marquette and Joliet drifted out of the mouth of the Wisconsin to enter the broad expanse of the Father of Waters. The explorers had left the little mission of St. Ignace on the Straits of Mackinac on May 17 and, accompanied by five white companions, the group floated via waterways which vein the landscape toward the Mississippi. At what is now Portage, Wisconsin, two Miami Indians guided the tiny expedition, traveling in two birch-bark canoes, on "a portage of 2700 paces" between the Fox and Wisconsin Rivers, and then, Marquette continued in his journal, the guides "returned home, leaving us alone in this Unknown country, in the hands of providence. Thus we left the Waters flowing to Quebeq, 4 or 500 Leagues from here, to float on those that would thence forward Take us through strange lands."

What a hauntingly poignant description Marquette wrote of this episode in the history of the Mississippi and of exploration in the New World. Looking back over the long years, more than three centuries later, we can scarcely imagine how the now settled and tamed Mississippi River Valley appeared to the early explorers. For them all was new, all was unknown. Marquette's words vividly capture that combination of anticipation and anxiety explorers and adventurers typically experience as they leave the familiar and set forth toward "strange lands" and a problematic future. Three days after the portage, the men entered the Mississippi "avec une joye que je ne peux pas expliquer": so awesome was this event for Marquette that even his eloquent pen could not record the joy he felt on reaching the great river. Down the waterway they continued, finally arriving at the Arkansas River where they ended their downstream trip, departing on July 17 for the return journey, which took them back to the north country, via the Illinois River, by late September after a 3000 mile adventure. So began the exploration of the Mississippi.

On the south side of the Wisconsin River, a back road to the west will take you to the Mississippi, where Wyalusing State Park affords splendid views down onto the river valley and the confluence of the two waterways. Established in 1917, Wyalusing—"home of the warrior"—includes some 15 miles of hiking trails, one along an old Indian route, another on a former covered wagon road, and yet another on a trail to a ferry once used by settlers heading westward. The little town of Wyalusing began in 1836 as Paper City, a site promoted by an eastern syndicate but never settled—truly a paper city—and later renamed by a Pennsylvania settler for an Indian warrior's home in that state. County Road X follows the Mississippi for part of the way down to Bagley, a tavern-rich village of some 300 people with wooden buildings lining the block-long commercial area. The old-time Bagley Hotel (608-996-2241) contains seven rooms, rather less elegant than those at a Motel 6, and a dining area sporting an advertising mirror touting Leinenkugel's beer, a Wisconsin brew. The road called X continues on its narrow way to nearby Glenhaven—Parson's Inn (608-794-2491) there offers bed and breakfast—through the back country, with the route tucked into the hillside above the river bottomland below. North Andover, a few miles east, took its name from Andover, Massachusetts, which supplied the machinery for an early flour mill, while nearby Beetown was named after a man named Cyrus

Alexander found a 425-pound lead nugget in a cavity opened when he overturned a bee tree in 1827.

North of Cassville lies Stonefield (Memorial Day weekend-Labor Day 9-5), replica of a farm village from a century ago. Operated by the State Historical Society of Wisconsin, the site includes nearly forty structures as well as the State Agricultural Museum, while perched on a hill across the road in Nelson Dewey State Park is the Dewey Home (F-Sun), a brick residence built after a fire in 1873 destroyed his earlier house. Dewey arrived in Cassville at age twenty-three in 1836, just days before organization of the Wisconsin Territory. Twelve years later voters elected the lawyer and land investor as the state's first governor. Weekends in August and September, Stonefield presents "Autumn on the Farm" events, with threshing demonstrations, sorghum making, and other such rustic activities. Although Dewey promoted Cassville as the state capital, the place today is but a sleepy Mississippi River town with a lost-in-time ambiance. Near the waterway rises the Denniston House, now an apartment building which has seen better days, opened in 1854 as a hotel by Nelson Dewey. An old fashioned soda fountain in the Korner Kard Shop also recalls bygone times. Cassville—a bald eagle watching area—boasts the *Charlie D.*, a ferry across the Mississippi to Iowa established by the village in 1988 as the latest in a long line of such services there. The first ferry, powered by horses on treadmills, began in 1836, and operated continuously until the 1940's. In the early 1980's a ferryman from Illinois ran a service for two years, and finally the city started operating a boat across the Mississippi in May 1988 (May and Oct F-Sun 9-9, June-Labor Day daily 9-9; car: $5; for information: 608-725-5180). The 1851 Geiger House (608-725-5419, closed Jan-March) in Cassville takes bed and breakfast guests. During third weekend of July, the town hosts the annual Twin-O-Rama, a festival first held in 1929, which attracts hundreds of sets of twins and triplets from around the country.

Near the Mississippi in southwestern Wisconsin and the northwestern corner of Illinois stretches an old lead mining district, which by 1840 produced almost half the nation's supply of the metal. At present day Potosi Indians worked a deposit called Snake Cave, discovered in 1690 by Europeans when French explorer Nicholas Perrot located the lode. In 1827, about the time commercial mining began in the area, a squatter named Willis St. John started operations at the cave, which he sold in 1848 to entrepreneur Nelson Dewey, better known as Wisconsin's first governor, who worked the mine until 1870 when it closed. In 1985 Bette and Harry Henderson, who for some twenty-five years lived in the Middle East as agricultural educators, bought the St. John Mine where they now offer tours of the historic facility (May-Aug 9-5, Sept-Oct weekends only). On the hill opposite the mine survive remnants of century and a half old "badger huts", crude stone structures where miners lived.

A cholera scare and the late 1840's California Gold Rush induced many residents to leave, but the mines revived during the Civil War. Although most closed by 1870, the last lead-zinc mine in the area continued to operate until about 1960. Potosi claims the world's longest main street, some three miles, with no intersecting cross streets, and the town also boasts that it is "Catfish Capital of Wisconsin", a claim reinforced with the annual Catfish Festival, held the second weekend of August, when some 2500 pounds of the Mississippi River delicacy are served. On the north side of town by the old Holiday Beer brewery, established in 1852—the "i" indicated by the image of a glass of brew—is the Snake Hollow Craft Shop, while farther north on a bluff overlooking the Mississippi stands the O'Reilly House (608-763-2386, closed Nov-April), a bed and breakfast establishment. The Grant River Recreation Area, on the Mississippi 2 ½ miles south of Potosi, occupies land near where in 1945 archaeologists found artifacts of the Copper Culture, Indians who lived along the river as early as 2700 B.C.

Adjacent to Potosi to the east lies Tennyson, originally Dutch Hollow, where the 1847 Dutch Hollow Rock House once hosted actor John Wilkes Booth, Lincoln's assassin. About twelve miles east, Wild Bill Hickok was born; his parents worked as lead miners. Platteville, also east of Tennyson, offers a mining museum, the Chicago Bears' football training camp (late summer), the Wisconsin Shakespeare Festival (early July-early Aug, 608-342-1298), and bed and breakfast accommodations at Cunningham House (608-348-5532).

At Dickeyville, farther south, bristle the curious rough-surfaced figures and formations built between 1925 and 1930 at the Holy Ghost Church grounds by Father Matthias Wernerus. The pastor used bits of glass, pottery, porcelain, shells, coal, quartz, rock, fossils and other fragments to confect bit by bit a grotto filled with monuments to "Religion" and "Patriotism", as signs atop crusty pillars state. Stony trees and flowers garnish the grotto, a bird house in the same style offers a rough shelter, while statues of Jesus, Columbus, and others occupy small pavilions. Another religious remnant survives at Sinsinawa—"rattle-snake" in Algonquin, "home of the young eagle" in Sioux—to the south. In the mid-1840's, missionary Samuel Mazzuchelli bought an Indian mound and established there a religious and educational center. A missionary school, convent, and other facilities operated at the mound, where the original 1846 stone building and later red brick structures, higher up, still stand. The Sinsinawa Dominican Sisters now occupy the complex.

At nearby Hazel Green—one of the earliest mining settlements, established after lead was discovered in 1824—two bed and breakfast places occupy century and a half old buildings: Wisconsin House Stage Coach Inn (608-854-2233) and De Winters (608-854-2768). On Highway 84 south of town stands a marker at a base point from which every land measurement in the state is calculated. At this point, Illinois lies a few miles away and Wisconsin's "West Coast", formed by the Mississippi, comes to an end.

WISCONSIN PRACTICAL INFORMATION

Wisconsin Division of Tourism Development, 123 West Washington Avenue, P.O. Box 7970, Madison, WI 53707; 603-266-2161; in-state 800-432-8747; surrounding states 800-372--2737.

For information on Wisconsin's four state parks along the Mississippi: Department of Natural Resources, Bureau of Parks and Recreation, P.O. Box 7921, Madison, WI 53707.

State Historical Society of Wisconsin: 608-262-9606.

State tourist offices along the Mississippi operate at La Crosse and at Prairie du Chien.

For information on cities along the Mississippi: Alma: 608-685-3351; La Crosse: 608-782-2366; Pepin: 715-442-2219; Potosi-Tennyson: 608-763-2221; Prairie du Chien: 608-326-2241; Trempealeau: 608-534-6615.

The Wisconsin Indian Head Country includes Mississippi River counties north of La Crosse: in-state 800-472-6654, 800-826-6966 elsewhre.

The state of Wisconsin operates a tourist office in Chicago at 342 North Michigan Avenue, Chicago, Ill. 60601; 312-332-7274.

From this hill Henry Rowe Schoolcraft discovered the source of the Mississippi on July 13, 1832.

Great River road highway markers indicate the route along the Mississippi from Minnesota to Louisiana.

For miles downstream from Lake Itasca the Mississippi remains a small stream.

Bemidji is the first city reached by the Mississippi.

The Mississippi enters its first metropolitan area at Minneapolis, where the St. Anthony Falls tame the river.

At Trempealeau, WI, a restored inn recalls early days on the river.

Barges headed downstream wait to enter Lock and Dam Number 9 at Lynxville, WI.

Marker to the first railroad bridge across the Mississippi (1856) stands at Rock Island, IL.

McGinnis produce market at Thomson, IL, evokes the waterway's agricultural and rural regions.

Rand Park at Keokuk, IA, offers splendid views up the Mississippi River.

River at Hannibal, MO, seems serene and pristine.

Marina hamlet not far north of St. Louis is at Peruque, MO.

The Goldenrod*, the grandest showboat ever built, is moored at St. Charles, MO.*

The St. Louis Arch reflects the city's role as "Gateway to the West."

Eads Bridge (1874) stretches across the Mississippi at St. Louis.

River gauges measure the Mississippi at the St. Louis water-front.

At Cairo, IL, the Mississippi (right) and the Ohio rivers merge to begin the 984-mile trip to the Gulf.

Flood wall at Helena, AR, advertises the Mississippi's presence.

Lookout tower at Warfield Point Park, just south of Greenville, MS, provides a view of the Mississippi's treacherous currents.

On July 4, 1863, Confederate gun emplacements on the bluffs above the Mississippi dominated the river.

Mississippi made its mark at the Vicksburg, MS, levee.

Structures such as this moss-framed country store at Church Hill can still be seen between Vicksburg and Natchez.

The Mississippi Queen *brightens the waterfront at Natchez, MS, and brings back a touch of old times on the river.*

Port Allen Locks in Baton Rouge replaced this 1909 facility, closed in 1961, at Plaquemine, LA.

From top of the Louisiana state capitol in Baton Rouge, the view includes the petrochemical installations.

Relic of the old days survives by the river at Edgard, LA, on the west bank between Baton Rouge and New Orleans.

Old time trolley connects attractions on the New Orleans riverfront.

Behind 1832 Fort Jackson is a monument to La Salle, who in 1682 claimed the Mississippi valley for France.

River and bar pilots live at Pilottown, the last inhabited settlement on the Mississippi, reachable only by boat.

3. IOWA

Iowa developed along its waterways. Mason City is the state's only town of any size not situated on a river. The earliest settlements dot the banks of the Mississippi, fronted by a series of attractive cities and some of Iowa's 680 small towns—more than any other state—with a population under 1000. A three hundred mile stretch of the Mississippi forms the state's eastern border, where the earliest settlers arrived. In *The Iowa Handbook for 1856* Nathan H. Parker noted that the bluffs bordering the Mississippi "and the rich alluvial bottoms that intervene, furnish the sites for the numerous cities that stand along the banks of the Father of Waters, like gems in the great area of commerce." After the Black Hawk War, when the federal government officially opened Iowa for settlement in 1833, newcomers—farmers and city dwellers alike—began to cross the river, which exerted a strong influence on the pioneers and their villages along the Mississippi. "As the first farmers settled as near as possible to the great river which was their highway to the outside world, so the first towns in Iowa were the Mississippi River towns", states Joseph Frazier Wall in *Iowa: A Bicentennial History*. "The river was to mold them and to give them a character unlike that of other towns in Iowa. Most of these river towns looked out and down the Mississippi to St. Louis, Memphis and New Orleans. The river culture, an amalgam of north and south, east and west, was their culture, distinct from and often antagonistic to the culture of their own state."

The River Road enters Iowa from Minnesota at the village of New Albin, where the diminutive one story white frame Town Hall (1895) sports an oversized belfry, while west of town on Route1 stands the twelve-sided century old Redburn Barn, listed on the National Register. South of town on Highway 26 stands the ancient Fish Farm Mounds, also Register-listed, so named as they occupy land formerly farmed by the Fish family. These formations comprise a few of the surviving one-quarter of the more than 10,000 Indian mounds which originally dotted the northeastern Iowa landscape.

At Lansing the road rejoins the river, spanned here by the webby, metal girder 1932 Blackhawk Bridge, which looms above wooden houses huddled below. Beyond the bridge, a three mile causeway continues on into Wisconsin above the Winneshiek Bottoms, a maze of wetlands filled with islets, marshes, and backwaters frequented by wildlife and fishermen. From atop 400 foot high Mt. Hosmer, a city park on the bluff—which affords good views as it stands closer to the river than most such rises—five lookout points offer extensive panoramas onto the Mississippi and parts of three states. Below lies picturesque Lansing, dotted with such National Register-listed limestone structures as the 1864 Old County Courthouse, a rather severe looking classic-style building, the 1864 Old Stone Schoolhouse, used for 110 years, and the early 1860's G. Kerndt & Bros. grain elevator, now a sports and gift shop, through which tons of Iowa crops passed for loading onto paddlewheelers. Just to the south of the old elevators stand turn-of-the-century warehouses, while next door to the north, the Waterfront Restaurant offers a deck overlooking the river. Traveling further south on Front Street, you'll find a large wholesale fish market. For a less common culinary delicacy, the Venison Marketing Center (800-247-2570), 201 St. John Street, sells deer meat and venison sausages. At 391 Main Street, which runs west from the river and retains an old-fashioned appearance, stands the 1861 Register-listed Kerndt Dry Goods Store and Bank Building, now occupied by a hardware retailer. At Lansing—where in 1832 Daniel Boone's son surveyed an Indian treaty boundary—S & S Houseboat Rentals (319-538-4454) offers ships for excursions on the Mississippi, while Backwater Cruises (319-538-4497) runs excursions on the river in a 49-passenger paddlewheeler. Bed and breakfast accommodations are available at Fitzgerald's Inn (319-538-4872) and at Lansing House (319-538-4263), located on the riverfront.

The River Road, X52, south out of Lansing continues through the unglaciated hilly area by the Mississippi known as the "Little Switzerland of Iowa". The hilly, winding road passes a power plant, then veers away from the river. A few miles from Lansing you'll pass the Wexford Church of the Immaculate Conception (c. 1848) a gothic-like limestone sanctuary which sports a small belfry, which was added later. In the peaceful country graveyard by the church repose parishioners whose ancestors originated in Ireland's Wexford County. Harpers Ferry, farther on, nestles below a series of bluffs which rise above the town to the east. The village began when David Harper started a ferry service across the Mississippi to Lynxville, Wisconsin. The town, which once served as a steamboat landing, now functions as a commercial and recreational fishing center. Since the early days, the Mississippi has yielded a plentiful supply of fish. When an adventurer named Peter Pond traveled from Connecticut to the Mississippi country in 1773, he related in his diary Iowa's first fish story, recounting how he put "Hoock and lines into the Water and Leat them ly all nite". This yielded at least one fish which weighed—so Pond claimed in his journal—104 pounds, enough to "Give a Meale" to twelve men.

At Harpers Ferry, Ralph and Diane Mohn operate a fish business of the sort occasionally found along the Mississippi, but which in recent years has become a waning activity on the waterway. Some forty years ago, the state of Iowa licensed 1200 commercial fishermen to operate on the Mississippi, while now fewer than a third of that number hold licenses. Mohn usually runs some 130 nets in the sloughs and backwaters, using cheese trimmings and soybean cakes as bait. The main catch often consists of carp and catfish, sold both wholesale and at retail in the Mohn's market, one of those typical little fish establishments sometimes found in small towns along the Upper Mississippi. The 6400 acre Yellow River State Forest three miles southwest of Harpers Ferry offers recreational fishing in trout streams, horseback riding, and other outdoor activities. A half mile south of town at Andy Mountain Campground on Highway 364 stands the Sherman Swift Tower, built in 1914 by Althea Sherman, Iowa's first female ornithologist, to study the habits of the chimney swift.

Indian mounds in northeastern Iowa recall the tribes which hunted in the region in ancient times. A survey conducted a century ago listed nearly 900 mounds in and around Harpers Ferry, some of them still remaining in City Park and elsewhere in the area. The state's most famous formations lie within Effigy Mounds National Monument (Memorial Day-Labor Day 8-7, rest of the year 8-5) on the River Road south of Harpers Ferry. The nearly 1500 acre preserve, which spreads along the bluffs high above the Mississippi, contains 191 known prehistoric burial mounds, 29 of them shaped liked birds and bears, and the rest conical or linear. Eleven miles of trails wind their way through the park, reached by a steep path to the top of the 300 foot high bluff. Fire Point Trail will take you past Little Bear Mound and out to Fire Point, an observation terrace overlooking the Mississippi. At this evocative spot, time and place weave a web of musings. Behind you, scattered across the landscape, rise the two millennium old tombs where the region's earliest settlers have reposed for centuries, while far below rolls the ever-flowing great river, a silent and permanent witness to the men who have come and gone over the long years.

The River Road continues south, tucked between the high limestone bluffs, railway tracks, and the Mississippi. At Marquette, the blue hued bridge gracefully arches across the waterway to Prairie du Chien, Wisconsin. Marquette and the nearby river town of McGregor occupy terrain which formed part of the Giard Tract, one of three Spanish Land Grants in Iowa. In 1800, sixteen years after Basil Giard, a trader in Prairie du Chien, took control of the area, the Spanish government confirmed his title and directed Giard to "preserve a good understanding between the Indian natives" and the King of Spain. If you overnight in Marquette, the well placed Mississippi Inn (319-873-3477), nestled among the trees perched on a bluff high above town, contains twenty-one rooms which sport balconies overlooking the river. Between McGregor and Marquette lies a visitor center of the Upper Mississippi National Wildlife and Fish Refuge, a 200,000 acre nature preserve, established by Congress in 1924, which includes two to five mile wide sections of the Mississippi River wetlands for some 260 miles between Wabasha, Minnesota to near Rock Island, Illinois.

A Scotsman named Alexander McGregor founded the town which bears his name in 1837, the year after he established a ferry from Prairie du Chien, when he bought part of the Giard Tract. The settlement became a thriving river port and railroad center, with the world's first and largest pontoon bridge, used from 1874 to 1961 for trains crossing the Mississippi. In 1870, a circus showboat which docked at McGregor delighted four brothers taken there with their family from Baraboo, Wisconsin, ten years before. After watching the parade and performance the boys produced an amateur production for the townspeople. So originated in McGregor—where harnessmaker August Ruengeling (as he spelled the name) and his family lived for twelve years—the very first performances of the Ringling Brothers Circus, established professionally in June, 1882, at Baraboo as the Carnival of Fun. During the time the Ringlings lived in the Iowa river town a Baptist preacher named William Russell Cary Wright and his wife, Anna Lloyd Jones, also resided in McGregor. When Albrecht Ringling and his brothers presented their boyish circus in 1870, perhaps one of the youthful spectators was the Wright's three years old son, later famous in his own right as the world renowned architect, Frank Lloyd Wright.

McGregor today—tucked away snugly between bluffs which hem the settlement in by the Mississippi—still retains an old time and even slightly seedy river town flavor. Century old commercial buildings line Main, which stretches west from the Mississippi for a few blocks only to meet a bluff. Over the door at 228 Main, a dentist's office indicated by a large white tooth image, appears a mural of the waterfront showing the *Golden Eagle* paddlewheeler. Down the street at number 322 one of McGregor's seven antique stores occupies the town's best preserved commercial building, its metal facade painted blue with white inset columns. Also on Main is River Junction Trading Company, which sells old-time garments from the West's early days. A pressed tin ceiling, an old-fashioned iron stove and other such touches lend a yesteryear flavor to the store. The Queen Anne-style 1890 mansion at 322 Kinney built by businessman William Huntting survives as the city's most impressive residential structure. The town museum (June-Oct 15, Tu, Th and Sat 2-5) on Main houses old clothes, furniture, photos and bric-a-brac along with a small display on the Ringling Brothers, including posters and pictures of early performers. Memories of the circus impresarios also linger at Ringlings, "A Rivertown Pub" installed in the three story brick and white bay window Alexander Hotel (319-873-3454), which occupies the 1899 Lewis Hotel building. Another old fashioned place to stay, Little Switzerland Inn (319-873-3670), a bed and breakfast establishment, occupies the 1862 former offices of *The North Iowa Times*, the state's oldest weekly newspaper. The original balcony at the picturesque old building, restored in 1986, offers a view of the nearby Mississippi. In the same area you'll find the Christina Winery, one of Iowa's thirteen such firms. Rivertown Inn (319-873-2385) in McGregor also offers bed and breakfast rooms, while Boatels (319-873-3718) rents houseboats for river excursions, and at Spook Cave, seven miles west of McGregor, electric boats take visitors through caverns on supposedly the world's longest underground boat tour.

Pikes Peak, located just south of McGregor, is named for Lieutenant Zebulon Pike, later commemorated by the more famous peak in Colorado. In 1805, Pike led an expedition from St. Louis up the Mississippi to map the river, study the adjoining country, obtain specimens of plants, animals and minerals, gather information about the Indians, and choose sites for two forts. One location Pike selected lay atop the peak on the west side of the Mississippi, opposite the mouth of the Wisconsin River. A 1000 acre park on the peak includes a trail which leads to a bear effigy Indian mound, stands of endangered plant species, and wooded areas. In one of the park's deepest ravines lies the "Pictured Rocks" formation, comprised of forty-two hues of sand favored by artists who use the material to create pictures. From the 485-foot-high bluff stretches a splendid view down onto the Mississippi and the point where the Wisconsin enters the great river.

It was these bluffs, along the Mississippi's west bank, which Marquette and Joliet spotted in June, 1673, as the French explorers emerged from the mouth of the Wisconsin into the Mississippi. "Here we are, then, on this so renowned river," noted Marquette in his *Narrative*, after which he entered the first written description of Iowa: "a la droitte on voist une grande Chaisne de Montagnes fort hautes"—"On the right is a large chain of very high mountains": not mountains, of course, but the rugged bluffs Pike later favored for a fort. Here, then, began the exploration of the Mississippi.

The River Road winds and climbs and dips its way past cornfields tucked into flattish areas between the hills. By the river, a mile off the highway, lies Clayton, an attractive little village with a few old buildings, including the turn of the century Peace Evangelical Lutheran Church and a two story 1860 stone structure which for a century served as a school. Hidden away in one of the riverside bluffs at Clayton, nestles an unusual storage area installed in some of the fourteen miles of huge tunnels excavated, beginning in 1945, when a mining company began extracting silica sand from underground deposits there. After the operation closed, the Ag Products Terminal Company bought the mine in 1983 and converted the 35-foot-wide, 60-foot-high tunnels, some more than a half mile long, into warehouse space which stores corn, logs, bulk fertilizer, old tires and other items. In the early 1960's the government supposedly outfitted the cavern with sufficient civil defense supplies for up to 44,000 people who might find shelter there in case of a nuclear attack. By the river at Clayton stands the oddly spelled Cklaytonian Bed and Breakfast Inn (319-964-2776), whose amenities include bicycles for guests and suites with views of the Mississippi.

Although the River Road continues south to Guttenberg, a short detour to the west will take you to Garnavillo, where the century old Congregational Church houses a history museum (May 1-Oct 15 Sat, Sun and holidays 1-5, 7-9) with documents dating to 1750, to 1858 Ceres Pioneer Rock Church, and to Elkader, named after Algerian nationalist Abd-el-Kader, whose struggles against the French inspired pioneers in far off Iowa to designate their village for him. Elkader's attractions include the 1877 Clayton County Courthouse, the 1888-9 Keystone Arch Bridge over the Turkey River, the 1893 restored Opera House, a history museum (Memorial Day to Labor Day Sat and Sun 2-4) installed in the 1850 Greek Revival-style Carter family mansion, the nearby six and a half story limestone Motor Mill, and five houses and four other buildings listed on the National Register. The Little House in the Woods, (319-783-7774) six miles north of Elkader, offers bed and breakfast accommodations in a Victorian era residence on a 1000 acre grain, beef, and dairy farm.

Unlike many of the old towns along the river, Guttenberg takes full advantage of its situation just by the Mississippi. The very narrow but mile long River Front Park affords good views of the waterway and a pleasant place to stroll alongside the river. French missionaries canoeing down the Mississippi called the site Prairie La Porte—door to the prairie. The French originally settled in the village, site of the first district court in Iowa and the first seat of Clayton County when its boundaries extended to the Canadian border.

German settlers later renamed the village for Johannes Gutenberg, the fifteenth century inventor of movable type, with the extra "t" added by a spelling mistake on the first plat. The Germans arrived in 1845 when the Western Settlement Society of Cincinnati colonized the town, with many of the newcomer intellectuals escaping military service in Europe. Until the turn of the century, the town kept German as its prevailing language. The settlement's early day cultural orientation survives in some of the street names: Goethe, Herder, Schiller, Lessing and Mozart. The new library houses a bust of Gutenberg above a replica of the printer's famous Bible, acquired at the original print shop in Mainz by the owner of the local Guttenberg Press when he served with the United States Army in Germany during World War II.

The modern library building seems quite out of keeping with the pre-Civil War limestone structures which dominate the town, whose downtown area is a National Historic District. These pleasingly pale-yellow buildings typify the many hand-hewn native limestone structures built in the late 1840's and early 1850's by German settlers in such Iowa Mississippi River towns as Lansing, McGregor, Guttenberg and, downstream, Dubuque and Bellevue. The honey-hued rough stone Register-listed Albertus Building (1852), the most distinctive of these structures, sports two balconies and tracery around the windows. Others include the 1845 Johannsen Building, 120 North First, built as a hotel, supposedly the town's first stone structure; the 1850 Fishback House, 230 South First, the old Meyer Cigar Company factory; the Friedlein Hotel (1885), 310 North Third, decorated with stone lentils above and below the windows; the Harter House (1858) and buildings, 302 North Bluff, the only farm in the town itself; and the old Jungk Brewery (1858), 402 South Bluff, recently restored to house an art gallery, antique shop, and wine store.

Back down on the river stands the U.S. Aquarium and Federal Fish Hatchery (May-Sept 8-8), with displays of fish, mussels, turtles, and other marine life found in the Mississippi. The adjacent state fish hatchery produces from late March through mid-May some ten million sacfry (northern pike) annually for restocking Iowa rivers. Just north of the aquarium lies Lock and Dam Number 10, built over a three year period at a cost of $4.8 million. An observation platform affords a view onto the 1.2 mile long dam, completed in 1936, and the lock, finished the previous year, which makes about 7000 lockages a year.

In August, 1979, President Jimmy Carter arrived at Guttenberg's waterfront on the *Delta Queen*, the old fashioned paddlewheeler that plies the Mississippi. As a crowd gathered, the President asked his aids, "Hey, is this Iowa?" The locals who overheard shouted, "Yes," whereupon Carter delivered an inspired tribute to the great state of Iowa and all its citizens. For some time after the President's visit the phrase, "Hey, is this Iowa?" become a common greeting in Guttenberg, to which the standard response was, "Yeah—and who's that, Teddy Kennedy?"

The Diamond Jo Warehouse, named after the old Mississippi River freight line, offers meals overlooking the waterway, and the Schmitt House (319-252-3248) provides "b and b"—bed and bath—accommodations in a century old renovated residence. Lawson's Landing (319-252-1717) rents fishing boats and other craft for river excursions.

A few miles south of Guttenberg, a scenic overlook provides a splendid view of the river's full sweep across the land. Layered limestone strata of the bluffs reveal the the area's age old geologic history. The rise where the observation point perches contains rich deposits of the Galena Group of rocks, lead ore of the type mined in the region for three centuries. The River Road winds along above the river valley, with red barns, white farmhouses, and green fields of various shades painting picture-perfect scenes of the Iowa countryside. County Road C94 starts at the Turkey River Indian Mounds. Popularly known as Balltown Road, the route curves and climbs through an alluring stretch of scenery on the fifteen mile ride from North Buena Vista to Dubuque. The road drops down to North Buena Vista, where a car ferry links Iowa with Cassville, Wisconsin (for schedule information: 608-725-5180), then the route climbs and veers away from the river. A series of lovely panoramas onto the farms that stretch across the rolling hills unfolds as you continue south. Roads and rows of trees stitch together the quilt of green fields that blanket the area. Some of the corn fields range across slopes like terraced rice paddies in the Far East. At Balltown, a hamlet perched atop a rise, Breitbach's Country Dining, installed in an 1852 building, offers meals in a delightful old time heartland ambiance. On the front porch hang old farm implements, while inside old quilts and craft items lend rustic touches. The Breitbach family has owned the establishment—which boasts Iowa's oldest bar in continuous service, Prohibition years included—since 1892. The centerpiece of the restaurant is a mural painted in 1934 by a Gypsy artist named Alberto in exchange for $15 and two weeks' room and board for his band of roamers. Hidden under paneling for years, the mural—uncovered only in 1989—pictures a view of fields and woods bordering the Mississippi. If you want to linger in this scenic area the Cottage Hill Guest House (319-552-2551), west of Balltown on U.S. Highway 52 (about halfway between Rickardsville and Holy Cross) offers bed and breakfast rooms at the site of the now vanished nineteenth century settlement of Cottage Hill.

The River Road continues on south of Balltown into Dubuque, Iowa's oldest city, named for the French-Canadian fur trader Julien Dubuque, who in 1788 received permission from the Fox Indians to extract lead from what he called The Mines of Spain, for he also obtained Spanish approval. After Dubuque's death in 1810, the Indians buried him with great ceremony atop a bluff overlooking the Mississippi on a site at The Mines of Spain, marked by a circular, medieval-style, crenellated limestone monument, listed on the National Register, erected in 1897. The 1380 acre The Mines of Spain Park, where the marker stands, includes historic areas, hiking trails, and the state-managed Lyons Prairie Woodland Preserve. Nearby Louis Murphy Park, just to the north, also overlooks the Mississippi.

Dubuque's river heritage survives at the lively waterfront area where Mississippi-related attractions abound. At the Port of Dubuque stands the Corps of Engineers former dredge William M.Black (May-Oct 10-6:30), a sidewheeler maintained as in its working days. In 1979, workers removed the huge 85-foot-wide paddle, displayed separately, so the ship could fit through the 74-foot flood wall gate at Ice Harbor. The nearby Woodward Riverboat Museum (May-Oct 10-6:30, Nov-April Tu-Sun 10-4)—whose donors appear as "Captains", "Pilots", and "Mates" on a plaque by the door—houses such displays as a simulated lead mine, a pilot house, a cutaway model of the steamer *Dubuque*, a lifesize scene of Marquette and Joliet in their canoe, and a diorama of Ice Harbor at the turn of the century. Not far away a shopping mall called Harbor Place occupies an old building which served as the home of the Iowa Iron Works and then the Dubuque Boat and Boiler Works, the nation's biggest inland waters boat building firm, which in 1901 constructed the *Sprague*, the world's largest steam towboat, and later the *Herbert Hoover*, the largest diesel towboat. From Ice Harbor two boats depart (May-Oct) : *The Spirit of Dubuque* and the *Mississippi Belle II* excursion boats operated by Roberts River Rides (319-583-1761 and 800-426-5591). In April, 1991, Roberts began cruises on the *Dubuque Casino Belle,* the nation's first vessel licensed for casino gambling. The 3000-passenger old-style but newly built ship, longer than a football field, leaves on brunch or lunch and dinner cruises daily, year-around, and features entertainment, gaming tables and gambling machines. The less glitzy, sleek white yacht *Island Princess* which leaves from the Dubuque Yacht Basin beneath the new (1982) bridge across the Mississippi to Wisconsin (the first span at Dubuque, for trains, opened in 1868) also offers river cruises (May-Oct, 319-556-6175 and 800-747-6175), while Family Marine (319-583-8848), located at the Dubuque Marina, rents houseboats.

The newest attraction in the Port of Dubuque Ice Harbor area is the National Rivers Hall of Fame (May-Oct 10-6:30, Nov-April Tu-Sun 10-4), established in 1989 in a former train station. A small but worthwhile series of displays evokes the history and lore of the river. Sheet music of such ditties as "'Sippy Shore", "Mississippi Days", "Floatin' Down the Mississippi", and "Come Back to the Mississippi Shore" strike a nautical note. One exhibit recalls the Diamond Jo Line, established in 1862 when Joseph "Diamond Jo" Reynolds bought a small sternwheeler steamer to run between Lansing, Iowa and Prairie du Chien, Wisconsin. In 1874 he transferred the headquarters from McGregor to Dubuque, and soon the line, which by then operated five steamboats and some twenty barges, became the Upper Mississippi's leading grain shipper. Frequent low water—common in the days before the Corps of Engineers—established the nine foot channel in the 1930's—impeded the heavily laden ships, and by the turn of the century, the Diamond Jo Line derived nearly three-quarters of its revenue from passenger traffic.

A huge mural photo on display at the museum shows a steamer dining room set for a meal, with elegant tables, elaborate fixtures, and waiters attired in crisp white uniform standing by—a picture of a vanished era. In the Hall of Fame theater—where a twenty-five minute slide show presents a history of the Mississippi and other waterways—displays tell the story of various river-connected figures, including engineer James B. Eads, the exploring duos of Marquette and Joliet and Lewis and Clark, and Mark Twain. Also included is Mary B. Greene, who started working on the Mississippi in 1890, and with her family owned Greene Line Steamers, which in 1946 acquired the *Delta Queen*. A great river lover, Mary Greene used to say:"There's nothing like the feel of a good boat under you." Every May the National Rivers Hall of Fame hosts a gathering of people interested in the nation's waterways (for information: 319-557-9545).

North of the downtown area, Eagle Point Park occupies 164 acres overlooking the Mississippi and Lock and Dam Number 11, completed in 1937. Designated the General Zebulon Pike Lock and Dam, the installation—like the Ford Lock and Dam Number 1 in Minneapolis, named for the old Ford Motor plant on the St. Paul side of the river—is one of the few of the twenty-nine Mississippi locks and dams with a name as well as a number. A nearby recently installed (1990) sidewalk enables visitors to stroll along the river levee, part of a five mile barrier built at a cost of $13 million by the Corps of Engineers starting in 1973 after devastating floods in 1951, 1952, and 1965 innundated Dubuque. A covered observation deck provides views of the lock and dam, which offers tours (mid-May-Labor Day Sun at 2). The Tollbridge Inn restaurant, perched atop a limestone footing that once supported part of a toll span, overlooks the lock and dam. Below Eagle Point Park stands the Mathias Ham House (May-Oct 10-5:30, Nov-Dec 12-4), a thirty-two room limestone Italian Villa-style residence with antique furnishings and decorative plaster details. Ham, one of the first settlers to cross the Mississippi into Iowa after the territory opened, established mines and a smelting furnace at Eagle Point by the river in 1833. Near

Ham House stand a one room school and Louis Arriandeau's 1833 two-sectioned log cabin, Iowa's oldest building.

Other Dubuque attractions—all listed on the National Register—include the Five Flags Theater, built in 1910 and modeled after Paris music halls. The theater occupies a site where a playhouse has stood since 1840, the oldest continuous theater location west of the Mississippi. The delightful Fenelon Place Elevator (April-Nov 8-10), the world's steepest, shortest funicular, was built in 1882 to connect the business district via a 296-foot-long track to the bluff top residential area 189 feet above. The 1858 Dubuque City Hall offers a rare surviving example of a combination market, which once occupied the ground floor, and public office located upstairs, a common arrangement in the Middle Ages. The gold dome-topped 1893 Dubuque County Courthouse towers above the adjacent 1858 Old Jail, closed in 1971 and now the Museum of Art (Tu-F 10-5, Sat and Sun 1-5), one of the few Egyptian Revival-style structures in the country. The old German Bank Building, 342 Main, now the Silver Dollar Bar, sports elaborate fluted columns on the facade, while Cathedral Square, contains St. Raphael Cathedral and figures representing a lead miner, a priest, a farm couple and a river hand. Near the waterfront stands the 1855 Shot Tower, a place where workers dropped melted lead through a screen at the top to form pellets which cooled as they fell and solidified into rifle shot when they dropped into water at the base. Near the Shot Tower, the Dubuque Brewery, Iowa's oldest, founded in 1898 as the Star Brewing Company, offers tastings of such brands as Erlanger Rhomberg, Golden Star Light and Xele Panaches (June-Sept 11-6, May and Oct weekends only). The Dubuque Arboretum and Botanical Gardens (May-Nov 8-sunset, Dec-April 9-12) occupies sixteen and a half acres of a former farm, while the Barn Community Theater (319-588-1305) occupies the 1890 Grand Opera House where such stars as George M. Cohan,

Lillian Russell, Ethel Barrymore, and Sarah Bernhardt performed.

Some of Dubuque's old mansions—built a century and more ago by the city's lead, flour and lumber tycoons—now serve as restaurants or inns. The 1873 Italianate Ryan House, where Ulysses S. Grant and other notables were entertained, houses a restaurant. The imposing 1890 red sandstone Richardson Romanesque Stout House, for seventy-five years the archbishop's residence, and the Register-listed 1894, Redstone Inn (for both: 319-582-1894), given by wagon builder A.A.Cooper to his daughter as a wedding present, take bed and breakfast guests, as does the Register-listed Hancock House (319-557-8989), built in 1891 by grocery distributor Charles T.Hancock on the bluff with a splendid view of the city and the Mississippi.

Other bed and breakfast places in Dubuque include L'Auberge Mandolin (319-556-0069), with river views; B.B. & C. Guest House (319-582-8045), with stained glass windows, leather walls in the dining room and other decorative touches; Collier Mansion (319-588-2130), in a well wooded 1895 lumberman's residence; Kloff House (319-588-1996); the slightly spooky Queen Anne-style Stone Cliff Manor (319-588-2856), with a turret-like tower tucked into the flank; and 1883 Richards House (319-557-1492), brightened with nearly ninety stained glass windows. The Julien Inn (800-798-7098) downtown—rebuilt after a fire in 1913 on the site of the four story 1839 Waples House, an early day skyscraper visible to travelers crossing the Mississippi—belonged during Prohibition to gangster Al Capone, who used the hotel as a hideout. Farther afield, bed and breakfast places outside Dubuque or in the country include Juniper Hill (319-582-4405), on a farm first homesteaded in 1833; Martin Anthony (319-583-5336), with accommodations in a converted barn; Oak Crest (319-582-4207); and Paradise Valley Log Home (319-552-1034).

From Dubuque to Dyersville to the west, the twenty-six mile Heritage Trail along the abandoned Chicago and Great Northern Railroad line passes old mining and mill villages through the 450-foot-deep Little Maquoketa River valley. Dyersville, a town of 4000, offers a number of attractions, including the National Farm Toy Museum (8-7), opened in 1986, the Ertl Toy Manufacturing Company (tours at 10 and 1), the century old Gothic-style St. Francis Xavier Basilica, and the "Field of Dreams" (April-Nov 10-6), the baseball diamond installed in a cornfield at Don Lansing's farm where the movie of that name was filmed in 1988. Off Highway 151, twelve miles southwest of Dubuque, lies the splendid stone Gothic-style New Melleray Abbey, established in 1849 by Irish Cistercian monks. In this dreamy hilly religious enclave, some forty-five members of the order cultivate 3000 acres of Iowa farmland.

Back on the River Road, thirteen miles south of Dubuque on Highway 52 lies the village of St. Donatus, founded in the early 1840's by settlers from Luxembourg. Although they left the old country for the New World, the newcomers clung to their original way of life—even starting a newspaper, the *Luxembourger Gazette*—and constructed in the hilly Iowa area a village which to this day resembles a Luxembourg town. Long, eavesless, two story dwellings and European style religious structures fill the tiny town (population: under 200), a National Historic District which includes thirty-five buildings. The Way of the Cross, built in 1861 as the nation's first such route, passes fourteen brick alcoves containing prints depicting Christ's path in Jerusalem to the Crucifixion. The walk leads up to the 1885 Pieta Chapel, a small stone sanctuary topped by a bulky belfry, modeled after the Chapel du Blichen in Luxembourg. On a rocky hillside opposite the chapel stands the red brick twin-spired Evangelical Lutheran Church of St. John, built about 1918, while elsewhere you'll find the 1858 St. Donatus Catholic Church, an engagingly simple structure. At the peaceful little cemetery in town the artful grave markers bear German inscriptions.

The twenty room Peter Gehlen House (1848), listed on the National Register, has served over the years as a post office, trading post, grocery store, and tavern, and now contains a doll museum, while the Gehlen Barn, also Register-listed—where Luxembourg settlers lived on the top floors while animals occupied the lower level—now houses antiques. Gunports on the barn's west side served to defend against Indians in the old days, an era when the area was called Têtes des Mortes (Heads of the Dead) after a nearby stream where a battle between two bands of redskins left dismembered scalped heads floating down the creek toward the Mississippi. The Stonehouse Bakery in St. Donatus occupies a boys' high school building, and the blacksmith shop (open weekends) remains little changed from when it opened in 1885. Kalmes Restaurant and Olde Tavern, which began as a family business in the early 1850's, offers home cooked meals and also a gathering place where older St. Donatus residents meet to speak the Luxembourg dialect, taught at Kalmes during the winter.

At Bellevue, ten miles south of St. Donatus, the River Road returns to the Mississippi, where Lock and Dam Number 12 can be viewed from an adjacent park-like observation area, or from the heights of Bellevue State Park, which also boasts the Butterfly Gardens. Here special flowers, shrubs, and plants have been installed to appeal to both migrant and resident butterflies. The foliage attracts some sixty species. Down on the Mississippi, a ten-room, century old native stone house contains the Young Museum (June-Oct Sat and Sun 1-5), filled with 4000 china, crystal, silver,and other pieces along with old maps and photos. The 1848 Bellevue Elementary School, listed on the National Register, originally served as the Jackson County Courthouse, while just south of town stands the Register-listed Dyas Round Barn. Four miles west of Bellevue in Paradise Valley lies Paradise

Farm, the home of an independent fellow named Elbridge Gerry Potter, who established the farm on Big Mill Creek after his arrival in the area in 1842. He called the property "Paradise" because, as Potter explained, one had to pass through purgatory to get there, so bad were the country roads back then. Potter, a crusty old character, established on the property the first private lending library west of the Mississippi, set aside a hillside burial ground for "infidels", and once helped raise funds for a monument to fiery Revolutionary War tract writer Thomas Paine. In 1843, Potter built the Jasper Flour Mill at the mouth of Big Mill Creek near the Mississippi. From a six story native stone structure, supported with massive walnut and oak timbers, he shipped flour down the Mississippi to distant markets, and later to Union troops during the Civil War. After flour milling ceased in the early part of this century, the facility served to grind feed and grist until 1969, and now the attractively restored Register-listed mill houses a restaurant.

Bellevue residents have also recycled other old buildings, many of them now bed and breakfast establishments. The 1850 Spring Side Inn (319-872-5452), laden with "gingerbread" trim, overlooks the Mississippi, as does Mount Rest (319-872-4220), an angular tower-topped place built in 1893 and lost by the owner two years later in a card game. Others include Pillar House (319-872-4396), Dyas House (319-872-5612),on a farmstead settled in 1833, and Riverview Hotel and Restaurant (319-872-5953), built as a store and house on the Mississippi in 1844 and later converted into the Central House Hotel, owned by the Weck family for nearly a century until 1960, where Ulysses S. Grant used to stay on his trips from nearby Galena, Illinois. Out of town the Log Cabin Resort (319-872-4320) offers cabins on the Mississippi. The Country Cupboard, a gift shop, includes an old fashioned candy counter with treats displayed in an antique glass case. Windy's Mississippi Lounge, two miles northeast of town on Spruce Creek Park Road, serves meals in a dining room with views onto the waterway, while Riverview Rides (319-872-4729) offers cruises as well as trips over to Galena and passage through Lock Number 12. Back in the late 1830's the locals used the river to send away a gang of horse thieves from town. They were captured after the so-called Bellevue War, an encounter which saw four outlaws and four vigilantes killed before authorities apprehended the thirteen surviving bandits. The posse voted to decide whether to hang the captives or simply to whip and exile them. The whippers won, and they thrashed the men and then set them adrift on the Mississippi with three days' rations and ordered the na'er-do-wells never to return to Bellevue.

Eight miles south of Bellevue by Highway 52 lies the 3500 acre Green Island State Wildlife Refuge, with trails and scenic overlooks, backwater bayous, and the nation's most northerly stand of pecan trees. The road continues on to Sabula, an island city reached by a causeway. The narrow oval-shaped patch of land in the river was severed from the mainland after construction of the lock and dam system in 1930's. On River Street, which borders the Mississippi, stands a boulder bearing a metal plaque which notes that in 1835 Isaac Dorman, the town's first settler, arrived from the Illinois shore after he "crossed the river on a log and landed on this site." While still connected to the mainland, Sabula—so named in 1846 for Sabula Wood, wife of an early settler—thrived from such commercial activities as fishing, sawmills and pork production, with the goods shipped out on Mississippi River steamers. The Iowa Packing Company, established in 1879, made the town the state's fourth largest meat packing center, while in the 1870's the Octennial Oat Mill produced Sabula Oatmeal. At one time a State Fish Rescue Station, the only such facility in Iowa, operated at Sabula to recover after the spring floods and return to the river fish stranded on the banks when the high waters receded. On Pearl Street stands an old fashioned post office in a white frame building, and also the old-time Mississippi Mercantile antique store (F, Sat and Sun 10-5 through Oct), while the Jeremiah Wood House, listed on the National Register, overlooks the Mississippi from River Street. Sleepy Sabula also boasts one of the river's few remaining swinging railroad bridges, which pivots to give entry to the four story high barge tows hauling commodities.

Hauntown, which once existed five miles south of Sabula on U.S. 67, the River Road, was named for William Haun. The name serves as an appropriate designation for the vanished ghost town where Haun established Clinton County's first mill and later opened a whiskey distillery. When the railroad bypassed the village, which once claimed 115 citizens, the inhabitants all abandoned the place for greener pastures.

Just above Lock and Dam Number 13, at the north side of Clinton, the Mississippi and its adjoining marshes extend between the Iowa and Illinois shores for nearly four miles, believed to be the widest point on the entire river. Just after you enter Clinton, a turnoff to the east takes you to Eagle Point Park, a 200 acre enclave by the Mississippi with an observation tower overlooking the river. The waterway exerted a major influence in the development of Clinton, originally called New York, where in 1835 Elijah Buell began operating a ferry. In 1855 the Chicago, Iowa and Nebraska Railroad acquired the site and renamed it for DeWitt Clinton, one time governor of New York and promoter of the Erie Canal. The following year saw the rise of the elegant Randall Hotel, which featured a five story brick outside privy accessible directly from each of the floors. Although skeptics dubbed the hotel Randall's Folly, the establishment thrived as Clinton rapidly developed. Some developments disappeared, however: the elevated, stilt-supported, wooden sidewalks the town installed tended to wash away and float down the Mississippi during floods.

The most rapid growth took place in the 1880's when five sawmills, processing timber from log rafts sent down the

Mississippi from northern forests, made Clinton the world's largest timber producing city. William J. Young of Clinton became the first major sawmill operator on the river to use not only the Mississippi's currents but also steam power to move timber. In 1864, a steamboat pushed a log raft to his mill, and soon all logs sent down the river traveled with the help of steamers. Between 1865 and 1892, the production of lumber in the Clinton area increased nearly tenfold to almost 200 million board feet, with the mills spitting out so much sawdust that great piles of it, up to twenty feet high, lined the shore. The townspeople used some of the waste material to fill in sloughs and wetlands, so parts of nineteenth century Clinton stood on sawdust underpinnings. The last log raft arrived from the north in 1906, and so ended the great lumber era which created most of Clinton's late nineteenth century millionaires. Along 5th, 6th and 7th Avenues South the moguls built elegant mansions, most of them by now fallen onto hard times or disappeared. At 420 Fifth, however, survives the National Register-listed dark red brick house, embellished with terra cotta trim and stained glass windows, constructed by George M. Curtis, a founder of a sash, door and millwork company which operated in Clinton for a century. Farther down Fifth, in the business district, stands the splendid Register-listed 1914 Van Allen Building, which for seventy-five years housed Clinton's major department store. Designed by the renowned architect Louis Sullivan, the cube-shaped structure—its horizontal brick strips crossed by vertical sections whose ends sport colorful leafy motifs—is under development as an architectural center and a Sullivan museum.

At the foot of Fifth Avenue South, Clinton's main street, lies the waterfront area. Here you can drive on top of the levee through Riverview Park. In the park, the municipal band presents concerts at the bandshell in the summer (May-Aug) and the Clinton Giants Class A baseball team plays in the diminutive green-walled stadium. The levee road passes three blue and white lighthouses and the land-based showboat—its engines and other machinery gleamingly restored—where summer stock companies perform in the Lillian Russell Theatre (319-243-1260), named for the famous actress born (under the name Nellie Leonard) on the second floor of the old Hotel Clinton in 1861. Russell, whose father Charles Leonard was founder and editor of the *Clinton Herald*, returned to Clinton in 1908 for a hometown appearance.

Back in 1856, a waterfront drama involving a vessel other than a showboat played out when the steamer *Envoy* escaped a lien server, seeking to obtain repayment of debts owed by ship owner N.C. Roe, by pulling away from the dock at Clinton while still tied to the wharf. The crowd at shore looked on transfixed as the slack gradually disappeared and the rope tightened. Suddenly a great jerk pulled the ship to one side, almost capsizing it, until the mooring post finally ripped away from the ground. The steamer proceeded to Dubuque where authorities seized the boat and removed the piston heads from the engine. Roe crafted substitute pistons out of oak, and soon, much to the surprise of the officials, the *Envoy* took off. For some time the rogue boat sailed the Mississippi, dodging creditors as well as submerged trees and other hazards.

Other attractions in Clinton include Smith Brothers General Store, 1016 South 4th, with old fashioned wares; the Historical Society Museum (Sat and Sun 1:30-4:30) in Root Park, with displays on Mississippi riverboats, the nineteenth century lumber and millwork industry which so enriched Clinton, and old time firefighters; and the Bickelhaupt Arboretum (dawn to dusk), a thirteen acre spread of plantings established in 1970 by Frances and Robert Bickelhaupt on grounds around their home. Devastation caused by the Dutch Elm disease, which destroyed most of the six thousand elms planted in 1855 along Clinton's residential streets, partly inspired the couple to create the arboretum. For river activities, *Lady D.* (319-243-3611, ext.466), the "Belle of Clinton", cruises the waterway, Bill's Bait and Tackle Shop

(319-243-4696) offers fishing excursions on the Mississippi, and houseboat rentals are available at Seesen's Rent-A-Cruise (319-243-1111) at the marina in the adjacent community of Camanche, where the 1899 depot (Sun 1-5) and a restored 1951 Milwaukee Road caboose contain railroad exhibits. Camanche received its name in 1835 when Dr. George Peck, who walked to Iowa, designated a high bluff on the Mississippi for the Indian tribe Comanche, which he misspelled. A ferry soon started up between Albany, Illinois and Camanche, designated in 1840 the first county seat.

On the south side of Clinton—where Rocking Horse Bed and Breakfast (319-242-6733) takes overnight guests—puffing smoke stacks call attention to the town's industrial area, with a grain terminal, the Chicago and Northwestern shops and a large Du Pont complex. A few miles beyond Camanche, Bluff Road (County F33) leads west from Highway 67 out to the "Buffalo Bill" Cody Homestead (April-Oct 9-6), a native limestone house on a seven thousand acre farm. William F. Cody, the famous frontiersman and showman, born (1846) not in the Wild West but in the mild Midwest, lived at the homestead until the family moved to Kansas when he was eight. The house occupies a lovely, lonely spot on a slight rise with a view across the prairie where cattle and buffalo graze. A certain sense of isolation prevails, and the residence somehow seems lost in both time and place, as if still existing in the old days when steamers plied the Mississippi and pioneers ventured into the little known lands west of the river. Relics which recall that era survive at the Walnut Grove Pioneer Village (April-Oct 8-sundown) at Scott County Park, a few miles west, which includes fourteen historic buildings, among them the c. 1860 red wood Ehlers Blacksmith Shop, which operated for nearly a century, a c. 1870 schoolhouse typical of the more than five thousand one room schoolhouses in nineteenth century rural Iowa, a pioneer cabin (c. 1837) which housed a family of six in one room, and the c. 1853 St. Ann's Church. At the First Christian Church graveyard in the town of Long Grove—near where A Night On the Farm (319-285-4377) offers bed and breakfast—lies the grave of Buffalo Bill's brother, Sam Cody. You'll also find bed and breakfast at the Woodlands (319-289-3177) in Princeton on Highway 67, the River Road which lies back to the east.

Further Cody memories linger at Le Claire, on the Mississippi south of Princeton. At 1034 North Cody Street stood another Cody family house, later moved to the Buffalo Bill Historical Center in Cody, Wyoming. Le Claire also boasts the Buffalo Bill Museum (May 15-Oct 15, 9-5, winter 9-5 Sat and Sun only), with exhibits on Cody's Iowa roots and his later career as a Pony Express rider, Union Army soldier and Wild West show impresario and performer.

The museum also contains displays relating to Le Claire's river history. During the mid-nineteenth century, the town served as home to many workers connected with the steamboat industry, including captains, engineers, and rapids pilots hired on ships to steer them through the treacherous fourteen-mile-long Rock Island Rapids which once vexed traffic on the Mississippi. Fourteen old Le Claire dwellings once occupied by the town's pilots, ship captains, and boat builders are listed on the National Register under the description, "Houses of Mississippi Rivermen". The old Marine Railway boat repair yards began operation at Le Claire in 1856, and in the village lived Colonel Thomas Clark Eads and his wife Ann, owner in the 1830's and 1840's of the Hotel Berlin, across the street from Isaac Cody's house. They were the parents of James B. Eads (see the St.Louis passages in the Missouri chapter), builder of St.Louis' Eads Bridge and other important Mississippi-related projects.

On the waterfront next to the museum stands the now grounded wooden hulled sternwheeler *Lone Star*, believed to be the last working steamboat on the Upper Mississippi. Adjacent to the *Lone Star* also rests after its labors the white and blue hued

City of Baton Rouge excursion boat. For present day river trips, the *Twilight* and the *Julia Belle Swain* depart daily from Le Claire on two day cruises (800-331-1467), late May to mid-October, to Chestnut Mountain Resort, where passengers may overnight, near Galena, Illinois. Near the display ships on the Le Claire waterfront stands a plaque to the elm, removed in 1964, where Buffalo Bill played as a boy and which became famous all up and down the river as the Green Tree Hotel. The stately elm, which cast a pool of shade a hundred feet in diameter, served as a haven for impoverished rivermen from near and far along the Mississippi. There by the steamboat landing, the Mississippi men slept on blankets and cooked their meals beneath the tree's sheltering limbs.

Other activity took place under the famous tree. Antoine Le Claire, one of early Iowa's most colorful characters, parlayed with the Indians here. Half French Canadian and half Indian, the 5 foot 8 inch Le Claire weighed in at more than 350 pounds. The Iowa State Bank squeezed his likeness onto the $5 bill in the late 1850's, and the first railroad locomotive to reach nearby Davenport in 1855—the beginning of the end for steamboat traffic—was named for him. After the 1832 Davenport meeting to end the Black Hawk War, at which Le Claire served as an interpreter, he received two sections of the land ceded by the Indians, one parcel in Davenport and the other now occupied by the town of Le Claire.

You'll also find the restaurant Sneaky Pete's in Le Claire. It offers attractive views of the river, and specializes in wood-cooked meats, which are served in an eccentric ambiance, featuring kerosene lamps, drinks in fruit jars, a salad bar installed in an antique bathtub, a wall papered with business cards, and the bottoms of amputated ties dangling from the ceiling of the century and and a half old building, the town's oldest commercial structure, originally a hotel. Three bed and breakfast establishments in and around Le Claire overlook the river: Monarch

Inn (319-289-3011), on the Mississippi where the fearsome rapids once began, Sunrise (319-332-9203), and Mohr Haus (319-289-4503). Other bed and breakfast places include Latimer (319-289-5747) in the center of town, and the Country Inn (319-289-4793) north of town. The new (1989) Mississippi Valley Welcome Center, by Interstate 80 just south of Le Claire, includes a scenic overlook to the river, provides tourist information, and also contains displays, including nineteenth century photos, on the area's nautical history.

A few miles south of Le Claire, Highway 67 curves to afford a good view of Lock and Dam Number 14, and at Riverdale, on the outskirts of the Davenport metropolitan area, the River Road passes a huge Alcoa factory—one of the biggest industrial installations on the Mississippi—which extends along the waterway for about a mile. Established in the late 1940's, the plant, where three thousand workers produce two million pounds of metal a day, is the world's largest aluminium sheet and plate rolling mill.

From the adjacent town of Bettendorf, one of the Quad cities, the *Quad City Queen* offers area excursions on the river, while the *Mississippi Belle II* departs at 7 a.m. to travel some hundred miles upriver to Dubuque (for reservations on both boats: 800-527-3152). The newest Mississippi attraction at Bettendorf—named for the Bettendorf Axle and Wagon Company, in its day the largest railroad car shop west of the river—is Steamboat Landing, a $57 million riverfront development project, home port of the lavish old-style but new *Diamond Lady* (800-448-7540), which departed on its first casino cruise to Iowa port cities on April Fool's Day, 1991. Plans for the Landing, located on terrain once occupied by the J.I. Case farm equipment factory, include a hotel, an indoor theme mall, a factory outlet retail center, and a riverfront walkway along the Mississippi. At Bettendorf's Children's Museum (Tu-Sat 10-4:30, Sun 1-4:30), youngsters can appear on TV station KIDS, drive mini-cars through Traffic Town, take machines apart on the Disassembly Line, and cook up fun activities in a 1915 farm kitchen. For more modern day fare, a restored gas station in Bettendorf houses the Waterfront Deli. The 1914 St. Francis Monastery (tours by appointment: 319-355-0291), home of Franciscan monks and a religious retreat which recalls those in the Italian hill towns, includes gardens with vistas onto the Mississippi and the Quad Cities area.

Adjacent to Bettendorf lies East Davenport, an old-fashioned river village established in 1851, tucked into sixty square blocks with some five hundred houses and commercial buildings, many from the nineteenth century. Here at the only place where the Upper Mississippi runs directly east to west for any distance, the river's current scoured an eddy at the foot of the Rock Island Rapids, one of the world's longest such hazards, which began at Le Claire, fourteen miles north. Zebulon Pike stopped here in August, 1805, during his expedition up the Mississippi before he attempted to brave the rapids, surveyed in 1837 by Robert E. Lee, then a recent West Point graduate. Near the eddy settled a soldier named Captain James Stubbs, a hermit who lived in a cave, and soon the site became known to river travelers as Stubbs' Eddy. During the Civil War, the Union Army established a training post called Camp McClellan at present day Lindsay Park, named for a lumber tycoon, which overlooks the Mississippi. On the third weekend in September the park reverts to a Civil War encampment when some five hundred men, clad in period uniforms, re-create battles at the colorful Civil War Muster and Mercantile Exposition, started in 1973, which includes an 1860's tea party, a Military Ball with costumed participants, and other gala nineteenth century events. After the war, logs sent down the river from northern forests fed the town's sawmills, which produced lumber shipped west by rail to settlers who could then build wood rather than sod dwellings. Near Mound Street rises the 1877 wood railroad trestle, remnant of the early days of train traffic west of the Mississippi. After the turn of the century a riverfront fire and the end of the lumber era turned East Davenport into a declining backwater, but in the early 1970's began a movement to restore and preserve the old town, named a National Historic District in 1980.

The commercial area, clustered in a few blocks by the Mississippi, includes a number of old buildings recycled for present day use. At 1029 Mound stands the old 1880's Kuehl Hotel, a limestone and brick structure on the site of the mound where Captain Stubbs occupied his cave. Another hotel, St. Paul House, which once catered to river rapids pilots and raftsmen, stood at the corner of Mound and East 11th. At the corner of East 11th and Jersey Ridge Road—named for the cows which took this path from the pasture to the barn at milking time—stands the early 1860's Boyler's Blacksmith shop, with an ornamental metal sign and, on the flank, a painted ad for "Genuine 'Bull Durham' The old reliable Smoking Tobacco, standard of the world", with the bull image by now blending into the old brick. Atop a rise perches the 1899 Register-listed Pierce School No. 13, which now houses shops. Next door stands the Italianate mansion built by Robert Christie, who arrived in East Davenport in 1854 to establish a sawmill on the river. Not far away, at 2301 East 11th, the International Fire Museum (May-Oct W and Sat 10-2) occupies a restored vintage firehouse. At 1329 College Avenue, outside the business area, Claim House survives, originally built along the river near Bettendorf in 1832 by the son of Davenport founder George Davenport as the first residence west of the Upper Mississippi, and moved to its present site in the late 1860's. On College Avenue in 1836 the Sac and Nation gathered for the last time to sign the "Keokuk Purchase Treaty" by which the Indians relinquished their lands along the west side of the Mississippi.

As you continue along the Mississippi on the East River Drive into Davenport, a hilly area of mansion-lined steep streets which rise to the right includes the late nineteenth century Bridge Avenue and Prospect Terrace residential districts, where historic houses recall the city's early days. At 1017 Mississippi Avenue, you'll find U.S. Congressman Joe Lane's residence (1890), topped by an octagonal tower—typical of the turrets, verandas, and other lookouts which afford river views—sported by many dwellings in the neighborhood. Lumbermen occupied some of the mansions (901 and 945 Mississippi, 225 Prospect Terrace, 911 and 1192 College), while the imposing 1871 Italianate-style place at 1206 East River Drive belonged to Ambrose C. Fulton, known as "Locomotive in Boots" the first person to propose a railroad bridge at Davenport. This bridge, finished in the spring of 1856, was the first span across the Mississippi south of the Minneapolis-St. Paul area. It left Davenport at Federal Street, a short distance downriver from "Locomotive's" house and not far from the present 1894 Government Rail-auto Bridge, built to pivot a full 360 degrees when letting boats through.

The completion of the 1856 bridge, which marked the beginning of the end of the steamboat era, exerted a profound influence on the Mississippi. The first railroad to reach the Mississippi, the Rock Island and Pacific line, extended from Chicago to Rock Island, Illinois, reaching that point on the river's east bank across from Davenport in early 1854. Work to continue the line westward from Davenport soon began, and on July 19, 1855 a flatboat delivered to Iowa the first locomotive, named "Antoine Le Claire". Before long the railroad interests organized a company to build a bridge across the river to connect the lines. Only a few short years before this bold concept seemed so remote and unlikely that in 1851 an Iowa wit versified: "I dreamt that a bridge of a single span / O'er the wide Mississippi was made. / And I also dreamt like an insane man / That the railroad there was laid." The project once only dreamed of, proceeded. Construction began, however, with vociferous complaints from the steamboat industry, a seeming repeat of the bitter opposition mounted by the rivermen when the first bridge across the Ohio at Wheeling, West Virginia was constructed in 1849. After completion of the bridge at Davenport in the spring 1856, the controversy between the river and rail interests continued to rage for, as Marquis Childs noted in *Mighty Mississippi,* the conflict embodied "the whole opposition between the river system and the railroad system, between the individualistic, chaotic South and West and the corporate, efficient East." The outcome of the bridge battle would thus determine which form of transportation, trains or ships, and what sort of culture would prevail along the great waterway.

On May 6, 1856, shortly after the span joined Iowa and Illinois, the steamboat *Effie Afton,* headed upriver for St. Paul, crashed into the bridge's piers, touching off a fire which burned the wooden construction. Less than four months later, however, the railroad completed a new bridge. J. S. Hurd, the *Effie Afton's* captain, sued the train company, arguing that the bridge created an obstruction to navigation. T.D. Lincoln, an attorney from Cincinnati, served as one of Captain Hurd's lawyers, while the railroads retained a less renowned Lincoln from Springfield, Illinois named Abraham. On September 22 and 23 the *Chicago Daily News* reported Abe Lincoln's arguments, noting that the Illinois attorney stated he "had no prejudice against steamboats or steamboatmen," but "there is a travel from east to west, whose demands are not less important than that of the river." The railroad's attorney cited figures on the heavy traffic across the span, which "shows that this bridge must be treated with respect in this court and is not to be kicked about with contempt." Lincoln discussed the collision, which he suggested was intentional, and he then dismissed the possibilities of a tunnel or higher bridge. Next, he uttered the most welcome words any lawyer can speak: "He said he had much more to say, many things he could suggest to the jury, but he would close to save time." Perhaps this brevity impressed the court, but—for whatever reason—Lincoln's arguments carried the day and, after further litigation which ended with an 1862 U.S. Supreme Court decision, the judiciary finally determined that bridges across the Mississippi did not present navigational hazards and could be allowed to stand. Years later, in July, 1928, dredgers recovered from the bottom of the Mississippi the bell of the *Effie Afton*—a relic of the long vanished era, before the Civil War, when the great paddlewheelers, now virtually extinct, ruled the mighty Mississippi.

In 1808, half a century before the bridge at Davenport changed the course of the Mississippi's development, settlers began arriving in the area, then occupied by Indians. Conflicts between the pioneers and the Indians led to the Black Hawk War, settled on September 30, 1832 by a treaty signed near the present day intersection of 5th Street and Pershing Avenue. The Putnam Museum (Tu-Sat 9-5, Sun 1-5), on a bluff above the Mississippi, houses the historic treaty, as well as the "River, Prairie and People" exhibit, which traces the development of the area from prehistoric times to the present. The Davenport Museum of Art (Tu-Sat 10-4:30, Sun 1-4:30) next door contains a large collection of Haitian paintings, Mexican colonial art, and a regionalist collection featuring works by Thomas Hart Benton of Missouri, Kansas' John Steuart Curry, and Iowa's "artist laureate" Grant Wood. The unusual Catich Gallery (M, W, F 1-3, Sun 1-4:30) at St. Ambrose University displays calligraphy, slate-incised sketches, and other works by Father Edward M. Catich, an authority on the alphabet of ancient Rome,while another offbeat museum in the library at Palmer College of Chiropractic, founded by D.D. Palmer, in 1895 originator of the discipline, includes displays of human bones and skeletons.

The nearby solid looking rough hewn stone Episcopal Cathedral, said to be the denomination's oldest cathedral (1867) in the United States, contains in its wall a stone from Canterbury Cathedral in England. The local Episcopalians arrived in

Davenport in 1837. They greeted their first bishop in 1854. He was a true heavyweight, the three hundred pound Reverend Henry Washington Lee, and made a great impression around the diocese, as any number of carriages, chairs and bedsteads collapsed under him. An even weightier historical figure, the famous slave Dred Scott, once lived in Davenport, having been brought to the area from St.Louis in 1835 by his owner, Dr. John Emerson, who built a house at 217 East 2nd Street. Emerson, buried in the old City Cemetery, later took Scott to Fort Snelling, the Mississippi River outpost at Minneapolis. Based on his presence there and other free areas, including Iowa, the only state west of the Mississippi to ban slavery, Scott in 1854 sued in St. Louis for his emancipation, a case he finally lost in the U.S. Supreme Court three years later.

Downtown Davenport includes such noteworthy structures as the Public Library (1968), a low white well-windowed building designed by renowned architect Edvard Durrell Stone; across the street, 1853 St. Anthony's, the city's first church; the 1934 art deco Mississippi Hotel; the Davenport Bank, downtown's tallest building, with an old fashioned interior decorated by paintings depicting the area's history; and nineteenth century red brick buildings in the 400 block of Brady Street which house antique stores and Trash Can Annie, claimed to be one of the nation's largest antique clothing emporiums, with more than 10,000 items dating back to the Civil War era. Davenport Riverboat Gallery, 110 West 3rd, sells ship models, nautical wares and river-related art works.

Along the waterfront stretches Le Claire Park, retirement home of the 1932 *Sainte Genevieve*, a river dredge emplaced there in 1985. At the park in the last week of July the Bix Biederbecke jazz festival takes place, honoring the local musician born (1903) and buried (1931) in Davenport. At age sixteen Bix sat on the levee and listened to Louis Armstrong play, and soon began tooting his own horn on showboats. A bit upstream lies Lock and

Dam Number 15, the nation's largest roller gate dam, complete with a Visitor Center and observation deck. In the Mississippi south of town lies Credit Island. Now a park, the island was named for an early British fur trading post that sold supplies to Indians on credit, receiving repayment with pelts delivered after the winter trapping season. In August, 1814, three hundred and thirty-four American soldiers under Major Zachary Taylor, later U.S. President, arrived at the island from St. Louis in eight keelboats in order to punish the Indians for their attacks on American installations. Aided by about one thousand braves, some fifty British troops defeated the Americans on September 5 in the only battle Taylor ever lost, forcing the Yankees to retreat back down the Mississippi. Later, in September, 1837, another army officer, lieutenant Robert E. Lee, arrived in the area to survey the river from Davenport north to Le Claire.

From the new President's Landing, inaugurated April 1, 1991 with the first departure of the *President*, that ship sails on daily breakfast, lunch, and dinner gambling cruises (800-B0AT-711). Completed in 1933 and recently converted into the world's largest casino vessel, the *President* houses an on-board river museum which includes the old steam engines of the five-deck-tall sidewheeler, a National Historic Landmark, once the largest overnight passenger steamer on the Mississippi. For less chancy activities, the Fejervary Park Zoo (May-Labor Day) features plants and animals native to the Upper Mississippi Valley. The bucolic Duck Creek Parkway forms a trail along the creek—used by explorers and frontiersmen as it runs parallel to the Mississippi but flows in the opposite direction—which connects a series of parks in north Davenport. For an unusual restaurant, Iowa Machine Shed, decorated with antique farm tools and implements, serves family-style meals and asks "Have you hugged your hog today?" Bed and breakfast places include River Oaks (319-326-2629), in a Register-listed 1850's house overlooking the Mississippi, and Village Bed and Breakfast (319-322-4905), an

1857 Greek Revival-style residence, also Register-listed and with a view of the river, while the 1871 Bishop's Inn (319-324-2454) formerly served as the Catholic bishop's residence.

As you leave Davenport the road takes you through an industrial area, with a large Ralston Purina plant and the boxy brick Oscar Mayer factory. Farther on, just south of the city limits, stand other facilities, including a Peavey grain installation, an Amoco asphalt plant and, at Buffalo, a huge riverside complex of brown buildings that comprise the Davenport Cement Company, furnished with quarried raw materials carried over the road in an elevated conveyor. In the mid-1830's Captain Benjamin W. Clark established at Buffalo one of Iowa's first public ferries across the Mississippi. In his *Notes on Wisconsin Territory*, published in 1836, Albert M. Lea deemed Buffalo "the most convenient place to cross the Mississippi that I have seen anywhere." The first ferries were crude flatboats propelled across the river by poles and oars. In 1833 the Illinois legislature licensed the ferries to connect that state with Iowa, which in the late 1830's and early 1840's issued charters for its own ferryboats on the Mississippi. Even after the advent of bridges, the boats continued to serve travelers, with the *W.J.Quinlan* operating between Davenport and Rock Island until 1946 (fare: ten cents), although by then three bridges spanned the river in the Quad Cities area.

Five miles south of Buffalo, at the north end of Montpelier, a former stagecoach station on the 1850's route between Davenport and Muscatine, the sign "Varner's Depot" indicates one of the most unusual bed and breakfast places anywhere (319-381-3652). Behind the house on a short stretch of train tracks, complete with a signal, stands a red and yellow caboose, outfitted with sleeping quarters for four and a kitchen. Farther on, near the River Road, Highway 22, lies Wildcat Den State Park, an area settled in 1838 by Benjamin Nye. Ten years later he built a grist mill on Pine Creek, a well preserved relic listed on the National

Register. Nearby stands a restored turn-of-the-century schoolhouse. Closer to Muscatine, you'll pass near the Fairport State Fish Hatchery (for tours: 319-263-5062), a one time U.S. facility now run by Iowa. Formerly called Jug Town, Fairport took its nickname from the pottery works supplied by clay hauled across the Mississippi from Illinois when the river iced over. At the Kent Research Farm (for tours: 319-263-8971) off the highway, Kent Feeds studies livestock and poultry nutrition.

At Muscatine, thirty miles west of Davenport, the river resumes its southward course. The town began in 1835 when James Casey started a trading post to sell fuel and supplies to river boats, whose captains referred to the new settlement as Casey's Wood Pile. The following year it took the name Bloomington, changed in 1850 to eliminate mail delivery confusion with the Bloomingtons in Illinois and Indiana. The new designation derived from the Mascoutin tribe which lived in the area. Muscatine, the world's only town with that name—no danger of mail confusion any more—became an active river port. In 1838 a ferry connection to Illinois began with the flatboat *Polly Keith*, the first of such services which ended in 1881 after completion of the High Bridge, so called as it rose one hundred and twelve feet above the river, high enough for the tallest steamboats to pass. The wood span survived intact until 2:30 a.m. June 1, 1956 when a one hundred and sixty foot center section collapsed. The repaired antique remained in use until completion of the new bridge in 1972. This span leaves Muscatine just below Mark Twain Overlook, a small hilltop park just north of downtown. Twain highly praised the colorful summer sunsets at Muscatine, but allowed that he did not rise early enough to judge the sunrise. Twain (Samuel Clemens) moved at age eighteen to the town in 1854 to join his widowed mother, Jane Clemens, and his brothers Henry and Orion, who put the newcomer to work as a printer and reporter at the *Muscatine Journal*. The Clemens family lived at a house located near the corner of Walnut and

Mississippi Drive by a present day dry cleaning store across the street from the Register-listed McKibben House, now an art gallery, an iron balcony-bedecked brick residence built by a lumberman and saloon owner. The nearby Riverside Park along the Mississippi includes a statue of an Indian brave looking out to the waterway, a monument given to the city in 1926, the plaque states, by the "Musquitine Tribe No. 95 Improved Order of Red Men".

Downtown Muscatine, which lies close to the Mississippi, still retains the flavor of an old time river town. Especially evocative are the block on East 2nd between Cedar and Sycamore, lined with brightly colored nineteenth century facades, and Iowa Avenue from 2nd to 3rd, where galleries and craft shops occupy vintage buildings. On Chestnut between West 2nd and 3rd stands an old brick building, now a laundry but originally a church where the parents of radio pioneer Lee de Forest, the famous inventor—who grew up in Muscatine—married. Along tree-shaded West 2nd and 3rd and the intersecting streets stand a number of imposing nineteenth century mansions which housed the era's leading Muscatine families. The plain brick house at 205-7 West 3rd belonged to Alexander Clark, a free black who settled in Muscatine in 1842 and sold cut wood to steamboats for fuel, eventually earning sufficient money to enter the real estate business. At age fifty-seven Clark became the second black—after his son—to graduate from the University of Iowa Law School. Later he served as minister to Liberia in West Africa, where he died in 1891. At 315 West 3rd lumberman William Huttig lived; in 1889 he served as president of the Muscatine Bridge Commission, which promoted the High Bridge. Materials for the classic-style 1853 house at 205 Cherry and for the 1880 Queen Anne mansion at 206 Cherry arrived by steamboat. Cherry dead-ends by these houses, perched high above the Mississippi, which stretches before you here in a splendid panorama.

Back down by the river on Mississippi Drive, south of

downtown, stands the 1907 red brick McKee Button Company factory. Established in 1895, the firm may well be the most river-related family-owned business on the entire waterway. The industry began in 1890 when John F. Boepple, a one-time buttonmaker in Germany who fabricated his product there from horn, cut his foot on a clam shell while swimming in the Mississippi. Boepple, a farm worker in Iowa, collected a few of the hard, pearly-hued shells and from them cut a dozen buttons—the first fresh water pearl buttons made in the United States—which he sold to a store in Muscatine for ten cents. Thus began the city's soon thriving river-based button industry. Until then, most of America's buttons were imported or came from sea shells, but after Boepple's find a clam rush developed in Muscatine. Hundreds of boats crammed the Mississippi, fires of clam boiling installations flared along the banks, and piles of shells littered the boom town. When a fisherman found a pearl he sold to a Chicago jeweler for $2000, even more fortune seekers flocked to Muscatine. By around 1910, at the height of the industry, forty-three local companies employing more than two thousand five hundred workers churned out some seventeen million gross of buttons. Just inside the McKee factory appears a display of twenty-four shells, the name of the firm and town written in letters formed by buttons, and an ear of corn image shaped with colored buttons. Along the hallway off to the right you'll see old photos of the original factory operations as well as a July 5, 1946 *Muscatine Journal* which pictures Ronald Reagan, "Warner Brothers motion picture star", holding a shot of the Pearl Button Queen, who he selected from photos sent to him. Although the clam beds eventually ran out, McKee remained in business, with the plant's hundred or so employees producing buttons made of polyester since 1958.

Muscatine offers some other attractions. Weed Park affords a view onto the Mississippi. The 1855 Octagon Place, out near Highway 61, occupied by the Sinnett family until 1934 now serves as an office. The Art Center (Tu-F 11-5, Th also 7-9), part of which occupies the fifteen room 1908 Musser mansion, contains exhibits which include the Great River Collection of paintings, drawings, prints and maps of the Mississippi and material relating to the local button industry. At the boxy, 1907 Muscatine Broom Factory building, 918 Colver—built with blocks formed by sand and gravel from the riverfront—three generations of Metzgers crafted handmade brooms from Mexican straw. In a residential area near this musty old cottage industry relic you'll see the more substantial and fragrant Heinz canning facility, established here in 1893 and by now the company's largest plant outside of Pittsburgh as well as the biggest canning plant between the Mississippi and the Rocky Mountains. In downtown Muscatine spread the facilities of the publicly-held office furniture manufacturer Hon (from Home-O-Nize) Industries, the town's largest employer, with some seventeen hundred workers. Out on Highway 61 to the north lies the campus-like headquarters of tire retreader Bandag, a New York Stock Exchange Company, while south of town operates a Monsanto factory which makes alachlor, the main ingredient in Lasso herbicide. Farther south on Highway 61, toward Fruitland, roadside stands sell the well known local watermelons, cantaloupe, sweet potatoes and other products cultivated in the Muscatine "Island" area, a thirty thousand acre spread formerly an island tucked into the bend of the Mississippi.

County Road X 61, the River Road—here gravel—continues south along the waterway to Toolesboro, site of the National Register-listed Hopewell culture Indian burial mounds. Dating from 200 B.C. to 400 A.D., these rise near where the Iowa River meets the Mississippi. Although most of the hundred or so mounds here disappeared when settlers started farming the area, by the Visitor Center (Memorial Day-Labor Day F-M 1-4)—which contains displays relating to the Hopewell—two such formations survive. Nearby spreads a half-acre Demonstration Prairie Plot, established in 1974. A few miles up the Iowa lies Wapello, established in 1836 and named for the Ioway tribe's peace-loving chief who met nearby with the truculent Black Hawk in an unsuccessful effort to prevent what became known as the Black Hawk War.

On June 25, 1673 at the Iowa River by Toolesboro landed Marquette and Joliet. As Marquette recorded in his *Narrative*, they then followed "a narrow and somewhat beaten path leading to a fine prairie." Suddenly the explorers came upon an Indian village where "the savages quickly issued from their cabins, " two of them bearing feather-decorated peace pipes which the braves offered to the explorers. The Frenchmen spent the night with the friendly Indians, who the next day—six hundred strong—escorted the travelers back to their canoes on the Mississippi, "giving us every manifestation of the joy Our visit had caused them."

Along the waterway just east of Toolesboro Burris City once flourished on the north shore of the Iowa River, a boom town founded in the late 1850's but soon washed away when the Mississippi flooded. The River Road continues south on Highway 99 through rather featureless countryside removed from the Mississippi. Near Sperry, off to the west, Grandpa Bill's Farm (May-Dec) operates on a century-old farmstead, featuring hay-rides, a children's playbarn, barbecue dinners and weekend performances of country music (319-985-2106). On the way into Burlington you'll pass on the left the J.I.Case factory, where a sign proudly proclaims, "Backhoe Capital of the World". Now a subsidiary of Tenneco, the company descends from the farm machinery firm founded in the mid-nineteenth century by Jerome Increase Case.

The pleasant town of Burlington remains much as native son Hartzell Spence described the place he called Riverton in his novel *One Foot In Heaven*: "Built on five hills overlooking the Mississippi River, Riverton was opulent with handsome homes set in expensive lawns, with clean stores, wide streets and many churches." Many of those old homes lie in the National Register-listed Heritage Hill Historic District, filled with nearly one hundred and sixty structures built in a wide variety of styles. In 1874, hilly Burlington introduced horse-drawn cars to take people to their houses in the high areas. After pulling the vehicles up the horses rested on the rear platform of the car as it coasted back down. Century old Snake Alley connects the Heritage Hill area with the business district fifty-eight feet beneath the hilltop. With seven curves over two hundred and seventy-five feet, the Alley rivals San Francisco's Lombard Street for the title "Crookedest Street in the World", as Ripley's "Believe It or Not" designated the Iowa artery. By the upper entrance of the sinuous street stands the Phelps House Museum (May-Oct Th and Sun 1:30-4:30), installed in a mid-nineteenth century mansion. A block from the bottom of the Alley the old German Methodist Church (1868) houses an arts center (Tu-F 12-5, Sat and Sun 2-5). Down in town, Jefferson Street between 4th and 8th includes a scattering of late nineteenth century commercial buildings, while over at 3rd and Columbia stands the 1850 Joshua Kopp House. Next door lies the site of Iowa's first capital, where in 1838 the Territory's initial assembly convened. A block up the street the Public Library stands, a striking Register-listed 1898 dark red stone structure with green copper gutter trim. The high-ceiling wood interior, outfitted with oil paintings and a fireplace, offers a pleasant setting for readers. The Register-listed First Congregational Church, in English Gothic style, dates from the 1840's, while out in West Burlington the Lady of Grace Grotto, a religious enclave, includes stones from around the country.

Central Burlington's site, tucked away between two ridges, required an unusual street pattern, with the main arteries running from the Mississippi rather than along it, as in most river cities. The main thoroughfares therefore offers views down to the waterway. Centerpiece of the riverfront—where in October 1858 Abe Lincoln arrived on a steamboat to deliver a speech in town—is the new (1988) Port of Burlington Welcome Center (April-Oct 10-6), installed in the 1928 Municipal Docks building renovated by funds from the state lottery. At the docks, barges could be loaded with coal carried by a conveyor directly from freight cars, an efficient technique which river interests thought would revive the Mississippi shipping industry. With its river-related displays, the Docks Welcome Center revives many Mississippi memories. "The Land, The River, and its People" exhibit includes a model of the paddlewheeler *Burlington*, while a pilot's cabin and wheel face a large photo of the river as it looks just outside at this point. A colorful mural by local artist David Garrison depicts historical vignettes, including Marquette and Joliet, the railroad bridge at Burlington, and steamboat era scenes. A canoe on display used in April 1984 by Valerie Fons-Kruger and Verlen Kruger recalls their record breaking twenty-three day ten hour and twenty minute float trip down the Mississippi's 2348 miles from the source at Lake Itasca to the Gulf of Mexico. On the boat's bow appears the inscription, "By your endurance ye shall gain your lives" (Luke 21:19).

Just south of the Port of Burlington, the *Julie* excursion boat offers trips on the Mississippi (May-Sept Sat and Sun, 319-753-5574). Near here stood the warehouse for the Diamond Jo steamship line, a freight service eventually overtaken by the railroad. By the nearby angular Frank Lloyd Wright-ish depot stands Chicago, Burlington and Quincy display engine number 3003. The line, which reached Burlington in 1855, built a railroad bridge in 1868 which the current span replaced in 1892. So powerful was the C.B. & Q. in southern Iowa that the area through which the line ran became known as "The Burlington Reservation". In addition to ships and trains, Burlington also boasts an early air connection, recalled by Art Hartman Drive near the airport. The name commemorates the man who, on May 10, 1910, flew a plane he built—Iowa's first recorded flight—after consulting with the Wright brothers. A block north of the Welcome Center, Big Muddy's Bar and Grill occupies the renovated (in 1987) 1898 Cedar Rapids and Northern Railway building, which lies within view of the Mississippi. The restaurant includes as decor photos of river scenes and of the adjacent MacArthur Bridge being built from 1915 to 1917. Just north of the bridge lies the recently developed Riverfront Park, while around the corner on Main an 1841 brick building, originally an inn, houses the Steamboat Stop Country Store, with Iowa crafts and wares and other gift items. Also on Main, south of downtown near the river, stands the 1924 publishing plant and office of *The Hawk-Eye*, "Iowa's Oldest Newspaper", as the masthead boasts. It succeeded a paper started in 1837 at Montrose, downriver, and moved a few years later to Burlington.

Mosquito Park, a tiny overlook high on a bluff tucked away behind the Heritage Hill residential district, affords an excellent view of the Mississippi, its islands bristling with trees. Off to the right stretches the bridge, while to the left tower the rounded, white Garnac grain elevators. Locals favor the scenic setting at Mosquito Park for weddings. A rambling white house with green trim just by the park enjoys one of the best residential sites on the entire Mississippi. At another park, South Hill, 6th and Elm, scientists gathered on August 7, 1869 at the most favorable point in the nation to observe a solar eclipse. In Perkins Park, the Apple Trees Museum (May-Oct Th and Sun 1:30-4:30), whose historical displays include a headdress worn by Black Hawk, occupies the surviving wing of the mansion built by Charles E. Perkins, president of the C.B. & Q. Railroad. His many philanthropic efforts included the gift of "The Garden of the Gods" to Colorado Springs, Colorado.

Along the Mississippi in the southern section of town stretches National Register-listed Crapo (pronounced Cray-po) Park, where in 1805 Zebulon Pike first raised the American flag on Iowa soil. A latter day (1909) log house, the Hawkeye Log Cabin (May-Sept Th and Sun 1:30-4:30), contains antique tools and implements. Crapo Park also offers unspoiled bluff-side views of the Mississippi and the Black Hawk Trails, named for the Sac and Fox leader who hunted on them with his braves. Black Hawk spent part of his afterlife in Burlington, to which he returned after his demise. Following the disappearance of the chief's body from its grave in 1839, the bones resurfaced a year later at the office of a Quincy, Illinois dentist. The relics later went on display at the Burlington Geological and Historic Society, which burned down in 1855, so cremating Black Hawk's mortal remains.

Burlington Steamboat Days, featuring music, cruises and a sailboat regatta, takes places along the waterfront for a week beginning the second Monday in June. Burlington boasts the office of MADRAC, the Mississippi Annual Down River Adventure by Canoe, a one week hundred and eighty or so mile canoe trip event, started in 1983, along the Mississippi (for information: 319-752-4142). Lakeview Bed and Breakfast (319-752-8735 and 800-753-8735) offers accommodation in a modern house built from a hundred and fifty year old country inn.

South of Burlington Highway 61 crosses the Skunk River. In the fall of 1884, reports surfaced of a huge sea monster said to have traveled up the Mississippi and into the Skunk. Stories in papers along the Mississippi described the beast, but the affair proved to be a hoax devised by an Iowa joker in league with a few editors. As you enter Fort Madison you'll pass the forbidding white and yellow hued stone walls of the medieval castle-like Iowa State Penitentiary, established in 1839 as the oldest penal institution west of the Mississippi. Some portions of the original building still stand. The complex enjoys a prime river-side site, but high walls prevent residents from enjoying the view. Facing the river not far beyond the state pen lies Sheaffer Pen (tours Tu and Th 9:30 on twenty-four hour notice: 319-372-3300), founded in Fort Madison in 1912 by Walter A. Sheaffer, a high school dropout who invented the fountain pen in 1907. Display cases in the lobby of the plant—which every year turns out more than twelve million units of three hundred different products—hold antique and historic pens, including a desk set used to sign the United Nations charter in San Francisco in 1945 and the instrument which signed the Japanese Peace Treaty.

By Sheaffer Pen stretches the triangular-sectioned 1927 Santa Fe Bridge, which carries both trains and cars. This is the world's longest double deck (vehicles above, trains on the lower route) swing span (five hundred and twenty-five feet) bridge. The original stone chimney of old Fort Madison, built in 1808-9 and burned in 1813, stands by the river just across from Sheaffer Pen. On the firm's employee parking lot workers by chance discovered the remains of the fort in 1965, the nation's first military outpost west of the Mississippi north of St. Louis. In Riverview Park a few blocks to the south the city erected a replica of the fort (mid-May-mid-Sept 10-5) crafted by volunteer workers imprisoned in the state penitentiary. On the limestone sections from the original fort which now comprise foundation facings of the three reconstructed blockhouses appear reddish burn marks left by the fire set when soldiers burned the outpost in 1813, just before they abandoned it and escaped down the Mississippi from attacking Indians. After the fort's fall the British and their Indian allies controlled the Mississippi down to St. Louis. Nearby rises the 1910 Santa Fe depot, used until 1968 and now a history museum (May-Oct Tu-Sun 10-4). The *Madi Lee* (319-372-3276), moored at "A" dock in Riverview Park, offers sailboat rides on Lake Cooper, as area residents call this stretch of the Mississippi upstream from the Keokuk Dam. *The Emerald Lady* riverboat casino (800-448-7450) regularly docks nearby; in mid 1991 the ship began cruises between Burlington, Fort Madison and Keokuk. On the riverfront to the north, opposite the rebuilt fort, rises the recently restored Kingsley Inn (319-372-7074), a bed and breakfast establishment in a century old building. The Morton House (319-372-9517) also takes bed and breakfast guests.

A few blocks west of the river lies the 1841 National Register-listed Lee County Courthouse, believed the oldest one in continuous use in Iowa. Inside the structure—rather unassuming, except for the four fat columns which front it—hang photos showing the March, 1911 fire which damaged the building. The old Lee County Jail next door houses a law enforcement museum. Across the street stands the Register-listed boxy brick 1858 Albright House, home of descendants of American flag maker Betsy Ross, whose daughter and her offspring repose in Fort Madison's City Cemetery. One of Ross' granddaughters married a Fort Madison merchant. On County Road X38 a few miles north of town Brush College survives (shown by appointment: 319-372-7661), a c. 1860 one room school outfitted with period furnishings.

With its state pen, Shaeffer Pen and the cattle pens which filled the old stockyards, Fort Madison can truly be called "the Pen City". Although the town did lack the Penn Central, the main line of the Santa Fe passed through Fort Madison. In the late 1940's a rodeo traveling from the southwest to New York City customarily stopped in town to rest the livestock in the stockyards. In 1948 the performers staged a show, called the Pre-Madison Square Garden Rodeo, forerunner of the Tri-State Rodeo held every year the weekend after Labor Day, no doubt the only such event on the banks of the Mississippi. Fort Madison boasts another river-related exclusive: the world's only calliope manufacturer, owned by former computer engineer David Miner, who makes twenty-five to thirty of the music machines yearly. Miner began with the Tangley Calliaphone originally manufactured in Muscatine in 1914. He later developed a model called "Excursion Boat Special" used on the *Delta Queen* and other Mississippi riverboats. In the fall of 1988, Miner exported a "Special" to Holland, the first new calliope sold abroad from the United States since the 1920's.

Memories of historic Mississippi events linger at Fort Madison. The *Ottumwa Belle* arrived at the town in 1915 with the very last log raft sent down the river from northern forests—the end of an era. And it was in Fort Madison where, at a July 4 celebration in 1838, the once feared Black Hawk delivered his last public talk. Under trees overlooking the Mississippi the crowd enjoyed a lavish feast, then the Indian leader rose to address the audience. "I loved my towns, my cornfields and the home of my people," he said of his beloved lands across the Mississippi to the north. "I fought for it. It is now yours," said the chief. Gazing at the river, he went on:"I have looked upon the Mississippi since I was a child. I love the great river. I have dwelt upon its banks from the time I was an infant. I look upon it now." The following September, Black Hawk fell ill, and on October 3, age seventy-one, he died at his lodge by the Des Moines River in the northeast corner of Davis County, about fifty miles northwest of Fort Madison. And so ended another era on the ever-changing Mississippi.

On the way out of Fort Madison you'll pass an industrial area with the Du Pont factory, which produces resins and thinners used in paint, the Dial convenience food plant, believed to be the world's largest meat canning facility when it opened in 1972, and the Climax Molybdenum installation, which manufactures compounds used in the steel and petrochemical industries. Nine miles south, the River Road reaches Montrose, where the Linger Longer rest area merits its name, for this point affords a splendid view of the broad Mississippi, here more than one and a quarter miles wide. On Highway 404 north of town lies the marked grave of Kalewequois, a Sac and Fox princess who died in 1837 of tuberculosis, a disease previously unknown to the Indians. Montrose lies in the so called Half-Breed Tract, where children of trappers,traders and soldiers who had lived with Indian women wanted their own land. In 1824 the Sac and Fox ceded to the United States about one hundred and nineteen thousand acres of their holdings between the Des Moines and Mississippi Rivers for the benefit of those mixed-blood offspring. From 1834-6 the first Fort Des Moines stood in present day Riverview Park at Montrose, then called Cut Nose for an Indian chief. Near the fort's location in February 1846 some two thousand Mormons arrived across the frozen Mississippi from Nauvoo, Illinois, after the assassination of prophet Joseph Smith, to begin their trek out to Utah. Montrose boasted Iowa's first apple orchard, planted by French-Canadian trader Louis Honoré Tesson after he received a land grant of some six thousand acres from the Spanish government. The Spaniards directed him to plant trees and to monitor the "savages" and "keep them in the fealty which they owe His Majesty,"the King of Spain. Thus did the Iowa Indians become subjects of the Madrid monarch. Following Tesson's sale of the property in 1803 to pay debts a series of suits developed over the grant, which the U.S. Supreme Court finally declared valid in 1852, so confirming Iowa's oldest land title. During the many land title disputes in the area New York Land Company lawyer Francis Scott Key, author of "The Star Spangled Banner", came to Keokuk where he drew up papers which settled some of the squabbles. At Montrose,which lies at the head of the formerly fearsome Des Moines Rapids, stands 1871 National Register-listed St. Barnabas Episcopal Church, constructed of blue-grey limestone removed during excavation of the canal built from Montrose to Keokuk to bypass the Rapids, covered by the Mississippi after construction of the Keokuk dam in the early twentieth century.

On a low rise within view of the river three miles south of Montrose perches a replica (1977) of Iowa's first schoolhouse, built on a site also now under water. Two wood benches and a chair hewn from a thick log furnish the tiny school, which opened in October 1830 with seven boys and one girl. Oiled paper, rather than glass, served as windows in the school, built by Isaac Galland, father of Eleanor, believed to be the first white child born (1830) in the Iowa Territory. Galland—who in his 1840 *Iowa Emigrant* described the Mississippi as a "truly majestic river"—was both a colorful and a shady character, a well-rounded fellow who worked as a land agent in the Half-Breed Tract, occasionally forging land warrants, practiced medicine and spiritualism, and for a time ran a counterfeiting operation which he gave up because of excess competition. Eight years after the appearance in 1850 of a booklet entitled "Villany Exposed", attacking his business practices, Galland died at Fort Madison.

The pleasant settlement of Keokuk to the south enjoys a certain down-home atmosphere which led Erskine Caldwell to observe, in *Afternoons in Mid-America*, that the city "comes closest to being as truly representative of life in America as any one place can possibly be." Keokuk retains a strong connection with the great waterway which flows by at the rate of fifteen trillion gallons a year. By the waterfront—where in 1907 President Teddy Roosevelt boarded a steamer for a trip down the river—stands the *George M. Verity* River Museum (April-Nov 9-5). It occupies a steamer built in 1927 at the Dubuque Boat and Boiler Works. This was one of four such ships which revived river transportation on the Upper Mississippi after the virtual disappearance of such traffic by the turn of the century. During the golden era of steamboating, from 1840 to 1880, nearly five thousand steamers plied the waters of the Mississippi and Ohio, but by 1900 barges handled little freight except for gravel and rock. On August 15, 1927 the *S.S.Thorpe*, the *Verity's* original name, left St. Louis for Minneapolis with three barges carrying nine hundred tons of New Orleans sugar and seven hundred tons of other freight—the first modern-day barge trip on the Upper Mississippi. In 1940 Armco Steel bought the steamer, using it on the Ohio until 1960, after which the company gave it to Keokuk to house a river museum. The Keokuk-based Midwest Riverboat Buffs (319-524-4269) started up in 1972 as an organization for people interested in the history of riverboats.

A plaque across from the *George M. Verity* honors Hugh Lincoln Cooper, the engineer who from 1910 to 1913 built the nearby Union Electric dam and powerhouse, at the time the world's largest electric generating plant (tours Memorial Day week-Labor Day week 10:30, 11:15, 12:45, 1:30, 2:15,3). This facility, the adjacent Lock Number 19, completed in 1957, and the nearby disused swing span car bridge, now an observation deck overlooking the river, comprise a complex of improvements aimed at taming the mighty Mississippi, an effort which began there in the early nineteenth century. Like the Rock Island Rapids between Le Claire and Davenport upstream, the Des Moines Rapids—which extended eleven miles from Montrose to Keokuk—intimidated and impeded early river traffic. As early as 1829, U.S. engineers examined the Rapids, as did Robert E. Lee, assigned to survey both the Des Moines and the Rock Island Rapids. He was directed to suggest a plan for improvements which would enable steamboats to continue up the river without having to transfer their cargo to shallow draft lighters, the only vessels able to pass through the hazard at Keokuk. No action developed until after the Civil War, when Congress authorized the Corps of Engineers to establish a four foot channel on the Mississippi north of St. Louis. Starting in 1866 — the beginning of the Corps' permanent presence on the Upper Mississippi — engineers took more than forty thousand soundings along the Des Moines Rapids before recommending a canal by the Iowa shore to bypass the hazard. Twelve years after the canal opened in 1877 the Corps completed the only dry dock on the Upper Mississippi.

As the turn of the century, a power company requested permission to build a dam across the Mississippi. Although the martyred Mormon leader Joseph Smith had in 1844 proposed a dam at Nauvoo, the head of the Rapids on the Illinois side, as late as the early twentieth century not a single dam stood anywhere along the entire Mississippi. Two years later after construction of the mile long Keokuk dam began in 1910, the old canal closed, replaced by a new lock completed in 1913. It was later succeeded by the existing twelve hundred foot Lock Number 19, opened in 1957 almost directly over the site of the original 1877 canal. The lock's twelve hundred foot locking chamber, the largest on the Upper Mississippi's six hundred and sixty-nine miles, exceeds the size of those on the Panama Canal, but is equalled by the brand new replacement Lock Number 26 at Alton, Illinois downstream. From November to March one of the largest concentrations of the estimated fourteen hundred Bald Eagles which winter along the Mississippi from St.Louis north gather in the Keokuk area, many of them near the lock and dam which keep the river from freezing and thus enable the birds to fish in the water there.

During the mid to late nineteenth century, ships delivered to Keokuk home builders a rich array of stained glass, furniture and other opulent objects used to outfit dwellings built in the growing city. These houses proved more elegant than the city's crude hewn log structures, erected by the American Fur Company in the 1830's, a neighborhood known as Rat Row. Less ratty historic homes include the residence at 119 North First, Keokuk's oldest surviving dwelling (1840's), and the place at 110-112 North Second, an 1840's house with a third level added in 1857 under the first two stories, jacked up to make room for the addition. At the twin-winged house at 116 Concert, now a gourmet restaurant and cooking school, runaway slaves hid in a concealed passageway; above the residence rises a tower—the highest point in Keokuk—from which the owner, a lumberman, watched his ships on the Mississippi. At 206 High Street lived Major General Samuel Curtis, a Congressman who resigned to command troops which won the crucial Battle of Pea Ridge, Arkansas for the Union. The Civil War reached Keokuk in the form of seven hospitals located there. Medical boats sailed up the Mississippi from southern battlefields carrying the wounded, some of whom died and repose in the National Cemetery, one of the original twelve designated by Congress in 1861 and the first one west of the Mississippi.

The National Register-listed Miller House Museum (Memorial Day-Labor Day Th-Sun 1-4) honors Samuel F. Miller, who practiced law in Keokuk from 1850 until Lincoln appointed him to the Supreme Court in 1862 as the first justice from west of the Mississippi. Next door (to the left) stands the 1880 house of Felix T. Hughes, grandfather of Howard Hughes, Jr., who occasionally visited his Keokuk family. According to local legend, he conceived the idea for the diamond-tipped oil drill bit here. In this house Howard Hughes, Sr. and his brother Rupert, a famous writer in his day, grew up. At 626 High Jane Clemens resided, mother of Sam Clemens (Mark Twain), who for some fifteen months lived in Keokuk where his brother Orion owned a job printing shop which in 1856 published the first city directory. Young Sam set most of the type for the work, in which he listed himself as an "antiquarian". Until they moved to California when their daughter was eighteen months old, Laura and David Maxwell occupied the house at 318 North Fourth with baby Elsie, known later in life as Elsa Maxwell, the famous international hostess.

To complete your visit to Keokuk and Iowa's Mississippi River region it's worth driving out appropriately named Grand Avenue to see the stately houses which line the lovely street. From their rear, the dwellings on the east side of Grand enjoy perhaps the most splendid views of the Mississippi found in any residential district along the entire waterway. At 925 Grand stands the early twentieth century colonial-style residence which Felix Hughes used as his so called summer house, while next door rises an eccentric looking place made of sharp stone building blocks. Grand continues on to Rand Park, where the statue of Keokuk—said to be a remarkable likeness of the chief—stands. In contrast to the militant Black Hawk, Keokuk counseled caution and cooperation with the whites. Influenced by Keokuk, Black Hawk signed the 1831 Corn Treaty, allocating his tribe an amount of the crop equal to that which his former lands would yield. The pact also designated Keokuk as the leader of the Sac and Fox nation, a position he solidified after Black Hawk's defeat the following year. The statue depicts Keokuk, buried here, with a blanket slung over his left arm, while in his right hand he holds the bowl of a long peace pipe. The inscription reads: "Sacred to the memory of Keokuck, distinguished Sac Chief, Born at Rock Island in 1788, Died in April 1848." He faces the Mississippi, which spreads below in a truly magnificent and majestic panorama as the great river winds its way past Keokuk, out of Iowa and down to the distant sea.

IOWA PRACTICAL INFORMATION

Phone numbers of tourist offices in Iowa's principal Mississippi River cities:

Bellevue: 319-872-5830; Bettendorf: 319-355-4753; Burlington: 319-752-6365; Clinton:319-242-5702; Davenport: 319-322-5142; Dubuque: 319-557-9200; East Davenport:319-322-1860; Fort Madison: 800-369-FORT; Keokuk: 319-524-5055; Le Claire: 319-289-4242; Muscatine: 319-263-8895; St. Donatus: 319-773-2405.

Other useful numbers for travel along the Mississippi include:

Iowa Bureau of Tourism and Visitors: 515-281-3100; Iowa Department of Cultural Affairs: 515-281-6258; Iowa Department of Natural Resources: 515-281-5145.

The Iowa Bed and Breakfast Innkeeper Association: P.O. Box 545, Bettendorf, IA 52722.

Bed and Breakfast in Iowa is a reservation service: 800-373-3148.

Heartland Bicycle Tours offers trips along and near the Mississippi: 319-653-2277.

Iowa operates Welcome Centers along the Mississippi at Burlington, Dubuque and Le Claire.

II.

THE MIDDLE MISSISSIPPI

4. Illinois

5. Missouri

4. ILLINOIS

Although the Great River Road in Illinois extends from East Dubuque to Cairo for some 550 miles—second in length only to Minnesota's route—only 50 miles border the Mississippi. Much of the waterway which forms the Prairie State's western boundaries remains little populated, largely unspoiled countryside and riverside areas where "great stretches of the Mississippi are lovely corridors of wildness that still honor original landscapes," as John Madson wrote in *Up On the River*. As elsewhere, however, the river—although tucked away between vast spreads of Middle-western farmland—exerted and still exerts a strong influence on the state. "That buffering ocean of grass and grain cannot prevent the arteries of motion from carrying away sons and daughters and bringing back new ideas, new moralities," observed William Carter in *Middle West Country*. "Worldly wisest of those arteries is the Mississippi River. Murky and meandering, shipping out whiskey and bringing in foreigners, handling bargefuls of industrial materials to the wide-open cities along its shores, its unpredictable current has long frightened and fascinated the right-angled towns of the hinterland."

In a certain sense, East Dubuque—tucked away in Illinois' far northwestern corner at the beginning of the River Road—was one of those "wide-open cities", but the town imported whiskey rather than shipping it out. During Prohibition, speakeasys and hard liquor supplied by stills in the hills and by Al Capone in the underworld kept East Dubuque well irrigated, giving it the nickname "Sin City". Dunleith, a Scotch name, appropriately enough, designated the original settlement, a Mississippi river hamlet where in 1832 Eleazer and Diadamia Frentress became the area's first whites to farm the prairie. They settled on land by

Frentress Lake, which still today bears that name. Around the middle of the century Captain Charles Hamilton Merry established a ferry, superceded in 1868 by the railroad which still uses the tunnel and bridge built then. Two decades later—ten years after the town took the name East Dubuque in 1877—the High Street foot and wagon bridge rose alongside the train span. In 1943 the 7392-foot-long Julien Dubuque Bridge opened, one of the longest of its type—tied arch and cantilevered—ever built. Atop the bluffs, with a view onto the gracefully arched bridge and the river, perches Zimmerman's Lodge (800-747-3181) and Supper Club. For more atmosphere but without the extensive view, The Captain Merry Guest House (815-747-3644) down in town offers bed and breakfast accommodations. The widow's walk atop the boxy brick and limestone house affords a view of the Mississippi, which once flowed by the limestone retaining wall at the front of the dwelling. When Captain Merry built the house in 1857, he included indoor plumbing and central heating, unusual for the era, as well as a canal beneath the residence to moor his boat. Guests and visitors at the historic house included Abraham Lincoln and Al Capone, although they did not attend the same functions. Not far from the Merry House stands the Hillman House, listed on the National Register, once the East Dubuque High School and now a retirement home.

South of East Dubuque lies Galena, preserved as it appeared a century or more ago. Lead mining and Mississippi River shipping enriched Galena; the rise of the railroads and decline of the deposits impoverished it. As early as 1690, French explorer Nicholas Perrot visited Indian lead mines on the Fever River at the site of present day Galena. The earliest application on record for a grant of lead mining land in the Upper Mississippi valley dates from 1769, issued for a claim on the Fever to a man named Duralde and signed by Bellerive, commandant at Fort de Chartres, the French built and British controlled outpost on the Mississippi in central Illinois. In 1816 Colonel George Davenport, founder of the Iowa town of that name, shipped the first boatload of lead ore down the Mississippi from Galena, and eleven years later steamboats began regular service from the city to St. Louis. The advent of steampowered vessels proved crucial, for lead weighed too much to ship by hand-propelled craft. Back then, ships could navigate the three miles from the Mississippi to Galena up the Fever River, which in the 1830's began to silt up. In 1845 lead production in the area peaked at fifty-four million pounds, more than eighty percent of the nation's supply. Residents opted to rename the Fever River—an off-putting designation—the Galena in 1854, the year the Illinois Central Railroad arrived in town. Before long the river trade began to decline, a trend accentuated during the Civil War when the north-south trade routes along the Mississippi—on the St. Louis, Memphis, New Orleans axis—gave way to the east-west pattern promoted by the railroads, centered in Chicago. The Fever silted up, the lead mines played out, and Galena wound down. As the years passed, time passed Galena by, leaving its buildings and ambiance intact as a nineteenth century enclave, some eighty-five percent of it now listed on the National Register. The pockets of lead lodes disappeared, but Galena now mines loads of gold from tourist's pockets.

Like the picturesque and well preserved Mississippi town of Natchez, Galena survives as a little changed picture out of the past unmarred for the most part by modern additions. By the Galena River at the far end of Main (601 South Main) the 1827 Phineas Block stands, the only surviving frame warehouse still on the levee (later improvements now conceal the original building). Down the street you'll see the flood gates, completed in 1951 by the Corps of Engineers to protect the city from the occasionally unruly Galena River. Over the centuries the waterway cut the hillside terraces on which the upper town perches. Farther along Main stands the De Soto House, a restored hotel built by local merchants in anticipation of the Illinois Central's arrival in 1854.

The De Soto (800-343-6562) retains its atmosphere of yesteryear, with old lobby fixtures, a pressed tin ceiling and a certain tone of recycled but faded elegance. The multi-use 1845 Old Market House (9-5) on Commerce served on the ground floor as a farmer's sales area until 1910, while the City Council met upstairs up to 1938. On nearby Diagonal, an ultra-short street, the 1828 John Dowling House, a rather dilapidated grey limestone structure erected as a trading post, survives as one of Galena's oldest buildings. The nearby Amos Farrar House—which stands on one of the nation's few remaining original cobblestone streets—once stood inside the stockade built in 1832 at the time of the Black Hawk War.

A later war focused national attention on Galena. In the summer of 1860, thirty-eight year old Ulysses S. Grant arrived in town on the steamboat *Itasca* and took a job for $600 a year as a clerk in his father's leather store at 120 South Main. Grant, his wife and four children lived at the modest brick house, fronted by a porch and with picket fence around the yard, up on Quality Hill at 121 South High Street. Nearby lies the peaceful old cemetery whose graves include those of Cornish miners attracted to Galena in the 1830's and 1840's by the lead boom. As a notice at the residence relates: "From this home Captain Ulysses S. Grant a citizen of Galena, Illinois went to the Civil War May 1861." Thanks to Grant, nine men from Galena—more than any other city of its size—attained the rank of general during the conflict. Among them were John A. Rawlings, named Union Army Chief of Staff and Secretary of War before he died at age thirty-seven, and Ely S. Parker, a full-blooded Seneca chief, refused admittance to the bar in New York State because he was an Indian, who moved to Galena in 1857. Grant and the two generals appear in Thomas Nast's famous "Peace in Union", a painting depicting Robert E. Lee's 1865 surrender at Appomattox, which hangs in the History Museum (9-4:30). The "Diggers, Smelters, Steamers" display, old photos and drawings on the Galena River, and other exhibits at the museum evoke the town's past. That era is also evoked at the Old General Store (June-Oct 10-4:30; May, Nov, Dec weekends only), a reproduction of a nineteenth century emporium with period wares and airs. When Grant returned to Galena after the war, some of the townspeople presented the hero with a spacious Italianate-style brick house which he occupied briefly until moving to the even roomier White House in Washington, where the general remained for two terms after his election to the presidency in 1868. Grant's heirs deeded the Galena dwelling to the city in 1904, but only in 1957—twenty-six years after Illinois acquired the property—did the house open as a State Historic Site (9-5). A few blocks away stands the handsome columned Elihu Washburne House, recently restored and also a State Historic Site, built by Grant's mentor, who served in Congress from 1852 until 1869 when he became U.S. ambassador to France. In the yard of Washburne's house Captain Grant drilled local troops before marching them off to the war.

More area history lingers at the old Vinegar Hill Lead Mine (June-Aug 9-5, weekends only May, Sept, Oct) six miles north of town. The mine consists of an ore vein struck in 1824 by John Furlong, worked by him, his son and great grandson, opened to tourists in 1967 by his great-great grandson, and since 1986 managed by his great-great-great grandson. Back in town, a restored 1840's grainery houses the Galena Cellars Winery, while the 1845 Peck Building, a steamboat provisioning warehouse, now provisions visitors as the Galena River Cheese Shop. More than fifty other old or rustic buildings in and around Galena—where in 1988 the *Field of Dreams* movie was filmed—serve as inns, guest houses, bed and breakfast establishments, and country homes which offer accommodations. These include, east of the Galena River, the handsome c. 1830 Federal-style native limestone DeZoya House (815-777-1203) and the nearby Aldrich House (815-777-3323), built about 1845 by Cyrus Aldrich, later

U.S. Senator from Minnesota, and enlarged eight years later by J. Russell Jones, who also built the antique filled Belvedere (April-Nov 9-5), Galena's largest mansion. West of the river you'll find the Captain Gear Guest House (815-777-0222), a nicely proportioned 1855 residence built by a lead mine owner, and Farmers' Home Hotel (800-373-3456), installed in an 1867 brick bakery and hotel building. Places up on Quality Hill with views down onto the town include the large c. 1850 hilltop Felt Manor Guest House (815-777-9093); the seventeen room Victorian Mansion (815-777-0675), built by lead smelter entrepreneur Augustus Estey, whose daughter spent a winter with Grant's family at the White House; and the 1895 Queen Anne-style Hellman Guest House (815-777-3638), with an angular and rounded section tucked into its corner. Out of town are the twenty-four room mansion Chicago food purveyor James M. Ryan built in 1876 on some hundred and twenty acres (815-777-2043), and two up-scale resorts: Eagle Ridge (800-892-2269 in Illinois, 800-323-8427 out-of-state) and, overlooking the Mississippi, Chestnut Mountain (800-397-1320), a ski area in the winter, where guests who take Mississippi River cruises from Le Claire, Iowa on the *Twilight* and *Julia Belle Swaine* (800-237-1660 in Illinois, 800-331-1467 out-of-state; see the Iowa chapter for details) spend the night.

The River Road heads southeast from Galena through attractive, hilly countryside, part of the so called "driftless area" unflattened by ancient glaciers. Illinois' highest point, 1235 foot high Charles Mound, lies to the northeast by the Wisconsin border. By the road, a half mile before the intersection with U.S. 20, stands the pagoda-like Long Hollow Scenic Overlook tower, which affords a splendid view of the exceptionally scenic rolling hills and Apple River valley below, where silos dot the landscape and white farm houses nestle in clusters of trees. The nearby Inn at Irish Hollow (815-777-2010), not far from the intersection of Rodden and Irish Hollow Roads, takes bed and breakfast guests in a former general store and post office. Off to the west, at 7351 West Blackjack Road, near the Mississippi, towers the AT&T Satellite Earth Station (for tours: 815-777-2400), one of seven such company facilities in the continental United States. Two 100-foot diameter dish-shaped antennas relay more than 22,000 telephone circuits and video signals via geo-stationary satellites. Slightly off the River Road, three miles east of the Overlook, beyond Apple River—more an unpretentious little creek than a river—lies Elizabeth, with a scattering of old buildings, including the 1888 depot and 1894 Commercial Hotel across the street, and bed and breakfast establishments at Amber Creek Farms (815-598-3301), Elizabeth Guest House (815-858-2533, no breakfast), Flint Hill Farms (815-858-3471), and Locker Knoll Inn (815-598-3150), installed in a 1921 country schoolhouse, its bell tower glassed in as a skylight. Stockton, farther east, boasts even more nineteenth and early twentieth structures, as well as the site of the nation's first Kraft plant, a creamery at 264 West Front Street purchased in 1914 by J.L.Kraft, who made the first Kraft cheese there. Maple Lane (815-947-3773), south of U.S. 20 between Stockton and Woodbine, takes bed and breakfast guests.

Back on the River Road—Highway 84, which heads south just beyond the Long Hollow Scenic Overlook—lies Hanover, established next to the Apple River in 1827 at the site of a Sac and Fox settlement. After the area lead mines declined, the town dammed the river—so inspiring the locals to describe Hanover as "the best town by a dam site"—and established a grist and later a woolen mill. In 1856 Delinda Boone Craig, frontiersman Daniel Boone's granddaughter, led a mob of sixty women to the local saloon and gambling den, which the group dismantled brick by brick until the walls collapsed. One of the women later moved to Guthrie, Oklahoma where she supposedly inspired her neighbor, Carry Nation, to carry on the temperance movement. At the beginning of the Civil War a shop worker traveled to Hanover from nearby Galena to deliver a morale-boosting speech to young Union Army recruits, who heard that day Ulysses S. Grant's first public address. Signs at Hanover's outskirts welcome you to the "World's Mallard Duck Capital", while the hilltop white water tower bears a flying duck emblem, references to the town's Whistling Wings operation. Near the Apple River in Hanover stands the firm's headquarters, a small neatly kept building which houses a glass display case filled with frisky, flighty two-day-old ducklings, a few of the 200, 000 mallards the company produces every year. In the processing area, visible through large windows, five metal incubators each hold 15,000 eggs brought there every week from breeding pens at Whistling Wings' nearby farm where 4,000 hens each produce some fifty eggs a year. When the business started in 1954 which came first—the duck or the egg? For Whistling Wings it was the duck—200 mallards, whose descendants the company sells for breeding, to stock hunting preserves, for research, and for food. A freezer case at the office holds a selection of prepared ducks and other game birds (for mail orders: 815-591-3512). Down the street and around the corner from the large Eaton Corporation plant stands the century old Sullivan's Hardware building, which includes a section devoted to a jumble of used clothes, antiques and bric-a-brac.

On the River Road farther south you'll pass the brick entryway, inscribed "The Pacesetter", of the 13, 000 acre Savanna Army Depot Activity. Known as SADA, the facility stretches along the Mississippi for some thirteen miles. The base opened in December 1918 with the mission of testing field artillery and ammunition. After World War I the facilities served to warehouse military vehicles and artillery weapons. In 1920 the army began construction of high explosive and ammunition storage magazines, built in an area surrounded by a six-mile-long unclimbable fence. During World War II, when the number of employees at the depot increased from 143 in 1939 to nearly 7200 in 1942, the War Department built additional magazines and a shell loading plant. It was that facility which outfitted planes with special bombs dropped by General James Doolittle on his famous raid over Tokyo. In the 1950's the army established an Ammunition School at the base, one of eighteen storage depots around the world. SADA today receives, stores and ships ammunition and explosives and serves as one of the nation's two testing facilities for those supplies. Some 620 people work at the depot, which includes nearly 1,000 structures, among them many earth-covered magazines, and 68 miles of railroad track for internal transfers of military material.

Near the Mississippi south of SADA you'll pass limestone bluffs which border the 2550 acre Mississippi Palisades State Park, established in 1929 and named for the similar cliffs along the Hudson River in New Jersey known as the palisades. The park, designated a National Landmark, includes 241 tent and trailer sites (for information: 815-273-2731) near the waterway and eight miles of trails, many of them close to the edge of the bluff from where views of the Mississippi spread before the hiker. Inside the north entrance to the park the road snakes around and up, then continues along the top of the bluff past trails and on to Lookout Point. A sign there states, "Before you lies the Upper Mississippi River National Wildlife and Fish Refuge". This refers to the 260 mile long, nearly 200,000 acre river bottoms set aside in 1924 for migrating birds, wildlife and fish. At Savanna, a few miles south, operates one of the Refuge's four district offices. A wood deck by a precipitous dropoff affords a view onto the river valley. Downstream, the lacy beams of the 1933 bridge (rebuilt in 1985) to Sabula, Iowa weave a pattern against the water, while just below you lie the River Road and the railway tracks which curve away gracefully to the south. Although a few houses cluster off to the right, the view out to the Mississippi, uncluttered with signs of human presence, reveals the river as it no doubt appeared centuries ago. Toward the south end of the park—today filled with trees, but a century ago stripped bare for wood to fuel steamboats—the craggy Indian Head formation emerges from the bluff, which lies toward the end of the 200-mile-long line of cliffs which rise along the east side of the Mississippi starting in Wisconsin.

The town of Savanna, three miles south of the Palisades' south entrance, survives as a low-key Mississippi River town. Its name stems from the grassy plains which extend south from here. In 1815 Harriet and Aaron Pierce settled on farmland along the waterway at the site where a port opened thirteen years later. The nineteenth century mansion at 1019 North Main, built by riverboat captain John B. Rhodes, stands on the site of the Pierce family cabin. The house built in 1865 by another early steamer captain, Stoughton Cooley, overlooks the Mississippi from its perch on a bluff at 4th and Jefferson Streets. Another relic, the Avenue School, has recently (1989) been remodeled into a theater, and more old commercial buildings line Main Street. These include the red brick Pulford Opera House (1890), opened in 1989 as an antique mall, and the venerable Hotel Radke, with an antique La Palina cigar display case at the old fashioned front desk. A model train over the door and train photos on the lobby wall hint that the hotel housed railroad workers, a function it continues to serve, although rail traffic has greatly diminished from bygone times. When the railroad arrived in 1850 Savanna began to develop as a major train center, with the Milwaukee Road and the C.B. & Q. operating extensive facilities in the town. In July 1862 the first passenger train left Savanna, and during the early years more than 100 freight and passenger departures took place daily. Between Savanna and East Dubuque the crack Burlington Zephyr used to open the throttle and run at 105 miles an hour, more than 15 mph faster than its average speed. At the south end of town by the railroad bridge stretches a large train yard crammed with rusting Soo and Milwaukee line boxcars. Tracks ripped up from the compound off to the left make the once-bustling yard seem rather forlorn. The steamboat came and went and so, it seems—at least to a certain extent—have the trains. In June 1990 the local Chamber of Commerce moved its office to one of sixteen remaining Milwaukee Road Hiawatha passenger cars—purchased by a local group for $3,000—used on the line between 1940 and 1956. Along the banks of the Mississippi lies Marquette Park as well as the newly developed F.A.S.T. Trail—named for the river towns it passes through: Fulton, Albany, Savanna and Thomson—which offers bikers, hikers and joggers a pleasant path through the countryside.

If time permits, it's worth a detour nine miles east to Mount Carroll, a delightful county seat town still—by appearances—living in the nineteenth century. Well preserved old architecture and historic places fill the picturesque settlement. Much of the commercial section comprises a National Historic District, while in 1980 Illinois designated Mount Carroll—in and near which operate four bed and breakfast establishments—one of the state's five "Main Street" towns, for its characteristic old downtown area.

The River Road continues south from Savanna to Thomson, nine miles away, where since 1882 McGinnis Melon Market (Jun-Dec) has been selling produce. At McGinnis a brightly colored sign decorated with images of pumpkins and a watermelon slice advertises "Pioneer Melon Growers". Even the nearby water tower, which rises above the old village hall and jail, bears a watermelon slice motif. Inside the corrugated metal store, wood bins overflow with a cornucopia of nature's bounty, while from the wood beam ceiling dangle old corn cobs. The firm, run by the third generation of the founding family, began when Joseph McGinnis settled on the banks of the Mississippi near Thomson. Inspired by the local saying that to grow melons "all it takes is a strong back and weak mind", he planted his first crop in the sandy soil, which hosts cactus and desert-type grasses and vegetation and must be irrigated to produce edible crops. At one time, local farmers shipped out twenty rail car loads of melons a day. Just as in the old days, workers still cultivate the labor-intensive crop mainly by hand. Next door to the market stands the cozy Water Melon Cafe, decorated with mounted fish, ducks and deer, which serves not only meals but a delicacy called a watermelon malt. The nearby restored century old Burlington depot, painted a rich dark red with green trim, houses railroad memorabilia (May-Oct, Sat and Sun 1-4). On Ideal Road at the point of the bluff two miles northeast of town, where the 1830's settlement of Bluffville stood, stands an 1852 house unique in the area for the grout—ground stone added to mortar, sand and shells—which forms the walls.

A spur road to the west about four miles south of Thomson leads out to Lock and Dam Number 13, which lies tucked away on the river three miles north of Fulton, named for Robert Fulton, inventor of the steamboat. Upstream, the Mississippi and adjoining wetlands spreads out to form one of the river's widest stretches, nearly four miles across, while below the dam the waterway quickly narrows. The F.A.S.T. trail extends south from the lock and dam into Fulton to Tenth Avenue, one of the access points for the three-quarter mile walking and biking path atop the levee along the river. By the bridge to Clinton, Iowa stretches Fulton's river terminal, while just up the street stands the old train depot—complete with a track crossing signal—which houses the city hall. Nearby you'll find the Antique Loft, containing three levels of shops. The now closed 1851 Martin Hotel on 2nd Street served travelers for more than a century.

At the north edge of town, near Cattail Slough, nestles Wierenga's Heritage Canyon, one of those unexpected off-the-beaten-track corners of America which occasionally materialize to delight back roads travelers. In 1967 Harold and Thelma Wierenga bought a twelve acre limestone rock quarry, worked from the mid-nineteenth century to 1954 and abandoned until 1967. The couple slowly and lovingly developed the facility into a village filled with reproduced and restored pioneer era buildings nestled in a thickly wooded canyon by the Mississippi.

After you pass by the entrance (April-Dec 15, 8-5; admission free, but donations appreciated, and deserved), where a sundial inscription advises, "Time is what life is made of", the path leads across a swinging bridge, truly a moving experience. You continue on into the narrow canyon to an old log cabin, cross a covered bridge lined with vintage advertising signs, then advance to a one room schoolhouse, a blacksmith shop and a diminutive church built with materials salvaged from old barns. Other structures fill the tranquil enclave, a pleasant place to linger and enjoy a quiet corner of the river, which flows by just across the street. A sign on a swatch of attractive land by the Mississippi there states: "This property *not* for sale".

Near Garden Plain, a hamlet southeast of Fulton, Rally Tree Farm (309-887-4646) offers rooms on a 500 acre working farm. At Albany, on the river back to the west, Indian burial mounds stand, while the Tri Township Heritage Museum contains local family historical objects, collectibles and antiques. A few miles south of Albany, nearly destroyed by an 1860 tornado, stretches a huge 3M plant, and farther on, four miles north of Cordova, a turnoff leads to the $260 million Quad-Cities Station Nuclear plant, put into service by Commonwealth Edison in 1973. An information center (Tu-Sat 9-5, Sun 12-5) houses a one room display area on nuclear power. The plant, which boasts 1.6 million kilowatts of generating capacity, one of the nation's largest, stands by the Mississippi where engineers constructed a three mile long canal to serve as a closed cycle cooling system. This proved unnecessary, as two 16-foot diameter pipes buried in the river bed suffice to discharge from the plant warm water heated to turn the turbines. Under each of the two nuclear reactors stretch 500 miles of condenser tubing through which about 1 million gallons a minute of demineralized Mississippi water flow to act as a coolant. The water, which reaches a temperature of 546° F. in the reactor system, is then returned to the river. Studies indicate that the Mississippi's water temperature rises 4° F. just below the discharge point, while within 600 yards downstream the emitted water thoroughly mixes with the river. Scientists monitoring the Mississippi's ecology in this area since 1968 are said to have detected no appreciable change in the river's ecosystem due to the plant's operations.

South of Cordova—where the sleek *Angelique* (309-654-2075) offers river cruises on a European-type canal boat—the River Road runs along next to the Mississippi. A sign at Port Byron, farther on, states "a port born from the river", not an idle remark, for the town began in 1828 as a fueling station for wood burning steamers. Before long, Indian trader Archie Allen established a ferry across the Mississippi, and later the Overland Stage from Chicago to Des Moines and on to Denver crossed the waterway here. Main Street borders the river, where a small park with benches offers a vantage point onto the Mississippi. The Ol' Lighthouse restaurant on Main overlooks the waterway. At Walnut and Main, a white frame building bears a yellow sign with fading green letters, "Wainwright's Real-estate office and barber shop"— a truly versatile establishment. On High Street stands the c. 1855 Olde Brick House (309-523-3236), once owned by International Harvester Company founder Cyrus McCormick, an inviting looking bed and breakfast place, with white wicker chairs on the spacious porch. In mid-August Port Byron hosts the Great River Tug, with teams on each end of a rope stretched across the Mississippi to Le Claire, Iowa. In 1988, the year the event began, a passing tug boat delayed the beginning of the tug-of-war competition. Farther on lies Hampton, founded as McNeal's Landing in the 1820's near a bend in the river where the Mississippi starts to head in a westerly direction. Once the area's leading trading center, Hampton now seems lost in the highly industrialized Illinois section of the Quad Cities metropolitan area. One relic from the past—Brettun and Black Historical Store and Museum (June-Oct Sat and Sun 2-4), installed in an 1849 building— serves to recall the old days.

The approach to the Illinois Quad Cities through scruffy East Moline introduces you to the area's industrial character. Just before Highway 84, the River Road, turns right on to 92 stands the John Deere foundry. Not far on looms the Case International Harvester plant (tours by appointment: 309-752-3000), the world's largest single farm implement factory, which makes combines. Alongside River Drive, which borders the Mississippi, runs the two mile long Ben Butterworth Parkway, a narrow strip of greenery which includes a walking path. At the south end the *Queen of Hearts* moors (800-521-3346 in Illinois, 800-227-9967 out-of-state), an old-style paddlewheel showboat which cruises the Mississippi from April to October. Nearby floats the Jubilee restaurant, a three story glass-enclosed establishment parked on the river.

Up in Old Town, centered around 19th Avenue and 7th Street in Moline—whose name derives from "moulin", the French word for "mill"—lies a touch of the old country, the Center for Belgian Culture (W and Sat 1-4), 712 18th Avenue. Yellow letters on the lace curtain-draped window proclaim "Centrum voor Nederlandse Cultuur van Belgic". One of the doors bears black and yellow hues with a red panel, colors which match those of Belgium's flag. Back toward the river but still up on the hill stand, on 11th Avenue, some spacious old houses in a pleasant residential area built in the nineteenth century by Moline's leading families. The Rock Island County Historical Society (May-1st Sun in Dec, Sun 1:30-4:30, Th 9-4:45) occupies an antique-furnished 1877 mansion with an old time kitchen, displays of Indian items, a period dental office, and a model of the 1880 steamer *Moline*, renamed the *Emerson* in 1905 when Captain Ralph Emerson bought the boat to push his showboat. Nearby lies the Butterworth Center, a mansion originally called Hillcrest, donated as a community meeting place. The grounds include formal gardens, while inside the library boasts a sixteenth century ceiling painting which until 1917 embellished the

Danielli family palace in Venice, later the Grand Danielli Hotel. Steps away from the Butterworth Center and across from the Historical Society perches on a high point overlooking downtown Moline, with fragments of the Mississippi also visible, the Deere-Wiman House (tours July and Aug Sun 1-4 on the hour, weekdays by appointment: 309-764-1121). Charles Deere, son of John Deere, founder of the famous farm machinery company, built the residence in 1873 as a wedding present for his wife. Their descendants occupied the property, which they called "Overlook", until 1976 when the widow of Charles' grandson died. The house—which contains Moline's oldest operating elevator and other antiques—was then opened to the public.

Seven miles southeast of downtown Moline stands the modernistic steel and glass Deere Company headquarters building (tours M-F 10:L30 and 1:30, building open 9-5 every day). This ranks among the most outstanding contemporary structures anywhere in the Mississippi River Valley. Beneath a huge oak near the entrance a plaque honors Eero Saarinen, who designed the Deere facility, opened in 1964, the renowned architect's last major project before his death. The building's dark brick and rusted steel sections recall the rich Midwestern prairie soil in which is rooted the beginnings and growth of the company, the world's largest farm equipment manufacturer. From within, the many-windowed structure—made light and open by the expanse of glass—seems almost to float. At the lower level stand bright green Deere farm vehicles, huge sleek and shiny machines which contrast with the antique equipment on display nearby. Along the length of one wall stretches an outstanding three-dimensional mural filled with more than two thousand historical items dating from 1837 to 1918, including documents, photos, advertisements, old farm implements and other period memorabilia which recall the development and culture of agriculture. One year after Vermont native John Deere moved to Illinois in 1836, he devised the "self-scouring" steel plow. Unlike the cast iron version designed for the light, sandy New England soil, Deere's device shed the thick, sticky Midwestern dirt. In 1847 Deere moved his fledging factory from the village of Grand Detour, seventy miles upstream on the Rock River, to Moline where the Mississippi offered water power and transportation. Ever since then the Deere Company, incorporated in 1868, has kept its headquarters in the city.

Some of the Deeres and their dear spouses repose in Riverside Cemetery, which lies on a hill you can reach if you turn right off 5th Avenue half a block before 34th Street, curve around around the Riverside Center and then enter the burial ground at a gate near a mausoleum. Take the first left up a narrow gravel road to a circle where a large rough-hewn stone cross bears the inscription "Deere". The reason for visiting the cemetery, however, is to see a little expected grave in this obscure corner of the Mississippi Valley—the last resting place of one of Charles Dickens' sons. In an area below the street off to the right rear of the Deere plot stands a square stone with a relief of a bearded man and the inscription, "In memory of Francis J. Dickens, Third, son of the renowned Author, Born Jan. 15 1844, Died June 11, 1886, 'Take ye heed, watch and pray for ye know not when the time is'. " Dickens fifth child, Francis left England for Calcutta in 1864, remaining for seven years in India where he served with the Bengal Mounted Police. Later, young Dickens worked in Canada as a Mountie. While visiting a friend in Moline one sweltering day he drank large quantities of ice water and died of paralysis of the heart, the only Dickens known to expire by imbibing just water.

John Deere's daughter, Emma, married a man named Stephen H. Velie, whose son Willard built in 1914 a palatial Moline mansion, hand-decorated by imported Italian craftsmen. The forty-six room show place included fourteen bedrooms and twelve bathrooms. For the "Villa Velie", Willard brought in trees and shrubs from the Mediterranean, imported from France twenty-one varieties of grapes he used to make his own wine, bottled with gold-leaf labels, and he also added a large greenhouse to grow bananas around the year. Velie, who for a time worked at Deere, left to start his own carriage firm, which in 1908 evolved into a motor car company. Of the two hundred and seventy or so automobile manufacturing companies in the United States in 1928, only Ford and Moline's Velie Motor Company were still controlled by their founders. After the family closed the mansion in 1928 it later opened as a club. B.J.Palmer, chiropractic inventor's son (see the Davenport section in the Iowa chapter), obtained the right to visit the villa the morning after big parties to offer treatment for hangovers. In 1945 the house became the Plantation Restaurant, and now it operates as Velie's, 3551 7th Street, just off John Deere Road. A glass-enclosed pavilion by the restaurant contains antique cars, including a 1917 roadster and a 1923 Phaeton, while the decor inside the museum-like eatery reflects the artful touches the Italian artisans added. Rather less elegant is Harold's On the Rock, 2600 North Shore Drive, a rustic restaurant at a tree-filled country-like site overlooking the Rock River. Specialities there include a large selection of unusual game meat, such as zebra and antelope.

Moline blends imperceptibly into the adjacent city of Rock Island, so named for the solid limestone island which stretches along the Mississippi for more than two miles. After the War of 1812, the government wanted to secure the nation's rivers, which then served as highways, to permit the country safely to expand to the west. In 1815 soldiers traveled upstream from St. Louis in keelboats to establish an outpost on Rock Island, named Fort Armstrong for the then Secretary of War. The new base retained English-born George Davenport as a sutler to supply the post. Davenport, the area's first white settler, brought provisions up the river in the *Flying Betsy*, his keelboat, and he later served briefly as a pilot on the *Virginia*, the first steamboat to reach Rock Island, in 1823. Ten years after that, using pine boards shipped from St. Louis, he built the first clapboard house in the Upper Mississippi valley, and the following year Davenport established one of the first ferries on the Mississippi. In his house Davenport, and others, platted the town of Davenport, Iowa, helped found the city of Rock Island, established the Chicago, Rock Island and Pacific Railroad, and planned the first railroad bridge across the Mississippi. All of Davenport's dreams and planning ended on July 4, 1845, when three robbers, members of a gang called the "Banditti of the Prairie", entered his house in search of money and murdered him. The heavily restored residence (May-Oct Sat and Sun 1-3) survives there by the Mississippi, the river which played such a large role in the life and career of Englishman turned Illinois pioneer George Davenport.

Near the Davenport house stands a monument made of stones from a pier of the original bridge. The plaque notes: "Near this spot and upon these stones rested the first bridge to span the Mississippi River. The first train consisting of a locomotive and eight cars passed over the bridge April 22, 1856". (For the history of this bridge, see the Davenport section in the Iowa chapter.) The original Fort Armstrong occupied a site by the tip of Rock Island, where a replica of the blockhouse stands. Nearby lies Lock and Dam Number 15, completed in 1934 as the first installation built for the nine-foot channel project, mandated by Congress to make the Upper Mississippi more predictably navigable. The barrier—the world's largest roller dam—comprises part of the system which includes twenty-nine dams on the Upper Mississippi. These facilities were designed to create a "stairway of water" so ships could descend the 420 foot drop between Minneapolis and St. Louis, beyond which the river flows through a channel deep enough to eliminate the need for dams. Here you'll find one of the Mississippi's best lock and dam Visitor Centers (9-5), opened in 1980; it contains river-related exhibits and an observation area with views onto the lock and dam.

Across from the Visitor Center stands the 1867 Clock Tower Building, completed as part of the Army Arsenal, a National Historic Landmark, which now occupies most of Rock Island. The Tower serves as headquarters for the Corps of Engineers Rock Island District, whose jurisdiction covers 314 miles of the Mississippi from Guttenberg, Iowa to Saverton, Missouri, a stretch of river which includes twelve locks and dams. The historic Arsenal—still an active factory facility, which manufactures artillery, small arms and gun mounts—includes such other sights as the fifty-two room 20,000 square foot Quarters One, the government's second largest single family home (after the White House). Completed in 1872, it still serves as the commanding general's residence. The island also includes a Confederate and National Cemetery, the site of a prison for captured Southern troops, and the Moline Navigation Locks built in 1906-7 as part of the Mississippi six foot channel project. The Arsenal Museum (10-4), the army's second oldest after the one at West Point, contains more than 1100 weapons dating back to pre-Revolutionary War times. The cracked bell on display, salvaged from the Mississippi in 1928 during dredging of the river channel, belonged to the *Effie Afton*, which smashed into and destroyed in 1856 the first railway bridge to span the waterway.

After the *Effie Afton* hit the bridge, the vessel's captain sued the railroad for obstructing navigation on the Mississippi, a case the river interests eventually lost. The arrival of the railroad at—and then across—the waterway greatly vexed the steamboat industry. The first train to reach the Mississippi arrived at Rock Island on February 22, 1854, with the last rail emplaced less than an hour before the celebrity-laden cars rolled up to the river.

At the ceremony commemorating the momentous occasion Henry Farnham, the line's engineer and contractor, said, "Today we witness the nuptials of the Atlantic with the Father of the Waters," adding that he "would rather build two railroads than make one speech." At 30th and 5th Avenue, north of downtown Rock Island, stands the 1901 Rock Island depot, successor to the first one in Illinois on the Mississippi (1854). The line closed the depot in 1979 when passenger service ended. Currently rather forlorn and empty, it may be restored. By the station, stands a three-sectioned monument to the historic Rock Island Line—the "first to erect a bridge over the Father of the Waters"—with maps showing the route of the first "Rocket" train (1852) from Chicago to Joliet and the more far-flung 1952 "Rocket" route from the Midwest out to Colorado, New Mexico, and Texas.

The current span across the Mississippi, the 1940 Centennial Bridge—which carries an average of 15,000 vehicles a day—leaves Rock Island at 15th Street and continues .88 of a mile to Davenport. Nearby, at 19th Street and 3rd Avenue, stands the National Register-listed Fort Theatre, decorated with bright tiles and a colorful relief of an Indian wearing a feathered headdress. Late nineteenth and early twentieth century houses line 19th Street between 6th and 9th Avenues, an area called Spenser Place. An 1816 treaty with the Indians allocated to them land north of 9th, formerly called Indian Boundary. The area extended from the Mississippi to the southern tip of Lake Michigan, a line meant originally to mark the Illinois-Wisconsin border. An Illinois assembly delegate, concerned the territory lacked sufficient people for statehood, and desiring to include in its borders enough northern sympathizers to keep it a free state, managed to move the line 2° farther north. Fred Kahlke resided at the rather modest, turn-of-the-century house at 831 19th Street. He was a boat builder whose yard constructed the *J.W.Quinlan*, the ship used as a ferry between Rock Island and Davenport until 1946. In the neighborhood from 38th and 40th Streets between 15th and 18th Avenues lie many of the two hundred cottage-like dwellings built during World War I to house some of the 13,400 workers employed at the Rock Island Arsenal.

Many of Rock Island's pioneers and early leaders lie at rest in the historic Chippiannock ("village of the dead" in Indian) Cemetery, 2901 12th Street. The ninety-five acre wooded burial ground occupies a hill not far from the Mississippi. Established in 1885, it survives as the oldest formal cemetery in western Illinois. A stone obelisk marks the last resting place of George Davenport, whose first resting place lay behind his house under a tree trunk-like marker—now emplaced near his present plot—"erected over the grave of Col. Davenport by friendly Indians". Others buried at Chippiannock include politician John Buford, "a public spirited citizen", one of whose sons chose the site for the Civil War battle at Gettysburg; John Wilson, who in 1837 bought the local ferry business from Iowa pioneer Antoine Le Claire for $1000 plus free rides for the seller; C.C. Knell, who in 1883 invented a recliner, the nation's first easy chair; and steamboat owner Captain A.J. Whitney, whose monument bears a bent anchor deformed when it served to retain one of his boats torn from its moorings during a storm. An elaborate Celtic cross stands at the entrance, carved by the father of well-known sculptor Alexander Calder, to memorialize Civil War naval officer W.H. Harte, buried elsewhere.

Up on a bluff, overlooking the Rock River, which borders Rock Island on the south, lies the Black Hawk State Historic Site. This area occupies a 208-acre spread inhabited by Indians as early as 10,000 B.C. For nearly a century, beginning in 1730, the Sauk and Fox dwelled here. Their city, called Saukenuk, grew to become one of the largest Indian settlements in North America. It included 11, 000 inhabitants at the time the Americans began building Fort Armstrong in 1816. The westernmost Revolutionary War encounter occurred in 1780, when an American force destroyed Saukenuk to retaliate for Indian support of the British. When Zebulon Pike visited the site in 1805, the explorer told Black Hawk, the Sac leader,that he should pull down the British flag and the American father would treat the Indians well, an offer the chief declined, for "we wished to have two fathers." A striking statue of Black Hawk stands next to the 1930's Civilian Conservation Corps stone lodge. His right hand grasps a blanket which drapes him as he peers out toward the Rock River which bordered his beloved homeland. Inside the lodge, the one-room Hauberg Museum (8:30-12, 1-4:30) houses Indian artifacts, a bark teepee, and displays on the amusement park—where the "chute-the-chute" ride was invented—which occupied the site from 1882 to 1927, when the state acquired the land.

From a terrace behind the building near the Black Hawk statue, the land drops off to the Rock River Valley below, where an unsightly gravel yard mars the view. The waterway begins in Wisconsin, sixty miles west of Lake Michigan, and then flows three hundred and thirty miles to this point, where it enters the Mississippi. From the mouth of the Rock up to the Green River, about twelve miles upstream, the waterway forms part of the mostly man-made, hundred-and-two-mile-long, eighty-foot-wide Hennepin Canal, used for navigation between the Illinois and Mississippi Rivers. Although shippers proposed the canal as early as 1834, construction began only in 1890, and the facility remained in service from 1907 to 1951. By using the canal, which included thirty-two locks, boats could travel from the Mississippi to the Illinois and then, via the Illinois and Michigan Canal, enter Lake Michigan at Chicago. This route, which reduced the water distance from the Upper Mississippi to Chicago by four hundred and nineteen miles, opened a commercial link between the Mississippi and the east coast. Construction of the Hennepin Canal—the first in the country built of concrete without stone facings—greatly influenced the building of later such constructions, especially the Panama Canal.

Two unusual excursions originate in Rock Island. Balloons Are Beautiful (309-788-3118) offers balloon flights over the Mississippi River Valley, and Huck Finn University (800-369-3061) runs three to five day tours, with days on the Mississippi and nights at bed and breakfast places. Cruise "graduates" receive "diplomas" at the end of the trip. Area bed and breakfast establishments include River Drive Guest House (309-762-8503), on the Mississippi in Moline, and, in Rock Island, Victorian Inn (309-788-7068). Top o' the Morning (309-786-3513), was installed in the eighteen room c. 1912 brick mansion built by Hiram S. Cable, president of the Rock Island line. The Register-listed 1907 Potter House (800-747-0339), was formerly occupied by owners of *The Argus* newspaper.

The River Road out of Rock Island, Highway 92, crosses the Rock River near where it enters the Mississippi. The route passes Milan, where on Andalusia Road across from Showcase Cinema, a marker recalls that in this area on May 8, 1832 Abraham Lincoln entered military service as a captain for the Black Hawk War. In later years, Lincoln enjoyed mocking his supposed heroics, and those claimed by more wily politicians who tried to exploit their participation in the campaign. Referring to 1848 Democratic Presidential candidate Lewis Cass, Lincoln joked: "If General Cass went in advance of me in picking whortle berries, I guess I surpassed him in charges upon the wild onion. If he saw any live, fighting Indians, it was more than I did; but I had a good many bloody struggles with the mosquitoes." From Andalusia, Clark's Ferry carried travelers to Buffalo, Iowa. This was the best known river crossing above St. Louis in the 1830's, where thousands of pioneers traveled over the Mississippi to settle in the Iowa territory and points beyond. Land promoters developed at Andalusia a substantial town, but only on paper—maps, plats and drawings which the hustlers used to peddle lots to gullible buyers on the east coast. Only a village ever developed there, a hamlet where a handful of families lived by making pearl buttons out of clam shells fished out of the Mississippi. Beyond Andalusia, not far from the river, lies the Snowstar Ski Area (309-798-2666).

Further on, the road reaches Illinois City, where the Hillbilly Corner store—with stacks of horse feed, a pool table in the side room, and a rather rural atmosphere—lives up to its name. At this point, the Mississippi ends its westward path, which began at East Moline, and bends to the south. Just north of New Boston, a spur road leads out to Lock and Dam Number 17, located on a remote stretch of the Mississippi. New Boston, a village of 731, seems little changed from its early days a century and a half ago, when Abe Lincoln surveyed the town in 1834. Yesterdays Cafe suggests the town's tone, for New Boston is definitely a "yester day" sort of settlement, isolated in time and place. At the foot of Main, where a sign by the Mississippi cautions, "Road Ends," the river laps at the little spur of pavement which reaches the waterway there. Few roads dead-end at the river: New Boston, an end-of-the-line back road backwater, merits the distinction. Opposite Yesterdays Cafe, the 1900 Doffenbarger Building houses the New Boston Banking Office, no threat to Morgan Guaranty. A museum inhabits the Levi Willitz brick residence (1856), painted a rich red hue, an exception to the unappealing peeling places which dominate the town. A wood frame structure up the street bears the black lettered designation "Abe Lincoln Hotel," now locked and crammed with a jumble of seemingly orphaned objects. All in all, however, there is something pleasantly haunting about New Boston, as if the hamlet—frozen on a century-old daguerreotype—had suddenly come to life, just barely, in the late twentieth century.

Indians have inhabited this area since time immemorial. When the Sac and Fox arrived in the eighteenth century, the newcomers referred to the region along the Mississippi from New Boston to Gladstone farther south as Yellow Banks, so named for the shore's sandy soil and russet bluffs. Early New Boston settler Levi W. Myers, who first spied the Yellow Banks area from atop a bluff, adjudged the pristine country "an earthly paradise." At New Boston, named Upper Yellow Banks by the Indians, the peace-loving Keokuk held a pow-wow with Black Hawk in 1832 in an unsuccessful attempt to prevent the Black Hawk War. After this, the victors forced the Indians to abandon their beloved Yellow Banks. Societies and settlements come and go and, all the while, the Mississippi relentlessly rolls along past Yellow Banks, the eternal waterway—so wrote Hart Crane—"a mustard glow/Tortured with history, its one will—flow!"

Six miles farther south in the Yellow Banks territory lies Keithsburg, which the Indians called Middle Yellow Banks. In 1837 Scotsman Robert Keith established Keith's Landing, where he operated a wood yard which sold fuel to steamships. Although Keith believed the settlement would grow to rival St. Louis, the town of less than a thousand now rivals only New Boston. In 1847, Keithsburg became the county seat, an honor it lost ten years later, but in the 1850's the town enjoyed a certain prosperity as a leading river port for the export of western Illinois grain and livestock. This commercial activity survives today with the Garnac Grain terminal operating in Keithsburg. Floods in 1848, 1851, 1853, and 1881 damaged the city, while the 1965 inundation completely irrigated the business district; the Mississippi crested at 20.26 feet. Finally, in 1979, engineers installed a levee to protect Keithsburg from the temperamental waterway. In 1986, some four blocks of downtown Keithsburg, including fifteen buildings, received designation as a National Historic District. The 1849 Commercial Hotel, listed on the National Register, survives as the town's oldest structure, while other relics—some restored, or at least repainted—include the c. 1900 brick Morgan building, the 1888 Bettler Building, which now houses a market, and the c. 1890 Keithsburg *News* Building, with old presses displayed inside. The 1966 former Keithsburg Grade School, closed for lack of students, now contains the city hall and a museum. Established in 1985, it holds such items as old newspapers, antique clothes, views of town a century ago, and a long, red wood "Loafer's Bench," the last such seat which stood in front of Jonesy's Tavern.

Three miles south of Keithsburg, the nearly three thousand acre Big River State Forest Reserve stretches out along the Mississippi, a remnant of the once-extensive prairie woodland border. When N.H. Patterson first found Patterson's Bindweed here in 1873 (now an endangered plant), this was the only known place in the world where that species grew. Farther south lies Delbar State Park, with a nature trail and paths leading to the Mississippi. In the winter, area residents enjoy ice skating and ice fishing here.

The town of Oquawka perches a few miles south by the Mississippi. Its designation derives from Oquawkiek, the Indian name for "Yellow Banks." The town began as an Indian trading post established in 1827 by Alexis and Stephen Phelps. Portable mills sawed timber cut on nearby islands and floated to Oquawka. For a time, the town served as a summer resort for Burlington, Iowa, and Monmouth and Galesburg in Illinois. In 1842, the Phelps brothers gave to Henderson County the cupola-topped Classic Revival-style brick courthouse, still in use. Here, in the early 1840's Lincoln opponent Stephen A. Douglas served as the first circuit court judge. The National Register-listed 1833 white frame green-trimmed Alexis Phelps House, under restoration, enjoys a splendid view of the Mississippi from a high point above the river. By the waterway at the end of Schuyler, the main street, stands Ye Old Fish House, a cozy little eatery. Up the street, the facade of the 1866 Graham Building, occupied by a pharmacy, bears a most unusual sign (does such a notice exist anywhere else in the world?) listing all owners of the site from 1836 to the present. Across from Hamilton's market—"Just good food," boasts a sign—a richly colored mural painted in 1986 for the town's 150th anniversary depicts Indians, Lincoln and the *Oquawka*, a paddlewheeler shown with black smoke frothing from its stacks. In May, 1990, Oquawka hosted an unusual dragon boat race on the Mississippi. It featured replicas of forty-foot long Chinese canoes manned by twenty-two paddlers plus a coxswain, drummer, and flag person to grab a banner from the water at the end of the course (for information: 309-867-2045). The sport, popular in Asia and Australia, derives from a 2000 year old Chinese tradition.

Oquawka's most unusual attraction lies near the swimming pool, not far from the town water tower—namely, the tomb of an elephant. A small stone wall topped by an elephant figure honors "Norma Jean Elephant Aug. 10, 1942-July 17, 1972. This memorial is dedicated in memory of an elephant named Norma Jean, who was killed by lightning at this location and lies buried here." A glass display case contains a photo of the animal taken on July 16th and another showing her lying on the ground just after her demise. Norma Jean—valued at $10,000 and uninsured—was tethered to a tree when the fatal bolt, which knocked the elephant's trainer, Larry "Possum Red" Harsh thirty feet, struck at 7:30 a.m. as the Clark and Walters Circus prepared for the evening performance at the Oquawka town square. Workers dug a twelve foot deep hole at the site and, with the help of a tractor and chains, rolled 6500 pound Norma Jean into her grave.

The Henderson Covered Bridge survives two and a half miles south of town. It was built in 1866 for $2125 and used until 1934. Seven years after gaining a listing on the National Register in 1975, the bridge washed away in a flood and lodged against the Route 164 span downstream. Workers salvaged and reconstructed the relic, using the original timbers and oak beams, but this time the bridge was raised three and a half feet. On the 104 foot long span appears a notice: "Five dollar Fine for leading or driving any beast faster than a walk or driving more than thirty head of cattle, mules or horses at a time on or across this bridge." Limestone quarries along Henderson Creek, which the bridge crosses, furnished some of the stone used in Mississippi River bridge piers in Illinois. Beyond the covered bridge lies Gladstone, platted in 1856 and settled by Irish, Swedish, and German immigrants. A spur road leads two and a half miles west out to Lock and Dam Number 18, like Number 17 located in a rather isolated area of the river. Tiny Gulfport, originally East Burlington, began in 1855 as a ferry port, but declined after bridges started spanning the Mississippi.

The River Road leads through sparsely populated back country down to Dallas City. So modest did English writer Jonathan Raban find the place that in *Old Glory: An American Voyage* he mocked that "'City' was a courtesy title." This discourteous dig is not strictly true, for in 1859 the settlement actually went to the trouble of getting the state legislature to change the name from Dallas Town to Dallas City. But, indeed, the "city"—named in the 1840's for U.S. Vice President George M. Dallas—seems at most a town, and is perhaps even better described as a village.

Dallas served under President James K. Polk, whose last name designates a Mississippi River island just offshore. Back in the old days, boys were allowed to skinny-dip out there in the Mississippi under cover of night, but only if, as the law provided, the lads waited until at least eight stars appeared in the sky.

Eleven years before Israel Atherton built the city's first house in 1836, occupied until the late 1960's, Hezekiah Spillman arrived in the area where he established a ferry and a woodyard which served steamers as a fueling station. At Dallas City on October 23, 1858 Abraham Lincoln delivered one of his sixty-three speeches, including seven debates with Stephen A. Douglas, in his unsuccessful campaign for the U.S. Senate. This event was memorialized in 1936 by a twelve ton boulder, with a commemorative plaque, placed at the foot of Oak Street by the Mississippi. On the waterfront stands the picturesque Walker Fish Company—one of those colorful little fish shops found in small towns along the waterway—whose sign states "Fur Buyer & Trapping Supplies," an evocation of the early days on the Mississippi. An old brick building by the train tracks bears on its flank the designation "Anguish & Wolfenbarger," the name of a Ford agency established in 1923 by W.F. Anguish, farmer, mayor, and president of the Dallas City Bank.

A few blocks away stands the rather spooky and definitely eccentric turret-topped stone high school, which a local businessman suggested should resemble a castle on the Rhine. Near the school runs a dividing line between Henderson and Hancock Counties, which places parts of Dallas City under two separate jurisdictions. After Lewis Burg moved his buggy factory to Dallas City in 1891, to take advantage of the railroad and Mississippi River access, he constructed three buildings at the east end of town, where in 1909 he started assembling automobiles. A car buff in Dallas City owns the only surviving example of the fifty or so machines Burg produced. The only Burg building still standing, which through the years housed a garage, mattress coil company, skating rink, and dance hall, now contains the regionally renowned Riverview Supper Club. It specializes in catfish meals, and is decorated with mounted animals, steamboat murals, cigar store Indians, and other such Americana. The 1850's Guest House (217-852-3652 or 217-755-4327) in Dallas City takes bed and breakfast guests. Six miles south of town lies a 1928 two level—one for cars, the other for trains—toll bridge, which boasts the world's longest swing span, to Fort Madison, Iowa. Its predecessor, which cost 25 ¢ for a horse and buggy, opened in 1888 after the Santa Fe Railroad agreed to finance the bridge.

To the south, the old Mormon town of Nauvoo occupies one of the most splendid sights on the Mississippi. Rarely does such a prime location along the waterway remain so uncluttered and undeveloped. In 1824, the Fox Indians relinquished this outstanding position, where the Mississippi sweeps gracefully around a promontory, for two hundred sacks of corn. Four years after a post office called Venus opened in 1830, the hamlet changed its name to Commerce. This proved to be a misnomer, as little commerce transpired there. Within ten years, however,

Nauvoo (as the Mormons called their town) grew to become Illinois' second largest city, with some eleven thousand inhabitants, only a thousand less than Chicago.

This transformation occurred after Mormon leader Joseph Smith led his people in 1839 from Missouri to the gently sloping terrain that rises above the river's curve. Here they built a thriving settlement described by army colonel Thomas L. Kane, who visited Nauvoo in 1846: "Half encircled by a bend of the river, a beautiful city lay glittering in the fresh morning sun; its bright new dwellings set in cool green gardens, ranging up around a stately dome-shaped hill." Unfortunately, this idyllic setting and picture-perfect town did not serve as the scene of a happy ending. A schism fractured the church, resulting in the arrest of Joseph Smith and his brother Hyrum, both killed by a mob at Carthage, southeast of Nauvoo, on June 27, 1844. Further internal conflicts, as well as disputes with non-church members, induced the Mormons to abandon Nauvoo. This undertaking began in February, 1846, as the first emigrants left across the frozen Mississippi to begin their 1400-mile trek to Utah. This Mormon exodus, led by Brigham Young, was the largest and best organized migration in the history of the trans-Mississippi expansion of the United States. After the Mormons left Nauvoo, it became a near ghost town, a skeletal settlement only slightly fleshed out from 1849 to 1856 by a small utopian communal society called the Icarians. Following this failed experiment, a few Germans arrived in the late 1850's and the 1860's. Only a century later, however, did the Mormons restore their old settlement, now a National Historic District.

Today a dozen or so attractively restored houses and commercial establishments—some built with lumber floated down the Mississippi from Wisconsin—stand along the grid-like streets where the original town stood. These structures include dwellings occupied by Joseph Smith, Brigham Young, and gunsmith Jonathan Browning, whose son John invented the automatic machine gun; the *Times and Seasons* newspaper office; Seventies Hall, a cultural and training center; Lyon Drug and Variety Store, filled with old-type merchandise; and the reconstructed Webb Wagon and Blacksmith Shop, which fabricated wagons for the 1846 westward migration.

At a high point up in the present day town, lies the site of the Nauvoo Temple, built between 1841 and 1846, the largest structure west of Cincinnati and north of St. Louis. It was damaged by fire in 1848 and destroyed by a tornado three years later. Nauvoo State Park, just south of town, holds one of the only two remaining "sunstones" (the other belongs to the Smithsonian) of the original thirty such ray-topped relief faces which decorated the temple, along with "moonstones" and "starstones." The park also includes Nauvoo's first vineyard, planted by the Icarians in the 1850's, as well as a museum (May 15-Oct 31, 1-5) with exhibits on the town's history. Two Mormon Visitor Centers vie for tourists' attention. The smaller one (Memorial Day-Labor Day 8-8, rest of year 8:30-5) belongs to the Reorganized Church of Latter Day Saints, headquartered in Independence, Missouri. It holds that leadership descended directly from Joseph Smith. The better known Salt Lake City branch, which maintains that after Smith's death the Twelve Apostles became the governing body, operates a large facility (8-7) with well-mounted exhibits, installed in 1990, including an excellent small-scale reproduction of Nauvoo in 1845. Outside stand thirteen bronze figures which form the Monument to Women.

Along Mulholland, Nauvoo's main street, stand various vintage buildings which lend the town a nineteenth century flavor. Even the laundromat sports an old fashioned hanging sign—a wash board in a big tub of sudsy water—of the sort which indicate the street's commercial establishments, among them pottery, wood working and other craft shops. The Hotel Nauvoo (217-453-2211, open from two weeks before Easter to mid-November) promises more than it delivers. The seemingly (from the outside) antique eight room hostelry appears rather ordinary inside, complete with a fake fire and a mundane looking main dining room (Tu-Sat 5-9, Sun 11-3), which features a buffet. You'll find wines available from Baxter's Vineyards (9-4:30, Sun from 12), run by the great-great-grandson of firm founder Emile Baxter, who in 1855 settled at the Icarian colony (recalled by the Icarian Living History Museum: 217-453-2437). Nauvoo Blue Cheese, made locally since 1937 in a former brewery building, joins with the winery to celebrate "The wedding of the wine and cheese" at the Grape Festival, held annually (F, Sat and Sun of Labor Day weekend) for more than half a century. In mid-August, players perform the *City of Joseph* pageant, a musical production that reviews the town's history. East of town, not far beyond the winery, Parley Lane (217-453-2277) Bed and Breakfast occupies a restored nineteenth century farmhouse, while two and a half miles south of Nauvoo, Mississippi Memories (217-453-2771) offers rooms overlooking the river.

Southeast of Nauvoo lies Carthage, site of the jail (8-5), now restored, where in 1844 a mob killed Joseph and Hyrum Smith. The River road, Highway 96, continues directly south from Nauvoo, bordering the Mississippi only a few feet above the water level. This is one of the river's most impressive stretches. A series of striking vistas unfold before you as you follow the waterway's curving course. Traveling so close to the mighty artery gives you a feel for its size and grandeur. Shortly after passing the Hoot Owl Ridge Rest Area, site of the vanished town of Montebello, first seat of Hancock County, looms the large, boxy Union Electric power plant. Then you reach Hamilton, home of Dadant & Sons, the world's biggest supplier of bee-keeping items. Founded in 1863 by Charles Dadant, who moved from a village near Dijon, France to Hamilton, the business soon became the nation's largest honey producer. In time it evolved into a bee supply company, now run by fifth generation family members. "Beekeeping," affirms the firm's catalog, "is a honey of a hobby." The operation occupies an old fashioned brick building which emits the faint aroma of honey, released from the beeswax processing area in the basement. Products turned out at the factory—one of four operated by Dadant—include candles and veils to protect the bee-handler's faces. A small shop sells honeycombs (you can eat the wax or chew it like gum), beeswax candles, and other related items.

Hamilton, established in 1852 by Artois Hamilton, served as the site of a sawmill, once powered by the Mississippi's Des Moines rapids until they disappeared after the construction of the Keokuk dam in 1913. The Kibbe Life Science Station, a Western Illinois University facility, perches on the river bluffs three miles south of town. From September through April, between one hundred and five hundred bald eagles reside here.

A large number of nineteenth century buildings at Warsaw, a few miles south, lends that river town—much of it a National Historic District—an old fashioned flavor. To protect supply ships on the Mississippi during the War of 1812, the government built Fort Edwards on the bluffs high above the waterway. The installation also served as an official fur factory—a trading post—up to the time when John Jacob Astor's Fur Company, which operated it until 1832, took over. Meanwhile, in 1824, troops vacated the fort, recalled today by a pillar erected in 1914 at the outpost's site. On the fifty foot tall granite shaft monument appears a metal relief of Illinois governor Ninian Edwards, whose name designated the post. A relief also commemorates Major Zachary Taylor, later U.S. President, who in 1814 constructed Fort Johnson, a previous installation on the bluffs. From this strategic high point a view extends upriver to a fragment of Keokuk, Iowa, and then across the waterway to Alexandria, Missouri. Warsaw locals enjoy pointing out that the view here looks onto three cities whose names all begin and end with the same letter.

When settlers first established Warsaw in 1834, they gave it the colorful name Spunky Point, as the Indians there produced "spunk water" ("fire water"). In 1841, the Mormons tried to establish a new town next to Warsaw, which annexed the land to keep the unwelcome newcomers away. Anti-Mormon articles in *The Warsaw Signal* incited the public against the sect, and eventually led to the murder of Joseph Smith at the jail up at Carthage. The Print Shop Museum contains antique printing equipment of the type Thomas Sharp used to publish the newspaper, often filled with sharp attacks on the Mormons. At 130 Main, stands (the brick portion) the old Warsaw House Hotel (1835) where the crowd which stormed the Carthage jail gathered. The nearby Warsaw Historical Museum (May-Oct Tu and Th 1-4), contains the desk supposedly used by Zachary Taylor when he served as commander of Fort Edwards, a model of which is on exhibit, and a piano the city presented to the steamer *Warsaw* in 1858. According to local lore, young Sam Clemens (Mark Twain) worked in the print shop at 204-6 Main, which in 1840-1841 published the *Western World* weekly, while 412 Main contained a bakery owned by Conrad Nagel, grandfather of the early silent movie star of the same name. The house at 220 Crawford supposedly consists of stones from the Nauvoo Mormon Temple ruins. A c. 1814 log cabin survives at the west end of Crawford.

At 185-7 Clay stands the double house (1841) where John Hay, son of a local physician, lived (west side) as a boy. In the 1840's young Hay attended classes at the nearby 1835 Little Brick School, the city's first public school, which closed in 1903. Hay graduated from Brown University, then studied law in Springfield, the capital of Illinois. There he met Abraham Lincoln,who in 1861 appointed the Spunky Point native as his assistant private secretary in the White House. Hay, at the President's bedside when he died, went on to serve as editor of the *New York Tribune,* as well as ambassador to England, and

Secretary of State under William McKinley, who, like Lincoln, was also assassinated. Hay, who died in 1905, also co-authored a respected ten-volume biography of Lincoln, and is no doubt the only U.S. Secretary of State whose poetry appears in anthologies. His dialect-filled verse tells of various Midwestern characters, some of them rivermen like Jim Bludso, an engineer of the *Prairie Belle* who saved passengers from the burning steamer: "And, sure's you're born, they all got off/Afore the smokestacks fell,—/And Bludso's ghost went up alone/In the smoke of the Prairie Belle." During the second weekend of October, Warsaw celebrates its annual Hay Day On the Mississippi with music, games, food, and crafts.

Some other early Warsaw lads, the brothers Henry and William Leyhe, also made their mark on the world. In 1861, at ages twenty and eighteen, they launched their first steamboat, the *Young Eagle*, at the base of the bluff below Fort Edwards. So began the Eagle Packet Company, which in 1863 added the *R.E. Hill* and the *Eagle*,in 1864 the *Amorath*, and in 1865 the *Grey Eagle*, all built at Warsaw. In 1874—about the time three trains started offering daily service to Warsaw—the Leyhes moved the company offices to St. Louis, where the firm survived for more than a century, although not always as a steamship company. Another local enterprise began in 1861, when Rudolf Giller established the Warsaw Brewing Company, whose abandoned, castle-like 1910 brewery complex still stands by the Mississippi at the north side of town. During Prohibition, the plant produced a rather hardy and hardish soft drink, supposedly almost like beer. Federal authorities found it so near beer that the brew proved stronger than just near beer, and they closed the brewery. It reopened in 1936 and continued until 1972. On the way out of town to the south, a steep descent to the Mississippi takes you past the Warsaw grain elevators and onto Water Street, which parallels the river. At 300 South Water stands a mill building, reconstructed in 1856 after a fire and named Grace Mills, as the owner said that only by the grace of God would he be able to start over. The solid-looking limestone house (1828) at 900 South Water belonged to Major John R. Wilcox, first commandant of Fort Edwards, the only officer to remain in Warsaw, of which he was one of the founders. The four story 1866 brick Warsaw Woolen Mill remains at 1401 South Water. It manufactured cashmere, and later housed a shoe (1905-1930) and (until 1979) a battery factory.

The River Road continues south to Lima, a hamlet of 125 with a one-time general store that retains a few traces of its former function and flavor. The screen door bears a "Butter-Krust Bread" metal plate. Look inside the musty shop and you'll see canned goods and other staples vie with old dishes, toys, postcards, and other bric-a-brac for customers' dollars. Across the street, a bright, red, apple image decorates the now-closed white Reed Orchards building, and nearby stand the peeling frame Lima Christian Church, along with a porcelain doll shop. Its nearly paintless dull wood contrasts with the adjacent, bright Citgo gas sign. Lima's odd little cluster of unpeopled structures somehow seems surrealistic as if, say, it were a still-standing movie set for a long-abandoned production.

Realism returns as you head south, past the turnoff to the toll ferry to Canton, Missouri and then on into Quincy, a once bustling river port. "Quincy boomed with the coming of the steam-boat," wrote Albert S. Tousley in his 1928 *Where Goes the River*, "and it is still a steamboat town in spirit." For twenty years, a century ago, Quincy remained Illinois's second largest city, with a peak of 72,000 people in the 1880's, 30,000 more than the present population. The town once boasted the Mississippi's most northerly post office, opened in 1825. During the steamboat era, as many as 2,500 ships a year put in at Quincy, a port of entry for foreign goods. Quinsippi Island, a long strip of land offshore, created Quincy Bay, the largest natural harbor on the Mississippi. Arching over the southern tip of the bay is a slim-lined bridge with web-like struts, the Mississippi's newest span (1987). The wire ropes—components of the cable-stay system developed in Europe—hold the bridge deck from two main support towers, so eliminating shore anchorages and allowing a long span (here nine hundred feet) between the towers.

In 1822, John Wood, later governor of Illinois, along with a few other pioneers, established a settlement called The Bluffs, a name later changed to Quincy. The town square was designated John's Square when the legislature created Adams County in January 1825, all to honor John Quincy Adams, the newly elected President. The handsome, columned, Greek Revival-style, fourteen room 1838 John Wood Mansion (Sat and Sun 1-4), listed on the National Register, contains period furnishings and other early artifacts. The Osage Orangerie shop (M, W, F, Sat and Sun 1-4) at the mansion sells locally made craft items.

On Maine, Quincy's curiously named main street, lies John's Square, since 1857 called Washington Park. There you'll find a statue of the full-bearded John Wood, and also a bronze relief by Lorado Taft depicting the sixth of seven debates, held at the park on October 13, 1858, between Abe Lincoln and Senator Stephen A. Douglas; some 12,000 people attended. The scene shows Lincoln standing by the podium, left hand on his lapel, while to his right sits the pensive looking Douglas. His arms are folded, and his legs—which emerge from the vignette—crossed; the right shoe, brightly polished by the touches of countless hands, gleams. Quotations note Lincoln's point about slavery "that it is a wrong," while Douglas, who won the Senatorial election, said that the slave owners "are civilized men" who should decide the issue for themselves.

Quincy boasts a large number of noteworthy old buildings which lend it the flavor of a nineteenth century town. The Gardner Museum of Architecture and Design (Sat and Sun 1-5), the nation's only private architecture museum, features examples of local decor and ornamentation. The museum occupies the

1888 Richardson Romanesque-style former library. The Quincy Museum of Natural History and Art (weekends and by appointment: 217-224-7669), featuring antiques, Indian artifacts, and a miniature circus, occupies the 1891 Register-listed Newcomb-Stillwell mansion, a ponderous stone pile. The somewhat whimsical 1887 Lorenzo Bull home carriage house hosts the Quincy Art Center (Tu-F 1-4, Sat and Sun 1-5). Brick streets with a grassy median and attractive old houses, each a different style, enhance Park Place, between South 12th and 14th. Calftown (York to Jackson, 5th to 13th), was named as such because early settlers from Germany found enough land to keep cattle in the backyard, rather than, as in the old country, inside the house. The restored dwellings which survive there date from 1840 to 1870. The more than 10,500 Germans who settled in Quincy then accounted for some 40 percent of the city's population.

Register-listed Villa Kathrine, quite the oddest building in town, rises atop the bluffs overlooking the Mississippi at one of the waterway's prime residential sites. A magnificent view is to be had here. This fanciful, Moorish-style stucco structure, seemingly a stray from *The Desert Song* or *Casablanca*, may be the only such building of its type on the entire Mississippi. In 1900, George Metz, inspired by a villa he saw in Algeria, built Villa Kathrine, now Quincy's tourist center. Here, he lived alone with his dog Bingo, the pet supposedly buried with a diamond-studded collar in the rose garden. So far, fortune hunters, digging there, have failed to find the canine necklace.

Other Quincy museums include the Lincoln Douglas Valentine Museum (M-F 10-2), with a display of old and unusual valentines; the Pharmacy Museum (May-Sept Sat and Sun 1-4), a century-old drug store; the Quinsippi Island Antique Auto Museum (Sun 11-5); and the All Wars Museum (W-F 1-4, Sat and Sun 9-11, 1-4). The last is replete with maps, medals, uniforms, vehicles and a huge photo of General Douglas MacArthur signing the World War II Japanese surrender. These many items are all housed in a building on the grounds of the Illinois Veterans Home, whose rough-hewn stone block structures seem rather forbidding. Out on Quinsippi Island stands Adams Landing, a village of log houses and other buildings used by pioneer families. James Frazier built the 1828 cabin there for his new bride, Emelia, who lived over in Palmyra, Missouri. Because of this situation, he was forced to swim the Mississippi on horseback, before they married, whenever he wanted to see her.

A series of parks lines the river north of the bridges. Nearby, in the lower part of Quincy, a scattering of old commercial buildings survive. The Burlington Northern tracks run alongside the river. This railroad succeded the Chicago, Burlington and Quincy line, which served the city after the steamboat era. Riverview Park, up on the bluff, contains a bronze statue of George Rogers Clark. This intrepid Revolutionary War officer seized Kaskaskia, on the Mississippi in Illinois downstream, so earning the inscription, "The Son of Virginia; The Sword of Kentucky; The Savior of Illinois." The *Princess* (217-228-2400) offers cruises on the Mississippi, and Kaufmann House Bed and Breakfast (217-223-2502) offers rooms, as does the old fashioned Elkton Hotel (217-222-5660).

As you leave town, you'll see the huge elevators of the Quincy Soybean Company rise over the river, while the Huber Company underground warehouse occupies openings cut into the bluff. About fourteen miles south, the River Road passes the Fall Creek Scenic Overlook. Here survives a late 1850's native stone bridge, used until 1949. A large keystone arch supports the structure. At Kinderhook, which boasts 250 inhabitants, most of the few commercial places seem closed, but the still-functioning post office occupies a diminutive stone structure by the tracks. At nearby Hull,the old bank building houses a local history museum. Highway 96, the River Road, continues south to Rockport, founded in 1836, where the Rockport Cafe, with its porch plank benches, wood floor, overhead fan, and pressed tin ceiling, offers a picture out of the past. The head of a buck killed by a local boy with his first shot hangs on the wall of the cafe. At the junction of Highways 96 and 54 in Atlas, Pike County's oldest town (1820), stands an 1823 brick house built as a trading post on the old Keokuk to St. Louis trail. In this dwelling Mormon leader Brigham Young lived for seven weeks, and it also served as an inn and stagecoach shop. In 1833, Atlas lost the county seat to Pittsfield, where *Free Press* journalist John George Nicolay became the first person to suggest Abraham Lincoln for the presidency. After winning the office, Lincoln rewarded Nicolay by appointing him as private secretary. At Pleasant Hill, farther south, the Bowman and Springer Feed Store offers a Norman Rockwell-like picture of Americana.

The River Road enters Calhoun County—established in 1825 and named for U.S. vice president John C. Calhoun—a completely rural peninsula tucked between the Mississippi and Illinois Rivers, and inhabited by fewer than 6,000 people. "Every man and woman is in love with Calhoun County," claimed Mary Hartwell Catherwood in her booklet *Lower Illinois Valley Local Sketches of Long Ago*. In fact, it is easy to like this secluded enclave, one of Illinois's most isolated areas and the state's only county without a railroad. Calhoun formed the lower edge of the Military Tract, the territory between the two rivers up to Rock Island County allocated by the federal government to veterans of the War of 1812. The handful of soldiers who chose to settle in Calhoun engaged in lumbering or farming.

Highway 96 turns away from the Mississippi, and heads east to Kampsville on the Illinois, where the Kampsville Archeological Museum (May-October Tu-Sun 10-12, 1-5) contains exhibits on the various Indian cultures which existed in the central Mississippi River Valley over many centuries. One display pertains to the famous Koster Site, named after the farmer who owned the now filled-in dig, located across the Illinois River. At this site, Northwestern University archeologists excavated more than a dozen strata, the earliest dating back to 8000 B.C., one of the oldest traces of civilization yet found anywhere in the world. The museum belongs to the Center for American Archeology at Kampsville (618-653-4316), which runs summer educational excavation programs for high school students. The cozy Kampsville Inn restaurant stands by the ferry landing, one of four (plus one bridge) which connect Calhoun County with Missouri and the Illinois "mainland."

The River Road now follows the Illinois River to Hardin, which boasts the isolated county's only bridge (1932) as well as the courthouse, a two story red brick building with an outdoor staircase up to the second floor courtroom, while to the rear stands a limestone jail. Although the River Road crosses the bridge here, an alternative route will take you due south to the antiquated Wittmond Hotel at Brussels, a former stagecoach stop that remains a true period piece (1847) (618-883-2345). The hotel's home cooked meals feature fried chicken and apple pie. You might then proceed to the *Golden Eagle* ferry (mid-Feb to Mid-Dec, 5:30 a.m.-8 p.m., weekends and holidays 8-7; 618-883-2217) in order to cross the Mississippi to the St. Louis area on perhaps the waterway's only paddlewheel ferry. Kinder's restaurant by the landing overlooks the waterway. Another route takes you on to the twelve car Brussels ferry, six miles south of the Wittmond, to cross the Illinois and return to the River Road. Via either Hardin or the Brussels ferry you'll end up east of the Illinois, where the nearly 8,000-acre Pere Marquette State Park stretches along the river. A large white cross on Highway 100 east of the entrance marks the place where Father Jacques Marquette and Louis Joliet landed in 1673 during their trip back up the Mississippi after their pioneering journey down the river. In the reception area at the rustic National Register-listed lodge—built of stone and wood beams in the 1920s by Civilian Conservation Corps workers and recently (1988) remodeled—appears a painting of Pere Marquette in a birchbark canoe paddled by two Indians. The spacious lobby, with the original 1930's furnishings, includes a huge stone fireplace and a twelve foot square board with pieces some four feet high; this is supposedly the world's largest chess set. Lodge accommodations include fifty rooms and twenty-two stone guest houses (618-786-2331), while the park offers trails, horseback riding, and other outdoor activities.

Grafton, five miles south of the park, lies at the confluence of the Mississippi and the Illinois. Where the Upper Illinois reaches La Salle, named for the famous Mississippi explorer, the hundred and twenty mile Illinois-Michigan Canal begins. Built in 1848, it extends to the mouth of the Chicago River at Lake Michigan, so linking the Great Lakes with the Mississippi River system. Named for the Massachusetts hometown of James Mason, who founded the settlement in 1832, Grafton offers a scattering of antique shops. Other attractions include the Chateau Ra-Ha winery; the Fin Inn restaurant, where river fish occupy three aquarium tanks from which they eye their less fortunate cousins on dinner plates; and the *Belle of Grafton* (618-786-2318), which in mid-1990 began river cruises on the Mississippi and the Illinois.

When Marquette and Joliet returned from their ground-(or river-) breaking trip down the Mississippi to the Arkansas River in 1673, they entered the Illinois at Grafton for the journey north to the Great Lakes. At Grafton's Shafer Wharf Historic District, the Nancy Kirkpatrick Guest House and Shafer Wharf Inn (for both: 618-786-2328 or 618-374-2821) offer bed and breakfast rooms overlooking the Mississippi; Grandview Guest House (618-463-6864) and Tara Point Inn (618-786-3555) also take bed and breakfast guests, as does Wildflower Inn (618-465-3719) east of town. Just beyond Grafton, you'll reach the fourteen mile long Palisade Parkway, one of the finest stretches anywhere along the Mississippi. The road—bordered by the Sam Vadalabene bicycle trail—runs between magnificent limestone bluffs which rise steeply, and the wide river which ripples and sparkles in the sunlight. "No other stretch of the Great River Road, from Itasca to New Orleans, offers such ready access to such a superb riverscape to so many people," states John Madson in *Up on the River*.

A few miles down the highway you'll pass Chautauqua, a National Historic District founded in the nineteenth century, when such cultural meeting places were popular. Chautauqua now serves as a private vacation home enclave. An old lighthouse stands on the Mississippi here. Farther on lies Elsah, a vintage village—the first entire community listed on the National register—tucked into a narrow opening in the bluffs. Elsah survives as a virtually unchanged century-old settlement, one of the Mississippi's most delightful corners. Six years after the first settler started selling cord wood fuel to steamboats, former Senator James Semple acquired the site and offered to give a lot to anyone who would build a stone house on the land. In 1888, railroad tycoon Jay Gould planned to build a bridge at Elsah, but he abandoned the idea after receiving permission to use St. Louis's Eads Bridge for his line. The village thus remained a delightful backwater untouched by progress. Old brick and stone structures cluster at the picture-perfect hamlet nestled in the narrow valley by the Mississippi, while on the bluff high above lies Principia College. This Christian Science school moved from St. Louis in 1935 and now occupies an English village-like Tudor-style campus which offers views down onto the Mississippi. Because an honor system prevails, all doors lack locks, so the school allows only drive-through tours at certain times (618-374-2131). Elsah's Landing Restaurant in town serves meals and much-appreciated pies in an old-time ambiance. Bed and breakfast places include Green Tree Inn (618-374-2821), with a nineteenth century mercantile store on the first floor, Corner Nest (618-374-1891), and Maple Leaf Cottage Inn (618-374-1684).

Just before you reach Alton, you'll pass on the left a reproduction of the fearsome fanged and sharp-clawed Piasa bird, an Indian painting—destroyed by quarry activity in 1870—on the bluffs overlooking the Mississippi. These figures (two of them then existed) greatly impressed Marquette when he saw them in 1673: "These 2 monsters are so well painted that we cannot believe any savage is their author; for good painters in France would find it difficult to paint so well." Thus originated Illinois' first art criticism.

St. Louis postmaster and land speculator Rufus Easton promoted Alton in 1818, naming the new river town for his oldest son. The settlement began to develop just as the steamboat era did, and Alton became a thriving riverport which for a time rivaled nearby St. Louis.

One early-day riverman, an Alton ferryboat owner, attached a pair of millstones to the engine of his steam-powered vessel so he could grind meal as the ship traveled. Even this ingenious arrangement takes second place to what was no doubt the Mississippi's most unusual ferry, described by river pilot Frank J. Fugina in *Lore and Lure of the Upper Mississippi River* as a "wolf-powered ferry" whose owner "captured two wolf cubs and trained them to swim the river. He made a harness for them and hitched them to a rowboat. Those wolves, when full grown, pulled that boat across the fifteen hundred feet of river...There are fish stories...but this is a wolf story and a true one. As a boy I was one of the passengers."

The Alton Museum of History and Art (Th-Sun 1-4)—which occupies two nineteenth century townhouses on Broadway near many of the city's antique shops—contains exhibits which provide a good overview of local history. Four River Rooms house the story of the Mississippi at Alton, while the Alton Room covers the city's industrial development, including the Owens-Illinois Company plant, once the world's largest bottle manufacturing facility. The Lincoln Room recalls the seventh and last Lincoln-

Douglas debate, held October 15, 1858 by the Mississippi just down the street, where a pink granite marker commemorates the event. On the huge Con Agra grain elevator nearby appears a mark indicating the level reached on April 28, 1973 by the flooding Mississippi. When Mary Todd, Lincoln's future wife, insulted state auditor James Shields in 1842, the official demanded a duel, held at Alton on a Mississippi sandbar where the two men (Lincoln standing in for his lady) settled their differences just before the affair began.

The Lovejoy Print Shop at the museum memorializes Elijah P. Lovejoy, publisher of the abolitionist *Observer* newspaper, killed in 1837 when a mob seized his press—the fourth destroyed by pro-slavery ruffians—and threw it into the Mississippi. Workers dredging the river more than a century later found a piece of the press, now on display at the *Alton Telegraph* near the museum. At the City Cemetery stands a slim ninety-three foot granite column, supposedly Illinois's tallest monument, dedicated in 1897 as a memorial to Lovejoy, America's first press martyr. A life-size photo at the museum pictures 8 foot 11 inch tall Alton native Robert Wadlow, the tallest person in history, also commemorated by a marker at his long narrow tomb in Upper Alton Cemetery. He is also remembered by a full-size bronze statue—"He was known for his positive attitude and gentle manner," reads the inscription—on the campus of Southern Illinois University Dental School, originally Shurtleff College, founded in 1832 (as Alton Seminary), the state's oldest college. Loomis Hall, the original building, still stands, while the library contains the Conant painting of a smiling Abe Lincoln, believed to be the only portrait for which he actually sat.

At the corner of Broadway and Williams, a remnant of a cell block wall recalls the 1833 prison, Illinois's first penitentiary, which stood there. After social reformer Dorothea Dix criticized its conditions, Illinois closed the penitentiary and in 1860 moved the inmates to a new prison at Joliet. During the Civil War, when the Union army reopened the Alton penitentiary to hold captured Confederate soldiers, a smallpox epidemic erupted and officials installed a hospital and cemetery on "Smallpox Island" in the Mississippi. Others of the estimated 1,354 dead were buried in the Confederate Soldier's Cemetery in Upper Alton, where a monument lists the names of the deceased. During the Mexican-American and Civil Wars, women in Upper Alton continued a tradition started in 1846 of baking pies for soldiers encamped in the neighborhood, thus giving the area the nickname Pietown. The Haagen House (618-462-2419), in the Christian Hill Historic District, offers bed and breakfast in an 1868 antique filled mansion, and Watson House (618-462-3914), a. c. 1880's Victorian residence, also takes bed and breakfast guests. The Midtown restaurant, at 17th and Central, one of Alton's highest points, occupies one of the city's oldest buildings, which houses a painting of the Mississippi. A bridge now under construction and scheduled for completion in late 1993 — to connect Alton with Missouri — will be the Mississippi's newest span. In November 1991, workers digging footings for the bridge discovered a 22-foot-long section of a pre-Civil war sunken sidewheeler embedded in the muck 40 feet below the surface of the Mississippi. Only nine of the more than 600 steamboats wrecked in the 200 mile Mississippi stretch between St. Louis and the Ohio River have been recovered. In September 1991 the riverboat casino *Alton Belle* (800-336-7568) began gambling cruises out of Alton, the first such excursions in Illinois.

As you head out of Alton, along the river, the levee blocks your view of the waterway, but a road under the bridge at the flood doors leads to Lock and Dam 26, soon to disappear when a new version two miles downstream replaces the facility. Because the old locks, completed in 1938, extend only up to six hundred feet, long barge tows had to be divided into two sections and locked through separately, a procedure which created delays of some fifteen hours. To eliminate the bottleneck, Congress authorized a 1,200 foot lock, long enough to take entire tows. An observation area overlooks the new project, started in 1979 and now near completion. A Visitor Center will be added to the complex, and perhaps also a hydroelectric plant. It is both awesome and moving to see this mammoth construction—as it was a-building and as it appears now in its nearly final stage—which represents an attempt by man to control the mighty Mississippi. Even the most complete human intervention, observed Major R. Raven-Hart in *Down the Mississippi*, an Englishman who floated down the river in a kayak in 1937, "cannot tame that lawless stream, cannot curb or confine it, cannot say to it, Go here, or Go there, and make it obey; cannot save a shore which it has sentenced, cannot bar its path with an obstruction which it will not tear down, dance over, and laugh at."

Wood River, just beyond East Alton, began in 1907 when Standard Oil of Indiana (now Amoco) established a town and petroleum installations on the sandy, muddy floodplain to gain access to river transportation. Amoco tank farms stretch away to the east off Highway 3, the River Road's designation from here for virtually the entire distance to Cairo at the southern tip of Illinois. About where Lewis and Clark Boulevard intersects Highway 3, the famous expedition led by those two explorers departed to cross the Mississippi and begin the eighteen month trip up the Missouri. "I set out at 4 o'clock P.M. in the presence of many of the neighboring inhabitants, and proceeded on under a jentle brease up the Missourie," wrote William Clark in his journal account of the expedition's departure on its great adventure. Two miles after you pass the Hartford water tower, a spur road off to the west leads to a monument commemorating Lewis and Clark's epic journey. Eleven plaques, one for each state the expedition visited, note their progress across each area, while an inscription in the center of the circular pavilion summarizes the undertaking: "Near here at Camp Dubois the Lewis and Clark detachment spent the winter of 1803-04. They left on May 14, 1804, and ascended the Missouri River to its sources, crossed the Great Divide reaching the Pacific on November 7, 1805. They returned to Illinois on September 23, 1806, having concluded one of the most dramatic and significant episodes in our history."

This site is the only easily accessible place where you can conveniently see the confluence of the Mississippi and the Missouri. Just north of a wooded island, which diminishes the Mississippi's size here, the Missouri curves into the larger waterway after the long journey from the far reaches of the continent. This evocative point where North America's two great rivers meet—an ever-moving junction, rich in history and geographically unique—stirs time-haunted images of the watery arteries' importance over the long years. Past this point Marquette and Joliet floated in 1673, and from here Lewis and Clark began their trek west. Here hunted Indians of old, and by this spot once chugged majestic steamboats and now glide mile-long freight barges. Rivermen, explorers, pioneers, adventurers, farmers, the renowned, the obscure, the colorful, and the shady—a great ghostly parade of characters—passed by on the fast-flowing waters and passed on, leaving behind the age-old rivers which ran long before man appeared and which will roll on and on forever.

A mile south of the Missouri's mouth, on the Illinois side of the Mississippi, the Chain of Rocks Canal begins. You can see it at the Granite City Corps of Engineers Visitors Center just off Highway 3, about five miles beyond Interstate 270. (If you follow the River Road sign onto I-270 you will miss some river-related sights reached via Illinois 3.) Ever since the earliest days of navigation on the Mississippi, the Chain of Rocks Reach, a series of rock ledges extending into the waterway, has presented a hazard to river traffic. Between 1946 and 1953, the Engineers built an 8.4 mile long canal to bypass the treacherous Reach. Dam Number 27 lies on the Mississippi a few miles upstream, while Lock Number 27 fits into the canal toward its lower end.

This is the traveler's last chance to see a Mississippi River Lock, for below this point the river runs free. Upstream—starting at Minneapolis—lie a total of twenty-eight other locks and dams, most of them completed in the 1930's after Congress mandated a nine foot navigation channel for the Upper Mississippi. Outside the visitor center (M-F) stands the huge orange blade section from the dredge *Kennedy*, used by the Corps for more than forty-five years, while inside a display device enables would-be lock masters to simulate locking through a ship, an exercise which yields the operator a message of "Congratulations."

As early as 1815, farmers from the south settled in Granite City, named for the granite ware once made there. In 1891, St. Louis industrialist William F. Neidringhaus bought three thousand acres near the river where he established the following year the National Enameling and Stamping Company plant, forerunner of Granite City Steel, Madison County's largest employer with 3,500 workers (for tours: 618-451-4148). In 1943, Nestle Food Corporation opened a plant which produces instant tea and coffee (for tours: 618-876-6400), while the A.O. Smith factory manufactures automobile frames for Ford cars. This highly industrialized area has fairly well swallowed up most remnants of the past, but the restored old Six Mile Hotel, named for its distance from St. Louis, houses a historical museum. Highway 3 continues on through a scruffy wasteland of unkempt fields, train tracks, rusty metal structures, mobile homes, and other less than scenic sights. A crazy-quilt of towns checkers the map here. Madison began when early settlers rented out skiffs to cross the Mississippi. Larger boats, big enough to carry a horse and rider, later entered service, and for a few decades this remained the main business in town. In the late 1880's a syndicate of St. Louis industrialists constructed a trolley car bridge over the river to reduce the cost of shipping Illinois coal into the city, and soon after the American Car and Foundry Company built a railroad car plant in Madison, which then rapidly industrialized. The adjacent town of Venice—no compliment to its namesake but thus named because in the pre-levee era its streets often flooded—originated with a ferry landing established in 1804, while the next town, Brooklyn, platted in 1837, was originally called Lovejoy in honor of the martyred Alton abolitionist editor.

National City consists for the most part of the colorful National Stockyards facility, founded in 1873. Within ten years 350,000 head of cattle, 1.2 million hogs, 130,000 sheep, and 6,000 horses passed yearly through the yards, which spread over 100 acres. Eleven packing companies operated in adjacent areas, and the livestock market boasted Illinois's largest bank outside Chicago, thirty-six miles of railroad, and its own mayor, as National City is a separate jurisdiction. Only the mayor remains, for most of the pens now stand empty, with the weekly average of 1,200-1,500 cattle, 11,000-15,000 hogs and 500 sheep a mere trickle compared to the old days when National ranked second in the nation to the Chicago stockyards. The abandoned and wall-less Armour plant and a certain deserted feeling—broken only by the occasional squeals of the unknowing condemned—symbolize the stockyards' decline. Auctions, however, still take place—cattle Thursdays at 9:30; pigs Tuesdays at 1:30; sheep Wednesdays at 1—and the Stockyards Inn, rebuilt after an 1986 fire, still serves up prime steaks. Meanwhile, at the more earthy and colorful Stockyards Cafe, farmers and cattlemen gather to chat and chow down.

Highway 3 enters East St. Louis, nationally known as one of the country's most desperately poor and troubled cities, truly a study in urban decay. From a peak population of 82,000 in 1960, East St. Louis declined to 40,000 in 1990, with half of its residents unemployed, three-quarters of them receiving some sort of public assistance, and a per capita income of about one-third the U.S. average of $16,000. East St. Louis does offer a few attractions: the Katherine Dunham Museum, devoted to the famous black dancer; the Pennsylvania Avenue National Register

Historic District, in the 1000 block of Pennsylvania; and the Register-listed Majestic Theatre, 240 Collinsville Avenue.

The town did not always suffer from such impoverished conditions. The settlement began in the closing years of the eighteenth century when Captain James Piggott started a ferry service, and in 1816 land speculators sold lots near the ferry station for the new city of Illinoistown. Coal mined nearby and hauled to the river by horse-drawn wagons on wooden rails, starting in 1837, established Illinois's first railroad, forerunner of the ten train lines which arrived at Illinoistown between 1855 and 1865, making the city a leading rail center. Before Eads Bridge opened to rail traffic in 1874, trains crossed the Mississippi on vessels owned by Wiggins Ferry Company, successor to the original Piggott Ferry. When English novelist Charles Dickens visited the area in 1842 to see prairie land to the east, a Wiggins Ferry carried him across the Mississippi. Today, two centuries after its beginnings, Wiggins, a subsidiary of the Terminal Railroad Association, owns all the land along the Mississippi in East St. Louis. The Jefferson National Expansion Memorial—the St. Louis Gateway Arch just across the river—has developed plans to extend the national monument to a 100 acre riverside site in East St. Louis. With the arrival of the railroads East St. Louis, so named in 1859, began to develop. Between 1890 and 1920, its population increased from 15,000 to nearly 67,000, the fastest growth in the state, and its industrial output ranked third in Illinois, behind Chicago and Peoria. A 1903 flood which damaged the city led to the formation in 1907 of the East Side Levee and Sanitary District, which built 45 foot high barriers along the river, 3 ½ feet above the highest recorded water level, reached during the great inundation of 1844.

In *My Own Times* early 1830's Illinois governor John Reynolds described a scene at the often-flooded muddy American Bottom, the name given to the rich lowland along the Mississippi for about a hundred miles between Alton and Chester. He notes that a passer-by saw "in the American Bottom a hat on top of the ground. He got off his horse to pick up the hat, but found a man's head in it. The man under the hat said, under him was a wagon and four horses mired in the mud; that he was safe, but he supposed the horses and wagon were in a bad fix." But during the drier times the American Bottom offered superb soil, for it was "probably the richest tract of land in the United States," commented a traveler named William Blane, who toured southern Illinois in 1822. "The fertility of the 'American Bottom' is truly astonishing, and the stalks of Indian corn which I saw standing might have almost tended to remove one's doubts, as to the height of Jack's wonderful Bean." Civilization and culture as well as agriculture thrived in the American Bottom, as "this small strip of territory has become the most historic in all the state, " stated Clarence Walworth Alvord in *The Illinois Country 1678-1818*. "In the days before recorded history began it was the cradle of the most highly developed Indian culture in the state... Along its narrow plain were scattered the first permanent villages of the white men... Here was written the romance of early Illinois; in this small area were enacted scenes that marked the passing of empires."

The historic French villages, where the first settlers arrived, lie to the south along the Mississippi, while remains of the early Indian settlement survive a few miles to the east. Highway 3, just beyond the National Stockyards, reaches Interstates 55-70, which will take you out to Cahokia Mounds Historic Site, one of only some 125 places around the world designated by the United Nations a World Heritage site. Some sixty-five earthen Indian mounds dot the landscape in the 2,200 acre park, which occupies the core of the thousand year old Mississippian Culture city where 20,000 inhabitants lived. The Indians settled here, six miles east of the Mississippi, and put down roots in the fertile American Bottom (better described back then as the Indian Bottom) where they established a sophisticated society which survived until about 1400 when, for reasons unknown, the civilization disappeared. Monks Mound—so called for the French Trappist monks who planted gardens and orchards on its terraces around 1809—remains as the ancient town's most imposing remnant, the largest prehistoric earthen construction in the Americas. It took the Indians three hundred years and 22 million cubic feet of dirt to build the four-tiered hundred foot tall ceremonial mound. One hundred and forty-two steps now take you to the top, from where there spreads out before you the once-great city's now-empty territory. Beyond bristle the buildings of downtown St. Louis, angular against the graceful curve of the Gateway Arch. Across the way lies the new (1989), low-slung Interpretive Center (9-5), a museum with well-mounted exhibits, including a model of Monks Mound, a huge mural depicting the city about 1150 A.D., and life-size scenes showing daily life back when Cahokia was bigger than London.

From Cahokia Mounds, it's convenient to proceed west a mile or so toward Collinsville—horseradish capital of the nation and location of Maggie's Bed and Breakfast (618-344-8283)—and take Expressway 255 south to Highway 157. This leads to the town of Cahokia (not to be confused with Cahokia Mounds), the earliest of the French villages—and the oldest permanent settlement in the Upper Mississippi Valley—in the riverside region where Illinois began. Off to the right, just before you reach Highway 3, the River Road, lies Parks College, the nation's first federally licensed school of aeronautics. During World War II, one tenth of all U.S. Army Air Corps pilots received their training at Parks, now a unit of St. Louis University.

Three Canadian missionaries founded Cahokia ("wild geese" in Indian language) in March, 1699. Although only twelve Europeans lived there three decades later, Cahokia eventually grew to 3,000 residents, the largest of the French towns along the Mississippi. After France lost the Illinois Country (and Canada) to England in 1763, many of the French crossed the river and helped establish a new settlement at St. Louis, founded in 1764. Even after Cahokia fell to the Americans in 1778 during the Revolutionary War, the town retained its French flavor, an ambiance that survived for another century.

Today, three old buildings remain from the colonial era. The 1799 National Register-listed Church of the Holy Family is considered to be the oldest church west of the Alleghenies, while the nearby 1810 Jarrot Mansion survives as supposedly the oldest brick house in Illinois. The Cahokia Courthouse (9-5), built as a residence in 1737, was converted half a century later into a judicial and administrative center for the huge Illinois Territory, which extended north to Canada. In this building—a typical French palisade-type structure, with vertical timbers—Illinois's first United States court sessions and first election took place. After the county seat moved to Belleville in 1814, the courthouse became a town hall, storage area, saloon, and once again a home. At the 1904 St. Louis World's Fair, where the building served as an exhibit, some timbers from the courthouse were cut up into wooden cigars as souvenirs. After the Fair, the building was sold to the Chicago Historical Society and reconstructed in Jackson Park, where it stood until finally returning to Cahokia in 1939. Believed to be the oldest private dwelling in the Midwest and courthouse west of the Alleghenies, the much-moved structure is certainly the best traveled. The heavily restored relic now houses period furniture, old photos, and rather discordant modern reproductions of old-type artifacts and plastic plaques bearing quotations from early area settlers and travelers. The Visitor Center—whose restrooms bear "Hommes" and "Femmes" designations—displays objects salvaged from the Jarrot Mansion and a copy of a 1766 French map of the colonial area along the Mississippi.

Dupo lies nearby. An abbreviation of its original name, Prairie du Pont, the town was named for the bridge which spanned a creek there during the French era. The c. 1790 Pierre

Martin house, built by a settler from Quebec, also evokes the colonial period. At Dupo, 4 ½ miles long and for most of its length about a quarter of a mile wide, the nation's second largest rail switch yards once operated. The Missouri Pacific marshaling complex included nineteen pairs of tracks and a "hump", down which gravity-pulled cars glided during the sorting process. The town served as a bedroom community for railroad men, with many of the one-story frame cottages sporting two front doors, one used by the night shift worker so he could leave without disturbing the other occupants. As every trainman had to test his watch once a month, a number of jewelry stores formerly operated at Dupo, which is these days a laid-back and less time intensive town.

The River Road—the by now familiar Highway 3—continues south to Columbia, originally settled before 1800 by veterans of George Rogers Clark's Revolutionary War troops. In 1778, they captured Cahokia and Kaskaskia, downstream. In the mid-nineteenth century, German immigrants settled at Columbia and elsewhere nearby, as indicated by such area town names as New Hanover, Wartburg, Millstadt, and Freeburg (where Westerfield House offers bed and breakfast: 618-539-5643), which lie near Belleville, Sauget, East Carondelet and Dupo ("Du Pont"). Here, then, the French and the German cultures interface and mingle, with the towns and their names serving as avatars to symbolize both the eighteenth century colonial era—when Paris served as the first capital of Illinois—and the nineteenth century age of immigration, when the Germanic way of life developed. Columbia's well-known former Eberhard's restaurant, sold a few years ago and renamed Columbia House, reflects the German influence, with sayings in that language on the facade ("Gruss Gott"). Inside, you'll see a collection of beer steins and ceiling lamps made from the mugs. On Highway 158 toward Millstadt—named by Saxon immigrants Mittelstadt (Centerville), as it lay halfway along a stagecoach route, but incorrectly recorded by an official—the Farmers Inn restaurant serves meals popular with area residents.

The River Road follows the old Cahokia-Kaskaskia Trail as it continues south to Waterloo, believed to be the oldest American settlement in the Northwest Territory. The village began as Peterstown in 1781 or 1782 adjacent to the small French settlement of Belle Fontaine, which still exists as an area in south Waterloo. The two merged, and in 1815 took the name Waterloo to commemorate Napoleon's defeat near that Belgian town. At the north edge of Waterloo stands the Register-listed Peterstown House, a two story white frame building—the only remaining stagecoach stop on the old Trail—constructed in the 1830's by Peter Rogers, for whom Peterstown was named. More than two hundred old buildings comprise Waterloo's National Historic District, including the Monroe County Courthouse and the century-old Morrison-Talbott Library, built as a house for Congressman William R. Morrison. The Waterloo Winery (12-5) in town offers tours and samples. At the hamlet of New Design, south of Waterloo—where the Senator Rickert Residence offers bed and breakfast (618-939-8242)—stood the first English-speaking school and first Protestant church in the Illinois country. Farther south lies Red Bud, named for the trees which once brightened the area. Earlier, it was called Horse Prairie, as ponies that escaped from the eighteenth century French settlers became wild and roamed the prairie until captured by the new American pioneers. A National Historic District (approximately between Main and Market) in Red Bud includes the rather heavyset Germanic City Hall. At Ruma an old convent, St. Patrick's church, and O'Hara Cemetery recall early Catholic settlers. A more interesting and scenic route, closer to the Mississippi, begins just past the turnoff to Columbia, as you leave the River Road and enter Bluff Road toward Valmeyer. This offers occasional glimpses of the Mississippi as you travel through a farm area. Along the left side of the narrow blacktop road stands a low wooded limestone bluff, punctured by a few caves; its rock face presents a series of chaotic shapes and tones. Just after a sharp left turn, a small concrete pylon rises, dedicated to Shadrack Bond, a soldier with George Rogers Clark's Revolutionary War army, which dominated this area in 1778, capturing Kaskaskia, Cahokia and other English strongholds. Along with other members of Clark's unit, Bond settled here in 1782. He was later joined in 1794 by his nephew of the same name, later Illinois's first governor.

At Valmeyer—where quarry-excavated angular openings disfigure the bluff — you can take the gravel lane atop the levee, or continue on the Bluff Road toward Fults. Either way it's well worth a short detour over to the delightful hamlet of Maeystown, one of those lost-in-time villages hidden away in the Mississippi River Valley. Founded in 1852, the town enjoys the distinction—along with Elsah, on the Mississippi north of Alton—of being one of Illinois's two villages listed in its entirety on the National Register. The town of 150 residents presents a picture-perfect image of a nineteenth century Midwestern hamlet unchanged from its early days. Crowning the crest of a rise, St. John's church (1867) perches above the village. Until 1943, some services at the sanctuary were held in German. Scattered on the hillside below, integrated into the contours and configurations of the landscape, stand some of the settlement's sixty structures dating from the old days. These include the 1858 Zeitinger's Mill, proposed site of a future visitor center; the 1865 Jacob Maeys House, built by the town founder; and Hoefft's Village Inn (M and T 6-3, W-Sun 6-9), an old tavern and cafe with a long antique wood bar and mounted fish and deer heads on the wall. Across the way stands the newly restored (1989) Corner George Inn (618-458-6660), a bed and breakfast establishment, and the 1884 General Store (open weekends).

Back to the west of Maeystown, the Bluff Road, which follows the old Kaskaskia Trail route, takes you south past

Renault. This town was named for Phillipe François Renault, director-general of mining operations for promoter John Law's so-called "Mississippi Bubble," a speculative enterprise he organized in France to exploit North America's mineral resources. Although the "Bubble" burst in 1720, nearly breaking the Bank of France, the five hundred or so slaves Renault imported from the French West Indies to work the lead mines near the Mississippi settled in the area. For two centuries afterward, the workers' descendants continued to speak a French patois and cling to French customs.

The French presence and power in the middle Mississippi Valley centered on Fort de Chartres, not far to the south. In 1756 the fort's third version, which succeeded the flimsy 1720 and 1732 attempts, rose by the banks of the Mississippi, a massive and impressive stone structure. But two years after the 1763 Treaty of Paris, by which France ceded to England all its territory east of the Mississippi except New Orleans, the British took control of the base. After the English abandoned the outpost in 1772, it fell into disrepair as the Mississippi flooded the fort and area inhabitants plundered it for building materials. In 1913, the state of Illinois acquired the greatly deteriorated relic, reconstructed it, and restored the powder magazine, the only original section, and one of the state's earliest surviving structures. As you walk across the field from the parking lot to Fort de Chartres (8-5), it is not difficult to visualize how the stark, grey, stone walls of the fortress looked to Indians, English, or other enemies considering an assault. At this rather lonely and now forlorn spot, one can well imagine the small band of Frenchmen clustered there behind the walls trying—in the end, unsuccessfully—to carve out an empire in the middle of the New World, an ocean and a half a continent from home. The Peithmann Museum, inside the compound, contains displays on the French colonial era and such martial leavings as uniform buttons, shot, gun parts, and bayonets. An exhibit on the fur trade notes that sixteen beaver skins bought one gun, while a tomahawk sold for three beaver pelts.

Prairie du Rocher (Rock Prairie), a town of seven hundred, four miles east of the fort, survives as one of the rather rare remnants of the days of empire. Although the French era left few material traces behind, "it has thrown a gleam of the romance and chivalry of old France across the pages of Illinois history," noted Theodore Calvin Pease in *The Story of Illinois*. Such is the case at Prairie du Rocher, still imbued with a French tone. Some of the French colonists drawn to the valley by John Law's "Mississippi Bubble" remained after the speculation failed in 1720. Two years later they founded Prairie du Rocher. Even after France lost the region to England, Rocher—as the locals call it, pronouncing the terminal "r"—survived as a Gallic island surrounded by American and German settlers. As late as 1900 the residents still spoke French. To this day, the town celebrates "La Guignolée" (or "Guiannée") on New Year's Eve. The holiday features a wandering troupe of costumed singers and musicians serenading the townspeople, who invite the performers in for refreshments. The c. 1800 Register-listed Creole House, fronted by an arcade lined with ten square pillars, remains as the earliest French-influenced residence. However, the Melliere House, located out toward the cemetery—a white frame dwelling on a stone foundation, chimney peeking above the double slanted tin roof—dates from the late eighteenth century, one of Illinois's oldest houses. The latter-day (1976) post office and village hall at the opposite end of town occupy a reproduction of a French palisade-style (vertical timbers) building, while St. Joseph's church bears brick-designed details and its adjacent facility sports an iron balcony reminiscent of New Orleans. La Maison du Rocher restaurant—"Blending French flair with country heartiness" —occupies a restored 1885 structure with interior walls made of the same limestone used to build Fort de Chartres. Two guest rooms offer bed and breakfast accommodations (618-284-3463). In 1991 a ferry (M-Sat 6-dusk, Sun 7-dusk) started operating to connect the Prairie du Rocher area with Sainte Genevieve, Missouri, on the west bank.

An indentation hollowed into the rough, yellow-white limestone ridge bordering the road a few miles south of Prairie du Rocher marks the site of an ancient Mississippi Valley civilization. When an observer noticed tinges of smoke on the rock face archeologists began digging there in 1952, and after excavating evidences of five cultures, the workers unearthed, between the twenty to twenty-six foot levels, traces of a culture determined by radio-carbon to be 10,000 years old. The bones and other leavings recovered from the Modoc Rock Shelter, listed on the National Register, represent the earliest known society east of the Mississippi and the oldest human remains ever found in the United States. As early as 8000 B.C., nomadic Indians camped beneath the sheltering bluff, where they would come regularly for the next six thousand years. More recent tribes and, even later, pioneers also favored the bluff for shelter. Farther south on a side road stands a marker commemorating Dr. George Fisher, who in 1808 controlled a smallpox outbreak by vaccinating Indians and whites, and who established Illinois's first hospital near here.

A road out of Roots, to the south, takes you down to the lock and dam near the mouth of the Kaskaskia River. Within fifteen miles of the southern section of the Kaskaskia, which rises near Champaign-Urbana and flows 325 miles southwest to the Mississippi, lie coal deposits. The world's largest shovels mine the reserves, estimated to comprise almost 2 billion tons. In order to provide an efficient route for shipping coal on the Mississippi River waterway system, Congress authorized creation in 1962 of a nine foot channel on the Kaskaskia from its mouth to Fayette-ville, thirty-eight miles upstream. By eliminating "oxbow" bends, the project, completed in 1974, shortened the river's distance from the original meandering fifty-two miles it took to reach from Fayetteville to the Mississippi.

The route east out of Roots returns you to Highway 3, the River Road, which continues south to Fort Kaskaskia State Park, an historic enclave with splendid views onto the Mississippi. Old Kaskaskia, founded in 1703, lay at the southern end of the territory along the Mississippi settled by the French starting in 1699 when they arrived at Cahokia, fifty miles up the Mississippi at the colonial district's northern edge. Kaskaskia became the major settlement in the French Illinois Country, prospering as a business, religious and political center. When, in 1759, the thriving town asked the French to build a military outpost to protect the area against the British, Fort Kaskaskia was installed on the bluff high above the town. The British gained control of the area in 1765 but lost Kaskaskia to the Americans on July 4, 1778 when George Rogers Clark entered the city unopposed. When Clark arrived, he found a party in progress. Although his appearance panicked the revelers, the American "bade the crowd to go on with their dancing, but to take note that they now danced not as subjects of King George, but as Virginians," as James K. Hosmer described the bloodless victory in *A Short History of the Mississippi Valley*.

Kaskaskia, strategically located on the Mississippi at the westernmost frontier of the United States across from Spanish Missouri, continued to prosper from fur and shipping, and when the town became the territorial capital in 1809 and the first state capital in 1818, it developed even faster. But the growth of St. Louis and removal of the seat of government to Vandalia in 1820 resulted in a decline hastened by a devastating flood in 1844, and concluded in 1881 when the Mississippi changed course, virtually destroying the town. Each recurring spring flood ate away more land until finally the last traces of old Kaskaskia disappeared into the Mississippi, and now fish swim over the site of Illinois's first important city and one time state capital.

"This great, this magnificent Mississippi...is a very bad neighbor," French historian and political thinker Constantin Volney observed about the waterway's turbulence and temperamental behavior in his 1796 *View of the Climate and Soil of the United States of America*, a sentiment the inhabitants of old Kaskaskia would surely endorse. At Fort Kaskaskia State Park—overlooking the site of the submerged city and the remaining Kaskaskia, an Illinois island isolated on the Missouri side of the river—the posted poem "To a Sunken City" laments, "O Mississippi, monarch of the plain, / Despoiler old! We mourn your victim low. / Now stay the mighty minions of your train, / That this poor vale may no more havoc know." At the park, a few grassy mounds mark the 1759 fort's site, while the nearby Garrison Hill Cemetery contains graves moved from Old Kaskaskia down in the flood plain up to the heights where now rest, a notice states, "the early pioneers of the great Mississippi valley. They planted free institutions in a wilderness and were the founders of a great commonwealth." Tucked away by the river below the bluffs nestles the handsome and beautifully preserved French colonial house (9-5), built around 1800 by Pierre Menard, Illinois's first lieutenant governor. Called the "Mount Vernon of the West," the lovely residence contains at the lower level a small museum with some of Menard's personal effects. They include his ledger listing the 5,600 acres of farmland he owned in 1843, a model of the ferry he operated across the Kaskaskia River beginning in 1805, and the silk slippers worn by his daughter at a ball given for the Marquis de Lafayette, the French general who fought for the Americans in the Revolution, during his 1825 visit to Kaskaskia.

Present-day Kaskaskia occupies an island formed when the rampaging Mississippi cut a new channel in 1881 and severed the area from the Illinois mainland. The Illinois enclave, mainly farmland, lies just offshore from Missouri west of the Mississippi, and can be reached only through that state after crossing the river on the bridge at Chester. Only in 1970 did the U.S.

Supreme Court finally determine that Illinois, rather than Missouri, owned the island. At St. Marys, Missouri, on Highway 61, a turnoff takes you across the former Mississippi channel, now an overgrown ditch, and out to the 14,000 acre island, protected by a levee. Fewer than a hundred people live in the enclave's sole village. The brick 1843 Church of the Immaculate Conception, successor to the 1675 mission established by Father Marquette, Joliet's exploring partner, was moved brick by brick in 1894 to escape erosion by the encroaching Mississippi. A small shelter next door houses the so called "Liberty Bell of the West." Eleven years older than the Philadelphia Liberty Bell, the local version—cast in France in 1741 and given to the church by King Louis XV—sounded out on July 4, 1778 when George Rogers Clark captured the town from the British. It took boatmen more than a year to tow the 650 pound bell up the Mississippi from New Orleans by walking along the river bank pulling the barge by ropes. Just up the street at the new Old Kaskaskia Trading Post (1990), which sells crafts, hang early photos of the town, including pictures of the residence that housed the first state capitol and of the hotel where the Marquis de Lafayette was entertained during his 1825 visit. Twenty years before, William Morrison—a Kaskaskia trader and partner with Pierre Menard in the fur business—supplied a trading expedition sent to Santa Fe, the first American convoy to travel over the route which later became the Santa Fe Trail.

The road along the river from the Pierre Menard House into Chester passes the mustard-colored stone Menard Penitentiary, well garnished with barbed wire, watch towers, and spotlights. Over the main entrance an emblem appears, representing a key—perhaps the three thousand inmates' most desired, but least available, object. Built in 1877, the maximum security self-supporting prison occupies 2000 acres of pastures and farms worked by the prisoners, who publish the respected in-house *Menard Time*, the nation's first penitentiary paper. It enjoys a circulation not only to what might be called a captive audience but also to readers outside the walls.

Eleven years after a Cincinnati land company founded Chester in 1819 as a commercial rival to Kaskaskia, a settler named Richard B. Servant started operating presses to extract oil from castor beans, a liquid used for lubrication until the discovery of petroleum. Before long, businessmen in Sparta to the north-east established competing presses, and for some years the two towns engaged in a spirited castor oil rivalry. This competition accentuated in 1847 when they vied for the county seat. Chester won the vote, and also a rematch held before erection of the present 1974 courthouse, atop which a glassed-in observation room with an expansive view onto the Mississippi perches. Off to the right a web-like bridge stretches, beyond which the river curves in from the north. Next door to the courthouse stands the rather odd-looking mock Gothic-style stone structure (1864) which houses the Randolph County Museum and Archives, with French colonial records dating back to 1706.

In a tiny park by the bridge stands a six foot bronze statue of the cartoon character Popeye. The image depicts his characteristic knobby knees and puffy cheeks, and he puffs on his pipe, which is, as always, tilted at a jaunty angle. The character was created in 1929 by Chester-born Elzie Crisler Segar, who modeled the cartoon character after Frank "Rocky" Fiegel, a local roughneck. Other Chester residents became Olive Oyl and Wimpy, the hamburger gourmand. The weekend after Labor Day, Chester holds the annual Popeye's Picnic (spinach, his favorite food, is on the menu) to honor the town's most famous native son and leading philosopher, who once observed: "They ain't no myskery to life. Ya gits borned and that's all they is to it."

A monument at Evergreen Cemetery honors another local celebrity, Shadrach Bond, Illinois's first governor. This monument was moved to the graveyard from the burial ground at

Kaskaskia. The nearby 100 foot long Mary's River covered bridge—built in 1854 and used until 1930 on the old plank tollroad between Chester and Bremen—still stands near Chester. In town on a high bluff overlooking the Mississippi lies the ten room white frame Cohen Memorial Home (1855), with blue tinted glass in the upper half of the windows, now used as a community center. Nearby stands SugarWood (618-826-2555), a bed and breakfast house above the river. In 1844, the Mississippi so flooded the town that the steamboat *Belle Air* took a shortcut straight through it, hit a building whose third floor toppled into the water, and then rammed a stone mill, bounced off a few other structures, and levelled the town jail before finally returning to the Mississippi's main channel.

Occasional panoramas onto the waterway appear as you continue south on Highway 3. The road crosses Mary's River, at whose mouth by the Mississippi in early 1682 the French explorer La Salle camped, to Turkey Bluffs Scenic Outlook, a few miles from Chester. The spot offers a splendid view of the Mississippi. Rockwood, a way-station for slaves escaping across the Mississippi via Liberty Island, once thrived as a supply point for wood used to fuel steamers and as a flatboat building center. Highway 3 makes its way along and through the edge of Shawnee National Forest, a quarter of a million acre preserve spread across 115 miles, extending over to the Ohio River. Trails, wildlife areas, scenic landscapes, and historical attractions fill the Forest. An alternative route on Highway 127 into part of the forest will take you through Murphysboro, which features a museum (Sat and Sun 1-4, June-Aug also M, W, F) devoted to General John A. Logan, Civil War officer, U.S. Senator, and founder of Memorial Day; the picturesque, old-time general store at Pomona; and at Bald Knob antique shops, the Alto Vineyards and Winery, whose first production took place in 1988, and an 111 foot high cross, the nation's tallest Christian monument.

You'll also journey through Cobden, which claims the world's widest main street. Once called South Pass, the town was renamed for Sir Richard Cobden, the English politician who led the movement to repeal the Corn Laws, after his 1859 visit to inspect the Illinois Central line for which he raised British capital. Cobden once served as the nation's largest tomato shipping town; in 1858 the country's first refrigerated car shipment departed from here, a load of strawberries packed in ice bound for Chicago. Along the way you'll also find Trail of Tears State Park, site of a World War II prisoner of war camp. During the winter of 1839 nearly 2000 of the 13,000 Cherokee Indians en route on the trail from Georgia to their new reservation in Oklahoma died while they stopped here until the ice-clogged Mississippi cleared. Anna, hometown of "Moon Mullins" cartoon creator Frank Willard, boasts the modernistic limestone Stinson Library designed by one of Frank Lloyd Wright's students, and also the tomb of King Neptune, a Navy mascot pig auctioned for the war effort in the 1940's for $19,000 in war bonds. Nearby Jonesboro was the site of the third Lincoln-Douglas debate, held September 15, 1858, attended by the series' smallest and most pro-southern crowd, fewer than 1000 people. Also at Jonesboro stands the delightful and diminutive 1860 National Register-listed Koranthal church, which houses a pulpit modeled after the one in George Washington's Alexandria, Virginia place of worship.

If you choose the River Road route, Highway 3, you'll head on toward Grand Tower, passing an old cemetery south of Gorham where relatives of frontiersman Daniel Boone lie at rest. Just north of Grand Tower lies Devil's Backbone Park, an historic enclave by the Mississippi. In 1803, a U.S. cavalry unit led by Colonel Zebulon Davis, uncle of Confederate president Jefferson Davis, camped here while they eliminated a nest of pirates who had menaced river travelers. Two now-vanished iron furnaces utilizing iron ore from Missouri and coal from Murphysboro once operated at the site, which Andrew Carnegie supposedly considered turning into a Pittsburgh of the west. Grand Tower took its name from the sixty foot high limestone pinnacle which rises from the Mississippi just by the Missouri shore. The churning waters which swirl by the rock have for years made this a hazardous stretch of the river, part of the run pilots dubbed with the ominous name "The Graveyard." This is no exaggeration, for an 1867 survey recorded 133 sunken hulks between Cairo and St. Louis. Not far north of Tower Rock—which President Ulysses S. Grant ordered preserved as a possible bridge pillar when federal engineers cleared the waterway of navigation hazards in 1871—a pair of nearly 3700 foot natural gas pipes stretches across the Mississippi on the world's longest pipeline suspension bridge.

The 1870 Huthmacher House—a boxy wood residence with a large porch—survives from the time the town enjoyed greater prosperity, but today Grand Tower seems light years away from upstate, upscale places as Chicago's Tribune Tower or Sears Tower. This part of the state, as Baker Brownell put it in *The Other Illinois*, lies "south of the big-time Illinois" and "somewhat south of prosperity." Known as Little Egypt, the area supposedly acquired that designation when after the long winter of 1830-1831 farmers, like the sons of Jacob "going down to Egypt for corn," had to travel south to procure animal food. The region lacks population as well as prosperity. In *Legends and Lore of Southern Illinois*, John W. Allen observed: "The advent of the steamboat and the development of trails and roadways soon led immigrants to bypass the southern part of the state. It thus was left a somewhat isolated region, a kind of historical eddy." Fewer than 800 people live in the Mississippi River village, but many outsiders temporarily swell the town's population by coming to eat at Grand Tower's grand Ma Hale's Boarding House Restaurant. The establishment was founded in 1940 by Melissa Hale after a river captain who boarded with the Hale family found her food so tasty that he asked Mrs. Hale to cook for his entire crew. After her death in 1971, her son ran the restaurant until a

Mississippi ship pilot bought the eatery in 1979. Outside the restaurant stands a statue to Mrs. Hale, with the inscription noting that for more than thirty years she served some 1 ½ million home-cooked meals, and concluding: "Those of us who enjoyed her cooking affectionately dedicate this plaque to her." Old photos and family mementos decorate the restaurant (Tu-Th 8-3:30, F and Sat 8-7, sun 11-6; 618-565-8384) where friendly waitresses deliver some fifteen dishes and platters of food at prices equal to only the tax in fancier eating places. Hale's truly offers Hale and hearty fare, with no need for "boarding house reach."

Thebes, farther south, still evokes Ward Dorrance's thumbnail description of half a century ago in *Where the Rivers Meet*—"oldish and pleasantly crumbly." The hamlet (fewer than 500 inhabitants) saw less crumbly times back in the mid-nineteenth century when it began as Sparhawk's Landing. The name came from the Sparhawk brothers, who established a port to ship poplar logs down the Mississippi to New Orleans for making funiture. The restored former courthouse, an 1848 sandstone and hewn timber portico-fronted building, perches high on the bluff. Listed on the National Register, it served as the seat of Alexander County until 1864 when Cairo succeeded Thebes as the center of government. A two-sectioned dungeon—one for men, the other for women—beneath the courthouse once supposedly briefly held Dred Scott, the slave whose famous suit for emancipation the U.S. Supreme Court finally decided against in 1857.

It was at Thebes where Captain Andy Hawks of the *Cotton Blossom* in Edna Ferber's *Show Boat* lived. Or, rather, his residence stood there, but his home and perhaps his heart were elsewhere, for "Despite the prim little house in Thebes, home, to Andy, was a boat." His daughter Magnolia, however, did live in the "little white house at Thebes," and there, after dusk fell, she would look longingly at the river and the passing showboats, "their lights shining golden yellow through the boat's many windows." It's pleasant to pause a time by the Mississippi in Thebes and imagine Magnolia gazing at the ships chugging by in the darkness. The night-shrouded waters would now and again brighten as the lights of a passing steamer, its paddlewheel churning and splashing, cast gliding golden rectangles onto the river. Then, soon, the lights would disappear, leaving the waterway once again in darkness and solitude as "Old Man River" rolled on through the night toward the distant sea.

Beyond the Horseshoe Lake Conservation Area—a Louisiana bayou-like wildlife preserve where Canada geese winter—Highway 3 passes through Klondike, a huddle of houses straggling along the road, and then finally ends after following the river all the way south from Alton. Before proceeding to nearby Cairo, it's worth driving over to Mound City,an old Ohio River port town. On the way you'll pass the National Cemetery, where nearly five thousand Union and Confederate soldiers—more than half of them unknown—are buried. Also here lie about fifty nurses who ministered to 2,300 wounded brought after the battle of Shiloh to the federal Naval Hospital in Mound City.

The southern section of a still standing brick building—formerly used as a warehouse, opera house, and court house—by the Ohio River levee was converted into the largest U.S. naval hospital on the western rivers in 1861. A road leads up to the top of the levee which affords an excellent view of the Ohio, soon to disappear into the Mississippi at Cairo. During the Civil War, Mound City served as the nerve center for the Western Rivers Fleet, with the naval depot and the Marine Ways, a construction and repair yard where 1,500 workers built the gunboats *Mound City*, *Carondelet*, and *Cincinnati*, and converted steamboats into warships. Still today the Marine Ways, reached on South Fourth Street, exist. The C.G.B. Marine Services company operates at the riverfront site, used to change towboats on barges heading to or from the Mississippi. A rusting anchor lies on a concrete slipway—perhaps remnants of the old Civil War facility—which descends to the Ohio. In 1861, the federal government took over Marine Ways, built as a steamboat repair yard in 1859 by Emporium Real Estate, a Cincinnati company which hoped to develop the area into a major river town.

On the way down to Cairo (rhymes with "pharoah"), the road passes Future City, whose few modest frame houses and mobile homes mock the settlement's optimistic name. At Future City, named for a black resident of French descent named Futura, free blacks lived, while in adjacent Cairo they still remained slaves. "The history of Cairo is among the most complex and fascinating of any municipality in Illinois, rife with schemes, skirmishes, potential growth and almost equally phenomenal decline," states the National Register of Historic Places description of the city. As early as 1721, the French Jesuit priest Charlevoix observed that the strategic area at the confluence of the Mississippi and Ohio was destined to be a key corner of the country. In 1818 the Illinois Territorial legislature at Kaskaskia incorporated Cairo, a paper city left as such when promoter John Gleaves Comegys died a few years later. His unusual name for the proposed town—so designated as its riverside site recalled the Cairo in Egypt—was not completely far-fetched. A connection between the Nile and the Mississippi developed in 1884 when the British government, wishing to hire the best river pilots available for an expedition up the Nile, engaged four boatmen from the Upper Mississippi. In 1837, an eastern promoter incorporated the Cairo City and Canal Company, which developed plans for levees, canals, factories, and warehouses. The policy to lease, rather than sell, land retarded development but not the sale of bonds to English investors—among them novelist Charles Dickens—through the London banking firm of John Wright & Company, which failed in November 1840. On April 9, 1842 Dickens visited Cairo, which he found "desolate" and "dismal"—a judgement no doubt colored by his financial losses in the Cairo junk bonds—

while the Mississippi he adjudged "hateful" and "a slimy monster hideous to behold."

With completion of the Illinois Central Railroad from Chicago to Cairo in late 1854 (the nation's longest line at the time), the town began to prosper. This line along the nation's central corridor not far from the Mississippi might well have served as the Middle West's leading trade route, with Cairo as the nexus of rail and river traffic. The Civil War, however, then intervened, blocking shipments down the Mississippi. Shippers diverted industrial and agricultural products originating in the Midwest to Chicago, a restructuring of trade patterns which eventually left Cairo as a backwater.

When the guns boomed during the Civil War, so did Cairo. In September, 1861, Ulysses S. Grant established his headquarters in the strategically placed city to mass forces for his advance into the South, which began in early February, 1862. During the war, an estimated million Union troops passed through the city, which served as headquarters for the federal fleet. After the war, Cairo continued to prosper, with 3,700 steamboats docking in 1867. Within two decades combined river and rail shipments valued at $60 million gave the town the nation's highest per capita commercial freight traffic. Changing traffic patterns, the increasing dominance of the railroads, the advent of motor vehicles, a somewhat unhealthy climate—"at Cairo the old firm of Fever & Auge is still setting up its unfinished business," wrote Herman Melville in "The Confidence Man"—and occasional floods weakened the city's hold on prosperity. By now, the two-river town, overtaken by the twentieth century, has settled into a Southernish somnolent state, a languid remnant of its once-lively, steamboat-stoked days of glory.

A scattering of attractions around town recalls Cairo's nineteenth century peak period. The elegant residential area in the 2700 block of Washington includes such National Register-listed mansions as Magnolia Manor (M-Sat 9-5, Sun 1-5, closed

Jan-March M and Tu), built in 1872 by Charles A. Galigher, who made his fortune selling flour to the government during the Civil War. In 1880, Galigher hosted there a glittering reception for former President Grant. The 1876 Windham (618-734-3247) is a bed and breakfast home next door. Across the street, you'll find the stately 1865 Riverlore, with a frilly metal fence and front gate flanked by two columns. It was built by former riverboat captain William Parker Halliday, whose career inspired him to add atop the roof a "widow's walk" lookout, with views onto the Ohio and Mississippi. At the corner of Ohio and Second Streets stood the 1859 Halliday Hotel (then the St. Charles), burned down in 1942, where General Grant occupied room 215, from which he could monitor his troops and the gunboats at the confluence of the two waterways. In 1906 Captain Halliday's family and widow, Mary, gave to Cairo "in token of his unswerving faith in her destiny" a statue named "The Hewer" which stands in a small park at North and Washington.

A few blocks up the street lies the handsome, Register-listed, 1872 beige limestone Custom House, while in St. Mary's Park, in the residential district, the round, 1876 green-roofed pavilion served as the site of President Theodore Roosevelt's address during his 1907 visit to Cairo. In a small, triangular patch of ground south of the park behind Riverlore stands the flagpole from the Union ship *Tigress*, which in April, 1862, carried Grant up the Tennessee River to the Battle of Shiloh. A year later, when the vessel sank while attempting to run the Confederate shore batteries at Vicksburg, the crew salvaged the flagpole and returned it to Cairo. The solid looking red brick 1883 Cairo Public Library seems as much a museum as a book place. The establishment houses antiques, paintings, an 1876 model of the *City of Cairo* steamer, a large oak steamboat gambling table with a hole in it to collect the winnings, and President Andrew Johnson's desk. Churches include the 1894 St. Patrick, a Romanesque-style stone structure listed on the National Register; Cairo

Baptist, with a vaguely Middle Eastern-type cupola; and the 1886 Church of the Redeemer, a heavy-set, rough textured, stone pile. This church boasts a bell, supposedly cast from a thousand silver dollars, that once hung on the Civil War transport ship *James Montgomery*, sunk in 1861.

Outside the flood gate at 8th Street and Ohio, a sign atop the levee greets visitors with the phrase, "Welcome to Historical Cairo, Gateway to the South." Few people, however, arrive by boat any more. A webby steel beam bridge off to the left stretches across the Ohio, while to the right another span stands at the waterway's mouth. Notations on the flood wall indicate high water marks: 55.7 feet in 1973, 56.5 feet in 1975, and 59.5 in 1937. The flood wall rises 65 feet, the peak point reached by the extraordinary 1837 inundation. During the 1937 flood, when the Ohio swelled to record heights, the river inundated Paducah, Louisville, Cincinnati, and dozens of other towns. As the bloated waterway rolled downstream toward the Mississippi, photographers and newsmen from around the country hurried to record the collision of the two rivers at Cairo. The waters rose to nearly the top of the wall, held there a time and then began to recede, so sparing Cairo. The protective border encircling it makes the river-flanked enclave the nation's only walled city.

By action of accretion over the past century, the two rivers have added about a mile to the southern tip of Illinois, which extends into the confluence point. During the Civil War, Grant's headquarters stood where the Southern sympathizing Cairenes years later decided, supposedly by design, to construct the waste water plant you will pass on the left as you head south out of Cairo to so called Fort Defiance, a little frequented park. A road near the 1938 Ohio River bridge over to Kentucky descends into the park by the confluence. A concrete, three-level, ship-shaped observation tower, the Boatmen's Memorial, commemorates rivermen who lost their lives on the waterways. From the top deck, you can easily see the meeting of the waters some fifty yards away. Here the Ohio has flowed for 981 miles from Pittsburgh, while the Mississippi has traveled 1,360 miles from its headwaters at Lake Itasca in northern Minnesota, and it flows on from here—point zero, where the Upper Mississippi ends and the Lower begins—to Head of Passes, 964 miles south, the Lower river's point zero, and then on for another twenty miles out to the Gulf of Mexico.

For centuries, Indians used the two great rivers as highways for trade and for war. Marquette and Joliet were the first Europeans to pass this point, in 1673. In 1778, following the capture of Kaskaskia, George Rogers Clark stationed armored boats here to guard against attacks on the Illinois Country by British or French forces. In 1811, the *New Orleans*, the first steamboat to cruise the lower Ohio and Mississippi, moored here during three nights of the New Madrid earthquake. The Illinois Central ran a track down the levee to the point, at 268 feet above sea level, the state's lowest spot. In April, 1861, the federal government established at the confluence Fort Defiance, from which Grant launched his surprise flanking movement, thrusting into Tennessee toward Shiloh, farther west, rather than, as expected, advancing down the Mississippi to Memphis.

Near the confluence a triangular orange navigation marker rises, beyond which, littered by the shore, lie rocks which provoke uneven footing. You can make your way across the rocks and out to the very place where the bluish Ohio meets the darker-hued Mississippi, and there you can dip your hand into the waters. There is something primeval about this liquid corner, one of the continent's greatest single scenic and historic spots. Any traveler who happens to be at that evocative place will see the same ever-moving waterways as did the Indians and explorers, the rivermen and warriors of old. The rivers have flowed here since time immemorial and will no doubt roll on forever, rolling their roiling waters along in a ceaseless, endless rhythm. Occasionally a log or a branch or bit of debris, borne along by the current, spins and dips a moment, then flows onward to complete the long journey to the distant, waiting sea.

ILLINOIS PRACTICAL INFORMATION

Phone numbers of tourist offices in Illinois's principal Mississippi river cities: Alton: 618-465-6676 and 800-258-6645; Cahokia: 618-332-1782; Cairo: 618-734-2737; Chester: 618-826-3706; Fulton: 815-589-4545; Galena: 815-777-0203 and 800-747-9377; Granite City and nearby: 618-876-6400; Quad Cities (Rock Island and Moline): 309-788-7800 and 800-747-7800; Quincy: 217-223-1000 and 800-458-4552; Savanna: 815-273-2722; Warsaw: 217-256-4413.

Other useful numbers for travel along the Mississippi River include: State of Illinois Office of Tourism: 217-782-7139. State Tourist Information Offices in Chicago: 310 South Michigan, 312-793-2094; at Sears Tower, Midway and O'Hare Airports, Union Station, and the State of Illinois Center, 100 West Randolph. The state also operates one other tourist information center at Marion, thirty-three miles east of Highway 3, the River Road, in southern Illinois: 618-997-4371. An Illinois Welcome Center is located on Interstate 80 near Moline: 309-496-2145.

For information on historic sites: Illinois Historic Preservation Agency, 217-782-4836. For information on outdoor areas: Illinois Department of Conservation, 217-782-7454. Two state lodges with overnight accommodations lie near the Mississippi: Pere Marquette, north of Alton, 618-786-2331, and Giant City, south of Carbondale, 618-457-4921. The Illinois Bed and Breakfast Association: 618-683-4400. Regional information offices include: Western Illinois, 309-837-7460 and 800-232-3889; Southwestern Illinois, 618-654-3556 and 800-782-9587; Southern Illinois, 618-997-1005 and 800-342-3100; South Central Illinois, 618-634-2201.

5. MISSOURI

The Mississippi forms 490 miles of Missouri's eastern boundary, with the Des Moines River demarking the state's northernmost twenty miles. For the entire eighteenth century, the Mississippi served as an international border. In 1698, La Salle claimed the vast river valley for France, which held the territory until ceding most of the area west of the river in 1762 to the Spanish, who retained it until the turn of the century. Missouri thus remained, for a century, a foreign territory at the western edge of the United States. So it was that when the new state finally entered the union in 1821, "Missouri opened into a second America, as if the Mississippi River divided the nation into two great communities," wrote Paul C. Nagel in *Missouri: A Bicentennial History*. "In a sense the new State seemed to be located on the edges of two American civilizations that joined at the Mississippi." The river soon served to integrate rather than separate the country's two sections, and along the Mississippi in Missouri typical Midwestern settlements developed—including Twain's Hannibal, that quintessential archetype of small town America—which greatly outnumber the colonial era's few remnants, such as French-founded Sainte Genevieve and New Madrid, Spanish at least in name.

The Mississippi almost formed the entire eastern border of Missouri rather than all but twenty miles of it. Just as Missouri's Boothill in the southeast corner extends intrusively into Arkansas, so does Iowa push down into the northeastern edge of Missouri—a curious sort of geographical symmetry. In 1839 a boundary dispute arose between Missouri and Iowa, involving the location of the Des Moines Rapids, fixed by Congress in 1820 as the border dividing the two states. Iowa claimed the rapids lay at a southern point where the Des Moines joined the Mississippi, while Missouri argued that they started nine to thirteen miles farther north. In the disputed territory groves grew of so-called honey trees, in which bees nested. Pioneers coveted honey not only for use as a sweetener—the only one available on the frontier—but also used the beeswax for candles and sealing wax. Occasionally, the honey served as currency, called "yellow boys." Honey trees became private property, for finders carved their initials on the valuable producers.

When a Missouri sheriff in late November, 1839, tried to collect taxes on the trees in the disputed territory, an Iowa sheriff arrested him and jailed the official in Muscatine, so touching off the Honey War. Missouri mustered 2,300 soldiers who soon faced 1,200 members of the Iowa militia, some of them armed with crude swords cut from sheet iron. At least one trooper wielded an Indian spear decorated with red ribbons. One six-wagon convoy of provisions carried an essential supply item in five of the vehicles—liquor. A woman who owned land in the border area sided with the Iowans, as she claimed the Missouri climate was less favorable for crops. Referring to Iowa governor Robert Lucas, a Missouri wit derisively wrote: "We'll show old Lucas how to brag,/And seize our precious honey!/He also claims, I understand,/Of us three bits in money." In early December, the combatants—without shedding any blood, or honey—signed a truce treaty, then submitted the issue to the courts. In 1849, the U.S. Supreme Court decided the matter in favor of Iowa. So it is that the Des Moines River bridge just south of Keokuk takes you from Iowa into Missouri, whose eastern Mississippi River boundary begins here and not farther north.

Scruffy Alexandria hardly presents an attractive introduction to Missouri's Mississippi country. The forlorn village of some four hundred people huddles by the Mississippi, which lies out of view beyond the levee, completed in 1968. Near the boxy brick post office stands the town's sole noteworthy structure—and that only by default: a house whose now peeling white columns hint at some former minor grandeur. Alexandria once enjoyed better days. From 1847 to 1854, the town served as seat of Clark County, named for the co-leader of the famous Lewis and Clark expedition up the Missouri River in 1804-1806. In the mid-nineteenth century, Alexandria, which took its name from a Mississippi ferryman who established the settlement in 1834, rivaled St. Louis as a pork packing center, with more than 42,000 hogs processed in 1870, its peak year. These days, however, the town resembles the Missouri metropolis downstream only by its riverside location on the Mississippi.

From Alexandria the River Road, Highway 61, heads due west seven miles and then turns south to travel parallel with the Mississippi. Before following the route down to Canton, you may want to explore a few nearby places in Clark County. On the Des Moines River to the far north lies the site of Athens, now a state park (April-Oct 7-10, Nov-March 8-9). A village once stood here, where on August 5, 1861 erupted one of the two northernmost Civil War battles (the other occurred at Salineville, Ohio in July 1863). At the quiet little enclave stand the old Smith's Hotel and the Benning House, still perforated with holes opened by a cannonball shot. During the brief encounter at Athens, Union Colonel David Moore led a bayonet charge to rout a Confederate force which included his own two sons. The next reenactment of the battle, held every three years, is scheduled for 1993.

At Kahoka—named for the old French town of Cahokia in Illinois, just across the Mississippi from St. Louis—the diminutive silvery-domed 1871 Clark County Courthouse, listed on the National Register, houses an old-fashioned courtroom upstairs. On the town square stands the restored, Register-listed Kahoka State Bank, its building once the opera house. Just north of town, on three acres of a former farmstead six buildings comprise Gregory's Antiques (8-5), one of the Midwest's largest dealers in collectibles. The establishment seems as much a museum as a commercial enterprise. It contains old glass, furniture, cans and crates, wood trim, books, dishes, clothes, toys, and dozens of other once-coveted possessions, the residue of vanished households. Not far north of Gregory's, the Otte family takes bed and breakfast guests at their working farm (816-727-3533). On Highway C northwest of Saint Francisville—site of Fort Pike, built on the Des Moines during the Indian Wars, and of an 1853 Baptist church—the restored, National Register-listed Sickles Tavern once served as a stopover for covered wagon convoys and livestock herders who traveled the trail.

Farther south, tiny Saint Patrick (population:53), established in 1833 by Irish settlers, claims to be the world's only town to bear the name of Ireland's patron saint. A tiny post office, which on St. Patrick's Day affixes special cancellations, occupies a cubicle in the back of the 1914 Kirchner General Store building, whose roof sprouts green shamrock emblems. Nearby stands a statue of green-robed St. Patrick as well as the shrine of St. Patrick, a rough-surfaced, granite sanctuary modeled on a church in Donegal, Ireland, with a shamrock-shaped window and a tall, round, stone belfrey characteristic of Celtic churches.

Highway 61 leads south to Canton, a quiet Mississippi River town connected to Illinois by a ferry (mid-March to mid-Dec 7-6:45 summer, to 5:45 winter, Sun from 8), the latest version of the service which has linked the two states across the waterway since 1843. Near the ferry landing stands the Lock and Dam Number 20 complex, where a quartet of concrete towers loom above the 2144-foot-long barrier, completed in 1936. In the late 1980s the Corps of Engineers carried out at the site the first rehabilitation project on a Mississippi lock and dam. The Corps removed and replaced deteriorated concrete, reworked miter gates, and replaced gate machinery and the lock's electrical system. In order to perform the repairs the Engineers emptied the lock of water in January and February 1987; structural repairs on the dam and replacement of its gate machinery took place later. North Riverfront Park near the lock and dam affords the best place to see the Mississippi in Canton, where for the most part the river remains a rather hidden presence. At Canton the waterway reaches its most westward point along its entire length south of Minnesota.

Named for Canton, Ohio, the town spreads across attractive hilly terrain which rises just west of the Mississippi. From the campus of Culver-Stockton College, which perches above the city, an expansive view stretches across the wide, sloping lawn and on to the river in the distance below. Founded in 1853 as supposedly the first co-educational institution of higher learning west of the Mississippi, the thousand student school remains as one of the nation's few colleges which accepts no direct federal or state financial assistance. Silvery-domed, white-columned Henderson Hall, the Register-listed administration building, stands near the center of the tree-garnished 111 acre hilltop campus, where Union soldiers encamped during the Civil War. Another historic Register-listed local educational institution, the one room Lincoln School, operated from 1887 to 1952 for "colored" children; the building survives as one of Missouri's few such remaining segregated schools. Across the street, on South Third in Martin Park, stands the African Methodist Episcopal church where black children attended class before 1877.

In downtown Canton, the second floor of the 1890 Rice Building houses an art gallery with changing exhibits. The nearby one room Lewis County Historical Society also contains a few exhibits. With carefully calculated precision worthy of an actuary, the Society offers a life membership starting at age forty for $135 and declining by $3 every year until the fee reaches $30 at age seventy-five. The Golden Eagle Showboat Dinner Theatre, a land-locked replica of an old time steamer inaugurated in 1978, presents stage shows from late May to early September (314-288-5273). Out Route B a mile south of Canton—where J.S. Thompson Bed and Breakfast takes guests (314-288-5769)—the Remember When Toy Museum (June-Aug M-Sat 9-5, Sept-May Sat 9-5 or by appointment: 314-288-3995) displays more than 10,000 antique toys at the Golden Age Toy manufacturing plant. Its products include items manufactured from original Marx Toy Company molds and dies. A tour shows you dozens of miniature train systems, Wild West towns, ranches, circuses, farms, villages, animal and people figures, mechanical pieces and Marx prototypes, including an Alamo scene with tiny cannons which work.

Route B takes you along the Mississippi down to LaGrange, a rather scruffy river town well supplied with bars, taverns, and other such watering holes. About 1795 Frenchman Godfrey Le Sieur (or Lesseur) built a hut here in Spanish territory where he lived during the summer and fall when he traded with the Indians. In 1819 John Bozarth from Kentucky settled on some twenty acres with his family of eighteen, including his slaves. An account by Bozarth's son recalled how the buckskin-clad pioneers all lived in one room with a hearth in the middle and no chimney, but only an open roof to allow smoke to escape. On Sunday the family would visit the neighbors, not a convenient diversion as they lived twenty miles away. LaGrange enjoyed a certain prosperity as a port town, shipping out pork, whiskey, flour, tobacco, and other local products. The Civil War and, later, railroads, diminished the river trade, and—as with so many other early Mississippi towns which suffered from the same problems—the settlement declined. Near the corner of Jefferson and Third in upper LaGrange Thomas Riley Marshall, U.S. vice-president under Woodrow Wilson, lived as a boy in the late 1850s. Marshall—who returned to Indiana with his family after Southern sympathizers threatened his abolitionist father, Daniel M. Marshall, a country doctor—coined the phrase, "What this country needs is a really good five cent cigar." Wakonda State Park three miles south of LaGrange includes a seventy-five acre lake with a large sandy beach and overnight water-side cabins (314-655-4827).

Just past Taylor the divided highway which leads south toward Palmyra crosses the Fabius River. In July, 1841, at its mouth by the Mississippi a few miles east, Southern sympathizers arrested Alanson Work and two theological students, abolitionists from Quincy, Illinois, across the river, who were trying to help some slaves escape. At a trial in Palmyra the slaves testified against their benefactors, even though the law disallowed evidence given by blacks against whites. The judge ruled, however, that testimony presented by the slaves through their masters could be admitted. The jury—one of whose members was John M. Clemens, Mark Twain's father—voted to convict, and the defendants received prison sentences. Work's son, Henry Clay Work, later composed the anti-slavery song "Marching Through Georgia." Civil War era passions ran especially deep in this part of northern Missouri, known as "Little Dixie" because a majority of the settlers originated from the South, especially Kentucky and Tennessee. On the Marion County Courthouse lawn in Palmyra stands a monument to an episode which typified the bitter battles between Union and Confederate sympathizers—the shooting of ten Southern prisoners in October 1862, ordered when a Dixie colonel refused to return a captured pro-Union citizen. The 1907 monument to the so called "Palmyra Massacre" includes a soldier whose rifle reaches from the ground nearly to his chin and names of the ten victims. French, Spanish and British flags on the courthouse lawn recall the area's colonial era. A colorful mural on the flank of a building on Lafayette Street across the way illustrates local history. It depicts Marquette and Joliet in a birchbark canoe, a Mississippi River steamboat, historic buildings and a Pony Express rider.

The last figure refers to William H. Russell, whose firm started the famous mail delivery service at St. Joseph, Missouri in April 1860. Russell, who died in 1872, reposes in the local cemetery at the north edge of town. His monument notes that "He was a member of the firm of Russell, Majors and Waddell, founders, owners and operators of the Pony Express." Above appears a relief of a rider and a map of the route from St. Joseph via Fort Laramie and Salt Lake City to Sacramento, while the other side of the marker exhibits reliefs of the three partners and the text of the Pony Rider's Oath. Also buried in Palmyra is Pennsylvania-born George "Peg-leg" Shannon, a private with the Lewis and Clark Expedition, who lost his leg when he suffered wounds in a skirmish with Indians after the trip. Shannon returned to Philadelphia where he helped Nicholas Biddle edit the Lewis and Clark journals. He later moved to Missouri where "Peg-leg" served as U.S. District Attorney before dying suddenly in court at Palmyra in 1836.

Established in 1819, Palmyra was named for the remote Syrian desert city, perhaps because the Missouri town also began at a site distant from civilization. For some years, Palmyra remained the northernmost town on the Salt River Trail from St. Charles—the first capital of Missouri, on the Missouri River just west of St. Louis—to the Des Moines River. Prior to the arrival of white settlers, the site served as an Indian trading post and, earlier, as a hunting ground—the so called "Elm Lands," an elm forest—and council area favored by the Sac and Fox, whose rival leaders, Keokuk and Black Hawk, often visited the region. Some carry-overs from the past recall the town's early days: the old jail; the 1829 First Methodist Church, where ministers gathered in 1866 to revive the denomination after the Civil War; c. 1828 Gardner House, built as a hotel and stagecoach stop and later a saloon, school and residence and, currently, the visitor information center; and the Liberty Tree, a 300 year old fifty-five foot tall specimen with a sixty foot limb span. On Main near the Gardner House—one of the city's two hundred pre-Civil War buildings—are the offices of the *Spectator*, established in 1839 by Jacob Sosey, for more than a century Missouri's oldest newspaper continuously owned by the same family, and by now the state's oldest weekly. For just as long, a barber shop has occupied the space next door at the corner, where tall red, white and blue fluted columns—stylized versions of a barber's pole—flank the door.

On the Mississippi east of Palmyra promoter William Muldrow launched a grandiose plan in 1835 to establish a great port metropolis called Marion City. Although floods often inundated the lowland, Muldrow devised a scheme to deepen a slough into a canal which steamboats could enter to sail into town. In the fall of 1835 surveyers laid out and partly graded the first railroad lines in Missouri, from Marion City to Philadelphia, west of Palmyra. The following spring settlers began to arrive, many of them from the east where the extensive sale of Marion City lots inspired an emigration referred to as the "Eastern Run." Although the Mississippi spring floods soaked the new town in 1836, the promoter persisted and Marion City developed into an active port and distribution center. Floods in 1844 and 1851, however, deterred further growth, and eventually the townspeople moved away, finally completely abandoning the community, later covered by the Mississippi and melted away into the swampland. Muldrow also promoted Philadelphia, site of Marion College, a Presbyterian institution established in 1831 as the state's first Protestant school. It was later moved to Lexington, on the Missouri River toward Kansas City, and reopened in 1847 as a Masonic college.

The region's first settler, a Frenchman named Maturin Bouvet, arrived in 1795 at the Bay de Charles, three miles north of the site of Hannibal, where he worked as a trapper and fur trader and shipped salt from the salines along the Mississippi. Some French Canadians soon joined Bouvet, and a small trading post developed. There, on a balmy spring day or a crisp Indian summer morn, perhaps a hundred Indian bark canoes laden with skins and furs would arrive. Rumors circulated that Bouvet's enterprise so prospered that he amassed a barrel of gold, which he had supposedly buried near his house. In 1800 Bouvet disappeared, killed by Indians, some said, while others claimed he had floated by canoe down to New Orleans with his treasure. For some time afterward the ground near Bouvet's burnt-out house was pocked with holes dug by fortune hunters seeking the gold.

Of all the towns which lie along the great waterway, from Bemidji in Minnesota to Pilottown, Louisiana, none better evokes the olden days of life on the Mississippi than Mark Twain's Hannibal, that "white town drowsing in the sunshine" with "the great Mississippi, the majestic, the magnificent Mississippi, rolling its mile-wide tide along, shining in the sun." Neither the late twentieth century modernisms nor the thick overlay of touristy, Twain-related attractions and distractions manage to suppress Hannibal's underlying old time river town atmosphere which the author so vividly captured in his works. Major R. Raven-Hart found at Hannibal, where in 1937 the Englishman began a kayak float *Down the Mississippi*, as he entitled his account, "much Mark Twainery," but Raven-Hart nevertheless adjudged the town "a loveable place." More than half a century on, this description still holds true, for beneath the excessive "Twainery" survives a certain unspoiled small town flavor which even today young Sam Clemens might recognize.

Sam was born on November 30, 1835 in a two room shack-like cabin preserved at the Mark Twain Birthplace State Historic Site in Florida, twenty-seven miles southwest of Hannibal. A museum at the site (M-Sat 10-4, Sun 12-5) contains a handwritten manuscript of *Tom Sawyer*, family possessions and other exhibits relating to the famous author. In 1839 the Clemens family moved to Hannibal, where in 1847, after his father died, Sam left school at age twelve to work as a printer's apprentice. Later he worked for his brother, Orion, as a printer on the *Western Union*, which on January 16, 1851 carried Sam's first published writing, an account of one Jim Wolfe's action during a fire in the printing office. "Our gallant devil" removed from danger a broom, wash-pan and dirty towel, then returned to the room, "threw his giant frame in a tragic attitude, and exclaimed, with an eloquent expression: 'If that thar fire hadn't bin put out, thar'd a 'bin the greatest confirmation of the age!" So began the writing career of Samuel Langhorne Clemens, then aged fifteen, in a style already imbued with vernacular language and humor. In June, 1853 Clemens, age 17 ½, left his hometown to make his way in the world.

Sam's memory-filled years in Hannibal so haunted the boy who became Mark Twain that he spent the rest of his life trying to recapture that elusive, will-o'-the-wisp feeling of bygone times in a dreamy little Midwestern town on the banks of the Mississippi River. Thanks to Twain, Hannibal seems larger than life, for his writings add a time dimension to the town by preserving forever the yesteryear village of Tom and Huck and Becky, a locale and townspeople now familiar to all the world. There must be no other place anywhere which so vividly evokes fictional characters and settings as does Hannibal, still drowsing there by the Mississippi, which, as ever—as in Twain's time—rolls its mile-wide tide along. In *Lanterns on the Levee*, a memoir of his life in the Mississippi River town of Greenville, Mississippi, William Alexander Percy wrote that "There is no sound in the world so filled with mystery and longing and unease as the sound at night of a river boat blowing," a lonely whistle whose echo "hangs in your heart like a star." Similarly, along the great waterway there exists no place so filled with a haunting and, in some ways, sad tone and tincture of nostalgia—of vanished, unredeemable time—as Hannibal, a town which, once seen, "hangs inside your heart like a star."

Hannibal began in 1818 when Abraham Bird of New Madrid, the southern Missouri town on the Mississippi, received a certificate entitling hin to 640 acres to replace land he lost in the New Madrid earthquakes of 1811 and 1812. Bird chose an area tucked between two riverside bluffs, and by the time John M. Clemens moved his family there in 1839 a town with about 450 inhabitants had developed along the waterfront. Along one block of Hill Street stand the original buildings (the display places are open April-Aug 8-6, Sept-Oct 8-5, Nov-Dec 9-4, Jan-Feb 10-4, March 9-4) which existed when young Sam lived in that block. Next to the newly restored (1991) boyhood home (1844), a modest white clapboard frame house with green shutters, stretches the famous fence which Tom Sawyer tricked his chums into working on. "Does a boy get to whitewash a fence every day?" Tom teasingly tempted his pals, a coaxing no longer needed, for during Hannibal's annual Tom Sawyer days, held Fourth of July weekend, youngsters from far and wide flock to the fence, which they avidly—and messily—paint.

The stone block museum next to the house contains the cherry wood table on which Twain wrote part of *Tom Sawyer*, the first known photo of Clemens, taken when he was working as a printer's devil about the age of fifteen, and fifteen of the series of sixteen oil paintings Norman Rockwell executed for editions of *Tom Sawyer* and *Huckleberry Finn*. Across the street lies the Clemens law office, where John Clemens, who died of pneumonia in 1847, served as justice of the peace. Clemens helped organize the Hannibal and St. Joseph Railroad, which in February 1859 connected those two cities, thus becoming the nation's first line to cover the distance between the Mississippi and the Missouri Rivers. On April 3, 1860 a train departed from Hannibal carrying mail delivered to St. Joseph for the first Pony Express run out to Sacramento, California. Later that year the rail line used the nation's first mail car, built at Hannibal shops, which in 1865 also manufactured "General Grant," the first locomotive made west of the Mississippi.

At the 1830s Pilaster House down the street, so called for its wooden Greek-style columns, the Clemens family lived in 1846 and 1847 with Dr. and Mrs. Grant after John Clemens fell on hard times when forced to pay a loan he had guaranteed. The old time Grant apothecary occupies the ground floor. A display includes old steamboat spitoons weighted on the bottom so they would not overturn during rough waters. Fabricated in Cincinnati, the Pilaster House was floated down the Ohio and up the Mississippi bound for Marion City, promoter William Muldrow's town on the river north of Hannibal, but a flood there diverted the pre-fab dwelling to Twain's town. Along Main for a block or two stand nineteenth century commercial structures whose old-style facades lend a vague feeling of yesteryear. An antique store sign on Main states with Twainian humor: "Browsers welcome, buyers adored." Farther on, near the cobblestone levee at the foot of Broadway, the *Mark Twain* excursion boat (May-Oct, 314-221-3222, 800-621-2322), white with red trim, moors. In late 1992 the Army Corps of Engineers will complete a $7 million earthen and concrete levee, Hannibal's first such flood control facility. Up Broadway lies the Register-listed former Federal Building, which now houses the Missouri Territory Restaurant. In a nearby park stands a statue of Henry Hatch, a Congressman who sponsored the law creating the office of Secretary of Agriculture. For a century and a half Schaffer's Smoke House operated at 308 Broadway. In a back room at the tobacco store, which boasted a tin wall and ceiling, local characters—including, according to tradition, Sam Clemens—gathered to play pinochle while they traded small talk and tall tales. Not everyone in town appreciated Sam's patter: according to one local, "Sammy is a well of truth, but you can't bring it all up in one bucket."

Back the other way, at the end of Main rises Cardiff Hill, originally Holliday's Hill. It was so designated for a woman who once lived at the summit, where every night she lit a lantern as a guide for river pilots. Twain renamed the hill in his works, as the rise reminded him of an elevation in Cardiff, Wales. At the foot of the hill stand bronze portrayals of Huck and Tom, the nation's first statues to literary figures. From the top, as Twain recalled late in life, appears a "magnificent panorama of the Mississippi River, sweeping along league after league, a level green paradise on one side, and retreating capes and promontories as far as you could see on the other, fading away in the soft, rich lights in the remote distance...the most enchanting river view the planet could furnish."

Scattered around the fringes of Hannibal, outside the central section, you'll find such nineteenth century National Register dwellings as the Garth Woodside Mansion, a show house (Memorial Day-Labor Day 11:30-3) and bed and breakfast establishment (314-221-2789), and the Rockcliffe Mansion (March-Nov 9:30-5, Dec-Feb 11:30-3:30), where in 1902 on his last visit to Hannibal Twain addressed three hundred townspeople gathered around the stairway. A few days later, on June 4, while delivering the commencement address at the University of Missouri, Twain said of his hometown visit, "I was profoundly moved and saddened to think that this was the last time, perhaps, that I would ever behold those kind old faces and dear old scenes of childhood."

In addition to Woodside, bed and breakfast places include the 1854 Admiral Coontz House (314-221-7244), named for World War I naval officer Robert E. Coontz; Queen Anne's Grace (314-248-0756); the Register-listed Fifth Street Mansion (314-221-0445); and the Bordello (314-221-6111), installed in a 1917 house of ill repute, and still boasting "A reputation built on satisfaction." *The Reflections of Mark Twain* (late May-early Sept, 314-221-2945), a two hour pageant presented on a set depicting Hannibal in 1848—with a pond performing the role of the Mississippi—tells Twain's story. Stage shows also take place at a dinner theater called The Molly Brown (314-221-8940), named for Margaret Tobin, born at Hannibal in a house which stands at the corner of Butler and Denkler Alley. In 1884 Margaret followed her family to Leadville, Colorado where she married gold mine owner James Brown. She later survived the sinking of the *Titanic*, so earning the name "the unsinkable Molly Brown."

Hannibal offers such other Twainian sights as, downtown, a "haunted house" and wax museum with family and fictional figures; a museum with sixteen miniature carved scenes depicting Tom Sawyer episodes; the Becky Thatcher bookshop, which occupies the house where Sam Clemen's childhood sweetheart, Laura Hawkins, lived; and, outside town, Mark Twain Cave (June-Aug 8-8, spring and fall 9-6, Nov-March 9-4), setting for some of Tom and Huck's adventures. At Mount Olivet Cemetery, on Fulton Avenue south of town, repose John and Jane Clemens, Twain's parents. Also there lie his brothers Orion and Henry, the latter killed in 1858 when the steamer *Pennsylvania* exploded near Memphis, Tennessee (Twain himself, who died in 1910, lies at Elmira, New York with his wife and children). In the Renssalear graveyard, ten miles west of Hannibal, rests Laura Hawkins, who died in 1928. Hawkins' marker bears not only her name but the name "Becky Thatcher," who lives on.

To conclude your visit to Hannibal—perhaps at dusk after a day's sightseeing—it is pleasant to drive out to Riverview Park, high on the bluffs north of town. In the well-wooded 250 acre park stands a statue of Mark Twain—his features seemingly softened by countless rains and winds—now forever gazing out at his beloved Mississippi far below. Off to the right appears the railroad and the car bridges—symbols of the post-steamer age Twain lived to see—while upstream the tree-lined river curves into view. On the pink granite pedestal beneath the statue of Twain, on whose face appears a solemn and perhaps even sorrowful look, is written: "His religion was humanity and a whole world mourned for him when he died." At day's end twilight begins to shroud the great river, which gradually fades into the darkness. The vanished hours, the Twain figure, the setting and the setting sun serve to recall the words of an old folksong the hometown boy grown old remembered in *Villagers 1840-3*, a time-haunted reminiscence of his long lost youth in Hannibal: "The day goes by like a shadow on the wall, with sorrow where all was delight." It is that sort of bittersweet sense of the slow flow of time, of time passing and passed, that a visit to Mark Twain's Hannibal leaves with you as you linger there in the still dusk on the bluffs high above the great rolling river.

As Highway 79 heads south out of Hannibal—past Saverton, site of Lock and Dam Number 22—the road follows a scenic route "which edges around hills, and occasionally offers a view of the tawny Mississippi working its stubborn way southward, dotted with islands like little green ships afloat," so Mackinlay Kantor described this stretch in *Missouri Bittersweet*. About fourteen miles south of Hannibal appears the first of three turnoffs to viewing areas overlooking the Mississippi. Last of them is unusual as it lies a few miles from the waterway, thus affording a more extensive perspective onto the river valley by including a wide landscape. Farther on lies the 1,300 acre DuPont Reservation, a hilly, timbered riverside recreational area given by that corporation in 1938. Another preserve, the adjacent 11,000 acre Ted Shanks Wildlife Area, borders the Mississippi. About 1818 pioneers settled along the nearby Salt River, where they extracted salt from the salines by the waterway.

Farther on you'll reach Louisiana, an attractive old river town named for Louisiana Basye, supposedly the first child born in St. Louis after the Louisiana Purchase. When the family moved up the river to Pike County in 1818, the year the early residents began laying out the new town, they named it for the fifteen year old Basye girl. Louisiana echoes the Southern flavor suggested by its name with some of its street designations—Tennessee, South Carolina, North Carolina, Alabama and Georgia. A few blocks of Georgia—lined with old commercial buildings, some of them housing a number of Louisiana's many antique shops—comprise a National Historic District, part of what a state agency has called "the most intact Victorian streetscape in the state of Missouri." At 1401 Georgia stands the Register-listed pillared mansion once occupied by Lloyd C. Stark, governor of Missouri from 1937 to

1941. Stark belonged to the family established at Louisiana in 1816 when twenty-four year old James Hart Stark arrived in northern Missouri from his native Kentucky. In his saddle bags Stark carried bundles of apple cuttings which he grafted to wild crab apple trees to produce some of the first cultivated fruit west of the Mississippi. The newcomer soon expanded his budding fruit farm by planting apple orchards, and so began the Stark Brothers Nurseries, now more than 175 years old. Members of the sixth generation manage Stark, one of the nation's oldest firms continuously owned and operated by the same family.

On the west edge of Louisiana the Pioneer Stark Cabin survives. James Stark built the rustic structure, moved there from its original site in 1952. A classic-style structure building across the road houses the firm's retail sales facility (for catalogs: 314-754-4525). A display case in the sales room contains photos of famous plant scientist Luther Burbank, retained by Stark Bro (as the company calls itself) in 1893 as an advisor to help develop new types of fruit. The case also includes a copy of one of the first U.S. plant patents, a credential originated after the Stark firm, helped by Burbank and inventor Thomas A. Edison, persuaded Congress to amend the original patent law in 1930. North of the sales building, beyond the company's nearby home office, stands an old barn bearing a silhouette of a bear with the firm's slogan: "Stark Trees Bear." The company's best known trees are those which produce the Red Delicious, discovered in 1893, and the Golden Delicious, introduced in 1914, the world's two most widely planted apple varieties. Also west of town, on Highway 54, you'll find the Phillips Museum, a large round tile farrowing barn with displays of old toys, Indian objects, antiques and one of the largest collections of animal horns in existence.

Down by the river, huge venerable trees garnish an overlook area, while on nearby Water Street an old four story brick building labeled "The Nord-Buffum Pearl Button Co" bears a more recently painted designation, "American Shell Company,

Inc." At 220 North Third the four-column white brick 1856 Luce-Dyer residence, listed on the National Register, stands. Other nineteenth century dwellings offer bed and breakfast accommodations: Serando's House (314-754-4067), Baronial Orthwein Mansion (314-965-4328), and Louisiana Guest House (314-754-6366). Henderson-Riverview Park occupies a wooded knoll overlooking the Mississippi, spanned just to the north by the 1928 Champ Clark Bridge. It was named for the Speaker of the House of Representatives, who taught school and practiced law in Louisiana before moving to nearby Bowling Green, the county seat, where Honey Shuck, Clark's house, is open for tours on summer weekends. Also at the north end of Louisiana lies the peaceful Riverview Cemetery, with panoramas onto the Mississippi.

Just south of Louisiana you'll pass a huge Bunge grain elevator, nearby sprawls a large chemical factory, and further on, not far north of Clarksville, lies the Dundee Cement plant, a bit incongruous there in the rural countryside. Clarksville, a town of nearly six hundred people—about the same size as just before the Civil War—lies right on the Mississippi, near which tower abrupt bluffs. The Sky Ride (Memorial Day-Labor Day 9:30-5:30, to 7 Sat and Sun, weekends only May, Sept and Oct), established in 1960, takes you to the top of the six hundred foot high bluff, said to be the highest point on the Mississippi. From the top, a view over eight hundred square miles spreads before you. A nature trail from Lookout Point winds through the woods to an Indian burial area. Just north of town Lock and Dam Number 24, completed in 1939, stands. Numerate travelers may notice that the nearest such construction upstream bears the number 22. No Number 23 exists, as the Corps of Engineers, which numbered the locks and dams before building them, determined after completing Number 24 that Number 23 should be eliminated. Through the lock as much as thirty-four million tons of freight passes annually, considerably more than the two million tons a year carried by the steamers a century ago. By the lock and dam stands the new (1990) Adler Restaurant, whose name ("eagle" in German) recalls that Clarksville is one of the best places on the river to observe bald eagles, which feed in the ice-free waters below the dam. Many of the birds, found in the area from December to late February, perch on 818 acre Clarksville Island, one of the few remaining blue heron and American egret rookeries on the Mississippi north of the Ohio River. The Nature Conservency purchased the island in 1981.

Although settlers arrived in the area as early as 1808, an Indian massacre four years later delayed development of Clarksville, named in 1817 for William Clark, Lewis' exploring partner. Clark spent the winter of 1815 at the site when the Mississippi iced over as he headed north from St. Louis to Prairie du Chien, Wisconsin. Although the *General Putnam* became the first Mississippi steamer this far north in 1820, in the next few years only lowly flatboats served to ship out from Clarksville hogsheads of tobacco, sent down to New Orleans for export to Europe. In the middle part of the century rivermen dubbed the settlement Appletown because of the large amount of that fruit shipped every autumn. This trade is recalled by The Apple Shed, a former storage facility acquired by the Raintree Arts Council, a cultural group, and converted to a fine arts center, which hosts musical events, exhibits and theater productions (for information: 314-242-3264). An earlier performance hall, the 1892 Blake Opera House, stood near the river on the site now occupied by the Swetman apartments, while at the levee docked the *Cotton Blossom* and other showboats which brought leading performers to town.

A new paddlewheeler-like building overlooking the river houses a one room historical museum, with antiques, period dresses, vintage farm items, photos of century old river scenes, and other relics. One notice recalls that in 1886 Clarksville hosted the world championship bike races. Upstairs in the visitor center a case holds a model of the 1895 *Belle of Calhoun*, an apple and produce freighter which sank twice, was raised both times but then burned.

When Clarksville's old Carrol Hotel burned in 1941, the commercial dominance of the waterfront began to decline. The area gradually decayed until the 1887 Clifford Bank building, now an antique shop, became the town's first major restored commercial structure after the firm moved to a new office in 1972. The 1865 Pollack-Huber Building houses an art gallery, and the National Register-listed Clifford-Wirick House contains a shop selling glass and china. The 1877 Russell-Carroll House (314-242-3854) in town offers bed and breakfast, as do the Daniel Douglas House (314-242-3939) and the boxy brick thirty room Falicon Estate (314-242-3264) on Highway W four miles southwest of Clarksville.

Eight miles south of Clarksville lies Annada, named for Anna and Ada Jamison, daughters of an early settler. A cottage-like post office serves the hamlet's some seventy souls. A mile east of town the Clarence Cannon National Wildlife Refuge occupies about 3,700 floodplain acres. The refuge is drained in the summer to stimulate plant growth, then flooded in the fall to attract migrating waterfowl tempted by the combination of wetlands and seed food, as well as by cavity-ridden trees where the birds can nest. More than two hundred species enliven the enclave, most of them in October-November and March-April. Gravel roads afford access to the Cannon Refuge, purchased in 1964 with proceeds from the sale of federal duck stamps and added to the Mark Twain National Wildlife Refuge. This group of nine similar areas encompassing 25,300 acres in Illinois, Missouri and Iowa lies along some two hundred and fifty miles of the Mississippi Flyway, one of the nation's most important waterfowl migration routes. The Twain unit, in turn, forms part of the system of more than four hundred national wildlife refuges around the country, a network of nature reserves begun under

President Theodore Roosevelt in 1903. The Cannon Refuge memorializes Congressman Clarence Cannon of Elsberry, located just to the south, home of the Champ Goodwood model dairy farm and the 1896 Old Calaboose jail.

Farther on, at Winfield, site of Lock and Dam Number 25, an eight car ferry links Missouri with Batchtown, Illinois. Near where the Cuivre River—a baffling name, as no copper ("cuivre" in French) exists in the area—enters the Mississippi, just south of Winfield, a hamlet of sixty people called Cap au Gris (from "grès," for sandstone) once existed. Residents of Cape Girardeau, a Mississippi River town south of St. Louis, like to claim the world's only inland "cape" town, but Cap au Gris once also boasted the name, and so does Cape Fair, a hamlet in Missouri on the northern branch of Table Rock Lake in the Ozarks. The Cuivre (pronounced locally to rhyme with "river") marks the southern border of Lincoln County, named not for the President but so designated in 1818—when Abe was only nine years old—for Revolutionary War General Benjamin Lincoln, who served as Secretary of War for the Continental Congress from 1781 to 1783. Major Christopher Clark, a member of the Missouri Territorial Legislature, suggested the name in a two sentence speech to the group: "Mr. Speaker, I'm in favor of the new county. I was born in Lincoln County, North Carolina; I have lived a year or so in Lincoln County, Kentucky; and I want to live and die in Lincoln County, Missouri."

After the River Road south of Winfield reaches Interstate 70 that highway takes you a few miles east to St. Charles, a Missouri River town which served as the state's first capital. At the riverside site stand the first hills west of the Missouri's mouth at the Mississippi twenty miles downstream. There, on the high ground, French-Canadian settlers established a village in the 1770s. Fertile bottomlands, soon cultivated, spread away from the hills, while the river afforded a connection with the nearby Mississippi. In 1787 August Chouteau, a founder of St. Louis, surveyed the town, and before long the Spanish, who then possessed the lands west of the Mississippi, formed the District of San Carlos, a modest little unit which extended west to the Pacific Ocean. Around the turn of the century Daniel Boone, seeking "more elbow room," arrived from Kentucky and settled in a house (still standing and open to the public) he and his son built not far west of St. Charles. Between May 16 and 21, 1804 the Lewis and Clark Expedition stopped in St. Charles, the last civilized settlement on the Missouri, to make final preparations before heading west up the river. Two years later, Zebulon Pike started off from the town on his trek west to Colorado and the peak which now bears his name. When Missouri entered the union in 1821 St. Charles, already the Territorial Capital, became the state's seat of government until 1826, when Jefferson City, one hundred and twenty miles west on the Missouri River, captured the honor. Along Main Street, which parallels the Missouri two blocks away, stands the original capitol (M-Sat 10-4, Sun 12-5), a two story brick commercial building which also housed a general store. Vintage houses as well as shops, restaurants and old-type emporiums which occupy nineteenth century structures line Main, part of Missouri's largest National Historic District. This attractively restored street suggests the flavor of an early river town. The Vintage House Restaurant on South Main offers a delightful outdoor wine garden. Also on South Main, Saint Charles House (314-946-6221) and Boone's Lick Trail Inn (314-947-7000 and 800-366-2427) offer bed and breakfast as does the Lococo House (314-946-0619) up on Fifth.

Up on the hills on North Second Street lies the antique shop area known as Frenchtown, so named when the early French community moved to its own neighborhood after Germans began to arrive around 1835. The Germans settled in St. Charles and all along the Missouri River to the west in countryside which reminded them of the Rhineland. Sibley Hall (1857) at Lindenwood College, established in 1827 as the second oldest school of higher education west of the Mississippi, merits National Register listing. The Academy of the Sacred Heart, which dates from 1818, still uses its first permanent building, erected in the mid-1830s. St. Charles Borromeo Cemetery, named for the church which originally stood on the site of the Academy Chapel, includes the graves of many early-day settlers.

Back on the river, the *Spirit of St. Charles* (314-946-7766 and 800-322-3448) offers cruises on the Missouri, while the 1930s Corps of Engineers dredge *Sainte Genevieve* houses a new (1991) river museum. In the spring of 1991 the splendid old *Goldenrod* showboat resumed operations at the St. Charles waterfront. The city brought the ship there the previous August from the St. Louis levee, its home for fifty-three years. According to legend, Edna Ferber lived on the ship while researching her 1926 novel *Show boat,* supposedly based on the *Goldenrod,* a genuine 1909 relic of the river era, which Ferber called *Cotton Blossom* in the book.

The *Goldenrod,* a National Historic Landmark, is the biggest (200 feet long with a capacity of 1400) and the most ornately decorated showboat ever built. The old dowager survives as one of the nation's only two original showboats (the other, a smaller 1923 vessel named the *Majestic,* hosts summer-stock shows at Cincinnati). As for most showboats, the pilot's house which perches atop the ship served a purely decorative function, for the vessels traveled the waterways pushed by tugs. The first showboat, a keelboat named *Noah's Ark,* originated in December 1817 when a group of actors performed on the ship moored on the Mississippi at Natchez, Mississippi. The first vessel especially built to serve as a show ship, the 1831 *Floating Theatre,* plied the Ohio and Lower Mississippi until it sank in 1847. Through the years fifty-three showboats on the Mississippi and its tributaries—including such colorfully named ships as *Banjo, New Sensation, Great American Water Circus, Sunny South* and *Wonderland*—continued the tradition. As late as the 1914 to 1918 period some eighteen showboats served cities on the Mississippi River system.

Like other sorts of river ships, showboats inspired any number of stories and anecdotes. William Chapman, who built the *Floating Theatre*, once provoked unwanted laughter when he played the Ghost in *Hamlet* while still wearing spectacles, and in 1930 portly Captain William Menke of the *New Sensation* inserted himself into a hole opened in the hull when the ship hit a submerged piling and remained there as a human plug until the crew built a partition over the opening. By now the shrill, alluring siren song of the calliope no longer calls eager audiences to the magical world of the showboat, but the old *Goldenrod*, which does present performances, survives as a monument to one of the Mississippi's most colorful eras.

On the Mississippi north of St. Charles lies the landing for the *Golden Eagle* (618-883-2217), perhaps the river's only paddlewheel ferry, which connects Missouri with Calhoun County, Illinois. From St. Charles, Highway 94 to the east leads through the narrow peninsula which lies between the Missouri and Mississippi Rivers. A short spur takes you out to Portage des Sioux, a tiny (under 500 people) but historically significant settlement named for the episode when a band of Sioux braves floating down the Mississippi cut across the tongue of land on a two mile portage to bypass the mouth of the Missouri, where enemy Missouri tribesman lurked. Because the portage saved twenty-five miles of river travel, Portage des Sioux became a military and commercial point. In 1799 the Spanish established a fort at the strategic site, while in November 1804, the year after the territory passed to the United States under the Louisiana Purchase, federal authorities concluded with the Sac and Fox the first of a series of treaties by which Indians conveyed their Missouri lands to the Americans. Black Hawk, protesting that the chiefs who signed the agreement lacked authority, incited his tribesmen to harass white settlers in the War of 1812, during which Portage des Sioux served as the center of military operations against the Indians. In the summer of 1815, after the war, nineteen Indian tribes came to the village to conclude treaties and receive $30,000 worth of presents distributed by the American delegation. This distinguished group included Illinois Governor Ninian Edwards, Auguste Chouteau, St. Louis founder Pierre Laclede's right-hand man, and explorer William Clark, then governor of the Missouri Territory. Portage des Sioux eventually lost its importance, but not its rivers-related connections. When a 1951 Missouri River flood flowed over the peninsula and entered the Mississippi, the priest at St. Francis Church in Portage des Sioux asked his parishioners to pray that the town be saved. In gratitude for the waters receding without harming the hamlet, residents erected on the Mississippi a twenty-seven foot fibreglass Shrine of Our Lady of the Rivers, lit at night. In July a colorful Blessing of the Boats ceremony takes place at the statue, whose feet, perched atop a seventeen foot pedestal, felt lapping waters during the 1973 flood which inundated West Alton, a town of about 400 people nine miles east. The new (1992) Riverlands Environmental Demonstration Area lies along the Mississippi across from Alton, Illinois. Boardwalks and trails criss-cross the re-created 1,200 acre prairieland nature preserve.

Near West Alton, a bridge takes you across the Missouri about four miles above its mouth. At this point the river has nearly completed its 2,316 mile journey which begins at Three Forks, Montana. Carrying some 100 million tons of silt into the Mississippi every year, the Big Muddy's waters remain—as river dwellers describe it—too thick to drink but too thin to plow. Because silt carried by the shallow and sandy Missouri would clog locks, none exist to facilitate navigation, but the Corps of Engineers maintains a nine foot channel on the 732 mile stretch from St. Louis to Sioux City, Iowa. On the upper river, six huge hydroelectric dams (in Montana and North and South Dakota), along with seventy-five others on tributaries, serve to control flooding, a habit of the unruly waterway a Sioux City editor satirized in 1868: "Of all the variable things in creation the most uncertain are the action of a jury, the state of a woman's mind, and the condition of the Missouri River." Old time riverboat pilots on the "Big Muddy" used to taunt boatmen on the supposedly more easily navigable Mississippi by claiming that at the mouth of the Missouri were separated the men from the boys, with the latter clinging to the Mississippi's more hospitable waters. So treacherous was the Missouri that the St. Louis to St.Joseph run, across only one state, Missouri, took about as long as the trip on the Mississippi from New Orleans to St. Louis.

Father Marquette, the first white man (along with Joliet) to see the Missouri's mouth, during his 1673 expedition down the Mississippi, found it a formidably terrifying sight: "As we were gently sailing down the still clear water, we heard a noise of a rapid into which we were about to fall. I have seen nothing more frightful, a mass of large trees entire with branches, real floating islands came from Pekittanoui, so impetuous that we could not without great danger expose ourselves to pass across. The agitation was so great that the water was all muddy, and could not get clear." Although Marquette called the river by its Illini Indian name, which meant "muddy water," after his trip the explorer sketched a map—now in the archives of St. Mary's College at Montreal—noting at the confluence ten Indian villages, including one shown as "Ou-Missouri." Cartographers later showed the waterway as "Rivière des Missouris," for the Missouri Indians who dwelled near the river's mouth at the end of the seventeenth century. Although the Fox called that tribe the "Missouri," meaning "People with Big Canoes," the Missouri designated the river not with their own name but "Nishodse," or "Muddy Water." The Fox prefix for "big," "miss" (originally "mesisi"), also forms part of their word "mesisi-piya"—"Big River." So originated the names of the two great waterways which merge just above St. Louis.

It is surely remarkable that the citizens of St. Louis have failed in any way to set aside, mark or provide access to the point where the famous rivers meet. This junction, the most significant on the entire Mississippi, remains uncommemorated and unreachable—a curious omission for a city so linked with the Mississippi as St. Louis has been since its very beginnings in 1764. Only from across the river near Hartford, south of Alton, can the confluence be seen (see the Illinois chapter), and none too well at that. After you cross the Missouri and enter Lewis and Clark Boulevard, Highways 67 and 367, turn left about 3½ miles beyond the river onto Parker Road until it meets Bellefontaine where you again turn left. You soon turn right on Columbus for a block, then left onto Spanish Pond Road, which takes you toward the Mississippi at the far northern edge of St. Louis.

Bellefontaine Road takes its name from the first American fort built west of the Mississippi after the 1803 Louisiana Purchase. The first version of the outpost, tossed together with green logs still covered with bark, occupied a site on the bottoms near the mouth of Coldwater Creek. This make-shift installation soon rotted, and in 1810 troops built a new fort atop the bluffs at the end of present day Bellefontaine Road, where the original powder house still stands. From here a stair-case built in 1938 by W.P.A. workers leads down the rockface from the top of the bluff to the Missouri River bottomland. Lewis and Clark and Zebulon Pike stopped at the fort—where James Whistler, grandfather of the artist of the same name, ran a trading post—as the explorers began their westward excursions in the early nineteenth century. After the War of 1812, the frontier moved west, passing the outpost by, so the army abandoned Fort Bellefontaine in 1826 and moved its troops to Jefferson Barracks on the Mississippi at the far southern edge of St. Louis.

Prior to the construction of Fort Bellefontaine, the Spanish built Fort Don Carlos on the Missouri River bottoms, installed in 1767 to protect the territory then controlled by Spain from the

English and Indians. During the Revolutionary War, the Spanish abandoned the base and moved its guns to St. Louis. Atop a hill at the east side of Spanish Lake, which you pass on Spanish Pond Road, once stood the house built by Louisiana Territory Lieutenant Governor Don Zenon Trudeau, who in 1794 came to St. Louis to establish a fur trading operation for Spain. Not far beyond Spanish Lake, the street of that name curves into Strodtman Road which continues down to the bottom-land. The street becomes Madison Ferry Road, which leads to the Mississippi. Unfortunately, however, a gate bars the way here, for the inaccessible area by the confluence of the Mississippi and Missouri serves as a cornfield: thus does one of the nation's most historic corners, a unique geographical feature on the North American continent, remain devoted to producing animal fodder. You must therefore turn right and continue south on Columbia Bottom Road, which beyond Interstate 270 becomes Riverview Drive.

Riverview borders Chain of Rocks Park, perched above the road just to the west. The park was named for the navigation-vexing rock outcroppings which forced the Corps of Engineers to create a bypass on the Illinois side of the river (see the Illinois chapter). The narrow, two-lane 1929 Chain of Rocks Bridge spans the river above where the waters roil over a stretch of the submerged rock formation. The city of Madison, Illinois, owns the bridge, closed in 1968 after completion of I-270 across the river just to the north. A gas pipeline company now leases the span, where in 1980 moviemakers filmed scenes for *Escape from New York*. A developer once proposed converting the bridge into an enclosed shopping mall, but nothing came of the idea and the span rusts away there above the rocky river channel.

Paths in nearby North Riverfront Park, which stretches along the waterway, offer close views of the Mississippi, here still pastoral as the metropolitan area seems rather removed. A walking trail along the Mississippi leads from here to just beyond

Bellerive Park in south St. Louis. To continue along the river, you curve left from Riverview onto Hall, restricted at night to commercial traffic which serves the many trucking company terminals along the street. Their loading docks are latter-day analogues of the docks and wharfs where steamers of a bygone era once handled their cargoes. Modern day traffic still plies the river at St. Louis, the northernmost point on the Mississippi that usually remains free of ice and navigable. Between sixty and a hundred barges—which carry a total of some 26 million tons of freight a year—arrive or depart daily from the Port of Metropolitan St. Louis, where ten shipyards and repair facilities handle the river traffic. Size limitations at the Mississippi's locks restrict their capacity, so towboats headed up-river push no more than fifteen barges north of St. Louis; south of the city, however, the boats can push up to forty-five barges. The route to the center continues south on Hall. By the river, out of view a few blocks east, tower the ADM grain elevators, and farther on, at the corner of East Grand where Hall ends, a huge Proctor and Gamble manufacturing facility sprawls along both sides of the intersection.

Although nearby Broadway takes you south into the city center, and then beyond to the far edge of the metropolitan area, a short detour in this part of north St. Louis includes some historic and river-related sights. A left turn on Blair, just beyond the Interstate, a few blocks below a free-standing 154-foot Corinthian 1871 water tower, designed by Thomas J. Whitman, brother of poet Walt Whitman, the road leads to another such disused installation. This 1889 206-foot brick and stone campanile closed in 1913. Nearby, you'll also find St. Louis's oldest dwelling, the square-columned 1830 Lewis Bissell house. Now a restaurant, it was built by an army captain from Connecticut on Bissell's Point, a bend on the river a century and a half ago.

From here it's worth backtracking, via East Grand and then north on West Florissant, to Bellefontaine Cemetery, where many Mississippi River figures lie at rest. The graveyard occupies the long Bellefontaine Bluff, once an Indian camp with a trail connecting it to the nearby river. Later, the old military road leading to Fort Bellefontaine on the Missouri River passed through the property, opened as a cemetery in 1849. A drive along the curvy roads, many so aligned to save trees and to afford views of the hilly wooded area and the river, takes you to the graves of: Henry M. Shreve, who invented the snag boat which cleared the Mississippi of hazardous obstructions (see the Tennessee section); Manuel Lisa, an early day fur merchant whose trading post stood on the banks of the river in downtown St. Louis; Stephen W. Kearney, who in 1820 explored the Mississippi up to Camp Cold Water, later Fort St. Anthony at Minneapolis; Sol Smith, whose tomb inscription—"All the world's a stage / And all the men and women merely players. / Exit Sol"— recalls his career as a showboat proprietor and a theater impresario who brought to river towns traveling stage companies transported by ship; Dr. William Beaumont, who at Fort Crawford in Prairie du Chien on the river conducted famous experiments on the digestive process (see the Wisconsin chapter); Commodore John McCune, director of the Keokuk Packet Company in the 1850's; Captain Thomas H. Griffith, a founder of the Northern Line, which merged with McCune's firm; Samuel Gaty, partner in the Keokuk line, and the first steamboat machinery manufacturer in the West; Adolphus Busch, whose brewery near the river in south St. Louis (see below) tapped the Mississippi's waters to produce the company's beers; James B. Eads, builder of the pioneering Eads Bridge in downtown St. Louis (see below) and other river constructions; Captain Isaiah Sellers, a renowned pilot who in thirty-five years completed 460 round trips between St. Louis and New Orleans, whose grave bears a relief of him at a ship's wheel; George C. Wolff, who operated thirty bars on Mississippi steamboats, whose marker bears a silhouette of the steamer named after him; Senator

Thomas Hart Benton, the great proponent of the nation's trans-Mississippi expansion, who in an 1849 oration on extending the railroad from the Mississippi west to the Pacific delivered the famous phrase, "There is the East; there is India"; and, finally, William Clark, who explored the Missouri with Meriwether Lewis, served as Superintendant of Indian Affairs and as governor of the Missouri Territory, who rests beneath a granite obelisque overlooking the Mississippi which flows along not far from the graves of so many characters whose memories haunt the great waterway.

At neighboring Calvary Cemetery, the Catholic burial ground established in 1864, rest: Civil War General William Tecumseh Sherman; slave Dred Scott, famous for his suit to obtain freedom (see below); Auguste Chouteau, one of St. Louis's founders (see below); Alexander McNair, Missouri's first governor; and a more recent arrival (1983), playwright Tennessee Williams.

Returning to Broadway, the street heads south toward downtown, passing the Mallinckrodt Chemical works, an old St. Louis facility, and the O.T. Hodge Chili Parlor, which since 1904 has served its specialty. Farther on stand old industrial and commercial buildings, some bearing fading signs and fancy or fanciful architectural details. Soon the Gateway Arch looms into view and not far on, just before Broadway crosses I-70, a left turn on Cass takes you into a partly-abandoned area of old warehouses and distribution centers lining brick-paved streets. At 244 Dickson in this area stood the machine shop where in 1886 William Seward Burroughs invented the adding machine. You can thread your way through this section to the restored Laclede Landing's area, named for St. Louis's founder, which lies between two bridges. Listed on the National Register, the Landing includes renewed, late nineteenth century commercial structures. Starting in the mid-1970's, developers recycled these into offices, restaurants, night spots, shops, and other establishments. Historic buildings, many of them fronted by cast-iron facades, include the 1870 Bronson Hide facility, one of the riverfront's fur firms, where the company operated until 1983; Register-listed 1873 Raeder Place, a six story former tobacco company headquarters; and the 1874 structure, originally occupied by a stove enterprise, where Switzer Candy Company manufactured licorice. St. Louis began using cast-iron construction, introduced in New York City in 1848, after the devastating 1849 waterfront fire which spread from the burning *White Cloud* steamship, moored by the levee, and destroyed fifteen downtown blocks. A small branch of Boatmen's National Bank bears the steamboat logo of the company, founded in 1847 to handle the financial needs of rivermen and now the state's largest banking firm.

Just by Laclede's Landing, bordering it on the south, stretches the splendid Illinois-St. Louis Bridge, the official name of the great span known since the day of its dedication on July 4, 1874 as Eads Bridge. Although James Buchanan Eads, born in 1820 and named for his mother's cousin, future U.S. President James Buchanan, never attended school, the self-educated engineer became one of the greatest figures ever connected with the Mississippi River. As a boy, he designed a model steamboat powered by a rat on a treadmill. At age twenty-two, the St. Louisian converted a forty-gallon whiskey barrel into a diving bell, which he then used to recover a cargo of sunken lead. This proved to be his new salvage business's first job. In 1855, the enterprising Eads bought five snag boats and organized the Western River Improvement Company. Shortly after the Civil War started, the riverman built at his shipyard in Carondelet, on the south edge of St. Louis, seven ironclad gunboats. These saw service at Columbus, Kentucky, Island Number 10 near New Madrid, Missouri, Fort Pillow, Tennessee, and other Confederate river strongholds which later fell to federal forces in 1862. After the war, Eads promoted a convention, held in St. Louis in 1867, to consider improvements on the Mississippi, that "giant stream, with its head shrouded in arctic snows, embracing half a continent in the hundred thousand miles of its curious network," he told the delegates with a certain dramatic exaggeration.

At about this time, Eads began to promote the idea of a railway bridge across the Mississippi at St. Louis, a project bitterly opposed not only by steamboat interests but also by Chicago, a rival rail center, and also by the Wiggins Ferry Company which enjoyed a monopoly for all services crossing the waterway at St. Louis. Undeterred, Eads proceeded with the project in 1869, using many innovative techniques, some appropriated by Washington A. Roebling, who soon began work on the Brooklyn Bridge. In June, 1874, when the 6,220 foot span neared completion, General William Tecumseh Sherman rode on the first locomotive to cross the new tracks which connected Illinois and Missouri. To convince skeptical observers of the construction's safety, Eads arranged for an elephant to walk over the bridge, and then he ran fourteen train engines back and forth on the tracks as on-lookers watched to see if the span would collapse. Finally, on July 4, 1874, President Ulysses S. Grant attended the dedication of the new Mississippi marvel, the first bridge in the nation piered in pneumatic foundations, the first in the world to use extensive amounts of steel and tubular chord sections, and the first whose superstructure depended entirely on the use of the cantilever. These features led the 1886 *Encyclopedia Brittanica* to describe the span as "one of the most remarkable structures in the world in character and magnitude."

In 1881, the Missouri Pacific line bought the bridge, then sold it eight years later to a group of railroads belonging to the Terminal Railroad Association, which still owns the National Register-listed structure. As for Eads, he continued his engineering feats on the river, with his main project a series of jetties constructed near the mouth to deepen the waterway and clear its channel of sediment, enabling ocean-going ships to freely navigate the Mississippi there. Eads wrote in a letter describing his jetty project, "[Man is] capable of curbing, controlling and directing the Mississippi, according to his pleasure, from the Gulf of Mexico to the most attenuated rivulet." The great engineer lived by this credo until his death on March 8, 1887. He was laid to rest in Bellefontaine Cemetery on the low hills overlooking the river he did so much to curb, control, and direct.

Until the striking stainless steel Gateway Arch rose on the St. Louis waterfront in the early 1960's, Eads Bridge remained the area's most imposing construction, but now the 630 foot high Arch, the nation's tallest monument, overshadows everything else on the levee. By the 1930's the historic waterfront had fallen on hard times. The area mostly contained dilapidated old buildings and unsightly streets, an eyesore which Luther Ely Smith, a public-spirited St. Louisian, decided should be eliminated in favor of a monument to memorialize the city's role as "gateway to the West." Between 1929 and 1942, the city demolished the blighted buildings. Next, in 1947, Eero Saarinen's catenary arch design won the contest for the new memorial. In 1959, work began to remove the Terminal Railroad Association's riverside tracks, and in June, 1962 construction finally began on the Arch. It was completed in October three years later. The foundations sink fifty feet below ground level. Each leg contains 1,076 steps, and a forty passenger, eight-car train which rises to the upper reaches of the Arch, topped by a small observation deck with thirty-two small windows which afford views onto thirty mile panoramas. Some 2.5 million people a year visit the Arch, below which an underground section includes the *Monument to the Dream* film on the memorial's construction; the Museum of Westward Expansion (Sat before Memorial Day-Labor Day 8-10, Sept-late May 9-6), with exhibits on the Lewis and Clark Expedition, the St. Louis levee, and other "gateway to the West" history; and capsule-car trams (Memorial Day-Labor Day 8:30-9:30, rest of year 9:30-5:30), which come complete with a device to keep the seats level as the conveyance rises on the four minute ride to the top.

Just to the west of the Jefferson National Expansion Memorial, the park's official name, the Old Courthouse (8-4:30) fronts the small park which commemorates Luther Ely Smith. Part of the National Memorial, the 1839 Old Courthouse features exhibits on the history of St. Louis, dioramas, movies on the old West, a restored mid-nineteenth century courtroom, and a display on slave Dred Scott, who in 1847 sued here for his freedom. Scott was represented by abolitionist attorney Roswell Field, father of poet Eugene Field, who grew up at a nearby 1845 house which is now a museum (Tu-Sat 10-4, Sun 12-4). Scott died a free man in St. Louis in 1858. Although the United States Supreme Court decided against him, Scott's owner released him two months after the decision. As previously noted, Scott lies in Calvary Cemetery in north St. Louis. A plaque below the Old Courthouse steps recalls that Joseph Pulitzer bought at a public auction on the site in 1878 the *St. Louis Dispatch*, forerunner of the *Post-Dispatch*, a paper still controlled by the Pulitzer family.

Back toward the arch stands the Old Cathedral (museum open 10-5), a mid-1830's stone sanctuary which rests on the site of St. Louis's first church. The site was consecrated in 1770, six years after Pierre Laclede and August Chouteau founded the city on the waterfront below where the Arch rises. After the New Orleans firm of Maxent, Laclede, and Company received exclusive rights to the Mississippi River Valley Indian trade, Laclede traveled up the waterway, and wintered at Fort de Chartres on the Illinois side (see the Illinois chapter). In February, 1764, he sent 14-year-old Chouteau to the far shore to begin construction of shelters and storage sheds. A small marker by the steps below the Arch commemorates this event. Another memorializes Robert E. Lee, whose "engineering genius was responsible for moving the Mississippi River channel back to the St. Louis shore preserving the city as a riverport." Lee undertook this project in 1837-1839, when the young lieutenant built jetties and revetments by Bloody Island, a dueling spot of the era. Also honored is the city's

Flood Control Association, organized in 1948. In the mid-1950's the Corps of Engineers began construction of the St. Louis Flood Control Project, which includes twenty-eight pumping stations, four miles of levees, and seven of floodwalls. It extends along the riverfront from Maline Creek at Chain of Rocks Road to Chippewa Street south of downtown.

Along the cobblestone levee near the Arch a rather discordant flotilla of ships and ship-like establishments is moored. These include a Burger King dubbed *Spirit of the River*, a McDonald's bereft of its arch so the symbol does not upstage the Arch, the Robert E. Lee restaurant, and the *U.S.S. Inaugural* (April-Oct 10-dusk) World War II minesweeper. You can also visit there three smallish excursion boats—*Becky Thatcher, Huck Finn* and *Tom Sawyer*—as well as the new (1991) *Belle of St. Louis*, a $7.5 million, 2,000 passenger vessel, with a forty-three note calliope. The ship also possesses the world's largest illuminated ship sign, complete with nine-foot-high red letters spelling out its name (for information and reservations on these four boats: 314-621-4040 and 800-878-7411). From the Fostaire Heliport (314-421-5440) helicopters depart which show you the river from altitudes even higher than the soaring Arch's lookout room.

The free Levee Line shuttle bus which runs along the waterfront travels through downtown out to the restored St. Louis Union Station, a shopping mall on 18th Street across from the 1930 Carl Milles "Meeting of the Waters" statuary fountain. The installation symbolizes the confluence of the Mississippi and Missouri. The line passes the main post office, whose philatelic store occupies The Trading Post, modeled after a frontier fur center. The nearby St. Louis City Hall, modeled after Paris' Hotel de Ville, houses in the Mayor's Reception Room murals of early day area scenes along the Mississippi. On the grounds stands a statue of Pierre Laclede, shown just after he landed to found the city.

River-oriented places within walking distance of the Arch include the Clarion Hotel's Top of the Riverfront, a revolving restaurant with views onto the waterway. Two murals in the new Metropolitan Square Building lobby depict historical and geographical journeys down the Mississippi. The offices of the *Waterways Journal*, 319 North 4th (312-241-7354), house a weekly established in 1887, published for the Mississippi basin's shipping industry; the paper is filled with news, lore and anecdotes about the river. The St. Louis Mercantile Library, a private library, is the crown jewel of the city's cultural institutions. Tucked away on the sixth floor of the old First National Bank Building, 510 Locust (314-621-0670), the institution, founded in 1846, offers a treasure trove of historical information, including the Herman T. Pott National Inland Waterways Library.

Farther afield, the Missouri Historical Society (Tu-Sun 9:30-4:45) in Forest Park includes the "Where Rivers Meet" exhibit, on the development of St. Louis. It contains steamboat whistles, a pirogue, and models of flatboats, keelboats, side- and stern-wheelers, and the pilothouse of the old *Golden Eagle*. The little-known Golden Eagle River Museum (May-Oct W-Sun 1-5; for directions: 314-846-9073) in off-the-beaten track Bee Tree Park occupies a mansion overlooking the Mississippi. Named for the last St. Louis-based passenger ship, the museum houses photos, steamer models, ship bells and whistles, memorabilia of the inland waterways, and the Oliver C. Parmely Library of maritime materials. The National Museum of Transport (9-5) in suburban Kirkwood, mainly a train museum, displays a few river-related items, including a 1933 diesel towboat used on the Mississippi. The new (1991) Riverlands Association (314-436-7487) in St. Louis attempts to promote historical and environmental activities along the nation's waterways.

As you proceed south on Broadway, away from downtown, the large red-and-white checkerboard sign indicates the home office of Ralston Purina Corporation. Farther on lies a less sophisticated food operation, the venerable Soulard Market, established about 1779 and by now the oldest public marketplace west of the Mississippi. Frenchman Antoine Soulard, who emigrated to escape the revolution in his home country, arrived at St. Louis by keelboat in 1795. Soon after, he married the sister of August Chouteau's wife. Appointed by the Spanish, who then controlled St. Louis, as Surveyer General of Upper Louisiana, Soulard received in payment for his services riverside land where he established fruit orchards. On the death of his wife Julia in 1845, twenty years after Soulard's demise, she willed part of her land for use as a public market, thus allowing the previously established operation to continue. After a tornado destroyed the 1896 market building (successor to the 1843 version) in 1928, the city of St. Louis, owner of the property, built a new structure based on the Foundling Hospital by Brunelleschi in Florence, Italy. The open-sided display areas are brimming with colorful produce sold at stands, some of them operated by families who have rented stalls there for three generations. On Geyer, just south of the market, stand old brick row houses, some restored, and also commercial buildings occupied by bistros, cafes, and saloons.

Before modern refrigeration, caves under the Soulard District were filled with ice harvested from the river in the winter, and used as storage areas in the summer to keep beer cool. Back in the mid-nineteenth century, a number of breweries operated in south St. Louis, but these days only Anheuser-Busch, the world's largest beer company, survives. The firm's home office and brewing complex sprawl over seventy city blocks just off Broadway not far from the Mississippi, whose waters the facility taps to process the 13 million barrels of brew produced here annually.

In 1855, soap manufacturer Eberhard Anheuser lent money to a firm which acquired a small, failing beer maker the investors named Bavarian Brewery. When the company went under two years later, Anheuser took over, and soon he hired his son-in-law, Adolphus Busch, to oversee the firm, which in 1880 was named The Anheuser-Busch Brewing Association.

Displays at the new Visitor Center trace the history of the brewing giant, while tours (May-Oct M-Sat 10-5, Nov-April M-Sat 9-4) take you past the 1868 Lyon School, closed in 1907 and later converted by the company into its executive offices. You'll also see the 1891 Victorian Gothic Brew House and Adolphus Busch's 1885 private stable, now home to the famous Budweiser Clydesdale horses. All three buildings are listed on the National Historic Register. The nearby thirty-one acre packaging plant produces more than five million bottles and nine million cans of beer a day. Whimsical fox figures perch at the corners of the so-called Bevo Building, their legs crossed, each image munching on a chicken leg and holding a mug of Bevo, the non-alcoholic beverage introduced by the firm during Prohibition.

In the park on Broadway, a statue depicts Civil War General Nathaniel Lyon, who captured Fort Jackson in May 1861 to put St. Louis in Union hands. Directly below stands the secretive Defense Mapping Agency. Surrounded by barbed wire, this high security facility employs 2,600 workers who produce 12.5 million aerospace charts annually and also maintain data on some 43,000 airports worldwide. Arsenal, which borders the agency, leads to the Corps of Engineers Service Base, established in 1882. Nearby stands the engine house for the brewery's Manufacturers Railway. Just beyond I-55, a few blocks away, two historic houses stand side by side. The Lemp Mansion, now a restaurant, was built in the early 1860's by John Adam Lemp, a German immigrant who in 1840 established what is believed to be St. Louis's first brewery. By 1870, it grew to become the city's largest beer company. Lemp's daughter, Hilda, married into the Pabst brewing clan of Milwaukee, but his other children died, one mysteriously and two apparent suicides. The firm then failed during Prohibition, and in 1922 the ten-block brewing complex was sold to International Shoe Company, whose white lettered "ISCO" still remains on a smokestack near the mansion.

The Chatillon-DeMenil Mansion (Tu-Sat 10-4) next door escaped destruction when the Landmarks Association persuaded highway planners to reroute I-55. The structure originated in 1863, when Frenchman Nicholas N. DeMenil renovated an 1848 four-room brick farmhouse built by woodsman and western guide Henri Chatillon. Chatillon, a hunter for the American Fur Company, served as guide for Francis Parkman, Jr., author of *The Oregon Trail* and other works on the nation's early development. After Chatillon's first wife, Sioux Indian squaw Bear Robe, died he married his cousin, Odile Lux, who owned land near the Mississippi on which they built their farmhouse. In 1945, DeMenil's descendants sold the mansion to Leon Hess, operator of Cherokee Cave, a south St. Louis tourist attraction once used to store Lemp and Minnehaha brand beers. In the 1960's Landmarks acquired and restored the old house, outfitting it with period furnishings. A pleasant restaurant by the garden serves lunch (Tu-Sat 11:30-2:30). Just to the west, Cherokee Street between Lemp and Jefferson Avenues is lined for six blocks with more than fifty antique and art shops.

A few blocks south, at 3835-7 South Broadway, Geandaugh House (314-771-5447)—once owned by William Clark's cousin and supposedly used in the early days to house boatmen—takes bed and breakfast guests. For other such accommodations in Missouri, River Country Bed and Breakfast is a reservation service: 314-965-4328 and 800-728-0721. In the 4400 block of Ohio Avenue near I-55 you'll find one of two survivors of the original twenty-six Indian mounds which dotted the landscape at St. Louis, known as "The Mound City." Farther on, Broadway passes a row of retire-ment houses on the bluff above the Mississippi, including the Altenheim, whose name recalls south St. Louis's once large German population. Small Bellerive Park, overlooking the river, occupies a site near where settlers farmed the Common Fields, medieval-type land arrangements which ran in long narrow strips from the river inland, so giving every occupant access to water, bottomlands, and wooded hills. Called "Vide Poche"—empty pocket—for its early-day lack of prosperity, the settlement took the name Carondelet in 1794, for the Spanish governor. In the mid-nineteenth century, an industrial area developed, including James B. Eads' shipyard where, as previously mentioned, he made the gunboats Union forces used to good advantage during the Civil War. Three years after St. Louis annexed Carondelet in 1870, Susan Blow established at the neighborhood's Des Peres School the nation's first public school kindergarden. The school took its name from River Des Peres, farther south on Broadway, so called as in 1700 Jesuit Fathers established at the waterway's mouth on the Mississippi the St. Francis Xavier mission, Missouri's first settlement. Indians from the Illinois side of the Mississippi joined the Jesuits, but the new town failed to take hold and by 1703, the missionaries abandoned the site. The Museum of Western Jesuit Missions (Tu and Th 10-3, Sun 1-4) in suburban Florissant houses displays on early religious activity in the Middle West.

Beyond River Des Peres, Broadway bends to the left into Grant Road. Here you enter Jefferson Barracks Park, established in 1950. The site originally served as an army post which occupied 1,700 acres of "common fields" conveyed in 1826 by Carondelet to the federal government for the base, which replaced Fort Bellefontaine on the Missouri (see the beginning of the St. Louis section). Throughout its 120 year existence, from early frontier days to World War II, Jefferson Barracks played a part in the nation's military activities. In 1829, troops from the base provided the first armed escort for Santa Fe Trail caravans. After the 1832 Black Hawk War, soldiers brought the defeated Indian leader to the post, where Washington Irving interviewed Black Hawk, and George Catlin, the famous Western artist, painted the captured chief's portrait. In 1843, Jefferson Barracks became the nation's largest military post, and in 1861, its troops fought in the Camp Jackson encounter, which saved Missouri from Southern control and probably secession. In 1912, the first successful parachute jump took place at the fort. In both World Wars, the base served as an induction center. Finally, in 1946, the government vacated the historic post, where Ulysses S. Grant, Jefferson Davis, Robert E. Lee, Zachary Taylor, William Tecumseh Sherman, and many other famous military figures have served over the years.

Apart from three mid-nineteenth century stone structures—a powder magazine, stable, and dwelling which housed civilian laborers—little remains from the fort's historic past. Along Hancock Road, however, the Air National Guard still uses a few century old verandah-fronted buildings. A turnoff at Scenic Circle, flanked by cannon barrels and a metal fence fragment, leads to a terrace with views onto the Mississippi. Farther on along Hancock, you'll reach the office and museum of the National Association of Civilian Conservation Corps Alumni (M-F 8-4). The 28,000 members served with the Depression-era public works agency, which from 1933 to 1942 developed 800 state parks, restored 4,000 historic structures, built 204 lodges and museums, planted three billion trees, constructed 27,000 miles of fences, and added any number of other improvements to the nation's infrastructure. More than three million men—and one woman, Mildred Blanche, who issued tools and supplies to CCC workers at a camp in Nebraska—at some 4,500 CCC camps participated in the program, which ended after World War II eliminated unemployment.

Just to the south lies Jefferson Barracks National Cemetery, established in 1866 as one of the nation's 110 such burial grounds. More than 100,000 veterans and their families are buried here. Row after long row of low, white grave markers parade across the rolling terrain there by the Mississippi, last resting place of many noteworthy souls: Zebulon Pike's two-year-old daughter, Fort Bellefontaine commander Major Russell Bissell, Colonel Thomas Hunt who fought at the April 1775 Battle of Lexington and Concord in Massachusetts, two German and five Italian World War II prisoners of war, 1,140 Confederate Civil War dead, as well as other warriors from yesteryear's battles. At the eastern edge of the cemetery, low, bright, white gravestones line the hillside, which falls toward the Mississippi. Beyond a row of trees, the river rolls on, eternal and oblivious to the dead heroes who fill the graveyard.

By Jefferson Barracks, Broadway becomes Telegraph Road. It received its name because in 1853 the first telegraph wires between St. Louis and Nashville were strung on trees along this route. Three years later, the New York and Mississippi Valley Printing Telegraph Company, established in 1851 at Rochester, New York, changed its name to Western Union, after the owners merged various eastern systems into a single firm and linked them with a line running to Missouri, so creating a communications union between the Mississippi Valley in the west and the east. Telegraph Road crosses the Meramec ("catfish" in Indian language) River and then reaches Highway 61 (also 67 here), the River Road through southern Missouri. Between here and New Madrid, Highway 61 for the most part follows the route of El Camino Real, laid out by the Spanish in 1789 on the traces of an age-old Indian trail and hunting path used by early-day traders. Along the historic trail passed Sac and Fox, Sioux, Missouri, Osage and other tribesmen, and over it pioneers hauled provisions from trading posts. Along the route trappers carried pelts to fur buyers, on the path Audubon roamed while bird watching, and, years later, Civil War troops trod the well-traveled way. In 1808 Territorial Governor Meriwether Lewis, Clark's exploring partner, designated the "Royal Road," or King's Highway—one of the oldest thoroughfares in the Mississippi Valley—a public way and ordered it re-marked and cleared to a width of twenty-five feet: a land-based version of the 1930's Corps of Engineers nine foot channel project for the Mississippi. The Kingshighway Streets which still exist in St. Louis, Cape Girardeau, Sikeston, and other cities, approximate the Camino Real route.

Just west of Imperial, south of St. Louis, lies Mastodon State Park, which contains a new (1988) museum (M-Sat 9-4:30, Sun 12-4:30) featuring displays of 12,000 year old bones and a full scale ten foot tall replica of the prehistoric beast. Mastodon bones first surfaced on this site, listed on the National Register, in the early nineteenth century, followed in 1839 by the initial excavation of the elephant-like creatures. Scientist Albert C. Koch, who thought he had discovered a new species, named it the "Missouri Leviathan." However, the find was simply a plain, every-day, garden-variety, 12,000 year old mastodon. The British Museum in London still displays a skeleton made of bones acquired from Koch which the institution correctly identified as mastodon pieces. During the early 1900's, workers excavated bones from more than sixty mastodons, and in 1979, archeologists discovered in the stone beds—an ancient swampy mineral lick where the beasts often became mired in the mud and died—Clovis-type spear points which established for the first time the existence of humans in North America contemporaneous with the mastodons. A short trail leads from the museum out to the Kimmswick Bone Bed, where scientists unearthed the skeletal leavings and spear points.

A few miles south lies the hamlet of Kimmswick (population: under 300), founded by German immigrant Theodore Kimm in 1859. The town, which enjoyed both rail and river transportation, thrived until around the turn of the century, when the new-fangled horseless carriages on new roads passed the village by. Kimmswick dozed and decayed away—in the late 1930's Ward Dorrance, in *Where the Rivers Meet*, wrote of "tiny Kimmswick, whose inhabitants complain of its chief charm—green and leaf-smothered torpor"—until 1970 when Lucianna Gladney Ross, daughter of a Seven-Up Company founder, led a restoration effort. This revitalized the salvaged but still vintage village, which evokes a late nineteenth century Mississippi River settlement. Preservationists moved six venerable log houses to the town, including a c.1770 trading post and stagecoach stop, frequented by Ulysses S. Grant and his fellow officers from Jefferson Barracks, now the Old House Restaurant. These supplemented Kimmswick's original buildings, among the oldest of them the 1866 Ruess-Terry House at the corner of Market and 3d. Just after the road into Kimmswick crosses Rock Creek, lies a red granite boulder erected in 1917 to commemorate El Camino Real. Down on Front Street stands the c. 1912 post office, a delightful relic with metal "P.O." initials on the antique counter window grill. Just to the south a new, characterless, concrete bridge, by the rickety 1874 iron span across Rock Creek, leads out past a row of attractive summer resort houses to a marina where the Mississippi, hidden from view in Kimmswick itself, appears. On the river at Kimmswick Windsor Harbor once operated, supposedly named for a federal gunboat sunk there during the Civil War. As late as the mid-1970's, locals claimed they could see the wreck during low water.

South of Kimmswick lies fancifully named Herculaneum, so called by Moses Austin when he established the town in 1808. Smoke from his lead smelters there evoked the fumes emitted by Italy's Mount Vesuvius, whose lava covered the nearby ancient Herculaneum in 79 A.D. In 1797, Austin obtained a concession from Spanish authorities to extract lead at Mine à Breton, later Potosi, named for the Mexican silver mining town San Luis Potosi. Here, a Frenchman named Breton had discovered the deposits in 1774 while hunting in the area. In 1799 Austin, the area's first mining entrepreneur, moved his family into Durham Hall, an elegant manor house which recalled those in Virginia, where ten years before he had operated lead mines. Like Daniel Boone and others who settled west of the Mississippi in the late eighteenth century, Austin gave up his American citizenship to become a Spanish subject. Austin founded Herculaneum—where in 1809 he built a shot tower on a bluff overlooking the Mississippi—to serve as a shipping point for lead mined at Mine à Breton (Potosi). In May, 1820, Austin left Potosi on horseback for San Antonio, in the Spanish province of "Tejas", where he sought permission to open the lands for settlement. Austin's return trip to Missouri proved adventurous, for he was attacked by panthers, lived on roots and berries, swam streams, and faced other rigors which so exhausted the pioneer businessman and promoter that he died of pneumonia on June 10, age fifty-nine, in Potosi, where he is buried. His son, Stephen, however, carried out Moses Austin's idea, and in 1823 established Texas' first American town, San Felipe de Austin, settled primarily by Missourians. So began what became the state of Texas.

The mining industry started by Moses Austin originated in an area which developed into the world's largest lead mining district. Scattered across the landscape, not far west of the Mississippi, lie such towns as Valles Mines, Mineral Point, Leadwood, Rivermines, Leadington, Old Mines, and others which evoke the area's lead extraction operations. Highway 67, which branches off from 61 south of Herculaneum, passes through De Soto, named for the discoverer of the Mississippi—the nation's population center in the 1980-1990 decade, the first time that point lay west of the Mississippi—and continues south into the heart of the lead district. At tiny Mine La Motte on the southern edge of the district, the French established the area's first lead mine in 1720, exploited by Phillipe François Renault, an agent of France's Company of the Indies. In 1988 at Flat River the Missouri Mines State Historic Site (Tu-Sat 10-4; Sun 12-6, to 5 in winter) opened, a lead mining museum installed in the powerhouse of a former St. Joe Lead Company mill complex. At nearby Bonne Terre— where Mansion Hill Country Inn (314-731-5003) offers bed and breakfast—the National Register-listed Bonne Terre Mine (9-5) operates tours through the world's largest excavated caverns, where mining operations ceased in 1962. Ten years later, all lead mining in the original lead belt ended, but the Doe Run Company, the nation's largest lead producer, a subsidiary of Fluor Corporation, works six mines southwest of the old lead area. These mines can annually produce about 240,000 tons, nearly half the total capacity in Missouri, which supplies more than 90 percent of the nation's lead. Doe Run also operates a smelter at Herculaneum, called "Herky" by its residents. This facility succeded the 1892 facility built by the St. Joe Lead Company, formed in 1864, when it began to develop the river settlement into a company town. A plaque at the local Methodist church in "Herky" notes that "In 1798 John Clark, pioneer Methodist minis-ter preaching from a boat, gave the first Protestant sermon west of the Mississippi River at the mouth of Joachim Creek near present Herculaneum." The Dunklin and Fletcher Memorial Park overlooking the Mississippi—near where three shot towers on the bluffs formed ammunition balls by dropping molten lead through gates into the river—honors Daniel Dunklin, a governor (1832-1836) known as "the father of Missouri's public schools," and Thomas C. Fletcher, the state's first native-born governor (1865-1869), from Herculaneum. The riverside cliffs near "Herky" served an unusual function in 1919 when the St. Louis Zoo, wishing to build its concrete bear pits to resemble real habitats, took rock patterns from the limestone bluffs by the waterway.

Crystal City, another former company town, lies on the Mississippi not far south of Herculaneum. In 1868, a group of Englishmen visited Plattin Creek to examine the high quality sand rock which they planned to use for making glass. A Detroit capitalist bought the silica deposits from the English, and in 1871 started the American Plate Glass Company at New Detroit, later named Crystal City. The operation greatly impressed poet Walt Whitman who, after his 1879 visit to the city, wrote a friend: "What do you think I find manufactured out here and of a kind the clearest and largest, best and most finished and luxurious in the world? Plate glass!" In 1895, the Pittsburgh Plate Glass Company acquired the entire town for $25,000 and expanded the works to a 230 acre manufacturing complex. At its peak in the 1940's and 1950's, the new complex employed more than 4,500 workers, a considerably larger force than the 275 at the factory, which produced two million square feet of glass a week, when it closed at the end of 1990. Diagonally across from the former main office at Mississippi Avenue and Bailey Road stands the bank once run by Warren Bradley, father of Rhodes Scholar and New Jersey Senator Bill Bradley, who grew up in Crystal City.

The River Road winds its way south through attractive hilly countryside. Near Sainte Genevieve the road reaches the dusty Mississippi Lime Company plant, one of the world's largest producers of the material, which is extracted from limestone quarried at nearby deposits. Sainte Genevieve, founded in the second quarter of the eighteenth century (the exact date remains unknown), claims to be the oldest permanent settlement west of the Mississippi. The town began as a lead shipping port, salt center, and agricultural area where French pioneers farmed "Le Grand Champ," the Big Field in the fertile floodplain. After the 1763 Treaty of Paris transferred the Illinois Country east of the Mississippi from France to England, a few residents of the early 1700's French river villages—Cahokia, Kaskaskia, Fort de Chartres, Prairie du Rocher (all still exist: see the Illinois chapter)—left the area newly controlled by the English and crossed the waterway to live in Sainte Genevieve. It remained French in spirit although by then the town was, in fact, located in Spanish territory.

After a flood damaged the original settlement in 1785, the townspeople moved to a higher area four miles northwest, and the new town soon began to develop. In his journal for March 25, 1797, Moses Austin noted that "When the Lead Mines are properly worked, and the Salt Springs advantageously manag'd, St. Genevieve will be a place of as Much Wealth as any on the

Mississippi." For a time, in fact, the town boasted a population larger than St. Louis. That, however, was in the 1770's, an era during which originated some of the still surviving French colonial houses that give Sainte Genevieve its pronounced old world flavor. Some thirty late eighteenth and twenty-five early nineteenth century structures remain in Sainte Genevieve. Among them are six restored showplaces open to visitors (others open during festival and special times), including the c. 1770 Bolduc House (April-Nov M-Sat 10-4, Sun 11-5), regarded as the nation's most authentically presented Creole (colonial) residence, the architecturally distinctive 1770 Amoureaux House (10-5), the 1790 Green Tree Tavern (Sat and Sun 10-5), and the 1818 Felix Valle State Historic Site (M-Sat 10-4, Sun 12-5), built by Philadelphia merchant Jacob Philipson, believed Missouri's first Jewish settler (1808). He later sold it in 1824 to Jean Baptiste Valle, the city's last civil commandant. In 1790 John Price, operator of a Mississippi ferry boat constructed the first brick building, now a restaurant, west of the Mississippi. According to tradition, the bricks used for the structure—foreclosed on and auctioned off in 1806 by sheriff Henry Dodge, later U.S. Senator from Wisconsin, the first sheriff's sale west of the Mississippi—served as ballast on ships which sailed from France. The state's first ferry, 1780, crossed the Meramec near the Mississippi south of St. Louis. Missouri's newest ferry, which started operations in 1991, connects Sainte Genevieve with its sister French cities across the Mississippi in Illinois (M-Sat 6-dusk, Sun 7-dusk).

The Historical Museum (April-Oct 9-4, Nov-March 12-4), in the 1821 courthouse, contains an iron safe from the local bank supposedly robbed by Jesse James on May 26, 1873. It also houses birds believed mounted by John James Audubon, who lived in Sainte Genevieve in 1810 when he started a store which soon failed. On Du Bourg Place stands an 1880 Catholic church (6-6), the third sanctuary there where Missouri's first congregation worshipped. Along the square's south side ran the state's earliest European-built road, a route used to transport lead and later (1851) converted to a forty-two mile plank road, the longest highway of its type in the U.S. On the wood way, oxcarts hauled ore to the Mississippi from Iron Mountain, to the west, until completion of the railroad from the Mountain to St. Louis in 1858. On the flank of the Rozier store, Third and Merchant (ancestor Ferdinand Rozier, the town's first mayor [1827], was Audubon's business partner in the ill-fated venture), a mural appears depicting an Indian, soldier, and fiddler. These symbolize Saint Genevieve's past, populated in the early days by personages who now lay at rest in the nearby cemetery. This enclave constitutes the state's oldest burial ground, used from 1787 to 1833; French-inscribed tombstones fill the graveyard.

Those early settlers brought to the area "La Guignolée," a still-performed festive New Year's Eve revel featuring costumed roving musicians, a ritual portrayed in a mural at the post office. The new (November 1988) cedar-fragrant tourist office, which is called the Great River Road Visitor Center and occupies a French colonial-style structure, houses a gallery with attractive drawings of old Sainte Genevieve by regional artist Roscoe Misselhorn. A half dozen or so antique stores in town offer leftovers from the past. The Sainte Genevieve Winery sells wines named after the old local dwellings, some of them bed and breakfast establishments, including Captains Retreat (314-883-7108), Creole House (314-883-7171), Dr. Walter Fenwick House (314-883-2344), Inn St. Gemme Beauvais (314-883-5744), Merchant Street Inn (314-883-2233), Southern Hotel (314-883-3493), and Steiger House (314-883-5881).

The road south out of Sainte Genevieve takes you past Saint Marys, gateway to an odd little Illinois enclave west of the Mississippi called Kaskaskia Island (see the Illinois chapter). This is an isolated and sparsely populated lowland near the even lower lands—now under water—occupied by Illinois's first capital in drier days before the river flooded and washed away the original settlement. At a salt spring off to the west, toward the hamlet of River aux Vases, Missouri's first white settlement developed. French pioneers from Kaskaskia, then east of the Mississippi, established a salt works there around 1700. The operation continued for more than a century. Just past Saint Marys, the road enters Perry County, which boasts more than 10 percent of Missouri's five thousand known caves, more than any other state. A whole series of caverns, openings, and sink holes hollow the earth beneath the county, which calls itself "the sinkhole capital of the world," a seemingly unchallenged claim. The openings result when groundwater dissolves limestone or dolomite rock at or near the ground's surface, referred to in such fragile areas as karst terrain. In *Persimmon Hill: A Narrative of Old St. Louis and the Far West* William Clark Kennerly, nephew of explorer and territorial governor William Clark, told of how at "The Barrens"—the Catholic seminary in Perryville, named for the once treeless area near the town covered only with prairie grass—priests in the 1830's often took students to "a wonderful cave with many subterranean vaults and chasms" where the upperclassmen would catch bats and release them in the dorm when a new boy arrived. The 1837 pink-beige St. Mary's of the Barrens church—a one-third size duplicate of the Vincentian mother sanctuary in Rome—dates from the same year the Missouri legislature chartered the seminary. It is believed to be the oldest institution of higher learning west of the Mississippi.

Although the seminary—which educated the first bishops of St. Louis, Pittsburgh, Buffalo, and New Orleans—closed in 1986, the now student-less buildings house four unusual one-room museums (tours Sat and Sun 1 and 3, weekdays by request 9-4:30: 314-547-8343). The tour begins in the deserted library, where colorful window panes bear marks of early day printers. The Estelle Doheny Museum occupies a wood paneled room crammed with glass paperweights, porcelain, antique furniture, jade, crystal and other such decorative items. The nearby Rare

Book Room houses printed treasures, including a two-inch high German language Bible reader, a first edition of Sir Thomas More's *Utopia*, believed once owned by England's Henry VIII, and the Doheny collection of more than eight hundred first editions of American classics, some autographed. The Archives Room contains displays relating to the seminary's history, and the Bishop Sheehan Memorial Museum includes Asian items—hand-carved teak furniture, ivory, and jade—collected by the missionary when he served in China in the early 1930's.

The Register-listed Faherty House, the county's oldest dwelling (the original section dates from 1828, the later one from 1855), serves as the Perry County Museum. In Perryville, Highway 61, the River Road, bears the name Kingshighway, a reminder that along this route ran the old Spanish Camino Real. Just before you reach Longtown, seven miles south of Perryville, you'll pass on the west side of the road the tin-roofed, brick, Methodist York Chapel (1834), the second oldest church of that denomination west of the Mississippi. At Longtown a back road to the east, Highway D, takes you to Brazeau, where yet another early sanctuary, the boxy brick 1852 Presbyterian church (the congregation began in 1819) bears diamond-shaped metal stud pins. Inside, pressed tin walls and ceilings lend antiquated touches to the structure.

At Frohna, a few miles south of Brazeau, you'll reach the first of three small towns established in the late 1830's by Lutheran immigrants who left Germany to find religious freedom in the New World. In 1838, more than six hundred Lutherans sailed from Bremen to New Orleans, then made their way up the Mississippi to Missouri where the religious refugees bought some 4,500 acres of land in Perry County. Just outside Frohna, the Saxon Lutheran Memorial, listed on the National Register, recalls the settlers' early days. The memorial, on eleven and a half acres farmed by the Bergt family from 1839 to 1957, includes log buildings and the original farmhouse, filled with original furnishings. Among them can be found a Murphy-style folding wall bed brought from Germany in 1839. Down Highway C a short distance stands "Die Kleine Schule," as a sign over the door states. This "little school," which operated from 1898 to the 1960's, now preserves old photos, antique desks, and other reminders of how one-room schools appeared in the old days. Just east of Frohna lies "Stadt (city) Altenburg," as a welcome sign says. Neat frame houses and a certain lost-in-time ambiance typify the town, whose two hundred and eighty inhabitants make Altenburg the metropolis of the old Lutheran enclave near the Mississippi. Nestled under a protective shed is the original 1839 Register-listed log cabin that served as the first Evangelical Lutheran seminary, later moved to St. Louis. Across the way stands the 1867 Trinity Lutheran church. The original 1845 Trinity Church, just down the street, served for a century after the new sanctuary opened as the "Grosse Schule," and now the "big school" contains a small museum devoted to local history. The Old Timers Agricultural Museum (April-Oct 10-5) exhibits more than six hundred pieces of functioning antique farm equipment and also offers craft demonstrations. Trics, just outside town, dishes up tasty German-style meals.

Highway A east from Altenburg leads to Wittenberg, a remote Mississippi River settlement with a population listed as four, although even that modest claim may be overstated. Mobile homes by the waterway house the few residents, while the diminutive tin-sided post office, open two hours a day, seems the best-kept building in town. A metal plaque in the thickly wooded riverside recalls that Lutheran immigrants arrived at the Saxon Landing Place here in 1839 to establish their new homeland. Back up Highway A a short distance, a dirt and gravel road (it begins by the old "66" gas station sign) leads south through the woods along the Mississippi, past the nearly 3,700 foot white and red pipeline bridge. Supposedly the world's longest such span, it carries natural gas across the river on the Texas to Chicago route.

Farther on, you'll come to an overlook with a splendid view onto the Mississippi and historic Tower Rock, which rises just before you in the waterway. Past this famous river feature, lined with horizontal rock strata, the mighty Mississippi swirls and eddies as if agitated by the solid barrier that partially blocks its flow. Ever since Marquette and Joliet floated by the formation in 1673, the rock has been one of the Mississippi's best known landmarks. Artists portrayed it, riverboat pilots cursed it, travelers admired it. In 1871 President Ulysses S. Grant ordered that engineers clearing the channel preserve the rock for possible use as a bridge pylon. The order still stands, but not the bridge, and there towers Tower Rock, proud and solitary, as ever, in the great river.

Highway A takes you west from the river back to Highway 61 at Uniontown. A mile south is Appleton, a picturesque village on rustic Apple Creek, where the remains of an 1824 gristmill lie near a rustling waterfall. On the main—the only—street, stand the disused "Jos. F. Schnurbusch General Merchandise Store Since 1909," as the window sign states, and the 1821 Shoultz-McLane House. Travelers and Indians, including the Shawnee, frequented the house in the old days. Among them was the famous Tecumseh, whose main village, with French-style vertical log buildings, occupied a hill west of town until the tribe moved farther west in 1825. Five years later, President Andrew Jackson signed a bill authorizing the removal of another tribe, the Cherokee, from their homelands in North Carolina, Georgia, and Tennessee to reservations in the west. During the winter of 1838-1839, more than 13,000 Cherokee began a 1,200 mile trek along the "Trail of Tears," so called because the forced march killed a quarter of the Indians. In January, 1838, a band reached the Mississippi, which they crossed in bitter cold weather to land at Moccasin Springs, located in present day Trail of Tears State

Park, where a monument marks the supposed grave of Princess Otahki, who died after the crossing. The 3,265 acre enclave, Missouri's only state park located on the Mississippi, encompasses the Indian Creek Wild Area, a hardwood forest crossed by the ten mile Peewah ("come follow in this direction") trail, as well as two overlooks on the bluffs, which tower more than 175 feet above the river. A Visitor Center (9-5) contains exhibits relating to the forced resettlement of the Cherokee. Tucked away on County Road 638, which branches off from W southwest of the park, is the Black Forest (mainly for groups; open by appointment: 314-335-0899), an 1100 acre wooded spread with the German-type villages of Arnsberg and New Hanover. On W, the 5-H Exotic Animal Ranch (April-Nov), a supplier to circuses and zoos, maintains some six hundred head of camels, giraffes, and other specimens not normally found along the Mississippi.

Farther west, beyond Interstate 55, lies Jackson, with the National Register-listed 1840's Oliver House (May-Dec Sun 2:30-5), home of the woman who helped design Missouri's state flag. The 1905 Mueller Haus (314-243-7427) offers bed and breakfast. The solid stone courthouse, topped by a green dome sporting a quartet of clocks, stands at a high point chosen as the county seat site in 1814. From Jackson the colorful St. Louis, Iron Mountain & Southern Railway operates (mid-April to late Oct Sat and Sun, 314-243-1688), an old fashioned steam engine-drawn train which makes excursions to Gordonville, ten miles south. The line began in 1858 with a route between St. Louis and Pilot Knob, south of Flat River in the lead belt, where the Iron Mountain yielded ore. After the Civil War, the railroad built additional lines south through Missouri and into Arkansas. In 1877, rail tycoon Jay Gould gained control of the company, which expanded further until 1917 when the Missouri Pacific acquired the Iron Mountain road. The present excursion train, inaugurated in 1986, follows a branch of the line which ran to Belmont, Missouri, located on the Mississippi southeast of Sikeston.

About seven miles west of Jackson, the Bollinger Mill State Historic Site (Tu-Sat 10-4, Sun 12-5) includes an 1867 four-story grist mill and the 140 foot Burfordville Covered Bridge (1868). These make for an extremely photogenic duo at the Whitewater River. Between Jackson and Cape Girardeau on the Mississippi to the east lies Old McKendree Chapel (reached from Jackson via Old Cape Road and then left on Baimbridge which becomes County 620 out to the chapel about a mile on). The 1819 Methodist sanctuary, the oldest Protestant place of worship west of the Mississippi, occupies a pleasant wooded site slightly marred by noise from vehicles speeding along nearby I-55. A Methodist congregation began at the site in 1809 under the leadership of Bishop William McKendree. Services continued here until after the Civil War, when the church split into Northern and Southern factions. Parishioners gradually abandoned the chapel, which was later restored in the 1920's. Across the road lies an old hilltop cemetery, its gravestones standing along a ridge in a fixed, orderly arrangement which contrasts with the nearby interstate's rushing, erratic traffic flow.

A few miles to the east, beyond the interstate, Cape Girardeau occupies an attractive, hilly area by the Mississippi. Around 1720, Jean Baptiste Girardot, an ensign with French forces stationed at Kaskaskia across the river in Illinois, established a trading post on a rock promontory at the north edge of the present city, which took his name. Some seventy years later, another Frenchman, Louis Lorimier, arrived in the area to establish the first permanent settlement. The Spanish, who then controlled the territory, appointed Lorimier—married to a half-Shawnee woman—their local agent to deal with the Indians. The Spanish gave him the west bank of the Mississippi down to the Arkansas River. Near the waterfront, Lorimier—who wore his hair Indian-style in braids so long he used them to whip his horse—built La Casa Roja, the Red House, a residence and trading post which soon became a gathering place for whites and

Indians, a haven for travelers, a social center, and military headquarters for the District of Cape Girardeau, one of five units in Upper Louisiana established by the Spanish.

One visitor was a certain Captain Samuel Bradley, who during the French and Indian War in the 1760's had pursued Lorimier and grabbed his legs when the Frenchman started to escape into a French outpost. As Lorimier squirmed away, his trousers and moccasins slipped off into Bradley's hands. These trophies of war stood Bradley in good stead years later when he visited Lorimier at Cape Girardeau to return the leggings and shoes, at which time the Frenchman turned Spanish official presented his former adversary with a land grant. After the Louisiana Purchase, the United States Land Commission rejected Lorimier's Spanish land title, so clouding property ownership and retarding Cape Girardeau's development, which resumed in 1836 when, twenty-four years after the official's death, the federal government finally recognized his title.

Because the city occupies the first high point on the river from Cape to Cairo, where the Ohio enters the Mississippi, the Missouri town enjoyed an advantageous location as a port. The swampy riverside lowlands to the south impeded east-west traffic to and from the river. Goods and people funnelled through Cape, whose elevations made it a strategic point on the river during the Civil War, when Union troops occupied the city. In 1859, a Cape shipyard built the *Red Rover*, a commercial sidewheel steamer which the United States Navy converted in 1862 into its first hospital ship.

Memories of Cape's early days and later development linger in the pleasantly laid-back, hilly river town. By the Mississippi, a marker indicates the site of Lorimier's Red House, while a rough, red boulder memorializes El Camino Real, the Spanish road which ran along the river from New Madrid, to the south, to St. Louis. The Register-listed Old St. Vincent's stands adjacent, an 1853 Gothic-style structure, designated in 1977 a "Chapel of

Ease"—no longer a church but a cultural and religious center. Next door lies the exotic-looking 1928 B'nai Israel Synagogue, a Midwestern version of mideastern architecture. A few blocks away, on South Spanish, the 1883 Register-listed Glenn House (April-Dec W-Sat 1-4) includes a River Room, complete with navigation instruments, maps, a steamer whistle, and a model, complete with electric lights, of the first Cape Girardeau steamboat. A short distance away you'll find earthworks of Civil War Fort D, one of four such Union strongholds (the three others no longer exist). On a hill by the 1929 bridge survives the 1843 St. Vincent's College, formerly a seminary, whose buildings suffered damage in January, 1848 when the steamer *Seabird* caught fire, setting off an explosion of its cargo of powder. Local Congressman William B. Vandiver first introduced a bill to authorize the bridge in 1901. In a speech two years earlier at Philadelphia, Vandiver, who resembled fellow Missourian Mark Twain, questioned the accuracy of a previous speaker by saying, "I'm from Missouri and you've got to show me"—believed to be the origin of the "Show Me State" nickname.

Back toward the center, at the foot of both Broadway and Themis, openings give access to the waterfront beyond the concrete flood wall, constructed by the Corps of Engineers in 1964. By the massive Themis Gate, lines indicate high water marks in 1844, 1943, and 1973, with a black line near the top labeled "possible high water." The Port Cape Girardeau at the corner of Themis and Water occupies the 1830's building where Ulysses S. Grant established his local Civil War headquarters. Old photos of the river, the town, and steamboats decorate the restaurant's brick walls. Outside on the flank, an old sign, renovated in 1980, advertises Coca-Cola "3¢ plain" and, for big spenders, 5¢, the more expensive version containing a stimulant later banned. A mural at Water and Themis and a new one (1989) at Broadway and Spanish depict river scenes and sights around the city. An even newer (1991) mural on the river side of the flood wall portrays a steamboat and historical figures associated with Cape. At Main and Themis, one end of the first long distance telephone call west of the Mississippi took place. It connected Cape with Jackson on December 18, 1877. At Spanish and Themis, from 1878 to 1960, the nation's oldest millinary store (founded in 1859) in continuous service operated.

Crowning the crest of a steep, terraced hill is the 1854 Court of Common Pleas. You can reach it by steps which comprise the first concrete construction in Missouri outside St. Louis and Kansas City, with the cement shipped from England as ballast. From the courthouse, where Confederate prisoners languished in the basement, a view extends across the angular rooftops clustered downtown and out onto the river. The area behind the building served over the years as a produce market, slave auction, and site of religious services. Nearby, on Broadway, the 1868 Turnverein (gymnastics) and later Opera House, on the site of the 1806 hotel, one of the earliest west of the Mississippi, now contains the Royal N'Orleans Restaurant. The 1925 *Southeast Missourian* office across the street is a splendid tile-bedecked Moorish-style structure. It stands where in 1793 the Spanish established the first organized government west of the Mississippi. On the building's flank, two brightly colored tile murals depict "The Art of Printing" and "Gathering & Disseminating News," the latter portraying such Cape visitors as preacher Billy Sunday, bandmaster John Phillip Sousa, and Harry Truman. The Cape River Heritage Museum (March-Dec Sat 11-4 or by appointment: 314-334-0405), located in the former police and fire department building, contains the Lorimier Room, with displays on the town's early history, a room with murals and Cape's nineteenth century development, and the River Room, which includes a video of travel on the Mississippi.

Farther afield, the Old Lorimier Cemetery includes the tomb of the "first settler and commandant of the post of Cape Girardeau under the Government of Spain," and the grave of Lorimier's wife, Charlotte (1808), whose marker is the city's oldest man-made object. A cousin of George Washington also rests in the burial ground. Off to the west, in the northwest corner of Capaha Park (Capaha: "downstream," the name of an Indian tribe), the display rose garden includes nearly two hundred varieties of the flower. At the park's southwest entrance stand columns topped by eagle figures taken from steamers run by the Eagle Packet Company, which always operated one ship named for the city.

Across hilly terrain to the north spreads the attractive campus of Southeast Missouri State University, known as SEMO. Its centerpiece, classic-style Academic Hall, resembles a state capitol. Opposite stands the 1966 Kent Library, which houses a splendid 1973 mural by art professor Jake K. Wells depicting such aspects of the city's history as the steamer *Cape Girardeau* at the landing, piled with cotton bales, and a cast of characters including Indians, farmers, pioneers, and preachers. Off the main lobby, display cases by the Rare Book Room contain a few of the more than 10,000 items which comprise the William Faulkner collection given to the University in 1988 by Louis Daniel Brodsky. Upstairs, thirty-seven glass panels from the original library bear printers' marks and scenes which commemorate the art of bookmaking, while others show a Mississippi packet, Mark Twain, and river explorer Jacques Marquette. The University Museum (M-F 8-12, 1-5) in Memorial Hall contains southwestern Indian arts and crafts, a collection of military items, and eleven statues copied from masterpieces in European museums and then exhibited at the 1904 St. Louis World's Fair.

North of town at Cape Park lies the city's most affecting site. In a tiny enclave above the river, a plaque atop a knoll recalls: "On this rock promontory, which originally projected into the river and formed a cape, Ensign Girardot, a Frenchman, established a trading post about 1733. From this site Cape Girardeau took its name." Although trees partially block the river view, directly ahead you can see the Mississippi, while from the road below the panorama widens. From the north, the waterway curves in with a majestic sweep, and as it passes before you the brown water ripples gently and emits a pleasant rustle. Apart from the train tracks and a green navigation signal, no signs of human habitation appear. Here you can linger alone with the Mississippi and the distant past at the cape where Cape Girardeau began.

At Cape Girardeau—where the Olive Branch (314-335-0449) provides bed and breakfast—the Mississippi, emerging from the wooded bluffs and limestone cliffs which intermittently border the waterway for many miles to the north, begins to widen and enter the flood plains which extend down to the Gulf of Mexico. Off to the west, the Ozarks abruptly descend toward the flat valley lowland, a bottomland made habitable in Missouri by an extensive network of drainage canals. Geologists call this area bordering the river the Mississippi Embayment. It was once a giant finger of the Gulf which in ancient times reached this far north until sediment deposited by the Mississippi gradually filled in the huge inlet. Beneath the Embayment lies a continental rift called the Mississippi Structural Trough, a fault which unleashed the 1811-1812 New Madrid earthquakes, named for the Missouri river town to the south. The 1845 "Report on the Submerged Lands of the State of Missouri" strikingly describes the major change in the lay of the land which alters the nature of the Mississippi River valley from here to the waterway's mouth:

> It is a remarkable fact, that there is a chain of low, level and marshy lands, commencing at the City of Cape Girardeau, in Missouri, and extending to the Gulf of Mexico; and between these two points there is not a rock landing except at the small town of Commerce, on the west side of the Mississippi River; there is, furthermore, only one ridge of

> high land from Commerce to be met with on the west side of said river, which is at Helena, in Arkansas.

While the Upper Mississippi's configuration necessitated locks and dams to regulate the flow and facilitate navigation, the Lower Mississippi, which borders a flood plain that often tempted its roaming waters, requires barriers to contain the tempestuous river, lined along its lower banks by some 2,200 miles of levees. The levee line on the west bank begins just south of Cape Girardeau and, except for gaps where tributaries enter the Mississippi, extends unbroken almost to the Gulf of Mexico. The longest continuous levee line in the world starts near Pine Bluff, Arkansas, and follows the south bank of the Arkansas River to its mouth, then continues down the Mississippi to near Venice, Louisiana, a distance of 650 miles. Also on the east bank a long line of levees, occasionally broken by bluffs, rises.

As you leave Cape Girardeau on Interstate 55, just south of Highway 74, the interstate crosses the Headwaters Diversion Canal, one of the many facilities which form the intricate network of levees, reservoirs, floodways, dikes, bank revetments, cutoffs, pumping plants, floodwalls, flood gates, and other constructions built to control the Mississippi and its tributaries. The exit for Scott City takes you east to Highway N. This road leads south to Commerce, the place where, as the "Submerged Lands" report quoted above noted, one would find the only west bank river access point south of Cape a century and a half ago. This advantage, however, hardly resulted in any lasting prosperity for Commerce, whose name mocks its present day inactivity. Virtually no commerce transpires there, for the only commercial establishments are auto garages. The hamlet, however, also boasts a diminutive white wood post office, decorated inside with old photos of the two streets, Main and Tywappity. (An Indian name, Tywappity designates the bottoms located in Scott County in Missouri north of the Ohio's mouth.) Laid out in 1822,

Commerce at one time enjoyed a certain affluence, with the county seat, moved there in 1864, a population of 600—three times the current number—and twelve stores, four hotels, two stave manufacturers, a pottery, a steam gristmill, a newspaper, and two churches. Now the village seems strangely vacant and forlorn. The three-story red brick school building, closed down, lacks life, and the city hall—a white frame, tin-roofed building, reminiscent of architecture in the Caribbean, raised on concrete blocks—stands alone and seemingly inactive in a park. A dirt road leads down to the Mississippi, about a hundred yards from town, which for some reason distances itself from the waterway. Some geologists believe that at this point, in ancient times, the Mississippi's mouth entered the Gulf over a 300 foot waterfall. Now the waters flow calmly past the unpeopled shore. Prime riverfront land lies empty at Commerce, but so does much else there. Other towns and villages and even hamlets maintain a certain presence by the river. Commerce, set back from the shore and laid-back in attitude, seems oblivious to the Mississippi, as does the waterway to it. Of all the settlements along the great river Commerce, more than any other, somehow possesses the feeling of an isolated frontier town, lost and lonely and forgotten in the vast reaches of the Mississippi Valley.

Highway N, a narrow blacktop, takes you south through little populated farm country, past turnoffs to the Cargill Buffalo's Island grain terminal, and then to Bunge's similar facility at Price's Landing, an early day shipping point. Farther on lies Charleston, a Southern-type town with old houses on tree shaded streets garnished with dogwoods and azaleas. Here, it might be said, begins the greater Mississippi River Delta area, whose heartland lies in Mississippi, known for cotton and imbued with an ambiance typical of the South. Although a few early settlers planted that crop, before 1924 the Missouri delta region grew mainly corn and wheat. A boll weevil infestation farther south the year before induced Southern planters to establish cotton in lower Missouri. The first settlers arrived in the area in the early nineteenth century. Abraham Bird, who settled at the site of Cairo, on the Illinois side, established in 1802 Birds Point, soon an active transfer port for freighters on the Ohio and Mississippi. After the Civil War a "transfer boat" outfitted with train tracks ferried "Cat" (Cairo, Arkansas and Tennessee line) cars from the landing across the Mississippi. An auto ferry later operated at Birds Point, reached in 1920 by the first concrete highway in rural Missouri.

In 1837, Charleston began on land a man named Thankful Randol sold to the town founder. Eight years later the town became the seat of newly-created Mississippi County. On the grounds of the red brick courthouse, which sports curved windows and a tin-topped white cupola, a local resident drilled for oil in 1916, with the stipulation that if he found none he would drill for an artesian well. As late as 1970, wildcat drilling took place in the area, but no oil or gas has ever been discovered. Stately old Victorian-era houses line the 300 block of Commercial, some stretches of East Cypress and especially North Main. There, just beyond downtown, the County Historical Museum (Tu 1:30-4:30) occupies the turn-of-the-century Moore House. On Main downtown, where for a short distance an old-fashioned-type arcade shelters the sidewalk, a one room museum devoted to former Governor Warren E. Hearnes contains plaques, trophies, cartoons, and other mementos of his two terms in office. Sikeston lies west of Charleston. Here the Dunn Hotel enjoys National Register listing and the colorful regionally-famous Lambert's Cafe features "throwed rolls." These are tossed to diners by employees, who also visit tables to heap hearty portions of side dishes on your plate.

South of Charleston, back roads criss-cross the area and pass through former swamplands, dried by drainage districts formed in the 1890's. This type of terrain gave southeast Missouri the nickname "swampeast." After the devastating 1927 flood, the

Corps of Engineers proposed a levee bisecting the county, with the lower section beyond the barrier to serve as a floodway for diversion of the Mississippi. Area residents opposed the plan for obvious reasons.

Near East Prairie, an agricultural town which originated as Hibbard in 1890 when a railroad laid tracks through this area, Highway 80 leads east to the Mississippi. Here the village of Belmont saw a nearly fatal and fateful Civil War episode involving Ulysses S. Grant. In early November, 1861, Grant sailed from Cairo and landed at Belmont with 3,100 troops. In his first direct encounter with Southern forces, he attacked a Confederate encampment. Guns from rebel batteries just across the Mississippi at Columbus, Kentucky (see the Kentucky chapter) fired on the Union forces. Grant recounts in his 1885 *Personal Memoirs* how, as the Northerners withdrew by boat from the fray, he rode through a corn field and suddenly glimpsed at the end of a row of stalks a band of Southern soldiers. Turning his horse away, Grant quietly retreated, then galloped on to the landing and, still mounted, boarded just as the boat began to pull away under a volley of enemy fire. During a brief truce the next day, Grant asked a Southern officer if he had noticed a lone Union soldier riding through the corn field. Yes, replied the man, and so had his commander, who said to his troops, "There is a Yankee; you may try your marksmanship on him, if you wish." But for some reason the men withheld their fire, so sparing Grant.

Just to the south lies Wolf Island, a Kentucky enclave west of the Mississippi where a teenager named Thomas Jackson worked as a laborer. During the Civil War he became better known as "Stonewall" Jackson, the famous Confederate general. On another island off Mississippi County, a Missouri big-game hunter released two wild male African lions in January, 1933 and, accompanied by beaters and other safari personnel and equipment, proceeded to pursue the animals, no doubt the only lion hunt ever held on the Mississippi. In the southern part of the county lies Towosahgy ("Old Town") State Archeological Site, a fortified Indian village dating from 1000-1400 A.D. You can also visit Big Oak Tree State Park, which contains twelve state and two national champions, a slippery elm and a pumpkin oak. Rooted in the rich alluvial soil of "swampeast" Missouri, the trees in the park preserve an example of the virgin bottomland hardwood forests which covered the landscape before settlers cleared away the timber and drained the terrain for use as cropland. The Hickman Ferry—which, unlike the river, runs erratically (usually daily, late March to early Dec)—affords a splendid ride over to Kentucky. The river here is truly magnificent in its size, sweep, and solitude. For Mississippi River travelers, a crossing on the Hickman Ferry provides one of the most memorable experiences available anywhere along the waterway.

Back to the west by Highway 61, the River Road, lies New Madrid (accent on the first syllable). The name, but not the present day appearance, suggests the great hopes old Madrid entertained for its New World empire. Spain obtained the region from France in 1762, but the French resumed possession of the lands west of the Mississippi in 1800. "After governing the province [Upper Louisiana] for nearly forty years the Spaniards left surprisingly few traces of their presence," notes William E. Foley in *The Genesis of Missouri.* "Except for a maze of unconfirmed land concessions and a few scattered place names, vestiges of Spanish rule quickly disappeared after the American take over." Spain had wanted the territory west of the Mississippi to establish a buffer between its Mexican colony and the English domain east of the river. In 1766, Don Antonio de Ulloa, the first Spanish governor, divided the area into Upper and Lower Louisiana; New Madrid was established in 1789 as capital of one of the five districts in Upper Louisiana.

During the 1780's, Spain closed the river to U.S. ships, fearing that American expansion after the Revolutionary War would spill over into lands west of the Mississippi. This greatly agitated Americans living along the waterway and its tributaries for, as James Madison stated: "The Mississippi is to them everything. It is the Hudson, the Delaware, the Potomac, and all the navigable rivers of the Atlantic states formed into one stream." To enforce the closing of the Mississippi to American commerce, the Spanish sailed a fleet of warships, called His Majesty's Light Squadron of Galleys, up the river, establishing on the waterway a fresh water navy. In the spring of 1794, three of the six galleys arrived at New Madrid to patrol the waterway, the first time vessels of that size had ever traveled so far north on the Mississippi. These machinations typified the eighteenth century European intrigues which dominated so much of the Mississippi's fate. The river's destiny back then was controlled by decisions made in the refined and gilded palace parlors and musty foreign ministries of Old World capitals, far removed from the turbulent waterway's roustabouts and rivermen. By the 1795 Pickney Treaty, Spain let the Americans resume navigation on the river, and three years later the Europeans withdrew their galleys from the Upper Mississippi, thus ending the Spanish armada episode on the waterway.

Later martial activities reached New Madrid in April, 1862. The town was the site of the Battle of Island Number 10, so designated as it was the tenth island below the mouth of the Ohio. Tucked into Kentucky Bend, where the river turns north nearly 180° toward New Madrid, the island served as a seemingly unassailable Confederate stronghold, manned by some 7,000 troops. The fortification greatly vexed Union General John Pope after he took New Madrid from the rebels; he was stalemated, as he could not transport his men or receive supplies via the river. Pope cut a channel across the peninsula to bypass the island, and managed to outflank the Confederates. After two large Union gunboats ran the island batteries under cover of night, the Southerners evacuated their positions and retreated to Tiptonville, Tennessee. The capture of Island Number 10 marked a major turning point in the river war, for the victory opened this strategic section of the Mississippi to federal forces.

Few traces of New Madrid's former naval and colonial importance survive. The river, however, still remains as an overwhelming presence which seems to dwarf the quiet town of 3,200. A new (1988) wood observation deck perches by the Mississippi. The river is so vast here, this being one of its widest ponts, that it seems like a lake. The New Madrid Museum lies nearby (M-F 9-4, Sat 10-4, Sun 1-4, Memorial Day-Labor Day to 5 daily). It occupies the 1886 Kendall Saloon building, its upper facade faced with pressed tin. The building once sported a sign warning "Last Chance" for departing passengers to imbibe and, on the river side, a notice advertising "First Chance" to those arriving on steamers. In December 1991 the museum opened a new annex.

A road atop the levee affords excellent views of the river and takes you past the 1843 Stepp House, the city's oldest dwelling, complete with a distinctive fan-like triangular roof section. You'll also pass the pleasant little River Park, and the Anderson Lumber Company. Steam-operated until 1980, it occupies a rickety metal building perched on wood beams. Over the door of the 1903 First Methodist Church on Mill Street appears the claim "Founded by Jesse Walker in 1810 Oldest Methodist Church [congregation] West of Mississippi." On the edge of town stands the 1860 Hunter-Dawson House, a State Historic Site (10-4, Sun 12-4). In this attractive fifteen-room white wood dwelling Union General John Pope supposedly headquartered during the New Madrid area campaigns. At the Lilbourne Indian mound west of town, site of a thousand year old tribal village, Spanish explorer Hernando de Soto supposedly held the first European religious service west of the Mississippi in 1541.

Quakeburgers on sale at Tom's Cafe downtown, t-shirts bearing the phrase "It's our fault," and other shaky witticisms refer to the famous 1811-1812 earthquakes named for New Madrid, located near the epicenter of the most severe tremors ever felt in the United States. The convulsions began suddenly at 2 a.m. on December 6, 1811, with the ground undulating like sea swells. Great fissures opened in the earth, the Mississippi for a time ran backwards, and shock waves radiated out as far as New Orleans, Canada, and Colorado. The vibrations awakened Thomas Jefferson at Monticello, rang church bells in Washington, and rattled crockery in Boston. When an area south of New Madrid caved in, Mississippi waters poured into the depression, creating Reelfoot Lake in northern Tennessee. An eyewitness, named Godfrey Lesieur, recalled how "the earth began to shake and totter to such a degree that no persons were able to stand or walk. This lasted perhaps for one minute, and at this juncture the earth was observed to be as it were rolling in waves of a few feet in height, with visible depressions between." Severe shocks agitated the area on January 23 and February 7, 1812, and lesser tremors continued for another year and a half until the New Madrid Fault finally came to rest. The last major quake in the zone occurred in 1895 near Charleston. Unlike the San Andreas Fault in California, which lies on or near the earth's surface, the Midwest geological defect burrows under 2,000—3,000 feet of river-deposited sediment, which allows shock waves to travel farther and with greater force than at other faults.

At the time the December, 1811, quake erupted, the *New Orleans*, the first steamboat ever to sail the western waters, was making its way down the Ohio toward the Mississippi, which it entered only to find in disarray all the familiar landmarks carefully noted by pilot Nicholas Roosevelt on his six month reconnaisance voyage by flatboat the previous year. Nearly a century earlier, in 1717, French colonial administrator Lamothe Cadillac had stated: "Is it expected that for any commercial or profitable purpose boats will ever be able to run up the Mississippi, into the Wabash, the Missouri, or the Red River? One might as well try to bite a slice off the moon." At the time the *New Orleans* gingerly made its way down the messy Mississippi, it seemed as if the New Madrid Fault was carving off a slice of the earth. The steamer proceeded through the scrambled riverscape, however, the very first of the hundreds of such ships which later proved the skeptical Cadillac wrong. The vessel put in at New Madrid shortly after the tremors, then continued on down the mixed-up Mississippi, mooring at Natchez by an island which disappeared overnight. Henry Schoolcraft, who in 1832 discovered the source of the Mississippi at Lake Itasca, Minnesota, traveled in the Missouri lead belt in 1818, after which he penned a poem on the New Madrid quakes entitled "Transallegania; or, the Groans of Missouri," with such verses as: "The rivers they boiled like a pot over coals,/And mortals fell prostrate, and prayed for their souls." This effort—which probably induced many groans in Missouri and elsewhere—no doubt did as much damage to American literature as the tremors did to the landscape.

South of New Madrid near Portageville—originally called Big Portage for a trail between the St. Francis and Little Rivers on the west and the Mississippi to the east—the Missouri Bootheel begins. This is an oddly-shaped appendage which thrusts south into Arkansas as if to compensate for the Iowa encroachment that invades Missouri's northeast corner. The 1,100 square mile Bootheel originated when John Hardeman Walker settled at Little Prairie in 1809 (called Lost Village, following the earthquakes) two miles south of present day Caruthersville. He petitioned Congress to extend Missouri's boundary southward. Walker, age seventeen when the quakes began, opted to remain in the area although many other early settlers fled, and after the tremors he acquired large land holdings near the Mississippi. Shortly before Missouri entered the Union in 1821, Walker pleaded to be included in the new state so that his property would not lie south of the proposed border in a wild no-man's land without law and order. After his testimony before the Congressional Surveying Committee in Washington, federal authorites agreed to move the boundary south, so creating the Bootheel. In 1857, at age sixty-three, Walker laid out the town of Caruthersville on part of his plantation. He rests in that town's Eastwood Memorial Cemetery. Tucked behind levees along the Mississippi, Caruthersville—seat of Pemiscot ("liquid mud") County—offers the Riverview Museum (open by appointment April-Oct: 314-333-1861). Installed in the 1915 Frisco depot, it features farm implements, old vehicles, a vintage river skiff, Indian relics, quilts, World War I and II items, and photos and documents relating to Harry Truman, a frequent visitor to the Pemiscot County Fair. At the mouth of Old Pemiscot Bayou once lay Lint Dale, a shipping port, three quarters of a mile south of which operated a warehouse known as Midway, as it stood exactly halfway between Cairo and Memphis.

The Mississippi forms the Bootheel's eastern edge—100 miles farther east than where the river entered Missouri—while the St. Francis marks its western boundary. Toward the St. Francis lies Kennett, whose Dunklin County Museum (March-Nov W and Sat 1:30-5, Dec-Feb Sat only), listed on the National Register, contains old maps, political memorabilia, "Birthright Letters" which former slaves and their owners sent to one another, and a collection of mechanical toys.

To the south, at Hornersville, William "Major" Ray is buried. He is better known as Buster Brown, the child symbol used by St. Louis's Brown Shoe Company. The 3½ foot tall Ray grew up in the Bootheel, an appropriate place for a shoe company representative. He later traveled with a circus, paired with his 3 foot 1 inch wife, Jennie; they were billed as "The World's Smallest Couple." Ray started working as Buster Brown in 1904, appearing at the St. Louis World's Fair and touring for the shoe firm until he retired ten years later; in 1936 he died.

Four centuries before Buster Brown, Hernando de Soto entered Missouri across the St. Francis River into the territory of the Pacaha Indians, whose lands extended north beyond New Madrid. The Spanish explorer rested his army near the Pacaha's principal town for about six weeks before traveling on. Here, where the discoverer of the Mississippi began the exploration of Missouri in 1541—the first European to reach the territory—ends our tour of riverside attractions in the state, whose history intertwines through the years with the great waterway which marks its eastern border.

MISSOURI PRACTICAL INFORMATION

Phone numbers of tourist offices in Missouri's principal Mississippi river cities:

Canton: 314-288-4413; Cape Girardeau: 314-335-3312; Clarksville: 314-242-9662; Hannibal: 314-221-2477; Jackson: 314-243-8131; Louisiana: 314-754-5921; New Madrid: 314-748-5300; Palmyra: 314-769-2223; St. Charles: 314-946-7776 and 800-366-2427; Sainte Genevieve: 314-883-7097; St. Louis: 314-421-1023 and 800-325-7962.

Missouri operates highway tourist information centers at Hannibal, New Madrid, and St. Louis. Missouri Division of Tourism: 314-751-4133. For information on state parks: Missouri Divison of Natural Resources, 800-334-6946.

Other useful numbers for travel along the Missis sippi include: Jefferson National Expansion Memorial St. Louis Arch: 314-425-4465. Army Corps of Engineers, St. Louis District: 314-331-8000. Missouri Bed and Breakfast Association: 314-965-4328 or 314-533-9299. River Country Bed and Breakfast is a reservation service: 314-965-4328 and 314-771-1993 (open M-F 10-2.)

III.

THE LOWER MISSISSIPPI

6. Kentucky, Tennesse and Arkansas

7. Mississippi

8. Louisiana

6. KENTUCKY, TENNESSEE, ARKANSAS

Kentucky

As the Mississippi winds its way through the Mid-South section of its 2,552 mile long journey from Lake Itasca in Minnesota to the Gulf of Mexico, the waterway remains removed from the River Road. Apart from Memphis and Helena, Arkansas, no cities of any size border the stream, which in Kentucky, Tennessee, and Arkansas remains rather "a secretive river," as Willard Price described the waterway in *The Amazing Mississippi*. "It is unknown to many people who live within a few miles of it. Over some stretches the road hugs the shore and magnificent views may be had of the river and its maze of islands. But for the most part," Price wrote about the entire River Road, "the highway does not attempt to follow the river's meanderings." Nowhere is this more true than in the trio of states which border the Lower Mississippi just after it merges with the Ohio.

The waterway impacts Kentucky less than any of the ten states in the Mississippi River Valley. Only three small towns front the stream, which flows by Kentucky for a mere fifty-four miles. Strangely enough, however, the commonwealth once almost seceded because of a controversy over the river. The September 1783 Revolutionary War Peace Treaty between the United States and Britain established the Mississippi as America's western boundary and provided: "The navigation of the River Mississippi, from its source to the ocean, shall forever remain free and open to the subjects of Great Britain and the citizens of the United States." Later in the 1780's, however, U.S. Secretary of Foreign Affairs John Jay offered to suspend the right to free navigation on the

Mississippi for twenty-five years if Spain, which then controlled the area west of the river, would grant America certain commercial concessions. Former Revolutionary War General James Wilkinson, a promoter and political manipulator, saw this as an opportunity to gain power and profits by separating Kentucky—furious at the intrigue which threatened to close the Mississippi to the territory's shipping—from the rest of the country. In a 1786 letter, George Washington warned that the "many ambitious and turbulent spirits" in the west "may become riotous and ungovernable, if the hope of traffic [on the Mississippi] is cut off by treaty." The following year, Thomas Jefferson, then Minister to France, wrote from Paris, "The navigation of the Mississippi was, perhaps, the strongest trial to which the justice of the federal government could be put." When James Madison inquired in January, 1787, if Kentucky would entertain any change in arrangements for the river, the territory's chief justice, George Muter, replied, "I have not mett [sic] with one man, who would be willing to give the navigation up, for ever so a short a time, on any terms whatever."

To demonstrate to Kentuckians the benefits which would flow from continued access to the Mississippi, Wilkinson in June, 1787, sent a flatboat to New Orleans laden with tobacco, hams, and butter. The schemer himself then traveled to New Orleans, soon returning to Kentucky with a four-horse coach, the first ever seen in the territory's wild west. Wilkinson, "in order to impress the people of the district with the advantages of a change of political relations, not less than from a natural love of vainglory, assumed increased magnificance in his equipage and stylish living, [and] dwelt profusely upon the advantage of navigating the Mississippi and of a commercial connection with Louisiana," wrote Thomas Marshall Green in his 1891 *The Spanish Conspiracy*. In November, 1788, a Separation Convention organized by Kentucky to consider secession passed a resolution "That a manly and spirited address be sent to Congress to obtain the Navigation of the River Mississippi." So acute was the crisis that in his September, 1796,

Farewell Address, Washington warned of sectionalism and cited the navigation controversy as a case in point, noting the suspicions raised among "people of the western country" by actions of easterners "hostile to their interests in relation to the Mississippi."

Sensing a chance to fish in troubled waters, in 1793 French ambassador Citizen Genet sent agents into Kentucky in an attempt to convince westerners that the federal government was plotting to deprive them of access to the Mississippi. Genet induced Revolutionary War hero George Rogers Clark to lead an army to conquer the Spanish-controlled Louisiana Territory west of the river, appointing the grizzled veteran as "Major General of the Independent and Revolutionary Legion of the Mississippi." In January, 1794, Clark issued a call to arms, proclaiming that the militia's goal was "the reduction of the Spanish posts on the Mississippi, for opening the trade of that river." Clark promised volunteers 1,000 acres of land or $1 a day, with "all lawful plunder to be equally divided according to the custom of war." Soon after Clark's proclamation, however, Arthur St. Clair, governor of the Northwest Territory, issued his own announcement warning all citizens to refrain from any fighting, and Clark soon abandoned the project. The proposed military campaign influenced the federal government to settle the Mississippi problem, concluded by the October, 1795, Treaty of San Lorenzo. Thomas Pickney signed this with Spain, opening the river to navigation. This satisfied the Kentuckians, now free to profit from the river's benefits, and ended the threat of secession.

Centuries earlier, Indians enjoyed the advantages of locating settlements along the Mississippi. Wickliffe is the first Kentucky town reached after you cross the Ohio at the point where it flows into the Mississippi at Cairo, Illinois. You'll find there the Wickliffe Mounds (March-Nov 9-4:30), one of the many ancient settlements in the river valley built by the Mississippian Indians, a culture which lived along the waterway from about 900 to 1600 A.D. Fully half a century after the mounds at Wickliffe were first studied,

Colonel Fain White King and his wife Blanche bought and excavated the site, which yielded many old artifacts. After completing the excavations in 1945, the Kings donated the property to Western Baptist Hospital in Paducah, which benefited from admission fees to the site until conveying it to Murray State University in 1983. At the village, thought to have served as a trade center, the Indians built some mounds for ceremonial purposes and others to serve as burial areas. Exhibits at the site trace the history and mound building activities of the Mississippian culture.

Centuries after the Mississippians disappeared, for reasons unknown, their descendants the Chickasaw occupied the western section of Kentucky, beyond the Tennessee River. This area includes the three counties which border the Mississippi, and a fourth which partially fronts the waterway. In 1816, the federal government commissioned General Andrew Jackson and Kentucky Governor Isaac Shelby to negotiate with the Chickasaw for the thickly wooded river-washed area. Within two years, the Indians agreed to sell their 4,600 square mile territory—known since then as the Jackson Purchase, or simply The Purchase—to the United States for $20,000 a year over fifteen years.

Wickliffe, established in 1860, took its name from Colonel Chester A. Wickliffe, a state legislator and nephew and namesake of Kentucky's fifteenth governor. He inherited land in the area his pioneer grandfather, Colonel Benjamin Logan, had received for Revolutionary War service. The courthouse, a handsome, cupola-crowned, classical-style, brick structure with a quartet of white columns, stands in the middle of a typical Southern small town county seat square, with wood benches on the lawn. Around the perimeter stand law and real estate offices, a church, a grocery-hardware store, a bank and the newspaper, the colorfully named *Advance-Yeoman*. At Wickliffe a revetment—articulated concrete mattresses—constructed in 1951 and extended in 1968 lines the river bank to prevent erosion. More than nine hundred miles of revetment work lines the Lower Mississippi, installed to prevent erosion of as much as six hundred feet of shore annually at any one point. When eroded sand and silt temporarily suspended in the water become too heavy, the river then drops the load, which forms sandbars and other navigational hazards.

Just south of Wickliffe, beyond the bridge, stood Fort Jefferson, established during the Revolutionary War by George Rogers Clark, in order to protect the claim of the new United States to a western boundary on the Mississippi. In 1781, the Chickasaw, agitated by the American encroachment and encouraged by the British, besieged the fort. They eventually forced the newcomers to abandon the outpost, thwarting the plan of Clark and Thomas Jefferson to settle and civilize the remote Kentucky Mississippi River country. Military activity again reached the area eighty years later, after Confederate forces seized Columbus, farther south on the Mississippi in Kentucky, in September, 1861, when Union troops established at the site of old Fort Jefferson one of four riverside supply bases to serve the Western theater.

A short distance farther on, smoking chimneys, mounds of wood chips, and log piles indicate the large Westvaco paper plant. Bardwell, to the south, includes along Front Street a row of brick buildings out of an earlier era; they lend the place an old time flavor. Vintage signs indicate "Joyner & Childress," the First National Bank, whose grey stone stands out among the brick, and the Bardwell Hardware Company.

At Bardwell, Ulysses S. Grant mustered a show of force in January, 1862, by sending 5,000 troops from Cairo, Illinois to impress the Confederates at their Columbus stronghold and to acquaint his forces with the lay of the land. The troops marched on to Milburn to the southeast and then returned to Cairo. By this maneuver, Grant also hoped to gain support from area residents who favored the Union cause. Kentucky was by no means a Southern state. Although 35,000 Kentuckians joined the rebel army, twice that many entered the federal forces, and when the war began, the state refused to join the Confederacy, declaring itself neutral. Both sides eyed Columbus as a strategic site from which to control the Lower Misssissippi. Ignoring Kentucky's profession of neutrality, Confederate General Leonidas Polk, a West Point graduate and nephew of former President James K. Polk, seized the town on September 4, 1861, the first move in the campaign to dominate the Mississippi. Polk held that Columbus would serve to anchor control of the Mississippi in Southern hands, well armed there on the heights overlooking the waterway. On the 200 foot high bluff at Columbus he emplaced 140 cannons in tiered rows, while across the river Polk stretched a mile-long thick-linked chain, armed with torpedoes, which blocked the waterway. Atop this powerful redoubt Polk perched, master of the Mississippi, which at the outset of the war the Southerners controlled from Columbus to New Orleans.

Ulysses S. Grant, headquartered in Cairo not far upstream, now faced the challenge of gaining access to the Mississippi. After a quick foray in November, 1861, to Belmont, Missouri, just across from Columbus, to wipe out the rebel camp there (see the Missouri chapter), Grant withdrew to consider his strategy. The general decided that instead of a direct assault down the Mississippi to attack the Confederate positions established at Columbus, Fort Pillow, Memphis, Vicksburg, and New Orleans, he would outflank the enemy, an approach the Southeners did not anticipate. Grant therefore sent his artillery boats up the Tennessee, followed by 17,000 men, to take Fort Henry on that river. It fell after an enormous bombardment on February 6, 1862. Afterwards, the Northern gunboats proceeded to Fort Donelson on the Cumberland, which surrendered on February 16. On February 22, federal ships shelled Columbus and Polk, threatened from the rear after the fall of Forts Henry and Donelson, decided to withdraw. He left Columbus to the advancing Union troops, and re-established his forces at Island Number 10, which fell on April 7 (see the Missouri chapter), while federal forces were inflicting a decisive defeat on the Southerners at the bloody Battle of Shiloh in western Tennessee. In May, the fearsome federal ironclad warships shelled Fort Pillow as Union troops advanced from the rear through Tennessee, forcing the Confederates to retreat a short distance south to Memphis. After government ramboats destroyed Southern ships moored at Memphis, the city fell on June 6. Thus ended the battle to control the northern section of the Lower Mississippi.

Meanwhile, the second thrust of Northern forces on the Mississippi developed at New Orleans when sea ships commanded by Admiral David Farragut forced New Orleans to surrender on May 1. Federal forces now controlled virtually the entire Mississippi—except for Port Hudson (see the Luisianna chapter) and Vicksburg, Grant's most challenging target on the river (see the Mississippi chapter). As for Columbus—the so called "Gibraltar of the West," which Polk had supposed would assure Confederate control of the Mississippi—the town served Union forces as a supply center during their campaign to take Vicksburg in May and June, 1863.

At Columbus-Belmont State Park (April-Oct) in Columbus you can see earthworks of the confederate redoubt as well as cannons, a short stretch of the chain which crossed the Mississippi, and an audio-video presentation on the Battle of Belmont. With this encounter began the great western campaign, which developed with the North taking control of the Mississippi and ended with the fall of Vicksburg and the advance of Union forces eastward to the sea. Apart from the park's historical significance, the 156 acre bluff-top enclave also offers one of the most magnificent views of the river found on the entire waterway. This not-to-be-missed panorama at one of the Mississippi's great vantage points shows the river in all its splendor, rolling in from the north. To the south, points of land project into the waterway in pleasingly symmetrical patterns. The park originated after the great flood of 1927. Red Cross agent Marion Rust came to Columbus at this time to help the town recover. He found remains of the Confederate garrison when exploring the area, all the while directing relocation of the settlement from its original site by the river up to the high land behind the bluff. From 1934 to 1937, Civilian Conservation Corps workers partly restored the fort, the first phase in the park's development.

Columbus began below the cliffs by the Mississippi, when Revolutionary War veterans, who had served in the west with General George Rogers Clark, received land warrants in 1784 and used them to settle at Iron Banks, so called as early French travelers dubbed the rusty looking bluffs there "les rivages de fer." In 1804, the federal government established a military post at the site at the time of the "Burr Conspiracy," the supposed plot hatched by Aaron Burr, James Wilkinson, and others to detach western areas from the United States and form a new territory. After the British burned Washington during the War of 1812, real estate promoters, noting that Columbus lay in the center of the nation (which it then did) spread the tale that the federal government planned to establish the new United States capital at the Mississippi River settlement. No government arrived, but in 1856, the Mobile & Ohio Railroad reached Columbus. This was the world's longest line under one management. By 1861, it connected the city with Mobile, Alabama. Four years after the Civil War, a ferry between the town and Belmont, Missouri started up to carry rail cars across the river. The 1878 catalog for Columbus College, founded four years before, boasted that "A most beautiful view of the river may be had," but this failed to entice students, and the school closed in 1884, a precurser of the town's imminent decline. The downfall began after the Illinois Central line built a bridge across the Ohio River at Cairo in 1889. A succession of fires and floods, culminating in the devastating 1927 inundation, did the town in—literally, for much of the place washed away into the Mississippi. After the disaster, Herbert Hoover, chairman of Mississippi Flood Relief, visited Columbus and endorsed relocation of the town to the upper area 200 feet above the river. House movers transferred 166 dwellings, using hydraulic equipment which kept the buildings so level as they moved that some families remained inside during the ascent up the steep road. Today, Columbus survives as a sleepy hamlet with such establishments as Bencini's Fish Market, in a white stone building below the water tower, and the (perhaps closed) Tickle-Bone Bar-B-Q. Down by the Mississippi—where until December, 1981 a ferry operated, the last of the boats which for a century and a half linked Kentucky and Missouri here—Great River Marine Services overhauls and repairs ships.

At a sharp curve on Highway 123 south of Columbus, a whimsical sign announces "Hailwell Elev. 312 ft." The weary, peeling farmhouse and adjacent grey wood building, both unwell, seem not to conform to the name. The same holds true for Oakton, where houses tumble into ruins at the nearly abandoned hamlet, established at the edge of a Cherokee village. It remained less disintegrated until rail passenger service ended in 1953. A short distance to the east lies Clinton, seat of Hickman County since 1929, when Columbus lost the honor. The 1884 National Register-listed courthouse succeeded the 1832 version, the first brick building in Kentucky west of the Tennessee River. In 1846 the Clinton Seminary started, the state's first high school west of that waterway. Clinton College, which operated from 1874 to 1913, and the Methodist-run Marvin College—from which in 1897 Alben Barkley, later U.S. Vice President, graduated—gave Clinton the name "Athens of the West." After the politician, who worked as a janitor while studying at Marvin, gained fame as a U.S. Senator, the school posted a sign boasting, "Barkley swept here." Four blocks north of the courthouse stands the Register-listed old Jewel Hotel, built in 1910 as a boy's dormitory for Marvin College, which operated from 1884 to 1922. The large, two-story brick residence a block southwest of Courthouse Square occupies the site of Clinton Seminary. Harper's Country Hams, which turns out hickory-smoked treats, welcomes visitors. Murphy's Pond, northwest of Clinton on Highway 703, includes a wide variety of wildlife native to the region in a primitive area untouched by modern times.

Cayce lies nine miles southwest of Clinton. It was named for local resident merchant James Hardie Cayce and established as "Caceys Station," the designation of the first post office (1860). The spelling error was corrected in 1874, while the "Station" was eliminated in 1880 and, completing the circle, the post office closed in 1965. At age thirteen, John Luther Jones, born in southeast Missouri, moved to Cayce in 1877 with his family, crossing the Mississippi by ferry at Birds Point, Missouri. Jones started work with the Mobile & Ohio Railroad as a telegraph operator in Jackson, Tennessee, and by age thirty he rose to become a passenger train engineer on the Illinois Central. In order to distinguish himself from the many other employees named Jones who worked for the line, he adopted the nickname "Cayce," spelled "Casey" after his death. Jones soon took over the "Cannon Ball Express," the crack train on the 188 mile Memphis to Canton, Mississippi, run. "The old girl has her high heels on tonight," the engineer would exclaim when hurtling down the line behind his new locomotive, introduced in 1898, which sported half a dozen six foot high drivers (wheels). Early in the morning of April 30, 1900, as Jones pushed the Express to speeds of nearly 100 miles per hour to make up for a late departure from Memphis, the "Cannon Ball" smashed into the end of a freight train parked at Vaughn, Mississippi, twelve miles north of Canton. By remaining with his train to keep it on the rails, Jones saved the passengers in the twelve coaches but he perished. The trainman is buried in Jackson, Tennessee, where engineeers in passing trains would salute his memory by sounding the whistle. At Cayce, a marker erected in 1938 honors the brave, one-time resident, noting that "the name Casey Jones lives deeply set into the hearts of American people in both tradition and song." The latter refers to the famous ballad, composed by a black railroad worker, which begins, "Come, all you rounders, for I want you to hear/The story told of a brave engineer." Only a few scattered houses at the crossroads where Highways 94 and 234 meet comprise Cayce, where just up 94 the Jones grocery stands, not connected with the famous hero. His childhood house, however, stood in a field just beyond the store—an old-fashioned place with a canopy-covered porch, furnished with blue benches—on the opposite side of the road.

North of Highway 94, which heads west to the port town of Hickman, Bayou Du Chien flows, a creek whose mouth lies just north of Hickman. Along the stream stood some of the Mississippi River Valley's oldest Indian mounds. A nearby five mile long canal, built by area tribesmen, connected Bayou Du Chien with Obion Creek to the north. The ancient canal saved a hundred mile voyage when the Bayou entered the Mississippi much farther south before the 1811-1812 New Madrid earthquakes rearranged the landscape. At Hickman, Kentucky's only truly typical Mississippi River town, the business district occupies a low area near the waterway, while the residential neighborhoods spread over the high elevations which rise near the river. In *Old Glory: An American Voyage*, Jonathan Raban judged that Hickman "looked so right: a real river town of old brick, old timber, old painted store fronts, stepped and huddled on its hill." The town, indeed, presents a picture of a nineteenth century settlement on the Mississippi. Vintage storefronts of various hues dating from the 1880's line Clinton Street downtown, part of a National Historic District. Here, the c. 1898 LaClede Hotel, once Hickman's social center, sports a distinctive keyhole arch entranceway. Opposite this row stands an unsightly and ponderous nearly mile long concrete flood wall, built to a height of 317 feet in 1934 and raised in the early 1950's and again in 1986 to its present 324 feet. The name of the Showboat Theater lends a nautical touch, while the white brick flank of a building at Kentucky and Clinton bears a painting of a paddlewheeler. In 1964, Hickman, the only still water harbor between St. Louis and Memphis, became Kentucky's first official river port. In 1978, the Riverport cargo handling terminal began operations.

Hickman started in 1819 as a shipping settlement called Mills Point, renamed by G.W.C. Marr for his wife's family when he bought the site in 1834. He later sold his interest to Samuel Wilson, nephew of Alexander Hamilton, whose parents James and Rebecca Hamilton Wilson are buried in the Hickman cemetery, located in the southeast corner of the upper part of town. Between the lower section of town and the bluffs above, four flights of steps rise 200 feet to the Buchanan Street National Historic District. The steps, built in 1937 by the Works Progress Administration, lead you to such sights as the c. 1903 Register-listed brick Fulton County Courthouse. This striking structure includes octagonal corner towers and pleasing, curvy, Dutch-style fringes atop two of the central facades. For years, area residents have marked time with hours sounded by the hand-wound, eight-day Seth Thomas clock in the courthouse's tallest tower. The First Christian Church at the corner of Tennessee and Buchanan bears architectural touches reminiscent of a Spanish mission. The garden behind the nearby residence (c. 1889) at 209 Buchanan is a miniature replica of the garden at "My Old Kentucky Home" in Bardstown, Kentucky. At Bardstown John Fitch lived, who in 1786 ran an experimental paddle-propelled steamer, considered the first such craft ever built. However, New York's Robert Fulton—from whom Fulton County takes its name—is credited with inventing the first functioning steamboat in 1807. From the area around the courthouse in the upper part of town, panoramas appear down onto the Mississippi in the distance.

Out on Moscow Avenue east of town—near two water towers which bear steamboat images—the Kentucky Kernel nut company (for mail orders: 502-236-2662) occupies an old fashioned facility whose facade advertises "custom cracking of your in-shell pecans." Inside, the firm—which specializes in wild pecans from trees found along the Mississippi—three Rube Goldberg-type machines operate which crack the nuts one at a time. At the Riverport just south of Hickman stand huge storage tanks of the River Grain Company, beyond which a spur road leads past the Bunge metal bin to the ferry. This particular business has operated continuously between Hickman and Dorena, Missouri since 1840. The Lattus family has owned the ferry for more than half a century. In the early days, horse drawn cables powered the craft, but now the 12-car ferry (April-Oct 7-6, Nov-Dec 24 7:30-5; for information: 502-236-3448) chugs along with updated propulsion. A crossing on the Hickman ferry provides one of the most splendid experiences on the entire Mississippi, here vast and muscular, its current clawing at the boat as the little ship makes its way over the great river. New Madrid and Interstate 55 lie about twenty miles west of the Mississippi.

Offshore, out of view of the River Road, Highway 94, which heads west out of Hickman, lies Island Number 8, one of the largest in the Lower Mississippi. Farther on—around the sinuous bend which sends the waterway due north—is historic Island Number 10, scene of a crucial Civil War episode (see the Missouri chapter), where Confederate soldiers fortified the strategically located land mass after they lost Columbus. Later, in April, 1862, Union General John Pope outflanked the outpost and forced the rebels to withdraw. The fall of the island opened the river and paved the way for the Northern conquest of Fort Pillow and Memphis in Tennessee not far downstream. Later during the war, the Union Army moved 1,000 ex-slaves to the island, by which in 1864 the federal transport *James White* hit a submerged Confederate gunboat and sunk so rapidly that sixteen deckhands sleeping in the hold drowned.

The Mississippi loop beyond Island Number 10 curves around New Madrid and back to the south for more than twenty miles, ten times as far as the distance across the peninsula, a detached part of Kentucky reached only via a road which passes through Tennessee for eight miles. This bulbous-shaped patch of land—variously called Madrid Bend, Kentucky Bend, Bessie Bend, Watson Point and other names—started as an inhabited area with a population of two about 1830. It gradually grew to 322 by 1890 when eight different landings competed to receive steamers and sell them wood fuel. In the early years, farmers grew corn and wheat, later adding cotton. All three of them, plus soybeans, are cultivated today by a handful (under forty) of residents who farm 12,000 acres of some of the richest soil in the United States. Settlers established the first church about 1832 and the first school in 1852 at Compromise, a steamboat landing community, now vanished. Its name was finally decided upon after Kentucky and Tennessee agreed to settle a boundary dispute involving the Bend. Although a levee seems to protect the peninsula on the east side, the barrier broke during the extraordinary 1937 flood and the inundation almost totally destroyed the area. A road runs alongside the levee. Blacktopped in 1979, the street follows the route of an old cow path or Indian trail running north from the Tennessee line to a point opposite New Madrid where a ferry once operated. Along Steppe Road in this isolated corner of Kentucky—which recalls Illinois's Kaskaskia Island west of the Mississippi—stands Madrid Bend Church. There is truly little else in the area except the fields, sometimes marshy, and Beaver and Long Sloughs. You can also find Washpan and Watson Lakes, the latter named for Daniel and Romena Watson, the first settlers, whose son Greenburg helped found Mills Point, later called Hickman, south of which—beyond Sassafras Ridge—lies Tennessee.

Tennessee

Except for a small area in the southeastern part of Tennessee, the Mississippi River system—through the Tennessee and Cum-berland Rivers and their tributaries, which flow into the Ohio—drains the entire state. Tennessee, however, pays little homage to the great river, for few roads and virtually no cities lie along the waterway north of Memphis. Some long side roads which dead-end at the Mississippi extend west from U.S. Highway 51, the main north-south thoroughfare in western Tennessee, but these lateral routes lead you only to forlorn hamlets.

The River Road enters Tennessee south of Hickman, Kentucky, and passes through Phillipy, an unincorporated hamlet with a few houses. Not far on, a turnoff to the east leads to the unusual Airpark Inn (901-253-7756 and 800-421-6683), an oddly angular, twenty-unit, state-run hotel perched on pylons in Reelfoot Lake. This 15,000 acre body of water originated during the 1811-1912 New Madrid earthquakes when water entered a sunken area created by the tremors. Reelfoot took its name from a gimpy Chickasaw chief who, according to legend, brought a kidnapped Choctaw princess to his village, which the wrathful gods soon inundated with waters from the nearby Mississippi. Reelfoot teems with wildlife, with more than 56 fish and 240 bird species, many found in the National Wildlife Refuge north of the lake. From December to March, daily eagle watching tours leave from the Airport Inn (901-253-7756). Reelfoot Lake State Resort Park comprises ten segments located along twenty-two miles of the shoreline, where on the south edge a Visitor Center (8-4:30) houses a museum. Behind it, a boardwalk trail leads to a stand of cypress trees which grow in the shallow (less than nine feet) lake.

Tiptonville, just west of Reelfoot, once stood on the Mississippi, which after the Civil War deposited an ever-growing sandbar at the site, in time distancing the town from its waterfront. The settlement lies on a high area called the Tiptonville Dome, a ridge never covered by flood water, although during the 1937 inundation the lowlands for miles around lay beneath the rampaging Mississippi. On one of the town's water towers a guitar image appears, a reference to native son Carl Perkins, the singer, whose weathered, wood, tin-roofed boyhood home stands by the highway at the south edge of town.

Ten miles south of Tiptonville and two miles beyond Ridgely, a right turn at Freddie's BBQ taks you west on Highway 79, which soon curves into 181 as you pass the familiar green pilot's wheel River Road sign. This isolated road, devoid of traffic and bordered by fields, takes you south and crosses over Interstate 155, which leads to the Mississippi Bridge just west, then continues on atop the levee to Highway 104. Here, a sign warns that 181 dead-ends eleven miles south, for the $3 million 1988 bridge over the Obion River to the south has collapsed. So much for the River Road, but a right turn onto 104 takes you west out to Heloise, a hamlet of a few houses and a metal storage building, and then on a mile or so along a gravel-dirt road to a large brown hued storage tank and conveyer pipe on the Mississippi. Here the river flows virtually unnoticed through open countryside, little marked with signs of human presence. With the waterway as his only companion, the visitor enjoys at this remote spot—one of the best places in northern Tennessee to see the river—a certain pleasing sense of solitude. As late as the mid-1970's, a ferry connected the Heloise area with Cottonwood Point, a pre-Civil War steamboat landing and village across the river in Missouri. From here it is necessary to return to U.S. Highway 51, near Dyersburg, thirteen miles east of the Mississippi. Located halfway between Chicago and New Orleans, Dyersburg began in 1825, seven years after Andrew Jackson and Kentucky Governor Isaac Shelby acquired the area from the Chickasaw Indians, the same transaction as "The Purchase" referred to in the Kentucky section above.The columned, white-domed courthouse occupies the lively town square, surrounded by commercial establishments, many of them outfitted with awnings. At the end of North Main stands the Byzantine-like First United Methodist Church.

South of Dyersburg lies Halls, just east of U.S. 51, where a grey caboose houses a new museum (1989), and on Main, the museum-like, turn-of-the-century Simmons Men's Shop operates. This is a true relic of a place, installed in a long, narrow space, with a peeling ceiling revealing the original tin beneath the paint. The Bank of Halls, which opened in 1899 in a grocery store, showed such staying power through wars, depressions, drought, and other hazards that locals called the tenacious firm the "Cockleburr Bank." West of Halls, out Nankipoo Road, lies the town of that name, so called after the son of the Mikado in the Gilbert and Sullivan musical popular when the post office opened in the 1880's. Roark Bradford, born near Nankipoo in 1896, was the author of Southern black-oriented stories, including the 1928 *Ol' Man Adam and His Chillun*, the basis for Marc Connelly's Pulitzer Prize-winning play, *Green Pastures*. Key Corner, which lies north of Nankipoo, was established on the Forked Deer River in 1785 by Henry Rutherford of North Carolina, who surveyed the Western Territory. His measurements controlled ownership of thousands of acres registered at land offices in his home state, which originally extended to the Mississippi. The place took its name for the large key Rutherford used to mark a sycamore, on which he also carved his initials, on Cole Creek Bluff above the Forked Deer River, so called for the plentiful game here and for its branches where the stream flows into the Mississippi. A bronze tablet near where the original tree stood commemorates the base survey point used by Rutherford. Farther west, out Highway 88, lies Hales Point, a transfer port for goods carried down the Obion River—which merges with the Forked Deer nearby—on flatboats or small steamers and reloaded here for shipment to New Orleans. Farmers in the interior complained that the boats on the tributary charged exorbitant fees, but pilots responded by claiming that the Obion presented difficult hazards. In 1874, the Corps of Engineers considered improving the river for navigation, but railroads soon diverted traffic from the stream and before long, no boats plied the Obion.

In 1822, Davy Crockett settled upstream on the Rutherford Fork of the Obion east of Dyersburg at a site marked by a reproduction of the frontiersman's cabin, built with logs from the original structure. In his whimsical (ghost-written) autobiography, Crockett tells of his encounter with the Mississippi, where in the fall of 1825 he went to build two boats to ship barrel staves down to New Orleans. Within less than a year, he recounted, he killed 105 bears near the waterway. After loading the boats with some 30,000 staves, Crockett and his crew set sail and "when I got into the Mississippi, I found all of my hands were bad scared; in fact I believe I was scared a little the worst of any; for I had never been down the river." When they tried a tricky night landing, boatmen on a passing ship shouted a warning and "We took their advice, though we had a good deal rather not," and further downstream when Crockett's craft careened out of control he sat in his cabin "thinking on what a hobble we had got into; and how much better bear-hunting was on hard land, than floating along on the water, when a fellow had to go ahead whether he was exactly willing or not." The ship hit an island and Crockett's crew rescued the would-be pilot, pulling him through a tight opening which peeled his clothes off "and I was literally skin'd like a rabbit." The ship then sank as the men escaped on a raft until a skiff from Memphis rescued them. On arrival at Memphis, Marcus B. Winchester, son of one of the city's founders and later mayor, became so charmed by Crockett and his humorous tales that the Memphian urged the frontiersman to run for Congress. Thanks at least in part to his Mississippi fiasco, Crockett gained a certain fame and the support of Winchester, and in 1827 won a seat in the U.S. House.

Back roads made mostly of gravel travel south of Hales Point and pass through Anderson-Tully Wildlife Area. These remote routes soon veer to the east and, via Arp, reach Highway 19, which heads west past Open Lake, formed by the same 1812 earthquakes that created Reelfoot Lake, owned by hunting and fishing clubs. You can avoid the hard-to-follow gravel roads by returning to U.S. 51 to pick up Highway 19. This road leads to Ashport, located in a former big bend of the river, which before the Civil War boasted several warehouses and a steam-operated sawmill. The town gradually declined—indeed, disappeared—as the waterway ate away the banks, and eventually the bend as well, but the river's straight stretch here still retains the name Ashport Bend. Farther west on the Mississippi lies Golddust, where a store or two and some houses elevated on stilts comprise the hamlet. It was named in the early 1880's by John Duncan who, while pondering what to call the new community, heard the whistle of the steamer *Gold Dust* signalling for a landing at Ashport, four miles away. In 1882, none other than Mark Twain rode as a passenger on the 1877 paddlewheeler—"She was neat, clean, and comfortable," he later wrote—when he traveled down the river to gather information for *Life on the Mississippi*. Some three months after Twain's trip, the *Gold Dust's* boilers exploded near Hickman, Kentucky, injuring fifty people and killing seventeen, including pilot Lem Gray, who Twain had found to be a great raconteur of river stories.

South of Golddust, the river bends around to Plum Point —"famous and formidable," Twain described it—where a tangle of snags, semi-submerged trees, sandbars, unpredictable churning currents and other vexations made this corner of the river the most feared stretch on the entire Lower Mississippi. This terrifying point wrecked many barges, flatboats, and steamers. Despite the inherent danger Captain Henry Shreve, a one time fur salesman, accepted the river's challenge. In December 1826, Shreve was appointed Superintendant of Western River Improvement. He invented a "snagboat," a vessel to clear rivers of debris, which he said could be built for $12,000, a fraction of the $1½ million lost from snags on the Mississippi the previous five years. Although officials in Washington viewed him as a crank, Shreve built at his own expense a small scale test boat which performed as he claimed, breaking off embedded trees and uprooting others. In June, 1828, the government agreed to support Shreve's idea, and in April, 1829, a shipyard at New Albany, Indiana, completed the snagboat *Heliopolis*. After a few preliminary tests Shreve took the ship to Plum Point, which he described as "the Most dangerous place on the Mississippi River," and, as he reported to the authorities, "In eleven hours the whole forrest of formidable snags, so long the terror of the Boatman (many of which were six feet in diameter) were effectively removed. All of them were broken off several feet below the surface of the sand at the bottom of the river." Washington was finally convinced. One of the Civil War's few naval engagements occurred at Plum Point when on May 10, 1862, seven lightly armed old steamers converted by the Confederates into iron-nosed rams comprising the "River Defense Fleet" smashed the Union gunboats *Cincinnati* and *Mound City* until they both sank. When the Union gunboats *Carondelet, Benton,* and *Pittsburg* arrived on the scene the rebel ships, lacking adequate firepower, retreated to Memphis.

Just south of Plum Point lies Driver Bar, bordered on the east by curved Crutcher Lake, formerly the river channel. Until Driver's Cutoff removed the Bar from the main channel in 1935, it formed Island Number 33. The formation was called Flour Island by early day rivermen as so many wrecked flatboats laden with flour barrels littered the land with the smashed containers. In 1820, a storm detained John James Audubon at the island, where he spent the interlude drawing a bald eagle he had killed near Caruthersville, Missouri.

Along the bottom edge of Driver Bar lies Fort Pillow State Park (8-10), site of a Confederate garrison built in September, 1861, to help Southerners control the Mississippi. After the fall of Columbus and Island Number 10 upstream to Union forces, they continued down the waterway where, as noted above, the Northerners encountered the Confederate River Defense Fleet at Plum Point, within sight of Fort Pillow, on May 10, 1862. This slightly delayed the Northern advance, but on June 4 the rebels, in danger of being cut off from their army, evacuated the outpost, perched atop Chickasaw Bluff Number 1, the first of four high bluffs overlooking the Mississippi in southern Tennessee. Union forces took the fort without a shot. The North held the redoubt, named for Mexican War hero General Gideon J. Pillow, until April, 1864, when Confederate General Nathan Bedford Forrest, a former slave trader, attacked Fort Pillow and supposedly engaged in overkill by massacring many of the defenders, nearly half of whom were black, referred to by Southerners as "home-made Yankees." The Northern press demanded an inquiry into the alleged atrocity, but the war ended by the time the investigation had begun and the public lost interest. The Mississippi changed course and now flows a mile west of the fort, where trails with interpretive signs wind past the well-preserved original breastworks dug to protect the gun batteries against land attacks. An interpretive center (8-4:30) contains exhibits on the installations.

Somewhere near Fort Pillow stood Fort Prudhomme, the earliest known European settlement in Tennessee, built by the French explorer La Salle in 1682 as he sailed south to the Mississippi's mouth. La Salle named the post for Pierre Prudhomme, the expedition's armorer, who left one day to hunt in the area and failed to reappear. La Salle sent out a search party which returned without Prudhomme but with reports of many Indians lurking in the area, so prompting the explorer to build the fort. Further searches later located Prudhomme, who stayed at the base with a few men while La Salle continued down the Mississippi. When the explorer returned he became ill here, and remained at Fort Prudhomme for forty days until he recovered. Just south of Fort Pillow, a group of land speculators founded a town named Fulton in 1827. It once claimed a population of 400, sustained by the steamboat trade, but now survives only as an overlook on the Mississippi with a few houses.

Highway 87 takes you east past the Fort Pillow Prison Farm—6,000 acres cultivated by the inmates, whose predecessors first arrived in 1937—to Henning, which lies just beyond U.S. 51. At Henning, a black youngster used to sit on the front porch of his family's house on summer evenings in the 1920's listening to tales told by his grandmother and other relatives about their ancestors. The stories told there in the Tennessee twilight and hot night inspired the boy when he grew up to research and write about his family and their forebears in Africa; thus did Alex Haley create his 1976 Pulitzer Prize-winning novel *Roots*. Now a State Historic Historic Site (Tu-Sat 10-5, Sun 1-5), listed on the National Register, the 1919 Haley House—-built by his grandfather, Will E. Palmer, head of a lumberyard, one of Tennessee's first black-owned businesses (1893)—contains a museum on the author's life and works. Members of Haley's family are buried at Bethlehem Cemetery a mile east of town (bypass the main entrance, continue on the road off to the right and follow it to the second entrance) in a small plot surrounded by a metal picket fence just outside the wire fence about 100 yards up from the parking area. A photo of "Chicken George"—seated in an oversized chair and wearing a white smock or gown—who led the family from North Carolina to Tennessee bears a quote: "Here they lie, from 'Chicken George,' grandson of the African Kunta Kinte, and on down the line to Kunta Kinte's great, great, great granddaughter, our mother, Bertha." On the far left stands a stone inscribed "Final resting place of 'Chicken George,'" and in a line off to the right parade seven other markers, the last commemorating Bertha G. Haley (died 1932), the author's mother. Haley (died 1992) reposes at the family home.

On Main Street, which parallels the Illinois Central tracks, a small Heritage Museum occupies the former Henning Supply Store, near Just A Small Town Restaurant. The C.S.O. Rice Cotton Gin, owned by the Rice family since 1928, occupies a boxy building five blocks to the north. Beyond a narrow tunnel under the tracks on McFarlin at the corner of Morris Ferry stands c. 1876 Belle Grove, a modest dwelling built as a summer residence by Dr. Bennett G. Henning, son of the town founder. In 1887 Dr. Henning diagnosed at Memphis the first case of yellow fever, the beginning of an epidemic which killed more than 5,000 people in the city. His wife Cornelia, member of a prominent Memphis family, disliked the laid-back life in the small town, once observing that she "would rather be a lamp post in Memphis than the belle of society in Henning." The marble and slate sections which pave Belle Grove's front walk came from Memphis' old Gayoso Hotel Lobby, across which Confederate General Nathan Bedford Forrest once supposedly rode his horse. At Nutbush, east of Henning, Annie Mae Bullocks grew up, called "teeny" as she was so tiny. "Teeny" began performing at the Nutbush store for pennies to feed her piggy bank, and later she started singing at church, picnics, and in the fields. She moved north and began a career as a professional singer, eventually marrying performer Ike Turner, and "Teeny" Bullocks became the famous Tina Turner.

At Covington, to the south, a lively courthouse square includes shops and commercial establishments on all sides. In the circle-shaped center section stands the Tipton County seat of government, with a dapper Confederate soldier statue on the lawn, thumbs hooked in his belt. The red marquee and neon lights of the Ruffin movie house and the green brick facade of the old Ritz cinema add theatrical touches, and the National Register-listed Lindo Hotel, a three-story, balcony-laden building with a curved corner section, now housing law and other offices, also adds a decorative touch to town. At Covington's Tennessee Gins, the world's second largest automated cotton gin, you can see (in season) how the area's leading crop is processed.

Nineteen miles west of Covington, out on Highway 59, the Mississippi flows by the place where the town of Randolph once stood. A boat dock, the modest, white, wood Turner's grocery store, and not much else comprise present-day Randolph. For a decade, however, the town, once Tennessee's largest river port, vied with Memphis for supremacy on the Mississippi. When the steamer era began to develop, the middle Mississippi needed a major port between St. Louis and New Orleans. The four Chickasaw bluffs along this stretch of the river offered some of the few feasible sites in the region. Randolph began in the 1820's on Bluff Number 2, north of the fourth rise where Memphis was founded about the same time. Only one of them would survive as the dominant city, and for a time Randolph enjoyed the advantage. At its peak in the mid-1830's, the town boasted twenty-two business houses and shipped out more cotton than its downstream rival. Much of Randolph's success came about because people shunned epidemic-ridden Memphis, which suffered from cholera in 1826 and 1832 and yellow fever in 1828. Furthermore, Memphis back then lay far removed from the state's mainstream, isolated in a little-populated, remote corner with Indian country to the south and a dense wilderness to the east toward Nashville. Davy Crockett proposed a canal from the Tennessee River to the Hatchie, which entered the Mississippi by Randolph, a project which would have assured the city's dominance. But the proposal failed, and meanwhile in 1829, Memphis managed to gain a three times weekly mail service to Jackson, and also a stagecoach line which connected the city with Nashville and Little Rock, Arkansas. In 1834, the purchase by the federal government of the remaining Chickasaw land in northern Mississippi gave Memphis access to a rich hinterland. The panic of 1837 severly affected the river counties and especially Randolph, their commercial center. In 1838, low water there diverted steamers and the cotton trade to Memphis, which began to upstage its upstream rival, so by 1840, the settlement on the lower bluff finally emerged as the dominant river city. During the Civil War, General William Tecumseh Sherman inaugurated his policy of total war by means of burning Southern settlements, later prominently carried out at Atlanta, when in 1862 the Union commander set Randolph aflame to retaliate after the town fired on the federal steamer *Eugene* at Richardsons Landing below the bluffs there. After the war, railroads and highways bypassed the fragment of a town which remained, in 1871 the bluff began to crumble away, and now the once-leading river center remains forgotten and forlorn, lacking even a place on Tennessee's official highway map.

Back on Highway 51, designated a Tennessee Scenic Parkway, you'll pass through Millington, site of the Naval Air Station, the world's largest inland naval complex. A road to the right (at Millington Square shopping center) leads nine miles west out to the Meeman-Shelby Forest State Park, located along the Mississippi where Chickasaw Bluff Number 3 rises. According to some accounts, La Salle's 1682 Fort Prudhomme stood here rather than on Bluff Number 1 to the north. The park was named in honor of Memphis newspaper editor Edward J. Meeman, who helped establish not only the preserve but also the Great Smoky Mountains National Park in East Tennessee. It includes a museum and nature center, as well as hiking and riding trails, some in the river bottoms, a campground, and six housekeeping cabins (901-876-5215). As you approach Memphis on Highway 51 (Danny Thomas Boulevard), about two miles south of the Highway 388 turnoff to Meeman-Shelby a right turn at the Salvation Army store just past Northgate Shopping Center (located on the left side of the road) puts you on Whitney, where you continue west past a pale, blue-green water tower and curve around the General DeWitt Spain Airport. You then pass the Continental

Grain and Bunge facilities on Second Street, turn right on Henry for two blocks, then left on Front, which goes by the aromatic Conwood snuff factory and the Mississippi flood control installation before entering Memphis' downtown area.

At Jackson and Front, on the oldest part of Memphis, stands the city's newest attraction, the just completed stainless steel thirty-two story Great American Pyramid. It cost nearly $2 million a floor, and houses a 22,000 seat arena and may eventually include such attractions as the American Music Awards Hall of Fame, the College Football Hall of Fame, the Memphis Music Experience sight and sound section, the Egyptian Experience simulated ancient tomb, and an Inclinator Ride outside the structure up to the observation tower.

The Pyramid stands by the Mississippi at the site of the first Memphis waterfront where, as early as 1783, Paddy Meagher established a presence. Forty years later he built a warehouse, next to which in 1829 rose the city's first brick structure. Soon after 1830, the river here began to silt up and the landing moved south to Market Avenue and below. Long before this, the Chickasaw occupied the bluff here, then in 1739 the first Europeans arrived. The French built a primitive outpost, which was soon dismantled, called Fort Assumption. Bluff Number 4 remained under the control of the Chickasaw, who the Spanish hoped would block American expansion to the west. In 1795 Gayoso, the Spanish governor of Louisiana, secured permission from the Indians to establish an outpost at the mouth of the Wolf River. This installation, named Fort San Fernando de Barrancas, the governor himself dedicated on May 30. So concerned were the people of Tennessee about access to the river after the Spanish arrived that at the January, 1796, Constitutional Convention in Knoxville, delegates inserted into the state constitution a clause providing that all citizens shall enjoy "an equal participation in the free navigation of the Mississippi" which cannot be "conceded to any prince, potentate, power, person or persons whatever."

The following year the Spanish evacuated the base, as they had agreed in a treaty with the Americans, who arrived to establish their own base, called Fort Adams and then Fort Pickering.

After acquisition of the region from the Chickasaw in 1818, Andrew Jackson, John Overton, and James Winchester laid the new city out, tempting prospective settlers with the claim that Memphis was "the only site for a town of any magnitude on the Missisippi between the mouth of the Ohio and Natchez." Little growth occurred during the early years, as Randolph to the north dominated the area. But in 1834, the first steamboat service started from Memphis to New Orleans. In 1843, a telegraph line between the two cities began. In 1857, the Memphis & Charleston Railroad arrived, which connected the city with the Atlantic coast, a milestone celebrated when the first train brought two hogsheads of ocean salt water and dumped them into the Mississippi. The citizens of Memphis looked on from Confederate Park downtown on June 6, 1862, as Union gunboats sank six of the seven defending Southern ships in an encounter which lasted only ninety minutes. It was followed by a demand of surrender, to which Mayor John Park replied, "The city is in your hands." Yellow fever epidemics in 1867, 1873, and 1878 retarded the city's development, but in 1892 the first railroad bridge south of St. Louis crossed the river at Memphis, followed in 1909 by Harahan Bridge, rebuilt in 1915-1916 (now disused), the first vehicle and rail bridge south of Cairo. These spans helped augment trade and led to the city's growth as a hardwood and cotton center. The manager of the Memphis Southern Association baseball team once promised to dive from Harahan Bridge into the Mississippi if his club didn't finish ahead of the Little Rock Travelers, but he left in mid-season, thus avoiding the leap.

Near the pyramid area, the oldest part of town, lies the Pinch District, so called in the 1830's for impoverished residents of the poor neighborhood nicknamed "Pinch Guts" as their belts contracted their scrawny, underfed midriffs. At the corner of

Auction (named for a slave market there) and North Front stood the early forts San Fernando and Adams, and a block south on Front rose Paddy Meagher's Bell Tavern, frequented by Sam Houston, Andrew Jackson, Davy Crockett and other early day notables. All distances from Memphis are measured from the zero milestone at the post office, 1 South Front. To the south down Front lie Confederate Park and below, by the riverfront, Jefferson Davis Park, memorializing the President of the Confederacy, who from 1867 to 1875 lived in a house which stood at 129 Court Avenue. Farther on along South Front stretches Cotton Row, with the c. 1924 Cotton Exchange (inside is a small exhibit on cotton production) founded in the mid-1870's and now the world's largest spot cotton market. Across the street lies the Carver Seed Company, a colorful 1920's-vintage establishment in an 1843 building, the last of the many Front Street seed and feed stores which served farmers who brought their produce to the big city.

On Adams by the waterfront a monorail connects with Festival (originally City and until 1991 Mud) Island (April-Oct 10-10, Nov-March 10-5), a 50 acre area opened in 1982, featuring a 2600 foot long, three-dimensional model of the Lower Mississippi. More than 840 gallons of water per minute flow through the mini-Mississippi, consisting of 1,746 five ton pre-cast concrete sections which show the vertical topography of the river valley and include on the banks black slate tiles (72,000 of them in all) forming twenty-one river towns. Some seventy-five descriptive plaques relating information about steamers, plantations, pirates, shipwrecks, the Civil War, and other river lore line the model waterway. As you stroll in a few minutes from Cairo to New Orleans, each thirty-inch step equivalent to a mile, it seems as if, for once, you can dominate the Mississippi, the real version of which flows by in its indomitable way just a few yards from the model. That interplay of the waterway and its tiny twin lends the walk a striking sense of drama: the real and the replica, visual echoes, seem to complement each other. A museum (April-Oct 10-7, Nov-March 10-3:30) on Festival Island—over which passes the gracefully M-shaped 1973 De Soto Bridge—highlights three centuries of boat history on the river, including a reconstruction of the 1870's packet *Belle of the Bluffs* grand salon, main deck, and pilot house.

The rivulet between Festival Island and downtown Memphis comes from the Wolf River, diverted to maintain a channel after the island developed. That addition to the Mississippi at Memphis accreted when an eddy deposited mud against the stern of the gunboat *Aphrodite* while the ship moored at the city for some six months in 1910 because of low water. At the foot of Monroe on the riverfront across from the World War II B-17 bomber *Memphis Belle* exhibited on Festival Island are the *Memphis Queen II* and *Island Queen* excursion boats (901-527-5694 and 800-221-6197). Not far south legendary Beale Street begins— "where the heart meets the soul," proclaims a billboard—now lined with music spots, restaurants, and other establishments which recall Beale's blues heritage. On Mulberry a few blocks south of Beale, the new (summer 1991) National Civil Rights Museum (Tu-Sat 10-5, Sun 1-6, Sept-May Sun 1-5) occupies the rebuilt former Lorraine Motel where in 1968 Martin Luther King was assassinated as he stood on a balcony in front of his room. Tom Lea Park by the river honors another black hero, who in 1925 used his small boat to rescue thirty-two people when the *U.S. Norman* sank. In November 1991 part of the park's new expansion along the Mississippi collapsed into the river, delaying completion of the additional terrain to be reclaimed from the waterway. South along Riverside Drive the Memphis Mississippi gauge functions. It serves as one of the thirty or so such Corps of Engineers mechanisms, first authorized by Congress in 1871, used to obtain readings for flood control and for navigation improvements on the waterway. Up on a nearby bluff stands the Unitarian Church of the River, with a splendid picture-window view onto the waterway, the most advantageously placed sanctuary on the Mississippi. Ashburn Park, by the river, memorializes General T.Q. Ashburn, who operated a river terminal for his barge line here, while Martyr Park, not far south, recalls the city's 1870's yellow fever victims. Beyond the 1949 Memphis-Arkansas Bridge, Interstate 55, lie De Soto Park, with views onto the river, and the adjacent National Ornamental Metal Museum (Tu-Sat 10-5, Sun 12-5), the nation's only museum devoted to that subject, with a lacy metallic gazebo affording a sweeping panorama of the Mississippi below.

Farther south along the river, beyond the petroleum docks, lies Presidents Island, a twelve mile long, 32,000 acre land mass, formerly the largest island in the entire waterway and now connected to the mainland. Presidents hosts docks and other facilities which comprise part of the Memphis Harbor, the nation's second largest inland port, with five public terminals and other private ones which handle more than ten million tons of cargo annually. Presidents' varied history has included farms, land owned by Andrew Jackson, a Civil War-era black colony sponsored by the Freedman's Bureau, a federal agency for former slaves, sunken steamers, the farm of Confederate General Nathan Bedford Forrest, who died after drinking impure water there in 1876, and moonshine stills. One time, when the river changed course years back, it washed out a cemetery on the island and undermined a Memphis saloon, carrying both coffins and liquor barrels downstream together.

Eleven miles south of downtown at McKeller Lake, a backwater extension of the Mississippi below Presidents Island, lies T.O. Fuller State Park. Officials changed the original name, Shelby Bluffs, to honor a Memphis clergyman and educator who favored interracial cooperation. When Civilian Conservation Corps workers began excavations for a proposed swimming pool in 1940 they unearthed traces of a prehistoric settlement, now partially reconstructed on four acres as Chucalissa ("abandoned house") Indian Village (Tu-Sat 9-5, Sun 1-5). Choctaw Indians in attendance along with a conical temple, a burial exhibit, thatched huts, and a trench through layers of successive settlements recall the Mississippians who occupied the area from about 1000 to 1500 A.D., while the C.H. Nash Museum contains early tools, pottery, weapons, and displays tracing the region's history from 10,000 B.C.

Bed and breakfast places in Memphis include the Greystone Inn (901-278-7897) and turn-of-the-century Lowenstein-Long House (901-527-7174), while Bed and Breakfast in Memphis (901-726-5920) offers a reservation service for accommodations in the city and elsewhere in Tennessee. Not far east of T.O. Fuller State Park runs U.S. Highway 61, which takes you south out of Tennessee and into the state named for the Mississippi.

Arkansas

Thanks to the Mississippi, Arkansas from its earliest days enjoyed a means of communication with the outside world, but—no thanks to the Mississippi—the great river has also constantly vexed the territory. "The Mississippi supplied the eastern lowlands along the banks with year-round navigation," states George H. Thompson in *Arkansas and Reconstruction*, "but brought with this advantage the hazards associated with a winding and treacherous course, falling banks, and frequent inundations." Moreover, notes Harry S. Ashmore in *Arkansas: A Bicentennial History*, "the great, meandering Mississippi River" served as "a barrier for those traveling east and west, and a means of passage for voyagers coming down from the north." Present day travelers through the Arkansas Delta—a ten million acre strip of rich agricultural land bordering the waterway the entire length of the state—will find similar vexations, for the River Road memorializes the Mississippi but seldom reveals it. Apart from Helena, virtually no cities in the six Arkansas counties along the river lie directly on the Mississippi, so views of the stream remain few and far between.

The Mississippi enters Arkansas not far northeast of Blytheville, six miles south of the Missouri line and eight miles west of the river. Porch-fronted houses and leafy trees line the residential streets in Blytheville, named for Methodist minister Henry T. Blythe who in 1853 built a residence and small church on high land far enough from the menacing Mississippi to escape the frequent floods. Around the sanctuary a village developed called Blythe Chapel, which began its major growth after the first cotton gin began to operate in 1888. Around the turn of the century, the town prospered with the arrival of rail lines and the lumber industry. In 1902, the first drainage district converted some of the lowlands from swampy soil to extremely productive farm country, now thick with rice, cotton, and soybeans.

One colorful early resident, physician and planter Benjamin A. Bugg, who cultivated the land near Blytheville, prided himself on his 20-year-old, 6 foot, 6 inch beard, which he sometimes wore while hunting wrapped around his neck like a scarf for warmth. Usually, however, Bugg tied the appendage in silk ribbons and tucked the end into his shirt. At the 1893 Chicago Columbian Exposition, Bugg encountered a rival who sported a beard one inch longer. This so disappointed the Arkansan that he returned home and cut his whiskers off.

At Blytheville's Mississippi County Community College you'll find the world's largest solar photovoltaic demonstration project, which generates sufficient energy from the sun to heat the campus. Eaker Air Force Base landed on the Defense Department's April, 1991, list of military posts targeted for termination, but if the Strategic Air Command B-52 facility remains open, visitors can take driving tours (by appointment: M-F 7:30-4: 501-

762-6794). Farther west lies Big Lake National Wildlife Refuge, a way-station for migrating waterfowl on the Mississippi Flyway. To the east on the river, Barfield Landing offers a county park with a splendid view of the waterway. The area took its name from George C. Barfield who operated a warehouse to store goods and produce brought by flatboats and keelboats from the Forked Deer River in Tennessee until the merchandise could be transferred to steamers for shipment down the Mississippi.

A gravel road south out of Barfield leads to Tomato, named when a postal official arrived in 1895 and asked a storekeeper who then handled all the mail what the proposed post office should be called. The shop owner referred the query to his daughter, just then stacking shelves with cans of tomatoes, which prompted her suggestion. In 1950, Tomato's post office moved to a 1923 smokehouse building, a culinary combination with possibilities. At Daniels Point, on the river beyond O'Donnell Bend to the south, engineers carried out some of the earliest experimental work for erosion control when they installed willow mat revetments along the banks which the Mississippi proceeded to wash away in 1891 and 1892. Subsequently built dikes off Daniels Point and concrete revetments on the Tennessee side proved more durable.

On Highway 61, the River Road through Mississippi County, lies Luxora, founded in 1882 by D.T. Walker, who built a one-room store on the river's shore and named the settlement for his daughter. Steamers served the village, and in 1899 the railroad arrived, but these days the village of some 1,700 people seems rather moribund, with the peeling, dark, red paint on the marquee of the Luxora Theater setting the tone for the town. Osceola (pronounced "Oh-see-ola") a few miles south began in 1830, when William B. Edrington bartered with Indians living at the site to acquire their land. To encourage steamboats to stop there he sold them firewood at especially low prices. Incorporated in 1838 as Plum Point, the town later took the name of the

Indian chief who fought white settlers in Florida during the 1830's Seminole Wars. Resourceful J.W. De Witt, the first postmaster, threw together a shanty with lumber salvaged from wrecked steamboats, many of them done in at nearby Plum Point, the highly hazardous stretch known as the most dangerous run on the Lower Mississippi (see the Tennessee section). On the lawn of the National Register-listed courthouse, a beige-brown brick building topped by a squat copper dome, stands a metal relief of native son Congressman William J. Driver—a vivid portrayal, showing him clad in a wrinkled coat and sporting a watch chain on his vest—who as a member of Congress's River, Harbors and Flood Control Committees promoted "the enactment of laws which curbed the mighty Mississippi, the St. Francis, and other rivers of this area and minimized the danger of devastating floods," states a plaque. Driver, it continues, was "recognized as the foremost authority on drainage and flood control" and "the St. Francis Basin's most valued citizen. His life was gentle, and the elements so mixed in him, that nature might stand up and say to all the world, 'This was a man!'" (The last sentence repeats Antony's praise of Brutus at the end of Shakespeare's *Julius Caesar*.) Three years after the establishment of Mississippi County in 1833, Osceola, hometown of Holiday Inn founder Kemmons Wilson, became the seat of government, but since about 1900 the county has maintained a second courthouse at Blytheville to serve the Northern District. Opposite the Osceola courthouse stand a few commercial buildings dating from 1875, while the Hale Avenue Historic District includes other vintage structures.

Osceola, which originally lay directly on the river, enjoyed a lively steamboat trade, but the Mississippi deposited a sandbar at the waterfront, blocking it. In the 1970's, the city established a new port south of town, the only place in the area where the Mississippi can conveniently be seen. You can reach the river on Highway 198 either via 239 south out of Osceola on Chestnut

Street, or off of U.S. 61 five miles south of town where a Cargill sign indicates the turnoff. On the way east on 198, you'll pass the pale yellow tanks of the Cargill grain shipping facility and the modern Viskase factory, which makes cellulose tubing meat packers use to contain hot dogs and sausages. You then reach the river at the Bunge installation, where the Mississippi flows along just before you, ripples and eddies blotching the moving water's surface. At Island Number 30, a few miles upstream the huge sternwheeler towboat *Sprague* suffered a major disaster in 1913, when Old Man River spun "Big Mama," as rivermen called her, into a chute behind the island, tipping its barges, which dropped tons of coal into the water. The Mississippi later ripped away the old stone dikes at the island and washed away the huge mounds of coal as the waterway opened a new channel through the chute. The *Sprague* resumed service until the 1940's when "Mama" retired to become a tourist attraction on the Vicksburg waterfront, but in 1974 a fire destroyed most of the ship. At Craigshead Point a few miles south of the Bunge terminal, Union General John Pope's army arrived on April 13, 1862, after his victory at Island Number 10, accompanied by the federal fleet of gunboats under Andrew Foote. Across the way loomed the heavily armed Confederate redoubt at Fort Pillow, which the commanders proposed to bypass by cutting a canal across Craighead Point, a plan not executed as Pope's superior ordered him to advance to another point. Foote, suffering from a wound which led to his death, departed. While his successor pondered strategy to attack Fort Pillow, the Confederates withdrew from the post.

Wilson, a town of 1,000 on Highway 61 to the south, serves as the control center for the south's largest family owned plantation. This 33,000 acre spread began in 1886 when Robert Edward Lee Wilson rented swampland near the Mississippi, cut timber there and, instead of abandoning the land as did most loggers, he drained the terrain to create farmable fields. Following Wilson's saw that "the plow should follow a saw," the firm continued to drain former timberland for agricultural use. After the founding father died in 1933, R.E.L. Wilson, Jr. succeeded him. In 1950 Wilson III took over and managed the properties—twenty-two farms, with 13,000 acres devoted to cotton and other fields planted with soybeans and some fifteen other crops, including strawberries, alfalfa, rice, and turnip greens—until his death in 1987, when his sons assumed the reins. Reins remain scarce, though, for the modernized, mechanized company operates some 180 tractors, uses mobile phones, scrapers to level the land, and other updated equipment. Back in the 1930's anyone traveling from West Memphis to Blytheville crossed property owned by the company, which enforced a policy against vagrancy by allowing transients to spend only one night in town and offering them a job which, if refused, required the drifters to move on. A rare example of a still functioning company town, diminutive Wilson includes the five story white Wilson Seed and Chemical Division building, Lee Wilson Insurance, Wilson Funeral Service, the Lee Wilson and Company general office, and other Wilsonian establishments. Brick sidewalks lend a cozy touch to the town, while most of the village buildings, including even the Exxon station, sport Tudor-style architecture. A cotton gin stands by train tracks opposite the town square, where a monument recalls patriarch "R.E. Lee Wilson pioneer-builder-leader." Behind the square and the thick-beamed, arcade-fronted, commercial row stretches a pleasant tree-shaded residential area, but the neighborhood off to the east beyond the train line appears to lie on the wrong side of the tracks. Hampson Museum State Park (Tu-Sat 9-5) at Wilson contains exhibits relating to the Nodena site, an Indian town dating from 1350 to 1700 excavated in the 1930's by James K. Hampson, who studied the site at his family plantation when the physician began examining skeletons of the tribe's deceased.

At Dyess west of Wilson country singer Johnny Cash grew up. He picked cotton and picked out tunes on a guitar, as he sang from his pick-up truck and at area socials. In 1934, William R. Dyess, the first director of the Works Progress Administration in Arkansas, divided 17,500 acres into 500 units to form a cooperative agricultural community, the first of sixteen such resettlement projects in the state intended to give impoverished farm tenants a new start. A museum (April-Oct Sat 10-4, Sun 1-4) at Lepanto, a few miles west, contains exhibits on the Delta and its agricultural heritage.

Trees line Highway 61 south of Wilson, where a rice mill stands a few miles on. Wilson Company tenant houses in the countryside traditionally bore red roofs and green paint. At Joiner, a village of 725, Gin Street leads to the shabby commercial area, where a tin-roofed, red wood shop displays garments on the front porch, while across the street stands a tiny City Hall. Highway 118 from Joiner to the east dead-ends at the Mississippi, where not far downstream stood Devil's Island, not a penal colony like the one in French Guinea but a punitively tricky run of the river at the so-called Devil's Race Course which pilots dreaded. Traveling down the Mississippi in the winter of 1820-1821, John James Audubon noted in his journal that he was hardly surprised to find the Devil "on this accursed river." In 1876, the Centennial Cutoff, a variance the river engineered in honor of the nation's birthday, eliminated the Devil's Race Course, a change which eventually led to other natural alterations that shortened the channel by some thirty miles.

U.S. 61 borders I-55 a few miles, then turns into Highway 77, the River Road, which gives access to the Wapanocca National Wildlife Refuge (Visitor Center M-F 7:30-4:30), where a seven mile nature drive winds through the Mississippi Flyway preserve favored in the winter by bald eagles, ducks (mainly mallards), herons, and some 230 other species of birds. A group of Memphis businessmen operated the once privately owned area as a hunting club, until the U.S. Fish and Wildlife Service acquired the preserve, now 5,500 acres centering on an oxbow lake, formerly the Mississippi's channel, now five miles east. Swamps comprise a quarter of the area's land section, with the balance divided between remnants of the bottomland hardwood forests and fields cultivated by farmers who harvest their share of the co-op crop and leave the Refuge's portion for wildlife to eat.

At Marion, just past Sunset eight miles farther on, you'll see the Crittendon County courthouse. Above it perches a squat, red cupola, while at the front stretches a lawn garnished with magnolias. Over the building's columned porticos (both front and back), it bears the slogan: "Obedience to the law is liberty," a phrase accentuated by the adjacent prisoner's exercise yard enclosed with a chainlink fence topped with razor wire. Along Main stand a few venerable columned brick buildings, among them the old bank and the former Marion Hotel, now an apartment but still signalled by a sign, white letters on a fading green background, out on the highway. At Redman Point on the Mississippi, four miles east of town, the nation's worst marine disaster occurred in April 1865 when the 776 pasenger *Sultana*, greatly overcrowded with 2,134 Union soldiers recently released from Southern prisons, exploded and caught fire, drowning more than 1500 victims. Not long before, a shipyard at Memphis, just downstream, had patched the boilers and sent the veterans, eager to head home, on their way. Instead, they perished in a disaster which exceeded the death toll for the *Titanic* (1,513), the *Lusitania* (1,198) and all other nautical mishaps before and after, until Soviet planes wrecked the German passenger vessel *Wilhelm Gustloft* in the Baltic Sea during World War II, killing 4,120 refugees.

As early as the 1830's, residents in this area tried to fend off the Mississippi's frequent floods. In his travel diary, William N. Wyatt tells how, after he crossed the river at Memphis in November, 1836, he rode to Marion and "Thence—on the levee which reaches from the Mississippi 18 miles west." He proceeded farther west "through the mud and on the levee," finally reaching an area beyond the St. Francis River, then observing, "Have seen no very desirable country from the Mississippi to this place."

Early settlers, however, found the area desirable. In 1794, Benjamin Fooy (or Foy), a native of Holland, moved to the Chickasaw Bluffs at Memphis to settle just across the Mississippi, where he served as Indian agent for Gayoso, the Spanish governor of Louisiana. After the Americans forced Spain to vacate its fort on the east side of the river, Gayoso withdrew his men to a point opposite Memphis and built Fort Esperanza there. In 1795, the Spanish moored at the site galleys sent from the high seas to patrol and control the Mississippi. A few years later, they withdrew, and Esperanza became known as Hope Encampment and then Hopefield, one of Arkansas's first towns. Fooy, wrote Josiah H. Shinn in his 1908 *Pioneers and Makers of Arkansas*, represented "the first of the mighty army of settlers on the Mississippi,... the connecting link between the vanishing barbarism of the wild woods and the rising civilization of modern times." Hopefield became a thriving river port, and in 1858 the Memphis and Little Rock, Arkansas' first railroad, began operating trains on thirty-eight miles of track between the town and Madison on the St. Francis River. (At Brinkley, thirty miles west of Madison, the delightful Great Southern Hotel, 501-734-4955, offers regional cooking and bed and breakfast in the restored 1915 hostelry which served passengers on the line when the railroad extended the track to Lick Skillet, the hamlet's original name.) Although Hopefield was burned during the Civil War and its charred remains washed away by the Mississippi, as late as 1890 a ferryboat crossed the waterway from Memphis to connect with the railroad, a service unnecessary after construction in 1892 of the first rail bridge south of St. Louis.

West Memphis, which lies near vanished Hopefield's site, sprawls south of Interstates 40 and 55, a clutter of fast food franchises, strip shopping malls, gas stations, and other such eyesores. Southland Greyhound Park offers dog races—a private section at the track sports the name The Kennel Club—while Delta Farm Tours runs excursions (April 15-Aug, 10, Sept-Dec 9:30 and 3, 501-732-3384) to such Arkansas Delta farms and facilities as soybean, rice and cotton plantations, the Crittenden Gin Company, which processes (Sept-Dec) up to 600 bales (each 480 pounds) a day and Shivers Flying Service, a crop duster. Established in 1910 as a logging camp called Bragg's Spur, the town changed its name to West Memphis when incorporated in 1927 in order to take advantage of premium prices overseas buyers paid for lumber identified as originating in the Memphis area.

A few miles west of West Memphis, a left turn off U.S. 70 onto Highway 147 takes you south past Simsboro, where logger John C. Claybrook established a sawmill, accumulated 300 acres, and by the 1950's had become one of the region's wealthiest black businessmen. The road circles around Horseshoe Lake, a resort frequented by Memphians, where Snowden House (501-339-3414) takes bed and breakfast guests. Highway 38 takes you west a few miles to U.S. 79, where you continue south to cross the tree-lined St. Francis River, which curves its way toward the Mississippi, flowing by the support pylons of a vanished bridge. Along the St. Francis lay the epicenter of the New Madrid earthquakes, the nation's most severe, estimated at 8.4-8.6 on the modern Richter scale. The tremors opened huge fissures along the river, creating depressions known as the "St. Francis Sunken Lands." After the quakes, membership in the Methodist Church in Arkansas increased by 50 percent. Farther on, a dirt road runs east for eleven miles out to the W.G. Huxtable Pumping Plant, believed to be the world's largest such facility. It boasts a pumping capacity of more than five million gallons a minute, used to divert the St. Francis River into a 20 mile long lake. This serves to protect the St. Francis River basin, Arkansas' largest levee district, from floods.

Marianna to the south—named for Mary Ann Harland, who with heirs of her first husband, sold the site where the town began—spreads out beyond a cozy square, here a rectangle, bordered on three sides by brick-paved streets. A slim square pillar topped by a Confederate soldier statue honors "the lost cause, " as Southerners came to call their struggle. At the far end of the square, the less than attractive grey stone and yellow-beige brick courthouse perches on a low rise. Also on the square stands a gazebo and a granite marker erected in 1970, centennial of the town's incorporation, comparing the population size (163 in 1870, 6,215 a century later) and commercial activities—agriculture in both eras, but by 1970, industry had replaced timber. Fire plugs around town painted as figures, their sides spouting arms, lend colorful touches to the town, whose population since 1970 has surged by five to 6,220. On West Main, two blocks from the square, the Marianna-Lee County Museum stands. Featuring an old general store, displays on cotton and pioneer history, it occupies a National Register-listed house where the Elks Club headquartered. Across the street stands the 1911 Register-listed McClintock West House, embellished with iron grill work, a quartet of fluted columns, and two magnolia trees in the spacious yard. Texas Street, which becomes Highway 44, leads out to a yellow wood house on the left side of the road, about half a mile beyond the south end of town. Here, a partially vine-covered marker indicates the home site and grave of pioneer John Patterson (born 1790, died 1886) who, as the inscription relates, was "Arkansas' first native born child of Anglo-Saxon parentage. The following riddle was often asked by John Patterson: 'I was born in a kingdom—Spain/ Reared in an empire—France/ Attained manhood in a territory,/ Am now a citizen of a state/ and have never been 100 miles from where I was born."

To proceed south, you can either return to Highway 1, the River Road, which south of Marianna passes a cotton experimental facility and continues on, via U.S. 49, to Helena, or follow 44 which eventually becomes the gravel Forest Road 1900. This route, one of the nation's seventy recently designated National Forest Service Scenic Byways, passes through St. Francis National Forest. A parallel road, 1901, connects with 1901B, a spur out to the confluence of the St. Francis and the Mississippi. In January, 1819, Thomas Nuttall, an English Arkanasas traveler who published the first comprehensive work on American botany, reached the St. Francis's mouth, where he found screeching parrots feeding on buttonwood seeds. The birds, killed over the years by hunters, no longer caw their calls, and now, at this remote corner of the Mississippi River valley, a peaceful silence reigns.

The St. Francis, which rises in the southeastern Missouri Ozarks 475 miles northwest, provided navigation until the New Madrid earthquakes of 1811-1812 caused the stream to clog up with driftwood, later removed. The 1941 Wappapello Dam at the headwaters regulates the river's flow, while some 300 miles of levees protect the lower basin from floods. In 1738 Bienville, governor of French Louisiana, built Fort St. Francis at the river's mouth as a base for a campaign against the Chickasaw. The French soon abandoned the outpost and moved north to establish Fort Assumption at the site of Memphis. In 1797, Sylvanus Phillips from North Carolina built a two story log cabin near here which soon became a popular way-station for travelers on the Mississippi. Phillips later founded Helena, which he named about 1820 for his daughter.

Upstream, east of the Huxtable Dam and Pumping Station, the St. Francis flows within about a mile of the Mississippi. On April 15, 1927, during the great flood, the larger river broke through the levee at the Whitehall Crevasse there, then threatened to reach the tributary and form a new confluence some miles north of the present one. A mile or two upstream from the existing mouth the Corps of Engineers completed the Hardin Cutoff in 1942, the last of thirteen such straightenings on the

Mississippi between Memphis and Baton Rouge authorized in 1933. After the cutoff eliminated the meandering loop known as OK Bend, the former Ship Island nearby found itself several miles inland. Somewhere beneath this now land-locked spot the remains of the steamer *Pennsylvania* crumble away. The ship exploded in June 1858, then drifted downstream where the blazing wreck lodged against Ship Island. Among the 160 or so fatalities, many of them German immigrants, was a young ship's clerk named Henry Clemens, who died in a Memphis hospital. His brother, a cub pilot on the *Pennsylvania*, escaped possible death by remaining behind in New Orleans when the ship sailed; thus did Sam Clemens survive to become Mark Twain.

Helena, Arkansas's only truly old time Mississippi River town, enjoys a laid-back nineteenth century ambiance where "long ago is not so far away," as the sleepy settlement of 21,000 (including busier West Helena) describes itself. Commercial West Helena, founded in 1910 on a former plantation, stands on Crowley's Ridge, a 100 to 200 foot high elevated strip which extends for more than 200 miles from southeastern Missouri through Arkansas to this point near the Mississippi. The rise was named for Benjamin F. Crowley, a War of 1812 soldier who established the first settlement near the northern part of the ridge. The formation originated in the post-glacier age when the elevation—once located between the Mississippi, then flowing to its west, and the Ohio, just to its east—survived the rivers' eroding action and caught wind-blown loess which built the rise to its present height above the Delta lowlands. Oakland Avenue winds down Crowley's Ridge toward the Mississippi. Along this attractive, divided parkway stands a small, marble pillar commemorating what was supposedly the first Christian service west of the Mississippi, held on June 25, 1541 by Spanish explorer Hernando de Soto shortly after he crossed the river. Farther on, a square, white marker recalls Father Jacques Marquette who, with Joliet, "terminated his exploration [of the Mississippi] in Arkansas [and] returned north 17 July 1673."

Down in town, more than twenty National Historic Register structures evoke Helena's past. Dwellings include the 1826 Estevan Hall (tours by appointment: 501-338-8247), believed to be the city's oldest building. Helen Keller's grandparents married here in 1845. You'll also see the curved-verandah 1904 Edwardian Inn, a 12 room bed and breakfast establishment (501-338-9155); the c. 1858 Allin House, since 1982 offices, fronted by tall shutters and a 2-story arcade; William Straub's 1900 residence, its French doors added just after his death in 1929 (the original doorways proved too narrow to accommodate his coffin); the richly colored 1892 Tappan-Cunningham House, splashed with blue-grey, salmon pink and yellow paint; the much photographed 1890's Pillow-Thompson House, piled with porch sections, a turret-like tower, and Queen Anne-style architectural touches; and the 1907 dwelling called Evelyn's Southern Charm (501-338-3250), named for the indeed charming Evelyn Pittman, who takes bed and breakfast guests and, by reservation, serves Southern-style meals, accompanied by her serenade of songs such as "Mighty Mississippi"—"Old Man River keeps on callin', And there ain't no place on earth I'd rather be."

Helena offers some additional Register-listed places. These include the Old Almer store, now an arts and crafts cooperative (Tu-Sat 12-4). Swiss immigrant Ulrich Almer built the structure in 1872 with wood recyled from his flatboat, and its cabin, he floated down the Mississippi to Helena. The 1905 Centennial Baptist Church is the state's only black sanctuary designed by a black architect. The 1921 cypress log American Legion Hut was built by World War I veterans to recall the cabins they occupied whil fighting in France. A small French freight car ("Train de la Reconnaissance Française") on the grounds also evokes the European campaign. The restored Classic Revival-style 1914 courthouse, which sports eight inset fluted columns, stands near the World War I "doughboy" statue, his right hand held aloft grasping a hand grenade. The likeable 1891 Phillips County Library and Museum (M-Sat 1-4), bears over the door old fashioned gold letters spelling out "Public Library."

A marker at 609 Perry recalls Helena's Fort Curtis, one of five fortified federal positions which, with the aid of the U.S. gunboat *Tyler*, held off a Confederate attack on July 4, 1863, the very day Vicksburg fell to Union forces. Soldiers nicknamed their Commander, Theophilus Holmes, "Granny" as the half deaf old man scarcely presented a commanding appearance. While defending Arkansas Post to the south the previous January, "Granny" ordered his forces to "hold the place until every man is dead," a do-and-die attitude received rather unenthusiastically in the ranks. On the north side of Helena lies Maple Hill Cemetery (closes at 5). On the steep hillside above a Confederate graveyard nestles, with moss-bearded markers in a shadowed grove and a pillar topped by a soldier statue. On the way down the terraced hill, beyond the treetops, appear occasional glimpses of the Mississippi in the distance. Out College Street, a hidden hollow holds tumbled tombstones and markers tilted at eccentric angles in another burial ground, Magnolia Cemetery, established in the 1850's.

In downtown Helena, which includes the Cherry Street National Historic District, a number of late nineteenth and early twentieth century commercial structures survive. The oldest is the c.1879 former Bank of Helena Building, 509 Cherry, and the tallest is the five-story 1880 Helena National Bank Building, which housed KFFA, home radio station for the famous King Biscuit Time blues program, recalled by the King Biscuit Blues Festival (held every October) kiosk up the street. The show, sponsored by King Biscuit Flour and first aired in November, 1941, featured local singer and harmonica player Sonny Boy Williamson, whose name the sponsor used to designate "Sonny Boy" brand corn meal, a product still sold in the area. Near the kiosk, Casqui Restaurant advertises on its front window "Home of the Bluesburger," a delicacy illustrated by a painted burger and orange-hued cheese slice. Along Walnut, just around the corner, lies the Blues Heritage Area, now rather forlorn, with the Penthouse Lounge, the Nouveau and other scruffy joints located not far from such cotton houses as Grauman, T.W. Keesee and, on a side street, Solomon and Gradus. Near the King Biscuit kiosk on Cherry—which became the main street after the Mississippi washed away the riverside Water Street in the late 1860's—a plaque notes that not far south of Helena on June 18, 1541, Hernando de Soto crossed the Mississippi, the river he had just discovered.

The nearly brand-new (November, 1990) Delta Cultural Center (M-F 9-5, Sat and Sun 10-6), housed in the Register-listed 1912 St. Louis, Iron Mountain and Southern depot, contains exhibits on the Arkansas Delta so influenced by the great waterway which borders it on the east. A well-mounted display called "The Arkansas Delta: A Landscape of Change," which winds through the restored building like a meandering stream, includes eleven sections, among them "River Country," "A Late Frontier," and others on the Civil War, immigrants, and Delta music. A photo taken during the flood of 1917 of the high school at Eudora, the Delta's southernmost town, bears the legend, "We're high and dry,/ And want you to know/ We're in no danger/ From the OVER-FLOW," while a nearby monitor shows films of the flooding Mississippi. A caboose attached to the depot building houses displays on the Delta's railroads, spurred by the area's extensive logging operations, and the music exhibit includes piped-in blues melodies and photos of the King Biscuit Time show, while a quote from Johnny Cash's 1975 autobiography rhapsodizes, "The music carried me up above the mud,the work, and the hot sun." The museum represents the first of five phases of a plan to redevelop the Helena waterfront, a project scheduled for completion about 1998. Other elements include a park with a Riverwalk along the levee—decorated near the museum with river-related murals—and a boardwalk across to a peninsula which fronts the river, a farmers market in an old train warehouse, retail shops, a bed and breakfast inn, an outdoor stage, archives and galleries, and other enhancements.

Along the river bank at Helena—still dominated by the waterway and once called "Arkansas' only seaport"—engineers installed in 1896 willow mat revetments to halt erosion. A few years later an embankment rose three feet above the highest known water level, the biggest building project anywhere on the Mississippi at the time. In the early 1970's, the National River Academy of America, a school some ten miles south of Helena, started up to train riverboat workers, offering fourteen different courses of study, ranging from cook to master pilot. Half of the instruction provided by the school, which closed in the 1980's, took place on the towboats themselves. Although the River Academy no longer exists, a new slack water harbor south of town, begun in the fall of 1989, promises to give old Helena a new lease on its Mississippi River heritage.

Highway 44 south of Helena passes curvy Old Town Lake, so called as the Arkansas Indians located one of their early settlements there. In this area in 1937 the Farm Security Administration purchased former plantation lands and converted them into ninety-five farms for black families, who formed Lakeview Co-operative to handle the supplies the new farmers needed. Near the river south of Helena, Gideon J. Pillow, for whom Fort Pillow north of Memphis is named, owned a plantation. In an earlier career Pillow practiced law in Columbia, Tennessee, with his partner James K. Polk, later President of the U.S. Highway 44 leads on to the village of Elaine (population: 1,000) where the vintage O. Demoret & Son General Mercantile Store and Museum presents a picture out of the past. The establishment recalls a nineteenth century emporium, and suggests some of the delights of pre-Wal-Mart, K-Mart, and other modern mart days. In early October, 1919, a riot erupted near Elaine; it developed when federal troops arrived in the area to quell previous disturbances created by black farm workers organizing a union. The rioters fired at Arkansas Governor Charles H. Brough, and they killed one soldier and wounded another. These acts resulted in the indictment of 122 workers, 73 of them charged with murder, with 12 sentenced to death and the others sent to prison. After the NAACP intervened, the matter eventually reached the United States Supreme Court, which in 1923 held in the landmark *Moore v. Dempsey* decision, written by Oliver Wendell Holmes, that the Constitution's "due process" clause could be used to apply standards of fairness to state criminal trials. This famous case served as the first in a series of decisions which liberalized rules enabling federal constitutional rights to apply to state convictions.

At a point east of Lundell, south of Elaine, Hernando de Soto arrived in Arkansas shortly after crossing the Mississippi in June, 1541. He brought along with him 400 men, the better part of 200 horses, and a pack of hogs, carried for food, from which supposedly originated Arkansas' famous razorback hogs. De Soto's band proceeded north to the Indian town of Casqui, believed to have been at the site of present day Helena, where the Spaniards arrived on June 24. The natives were friendly, with the chief presenting the newcomer with gifts of skins, shawls, and fish. When the explorer boasted that he was a child of the sun, with power over all lands he visited, the skeptical chief asked for proof, much as did an Indian leader who later challenged de Soto, "As to what you say of being the son of the sun, if you will cause Him to dry up the great river, I will believe you." At last report, the Misssissippi still flows; de Soto must have failed the test. The explorer continued farther north to an Indian settlement called Pacaha, connected to the Mississippi by a fish-filled moat. There he tried to form an alliance against the Casqui clan. After further intrigues with the Indians, he headed west to look for copper and gold, then spent the winter at Calion, near present-day Eldorado. On March 6, 1542, the expedition broke camp and headed south, but the weakened leader, who had contracted malaria over the winter, soon faltered and then failed. The great explorer expired by the banks of the Rio Grande, his name for the great river he had discovered. De Soto's comrades buried him near the Mississippi. However, fearing that Indians might resurrect and desecrate his remains, they disinterred the corpse, wrapped it in a shroud weighted with sand, and carried the mortal remains to the center of the river. There, they eased the body into the Mississippi, and over Hernando de Soto swirled the river's waters. Perhaps even today the currents still flow above his long buried bones.

To cross the White River, it's necessary to reach Highway 1, west of Helena. Nine miles northwest of the city, Indiana Quakers established Southland College in 1866, a school and orphanage for freed slaves. The institution operated until 1925, after which Masons took over the property, now owned by the African Methodist Episcopal Zion Church. At Marvell, the Tri-County Genealogical Society, organized in 1985 to assemble records of families in Lee, Monroe, and Phillips Counties, maintains an extensive archive (Th 1-4, Sun 2-5). On Highway 243, three-quarters of a mile north of Marvell, A.B. Crafts Shop (June-Aug 9:30-5, Sept-May Tu-F 1:30-5, Sat 9:30-5) sells cotton bale and boll decorations and other farm-based items, and also offers children a chance to harvest cotton in season. This is no place to tell your youngsters to keep their cotton pickin' hands off the plants. The Louisiana Purchase Historic State Park off to the west includes the base point from which, in 1815, began an official land survey of the vast territory (830,000 square miles) acquired by the United States from France in 1803 for $15,000,000, less than 3¢ an acre. Clarendon, farther west on the White River, is a photogenic town, with National Register-listed vintage buildings. It served as the setting for the 1983 movie "A Soldier's Story," and also for several other productions filmed there.

The River Road, Highway 21, crosses the White River southeast of Clarendon at St. Charles. A sign here honors Dean Watson, "World junior duck calling champion 1989," and also bears a cannon figure and the phrase "Historic St. Charles." These refer to the June 17, 1862, episode when a federal fleet of eight ships tried to sail upstream past Confederate shore defenses, which fired a cannonball at the gunboat *Mound City*. This was deemed the Civil War's single most destructive shot, for the blast hit the vessel's boiler, which exploded and killed nearly 150 Union men. The road through tiny St. Charles ends in the village at the Botts Access Area by the fast flowing White River, where a pair of oversized stop signs warn that the pavement is about to give way to the stream. The White River National Wildlife Refuge, established in 1935, stretches just south of St. Charles. The preserve includes 165 lakes and miles of streams, sloughs, and bayous totaling 10,000 acres of water and also some 100,000 acres of bottomland hardwood forest extending along the waterway for sixty-five miles at widths of three to ten miles. Until the early 1900's, when timber cutting began, the area remained untouched by modern times. Only a few commercial fishers and hunters living on shanty boats populated the primitive wilderness. Now restored to its primeval condition, the area is one of the largest remaining Mississippi River valley bottomland forests. Mallard ducks and Canada geese abound during the winter, while in the refuge, open to the public from March through October, an estimated 150-200 black bears prowl. They establish their dens high in trees to avoid floods which cover the area as much as six months a year.

The economy of DeWitt, named for the New York governor DeWitt Clinton, rests on rice. Three major rice mills—Producers, Riceland, and Cormier, whose building bears the slogan "Have a rice day"—operate in the town. The Riceland facility belongs to the cooperative owned by 21,500 farmers, founded in 1921, the world's largest processor of the commodity, handling more than 100 million bushels a year, about one-third of the total U.S. crop. Other Riceland grain receiving locations in Arkansas towns on or near the River Road include facilities at Marianna, Dumas, McGehee and Eudora, while the company's Mississippi River terminal operates at West Memphis. The River Road, which becomes U.S. 165 at DeWitt, passes by Gillette, "home of friendly people and the coon supper." Wide Main Street hardly needs amplitude, as dormant Gillette lacks traffic jams, and very nearly lacks traffic. The post office occupies a brick building with a nearly vanished coat of white paint, the rough stone Rollison Furniture and Appliance store, signed with fading black letters, hardly gives Levitz a run for its money, and sleepy Central Hardware, installed in a corrugated metal structure, seems no longer on its mettle. Out on the highway, the Rice Paddy Motel's name recalls the area's main crop.

The Arkansas County Museum (March-Oct W-Sat 9:30-4, Sun 1-4, Nov-Dec F and Sat only) lies about six miles south of Gillette. Various buildings house a variety of exhibits. The first edition of the state's first newspaper, the *Arkansas Gazette* for November 20, 1819, founded at nearby Arkansas Post, and a Civil War-era copy of the *Vicksburg Daily Citizen* printed on wall paper due to lack of newsprint—both on display—contain news so old by now that the reports seem interesting. The John L. Peterson Building houses antique farm equipment, a still, a model of the *Golden Eagle* steamer, and copies of Civil War uniforms, including the Confederate Butternut type, dyed with that tree's bark. A 1930's child's playhouse, half the size of a regular residence, with furniture, dishes, pots and pans and other contents on the same scale stands next to a c. 1877 log house moved from a bayou.

Centennial Drive by the museum leads to Arkansas Post National Memorial (8-5), an historic corner of the Mississippi

River Valley, with a great gulf between the site's storied past and its present day lack of remnants from the old days. Arkansas Post's story began one balmy day in 1682, when the French explorer La Salle arrived at the mouth of the Arkansas River after floating down the Mississippi. The expedition started in the cool northern climes, and as the men proceeded south, "More and more they entered the realms of spring. The hazy sunlight, the warm and drowsy air, the tender foliage, the opening flowers, betokened the reviving life of Nature," Francis Parkman recounted in *La Salle and the Discovery of the Great West*. "For several days more they followed the writhings of the great river on its tortuous course through wastes of swamp and canebrake." They soon arrived at the Arkansas' mouth, even that early an historic place, for from here in 1542 Hernando de Soto's men floated down to the Gulf, and at this spot in 1673 Marquette and Joliet reached their southernmost point, where they reversed course and worked their way back up the Mississippi. After La Salle granted his colleague Henri de Tonty trading rights to the region, Tonty in 1686 sent six men to build a trading post, the first European settlement in the Lower Mississippi Valley, near the confluence of the Arkansas and the Mississippi. Through the eighteenth century, first the French and then the Spanish coped with the wilderness, the Indians, and the caprices of a Nature less benign than the one described by Parkman. All the while Arkansas Post grew, declined, changed its location and, after the 1803 Louisiana Purchase, began to develop as an American frontier settlement. In 1819, Congress designated Arkansas Post the territory's first capital, but three years later the seat of government, along with much of the population and the *Arkansas Gazette*, moved to more central Little Rock, a new settlement just established on the Arkansas River farther north. Over the next half century the remote frontier town declined, and by now few evidences of its former importance remain in the 221 acre National Memorial.

Even if the quiet little enclave there by the Arkansas lacks ruins, it fairly teems with memories of the Post's past. A stop at the Visitor Center to see the exhibits provides an introduction to the area. One room, called the River Road, contains models of vessels used on the Arkansas and old steamboat bills of lading, while on tall panels in another section characters appear from the Post's early days, including a French trapper, Quapaw Indian, boatman, and other figures. Beyond the Visitor Center lies the now empty town site. Explanatory panels there relate the outpost's history and indicate the location of such once-thriving establishments as Notrebe's Cotton Gin and Press, the State Bank of Arkansas branch, the *Gazette* office, and Montgomery's Tavern, where the General Assembly met in 1820. Although nothing remains to be seen except the remains of a cistern at planter Frederic Notrebe's long-gone house, the mind's eye can conjure up a vision of the vanished capital. The walkway-patterned empty fields where the town once stood seem all the more poignant for their lack of any evidences of the past. Anyone given to meditations on the vicissitudes of time will find food for thought at Arkansas Post, for the once-bustling, now vacant capital city inspires contemplation.

A path through the woods leads out to a water-bordered point where the Arkansas and Post Bayou meet. Off to the left lies the canal, which leads via two locks past the White River's mouth, and on to the Mississippi. At this point the Arkansas has traveled on its journey from the Rocky Mountains for nearly 1,500 miles to the Mississippi. For about a century after the *Comet*, the Arkansas' first steamer, entered the waterway in 1820, boats plied the river, but a decline in commercial traffic ended dredging and snagging by the federal government. In the 1940's a revival of river transportation induced the Corps of Engineers to begin work on locks and dams and other facilities to improve the Arkansas with the 445 mile long McClellan-Kerr Navigation System. At Cypress Bend on the Arkansas a few miles upstream from the Post, a hamlet which existed until floods washed it away in the 1860's, lived Henry M. Stanley. Later the famous journalist who encountered Livingston in Africa, Stanley then worked as a storekeeper for his foster father until the Civil War. Between the mouths of the Arkansas and the White not far north Montgomery Point once stood, "one of the oldest and most widely known landings on the Mississippi," William F. Pope described it in his 1895 *Early Days in Arkansas*. At this site, first settled in 1766 by a French fur trader named Francois D'Armand, "Two large log warehouses, built upon piling, stood near the water's edge," wrote Pope about the early day put-in point.

For years, a ferry crossed the lower Arkansas at Yancopin ("lotus"), but now a bridge on U.S. 165, the River Road, takes you over the river just south of Arkansas Post. The highway passes through Back Gate, a backwater hamlet consisting of a few scattered houses, water tower, gas station, and used car lot. A few miles south, a marker by the road recalls the old town of Napoleon, seat of Desha (pronounced "De-Shay" by locals) County from 1836 to 1874, once located twenty-four miles east on the Mississippi. After the former French general and Napoleon Bonaparte subordinate Frederic Notrebe established Napoleon in the 1820's, the town developed into an important port filled with river roustabouts. In 1855, the federal government completed an imposing three story marine hospital at the settlement, but before long the Mississippi started to erode the town, which gradually lost both its land and importance, as people, the county courthouse, Jay Gould's railroad, and other facilities moved away, leaving Napoleon high and dry or, more precisely, low and wet. Finally, the river claimed the last traces of the town, which ceased to exist. When the Mississippi fell to an unusually low stage in 1954, remains of Napoleon became visible for a time among the sandbars. Then the waters rose and once again the village vanished from view.

Just north of Dumas, farther on, the Desha County Museum (Tu, Th, Sun 2-4) contains exhibits on the area's history. Across the highway rusty farm implements for sale seem to mimic the antique agricultural equipment parked on the museum grounds. Not far west of McGehee, a railroad town where in the late nineteenth century passengers dined at Colonel Abner McGehee's plantation manse while their train refueled, sinuous Bayou Bartholomew snakes along, the world's longest bayou, which extends south to Louisiana on its 300 mile long course. East of McGehee lies Arkansas City, founded about 1873 at a steamboat landing, which had existed there since 1834, when residents of eroding Napoleon sought a new settlement by the Mississippi. The location proved ill advised, for flooding harassed the town for years, culminating in the 1927 inundation when the 2,000 residents climbed to their rooftops as ten feet of water filled the streets. Levees built after the flood of 1927 protected Arkansas City, but the town then lost its riverfront when an island just offshore attached itself to the bank.

Isolated Arkansas City, a village of 668 inhabitants, still retains a pleasantly decayed old-time river town flavor. A road runs along the top of the grassy levee, part of the world's longest continuous levee line, which extends from Pine Bluff, Arkansas down the Arkansas River to its mouth and then down to the Mississippi near Venice, Louisiana, a distance of more than 650 miles. On eccentrically spelled Desota Avenue, which parallels the levee, a few vintage buildings stand. One block west lies Kate Adams Avenue, named—as are other streets in town—for one of the Mississippi steamers of yesteryear. A small, brick building houses the Arkansas City Museum, with photos of the 1927 flood of riverboats, but at last report the roof had caved in, making the displays inaccessible (for the current situation you can check at the house just behind the museum). The county courthouse up the street sports a frilly cast iron device above the entryway, and eyebrow-like fringes above the large windows on the second level. The recently built Yellow Bend Slackwater Harbor Port nearby may revive some nautical activity in the area, but sleepy Arkansas City—a backwater off the beaten track—will no doubt continue to doze away the days. In Arkansas City John H. Johnson grew up, founder and publisher of *Ebony* and *Jet* magazines. He tells in his 1989 autobiography *Succeeding Against the Odds* of the 1927 flood and how, when he completed the eighth and last grade available to local blacks, his mother made him repeat the grade rather than lose a year of schooling.

At Dermott, a few miles west of the River Road, Arkansas' largest gin, the 1886 family-owned Lephiew Gin Company, offers tours during the cotton processing season (Sept-Nov 8-5, by appointment: 501-538-5288), while in mid May the town celebrates its annual crawfish festival. South of Dermott curls 20 mile long Lake Chicot, the nation's largest oxbow lake, the Mississippi's former main channel, formed about 1350 when the river changed course. During the 1927 flood, the receding Mississippi deposited across the lake an earthen barrier, paved in 1948 as a road which in the summer of 1990 acquired a bridge, below which boats can now travel between the lake's upper and lower sections. When drainage patterns altered after construction of the levee in 1920 part of the upper lake filled with sediment, which threatened to turn Chicot into an oversized mudhole. In 1985, the Corps of Engineers completed the Lake Chicot Pumping Plant to intercept and divert silt-laden overflow water into the Mississippi. Near the lake's northern tip lies Lake Chicot State Park, garnished with wild pecan trees and knobby-kneed cypress, some of the natural features seen during cruises of the park's *Night Heron* (501-265-5480). Along pleasant Lakeshore Drive north of Lake Village, the yard of a two story house with a metal balcony contains a low pillar which recalls the first night flight made, in April 1923, by Charles A. Lindbergh, then an unknown 21 year old mail pilot. Experiencing engine trouble, "Lindy" had landed at a now-abandoned golf course on the old country club grounds here, and that evening the aviator took his host up for a moonlight flight down the Mississippi.

At picturesque little Lake Village, which perches just by Chicot, stands the Chicot ("stumpy" in French) County Courthouse. The county seat moved there after Villemont and Columbia both suffered erosion by the Mississippi. Across from the rather pedestrian courthouse lies the seemingly solid Bank of Lake Village, fronted by two huge stone pillars. Below the water tower rests a latter day version of New Hope Missionary Baptist Church, organized in 1860 by slave Jim Kelley and believed to be Arkansas' oldest black congregation. Nearby, colorful hot tamale shacks serve up home-cooked meals. South of town a state tourist office which stands on wood pylons in the lake uses solar panels to generate sufficient energy for about half the building's heat and all its hot water.

In 1895, a New York banker and land developer named Austin Corbin brought 100 families from Italy to grow cotton at Sunnyside plantation, located between Lake Chicot and the Mississippi. Although many of the Italians died of malaria, some survived, and their descendants still live in the area. Beyond the southern tip of Lake Chicot the 1940 bridge crosses the Mississippi to Greenville, Mississippi. When a gas company began paying rent for a pipeline built alongside the bridge structure in 1950, toll charges ended, but later the old toll booths served as quarantine stations to inspect traffic for the cotton-endangering boll weevil.

The River Road in Arkansas finishes up with a visit to the state's "Catfish Capital," an official designation awarded by the legislature in 1987 to Eudora, named for a plantation owner's daughter who died in 1851 at age four. The annual early May Catfish Festival celebrates the "capital's" specialty. Fading painted Dr. Pepper, 7-Up, and Royal Crown Cola ads vaguely brighten a few buildings around town. Near City Hall, which sports a curvy art deco label above the door, stands the 1900 Anderson home, and at the south end of Main you'll see the huge Producers Rice Mill complex. Out on the highway the Eudora Garment Company factory store sells an array of work uniforms, medical garments, and different kinds of off-beat clothes. After the 1927 flood, the government proposed that levees in this area should be lower than others so a floodway west of Eudora could collect and divert overflow, but protests by residents blocked the so-called "fuse-plug" levee. Cotton fields of rich soil around Eudora reach depths of more than a thousand feet, compared to the world average of seven inches. The River Road leads on south to Louisiana, through fertile, alluvial, farm land, the gift of the river, a moody Mississippi which over the centuries has bestowed its benefits on and brought grief to Arkansas as well as some of the other states washed by the great waterway.

KENTUCKY, TENNESSEE AND ARKANSAS PRACTICAL INFORMATION

Phone numbers of tourist offices or chambers of commerce in Mississippi River area cities and of other river-related sources of information:

Kentucky

Clinton: 502-653-6473; Columbus-Belmont State Park: 502-677-2327; Hickman: 502-236-3566; Wickliffe: 502-335-3531.

The Hickman ferry: 502-236-3448. Kentucky Department of Travel: 800-225-TRIP.

Tennessee

Covington and Tipton County: 901-476-9717; Dyersburg and Dyer County: 901-285-3430; Memphis: 901-526-4880, 901-576-8171 and 800-873-6282; Reelfoot Lake: 901-253-8144; Reelfoot Lake State Resort Park: 901-253-7756; Ripley and Lauderdale County: 901-635-9541; Tiptonville: 901-253-9922; Southwest Tennessee Tourism Organization, in Jackson: 901-668-9400.

Tennessee Department of Tourist Development: 615-741-2158; Tennessee Department of Conservation, Division of State Parks: 615-742-6667; for lodge reservations: 800-421-6683. Tennessee operates a highway tourist Welcome Center on I-55 south of Memphis.

Arkansas

Arkansas City: 501-877-2426; Arkansas Post: 501-548-2432; Blytheville: 501-762-2012; Eudora: 501-355-4436; Helena: 501-338-8327; Lake Village: 501-265-5997; Marianna: 501-295-2469; Marion: 501-739-3289; McGehee: 501-222-4451; Osceola: 501-563-2281; West Memphis: 501-735-2720; Wilson: 501-655-8311.

Arkansas Department of Parks and Tourism: 501-862-7777. Arkansas State Parks: 501-682-1191. Arkansas operates state tourist offices at Blytheville and at Lake Chicot.

7. MISSISSIPPI

William Faulkner, the great Mississippi fiction writer who lived in Oxford not far east of the river, once considered a book on the waterway, but in 1935 he decided against the project, telling a correspondant: "About the Mississippi River book. I don't believe I can do it. I am a novelist, you see: people first, where second. " But the river's "where" in Mississippi—the picturesque, historic cities and old-fashioned Delta farm country along the waterway's 410 mile length through the state—would have provided Faulkner with enough character and colorful characters to populate his book. In this area washed by the great waterway, Hernando de Soto discovered the Mississippi, frontiersmen traveled the Natchez Trace, cotton plantations boomed as did the guns of the Civil War, multi-decked steamers, as beautiful as a wedding cake but without the complications, as Mark Twain said, arrived at Natchez and Vicksburg. In the region, blacks invented the blues, and the rich, black, alluvial soil deposited there over the centuries by the river supported a culture and agriculture deeply rooted in old traditions, which still exert an influence on the territory which borders the waterway.

More than two-thirds of Mississippi's river frontage includes the Delta, an elliptical area some 200 miles long extending as much as 60 miles east of the Mississippi. The Delta, in the famous phrase of Greenville writer David Cohn, "begins in the lobby of the Peabody Hotel in Memphis and ends on Catfish Row in Vicksburg." The earthy Delta area, perhaps more than anywhere else along the Mississippi, evokes a sense of place, a "where" which—as even Faulkner would no doubt agree—applies "not merely in the historical and prideful meaning of the word, but in the sensory meaning, the breathing world of sight and smell and sound," as an article on Southern writers in London's *Times Literary Supplement* once observed.

The recorded history of Mississippi and the Mississippi began in 1541 when Spanish explorer Hernando de Soto discovered the great river he called the Rio Grande. The names of De Soto County, in the northwestern corner of the Mississippi just south of Memphis, and of Hernando, the county seat, commemorate the state's first European visitor. The courthouse in Hernando, which lies by Interstate 55 seventeen miles east of U.S. 61, the River Road, contains colorful murals depicting de Soto's expedition. They were removed in 1952 from Memphis's old Gayoso Hotel, where the pictures had hung since about the turn of the century. The two paintings on the stairwell depict "De Soto Embarcation in 1538" from Spain and "De Soto guided through the forests," with Indians leading the mounted Spaniard. Upstairs in the rotunda appear "Hernando de Soto discovers the Mississippi River" and "De Soto's burial in the Mississippi River," a spooky moon- and torch-lit scene showing the explorer laid out in a casket with a sword on his chest. Over the judge's bench in the courtroom hang two small murals portraying Marquette and Joliet traveling in canoes on the Mississippi, and in the corridor around the corner from the circuit clerk's office off to the left another painting shows Bienville, the French explorer and colonial administrator, making peace with the Chickasaw in 1739. On the square behind the handsome courthouse, the seemingly timeless H.A. McIngvale clock repair shop, a picture out of the past, stands as it has for some forty years. Hernando boasts the National Register-listed show houses Magnolia Grove, a column-fronted white wood residence, and the home of Felix LaBauve. He was an intellectual and publisher of the local newspaper, founded in 1839 as the *Free Press* and now the *DeSoto Times*, located across from the courthouse.

Highway 304 out of Hernando takes you west to the Delta country and the River Road, U.S. 61. Just to the south of 304 lies Arkabutla Lake, a popular sailing place considered the second windiest lake between Chicago and the Gulf of Mexico, while farther south at Como, Main Street Bed and Breakfast (601-482-5483) offers accommodations in a c. 1900 cottage. Beyond Banks, Mississippi, not on the Mississippi banks or even on the official state highway map, 304 reaches U.S. 61. Farther along on 304 lies the picturesque Hollywood Cafe (open weekends only), whose fried pickles, marinated catfish, frothy brandy alexanders, and other such delicacies attract diners from around the region. A few miles northwest lie the Hollywood Indian mounds and farther on, the Commerce Landing mounds, on one of which perches a plantation house. Some historians believe that in this area the ancient Indian village of Quizquiz existed (other scholars put it at nearby Clarksdale), where de Soto discovered the Mississippi.

A once-thriving river port named Commerce developed near the mound of that name, but after the Mississippi changed course in 1874 a huge sandbar built up, blocking the waterfront, and although the town survived into the twentieth century eventually it disappeared. About fifteen river miles north, just below the Tennessee line, the Confederate government established a customs point in 1861 at Norfolk Landing, so putting this part of the Lower Mississippi under the control of a foreign power.

Tunica County and the county seat of the same name vie with East St. Louis as the poorest area on the entire Mississippi. As bad as the Illinois city might seem, Tunica—which between 1970 and 1990 lost one-quarter of its population—ranks as the nation's poorest county, with nearly half of its 9,200 residents below the poverty level (compared to one-quarter of the Delta's 350,000 people and 13 percent nationally). This chronic unemployment rate is more than four times the nation's typical 5 percent, and the earnings less than half of the U.S. per capita income of $15,000. Just west of wide Edwards Avenue in the center of the town of Tunica runs a long concrete trough known as Sugar Ditch, a misnomer as the one-time blight hardly exuded sweet aromas. Along this former open sewer stood shacks which housed nearly 100 black families until they gradually moved out between 1986 and 1991, when the city finally razed the last shanty. At the south side of town stands a water tower bearing the legend, "We welcome industry," but based on the unemployment figures, industry does not seem to feel welcome in Tunica.

A narrow channel called Yazoo Pass once connected Moon Lake, farther south, with the adjacent Mississippi. When Ulysses S. Grant sought a way to attack the Confederate Mississippi River stronghold of Vicksburg downstream in 1863, he cut the Yazoo Pass levee, built in 1859 to keep the river out, and the Mississippi opened a navigation channel across Moon Lake and into the Coldwater River. Grant hoped the new canal would carry him to the Yazoo River so he could attack Vicksburg from behind, but the scheme failed. Uncle Henry's operates on the northeast shore of Moon Lake. The building opened in 1926 as an Elk's Club, later became a casino and now houses a popular restaurant specializing in Cajun cooking.

A few miles south of Moon Lake once existed the river town of Delta, washed away by the waterway. The seat of Coahoma County was located there until 1850, when the courthouse was moved to nearby Friars Point. There it remained until 1930, when the county transferred the seat of government to Clarksdale. Coahoma—"red panther" in Choctaw—originated in 1836 on lands acquired by the 1830 Choctaw Concession after the Treaty of Dancing Rabbit Creek. Friars Point, once a busy cotton center and port, declined as the steamer era ended and railroads passed the village by, but the town remains as the only surviving river settlement in this area from the 1830's. Originally called Farrar's Point, the town changed its name to honor the early settler and legislator Robert Friar. A museum (Tu 9-4, W and Th

9-3:30, F 9-5, Sat 1-5) contains an ecclectic selection of displays, including Indian artifacts, Civil War relics, and Delta area historical items. At Friars Point, which huddles below the levee just by the Mississippi, many buildings remain empty, but The Old Ice House antique shop occupies two places in different parts of town, one of them—true to its name—the former ice house. At Friars Point the first Italian immigrants arrived in the 1880's. Planters imported them to work on Delta plantations, an experiment which failed to develop to any degree.

A few miles from Jonestown, east of Friars Point and U.S. 61, James L. Alcorn lived. He served as governor of Mississippi from 1870 to 1871, and promoted a state levee system along the Mississippi. At Clarksdale, not far south, the Delta Blues Museum (M-F 9-5), installed at the Carnegie Library in 1979, recalls the musical heritage of the city, where such composers and performers as W.C. Handy, Muddy Waters, Ike Turner, and Charlie Patton lived. Blues landmarks abound in the town: at 317 Issaquena stood Handy's house, and the Riverside Hotel at 615 Sunflower hosted many famous musicians. Blues men gossiped and performed along Issaquena by the tracks, at a stretch known as "The New World." At 127 3d, Early "Soul Man" Wright, on the air since 1947, broadcasts blues and gospel music on WROX, which in the 1940's carried the famous King Biscuit Time show (see the Helena section in the Arkansas chapter). "Juke joints" around town such as Smitty's Red Top Lounge, Margaret's Blue Diamond Lounge and Red's South End Disco present blues performances. Another famous show business personality from Clarksdale, playwright Tennessee Williams, lived with his grandfather, the Reverend Walter Dakin, in the rectory of St. George's Church. Clarksville took its name from John Clark, orphaned when his father, an English architect, succumbed to yellow fever in New Orleans in 1837. Clark, only a teenager, made his way to the area, where he established a logging business. The city holds the distinction of having obtained the world's first franchised Holiday Inn, now the Beacon Inn. In 1944, the Hopson Planting Company south of Clarksdale grew and processed the first cotton ever produced entirely by machinery, from planting to bailing. Although William Faulkner demurred when asked to write a book on the Mississippi, his delightful house and the University of Mississippi at picturesque Oxford, sixty miles east of Clarksdale, are well worth the detour.

Rena Lara lies back to the west. On the way there you'll pass in Sherard a typical old time Delta country store, the yellow brick emporium labeled "J.H. Sherard 1874." From there a road leads out over the levee to De Soto Lake, originally the Mississippi main channel and now an oxbox lake formed by a 1942 cutoff which diverted and shortened the river. At Jackson Point, a swatch of Mississippi on the west shore, once existed a plantation owned by Andrew Jackson. A sign along the road indicates the way to the lake's Sunflower Landing, reached on a dirt and gravel way which takes you to a remote, tree-filled corner of the Mississippi River Valley. Not much of a landing exists there, just a small clearing and a short incline down to the still water. Here at this isolated and by appearance unremarkable backwater lies one of the great river's most evocative spots for, as a sign notes, "Spanish Explorer Hernando De Soto and his men discovered the Mississippi River near this spot, Sunday, May 8, 1541. They camped, built barges, & crossed the 'Rio Grande' on June 18, 1541." At the bottom appears the source for designating this as the discovery point—a document issued by a group appointed by President Franklin Roosevelt to study the matter: "Final Report of the United States Expedition Commission (De Soto) House Document Number 71, 76th Congress, 1st Session, Jan, 1939."

The "Gentleman of Elvas," one of the expedition's chroniclers, told how "The stream was swift, and very deep; the water, always flowing turbidly, brought along from above many trees and much timber, driven onward by its forces." These days, however, this quiet corner, cut off from the Mississippi, remains silent and calm. It is no less impressive—and perhaps even more so—for that. River travelers who visit this lonely, out of the way place will find Sunflower Landing one of the most haunting areas on the entire waterway. At this almost primeval spot—virtually ignored, untouched by commercialism, unspoiled and natural, lost in the back woods—one can well imagine that balmy May day four and a half centuries ago when the Spanish adventurers happened upon the river, never before seen by European eyes. Here, then, is where the story of the Mississippi began. This is the "Rio Grande," the great river which, in the fullness of time, became so closely connected with the continent's, the colony's and the country's history.

Highway 1, the River Road, continues on south from Rena Lara through the Delta country, which contains some of the nation's richest land and poorest farmers. A welcome sign calls Rosedale "the Delta city of brotherly love." At the north part of town stands 1877 Grace Episcopal, Bolivar County's oldest church, an attractive wood Gothic-style sanctuary, and on the scruffy square stands the one-story brick courthouse, its shabby appearance emblematic of the rather forlorn settlement. The White Front Cafe and Joe's Hot Tamale Place seem typical of Delta eateries, while grocery stores named Wong's, Buck Wong's and Charlie Sang's also reflect the area's heritage.

Chinese food shops may not seem in keeping with the rest of the Delta's culture, but in fact they are typical establishments there. Planters brought immigrant workers from China to replace the freed slaves after the Civil War. In early 1870, the first boatload of 200 Chinese workers arrived in New Orleans, where the newcomers immediately jumped ship and fled. Before long, however, other laborers brought from China reached the Delta, where they toiled on the plantations. A century later, the workers'1,200 descendants in Mississippi formed the South's largest Chinese population, most of them living in the Delta. By then, more than 90 percent of the families operated groceries.

The first store opened in Sunflower about 1872, then others soon started up. The Chinese established a cemetery in Greenville, and in Cleveland, next to the 1935 Chinese Mission School on Highway 8, they built a Baptist church (1957), behind which lies a Sino-Delta neighborhood. By 1980, more than half of Mississippi's 1,000 Chinese lived out of the Delta, and many of them by then no longer operated food stores. The trio of groceries still functioning at Rosedale recall the era when new arrivals from halfway around the world added an exotic element to the Lower Mississippi valley.

Although Rosedale now lies inland, the port south of town revives memories of the early days when the settlement, originally called Floryville, fronted the Mississippi at an important point across from the mouths of the Arkansas and White Rivers. Riverton, a rival port just to the south, boasted of its mule railway, but both towns eventually lost their positions on the water when the Mississippi deposited a sandbar along the shore. In the 1860's Riverton completely disappeared. Just south of Rosedale the nearly 800 acre Great River Road State Park, supposedly the world's longest park, stretches along the waterway and includes a four-level observation tower with views onto the Mississippi.

Not far south of Beulah on the west side of the highway lies land received as a fee in a famous 1840's Indian lawsuit by Charles Clark, Mississippi governor from 1863 to 1865, buried on the grounds of Doro Plantation there. At a former Choctaw settlement five and a half miles west on the Mississippi stood Prentiss, seat of Bolivar County from 1852 to 1863, when federal forces burned the town, which flooded out two years later. During a period of low water in 1954 the old town, like a ghost from the past, resurfaced for a brief while, then it disappeared again beneath the river. Benoit, not far south, began in the late 1880's when the Yazoo and Mississippi Valley Railroad arrived. The town took its name from A.W. Benoit, plantation manager for James Richardson, the world's largest individual cotton grower at the time, who established the headquarters for his agricultural operations in Benoit. The village of some 650 people occupies a rise called Egypt Ridge. The name originated during a grain shortage in the late 1880's—similar to the Egyptian famine described in the Bible—when Delta residents flocked to the area, the only place in the region where it was possible to produce a crop. Just outside Benoit, hometown of light-heavyweight champion boxer Archie Moore, stands the c. 1858 National Register-listed Burrus House, where in 1956 the movie *Baby Doll,* with Karl Malden, Carroll Baker, and Eli Wallach, was filmed. On the way out to the dwelling, a rather spooky two-story house standing alone in the fields (cross the tracks on Highway 448, turn right after 8/10 mile on a paved road just before the big white house on the left), you'll pass on the left the latter-day brick Union Church, established in 1843 as a united congregation of Baptists, Presbyterians, and Methodists who still alternate ministers every Sunday.

By the Mississippi, just west of Benoit, curls Lake Whittington, an oxbow body of water where the river's main channel ran until the Corps of Engineers rerouted the waterway with the 1937 Caulk Neck Cutoff. Lake Beulah, not far north, similarly developed when, during the Civil War, a Union navy commander engineered a cutoff across from the Arkansas and White Rivers to help federal forces control the mouths of those waterways. During floods in 1912 and 1913 the levee at Lake Beulah broke, allowing the Mississippi to inundate nearly one million acres of Delta farmland. Six miles south of Lake Whittington curves Cypress Bend, whose name recalls the now denuded stands of trees cut by early settlers. They used the bark for roof shingles and shipped the lumber downstream, a trade which artist John James Audubon criticized during his trip down the Lower Mississippi in 1820-1821 as involving "logs stolen from the Government's land."

Scott, six miles south of Benoit, serves as the company town headquarters of the historic Delta and Pine Land agricultural operation. The business began in 1911, when the Manchester, England Fine Cotton Spinners' and Doublers' Association trade group sought for its textile industry members a source of cotton other than the crop grown in politically unstable Egypt. Mississippi banker Charles Scott and a promoter convinced the English group to buy 38,000 acres of Delta land, and improvements on the property, for $4.5 million. The new owners established here a cotton plantation said to have been the largest in the world. No conifers ever grew in the rich Mississippi River-deposited soil, but in 1919 the company consolidated its operation with a previously existing corporation named Delta and Pine Land Company. The original owners kept the plantation until 1968, when England's Courtaulds, the world's largest rayon manufacturer, bought the property which they retained for ten years. Prudential Insurance Company later acquired the plantation operation, while a group of about 100 private American investors bought the seed business. Prudential's farm management subsidiary rents the 40,000 acres of cropland and catfish ponds to seventeen operators, one of them Delta and Pine Land, the world's largest supplier of cotton seed. The company uses its 2,000 leased acres to produce some eight varieties of seed. The other sixteen lessees grow cotton (13,500 acres), soybeans (18,000), wheat and rice (3,000 acres each), milo, and alfalfa, and manage 700 wet acres of catfish ponds, a fraction of Mississippi's 95,000 "aquaculture" acres in which the state produces 80 percent of the nation's catfish. Because the Queen of England supposedly owned a large share of Courtaulds, the story originated that the monarch herself controlled the world's largest cotton plantation in the remote Mississippi River Valley countryside around Scott. This vestige of British imperial colonialism provoked New Hampshire Senator Thomas McIntyre to claim that the $120,000 a year federal subsidy paid to the plantation feathered the royal treasury in far off London.

On the way to Scott, you pass through "a flat and monotonous landscape of broad cotton fields broken by clumps of woods and drainage ditches," as *Fortune* magazine described the area in a long article on Delta and Pine Land in the March 1937 issue. Green, oval "D & PL" logos decorate elevated tanks which rise in the fields and also the short brick wall which marks the entrance to the property. In the late 1980's, the company sold occupants their pleasant looking, tree-shaded, one-story houses which comprise the small residential neighborhood, but the firm retained ownership of the even smaller commercial area, including the store and the old headquarters building, which also houses the post office. Photos in the new office depict crop dusting, vintage farm equipment, and cotton fields as they looked back in the 1930's.

Cotton grown in the Mississippi Delta's rich riverside lands represented over the years not only the leading crop but also a way of life, one which has not altogether disappeared. As Robert L. Brandfor wrote in *Cotton Kingdom of the New South* "The people of the Lower Mississippi Valley have lived by the fate of their great river. The Mississippi River made their lands, and the remarkable fecundity of the Mississippi's alluvial lands was the source of a prosperous cotton agriculture, out of which was born, in the years after reconstruction, a new 'Delta' planter society." When the old planter society existed, before the Civil War, the connection between the steamer-serviced river and the agricultural lands along its banks was even closer. "Many of the great plantations in Mississippi lay close to the Mississippi River and its tributaries," observed Charles S. Sydnor in his 1938 *A Gentleman of the Old Natchez Region: Benjamin L.C. Wailes*, noting that "because the most fertile part of Mississippi was strung like a shoestring along the river... there was a close interdependence between the steamboats of the Lower Mississippi Valley and the...

civilization along its bank." Although cotton no longer remains king, the fiber retains much importance in the Delta, with Mississippi supplying nearly two million bales (each 480 pounds) of 1990's 15.5 million bale crop, sold for $5 billion. This is the largest amount in history by dollar volume, but three million bales less than 1937's record production.

The fifty-five foot Great Temple numbers among twelve Indian mounds found at Winterville Mounds Historic Site (W-Sat 8-5, Sun 1-5) located south of Scott. The formations recall the culture which dwelled at the site from 1200 to 1400. The bunker-like concrete block museum nestles in an earthen mound which harmonizes with the adjacent originals. East of neaby Metcalfe, an all-black town established by former slaves, lies Stoneville, where the Little Bales of Cotton store (800-748-9112) sells unusual cotton-themed lamps, clocks, bookends, and other such novelties. The village also boasts a branch of the Delta Wildlife Foundation, engaged in emplacing in the Delta by 1995 5,000 wood nesting boxes for ducks (601-686-4062). At Stoneville Jim Henson grew up, who based his famous Kermit the Frog character on aquatic creatures seen during his boyhood wanderings along Deer Creek. The artist lived here when his father worked for the well-known U.S. Department of Agriculture Delta Branch Experiment Station (for tour information: 601-686-9311), established in 1906. The adjacent little town of Leland echoes with the melodies of blues singers, past and present.

Although tree-shaded Greenville indeed enjoys much greenery, the Mississippi River port town takes its name from Revolutionary War hero Nathaniel Green, a good friend of George Washington, whose name designates the county. The settlement began in 1829 at Bachelor's Bend—so called for the hamlet of mainly single men across the waterway in Arkansas—a frequently flooded lowland about three miles from the present city, established there on the highest elevation between Memphis and Vicksburg after Union troops burned the original hamlet.

The new version of Greenville, now Mississippi's fourth largest town, has more than 40,000 people. It prospered from river traffic and from the eleven mile slack water harbor, the deepest such facility on the Mississippi south of St. Louis, at Lake Ferguson. The complex's name honors Corps of Engineers General Harley B. Ferguson, who planned and carried out two artificial cutoffs on the waterway. These projects, completed in the mid-1930's, eliminated the so called "Greenville Bends"—Rowdy, Miller, Spanish Moss, and Bachelor—and, along with a natural cutoff the river itself created, shortened its distance in the area by nearly thirty miles and formed Lake Ferguson, where in 1963 the Corps finished installing the harbor. This facility brought to Greenville a number of river-related activities, including the world's largest flat-bottom boat builder as well as companies operating more than 900 barges and some 65 towboats, all of which inspire the city to call itself "the towboat capital of the world."

Although ship companies, the Corps of Engineers, the Coast Guard, and boat builders all maintain facilities in Greenville, the city's most prominent river-related institution is the County Levee Board. This is installed near the local levee in the town's oldest commercial structure, built in 1883 for the organization and still used by it. Inside the white, marquee-fronted Board building hang photos of the 1903 and 1927 floods, showing scenes of inundated Greenville and nearby areas, a map of the 1927 flood, and a fascinating satellite photo of the Mississippi River basin and its tributaries. Scrapbooks contain articles and photos relating to floods, steamers, and other river subjects, while a small display upstairs includes old surveying and office equipment used by the Levee Board, which maintains more than 200 miles of levees in Mississippi and also parts of Louisiana and Arkansas. The levees, built by the Corps of Engineers and maintained by the Board, average thirty-two feet in height, equivalent to twelve feet above the line of the 1927 flood, which discharged a volume of nearly 2.5 million cubic feet per second. The additional height lies five feet above the theoretical "Project Flood," the greatest volume of water, more than three million cubic feet per second, which might occur over a thousand year period. The levees should thus withstand the flood of the millenium. Greenville's new (1990) 1927 Flood Museum (M-F 8-12, 1-5), a one-room display of photos, articles, booklets, and sand bags, recalls this century's worst flood to date. A posted quote from Pete Daniel's *Deep'n As It Come* book on the flood evokes the calamity: "Everyone who saw the water and heard it had that image branded in their minds forever, for it had the eeriness of a full eclipse of the sun, unsettling, chilling." The flooding Mississippi played the title role in William Faulkner's novel *The Old Man*, a story of a convict who, released, encounters the "heavily roiling chocolate-frothy expanse" when "the river was now doing what it liked to do, had waited patiently the ten years in order to do, as a mule will work for you ten years for the privilege of kicking you once."

Though Mississippi passed its first state levee legislation as early as 1819, appropriating the grand total of $8000, development of the barriers along the river remained sporadic. In the 1830's the state approved more complete legislation and authorized additional funds, and in 1858 it established the General Levee Board to direct and coordinate the 300 or so miles of levees from below Memphis to Vicksburg, and to integrate the efforts of the various district boards. During the Civil War, the levees deteriorated due to lack of maintenance and to damage suffered when Union troops cut large openings in them to flood the cotton producing lowlands. By the end of the conflict, the Mississippi had breached the barrier and reclaimed much of the countryside, forcing many planters returning home to travel in dugout canoes. After the August, 1865, state levee reconstruction convention determined that Mississippi should tax only areas which would benefit from new levees, rather than the entire state, a board of commissioners established in November of that year levied for the levees a charge of ten cents an acre and one cent per pound of cotton produced along the Mississippi. Arguing that since Northern forces destroyed much of the old barrier, the federal government should pay for the new ones, Mississippi managed to persuade President Andrew Johnson to send the Corps of Engineers to conduct a survey. In the summer of 1866, a Senate committee reported that if the U.S. government failed to take over levee construction, "a large extent of the country, supporting a numerous population of both races, must be abandoned and will speedily relapse into its original wild and uncultivated condition." After a proposed levee bill failed in Congress, Mississippi proceeded to build on its own a temporary 225 mile long levee. In 1879, the U.S. finally formed a permanent levee commission which eventually led to federal help for the state's flood control facilities.

The quiet waters off the foot of Main beyond the levee hardly look threatening these days. Metal mooring rings lie embedded in the sloping, rock-surfaced waterfront, by which float the Marine Restaurant and the large white Yacht Club. Heading up Main through downtown Greenville you'll pass the c. 1881 former *Delta Democrat-Times* building where editor Hodding Carter wrote his Pulitzer Prize-winning 1946 editorials advocating racial tolerance, and Cotton Row, where Dawkins & Company and V & M Cotton survive to recall the old days when the fiber enriched the city. The cube-like William Alexander Percy Library on Main, on the site of the old Elysian Club building, honors one of the many well-known writers produced by Greenville, which claims more published authors than any other town of its size in the country. In his poetically bittersweet 1941 autobiography *Lanterns on the Levee* Percy, uncle of the novelist Walker Percy, wrote with both awe and affection about "the river"—as anyone who lives on or near the waterway calls the Mississippi—for "though there are many, you mean always the same one, the great river, the shifting unappeasable god of the country, feared and loved, the Mississippi."

The Percy Library houses on the second floor a well presented exhibit on the lives and careers of fifteen local writers. Photos, manuscripts, first editions, and articles by and about such authors as the two Percys, Hodding Carter, Civil War historian Shelby Foote, regionalist David Cohn, literary agent and sometime author Ben Wasson (who represented William Faulkner and Dashiell Hammett), and others fill the tall glass cases. Why did so many renowned writers originate in the smallish Mississippi River town of Greenville? One theory holds that Harvard Law School graduate Will Percy's example as a literate and published figure, a local educated class, and a tolerant community inspired the various local authors. Percy, who died in 1942, is buried at the cemetery on South Main below Highway 82 by the odd, medieval knight statue he installed in memory of his father, U.S. Senator LeRoy Percy.

Elsewhere around Greenville stand such National Register-listed structures as the 1903 First National Bank and the Wetherbee (c. 1878) and A.B. Finlay (c. 1870) houses, as well as other unusual buildings, among them the fanciful c. 1890 Columbus & Greenville line depot, the c. 1908 Dutch-style St. Joseph Catholic Cathedral, and the c. 1905 Hebrew Union, more like a Greek than a Jewish temple, home to Mississippi's largest Jewish congregation. McCormick Book Inn, installed in an attractive, glassy and classy shop nestled beneath pecan trees, exudes a user-friendly atmosphere, with a rocking chair by a fireplace and an excellent collection of works by and about Mississippi authors, whose photos hang on the wall. The brown stone courthouse stands in a spacious tree-garnished city block. Out on Highway 82, the state Welcome Center tourist office (M-Sat 8-5, Sun 1-5) occupies a land-based, nineteenth century steamship-like structure originally built by the Great River Road Association as its New Orleans World's Fair Facility. Greenville boasts the nation's largest rice processing plant, the country's only Schwinn bicycle (until it closed in October 1991) and Axminister carpet factories, and the state's first Chinese restaurant, How Joy. Another notable eatery, Doe's Eat Place, which offers a down-home ambiance, specializes in steaks cooked at a kitchen installed in the dining area. On the third Saturday in September, the city hosts the annual Delta Blues Festival, started in 1978, held in conjunction with a week-long celebration of the blues.

About three miles west of Highway 1, a 38-foot observation tower in Warfield Point Park, managed by Washington County and the Corps of Engineers and located at a site named in 1831 by a river traveler, affords a good view onto the Mississippi. From the top of the six-flight tower, the back channel to Greenville stretches north to a grain elevator in the distance, while before you swirls the river, its currents visible on the water's surface. Along the bank signs warn, "Do not go beyond this point" and, rather inconsistently, "Go beyond this point at your own risk." Near the tower, a small, metal display steamer rusts away. Farther south, east of the river, lies Leroy Percy State Park, Mississippi's first such facility, a picturesque enclave with trees bearded by Spanish moss, an alligator pen, a Delta wildlife interpretive center, and eight cabins (601-827-5436). A few miles down Highway 1, you might consider turning west on one of the unmarked roads which lead a short distance away to nearby Lake Washington (one such turnoff lies just past the weathered wood building with "Erwin" written on it), where the National Register-listed, c. 1856 Italianate-style Mount Holly plantation house (601-827-2652) offers bed and breakfast. The road which borders Lake Washington—one of the Mississippi River's oldest oxbow leavings, formed some 700 years ago—leads to Glen Allan, a pleasant little town on the water, and then on to the Greenfield Cemetery two miles south where ruined St. John's Church (1856) stands as a mute but eloquent witness to the Civil War. After soldiers removed the sanctuary's window lead to melt down into bullets, the elements gradually deteriorated the church, which a cyclone finally destroyed in 1904, and now, only a few red brick walls, one pierced by a Gothic arch doorway, remain. Church vestrymen included two generations of Wade Hamptons, prominent planters whose "big house"—a plantation's main dwelling—stood near the junction of Highways 1 and 436. Family member Wade Hampton III served as a Confederate general and first governor of South Carolina after Reconstruction.

Out on the Mississippi near the Arkansas-Louisiana line, west of Glen Allan, rivermen—for reasons unknown—designated a curving stretch of the waterway with the whimsical name General Hull's Left Leg. William Hull was a Revolutionary War hero later court-martialed after he lost Detroit to the British during the War of 1812. Highway 1 leads to U.S. 61, dotted to the north by such colorfully named Delta hamlets as Panther Burn and Nitta Yuma. On the Mississippi, off to the west, lies Mayersville, whose 300 or so inhabitants make it the metropolis of Issaquena County. Mayersville also serves as the county seat, a somewhat dubious honor as Issaquena has no schools, no factories, and only a few scattered hamlets. In the late nineteenth century, Mayersville was the biggest cotton shipping point between Greenville and Vicksburg, but the railroad's arrival in 1882 diverted traffic and the town declined. In March, 1991 county voters approved gambling, so perhaps riverboats will one day once again stop at Mayersville.

Farther south on U.S. 61 lies Onward, a rather backward little place whose general store and not much else evidences its existence. A sign by the old-time, porch-fronted emporium depicts Teddy Roosevelt and a bear cub in the woods, a reference to the President's November, 1902, hunting trip in the area. Roosevelt arrived by train at nearby Smedes Plantation, whose owner arranged for the President to hunt for black bear in an area fifteen miles east now occupied by the Delta National Forest.

The chief executive failed to find a bear, so guide Holt Collier, a Civil War veteran from Greenville, obtained one on the Little Sunflower River and tied the animal to a tree, but "T.R." refused to shoot the bear. After a Brooklyn, New York, couple saw cartoons of the soon famous episode in the *Washington Post* they asked the President if they could name a stuffed bear after him, and so originated the Teddy Bear. Inside the Onward store hang photos, obtained from the Harvard University Archives, showing scenes of the bear hunt which, thanks to Roosevelt's forbearance, soon captured the country's fancy. Member of the party included Hugh Foote, grandfather of author Shelby Foote, and John McIlhenney, whose father invented Tabasco sauce. The store sells locally made teddy bears, as does (by mail) Mae Wilson (601-873-6804). In 1986, Onward began the annual Bear Hunt Reunion, held the third week in October (for information: 601-873-9283). On the store's left flank outside appears a colorful mural showing a mule-drawn cart brimming with cotton as the vehicle rides through fields of the white fiber.

At Redwood to the south, the appropriately named Yazoo—"river of death" in Indian language—marks where the Delta meets its end, although poetic license has put its southern limits at Vicksburg's "catfish row," a former stretch of black-occupied shanties, shops, and shacks. At the Yazoo the Old Natchez District begins, an early day territory which extended from the river south to the Louisiana line. Soon after, you'll pass on Highway 1 Margaret's Grocery, a weird red and white hued combination food store and religious shrine, posted with the notices,"The devil is on the run" and "All is welcome black and white...Jews and Gentiles." A turn onto Business Route 61 takes you alongside the Yazoo Channel, below the National Cemetery and by the site where the Spanish built Fort Nogales in 1791, succeeded in 1798 by the American outpost of Fort McHenry. After the French, harassed by Indians, failed to establish a military outpost and plantation in the area in the early eighteenth century, the

Spanish seized the Old Natchez District in 1781, but in March, 1798, they abandoned Fort Nogales and American settlers soon arrived. In 1819, one newcomer, a Methodist minister from Virginia named Newit Vick, planned a city he named Vicksburgh, which later dropped the "h" but gained importance as a Mississippi port. After Vick's death, his executor auctioned off lots at the "truly desirable" location, a place "superior to any other site on the Mississippi river above New Orleans," as the 1822 sale notice said, "having an elevation of fifteen feet above high water mark, gradual ascent back for near a half mile, and possesses a commodious landing." Even at Vicksburg's very advent, then, the river played a major role, as the waterway did over the succeeding years.

The settlement flourished as a port. "Vicksburg has always been a river town, its pulse timed to the flow of the water which swirls there at its feet," observed Peter F. Walker in *Vicksburg: A People at War, 1860-1865*. "The city was founded and settled as the steamboat was developed; the city grew as the number of boats on western waters increased. From the river, the city drew its life as skiffs, flatboats, and steamboats, laden with people and wares, tied up along its wharves." But, as usual, both benefits and burdens flowed from the river's presence. By the time of the Civil War, Vicksburg enjoyed a population larger than nearby Jackson, the state capital. There on the high bluffs overlooking the Mississippi the Confederates emplaced a fierce battery of guns which enabled the rebels to block passage of Union vessels on the waterway. In 1862, federal forces gradually dislodged Confederate positions upstream along the Mississippi at Columbus, Kentucky, and at Fort Pillow and Memphis in Tennessee (see the Kentucky and Tennessee sections), but fortified Vicksburg remained as the last and most vexing rebel outpost on the river. Lincoln knew that only by conquering Vicksburg, the control point for the Lower Mississippi, could his army defeat the Confederacy. "The Mississippi is the backbone of the rebellion; it is the key to the whole situation," the President observed. "While the Confederates hold it, they can obtain supplies of all kinds, and it is a barrier against our forces." Lincoln noted that Vicksburg was "the key" to the river country and that "The war can never be brought to a close until that key is in our pocket."

In mid-June, 1862, Admiral David G. Farragut sailed his deep water fleet up the Mississippi to Vicksburg where he hoped to gain control of the four mile stretch of river within range of Confederate guns, the only part of the entire waterway, except for Port Hudson in northern Louisiana, in the Confederacy—between Cairo, Illinois, and the Gulf—not in Union hands. But Southern ram ships and other vessels forced Farragut to withdraw, and on July 27 he headed downstream for New Orleans. Lincoln's favorite plan involved cutting a bypass canal across DeSoto Point, a project undertaken by Ulysses S. Grant even though the Union general deemed the idea impractical. On March 6, 1863, Grant reported that the canal was almost finished but the rising water then delayed the work, one of the various "providential failures" which, as Grant later recalled, forced him to try land routes that proved successful.

This famous campaign began soon afterward when the general landed some 40,000 Union troops at Bruinsburg, south of Vicksburg, an accomplishment for which he "felt a degree of relief scarcely ever equalled," Grant later wrote in his *Personal Memoirs*, for "I was on dry ground on the same side of the river as the enemy. All the campaigns, labors, hardships and exposures from the month of December previous to this time that had been made and endured were for the accomplishment of this one object." Grant's forces advanced toward Vicksburg, and after a forty-seven day siege, the city finally fell on July 4, 1863, a crucial victory which inspired Lincoln's comment: "The Father of Waters again goes unvexed to the sea."

After the war, the Mississippi continued to dominate Vicksburg's life and livelihood. In April, 1876, the river managed to accomplish what Grant and his 50,000 men had failed to achieve in 1863 with their canal project. The waterway washed away a narrow neck of land and surged across DeSoto Point to create Centennial Cutoff, which removed the Mississippi from the Vicksburg waterfront and deprived the city of its landing. More than a quarter of a century lapsed before the Corps of Engineers built a canal which diverted the Yazoo River into the Mississippi's old channel in front of Vicksburg and restored the waterfront. By then, the steamboat era had nearly reached its end, but at least ship traffic could again dock at the old river city, where a slack water harbor completed in 1960 by the Corps of Engineers attracted river-related commercial activity to Vicksburg.

Vicksburg boasts three important federal agencies directly involved with the Mississippi. In August of 1873, after the Office of Western Rivers Improvement in St. Louis decided to establish a branch in the Mississippi Delta or a nearby area, an army engineer opened an office in Vicksburg, forerunner of the present Corps of Engineers installation there. The Vicksburg branch, largest of the four Corps districts on the Lower Mississippi, bears the responsibility for a drainage area of 58,000 square miles. The other three Corps offices manage lesser domains: New Orleans, 46,000 square miles; St. Louis, 27,000; Memphis, 25,000. As early as 1821, the Corps of Engineers became involved with the Mississippi when the agency assigned two officers to make a reconnaissance of the waterway from St. Louis to New Orleans. Based on a report they submitted the following year, in 1824 Congress enacted legislation directing removal of snags and other obstructions, while in 1838 the Corps completed a study for improvements at the Mississippi's mouth to facilitate navigation by seagoing ships. In 1850, engineers surveyed the river to prepare a plan for flood protection. In 1861, Corps officers A.A. Humphreys and Henry L. Abbott submitted their now famous study—still the basis for river improvements—entitled "Report Upon the Physics and Hydraulics of the Mississippi River;

Protection of the Alluvial Region Against Overflow; and Upon the Deepening of the Mouths; Based Upon Surveys and Investigations." Construction of levees of various sizes and quality by local districts and lack of coordination in river surveys indicated the need for a central agency to direct improvements on the Mississippi, a need Congress met in 1879 by creating the Mississippi River Commission. Originally headquartered in St. Louis, the Commission's first members included Benjamin Harrison, elected U.S. President ten years later, and the renowned river engineer James B. Eads (see the St. Louis section in the Missouri chapter). It assumed responsibility for preparing surveys and plans to improve the river channel, control flooding, halt erosion of the banks, and facilitate navigation. In December, 1929, the Commission moved its headquarters from St. Louis to Vicksburg, where the agency has occupied since 1944 the imposing 1894 Richardson Romanesque former post office and customs house building, richly embellished with decorative medallions, terra cotta trim, artfully arranged brickwork, wrought-iron fixtures, and other well-wrought architectural details.

In this authoritative edifice—where a small, changing exhibit on the river occupies part of the lobby—operates the central authority charged with taming and controlling the unwieldly waterway, which drains thirty-one states over a total of 1,245,000 square miles, absorbs the output of 250 tributaries, carries an average daily flow of 300 billion gallons, and serves as the main stem of a 15,000 mile navigable inland waterway system. After the devastating 1927 flood—which killed 246 people, left 650,000 homeless, drowned 165,000 livestock, and inundated 26,000 square miles to a width of up to eighty miles from the main channel—the Corps of Engineers developed the Mississippi River and Tributaries Project, called the "Jadwin Plan" for the Chief of Engineers, a flood control program for the valley between Cape Girardeau, Missouri and Head of Passes at the mouth. Administered by the Commission, the Project involves levees (by now

1,600 miles of them), reservoirs, revetments, cutoffs which have shortened the river by 170 miles (some completed before the Project), dikes, dredging, floodwalls, floodgates, and other improvements, all aimed at controlling the great waterway. They also facilitate commercial navigation, a trade now nearly three centuries old, which started on the Mississippi when boatmen carried the river's very first cargo, a load of 15,000 bear and deer hides, floated downstream in 1705 from the Wabash River in Indiana to New Orleans for shipment on to France.

Some of the studies for improvements on the Mississippi take place at the unique Waterways Experiment Station, Vicksburg's third federal river-related organization, the Corps of Engineers principal research, testing, and development facility. Since the Corps established the Station in 1929 to test flood control plans for the Mississippi, the 685 acre installation, on the south edge of Vicksburg, has expanded to include six laboratories. At the Station, which in 1959 installed Mississippi's first computer, a staff of more than 1,600 researches some 1,500 projects sponsored by about 150 federal and state agencies which fund the studies they request. The main river-related unit, the Hydraulics Laboratory, studies locks, dams, levees, and dredging using field investigations, computer models, and three dimensional mock-ups of waterways. A Waterways Experiment Station installation at Jackson, Mississippi, includes the remarkable Mississippi Basin Model, the world's largest small-scale working model, a giant relief map whose 200 acres reproduces the 1,245,000 square mile area drained by the waterway. This miniature duplicate of the huge river system originated in 1942, when General Eugene Reybold, Chief of Engineers, directed the Station to construct the nature-replicating artifact. The army established half a mile from the project site a 3,000 man camp for German prisoners of war, most of them from General Rommel's Afrika Korps. The inmates included General Von Cholitz, wanted in Germany for ignoring Hitler's order to burn

Paris. As the prisoners roughed out the model between August 1943 and May 1946, Dutch war pilots training in Jackson amused themselves by buzzing the Germans. In 1947, civilian workers began the hydraulic portion, with concrete mouldings formed to represent the river's contours. All of life shrinks to diminished proportions at the model: a person's step equals about a mile, a gallon of water represents 1.5 million gallons on the river itself, and time compresses to the point that 5.4 minutes on the model equals one day. These scales follow the ones established at the earlier Lower Mississippi model built nearly two decades previously at the Waterways Experiment Station in Vicksburg.

A guided tour at the Station (M-F 10, on occasion at 2; for information: 601-634-2502) includes stops at the Coastal Research Engineering and the Geotechnical labs, and at the Niagara Falls model, the oldest (1953) of the presently existing seventy or so waterway models, the first of which—the Illinois River—workers dug with a grapefruit knife. Inside, beyond the Niagara installation, stands a display on the Mississippi River Basin Model in Jackson, while outside across the street Vicksburg's only outdoor model includes the Old River Control facility (see the Louisiana chapter), one of the Station's few Mississippi sections.

On and near the river in Vicksburg lie areas and sights which recall the city's close connection with the Mississippi. Navy Circle, a Civil War gun emplacement site, perches by the state tourist office which overlooks the waterway. Just north of the bridge, an observation point at Louisiana Circle, part of Vicksburg's vast National Military Park, contains a rise where a stubby cannon on display, the so-called "Widow Blakely," served to help Confederates control the waterway. The nearby Top O' the River, perched atop the bluffs by the Mississippi, specializes in "Catfish Exeptionale", and next door stands the more elegant Delta Point Pestaurant. Just to the north near here the Yazoo River, not the Mississippi, fronts Vicksburg. As you proceed into town along Washington, a left turn on Klein takes you to the only four of Vicksburg's ten vintage bed and breakfast houses which boast views onto the water (here the Yazoo): 1873 National Register-listed "The Corners" (800-444-7421); c. 1840 Cedar Grove (800-862-1300, in Mississippi 800-448-2820); 1860's Register-listed Floweree (601-638-2704) and the city's newest such establishment, 1876 Belle of the Bends (601-634-0737), opened in March, 1991. The last was named for the 1898 excursion boat which led the ship procession at the 1903 inauguration of the Yazoo Channel which restored Vicksburg's waterfront. Downtown on the levee, outside the floodwall—which bears lines indicating flood levels in eight different high water years, including the 56.2 foot 1927 inundation—moor the *Mamie S. Barrett* showboat and the *Spirit of Vicksburg* excursion ship (May-Aug 10, Mar-Dec also at 2; 601-634-6059).

Other attractions downtown include the Coca-Cola Museum (M-Sat 9-5, Sun 1:30-4:30) at the candy store where in 1894 Joseph Biedenharn became the first person to bottle the fountain beverage. You might also visit *The Vanishing Glory* movie on the siege of Vicksburg (on the hour from 10 a.m.), and the Toys and Soldiers display (M-Sat 9-4:30, Sun 1:30-4:30), featuring Civil War and other miniature figures in a c. 1840 building which housed a grocery store, the first business Ulysses S. Grant allowed to reopen after he captured the city. Next door stands the 1858 former Courthouse, closed in 1939 and reopened in 1948 as a museum (M-Sat 8:30-4:30, Sun 1:30-4:30), crammed with antebellum, Civil War, and river items, including the trophy antlers won in 1870 by the *Robert E. Lee* when the ship beat the *Natchez* in the most famous steamboat race ever held. The Vicksburg National Military Park (8-5), east of downtown, includes a Visitor Center with displays on the siege of the city, a sixteen mile driving tour through the area occupied by federal and Confederate forces, and the *U.S.S. Cairo* display (9-5) of artifacts recovered from the Union gunboat. It sank in the Yazoo River after Confederate shelling in December, 1862. Workers salvaged the ship in the early 1960s. More than 17,000 Union soldiers are buried at the Vicksburg National Cemetery, nearly 13,000 of them unidentified. They perished in the campaign to take the city; the Confederate dead lie in Cedar Hill Cemetery.

South of Vicksburg, an irregular section of Mississippi around Lake Palmyra shaped like a jigsaw puzzle piece lies west of the river. In 1818, a Natchez lawyer named Joseph Davis gave up his practice and bought land in the area, then east of the waterway. On 5,000 acres, he established a plantation called Hurricane. In 1835, Davis conveyed some of the land to his younger brother, who resigned his military commission in the U.S. Army and moved to the property in order to develop a plantation called Brierfield. An enlightened owner, Joseph Davis kept his workers well housed and well fed, and he established a court to hear their grievances. By the time of the Civil War, Davis' 345 laborers at Hurricane made him one of only nine men in Mississippi to own more than 300 slaves. Meanwhile, Davis' little brother developed his own operation at adjacent Brierfield until called away during the war for service with the Confederacy. When the winds of war began to blow, Hurricane's name described its fate, for the property suffered stormy times: the slaves scattered, intruders burned the cotton crop, and marauders looted the plantation mansion. At Davis Bend, Admiral David Farragut landed a Union raiding party which pillaged the owners' dwellings, shattering china and glassware with bayonets, slashing paintings, burning books, and igniting the "big house", which blazed with flames visible as far as Vicksburg, thirty miles north. After the federal government confiscated the properties, the Freedman's Bureau attempted to establish there a model colony run by former slaves. This experiment survived until floods, then drought and injuries suffered by leader Benjamin Montgomery in 1874, led to the communal colony's failure. Afterwards, Benjamin's son Isaiah founded a new black settlement called Mound Bayou, which still exists in the Mississippi Delta just east of Rosedale. Eventually, the original owners managed to recover their property, with Brierfield returned in 1878 to Joe Davis' younger brother—none other than Jefferson Davis, former president of the Confederacy. The meandering Mississippi gradually rearranged the Davis Bend peninsula, first cutting it away from the mainland to form an island, then filling the bendway in to leave only tiny oxbow Palmyra Lake, once Davis Bend. By now, all traces of the Davis brothers' once famous plantations have vanished.

Port Gibson on the River Road, U.S. 61, farther south, enjoyed a happier fate during the Civil War, for during the march north toward Vicksburg in May, 1863, Ulysses S. Grant found the town "too beautiful to burn." Thus did the Union general and future president of the United States coin for Port Gibson's chamber of commerce the perfect endorsement. But Grant hardly exaggerated, for the well-preserved town, much of which encompasses Mississippi's first National Historic District, presents a most attractive appearance. Along tree-shaded Church, one of the River Road's more handsome streets, stand some twenty vintage dwellings and religious sanctuaries, which give flavor of a civilized, old Southern settlement. Port Gibson boasted the state's first library, second newspaper, and third Masonic Lodge. The eight religious sanctuaries on Church Street include the 1859 First Presbyterian, its chandelier from the famous *Robert E. Lee* steamboat and its steeple topped by a golden hand whose index finger points to heaven. You'll also find the 1849 St. Joseph's Catholic, the city's oldest church, and the odd-looking 1891 Gemiluth Chessed ("gift of the righteous"), a Moorish-Byzantine-Romanesque temple, Mississippi's oldest existing synagogue. The first Jews arrived in Port Gibson, once home to about forty Jewish families, in the 1840's. The community held the last service at Gemiluth Chessed in 1978. Jewish settlers arrived in Mississippi's river country early, with the first services held in Natchez, not far south, in 1798. In the summer of 1990, archeologists heard of four tombstones with Jewish symbols entwined in tree roots near Grand Gulf on the river a few miles west of Port Gibson. They soon discovered forty more such markers dating from the yellow fever epidemic of about 1830. At Utica, thirty miles northeast of Port Gibson, the Museum of the Southern Jewish Experience houses photos, artifacts and other mementos of now vanished small town Jewish communities in the Deep South.

At the cottage-like c. 1825 Hughes house on Church Street, Erwin Russell lived as a boy. He was supposedly the first author (1870's) to use black dialect in his works. On a spacious, oak-garnished lot stands National Register-listed Oak Square (c. 1850), the town's largest residence, a bed and breakfast place (601-437-4350). The c. 1830 Gibson Landing (601-437-3432) also offers bed and breakfast. A few blocks south of Oak Square, on Church, the c. 1805 Samuel Gibson House, the town's oldest structure, now serves as headquarters for the annual Pilgrimage house tour held every spring (601-437-4351). Town founder Gibson rests in Wintergreen Cemetery, where assassinated Confederate General Earl Van Dorn, a dashing West Point graduate who fought in Mexico and against the Comanche Indians, is buried facing south. In the Catholic cemetery lies Rezin Bowie (at the front to the left of the entrance gate), inventor of the famous knife first used by his brother James in a duel at Natchez. Around the corner on Marginal you'll find the Jewish cemetery, established in 1870, before which Jews were buried in Natchez. Over on Main stand the 1840 Greek Revival-style bank, formerly a hotel, the Claiborne County Courthouse, and the 1820 Planter's Hotel. The last survives as one of the county's oldest buildings. In its day, the Planter's was one of the best known inns along the Natchez Trace, the famous trail which ran from the Mississippi River to Nashville.

On the Mississippi, northwest of Port Gibson, lies Grand Gulf Military Monument Park, established in 1962 by the state on what remained of the site where historic Grand Gulf stood. The French originally settled there in the early eighteenth century, and later the town developed as a cotton shipping port. In the 1830's, a railroad to the port replaced a rough wagon road from the interior, and in 1839, the Mississippi legislature chartered a freight line to carry cotton from the waterfront at Grand Gulf directly to Liverpool, England, but the service soon ceased. A yellow fever epidemic diminished the population of nearly 1,000, and between 1855 and 1860, the Mississippi washed away Grand Gulf's entire fifty-five block business section, after which the population dwindled to under 200. During the Union campaign to capture Vicksburg, Grant decided to land his troops at Grand Gulf, but the Confederates fortified the position, forcing the federal invaders to cross the Mississippi and arrive at Bruinsburg, farther south. A museum (M-Sat 8-12, Sun 10-6) at the park traces the history of Grand Gulf and of Grant's maneuvers in the area. Old gun emplacements recall the rebel's defensive positions, shelled on April 29, 1863, by Admiral David Porter's seven warships in order to prepare for Grant's proposed landing. After the war, the Mississippi changed course and eliminated the waterfront at the village, now recalled only by the little cemetery garnished with moss-draped oaks, a picturesque watermill near the Gothic-style wood church, a Spanish era-type house, and a few other relics. An observation tower atop a hill in the park, listed on the National Register, affords views onto the Mississippi, while not far away stands a huge, round, cooling tower, at 520 feet the state's tallest concrete structure. It operates Grand Gulf Nuclear Station where the Energy Central exhibit (M-F 8-5) contains information on the facility, including a simulated control room.

A number of off-the-beaten-track attractions lie on the back roads near the Mississippi between this area and Natchez. Carrol Street out of Port Gibson leads west, through sparsely settled countryside, to a modern (1960) replica of an 1801 log church built there in the wilderness by three South Carolina missionary ministers. Lookout Point at this rise provides a view onto Bayou Pierre, an isolated, backwoods waterway, named by French explorers for its many rocks ("pierres"), where advancing Union forces forced the Confederates to flee. The road winds through a thickly wooded area and soon reaches the ruins of Windsor, considered the state's handsomest house after planter Smith Coffee Daniell completed the mansion in 1861. Imported furnishings, a library of rare volumes, and lavish appointments endowed Windsor—so called for the strange music which sounded as the wind blew among the column capitals—with an elegant and refined ambiance. From the observatory atop the fifth floor, Confederate soldiers monitored traffic along the nearby Mississippi, while Union forces later used the house as a hospital. Windsor, listed on the National Register, survived the Civil War intact, but in 1890 a fire caused by a carelessly discarded cigarette destroyed the showplace and its contents. Only the twenty-three Corinthian columns still stand as haunting evocations of a vanished antebellum mansion and way of life.

Nearby, toward Bayou Pierre, lay Bruinsburg, a plantation founded in 1788 by Virginian Bryan Bruin and his son Peter. Prominent travelers on the Mississippi often stopped in at the Bruins' civilized little enclave there in the wilds of Mississippi. In January, 1807, Aaron Burr—former U.S. Senator, Vice-President under Thomas Jefferson, Alexander Hamilton's assassin in a duel, and reputed schemer to manipulate Western territories to secede from the Union—arrived with some sixty followers at Bruinsburg. He began his negotiations here to surrender to federal authorities, who later tried him for treason in a case resulting in Burr's acquittal. In late April, 1863, some 40,000 Union soldiers under Ulysses S. Grant crossed the Mississippi and arrived at Bruinsburg. The army then advanced along wagon roads to Port Gibson, defended by 5,000 Confederates, and eventually marched on to Vicksburg. Down the road, beyond

Windsor, stands Bethel Presbyterian Church (c. 1845), where a congregation organized in 1826 worshipped. A tornado carried away the sharply pointed steeple, and the slave gallery no longer exists inside the white, classic-style sanctuary; it seems rather lost and lonely out there in the countryside.

Further on (about a mile) you'll pass the old Canemount plantation property, founded in the early nineteenth century by Irish native John Murdock. A short distance beyond, a right turn (just past the small brick telephone sub-station) takes you to Alcorn State University, the nation's first state-supported institution of higher learning for blacks. The Mississippi legislature chartered the school in 1871 at the abandoned campus of Oakland College, started in 1830 by Presbyterians as a boys' school, which closed permanently when the Civil War began. School founder and president Reverend Jeremiah Chamberlain, who supposedly favored the Union cause, was stabbed to death in 1851 on the campus by a Secessionist. Hiram R.Revels, the first black U.S. Senator, resigned his seat to serve as president of the new college, named for Governor James Alcorn who budgeted $50,000 for the institution. The legislature changed the name to Alcorn Agricultural and Mechanical College in 1878 when it became the nation's first black land-grant school under the 1862 Morill Act, and nearly a century later the university adopted its present designation. Today, 2,700 students attend the institution.

White-columned Oakland Memorial Chapel, centerpiece of the park-like 1,700 acre campus, dates from the original 1830 college. Built by slaves of the early Presbyterians, Oakland Chapel sports wrought iron stairs salvaged from nearby Windsor after the mansion burned. At an 1888 ceremony in the chapel, listed on the National Register, Beulah Turner Robinson became the nation's first black female to graduate from a state supported college. The president's house, a white wood residence, stands by the sanctuary. Up the street, which borders a grassy park in the center of the campus, stands the 1851 Belles Lettres Building.

This chapel look-alike was supposedly built for the literary society.

A back road from Alcorn leads west to Rodney, a forlorn hamlet near the Mississippi too small to merit a place on the official state highway map. Rodney originated in the early nineteenth century at the foot of a bluff called Petit Gulf, analogue to Grand Gulf on the river to the north. By the beginning of the Civil War, the town rivaled Vicksburg and Natchez. In September, 1863, Confederate cavalrymen captured twenty-five officers and men from a Union gunboat moored off-shore. They had left their vessel to attend a service at the Presbyterian church in Rodney, whose residents still worship at another old sanctuary, the delightful Baptist church. In the 1880's, the Yazoo and Mississippi Valley Railroad began to divert freight from riverboats and the Mississippi started shifting to the west, leaving Rodney removed from the waterway. In 1935, the Corps of Engineers completed a cutoff which diverted the river even farther from the village, now inhabited by fewer than fifty people. About a mile south of town lay Rodney Landing, where the evocative opening scene of *The Robber Bridegroom* by Mississippi author Eudora Welty takes place: "It was the close of day when a boat touched Rodney's Landing on the Mississippi River and Clement Musgrove, an innocent planter with a bag of gold and many presents, disembarked." These days, however, no such dramatic vignettes enliven that remote and untrafficked corner of the Mississippi River Valley.

Just to the south, directly opposite Waterproof, Louisiana, General Zachary Taylor, elected President of the United States in 1848, owned a plantation near Ashland Landing. Shortly before dawn in February, 1849, Taylor awaited the steamer *Tennessee*, chartered to take the President-elect to Vicksburg for the first of many receptions that party leaders had arranged. The ship's whistle sounded in the night, then the vessel landed and Taylor boarded and retired to finish his night's sleep. As the boat advanced up the Mississippi, the general's assistant learned that the presidential party had boarded the wrong steamer, the *Saladin.* The group had been tricked by a ruse the pilot, twenty-four year old family friend Tom Coleman, Jr., had engineered to kidnap the President-elect. Taylor's aids dreaded revealing the deception to the old man, but when he awoke, the newly-elected chief executive seemed greatly amused by the prank.

At Lorman back to the west on Highway 61, the River Road, survives the 1875 general store (M-Sat 8-6, Sun 12-6). It is now for the most part a tourist attraction, installed in a century old building with wood floors, high ceilings, original fixtures, and a few antique items in the loft area where the emporium once stored barrels of meal, flour, and molasses hauled by oxcart from Rodney. The 1857 Rosswood Plantation just to the east of Lorman offers tours (M-Sat 10:30-5, Sun 12:30-5) and bed and breakfast accommodations (601-437-4215). The Natchez Trace Parkway runs west of Lorman, and takes you south for ten miles to the turnoff at Highway 553. The unspoiled parkway, developed starting in the 1930's, is administered by the National Park Service. It follows the route of the 450 mile long, 8,000 year old path originally cleared by buffalo, then trekked by Indians and later followed by traders, trappers, adventurers, and, especially, rivermen returning home to the Ohio River Valley after floating down the Mississippi in flatboats. The French showed the old trail on maps they drew back in the 1730's, and the British on their 1770's maps designated the route as "Path to the Choctaw Nation." In 1785, the first commercial shipment, a cargo of flour, landed at Natchez. This event marked the beginning of the extensive river trade which soon sent over the so-called Boatmen's Trail every year as many as 10,000 "Kaintucks," as area residents nicknamed the men who floated down the Mississippi from the north and returned home via the overland route. After Spain surrendered its claims to the area, the United States created the Mississippi Territory, with Natchez as its capital, and the Boatmen's Trail became the Natchez Trail. Mail service began along the trace in 1800. Over the next three years the army cleared the route, and for a time the trail served to connect the east with the remote Mississippi River country at the far southwestern corner of the United States. After the advent of the steamboat era in the 1820's, boatmen could return home via the Mississippi, which also afforded a route for military and other purposes. The disused trail, gradually overgrown with foliage, faded from view until the Mississippi Daughters of the American Revolution headed a campaign in 1909 to salvage and reopen the historic route, a project which led to the Natchez Trace Parkway. One of the show homes in nearby Natchez, Ravennaside, residence of the head of the state Natchez Trace Association, contains an extensive collection of memorabilia on the old trail.

A mile after the turnoff from the Parkway onto Highway 553 stands Springfield (1786-1791), a National Register-listed show house (10-5, to 6 in the summer, possible shorter hours Nov 15-Feb) and bed and breakfast establishment (601-786-3802) where Andrew Jackson married Rachel Robards in 1791. After the ceremony, the pair learned that the bride had not been legally divorced from her husband, Lewis Robards, so the couple tied, or retied, the knot in January, 1794, following the divorce. Farther on, beyond the 1840's Richland Plantation house, lies the Maryland Settlement, an area established in the eighteenth century by pioneers from Maryland around Church Hill, a rise topped by the delightful, small, Gothic-style, stone Christ Episcopal (1857), where Union troops once paused to play bawdy songs on the organ. Just across the way stands picturesque Wagner's Grocery, a true period piece, with faded, round Coca-Cola signs on the facade, a "Reach for Sunbeam Bread" ad in the window and, inside, plank floors, bare light bulbs, a tiny post office area, and a refrigerator tilted at a slant. Highway 553 winds its way past another four or five plantation mansions, some visible from the road, and passes near the eight-acre, 700 year old Emerald Mound, supposedly the nation's third largest Indian mound, before reaching U.S. 61, which continues on to Washington.

Between 1802 and 1820, Washington served as the Territorial and the first state capital, and the town also became the seat of Adams County, site of both the federal territorial court and land office and of Jefferson College, but even all these institutions failed to energize the laid-back settlement. "It is doubtful that there is another instance of a country hamlet, barely five years old, receiving such an array of governmental functions and responding so slowly to these stimulations to growth," wrote Charles S. Sydnor in *A Gentleman of the Old Natchez Region: Benjamin L.C. Wailes*.

Washington's Elizabeth Female Academy, founded in 1818 as supposedly the nation's first women's college, no longer exists, but buildings at Jefferson College (M-Sat 9-5, Sun 1-5) survive to recall the Territory's first educational institution, chartered in 1802 and opened nine years later. Ten year old Jefferson Davis studied at the preparatory school, as did the two sons of bird artist John James Audubon, who taught drawing classes there. Two years after Jefferson became a college in 1817, the boxy brick East Wing building opened, matched in 1839 by the West Wing, both still standing. Andrew Jackson camped on the historic campus while traveling to and from the 1815 Battle of New Orleans, the statehood convention met there in 1817, and the Marquis de Lafayette watched cadet drills at the school during his 1825 tour of the United States. Between 1838 and 1846, the college was headed by John Wesley Monette, author of the first of two proposed books on *The History of the Discovery and Settlement of the Valley of the Mississippi*. The second volume was left incomplete, as the scholar kept collecting additional data, an occupational hazard not unknown to authors who choose to write about the capacious, age-old Mississippi. After the institution reopened in 1866 following the Civil War, Jefferson operated as a preparatory school until 1964, when it closed permanently. A Visitor Center contains displays on the college, a marker bearing the first page of the state's first constitution honors the 1817 statehood convention, and a nature trail leads past Ellicott Springs, where in 1797 Major Andrew Ellicott camped before he surveyed the 31st parallel to delineate the border between the United States and Spanish territory.

It was Major Ellicott who in 1797, on orders from George Washington, defied Spanish authority and raised the American flag for the first time in the Lower Mississippi Valley at a low hill overlooking the Mississippi in nearby Natchez. On this rise in Natchez stands the c. 1798 Connelly's Tavern, the terminus of the Natchez Trace, now owned by the Natchez Garden Club and called the House on Ellicott Hill (9-5). Before that point in time, when the Americans wrested Natchez away from Spain, the area had frequently changed hands as the European powers struggled to gain a foothold along the Lower Mississippi. Not long after the local Natchez Indians killed some French traders and pillaged their trading post, France built Fort Rosalie in 1716, which by 1729 served to protect more than 700 people at the new settlement. In November, 1729, however, the Indians revolted, capturing Fort Rosalie and killing many of the settlers. Visitor Center displays and mounds at the National Historic Landmark Grand Village of the Natchez (M-Sat 9-5, Sun 1:30-5) east of town trace the history of the Natchez culture. The Indians, who originated about 1100-1200, called their chief the "Great Sun," symbolized by a perpetual fire tended by special attendants, executed if the fire died. The tribe reached its peak about the time of Hernando de Soto's explorations near the Mississippi in 1541. After the French arrived a century and a half later, the Natchez suffered a rapid decline, and they finally disappeared when in 1730 the Europeans killed most of them and sold about 400 into slavery in the West Indies. France ceded the area through a 1763 treaty which included Natchez to the British, who remained only until

1779 when the Spanish captured the city, which prospered under their rule. The Americans arrived in 1797 and the town, located in the country's extreme southwest corner, became the nation's most remote frontier settlement. The Spanish retained control of Louisiana, to the south and west, and only trails like the Trace through Indian country reached Natchez. Of course, the river offered access, and in January, 1812 the *New Orleans*, the first steamer, stopped off at the landing to pick up a small cargo for New Orleans, and so began the town's riverboat era. Before long, Natchez, the only port between the mouth of the Ohio and New Orleans, began to prosper.

The waterfront developed along Water, Middle, and Silver Streets. These ran for more than a mile, tucked into the steep bluff atop which stood elegant mansions and refined establishments of the upper town, which once supposedly boasted more millionaires than any other American city. The boisterous area beneath the bluffs, Natchez-Under-the-Hill, gained a reputation as the roughest, toughest hell-hole on the entire Mississippi, with gambling dens, houses of pleasure, flop houses, and taverns frequented by brawling river roustabouts. Building owners on Silver (the upper street) burrowed caverns into the bluff in order to hide contraband. On River, the establishments—jutting out over the waterway and perched above it on pilings—contained trap doors used by the dives to drop their victims into the Mississippi after fleecing them. Over time, the river gradually shifted to the east, carving away from the front of Natchez more than 160 acres. Now Natchez-Under-the-Hill seems more dowdy than rowdy. Only a short stretch of Silver Street, along with a few restaurants and shops, survive at the once fearsome riverfront. Perhaps with a little imagination a latter day visitor can visualize how the area might have appeared during the days when planters and pilots, painted women and plastered boatmen, swarmed through the lively and deadly trio of streets at Natchez-Under-the-Hill.

Back up on the bluff, above Silver Street, stretches a park-like area which affords good views onto the Mississippi. Spread out upstream is a splendid, sweeping panorama of the river, which curves gracefully as it approaches the city. Just to the south stands 1821 Rosalie, located by the site of the early French fort named for the Countess of Pontchartrain. The white- columned brick mansion, which served as Ulysses S. Grant's headquarters, occupies one of the most compelling residential locations on the Mississippi. Like a dozen or so other Natchez show houses, Rosalie remains open for tours throughout the year, while during the annual spring Pilgrimage (early March-early April), started in 1932, visitors can tour thirty houses, and during the fall Pilgrimage (October), organized in 1977, twenty-four mansions remain open. The twenty-five or so show places which offer bed and breakfast accommodations can also be seen off-season if you stay at them. For room bookings and Pilgrimage information: 800-647-6742.

The Evans-Bontura House stands north of Rosalie, on Broadway. At the residence spectators gathered to watch the 1870 *Natchez* and *Robert E. Lee* steamboat race. Across the street, above the river, lie the old Spanish Commons, an esplanade established when Spain controlled the town and still today, more than two centuries later, a public park. Markers in the park commemorate the Natchez Trace and the nearby nineteenth century depot of the Illinois Central, "main line of mid-America." Broadway takes you north, past the Natchez Pecan Shelling Company. A left turn on Madison leads to Clifton Avenue which, if you continue, becomes truly a dead-end. Erosion has washed away part of the 150 foot tall bluff, leaving the road impassable. The erosion, which began in 1951, started eating at the road in the mid-1970's, about when the Corps of Engineers took core samples to see if the fragile loess soil atop the bluff could be stabilized. The houses which stand along the east side of disappearing Clifton Avenue enjoy a splendid view onto the Mississippi, but if erosion continues they may someday lose their perch and tumble into the bottomlands by the waterway. The distinctive looking old residence fronted by four columns belonged to A.B. Learned, who owned timberland along the river and operated a sawmill just below the bluff here. Nearby stands the Riverside bed and breakfast house (601-442-3762), while farther north, on Cemetery Road, Weymouth Hall (610-445-2304), a handsome c. 1855 National Register-listed home overlooking the river, also offers bed and breakfast. Both the Natchez city burial ground and a National Cemetery, with the graves of more than 3,000 Union soldiers, lie along Cemetery Road.

In downtown Natchez, the restored 1927 Eola Hotel (800-888-9140) also offers views of the river from many of its rooms. Named for the daughter of Isidore Levy, who built the establishment, the Eola merits not only National Register listing but is also one of about sixty hotels in the country designated by the National Trust for Historic Preservation as an Historic Hotel. Other Natchez attractions include the Old South Winery (10-6), run by descendants of the Galbreath family, who brought muscadine vines from South Carolina to Mississippi in the early nineteenth century, and river excursions on the *Jubilee* (604-442-6639). Ten miles north of town Natchez State Park, on land once part of early plantations, offers nature areas and cabins (601-442-2658).

Highway 61 heads south out of Natchez and crosses Homochitto ("shelter creek") River, which flows into Old River Lake, a 5,000 acre oxbow body of water part of the Mississippi channel until the river formed a natural cutoff in 1776. Beyond the Buffalo River, the highway reaches Woodville, a picturesque town with more than 140 nineteenth century structures. Not far from quiet courthouse square stands the 1803 Baptist Church, Mississippi's oldest sanctuary, while the Methodist and Episcopal churches, both built in 1824, also recall early-day religious activity. In 1862, St.Paul's Episcopal contributed its bell to the Confederate cause for melting into a cannon, "hoping that its gentle tones that have so often called us to the House of God, may be transmitted into war's resounding rhyme." Judge Edward McGehee, who helped found the Methodist Church, financed the 1831 West Feliciana Railroad, the first in the state, second in the Mississippi Valley, and fifth in the country. Later acquired by the Yazoo and Mississippi Valley, the line—which ran twenty-seven miles down to St. Francisville, Louisiana—was among the earliest American railroads to adopt the standard gauge, and the first to issue freight tariffs. Rosemount lies just west of Woodville (March-Dec 15 M-Sat 10-4). To this attractive, verandah-fronted 1810 house two year old Jefferson Davis, youngest of ten children, moved with his family from Kentucky. The Confederate president's mother, Jane, who died here in 1845, is buried in the cemetery where other family members lie. Five generations of the Davis family lived at Rosemont, which contains many original furnishings. Hidden away on a back road a few miles southeast of Woodville remain three columns, the only surviving sections of the Bowling Green mansion built in 1831 by Judge McGehee. Federal forces burned the house in 1864, an episode his nephew, Mississippi novelist Stark Young, recounted in his 1934 *So Red the Rose*.

From Woodville, Highway 66 leads west past Indian Fields Plantation and on to Pond, where the picturesque 1881 country store, reopened in 1984 by Liz and Norman Chaffin after being closed for twelve years, contains old display cases, a wood plank floor, and a now disused post office area. By the store lies Pond's pond, which served as a watering hole for oxen, horses, and mules used to haul cotton and other cargo to Fort Adams, by the river four miles away, for shipment on steamboats. A gravel road through the rugged Clark Creek Natural Area leads out to historic Fort Adams, a hamlet whose present obscurity scarcely hints at its previous importance. A few modest houses, a small general store, a church, an abandoned one room schoolhouse, and all of two streets, Front and Back, comprise the near ghost town, once America's most southwestern military base. The French established a landing at the site in the early eighteenth century, and in 1763 the British arrived in the area. In 1798, the Americans established a garrison there called Fort Adams to protect the border with the adjacent Spanish controlled territory.

At Fort Adams, General James Wilkinson, a trouble maker in the Mississippi River Valley (see the Kentucky section), negotiated a treaty with the Choctaw for use of the Natchez Trace by Americans, and W.C.C. Claiborne departed from the base to become governor of Louisiana in 1803. Meriwether Lewis, of the Lewis and Clark Expedition, served at Fort Adams, as did Philip Nolan, "The Man Without a Country" in Edward Everett Hale's famous story of that name. Tried for treason, Nolan (the fictional character) cries out that never again does he want to hear of the United States, and this became his sentence. In exile, however, he hopes that after his death someone will "set up a stone for my memory at Fort Adams or at Orleans." In reality, the Philip Nolan stationed at the outpost, a protege of General Wilkinson, acquitted himself well and remained a patriot, not a traitor. Hale simply used Nolan as a character in the 1863 tale, which was based on the attempt by Wilkinson and Aaron Burr to establish their own empire in the Lower Mississippi Valley. Hale's tale was published in the *Atlantic* as a cautionary lesson on the evils of secession. In his 1876 novel *Philip Nolan's Friends*, Hale tried to rehabilitate the real Nolan's reputation, but the character's name still evokes the countryless man once stationed at Fort Adams. After the Louisiana Purchase, when the country's boundaries extended far beyond Fort Adams, the remote post lost its importance, and in 1810 the Americans abandoned the base. Later in the century the Mississippi's channel shifted away from the village, which gradually declined. The name still survives to evoke its one-time strategic significance.

A back country road takes you south from Pond to Pinckneyville, comprised of a scattering of houses with no commercial establishments. On the east side of the road stands 1810 Desert, while opposite stands the smaller whimsically named Oasis, a dwelling in a converted general store. Cold Spring lies farther on, also built in 1810, and constructed by John Carmichael, a doctor at Fort Adams. Not far south the road imperceptibly slips into Louisiana, the last state washed by the waterway, so leaving behind Mississippi's Delta and Old Natchez District areas, whose history the Mississippi has so influenced ever since Hernando de Soto discovered the great river at Sunflower Landing in 1541.

MISSISSIPPI PRACTICAL INFORMATION

Phone numbers of tourist offices in Mississippi's principal Mississippi River cities: Alcorn: 601-877-6130; Clarksdale: 601-627-7337; Greenville: 601-378-3141; Hernando: 601-429-4414; Lorman: 601-437-3661; Natchez: 800-647-6724 and 601-446-6345, and for Pilgrimage information, 800-647-6742; Natchez Trace: 601-842-1572; Onward: 601-873-6804; Pond: 601-888-4426; Port Gibson: 601-437-4351; Tunica: 601-363-2865; Vicksburg: 601-636-9421, out of state 800-221-3536; Washington: 601-442-2901; Woodville: 601-888-6809.

Other useful numbers for travel along the Mississippi River include: Mississippi Division of Tourism Development: 800-647-2290. Mississippi Department of Wildlife, Fisheries, and Parks: 601-364-2120. In Vicksburg the Waterways Experiment Station, 601-634-2504, and the Mississippi River Commssion, 601-634-7023. Lincoln Ltd is a reservation service for bed and breakfast places in Mississippi: 800-633-6477 and 601-482-5483. For bed and breakfast places in Natchez: 800-647-6742.

Mississippi operates highway Welcome Centers on I-55 fourteen miles south of Memphis, on U.S. 82 at Greenville, and in Vicksburg and Natchez.

LOUISIANA

The meandering Mississippi curves 305 miles through Louisiana as the waterway completes its long journey from Minnesota's north woods to the Gulf of Mexico. Over the past 10,000 years the silt-bearing river deposited sediment which formed the Delta area, while more recently—from 2600 B.C.—the restless waterway has swung back and forth across the state, always seeking the steepest and straightest route to the sea. After changing course four times, in 900 A.D. the Mississippi finally settled in its present path in Louisiana, along which three major control and spillway structures, diversion canals, and the lower stretches of the Mississippi's 1,600 miles of levees and flood walls, including the world's longest uninterrupted levee, protect the flood plain which comprises more than half of the state's area.

Pirates and counterfeiters once lurked on the Mississippi, east of where U.S. Highway 65, the River Road, enters Louisiana from Arkansas (the east bank itinerary from the Mississippi line to the river's mouth begins on page 448). They preyed on the rivermen who—if they managed to escape— deemed their luck "an act of providence," a phrase which gave a new name to nearby Lake Providence, formerly Stack Island Lake. Not far north of the lake—a six mile long, oxbow-shaped former bed of the Mississippi—the Panola Pepper Sauce factory, less known but producing a no less fiery concoction than Louisiana's famous Tabasco, takes visitors. The town of Lake Providence perches toward the lake's south edge, its name changed from simply Providence to avoid confusion with the Rhode Island city of that name. The ten or so colorful murals which decorate building walls in town portray local activities and landscapes, including two scenes entitled "Cotton, The Fabric of Our Lives" and "The

Growth of Cotton And Technology." These evoke the crop which generates one-third of East Carroll Parish's farm income. On Hood Street, just east of Lake, a dip in the road indicates where in 1863 Ulysses S. Grant cut part of the canal he hoped would enable federal gunboats to travel through a network of streams and bayous to bypass the heavily fortified Confederate Mississippi River stronghold at Vicksburg (see the Mississippi chapter). Thousands of conscripted slaves worked on the project, abandoned in March, 1863, but only in 1953 did the Corps of Engineers finally fill in the canal. Seven years later, the Corps completed on the Mississippi south of town the Port of Lake Providence. At 1841 National Register-listed Arlington, on the lake's north side, headquartered Union officers, including—supposedly—Grant during his visits to the area. The 1902 old Parish Courthouse and three dwellings along Lake Street also merit Register listing. On the way out of Lake Providence, near where the Mississippi reaches its widest point in Louisiana, 7,600 feet, stands the Minsky Pecan Market, which sells those nuts as well as the locally made Panola Pepper Sauce.

South of town the road passes near the port and the huge blue metal Bunge grain storage tanks, then continues on to Transylvania, its water tower decorated—or at least blotched—with a vampire image, while the general store windows bear a long-fanged figure clad in a black cape bidding visitors a welcome—"We're always glad to have new blood in town!" Although the village seems to enjoy its nominal connection with Count Dracula's Carpathian Mountain realm in Romania, the designation probably originated with the Transylvania Company, a property venture which in the mid-eighteenth century acquired 20 million acres from the Cherokee, the largest private land transaction in history. In 1826, settler Richard Keene named his plantation Transylvania, farmed for more than a century until a U.S. government agency bought the 10,000 acre property in 1938, and divided the land into parcels given to some 150 families. On a side road just off the highway (you turn at the elementary school) a lone remnant of the plantation era survives, a picturesque swayback, shack-like, wood structure, now the Twin Oaks Nursery, formerly a plantation commissary. Although Transylvania does not seem very ghoulish—no undertakers operate there, the last burial in town took place in 1852, and the beverages of choice are no doubt beer or booze, perhaps even bloody marys, but not blood—the general store sells a selection of Dracula-related novelties. At Halloween, the post office stamps its cancellation on some 500 envelopes especially submitted to get the unusual name affixed. Not far south of town, a spur road leads out to Goodrich Landing, site of a Bunge Corporation grain facility, which offers sweeping views of the Mississippi as it curves away downstream.

Poverty Point State Commemorative Area museum and grounds (W-Sun 9-5, grounds only to 7, April-Sept) west of Transylvania includes four earthen mounds and a six-ridged half-circle construction left by an advanced Indian culture which between 1700 and 700 B.C. occupied a trading settlement at the site, a National Historic Landmark. Highway 65 south of Transylvania passes through a short stretch designated Roosevelt, originally called O'Hara's Switch. Locals later named the place for Teddy Roosevelt, who in 1907 hunted bear in this area, an adventure the president recounted in his article "In the Louisiana Canebrakes." In letters to his children, he told of his journey to the area in early October "on a funny, stern-wheel steamer" down the Mississippi which flows "in a broad, swirling, brown current, and nobody but an expert could tell the channel." At nearby Tensas Bayou, the president shot a bear supposedly cornered by guide Ben Lily, a famous but illiterate hunter who signed his name by sketching a lily flower. Like Onward across the river, where five years earlier Roosevelt also tried to bag bear (see the Mississippi chapter), Louisiana claims that publicity resulting from "T.R.'s" hunt inspired the "Teddy Bear" toy.

Not far beyond Roosevelt, a road to the east through Talla Bena Plantation leads to another Bunge facility and dead-ends near the Mississippi, partly screened by trees near the shore. The nearby Madison Parish Port, developed in the mid 1970's, occupies Omega Landing, established by a pre-Civil War cotton plantation along the Mississippi here. A century or so ago, the steamer *Iron Mountain* started to sink here, forcing the crew and passengers to abandon the vessel. By the next day, the ship had completely and mysteriously disappeared: it neither rested on the river bottom nor had it floated downstream. Area residents later found the missing *Iron Mountain* in an Omega plantation cotton field where errant river waters had carried the ship through a break in the levee. On the waterway not far south lay Millikens Bend, a prosperous port town which in early 1863 General William Tecumseh Sherman occupied as a springboard for an attack on Vicksburg across the Mississippi. Although supported by a fleet of steamers converted to military use, Sherman's campaign failed. Ulysses Grant then began digging off to the south one of the various canals he excavated above and below Vicksburg in an effort to enable Union ships to bypass the city. Although low water in the Mississippi left the canal useless, the river's fall opened a land route Grant employed to march his troops from Millikens Bend south to a point where he crossed the waterway for his successful siege of Vicksburg (see the Mississippi chapter).

Tallulah, established in 1857, supposedly took its name after an official with the Vicksburg, Shreveport, and Texas Railroad routed the line through the plantation of a lady friend who then spurned his attentions, whereupon he gave the new town the name of his paramour back in Georgia. The handsome 1887 Parish Courthouse, white with green shutters and sporting four large columns, stands on the gazebo- and tree-garnished grounds near the block long track-side strip of arcade-fronted brick commercial buildings. In 1914, the United State Department of Agriculture moved its Bureau of Entomology to Tallulah to study how to control the pesky boll weevil, which destroys cotton. In 1916, the Bureau began experiments in dusting the crop from the air with calcium arsenate, an operation which led to formation in 1925 at Monroe, Louisiana, of Huff Daland Dusters, the world's first crop-dusting firm. The operation soon flew eighteen planes, the largest unsubsidized private fleet in existence. In the winter they serviced cotton fields in Peru, where the seasons were reversed. In June, 1929, the company began passenger operations between Atlanta and Birmingham, and thus originated Delta Airlines, which still holds its annual meetings in Monroe. East of Tallulah, toward the river, lies Mound, named such for the area's Indian mounds. The town of Delta also lies nearby. Winnie Breedlove, born near here in 1867, was the nation's wealthiest black woman when she died in 1919; her fortune derived from the lotion she invented to straighten blacks' hair. Once the parish seat, Delta lost the honor to Tallulah in 1883, with the residents of the new seat assuring its transfer by carrying away the official records one night.

Someone persuaded President Lincoln that a canal near Delta would enable Union ships to bypass Vicksburg, so the chief executive ordered Grant, skeptical about the concept, to dig the cutoff. In March, 1863 the rising Mississippi flooded and ruined the canal, forcing the general to persue his eventually successful plan to take Vicksburg from behind. The Tensas River National Wildlife Refuge west of Tallulah, established in 1980 on the largest privately owned bottomland hardwood tract on or near the Mississippi in Louisiana, includes a Visitor Center, a boardwalk trail, and woods teeming with black bear, alligators, and 400 other species of wildlife. On the east side of Highway 65 about twenty miles south of Tallulah, the whimsical Ben Burnside Franklin Plantation mail box stands atop a twelve foot high post. The huge container—its flag up and end open—is large enough to hold a small pony. If the postman were Paul Bunyan, he could reach the receptacle and store a year's supply of mail in it. On the Louisiana side of the river, off to the east, lies a section of Mississippi—relocated when the waterway changed course—where Confederate President Jefferson Davis and his older brother once owned and operated large plantations (see the Mississippi chapter).

A marble arch at the family cemetery on Highway 575 near Newellton bears a history of the Newell clan. From Newellton, a side road curves along Lake Joseph, the Mississippi's ancient bed, where La Salle, on his 1682 journey down the river, encountered the Tensas Indians. The road winds around to Winter Quarters State Commemorative Area (open by appointment: 318-766-3222), a rare surviving example of a pre-Civil War structure in this area. Multi-talented Dr. Haller Nutt—physician, architect, cotton researcher—bought the property in 1850 and to the three room 1803 hunting lodge he added virtual-ly a complete house, which served as headquarters for his 2,000 acre plantation. While the Union sympathizer was away during the Civil War, his wife, Julia Nutt, visited Grant at Millikens Bend to offer to feed and quarter Union soldiers if the general would refrain from burning the dwelling. Grant agreed, and although all the other fourteen area plantations disappeared in flames, the Nutt house remained intact. The National Register-listed residence, a long, low-slung, porch-fronted building, contains Civil War displays, period furnishings, and a c. 1845 billiard table. A roundabout route leads to nearby Lake Bruin State Park, located along a former Mississippi channel, once a fish hatchery, garnished with stands of old cypress trees. From near the lake's southern edge, a ferry crossed the Mississippi until 1979.

St. Joseph, to the south, nestles by a stretch of Tensas Parish's forty-nine miles of levees along the Mississippi, which moved half a mile west, leaving the former port waterless. Thanks—or no thanks—to the river's meandering ways, more than 5,000 acres of the parish lie on the waterway's east side. Once called the "Cotton Kingdom," the pastoral parish still produces 60,000 bales a year and claims only one non-farm production firm, a small furniture factory.

St. Joseph's National Historic District boasts some ninety old buildings, including the Plantation Museum (M-F 8-12, 1-5), with exhibits from the plantation era, and a library. Both occupy the attractive, c. 1858 brick and wood porch-fronted former hotel on Plank Road, a one-time wood-paved toll route. Across the street stretches a row of old commercial buildings. Not far south lies the town square, a rare example in the Deep South of a New England-type village green surrounded by a planned community. The striking 1872 ribbed wood, American Gothic Christ Episcopal Church stands by the live oak-garnished green, surrounded by houses and fronted by the Register-listed, 1906 Greek Revival-style parish courthouse, its corner sections protruding between columned facades. Along Second Street, back toward Plank Road, stand the 1852 Episcopal Rectory, originally the upper floor of Waveland Plantation on the Mississippi, and other old houses. On Levee (or Front) Street you'll find the pre-1850 Davidson House, nestled in a grove of trees.

U.S. 65, the River Road, leads south from St. Joseph to boastfully named Waterproof, founded in 1830 by pioneers on their way to Texas. They decided to settle in this fertile, alluvial area. The first three sites chosen for the town proved all too alluvial, but at its fourth location, a knoll, the settlement lived up to its name, which—painted on the bulbous water tower—perhaps also describes the tank. The long, narrow 1871 First Methodist Church stands near the tower. Parishioners moved the white wood sanctuary from the river's edge ten years after it was built. A mile or so north of town by the levee you'll find 1810 Myrtle Grove, a plantation house prefabricated in Louisville and shipped down the Ohio and Mississippi. Vacated retail buildings line Main Street, including boarded up Kullman Bros. Department Store, whose sign still boasts, "We buy and sell everything." In 1870 when the steamer *Mississippi* hit a snag and sank by the Waterproof port, the vessel's chandelier-lit cabin separated from the hull and continued on down the waterway, much to the astonishment of on-lookers who saw the stray section float past Natchez.

Fourteen years later, the river channel changed course and cut Waterproof off from its landing.

Some historians hold that Hernando de Soto, who in 1541 discovered the Mississippi (see the Mississippi chapter), was buried in the river at present day Lake Concordia, formerly the waterway's channel. This lies near the Indian village, now the site of Ferriday, where the Spanish explorer fell ill. U.S. 84 west from Ferriday follows Nolan's Trace, a late eighteenth century cattle trail to Texas blazed by Philip Nolan, "the man without a country" in Edward Everett Hale's famous story of that name (see the end of the Mississippi chapter). Nolan was killed in 1801 by Spaniards, who sent his ears to Chihuahua in Mexico as proof of his death and the end of his contraband trade with American Natchez.

After the Americans forced the Spanish out of Natchez, Don Jose Vida, an Old Natchez District official, established Vidalia on the Louisiana side of the river. Two years later, in 1803, the Louisiana Purchase transferred the area west of the Mississippi to the United States, and Vidalia soon became a growing river town. After completion of the Giles Bend Cutoff to the north in 1933, the Mississippi moved 1800 feet west, forcing Vidalia to follow suit, so the town mounted buildings on rollers and transferred the structures away from the encroaching waterway, which soon submerged the former river front. In the nineteenth century the Vidalia Sandbar just offshore served as a popular duelling site where, in September, 1827, James Bowie first used the "Bowie" knife his brother Rezin had invented. Below the 1940 bridge to Natchez lies the Sandbar Restaurant, named for the old duelling ground. On the river a few blocks north the West Bank Eatery perches, a weathered, grey, wood restaurant with a view across to Natchez atop the bluffs above the Mississippi in Mississippi.

Highways 131 and then 15 south from Vidalia lead through a little populated area of fields and farms, with sparse traffic and no commercial establishments. The grass-covered, earthen levee—reached by driveways which take you to the top for views of the river—blends into the surrounding green landscape. Apart from the occasional barge on the waterway, this remote and serene stretch seems like something out of the frontier era, when the Mississippi marked the nation's border with Spain. Only an outdoorsman's shop marks Deer Park, beyond which the highway leaves and then rejoins the levee, topped by a rocky, one-lane road from which you can see the Mississippi. For some miles, telephone wires are the traveler's only companion through this otherwise desolate area, which lacks virtually all signs of human habitation. Notices mark the entrance and exit of Black Hawk plantation—"Leaving Black Hawk, Have A Nice Day"—named for the point on the river where in 1837 the steamer *Black Hawk*, carrying government payroll money, exploded and sank.

The new Sidney A. Murray, Jr. Hydroelectric Power Station looms a short distance on. The plant was inaugurated in 1990, after thirteen years of conception, planning, and construction. Named for Vidalia's long-time (twenty-four years) former mayor, the privately financed power plant stands as a memorial to the remarkable and still lively Sidney Murray, whose vision and energy inspired the facility. When ever-increasing power costs burdened the citizens of Vidalia, forty miles north, Murray decided in 1977 to commission studies of possible alternative sources. The consulting engineers developed a plan to use part of the water diverted from the Mississippi to the Red and Atchafalaya Rivers at the Corps of Engineers Old River Control Project, just to the south. In this area, the Red/Atchafalaya and the Mississippi, connected by the Old River, flow five miles apart in a parallel, north-south direction. Depending on the two waterway systems' stages, the Old River connector would flow either east or west, with the Mississippi feeding into the Red /Atchafalaya to the west when the river was high, and vice-versa when the other two carried more water. The Mississippi came to enjoy its path through the Red/Atchafalaya, a route 175 miles shorter than its normal 315 mile meander to the Gulf of Mexico. By 1950, the river threatened to change its main channel, thus leaving Baton Rouge and New Orleans downstream cut off from the waterway. To stabilize the two river systems, the Corps of Engineers completed the Old River Control in 1963, an inflow channel designed to regulate the volume so that the Mississippi would carry 70 percent and the Red/Atchafalaya 30 percent of the system's total waters. Part of the waters diverted into the Red/Atchafalaya now serve to power the Murray hydroelectric plant, a twelve-story high, 456 by 144 foot facility—Vidalia takes 10 percent of its power and an electric utility the rest—prefabricated at Avondale Shipyards, 208 miles downriver in New Orleans, the largest structure ever floated on the Mississippi.

After the 1973 flood damaged the Old River Control's Low Sill Structure, which diverted the waters, the Corps of Engineers built the Auxiliary Control Structure, completed in 1986, to alleviate stress on the original facility and to better control sediment entering the Red/Atchafalaya system. The road south takes you past the Low Sill and Auxiliary Control Structures and then, for the first time since Minnesota, the Mississippi starts to flow through a single state rather than serving as a border between two jurisdictions. Not long after you enter Pointe Coupee Parish the striking Gothic-style 1859 brick St. Stephen's Episcopal Church rises like an apparition. The cemetery there includes the South's only Confederate unknown soldier monument.

Farther on, south of Innis, stretches the long, low Morganza Floodway, outfitted with 125 gates through which the rampaging Mississippi can be diverted into the Atchafalaya Basin. High water in the 1870's and 1880's breached the levee in this area, chosen in 1928, after the great flood the year before, as the site of the Floodway. Designed to siphon off 600,000 cubic feet a second of Mississippi overflow, the facility was first used in 1973 at less than a quarter of its capacity. At the nearby town of Morganza, named for landowner and legislator Colonel Charles Morgan, the flower-garnished grounds and color window-bedecked, white American Gothic St. Ann Catholic Church furnish a bright spot in town. At tiny Labarre (also spelled La Barre) stands a colorful old post office, which occupies a metal-topped, weathered, wood cabin, a primitive place compared to the elegant plantation homes near New Roads to the south.

A circular tour around twenty-two mile long False River—an oxbow lake severed from the Mississippi about 1700 near a neck of land the French called "Pointe Coupée" (cut point)—takes you to a series of old plantation houses. Just beyond the c. 1760 National Register-listed cottage, which houses the Pointe Coupee Parish Museum (M-F 9-3, Sat 10-3), lie such other Register-listed mansions as: 1750 Parlange, occupied by descendants of the Marquis who built the house on a land grant from the French crown and still a working plantation, perhaps the nation's oldest business operated by members of the original family; c. 1825 Pleasant View; 1760 Riverlake, birthplace of Ernest Gaines, author of *The Autobiography of Miss Jane Pittman*; and, toward the Mississippi River beyond False River, Glynnwood (1836 and 1875) on Highway 416 and 1840 Le Beau on Highway 414.

Highway 413 back along False River passes through an eleven mile long resort area known as "The Island," and leads to New Roads, where the delightful, castle-like courthouse includes two round turrets and pointy roof spires. Frilly grillwork fronts a nearby yellow-hued pawnshop, and the abandoned King Movie Theater sports regal-sized white letters. In the yard of the elementary school, a stone pillar marks the grave of Julien Poydras, born in France, "Lover of his adopted country. Faithful citizen and public officer. Munificent donor to charitable funds." Poydras emigrated to Louisiana about 1768, where he began working as a peddler along the Mississippi, eventually earning enough to build in 1789 the house at Alma Plantation, scene of a 1795 slave rebellion, still one of the South's few working sugar producers with its own mill. Elected to Congress at age sixty-five in 1809, Poydras traveled for six weeks to Washington by horseback. On his death in 1824, the lifelong bachelor left his fortune, which included 1,000 slaves and six plantations, to establish a hospital in New Orleans, a college—Louisiana's first—in New Roads, and a still-used dowry fund for impoverished brides. Plantation Country Tours (504-231-8597) offers excursions through the area, and Bergeron's Pecan Plant, one of the state's two such shelling and packaging facilities, offers tours (Oct-April, 504-869-3098). Accommodations at New Roads include three houses run under the name Pointe Coupee Bed and Breakfast (504-638-6254), and also Garden Gate Manor (800-487-3890) and Bonnie Glen (504-638-9004).

An entire network of back roads veins the countryside near the Mississippi south of New Roads. These roads funnel into U.S. 190 and then Highway 1, which parallels the Mississippi as it passes an Exxon lubricants plant and tank farm, and a Placid Oil refinery. The road then enters Port Allen, which lies directly across from Baton Rouge, the state capital. The Capitol, the nation's tallest, towers on the opposite bank. (The itinerary from the Mississippi line south to Baton Rouge and then on along the river's east bank to New Orleans begins on page 448.) At the foot of Court Street, an overlook near the old ferry landing provides views of the river traffic, including ocean-going vessels, the Baton Rouge skyline and the port, fifth busiest in the nation. The port, which lies about two hundred miles from the Gulf, is the nation's most inland such facility for sea-going ships. The Port of Baton Rouge, which boasts a seven million bushel grain elevator and an eleven million tank terminal, thrived after Governor Huey Long deliberately blocked the Mississippi with a bridge just low enough to keep ocean vessels from continuing north to Natchez.

The 1,200 foot long Port Allen Locks lie just south of the bridge. The largest free-floating structures of their kind, they occupy a man-made break in the levee. Completed in 1961, the facility enables ships to connect with the Intracoastal Waterway and the Gulf at Morgan City, sixty-four miles south, 160 miles less than the deepwater channel route down the Mississippi. The West Baton Rouge Museum (Tu-Sat 10-4:30, Sun 2-5), which occupies the squat, 1882, former West Baton Rouge Parish courthouse, features a restored c. 1840 bedroom, a model of a 1904 sugar mill, and a slave cabin relocated from the Allendale Plantation. Just north of Port Allen—where Poplar Grove (504-344-3913) offers bed and breakfast—the *New Orleans*, the first steamboat on the Mississippi, sank in 1814 when it became stranded on a huge stump after the water fell where the vessel moored overnight.

On the left side of Highway 1 after it passes over the Intracoastal Waterway stands the Cinclare Plantation, signaled with a large "C" on the water tower. The area includes a mill for processing sugar cane, one of the few which survive from the 1930's when West Baton Rouge and the two adjacent parishes boasted twenty-four such plants. During the processing season, which runs from October through December, Cinclare operates around the clock, handling 5,000 tons of cane a day. Although the facility does not take visitors, a display "dummy"—a small steam engine which conveyed the cane from fields to the mill—can be viewed on the grounds.

Brusly's St. John the Baptist Catholic Church, a nicely proportioned, 1907 wood sanctuary, faces the levee. At Main and Labauve Streets, west of Highway 1, between Back Brusly and Back Back Brusly, stands a 350 year old landmark oak tree. In the 1,900 square mile Atchafalaya Basin wetlands off to the west, about sixty professional fishermen each run 350 to 400 traps, which catch about two pounds a day of crawfish, that Louisiana specialty, during the season from early winter to about June. Highway 1 continues on through a commercial and heavily industrialized area, with tubes, pipes, and tinker toy-type towers indicating the Copolymer petrochemical complex. The Air Products and the vast Dow Chemical facilities sprawl nearby.

Plaquemine—from the Indian word for persimmon—lies on Bayou Plaquemine, first noted by the explorer and colonial official Iberville in 1699. For the next century and a half, the bayou served to give access from the Mississippi to the Atchafalaya basin waterway system. Longfellow's heroine Evangeline took this route as she traveled to the Cajun country in search of her lover Gabriel. Repeated flooding after the Civil War, including the 1880 disaster when a large part of the town fell into the Mississippi, inspired Plaquemine to build a levee, which closed off the bayou to traffic. In order to restore the link, Congress authorized a lock, designed by Colonel George W. Goethals, who later served as chief engineer for the Panama Canal and as the Canal Zone's first Civil Governor. Upon completion in 1909,the Plaquemine Lock boasted a fifty-one foot lift, the highest such freshwater facility in the world. The lock reestablished the shortcut from the Mississippi west via Bayou Plaquemine, which in 1925 became the northern terminus of the Intracoastal Waterway system. In 1961, the new Port Allen locks replaced the smaller Plaquemine facility and a levee built at the old installation closed off the Mississippi from the bayou. By the Plaquemine Lock, listed on the National Register, stands the delightful, step-roofed lockhouse, now a small museum (M-F 8-4). A nearby pavillion houses displays on old-time riverboats while a forty foot tower affords views of the Mississippi which flows just beyond the levee. Across the way stands the Register-listed, 1848, Greek Revival-style, former parish courthouse, later used as a city hall until 1985. It was replaced in 1906 by the rather ponderous, brown brick government center on well-named Railroad Avenue, bisected by train tracks. Tucked away by the Mississippi, just north of the lock, is the picturesque village of Old Turnerville, estabished in the late nineteenth century during the peak of the area's cypress logging era. Two old houses, Marietta's and Miss Louise's, each offer tours (M-Sat 10-4, Sun 1-4).

Just south of town stands 1857 St. Louis, a two-story, galleried house at a still working plantation. At Bayou Goula, just east of Highway 1, lived an Indian tribe of that name. At one time a busy steamboat landing, the village retreated four times from the encroaching Missisippi, along which at this point rose some of the river's first levees. Farther on, set back from the highway, stands 1859 Nottoway (9-5), the South's largest plantation mansion with some seventy rooms (ten used for overnight guests: 504-545-2730), 200 windows, 165 doors and more than 40,000 square feet. Between these two relics formerly stood some seventeen other old sugar plantation mansions, among them Retreat, Last Hope, Golden Rule, and Tally-Ho, part of the procession of "big houses" described by Louisiana author Harnett T. Kane in his 1945 *Plantation Parade*: "A century ago, along the Mississippi and its adjacent waters, the sugar and cotton plantations rose in a double file of splendor. For more than two hundred miles, beginning below New Orleans, hardly a foot of ground remained free from the hand of cultivation; for most of this distance it was not possible to travel the river and be out of the range of a great house, serene and proud and pillared."

On the south edge of the nearby town of White Castle, named for a palatial c. 1880 house which stood on a site now occupied by the Mississippi, you'll find the Cora Texas sugar mill, a maze of rusty machinery, conveyers, and large, metal buildings. In 1700, Iberville introduced sugar cane from the West Indies to Louisiana, but production failures in 1725 and 1762 almost eliminated the crop in the region. In 1795, Etienne de Bore, New Orleans' first mayor, risked his fortune on one last effort to produce sugar commercially, and when he succeeded, using new techniques, other planters tried again; Louisiana's sugar industry soon turned sweet. Many early experiments for the manufacture of sugar took place at the Cora Plantation, established in 1817, which remains a major producer of the crop.

Texas Road, alongside the mill, leads to Highway 405, which borders the levee just by the Mississippi. At White Castle one of the state's ten ferries operates. They criss-cross the river to connect the two sides of Louisiana which flank the waterway, also spanned in the state by nine bridges. At about where the road enters Assumption Parish, the precocious William Charles Cole Claiborne owned a plantation he established in 1811. Born in Virginia in 1775, Claiborne moved to Tennessee, where at age twenty he helped frame the new state's constitution. President Jefferson appointed him at age twenty-six to serve as governor of the Mississippi Territory, while later Claiborne became governor of the Territory of Louisiana and, in 1811, the state's first chief executive. Within a year after his election to the U.S. Senate in 1817 Claiborne, then forty-two, died. Farther south, at Modeste—indeed modest, with a small, white wood post office and little else—a small German community once existed named Hohen Solms, center of a sugar cane area, established in the mid-eighteenth century.

Donaldsonville, farther on, preserves in its National Historic District more than 600 vintage buildings. Through the town runs Bayou Lafourche, so named by La Salle in the 1680's as it forked into two arms near the Mississippi, where in this area some of the Acadians exiled from Canada began to settle starting in 1758. From his Viala Plantation one early area resident, pirate Jean Lafitte, would travel down Bayou Lafourche to the Gulf to prey on passing ships. Governor Claiborne's 1813 offer of $500 for Lafitte's capture supposedly prompted the buccaneer to immediately offer $5000 for the official's head. Lafitte called himself a privateer, not an outlaw but a lawful private businessman sanctioned by the authorities, who excused his transgressions in gratitude for the help given by Lafitte's band of brigands during the War of 1812 against the British.

Donaldsonville served as Louisiana's capital in 1830 and 1831, and later the settlement became a sugar country social and cultural center. The good times ended when Union troops burned the town to eliminate pesky snipers who fired at government ships on the Mississippi. Although a river town, the city changed the name of its main street to Railroad Avenue when the train line arrived in 1871. Along Railroad, whose sidewalk arcade gives the street a certain West Indies flavor, stand restored First United Church, fringed by jagged wood trim; the barn-like wood and blue brick Jewish synagogue (1850), now occupied by Ace Hardware; an 1870 residence which houses homey Ruggiero's

Restaurant; and at the top end of the street the First and Last Chance Cafe, its third location since opening in 1927, which gave train travelers their chance to dine. At the bottom of Railroad stands the splendid c. 1836 B. Lemann (pronounced "lemon") & Brothers firm, the state's oldest department store building. Now housing a hardware store, the structure is embellished with elaborate ornamentation, a cast-iron gallery, elegant long and slim windows on the north side, and other decorative touches. Nearby on Mississippi, the c. 1881 Bel House, now containing offices, sports a New Orleans-type iron balcony, while the c. 1911 First National Bank glistens with white terra cotta. On Chetimatches, named for the Indians who Governor Bienville expelled from Bayou Lafourche after they murdered French missionaries in 1704, stands the century old parish jail, now a food stamp office, and nearby stretches spacious Louisiana Square, laid out about 1806, fronted by the Ascension Parish courthouse, a rich red brick building. Across from the courthouse stood the structure where the state legislature met, later razed and its bricks used to control waves from the Mississippi at the bayou's mouth. The massive brick 1896 Church of the Ascension lies not far from the c. 1850 St. Vincent's Institute, one of the first hospitals north of New Orleans, now a Catholic school.

Along Bayou Lafourche—lined with plantation houses, including the handsome, 1846 Greek Revival-style, Register-listed Madewood (for tours: 504-524-1988)—runs Highway 1, supposedly the nation's longest stretch of road (107 miles) always within sight of a residence. Just below the Sunshine Bridge across the Mississippi—dubbed the span that "goes from nowhere to nowhere"—lies the c. 1800 Old Viala Plantation House, Jean Lafitte's lair, relocated to the site and in 1978 converted into Lafitte's Landing Restaurant. Just before the bridge, Highway 18 turns south to follow the levee alongside the Mississippi, and soon the road passes a Louisiana Power and Light facility and then Agrico, Freeport-McMoran and Chevron Chemical plants. Farther on stands the plain, brick Saint Jacques de Cabahanoce

Church, which serves a parish organized in the mid-eighteenth century. When Spain controlled the area, the diocese here fell under the jurisdiction of Havana, Cuba. At a site across the street, where one of Louisiana's characteristic above-the-ground cemeteries lies, so elevated to avoid the water-logged earth, the Acadians from Canada first settled in Louisiana in 1756 and 1757. A road to the west leads to the St. James Terminal, one of six Strategic Petroleum Reserve sites at which a series of caverns excavated in salt domes each holds some ten million barrels of oil. Down Highway 18 sprawls the St. James Sugar Cooperative facility, and across from the post office in the village of St. James stood Louisiana governor (1845 and 1852) André Bienvenu Roman's Cabahanoce Plantation home, washed away by the Mississippi. In 1837-1839 the governor's brother, Jacques Telesphore Roman, built a mansion which stands at the end of two rows of fourteen live oak trees, planted a century earlier. A lightning rod protects each of the twenty-eight trees, which dine on liquid fertilizer, and get pruned every third year. Interlacing branches provide a canopy over the quarter-mile long approach, one of the most dramatic and renowned vistas in the Mississippi River Valley. Although this perspective and the oak-garnished grounds represent the property's best elements, visitors can also tour the mansion (March-Oct 9-5:30, Nov-Feb 9-5), eat at the restaurant (9-3) and stay overnight in cottages (504-265-2151).

A mile and a half past Oak Alley stood the Valcour Aime Plantation mansion, a lavish property called "Little Versailles," built by supposedly the South's richest man. Aime, who operated his own private steamboat for trips to New Orleans, created here a kind of early-day Disneyland, with gardens garnished with exotic plants cultivated by thirty slaves, managed by a landscape gardener imported from France. He also maintained a menagerie of unusual animals, a miniature fort where children staged mock battles using oranges as cannon balls, grottos, lagoons, and a Chinese pagoda. Aime once won a $10,000 bet by serving a complete meal whose components—fish, game, fruit, nuts, coffee, wine, and cigars—all originated at the plantation, whose house burned in the early twentieth century.

The cigars stemmed from St. James Parish's unique "perique" tobacco, grown only in this area. About 1,000 acres produced 250,000 pounds annually of the tobacco, first cultivated by the Indians and introduced commercially in the late 1770's by Acadian exile Pierre Chanet, nicknamed "Perique." His descendants, and those of other early Acadians, continued as exclusive producers of the tobacco. The best crops of the strong, black perique—an expensive variety used for blending with milder types—grow on the vachery, or cattle land, an elevated area not far west of the river. In the old days, the curing of perique took so much preparation with months of fermentation under pressure to extract the tobacco's rich, winey juices—that the government required growers to obtain manufacturers licenses. A perique tobacco farm on Highway 642 offers tours of the curing barn and plantation (504-869-3098; the best months are June and July). The town of Vacherie on the River Road—settled over the years by Acadians, French, Spanish and Germans—recalls the early-day cattle raising region.

Just after you enter St. John the Baptist Parish a web of girders loom at a disused bridge which lacks its end sections. Beyond Wallace lies the c. 1840 Evergreen Plantation House, fronted by a striking, curved stairway. Although perhaps evergreen, the property includes a roadside picket fence not ever white; it needs painting. Even the solidly built brick privies behind the mansion sported Greek Revival-style architecture to match the "big house." Farther on stand the 1803 Bacas House and slave quarters, and then the 1814 Dugas House, both listed on the National Register. Just before Edgard you'll find the 1785 Columbia Plantation House, the parish's oldest dwelling, and the 1810 Columbia Sugar Mill, the oldest in the nation. At Edgard, seat of St. John the Baptist Parish, stands the venerable, saggyporched, brick E.J. Caire store building (1900), moved back from its original riverside site at Caire's Landing, founded in 1860. This extremely picturesque relic gives the flavor of old days along the Mississippi. Next to the nearby courthouse stands the brick Romanesque-style St. John the Baptist Church, which served parishioners on both sides of the river until 1864. The cemetery by the church, which gave its name to the parish, contains the grave of General P.G.T. Beauregard, a famous Confederate officer.

Beyond Lucy, which straggles along the road, two tall red and white metal towers and a large, round, concrete reactor building mark the Louisiana Power and Light 3,600 acre Waterford 3 plant, the state's first nuclear station. Supposedly the most productive of the nation's 108 nuclear power plants, the facility opened in 1985 at a cost of $2.73 billion. Highly industrialized Taft includes a huge Agrico chemical plant, and Occidental and Union Carbide chemical factories, both opened in the mid-1960's. Mazes of pipes, conveyers, connectors, and fixtures characterize the facilities. On the way into Hahnville you'll pass Register-listed 1790 Homeplace Plantation, a raised French colonial West Indies-style house.

Hahnville, seat of St. Charles Parish, took its name from Michael Hahn, Louisiana's Union governor who served concurrently with a Confederate chief executive after part of the state fell to the North in 1864. Hahnville hosted German captives at a World War II prisoner of war camp, but Germans first arrived in the area more than two centuries earlier, when some 200 immigrants settled near the Lac des Allemands (Lake of the Germans) in 1719. Two years later, a new group of German immigrants, led by Karl Friedrich D'Arensburg, founded a town at present-day Lucy on the "German Coast," a stretch bordering the Mississippi for forty miles through much of St. Charles and St. John the Baptist Parishes. Five years after the repressive Spanish regime took the area over from France in 1763, the seventy-six year old Arensburg led a revolt, the first North American revolution against a foreign power, forcing Governor Ulloa to flee to Havana. The Spaniards returned the following year, however, and executed most of the uprising's leaders. At the south edge of Hahnville stood the stylishly named Fashion Plantation, home of General Richard Taylor, son of President Zachary Taylor, a member of the 1861 Secession Convention and military commander of the Louisiana District from 1862-1864. Federal troops sacked Fashion in 1862 while foiling a plan to gather there animals and slaves for Confederate use.

The 1983 Hale Boggs Bridge soars across the Mississippi not far south, its cables weaving a web of huge triangles etched against the sky. Beyond the span lies Monsanto's Luling plant, located on land once occupied by Ellington Manor, a mid-nineteenth century sugar plantation house razed in the 1960's after the company acquired the property. Along the Mississippi near Luling rice as well as sugar plantations operated in the nineteenth century, with growers cutting flumes into the levee to siphon river water into the rice fields. When in 1884 one of these poorly refilled cuts, which tended to weaken the levee, gave way at the Davis Plantation a 1,000 foot wide crevasse soon opened, allowing the Mississippi to flood the area. Later sealed, the levee will once again be opened when, starting in early 1993, the Corps of Engineers begins construction of the Davis Pond Freshwater Diversion Structure. One of three such planned facilities on the Mississippi in Louisiana—the Corps completed the Caernarvon diversion project, fifteen miles downstream from New Orleans, in February 1991, and began the Bonnet Carré construction across the river from Taft in August 1991—the Davis structure will divert up to 10,650 cubic feet per second of fresh water to reduce the salinity of the wetlands (86 percent of St. Charles Parish consists of water and wetlands), blocked by the levees from receiving the Mississippi's natural overflow which brought essential nutrients to the watery low country.

Farther on, the American Cyanamid chemical complex occupies land in a residential area, while a stand of huge live oaks down the road at Thomas Jefferson Park garnishes the small enclave. Tchoupitoulas Plantation Restaurant, nestled in a grove of live oaks, pines, and pecan trees on the River Road, occupies an 1812 mansion once the center of a sugar growing property. On the wall of one dining room hang paintings of female nudes, supposedly the ladies of the night who gave their all for Norma Wallace, last of the famous New Orleans madames, a previous owner of Tchoupitoulas. Another room which originally stood on pillars was twice moved to escape flooding by the Mississippi, and then once again shifted, this time to come to rest as a ground floor. In the former kitchen, now a waiting area, rests an old fashioned, hand-operated, wood fan, one of the venerable dwelling's many antiquated touches. The road continues on to Bridge City, where Italian immigrants settled in the early twentieth century. The town adopted it name after completion of the Huey P. Long Bridge in 1935, truly well named, for it is the world's longest railroad span, nearly four and a half miles. On the second weekend of October, Bridge City hosts a festival honoring its title as "gumbo capital of the world."

In 1938, Avondale Marine Ways, on the site of the old Avondale Plantation, started operations where the shipyard could use the rails and ramp of the former Southern Pacific Railroad ferry. At the Avondale complex, which boomed during World War II, huge cranes and even bigger vessels under construction line the west bank of the Mississippi, here an industrial river, a far cry from its more pastoral guise not far upstream. So great a distance does the shipyard extend along the waterway that workers ride bikes to get around.

The road passes between the concrete and steel beam supports beneath the Long Bridge and continues on to a verdant area along the Mississippi which contrasts both with metallic Avondale shipyard and bustling New Orleans, out of view just across the waterway. Beyond the Nine Mile Point Louisiana Power and Light Plant, whose components—with their varying shapes, sizes, and colors—seem to form a giant abstract painting, lies Westwego, site of an Avondale fabrication yard. Before the days of the railroad bridge, trainmen would shout, "West we go" after they rejoined rail cars ferried across the Mississippi, and their call came to designate the town. Pacific Molasses Company tanks stand by the road, which passes through the light industrial district of Marrero, originally called Amesville for the Ames sugar plantation but renamed for L.H. Marrero, a prominent nineteenth century politician. The new (1989) West Jefferson Levee District Headquarters (M-F 7:30-4) houses four satellite color photos showing the New Orleans area, including the Mississippi and various canals which intersect the waterway.

One such artery, the 6.5 mile Harvey Canal, connects the Mississippi with the Gulf Intracoastal Waterway. The Corps of Engineers-built canal, which lies along the road beyond Hess, Texaco, and other oil tanks and terminals, occupies the site where in 1835 an early sugar planter, probably Noel d'Estrehan, dug a drainage and small boat canal. In 1845, Virginian Joseph Hale Harvey married d'Estrehan's oldest daughter, Marie Louise. Harvey deepened and widened the canal and constructed an ornate three story mansion nearby, his wedding gift to her, built in ninety days. Something more than love inspired him, however: the house was completed so quickly on a wager, which Harvey won. River pilots, who used the dwelling's two octagonal, ornamental turrets to take bearings, referred to the residence—which boasted above each turret an observatory affording views of the Mississippi—as Harvey's Castle. The Harveys occupied the "castle" until 1870, then the mansion served as the Jefferson Parish Courthouse from 1874 to 1884. In the early 1920's the family sold the canal and the house for $425,000 to the federal government, which demolished the building and constructed the present canal, opened in 1934. The Harvey Canal links the Mississippi River and the New Orleans port, the nation's second largest, with the 1,450 mile long Gulf Intracoastal Waterway. Conceived in 1905, it consists of a series of 12 foot deep and 125 foot wide canals cut through the Gulf coast marshlands extending from the Mexican border at Brownsville, Texas to St. Marks, Florida, and then, farther on, from Tarpon Springs south to Fort Myers, Florida. Ships carry more than 100 million tons of cargo a year on the Waterway, which also connects with the Mississippi via a nine mile canal beginning at the Algiers lock, opened in 1956, about ten miles downstream.

Not far beyond the Harvey Canal lies Gretna, a laid-back town on the banks of the Mississippi, connected to downtown New Orleans by a ferry service which originated in 1838 with the St. Mary's Market Steam Ferry Company, which sold residential lots in the suburb. This promoted the development of Gretna, an amalgam of that village, along with Mechanickham, founded in 1836 by Noel d'Estrehan, and McDonoghville, established in 1815 by John McDonogh. His tombstone in the McDonoghville Cemetery bears the set of rules for living he propounded in 1804. The philanthropist ended his will, which left most of his estate for educational purposes, with a request that the school children nearest his grave annually plant flowers at the site. In 1913 the city adopted as its official designation its long-time nickname, which derived from Gretna Green in Scotland where lovers ran away to marry, as they did to McDonoghville.

Some 350 structures occupy Gretna's National Historic District, the largest in Louisiana after the one in New Orleans. Near the ferry landing stand: the commemorative arch to World War I dead; the City Hall, built in 1907 as Jefferson Parish's fifth courthouse; the Texas-Pacific and Southern-Pacific Depots; and the former parish archives building (1911), slated to house a cultural center relating to the area's German heritage, including the "German Coast" on the Mississippi, upstream from New Orleans. On Lafayette Street two blocks from the river stand the

c. 1845 Lilly White Ruppel and Kittie Strehle (Sun 1-5) houses and the picturesque 1859 David Crockett Steam Fire Company Number 1 (Sun 1-5), supposedly the nation's oldest continuously active volunteer fire force, founded as a bucket brigade in 1841. The Company's 1876 Gould #31 Steam Fire Pumper, separately listed on the National Register, is the only remaining such piece of equipment. Lacking funds for a horse, the volunteers had to pull the pumper by hand. Fire hydrants installed in the early 1890's drew Mississippi water so muddy that the firemen had to wait a few minutes for it to clear before spraying. At 10th and Lafayette lies the William Tell Hook and Ladder Company Cemetery, established in 1858 as a fireman's public burial ground and to raise revenue for fire fighting by the sale of plots. Farther afield, Gretna's Mel Ott Park honors the native son who in 1926, at age sixteen, joined the New York Giants, the youngest major league player in history. The 1899 Perpetual Adoration Convent, at 7th and Lavoisier, now a senior citizens center, bears a three-story, cast-iron gallery, and the nearby pale yellow, stucco, Spanish Baroque-style St. Joseph's Church (1926) sports reliefs, shell motifs, and twisty columns on the facade, which seems much busier than sleepy Gretna.

Algiers Point juts out a a short distance downstream, where the river makes a sharp bend. The area is a National Historic District with some fifty blocks of quiet, tree-shaded streets, lined by vintage houses. The village-like neighborhood lies by the levee just across the waterway from New Orleans' French Quarter but, seemingly, a thousand miles away from the big city. In 1719, France granted the west bank to Bienville, founder of New Orleans. Only nearly a century later, in 1812, did the first family, the Duverje, settle there, constructing a plantation house. The ferry service which still operates started up in 1827, and in the 1840's an iron foundry and warehouses along the river began operation. Although a fire in 1895 destroyed about 200 dwellings, a number of old houses remain, among them some "gingerbread"-trimmed cottages along Pelican and other places in the 300 block of Bermuda, where a line of metal fences presents a united front. Facing the riverfront stands the c. 1870's Renecky store, with colored windows and a two-story, wrap-around, cast-iron gallery. Back toward the ferry landing, on the site of Duverje Plantation House, stands the c. 1896 courthouse, a Moorish affair, with a square clock tower and onion-like knobs atop small columns on the balcony. On Brooklyn Avenue toward the bridge, a few blocks south of Algiers Point, Blaine Kerr's Mardi Gras World (9:30-4) offers one of the Mississippi's most unusual attractions. Tours through the cavernous warehouses take you to "carnival dens" where the firm, founded in 1947 and the world's largest float building company, confect the huge, fanciful figures which Krewes parade in the Mardi Gras and also other images which figure in various processions and celebrations around the world. Outside by the sign, a leering figure in purple shirt and green pantaloons greets visitors, while horses of different colors parade along the roof edge. The gift shop inside sells a wide assortment of novelties, including masks, mugs, faces, figures, and Mardi Gras favors.

From the Algiers Point-Gretna area via thoroughfares such as General de Gaulle Drive and Belle Chasse Highway lead to Route 23, which borders the west bank of the Mississippi to Venice, the end of the road near the Gulf of Mexico. The itinerary from New Orleans along both banks of the waterway south to the end begins on page 476. A description of the east side of the Mississippi in New Orleans begins on page 469 at the end of the itinerary—which starts in the next paragraph—from the Mississippi line south, via Baton Rouge, along the river's eastern bank.

The River Road, U.S. Highway 61, enters Louisiana from Mississippi and winds its way toward the picturesque river town of St. Francisville, twenty-four miles south. Five miles north of town stands The Cottage, the first of eight plantation mansions in the countryside around St. Francisville open to the public. A hundred foot long gallery fronts the Cottage (9-5; for bed and breakfast reservations: 504-635-3674), surrounded by ten original out buildings. Nearby Catalpa (Feb-Nov 9-5) houses antiques collected by five generations of the family, while across the highway, not far on, Afton Villa Gardens includes an approach lined by live oaks leading to the site of a Gothic-style mansion which burned in 1963. Highway 66, which branches off to U.S. 61 three miles north of town, leads out to Highland (504-635-3001) and National Register-listed Live Oak (504-766-7706) Plantations, both open by appointment, and to Greenwood (March-Oct 9-5, Nov-Feb 10-4), an imposing, Greek Revival-style house rebuilt in 1980 after a fire twenty years earlier burned the 1830 original. Twenty-eight huge columns surround the mansion, reflected in a pond dug by slaves to obtain material for bricks. Highway 66 leads out to Angola, where the Louisiana State Penitentiary, moved there from Baton Rouge in 1890, houses inmates who farm some 18,000 acres of land along the Mississippi. At Lake of the Cross in this area Iberville, founder of New Orleans, visited the Houma Indians. The following year, 1700, a Jesuit priest inspired the tribe to build a chapel, the first Catholic sanctuary in the Lower Mississippi Valley. A few years later, the Tunica pushed out the Houma, who settled near the river farther south. When Union fleet commander David Farragut made his first trip up the Mississippi in 1862, his flagship, the *U.S.S. Hartford*, ran aground at Tunica Bend here, an experience which provoked the admiral to observe that navigating the vexing waterway so unnerved him that he longed to return to the less challenging high seas.

Back on Highway 61 stands The Myrtles, supposedly haunted, which takes visitors (9-5) and bed and breakfast guests (504-635-6277). Rosedown stands nearby (March-Oct 9-5, Nov-Feb 10-4), where a splendid twenty-eight acre formal garden, garnished with oriental flowers, a long row of oaks, and many other plantings, front the 1855 mansion. In a park-like area just west of the highway lies the St. Francis Hotel, a modern, characterless place which, however, houses the Audubon Gallery. This gallery occupies a warren of small rooms, alcoves, and narrow passageways crammed with all 435 of the artist's "Birds of America" drawings from the so called "elephant" folio edition, reproduced in Amsterdam by photolithography. The hotel dining room resembles those found in old-time steamers. A mural portraying a riverboat gambling scene appears in the lounge, with a dapper gent about to play a card as his wary opponent scrutinizes the action.

Riverboat gamblers comprise part of the Missisippi's legendary history. In his classic account of games of chance on riverboats, *Forty Years a Gambler on the Mississippi*, published in 1887, George H. Devol told how, by living "off of fools and suckers," he could "make money rain." Devol—who observed, "Some men are born rascals, some men have rascality thrust upon them, others achieve it"—used to hire a spy to observe his opponent's cards through a peephole overhead and signal the holdings by a wire which ran to Devol's foot. Thus, for the pros, games of chance were not always chancy. Most professional gamblers carried a pistol, which "stiffened the moral fibre of a man about to turn bad loser," noted Irwin Anthony in *Paddle Wheels and Pistols*. Shady riverboat gamblers disgusted a prim English geologist named George W. Featherstonhaugh, who recalled of his trip on a Mississippi steamer in December, 1834: "I never saw such a collection of unblushing, low, degraded scoundrels, and I became at length so unhappy as often to think of being set on shore...rather than have my senses continually polluted." Even the pros sometimes relented, with Devol recounting how he once took all of a preacher's money, gold spectacles, and sermons, then "gave him his sermons and specks back"—but not the cash—as the gambler didn't want "to serve the devil (Devol)."

The National Historic District, which encompasses much of St. Francisville, includes nearly 150 old buildings that give the town a pronounced nineteenth century flavor. The settlement took its name from the saint revered by Capuchins who, about 1785, moved from the flood-prone lowlands across the Mississippi to higher ground on the east bank where the monks established a monastery and burial ground. The town began to develop about 1790, after British and American settlers received land grants from the Spanish government. Following the 1803 Louisiana Purchase, Spain tried to retain possession of the St. Francisville and Baton Rouge districts, claiming they belonged to West Florida, but in 1810 the residents rebelled and set up the "Republic of West Florida," a short-lived country annexed seventy-four days later by the United States. Strung out on a narrow ridge above the river, St. Francisville—the state's second incorporated city (1807)—became known as "a town two miles long and two yards wide." Down below, along the Mississippi, a rival settlement called Bayou Sara sprung up, named for the creek where flatboats found a safe anchorage. The village became the largest port between New Orleans and Natchez, but Civil War attacks, floods, and the arrival in 1842 of the West Feliciana Railroad—a twenty-eight mile route on the nation's first standard gauge track, built to carry cotton from Woodville, Mississippi—diminished the town. It was finally disenfranchised in 1926, then wiped out by the 1927 flood, and by now, the waterfront where Bayou Sara once stood has reverted to the same role it performed at the beginning—an unpopulated boat landing—where the St. Francisville-New Roads ferry docks.

On St. Francisville's Ferdinand Street stand a scattering of antique shops, nineteenth century houses, and the 1895 former hardware store, which houses a one-room historical museum, whose displays include a case entitled "When the South was West" and six mini-dioramas showing period rooms. Solidly built, Gothic-style Grace Episcopal, constructed in 1860 to house one of Louisiana's oldest Protestant congregations (1827), stands in a splendid yard garnished with oaks. Next door at a high spot towers Mount Carmel Church, where the Capuchins established their monastery and cemetery. The street descends toward the bottomland, passing on the way to the ferry landing the Corps of Engineers casting field where the unit makes revetments installed to stabilize the river's banks. The Corps began carpeting the shore in the 1890's with concrete blocks, asphalt, and willow mats. In the 1940's, the Engineers started using concrete mats, thirty-nine four by twenty-five foot slabs wired together. Twenty-three barge thousand foot long tows are manned by some 200 workers who lay the revetments for twenty hours a day from August to November. Each tow includes four bedroom units, a power and water treatment section, a sewage barge, units that carry fuel and bulldozers, and other specialized facilities. Barges on the lower river work along the 300 miles betweeen Natchez, Mississippi and Venice, near the mouth, while a second barge group travels the waterway from near Natchez up to Cairo, Illinois.

Back in town, other old buildings line Royal, which curves out off of Ferdinand. Next to the diminutive *St. Francisville Democrat* office (a hand-lettered sign warns, "Democrat parking only": is this a political statement?) stands c. 1814 Printer's Cottage (504-635-6370), a bed and breakfast house, as are adjacent Propinquity (504-635-6540), built in 1809, and Barrow (504-635-4791), where a white box labeled "Inn formation" contains rates and color photos. Farther down Royal stand the Greek Revival-style Virginia, begun in 1817 as a store, expanded into a cottage in 1826, and extended in 1855; the appealingly simple 1899 Methodist Church; and Audubon Hall, built in 1819 (the sign dates it two years too early) as a public market and later used as a theater, library, and, from 1947 to 1978, as town hall. Back out where Ferdinand abuts Commerce Street stands the St. Francisville Inn, a house embellished with frilly trim and tucked away among an oak grove, which offers bed and breakfast (504-635-6502).

Many local homes and gardens offer tours during the annual Audubon Pilgrimage, the third weekend in March. John James Audubon, who arrived in the area in 1821, painted more than eighty of his famous bird studies during his stay. The 100 acre Audubon State Commemorative Area (W-Sun 9-5, grounds to 7 April-Sept) southeast of St. Francisville includes 1799 Oakley House, listed on the National Register, where the artist resided for four months while teaching drawing to Eliza Pirrie, the owner's daughter. Some of Audubon's first edition prints, including the wild turkey he put at the beginning of his book, hang at Oakley, where the artist completed twenty-one bird paintings. Audubon drew additional specimens during the twenty-three months he spent visiting West Feliciana Parish through 1830. Other historic sites not far north include four State Commemorative Areas: Locust Grove Cemetery, where Sara Knox Taylor, wife of Jefferson Davis and daughter of Zachary Taylor, is buried; the Jackson and Clinton Cemeteries, Confederate burial grounds; and, adjacent to the graveyard in Jackson, the site of Centenary College, listed on the National Register, where displays in a professor's house and the West Wing dormitory recall the school which began as College of Louisiana in 1826.

Back on the River Road, U.S. 61 south of St. Francisville reaches a turn-off to Gulf States Utilities's River Bend nuclear plant, built between 1979 and 1985. Workers dug a hole 80 feet deep and 1,400 feet wide—large enough to accommodate two sports stadiums—and in the opening constructed by the Mississippi a reactor structure containing 312,000 cubic yards of concrete and 55,000 tons of steel. The nearby Energy Center (M-F 8-4) includes an animated Thomas Edison figure which talks about electricity, material on solar and wind power, and information about nuclear energy. Farther south another turnoff to the west takes you to Port Hudson State Commemorative Area (W-Sun 9-

5, grounds to 7 April-Sept), where six miles of trails lead past Confederate defensive positions occupied by the rebels during the forty-eight day siege by Union attackers. Situated high on the bluffs overlooking a river bend which forced passing ships to reduce their speed, the strategic site served as the southern anchor for Confederate positions along the Mississippi north to Vicksburg, 150 miles upstream. Admiral David Farragut failed to maneuver his fleet by the redoubt, which stretched four and a half miles along the river, when he tried to slip past in March, 1863, and 13,000 Union troops under General Nathaniel P. Banks proved insufficient to dislodge the 6,800 defenders in May and June that year. Food ran out as the siege continued into July, forcing the Southern forces to eat mules, horses, and rats. On July 3, Union troops at Gettysburg, Pennsylvania, blocked Robert E.Lee's invasion of the North. On July 4, Vicksburg fell and finally, on July 9, Port Hudson, the last Confederate stronghold along the Mississippi, surrendered. A new interpretive center, a lookout tower, a boardwalk by the original breastworks at Fort Desperate, so named by the besieged defenders, and the National Cemetery with 3,804 Union soldiers, all but 582 unknown—the Southern dead lie at rest in area churchyards and family graveyards—recall the historic encounter there on the bluffs above the Mississippi.

At Baker, just east of the River Road north of Baton Rouge, the Heritage Museum (Tu-Sat 10-4, Sun 1-4) preserves a Victorian era village, while farther on, a turn into Highway 408, Harding Boulevard, off U.S. 61 at Scotlandville, takes you west out to Southern University, parent campus for what is supposedly the nation's largest predominantly black university system. It is said to be the country's first state school of higher learning for blacks, although Alcorn State (see the Mississippi chapter) also makes this claim. Founded at New Orleans in 1880, the college in 1914 moved to Baton Rouge, where it occupies a prime, bluff-top spot overlooking the Mississippi. On Harding near a stadium stands the cage of Lacumba, "home of the fighting jaguar...Southern's live mascot," says a sign. The school acquired Lacumba ("heart of Africa") less than two months after the animal's birth at the Baton Rouge Zoo in May, 1971. The mascot, not declawed or defanged, dines on about two and a half pounds of food a day: don't get too close. Harding continues on to the bluff by the river where Joseph Samuel Clark (died 1944), the school's founder and first president, is buried. A small park overlooking the river occupies Scott's Bluff, believed named for Dr. William Bernard Scott, who in 1839 bought the property from Lelia Skipwith, daughter of Fulwar Skipwith, governor of the 1810 West Florida Republic, and widow of Louisiana Governor (1820-1824) Thomas Bolling Robertson, both residents at this attractive spot above the waterway.

At the north side of Baton Rouge, the Exxon Chemical complex lies along the road. Louisiana claims a quarter of the nation's chemical industry and a large portion of its transportation fuels, with many of those products processed in some seventy-five major industrial plants along the eighty-five mile stretch of the Mississippi between here and New Orleans. Beyond the Exxon facility, Gulf States Road west toward the river takes you past a wonderland of industrial plants, a strange metallic world filled with puffing stacks, pipes, tanks, tubes, twisting distributors, all fitting together in a maze of connections like some giant tinker toy or abstract sculpture. The metal curves and bends in a myriad of shapes and patterns, some forced, others graceful, some awkward, and many artful, but all mysteriously functional and purposeful. Ethyl, Exxon, the Gulf States power plant, and Formosa Plastics all operate facilities in this area near the river. The huge Exxon refinery—second in size in the U.S. only to the company's Baytown, Texas operation, with a daily capacity of 455,000 barrels of crude, almost two million gallons—sprawls along Highway 61 for the better part of a mile. Standard Oil of New Jersey, Exxon's former name, bacame the first major industrial firm to take advantage of Baton Rouge's deep water port facilities when in 1909, the corporation bought the N.S. Dougherty cotton plantation by the Mississippi for its refinery. The entire football team of Louisiana State University, now located at the south end of Baton Rouge, worked as boiler makers during construction of the refinery to help toughen the athletes' muscles. In 1924, Standard Oil established at its Baton Rouge operation the nation's first health maintenance organization, while more recently, in the late 1980's, the corporation spent $4 million to buy out 110 homes and businesses adjacent to its refinery and chemical plant to create an unpopulated buffer zone by the industrial facilities.

A right on Business 61, Chippewa, takes you past the Illinois Central Gulf Railroad freight yard and then around to the state Capitol area by the Missisippi downtown. Baton Rouge, named for the red pole on the river bank the Houma and Bayougoula tribes emplaced to demark their respective territories, began in 1721 when a Frenchman established a plantation. Later, in turn, England and then Spain controlled the territory, with the Spanish retaining Baton Rouge as part of West Florida even after the 1803 Louisiana Purchase. Two years later, they established a settlement called Spanish Town, where in 1930 workers excavating for the new state Capitol unearthed the old burial ground. The state reburied the bodies in a concrete vault at a site kept secret to deter fortune hunters from looking for swords, jewelry, and other relics reinterred with the Spanish Town deceased. In 1819, the United States, which nine years before had annexed the region, started a five building military complex called The Pentagon, a riverside base which became the Southwest Command headquarters, one of the nation's most important frontier posts. It was commanded in the 1840's during the Mexican-American War by Zachary Taylor, elected president in 1848 while living at his house in Baton Rouge overlooking the Mississippi. Steamers often tooted in salute or even stopped so passengers might catch a glimpse of the old man and "Whitey," his retired war horse which grazed on the grounds. Chosen the state capital in 1847, Baton Rouge fell to federal forces in 1862. Arrival of the state university in 1870 and, later, development of the port, opened in 1916 and now the nation's fifth largest, stimulated the city's growth.

The National Register-listed Pentagon Barracks (Tu-Sat 10-4, Sun 1-4), which survives from the the 1819 post, serves as a museum on the history of Baton Rouge. A statue of Louisiana native General Claire Chennault stands by the barracks. The Republic of China (Taiwan) erected the monument "in recognition of his service to the Chinese people" as advisor to the Air Force academy on the mainland from 1937 to 1941. A nearby marker commemorates another air milestone—the first official airmail flight between two U.S. cities, a feat accomplished on April 10, 1912, when New Orleans aviator George Mestache's monoplane carrying a thirty-two pound pouch of letters landed on the Louisiana State University campus, then located at and near the Pentagon Barracks. A huge moss-draped oak near the Barracks shades the spot where L.S.U. president (1896-1927) Thomas Duckett Boyd's house once stood. Nearby stands the statue of Louisiana's second most famous head of state—the first no doubt being Louis XIV, the "Sun King" whose name La Salle gave to the territory—who is buried beneath his dominating likeness, left hand on a model of the state Capitol, while below on each side reliefs of constituents huddle under the benevolent ruler. The inscription reads: "Here lies Louisiana's great son Huey Pierce Long an unconquered friend of the poor who dreamed of the day when the wealth of the land would be spread among all the people." At the nearby state Capitol Long commissioned, with thirty-four stories the nation's tallest, the former governor and then U.S. Senator met his end when an assassin shot Long on September 10, 1935, in a rear corridor which still bears bullet holes from the ambush.

Violence also struck the Senate chamber in the early 1970's, when a political protestor exploded a bomb which shot a sharply pointed pencil up to the ceiling. The pencil remains stuck there, still visible from below. Murals, old records, and artifacts, panels on bronze doors at the House and Senate and on elevators all include references to the state's history. One scene on the House door depicts the "arrival of the First steamboat, the 'New Orleans,' 1812." The House of Representatives cafeteria hidden away in the sub-basement offers low priced meals, while wide-ranging views extend from atop the Capitol. The new (1960) governor's mansion, which appears off to the east, is a replica of the famous Oak Alley plantation by the Mississippi's west bank. Along the river to the north spread the city's chemical and petroleum complexes. Downstream, next to the downtown area, moor the excursion boat *Samuel Clemens* (504-381-9606) and the tourist ship *U.S.S. Kidd* (9-5), a World War II destroyer, by which the Nautical Historic Center houses a large collection of ship models.

Along the Mississippi near the *Kidd* and *Clemens* stands the Louisiana Arts and Sciences Museum (Tu-F 10-3, Sat 10-4, Sun 1-4), installed in the 1920 Yazoo and Mississippi Valley line terminal, whose exhibits include a three dimensional model of the waterway. A few blocks east, the Museum-managed Old Governor's Mansion (Sat 10-4, Sun 1-4), a small scale version of the White House built by Huey Long, contains memorabilia of the nine governors who occupied the residence. A few blocks north, the Old Bogan Fire Museum (by appointment:504-344-8558) houses trucks and equipment from the early 1900's. Back to the south, near the river, stand the National Register-listed old State Capitol (Tu-Sat 9-4:30), a Gothic castle-like 1849 building, rebuilt in 1882 after it accidently burned during the Civil War and used as the seat of government until 1932. A stained glass dome colors the interior, illuminated starting in 1857 by the city's first gaslights, while outside runs the 1854 cast-iron fence decorated with fleur-de-lis, eagle figures, and pineapples, the symbol of welcome. Recently renovated and reopened in 1988, the Old Capitol hosted in 1852 the third Constitutional Convention held by Louisiana, whose eleven Constitutions since entering the Union in 1812 exceeds those adopted by any other state. Catfish Town, an old but now modernized corner of Baton Rouge along the Mississippi, includes a Food Court surrounded by restaurants featuring area specialties.

The 2,000 acre Louisiana State University campus stretches out near the river farther south. The university moved there in 1926 to afford more room for the "Old War Skule," L.S.U.'s nickname when it occupied the Pentagon Barracks near the new Capitol. Only the universities in the Mississippi's first and last states, Minnesota and Louisiana, lie along the waterway in cities which also boast the state capital, and only in those two does the river flow within the states rather than just bordering them. The school originally opened near Alexandria, in west central Louisiana, in January, 1860, under the presidency of none other than William Tecumseh Sherman, who resigned before the start of the second session to take command of the Union army. Meanwhile, the students joined the Confederate army and the school closed during the Civil War. In 1864, the State moved the unviversity to Baton Rouge, where it first occupied the school for the deaf, then in 1886 took over the Barracks, where some fifty buildings eventually housed the college. Named a land grant college in the early days, in 1978 L.S.U. also became a sea grant college—one of twenty-three universities holding both designations—under the 1976 National Sea Grant Improvement Act, for research on the use of the nation's marine resources. On a huge open field in the center of the campus stands Memorial Tower, which contains the Anglo-American Art Museum (M-F 9-4, Sat 10-12, 1-4, Sun 1-4), with English and American period rooms and decorative arts. Other museums at L.S.U. include Geoscience (M-F 8:30-4:30), with archeology and geology exhibits, and

Natural Science (M-F 8-4, Sat 9:30-1). The university also operates the Rural Life Museum (M-F 8:30-4) southeast of the campus, with a barn containing country artifacts, a nineteenth century-type working plantation, and seven buildings in venacular style.

Other reminders of the plantation era not far from the campus include Register-listed Magnolia Mound (Tu-Sat 10-4, Sun 1-4), a 1791 French-style elevated plantation house on a natural ridge facing the Mississippi, and Mount Hope Plantation (M-Sat 9-4), an 1817 antique-furnished dwelling which offers bed and breakfast (504-766-8600), while Southern Comfort Reservation Service (504-346-1928) in Baton Rouge represents bed and breakfast places around the state. (At Prairieville, a town not far southeast of Baton Rouge, Tree House in the Park, 504-622-2850, also offers bed and breakfast in a glass cabin perched on stilts above a swamp.) Not far east of Mount Hope the Jimmy Swaggart World Ministries organization operated, with 1,500 employees, which broadcast programs in 100 countries and collected $140 million a year in donations. On the grounds operates the Swaggart Bible College — its enrollment peaked in 1987 with 1,450 students — which by now may have changed its name. Baton Rouge "langniappe" (extras) include Frumbrussels, 3056 College Drive, with a "chocollage" of homemade candies; Maison Lacour, 11025 North Harrell Ferry, installed in a 1928 cottage decorated like a French country home, which serves venison, wild boar, and other specialty gourmet dishes; Fireside Antiques, 14007 Perkins Road, offers one of the city's most civilized experiences with its afternoon tea (Tu-Sat 12-3:30; for reservations: 504-752-9565); and the more raucous but no less enjoyable Blues Box Heritage Hall, 1314 North Boulevard, featuring bluesman Tabby Thomas performing in a dive with a peeling ceiling brightened with a wall mural depicting a hep-cat guitar-playing feline by the caption "Good Rockin' Tonight."

Highway 327 borders the Mississippi south out of Baton Rouge, but the gently sloping, grass-covered levee, where cattle graze, blocks the river from view. Manchac Bend, the sharp curve of the river as it doubles back to the west, takes its name from Bayou Manchac ("rear entrance"). This was explored in 1699 by Iberville, who hoped to take the waterway—which once connected the Mississippi with Lake Maurepas, next to Lake Pontchartrain—as a back entrance shortcut to the French outposts he established shortly before on the Gulf Coast. When France ceded to Great Britain in 1762 all of the Louisiana Territory east of the Mississippi from its source to Bayou Manchac (the French called it Iberville River), it became the border between Spanish Orleans and British West Florida. At the bayou's mouth, the British soon built Fort Bute, which the Spanish conquered in 1779. In 1828, American settlers in the area blocked the bayou with an earthen dam to keep its water from contributing to floods onto plantation lands to the south. Beyond the Highway 75 spur road out to the Plaquemine ferry landing stands the clean-lined, white, American Gothic St. Gabriel, the latest version of a sanctuary first built in 1769 by Acadian exiles from Canada and later used by German settlers who arrived from Maryland in 1784. Not far on, past the Ciba-Geigy plant, where 75 makes a sharp left, lies one of those characteristic Louisiana cemeteries where the boxy, white-washed tombs stand above the sometimes soggy ground.

A right turn leads west about two miles to the White Castle-Carville ferry landing, just beyond which lie a Federal Bureau of Prisons medical center and, next door, the 1857 Indian Camp Plantation house, which in 1894 became the Louisiana State Leprosium, taken over in 1921 by the U.S. Public Health Service. As early as 1766 the Spanish government established the first facility for victims of leprosy, while in the nineteenth century a hospital treated the lepers. In 1878 a "pest house" near New Orleans held the sufferers, in 1894 transferred at night on an old coal barge—trains and river steamers refused to transport the lepers—to the new state facility at Indian Camp by the Mississippi. Passing steamers took to sounding their whistles three times to greet the inmates, who waved and cheered in response. Now called the Gillis W. Long Hansen's Disease Center, the facility—the nation's only residential center for lepers since a similar place in Hawaii closed in the 1980's—is the world's leading leprosy research organization. Scientists study the mysterious malady—a bacterial infection that attacks the skin, flesh, and nerves, leading to deformities and disfigurement—using armadillos, which also carry the virus. Although up to 20 million lepers worldwide carry the disease, only about 6,000 cases exist in the United States, with 130 of them in residence at Carville. The facility, budgeted at $18 million a year, also treats ten to twenty outpatients. The old plantation house, white with green shutters, contains a Hansen's Disease Museum, while tours (M-F 10 and 1) take visitors through the spacious grounds, dotted with two story screened wood houses, which extend behind a chain-link fence that surrounds the mini-town. A century ago, when Carville started, it seemed more a prison than a treatment center, as the diseased could not marry or vote and had to notify the authorities whenever they crossed state lines, but now the fence serves to keep people out, not in, as the patients remain there voluntarily.

Between Geismer and Darrow to the south a highway off 75 to the east leads to 1841 Ashland-Belle Helene (9-4), in a certain way one of the Louisiana River Road's most evocative old plantation houses. Its decayed beauty and slightly spooky ambiance attracted movie makers who filmed such pictures there as "The Foxes of Harrow," "The Long, Hot Summer," "Band of Angels," "The Autobiography of Miss Jane Pittman" and "Mandingo." Moreover, since the mansion remains in the midst of a long-term, privately financed restoration, visitors can see some of the dwelling's innards, including the old mortar, confected of river silt, horsehair, and lime from burnt clam shells. Sugar planter and statesman Duncan Kenner named the house, surrounded by a colonnade of twenty-eight square pillars, for

Henry Clay's Kentucky residence. During the Civil War, Kenner, the Confederate minister to Europe, tried to raise a $30 million loan for his government, an activity which prompted federal authorities to confiscate the property, renamed by its second owner for his granddaughter Helene. His heirs still occupy the house.

A mile or so beyond Darrow lies Hermitage, another old house, named for the Nashville, Tennessee, mansion occupied by Andrew Jackson, under whom Marius Pons Bringier and his son Michel Doradon Bringier fought during the 1815 Battle of New Orleans. The elder Bringier built the column-surrounded house, which stands well back from the highway, for his son as a wedding present in 1812. Up the road a mile or so rises Bocage, a cube-shaped, all-white residence fronted by square columns. Bringier built it in 1801 as a wedding present for his daughter Françoise, wife of a Frenchman named Christoph Colomb, who claimed to be Christopher Columbus' descendant. The "plantation parade" along the Mississippi continues with nearby Houmas (Feb-Oct 10-5, Nov-June 10-4), surrounded by a columned portico and centered in grounds garnished by moss-hung live oaks and other plantings. Named for the Houmas Indians who moved here after the Tunica chased the tribe away from its lands by the Mississippi to the north, the 1840 mansion served as the centerpiece for the 20,000 acre plantation of Irishman John Burnside, known as the "Sugar Prince," who bought the property in 1858. Burnside, arguing his property should remain immune from damage as it belonged to a British subject, managed to persuade Union General Benjamin Butler to spare the house during the Civil War. After the turn of the century, the plantation fell into disrepair until New Orleans orthodontist Dr. George B. Crozat bought Houmas in 1940 and spent twenty-five years restoring the residence, scene of the film "Hush Hush, Sweet Charlotte."

On Highway 44 near Burnside, you'll find The Cabin

Retreat restaurant, installed in a 150 year old slave house papered with newspapers and filled with antique farm implements. Beyond the main dining room to the back, modeled after a "garconniere"—quarters for visiting, young, unmarried men ("garçons") at riverside Louisiana plantations—two more slave cabins and a restored 1865 brick school house stand by the courtyard. "Rock," an alligator carved from a century old sunken cypress log salvaged in 1988, adds a whimsical touch to The Cabin. The Burnside river terminal, with its welter of conveyers and unsightly stacks of coal, and the Du Pont plant contrast with nearby 1855 Tezcuco, a smallish showhouse (10-5) which also offers bed and breakfast cottages (504-562-3929) and a restaurant (11-3). Farther on, the huge Star Enterprise (Texaco) facility sprawls across the countryside east of the river near the webby steel girder Sunshine Bridge. The nearby village of Union recalls the plantation of that name occupied by a daughter of the Bringier family. A long row of huge storage elevators to the south bears large letters which indicate the owner's name, Zen-Noh Grain Japanese Co.—an exotic touch along the Louisiana Mississippi—and beyond lies the Agrico Chemical plant, a division of Freeport-McMoran Company, on the grounds once occupied by the Uncle Sam Plantation. Between 1837 and 1843, Samuel Pierre August Fagot built here a massive mansion and nearly fifty outbuildings, forty of them slave cabins where he operated one of Louisiana's largest sugar plantations. Until the Mississippi began eroding the cabins and the double row of live oak trees in the late 1930's, Uncle Sam remained one of the state's few complete original plantation properties, but all disappeared when workers demolished the buildings in 1940 to construct a levee. Nothing now remains except the name.

Convent, farther on, takes its name from St. Michael's, a convent French Sacred Heart nuns established in 1825. From 1848 to 1926, daughters of area sugar planters attended a school the sisters ran at the establishment, later used to house refugee

Mexican nuns and their pupils until abandoned as a school in 1932. Beyond the forlorn, old St. James Parish Courthouse, an abandoned brick building facing the river opposite the Delta Bulk Terminal installation, lies the c. 1870 picket-fenced, peach colored house (M-Sat 10-4, Sun 1-4) occupied by Felix Pierre Poché, Civil War diarist, politician, jurist, and a founder of the American Bar Association. Manresa, an imposing, many-columned Catholic retreat vaguely resembling the White House, occupies the grounds where 1831 Jefferson College once stood. After an 1842 fire, and withdrawal of financial support by Louisiana three years later, the college declared bankruptcy in 1855. However, sugar planter Valcour Aime, supposedly the South's richest man, bought the property at auction in 1859. Aime gave it to the Mariot Fathers, who reopened the school, which continued until 1927. Jesuits than acquired the facility in 1931 for use as a retreat, next to which stands the modern cubistic St. James Parish Courthouse.

At Lutcher, where a ferry crosses the Mississippi to Vacherie, operated a sawmill and later the Louisiana Perique Tobacco Company factory, which processed the unique, strong, black tobacco grown only in this area along the river. A plantation across the waterway in the uplands beyond Vacherie continues to cultivate the plant, found nowhere else in the world. Gramercy, where the large Colonial Sugar Refinery towers near the river, occupies part of the land, a one-time, Indian-French trading post, acquired in 1739 by Indian agent Joseph Delille Dupart. Farther on along the road stands the La Roche Chemicals plant, with its huge, brown, arena-like building and the Nalco Chemical Garyville complex. Continuing along, you'll see the 1857 Hope and 1882 Register-listed Emilie plantation houses, modest compared to the ornate 1856 San Francisco (10-4), one of the most famous old Mississippi River mansions, called "San Frusquin" (one's all) by Valsin Marmillion, the builder's son, as the project emptied the family's purse. The "Steamboat Gothic" house, which inspired Frances Parkinson Keyes' novel of that name, includes five painted ceilings inside. Outside, the latticed, overhanging roof and cypress cisterns topped by Moorish-like copper caps add fanciful touches, as do the semi-garish salmon-pink and Cerulean blue hues which brighten the exterior. The stately, old mansion's incongruous neighbor to the south, a Marathon Oil refinery, dilutes the antebellum ambiance with latter-day, industrial age overtones. At nearby Garyville, east of the river, however, a yesteryear flavor lingers in the old-time National Historic District, where sixty vintage buildings survive. At Reserve, where a ferry crosses to Edgard, the Godchaux sugar refinery no longer operates, but the 1790 Reserve Plantation house and the c. 1886 St. Peter's and its adjacent cemetery remain. A rose window at the Catholic church memorializes Jewish planter Edward Godchaux, descendant of the itinerant merchant, presumably a Godchaux, who, local lore holds, requested that the area be reserved for him until he could afford to buy it, so giving Reserve its name.

Beyond the Du Pont Pontchartrain plant, the highway reaches LaPlace, "Andouille Capital of the World," with the Cajun pork sausage featured at the annual festival held the last weekend of October. Half a century before the Andouille Festival began in 1972, frozen food pioneer Armand Montz built at LaPlace an ice and packing plant from which he shipped vegetables around the country. The Jeanne d'Arc church sports a Joan of Arc statue atop the central tower, with the cross relegated to a lower position. Other LaPlace area sights include the century old Woodland Plantation store and manager's house; Register-listed 1815 J.O. Montegut House; the diminutive 1898 Elvina Plantation House, white with green trim; and The John A. Reine Oak Tree, member of the Live Oak Society, whose members are the trees themselves, represented by their owners or sponsors. This might be the world's only organization comprised of inanimate members. More than 400 trees—each at least a century old with a girth of over 17½ feet measured four feet from the ground—belong to the Society, organized in 1934.

Highway 628 continues alongside the levee until it reaches Bonnet Carré Spillway, which you can circumvent by heading east to U.S. 61, then south for two miles over the floodway and then back to the west where an overlook affords a view onto the Corps of Engineers installation, completed in 1932 to divert Mississippi flood water into Lake Pontchartrain. Located thirty-three river miles above New Orleans, the long, low dam-like Spillway contains 350 bays which admit up to nearly two million gallons a second of river water which then flows over the 5.7 mile floodway that widens from 7,700 feet at the Mississippi to 12,400 feet by the lake. First opened during the 1937 flood, the facility has also served to protect New Orleans six other times, most recently in 1983. After each opening, the flood waters deposit some nine million cubic yards of sediment in the diversion channel which contractors take gratis to use as fill in the low-lying Louisiana Delta area. At one time, the Corps introduced more than 6,000 goats into the floodway to eat grass and weeds which might otherwise have clogged the waters' flow to the lake.

Norco lies past the Shell Chemical and Shell Oil facilities. Originally called Sellers, the town was named for the New Orleans Refining Company which in 1916 located its plant there. Four years later Shell acquired the facility. The c. 1790 Ormond Plantation, which yielded indigo, sugar, cane, and rice, offers tours (10-4) and bed and breakfast (504-764-8544) in one of the oldest mansions along the Lower Mississippi. Farther on, just before the 1983 Hale Boggs Bridge, stands Spanish mission-style, stucco St. Charles Borromeo, first built of logs about 1740, and rebuilt after fires in 1806 and 1921. Upon sighting the 1806 red-roofed version, a river landmark twenty-five miles above New Orleans, steamboat captains traditionally paid off their crews. Next to the church lies the old cemetery, with graves dating from the 1700's, its above-ground tombs showing their brick through the crumbling plaster overlay. Not far on stands among the grain elevators and oil installations 1787 Destrehan (9:30-4), the Lower Mississippi Valley's oldest documented plantation house, Greek Revival-style with a West Indies-type hipped roof. The Mexican Petroleum Company and later American Oil owned the plantation, whose nearly fifty buildings the firms razed to construct office and administrative facilities, with the surviving "big house" serving as the refinery manager's residence and as a clubhouse. Left vacant and vandalized for twelve years, in 1972 the mansion passed into the hands of the River Road Historical Society, which restored the property. According to local legend, pirate Jean Lafitte, a frequent visitor to Destrehan, buried part of his treasure on the plantation's property.

Beyond St. Rose, originally populated by Italian immigrants engaged in truck farming and dairying, lies Kenner, a suburb of New Orleans, named for Minor Kenner, son of William Kenner who owned the Cannes Brulées ("burnt canes") plantation here. Until 1945, the Cannes Brulées area around Kenner remained a major vegetable center, growing enough produce to fill sixty railroad cars a day. After the nearby New Orleans airport opened in 1946, a building boom paved over many of the fields. LaSalle's Landing by the river includes a statue of the explorer, who in 1682 put in at this point where he erected a cypress cross. The figure depicts him holding a scroll and sporting a wide belt across his chest and a foulard, while by La Salle stands a cloth-draped Indian holding a spear and a robed priest. Near this site on May 10, 1870, the nation's first world heavyweight boxing championship match took place in a makeshift ring behind William Kenner's old sugar house. Englishman Jed Mace beat fellow countryman Tom Allen in ten rounds, a bare-knuckle winner-take-all event with a $2500 purse.

A building across the street bears a mural depicting a steamboat era riverfront piled with cotton, while on adjacent Williams Boulevard stand the Louisiana Wildlife and Fisheries

Mueseum/Aquarium, the Saints football team Hall of Fame, the Freeport-McMoran Daily Living Science Center/Planetarium, the Louisiana Toy Train Museum, (all open Tu-Sat 9-5, Sun 1-5) and, on Minor a block away, the Kenner Historical Museum (open by appointment: 504-468-7274). A garish purple building near the Saints exhibit is the proposed site of the Jefferson Parish Mardi Gras Museum. Jefferson Highway, which connects Kenner with New Orleans, follows the sixteen mile route of the 1915 O-K (Orleans-Kenner) electric railway line, which ran until superceded by autos in 1931. Seven Oaks (504-888-8649) on Lake Pontchartrain in Kenner offers bed and breakfast accommodations.

Just after you leave the community of River Ridge, a right turn off Jefferson Highway onto Colonial Club Drive takes you down to the River Road, which borders the levee. The Colonial Country Club occupies part of the former 1,000 acre Tchoupitoulas Plantation, named for a local Indian tribe. The 1820 Soniat home, greatly remodeled in 1924 to serve as the clubhouse, hosted the pirate Jean Lafitte, who often sold his booty and smuggled his goods to Soniat. One day, when the buccaneer was casually displaying and touting his wares, none other than Governor Claiborne and his wife, Mrs. Soniat's sister, arrived, causing Lafitte to flee. The road passes under the Huey Long railroad bridge, the world's longest, then continues on to 1857 Whitehall, a plantation house occupied by Union troops, converted in the 1890's into a gambling casino, then a Jesuit retreat, and since 1935 a school. At Causeway Boulevard by the river stood Camp Parapet, established in 1862 as part of New Orleans' defenses. Federal forces instead attacked from the south and then used the post as a training camp for Union soldiers. A sharp right over the train tracks puts you on Leake Avenue, near the end of well-known St. Charles, where the huge, three-sectioned, modernistic Corps of Engineers facility stands along the river. Until the Corps, beginning in the 1950s, razed riverside houses to make levee improvements, hundreds of ramshackle, make-shift dwellings stood elevated on stilts between the barrier and the waterway. These picturesque old houses, which lined the banks between New Orleans and Baton Rouge, once occupied the batture (pronounced BATCH-er), a Louisiana expression for the thin strip of untamed, flood-prone land along the Mississippi outside the levee. Now only thirteen such structures, nestled in a sharp bend of the river in the nearby Carrollton section of New Orleans, remain. Tucked away by the Mississippi behind nearby Audubon Park lies the century-old Bisso Towboat Company, whose stubby, red tow vessels moor there.

The road into the park passes the zoo (M-F 9:30-4:30, Sat and Sun in the summer to 5:30) and reaches the river, where the sleek, white *John James Audubon* moors by a ticket kiosk (800-233-BOAT, in New Orleans 504-586-8777). The boat cruises the waterway to the new (1990) Aquarium of the Americas on the river, downtown near the French Quarter. Wood benches by the Mississippi along River View Drive offer excellent views in a tranquil setting far from the Quarter's crowds. Shipyard cranes jut into the air on the opposite bank, while upstream the Long Bridge stretches. If you continue on along the scenic riverside road, you'll suddenly reach the metallic installations at the Ryan-Walsh yard, which interrupt the park's green and serene ambiance. A left turn leads you to Tchoupitoulas Street, which continues near the Mississippi for much of the way downtown. Industrial buildings line part of the route on the right, while to the left lie rather seedy houses. After the rounded, red brick New Orleans Public Belt railroad structure, you pass the Harmony Street Wharf, then the First Street Wharf, a long, low, red building with the vague flavor of the old steamboat era. Along this stretch runs a high concrete flood wall occasionally breached by openings secured during high water with huge, blue-hued metal flood gates.

Just to the east of the river here, between Louisiana and Jackson Avenues, lies the Irish Channel, an historic but scruffy neighborhood bordered on the east by the more elegant and famous Garden District. A National Historic Register District, the Irish Channel contains a few warehouses and small-scale commercial buildings, but most of the neighborhood consists of dwellings built in a wide variety of styles between 1850 and 1900 for working class families, some employed at the nearby river wharves. Most of the houses remain rather dilapidated, but the 1000 block of Fourth includes a few restored places. At the corner of Rousseau and Soraparu an attractively redone building stands, embellished with fan-lights above the three doors and a small piece of cast-iron grillwork. At 436 Seventh a two-dormered house survives. One of downtown's oldest dwellings, it was built about 1835, just after subdivision of the nearby Livaudais Plantation, between St. Thomas and one block long Livaudais Street. The property was broken up after Celeste Marigny divorced François Livaudais and sold her part in 1832 for half a million dollars. At the foot of Jackson stands the 1980 ferry terminal for ships crossing the Mississippi to Gretna. The hospital at 625 Jackson originated in 1905 when women doctors unwelcome elsewhere founded the Sara Mayo Hospital. At 709 Jackson stands the c. 1865 Gates of Prayer, the city's second oldest synagogue building (no longer in use).

Closer to the center, the Riverwalk, a relentlessly commercial shopping arcade, stretches along the Mississippi, with a walkway outside the mall offering views of the waterway. From a dock behind Riverwalk the perky three-deck *Cajun Queen* (504-592-0560) departs on cruises along the Mississippi to historic houses and the bayous. At the nearby Canal Street Dock, where the Algiers ferry leaves and arrives, you'll find the *Creole Queen* (504-524-0814), which paddlewheels its way to historic areas along the waterway, and the *Voyageur* (504-523-5555), also an excursion boat. (RV River Charter of New Orleans, 800-256-

6100, established in 1989, offers unusual river trips on specially modified barges which carry recreational vehicles on cruises along the Mississippi and other waterways.) At the foot of Canal towers the thirty-three story World Trade Center, topped by a revolving lounge which affords extensive views of the Mississippi and downtown New Orleans.

In July 1991 the Louisiana legislature approved riverboat gambling, an enterprise expected to develop by late 1993 on five or six boats along the New Orleans waterfront. Plans for the 72-acre tract next to the Convention Center include several of the boats, hotels, a park, and other facilities. A fairly well-marked route starting by the new (1991) Convention Center next to Riverwalk leads to Robin Street Wharf, home port of the famous *Delta Queen* and *Mississippi Queen,* the nation's only remaining overnight steamboats. The National Register-listed *Delta Queen* began far from the Mississippi, as a passenger ship on the Sacramento River between San Francisco and Sacramento. A shipyard in Glasgow, Scotland, built the iron hull and machinery, then shipped them to California. There, in 1926, a yard assembled the vessel and its twin, the *Delta King*. In 1940, the Navy converted the *Delta Queen* into a shuttle ship for use in San Fransisco bay, and after the war Greene Line Steamers, predecessor of the Delta Queen Steamboat Company which now operates the two paddlewheelers, bought the ship for $46,250, five percent of its original cost, and towed it through the Panama Canal. The 176-passenger boat then steamed up the Mississippi and the Ohio to complete its 5,260 mile trip in Pittsburgh for conversion into the world's only original fully restored overnight steamer; it was inaugurated on the inland waterways in June, 1948. Her sister ship, the seven deck, 400-plus passenger *Mississippi Queen,* entered service in 1976 as the largest steamboat in history. With its gym, movie theater, elevators, and other amenities, only by exterior appearance does the vessel resemble the riverboats of old, among them the 4,800 steamers constructed in the nineteenth century by Jeffersonville, Indiana's Jeffboats, which built the *Mississippi Queen*. The present owner's predecessor company originated in 1880, when Captain Gordon C. Greene and his wife, Mary, also a certified river pilot and steamboat captian, started a freight line which they eventually converted into a cruise ship operation. Over the years, the Greene line owned and operated twenty-eight different steamers, the most famous of them being the beloved *Queens*. These regal ships travel the Mississippi and the Ohio, bringing the flavor of a vanished era to river towns.

Along the waterfront beyond Canal, two other excursion boats are moored. *The Natchez*, the ninth Mississippi vessel of that name, powered by a 1920's engine from the eighth, is the city's only day-trip steamboat, a splendid red and white paddlewheeler which at 11 and 2 offers a calliope concert. Down the way lies the *Cotton Blossom* (for both ships: 800-233-BOAT, in New Orleans 504-586-8777). Near the ships the Jackson Brewery stands, a century old beer factory recycled into a shopping center, which houses some seventy-five food, fashion, and other retail establishments. On the river a block away glistens the new (1990) Aquarium of the Americas (9:30-6), a fish-filled facility whose glossy, glassy, sea-green exterior makes the building look like a giant aquarium. Separarate sections feature aquatic specimens from a Caribbean reef, the Amazon rain forest, the Gulf of Mexico, and the Mississippi River. (The Louisiana Nature and Science Center, in eastern New Orleans, includes nature trails and exhibits on the Mississippi Delta area in Lower Louisiana.) Along the river in this area runs the Moon Walk, dedicated in 1976 to former Mayor Moon Landrieu. This pleasant path offers good views onto the waterway and its busy traffic, some leaving or heading towards the Port of New Orleans, the nation's second largest. The tiny Woldenberg Park on Moon Walk contains realistic seated bronze figures of liquor distributor Malcolm Woldenberg and a young man, a memorial to the local philanthropist who "prospered in New Orleans and left a legacy of caring and of confidence in the city of New Orleans." A lookout terrace farther on affords a panorama across to Algiers Point and the Mississippi's wide curve which inspired New Orleans' nickname, the Crescent City. Just below the terrace stands a sign noting, "La Salle Prend Possession de la Louisiane," a reference to the French explorer's 1682 claim of the Mississippi Valley for the French crown. Old-fashioned red-brown trolleys run through here along the waterway. They follow a mile and a half route recently opened to serve riverfront attractions.

Nearby, at the river edge of the famous Vieux Carre, or French Quarter, stretches the French Market, first established here next to the Mississippi in 1791. A flood wall, erected in 1953, protects the area. The legendary Cafe du Monde, opened in 1860, serves the traditional "cafe au lait" and beignets around the clock. The cafe occupies part of the original 1813 butcher's facility, the market's oldest building. Next door, you'll find the Bazaar, rebuilt in the 1930's after hurricanes destroyed the 1870 original, as well as the latter-day Riverside Market. The Jean Lafitte National Historical Park Visitor Center, in the alleyway between them, features exhibits on the Mississippi Delta. Nearby stand the reconstructed nineteenth century Red Stores, a three floor market which alternatively housed dry goods and seafood sellers. The 1823 Vegetable Market operates across the street, and the famous Farmer's Market, established in 1936, is located next door. In the 1820's, artist John James Audubon frequented the market's wild bird and game sellers in order to buy specimens as models for his paintings. A block away, beyond the flea market, stands the old United States Mint, now part of the Louisiana State Museum (W-Sun 10-5), with jazz and Mardi Gras exhibits. Here, in 1838-1862 and 1879-1910, the government coined money.

New Orleans originated in the Vieux Carre "Old Quarter" area in 1718, when Jean Baptiste le Moyne, Sieur de Bienville, plotted a new city at the river bend which connected via a portage and a small bayou with a large lake, named Pontchartrain for the French maritime minister. Bienville's advisors warned him that the chosen area would be vulnerable to flooding by the Mississippi. In 1722, chief engineer Pierre le Blond de la Tour claimed that the problem's solution lay in "Building a good dike of earth along the front of the city beside the river," and thus rose the waterway's very first levee, extended two years later to protect nearby plantations established on strips of land between the river and the lake. These early levees tended to wash away, so in 1732 King Louis XV authorized Bienville to levy a tax for streets and "the levees along the river," the first publicly financed flood protection project. Eight years after the six month long 1735 flood destroyed most of the levees, the governing council passed an ordinance threatening landowners with loss of their property if they failed to rebuild their levees. By 1810, the City of New Orleans had mandated the dimensions of levees—three feet above the waterline and at the base five to six feet wide for each foot of height. An 1822 Corps of Engineers report on a river survey from New Orleans to St. Louis led to passage two years later of the first law allocating federal funds for Mississippi River improvements. In time, levees extended on both banks of the river from below New Orleans to past Baton Rouge. The Orleans Levee District, one of Louisiana's eighteen levee boards, began operation in 1890 and now, its 350 employees manage an annual budget of $12 million, plus a separate capital improvement fund, to maintain 27.5 miles of levees and 103 flood gates on the Lake Pontchartrain shore and adjoining canals.

Beyond the French market, North Peters passes the yellow-orange Esplanade Avenue Wharf, then continues on by warehouses, freight firms, and other commercial establishments. The street then turns into Chartres, bordered by the Kentucky Warehouse and New Orleans Stevedoring Company, while off to the right lies the Louisa Street and then the Pauline Street Wharfs. Here in this quiet, river-related corner of town, the tourist-filled French Quarter seems far away. The street makes a sharp left and passes the F. Edward Hébert Defense Complex, a military personnel processing and naval facility. North Rampart Street takes you across the 1923 Inner Harbor Navigation Canal, a lock-equipped, five and a half mile link which connects the Mississippi with Lake Pontchartrain to the east. The continuation street, St. Claude Avenue, leads through Arabi—supposedly so called after an 1890's fire because the incendiary activities of an Arabian sheik then figured in the news—on to the Chalmette Battlefield (8:30-5) on the river six miles from downtown, a unit of Jean Lafitte National Historical Park. A mile and a half driving tour with six stops circles through the terrain where the Battle of New Orleans took place during the morning of January 8, 1815, the last encounter of the last war (so far) between England and the United States. During the War of 1812, fought in part to halt British-influenced Indian harassments on the Western frontier, the English decided that capture of New Orleans and control of the Mississippi's mouth would threaten the entire river valley and force the Americans to seek peace.

After England defeated Napoleon in the spring of 1814, some 9,000 battle-hardened British troops sailed for the United States, and in December of that year, thirty-six year old General Sir Edward M. Pakenham, the Duke of Wellington's brother-in-law, led a 10,000 man army on an attack at New Orleans. Assembling a motley band of 5,000 defenders, including some fifty of Jean Lafitte's pirates, Choctaw Indians, and a battalion of "Free Men of Color," General Andrew Jackson blocked the English advance, killing 700 attackers while losing only thirteen men. Enemy fatalities included Pakenham, fatally wounded as he rode forward to rally his troops. The English supposedly repatriated Pakenham's body, preserved aboard ship in a barrel of rum which soldiers on the homeward-bound vessel inadvertently imbibed.

The park's 1840 Beauregard House (9-4:30), fronted by a columned portico, is a former country residence which now houses such exhibits as "Life on the River," "The River Economy," and "The Mississippi River Delta." The nearby Visitor Center (8:30-5) also contains some displays. The tall, obelisque-like monument not far from the Visitor Center originated with a cornerstone laid in 1840, but construction began only fifteen years later, with completion in 1908. Next to the park just upstream, Chalmette Slip, a deep-water shipping inlet which cuts into the Mississippi's bank, covers the site of the Macarty House where Jackson made his headquarters. Along the other side of the park stretches the long, narrow Chalmette National Cemetery (8-5), established in 1864 for fallen Union soldiers. Although 15,000 veterans and their dependents, 6,773 of them unknown, are buried in the graveyard (closed for burials in 1945), only four fought in the War of 1812, one of whom participated in the Battle of New Orleans.

The Pakenham Oaks stand farther along the highway, beyond Chalmette and the huge Mobil refinery. They were supposedly planted in 1783 by Pierre Denis De La Ronde, a major general on Jackson's staff. The Louisiana Militia camped under the trees on December 23, 1814, the day the first encounter occurred between the combattants. The engagement included shelling of the British encampment by the Americann war schooner *Carolina* anchored on the Mississippi. Across from the Oaks rests a jagged-edged, red brick wall, part of De La Ronde's 1805 mansion, which burned in 1876. Pakenham used the residence as a hospital. The planter, whose nine daughters became known as the nine muses, intended to establish a city here called Versailles, along with a sister city on Lake Borgne to be named Paris, but the Battle of New Orleans interfered with his plans. At Violet, farther on, the 1901 seven mile channel begins, connecting the Mississippi to Lake Borgne, an inlet of the Gulf. It shortened the trip to the Port of New Orleans by about sixty miles, but these days ocean vessels now use the Inner Harbor Lock and Canal via Lake Pontchrartrain.

The nearby community of Poydras disappeared in 1922 when a crevasse opened in a levee an inspector had pronounced in top condition less than an hour before. The great break, which helped relieve flood waters threatening New Orleans, attracted thousands of curiosity seekers from the city, who were stopped at Violet and asked to contribute $1 for flood relief. On Highway 46 a mile and a half east, another unit of the Lafitte National Historical Park, the 1981 Isleno Center (9-5), traces the history of the 1,500 or so Canary Islanders who settled in the area starting in 1778 when the Spanish controlled Louisiana. The government gave the newcomers oxen, a four year supply of rations, and farming equipment, but the soil and climate proved unsuitable for crop cultivation. The Islenos turned to hunting, trapping, and fishing in the nearby swamp country, where they maintained their original culture and language until the present day. Just beyond Poydras on Highway 39, which borders the Mississippi's east bank for forty miles until the road ends, lies St. Bernard State Park (April-Sept 7-10, Oct-March 8-7), a quiet enclave with trails and lagoons only nineteen miles from the teeming French Quarter. In 1927, Caernarvon, like Poydras five years earlier, became the place where a break in the levee—here intentionally created—helped relieve flood pressure on New Orleans. In April, 1927 dynamite blasted a 2,600 foot crevasse in the levee, allowing the Mississippi to flow through the Delta and into Breton Sound. In February, 1991, the Corps of Engineers completed at Caernarvon the first of three river diversion structures (the other two will be built at Davis Bend and at Bonnet Carré, twenty-two and thirty-three miles upstream from New Orleans). These facilities are intended to flood the adjoining wetlands with fresh water to reduce their salinity and restore the swampy terrain to the condition it enjoyed before the levees blocked the Mississippi from periodically refreshing the lowlands.

Braithwaite, formerly English Turn, took its new name from the Lord who headed an English syndicate, which in 1901 acquired the Louisiana Southern Railway, whose line ran along the river down to Bohemia. The company also bought Orange Grove, a famous sugar plantation, turned into a marsh after the 1927 man-made crevasse, between Caernarvon and Braithwaite. Although the English group changed the town's name, the embarrassing designation still survives to indicate the sharp curve in the Mississippi called English Turn where, in September, 1699, seventeen year old Bienville and five companions floating down the waterway in canoes encountered a British ship headed upstream with settlers to establish an English colony on the river. The brash Bienville warned Captain Lewis Bond to turn around as a large French fleet approached to intercept the intruders. No such force existed, but the young man's bluff persuaded the English to turn and return to the Gulf. At the bend, nearly two weeks after the surrender at Appomatox, one of the Civil War's last naval engagements took place in April, 1865. The Confederate ram *William H. Webb*, its flag at half-mast to feign mourning for the assassinated President Lincoln, slipped past New Orleans and headed downstream, where the vessel encountered a federal gunboat at English Turn. The Southerners grounded their ship, burned it, and escaped into the Louisiana swamps.

The Chacuachas Indian Concession stretched two and a half miles along the river south of English Turn. In 1836, it was carved into three plantations called Mary, Stella, and "La Terre Promise." The last was named for the "promised land" promoter John Law described in glowing terms during his famous 1717 "Mississippi Bubble" colonization scheme which failed a few years later, nearly breaking the Bank of France. Law himself owned a place on the Chacuachas Concession, which he named Catherine for his Paris paramour. Such vintage dwellings as Mary, La Terre

Promise, and Knoblock Plantation houses still stand. Promised land—occupied for forty years, until 1966, by Leander Perez, Plaquemine Parish's famous long time political boss—now serves as the Promised Land Academy.

Nearby Port Nickel's name suggests the Amax nickel refinery by the Mississippi along this stretch, where a ferry connects the east bank with Belle Chasse. Ships' tops peeking over the levee as vessels travel along the river create a curious effect adjacent to the highway, which continues south through a sparsely populated area. A spur road leads to Phoenix, a hamlet with a few houses and weathered wood shops and taverns. The settlement's name originated when Edward Livingston, owner of St. Sophie Plantation, vowed after his manuscrpt of *A System of Penal Law* burned that, "like the Phoenix of old," the work would rise from the ashes. Livingston, later Senator, Secretary of State under Andrew Jackson, and ambassador to France, spent two years rewriting the book.

In 1699—the same year the French began to settle the middle Mississippi, establishing a mission at Cahokia in Illinois across from St. Louis—Iberville built Fort de la Boulaye about a mile north of present day Phoenix. Also known as Fort du Mississippi, it was the first of the six military installations the French established to protect the river's lower reaches. This outpost, which included five or six crude cabins and a battery of six small guns perched along a ridge, soon flooded. About 1711, the French abandoned the base, the Mississippi's first settlement south of the Illinois country, succeeded before long by New Orleans. Farther on lies Harlem Plantation House, listed on the National Register, and at Davant you'll find the Electro-coal Transfer Corporation facility, its storage yard piled with pyramids of the black fuel awaiting export to far furnaces.

Various versions explaining the origin of Pointe a la Hache's name exist. Some say the river bank there resembled an ax point, others that the designation refers to axes which cut wood used by steamers for fuel. Another story relates that one of Iberville's sailors dropped his hatchet into the Mississippi here. In 1839, Pointe a la Hache became the parish seat, with the present piebald courthouse—red and pale yellow brick, topped by a ribbed clock tower—dating from 1890. In this building Leander Perez occupied a succession of jobs, including district attorney from 1924 to 1960, between 1919 and 1967. A ferry (every half hour 6 a.m.-6:30 p.m., every hour 7-11) crosses to the west bank here. Before leaving the Mississippi's east side for the last time, however, you can complete the full journey by continuing south five miles to the end of the road. The highway ends at the Bohemia Wildlife Management Area, named for the old Bohemia Plantation. The paved road turns left, away from the waterway, but the route along the river, straight on, enters a gravel driveway which forks, the left branch posted as Exxon property and the right as the wildlife preserve. The rough route advances into the remote wilderness which borders the Mississippi, but for all practical purposes the river road along the eastern bank has finally reached the end.

The itinerary south out of New Orleans along the west side of the Mississippi begins at Belle Chasse, a "good hunting" area which originated as a plantation established in 1808 by Colonel Joseph Degoutin Bellechase. In 1844, the Bellechasse Plantation "big house" became the home of Judah P. Benjamin, one of the era's most brilliant lawyers. Born in the Virgin Islands in 1811, Benjamin studied at Yale then moved to New Orleans, where he established a law practice. During the Civil War he served as Attorney General, Secretary of War, and Secretary of State in the Confederate Cabinet, then fled when the federal government offered a $50,000 reward for his capture. Within ten years after settling in London, Benjamin built the largest appellate practice at the English bar. He later moved to Paris, where he died as a political refugee in 1884 and was buried in Pere Lachaise Cemetery. In 1968, Plaquemines Parish dedicated a monument to Benjamin topped by the plantation bell he ordered cast with 200 silver dollars "to sweeten its tone." At Belle Chasse you'll also see the Alvin Callender Field Naval Air Station, named for a New Orleans pilot who died in World War I while fighting with the Royal Flying Corps. During World War II, Navy bombers based at the field stalked German submarines prowling the Gulf of Mexico. Another air service at Belle Chasse, Southern Seaplane (504-394-5633), established in 1954, offers flights along the Mississippi and over the Delta's bayou country. The latter, a soggy area, contains marshes and waters which comprise more than 90 percent of Plaquemines' 895,000 acres.

The River Road, Highway 23, continues south along the last hundred of the 15,000 navigable miles which comprise the Mississippi River inland waterway system. Under a welter of pipes and fixtures at the Chevron Chemical Oak Point plant tank cars stand awaiting or delivering cargo. Farther on at Alliance, low white tanks and metallic spires mark the BP refinery, near which on the river parades a huge line of grain elevators. Jesuit Bend along this stretch takes its name from the early day missionaries. A Jesuit accompanied Iberville, and the priests later established religious and educational institutions until expelled from Louisiana by the intrigues of rival Orders. They returned in 1837 and started up a plantation along the Mississippi in this area. Ten miles south of Belle Chasse, the Judge L.H. Perez Memorial Park honors the Plaquemines Parish political figure with a statue, his boyhood home, moved from Ollie across the road, and a lagoon, shaped to mimic the Mississippi's configuration in the parish, bordered by sixteen whimsical historical markers. Great piles of coal dot the yards by the International Marine Terminals near Myrtle Grove. This was also the site of a huge sugar plantation, which bordered the Mississippi for fifteen miles, owned by the Wilkinson family for 125 years until it closed in 1921. A road to the right just past Myrtle Grove leads to Lake Hermitage, a picturesque area with an old cemetery and moss-draped trees. On this side trip you pass Woodland Plantation, which may look familiar, but hopefully not too much so, as the mansion appears on the Southern Comfort liquor label. Although you can see only the back of the house from the road, the front comes into view if you walk along the railroad tracks beside the residence.

On the River Road just south of the Lake Hermitage turnoff the Junior Plantation once lay. Near here the Junior Crevasse opened on April 23, 1927 when the *Inspector*, an outbound tanker rammed the levee. The captain tried to hold the ship's bow in the the opening to cork the gap, but the current swung the vessel's stern and the crevasse widened. When the flood waters finally receded from the lowland the river left behind a silt deposit which greatly enriched the soil. Farther south, near West Pointe a la Hache, where a ferry crosses the Mississippi—the last place you can reach the east side of the river—stood Magnolia Plantation, established about 1780 by two sea captains. In 1795 they built the stately "big house," constructed with hand-hewn lumber, native clay bricks, and hand-carved cypress wood, all worked by slaves. Magnolia, one of the state's most modern and efficient mid-nineteenth century sugar operations, served as the site of Louisiana's first Sugar Experiment Station, where the mechanical cane cutter, loaders, and other new equipment was developed. A similar facility, the Louisiana State University Citrus Research Station, south of West Pointe a la Hache, recalls the parish's thriving orange industry, which originated in 1860. In the twentieth century the citrus business prospered, but freezes in 1951 and again in 1962 and 1963, during which snow fell for the first time in memory, severely damaged the groves. Just as they started to recover, Hurricane Betsy in 1965 and then Hurricane Camille four years later destroyed the plantings, moved to safer areas farther north in the parish. By 1978, the industry revived.

Diamond, to the south, remains a diamond in the rough as the modest village straggles along the road. Port Sulpher, farther on, announces its presence by the mineral's distinctive odor. Freeport Sulphur Company built the town in 1932-1933 as a shipping and logistical support center for the Grande Ecaille Mine, the world's second largest, Frasch-extracted (superheated water melts the sulphur, then compressed air lifts it to the surface) deposit, located at Lake Washington, ten miles southwest. Production began at the mine in December, 1933, after construction of the plant in the difficult tidal marshlands, where workers installed 100,000 pilings—some sinking half their seventy-five foot length at the first touch of a pile-driver—to support the hot water plant and auxiliary buildings. To obtain fresh water required for the Frasch process, the company laid a pipeline from the Mississippi to the plant and built a fifty million gallon earthen reservoir to settle and clarify the muddy river water. By 1952, the peak year, the mine yielded nearly 1½ million tons, about ten times the first year's output. The company town of Port Sulphur, originally called Grandport, soon grew to include 300 houses, only a few of which remain, as well as the half mile long dock facilities along the Mississippi, visible from the road atop the levee. Here in 1960 Freeport pioneered the storage and shipment of liquid sulphur, conveyed in a 600-ton tanker especially built to handle molten cargo, shipped in a fleet of "Thermosbottle" barges which maintained the mineral's temperature above 240°F.

At Empire, where the Corps of Engineers completed a lock (1948) and waterway (1950) to connect the Mississippi with the Gulf via Adams Bay, a gracefully arched bridge offers from its high point views of the lock, the river, and seafood firms clustered below. The old road, an alternative route which borders the river starting just south of Port Sulphur, takes you across the more picturesque but less panoramic bright blue and yellow bridge. It then follows alongside the waterway down to Buras, where in 1860 Florentine Buras planted the parish's first large orange grove. Twenty years before, seven Buras brothers emigrated to the area from France, and soon the scattered settlements along the river here took their name. A rich ethnic mix settled at Buras, including not only French but Spanish, Slavonian, German, Dalmation, Chinese, and Filipino. Buras prospered from extensive seafood and citrus industries, although the hurricanes in the 1960's destroyed many of the orange groves. Area fishermen no doubt inspired the name of the Catholic Church at Buras, founded in 1864 as the parish's second such sanctuary—Our Lady of Good Harbor.

Across the river from Buras, at a hamlet called Ostrica, another aquatic trade developed, the cultivation of oysters. Recalling the oyster cultivation practiced in the old country, Slavonian settlers plucked seed oysters from Adams Bay and Bayou Cook beyond it, and planted the delicacies in new beds around Ostrica. The bivalves would attach themselves to a perch, usually another shell, and, after two years, be moved to a new bed nearer the sea to fatten and acquire the delicate flavor favored by gourmets, after which cultivators harvested the crop. To facilitate ship traffic between the Bayou Cook-Adams Bay area and Ostrica, in the late nineteenth century Captain M.P. Doullut developed connecting canals and locks on both sides of the river at Ostrica and at Doullut's Post Office, renamed Empire for an early day gasoline launch which towed oyster boats past the town. In 1952, the State of Louisiana opened a new lock at Ostrica to enable boats to travel from the Mississippi to the Gulf via Breton Sound. In 1956, the state Wildlife and Fisheries Commission developed the first successful technique for planting large quantities of "clutch," where the cultivated bivalves bed, by jetting clam shells off boat decks with high pressured water hoses.

Triumph, which lies south of Buras—where the Mississippi River Bank sports a pilot's wheel emblem—was once an orange wine manufacturing center where moonshiners thrived during

Prohibition. By the Mississippi a few miles on stands restored Fort Jackson, completed in 1832 to protect the mouth of the Mississippi. As early as a century before, a French officer recognized the site as an ideal defensive position. Vessels here were forced to slow by the four mile an hour current, and would tack to negotiate the bend, so the passing ships presented easy targets. In 1792, the Spanish built Fort St. Philip on the east bank and opposite they installed Fort Bourbon, where Fort Jackson later rose. In 1815, Fort St. Philip, then an American base, blocked the British fleet from joining General Pakenham's land forces attacking New Orleans. During the Civil War the Confederates virtually emptied New Orleans of troops, trusting the city's defense to Forts Jackson and St. Philip. The Southerners also blockaded the river here with a floating barricade formed by eleven schooner hulks chained together. This, along with the forts which bristled with batteries, seemingly secured the Mississippi. However, on the morning of April 18,1862 Union Admiral David Farragut arrived with twenty-four gunboats and nineteen mortar schooners which managed to breach the barrier while raining more than 8,000 shells onto the forts. Thirteen vessels passed by and continued upstream to take undefended New Orleans, so putting the lower reaches of the Mississippi under federal control. On April 28, the forts finally surrendered. Along the river's entire length only Vicksburg in Mississippi and Port Hudson in northern Louisiana then remained in Confederate hands.

Following the war, Fort Jackson served as a prison and as a training base until after World War I, when the government abandoned the base, finally selling it in 1927. In 1962, Plaquemines Parish opened the restored facility, listed on the National Register, to visitors (10-4). In the powder magazine nestles a one room—more like a cell—shop and museum, with a few military artifacts. The stained, patched brick around the pentagonal courtyard bears a patina of age. The concrete bunkers which face the river housed powder and shell magazines as well as lifts to raise and lower guns. A metal ladder affords access to a high point on the fortification which offers views of the Mississippi.

Fort St. Philip, used in bygone times as a hiding place for smuggled liquor, remains abandoned and inaccessible across the river from Fort Jackson, site of the annual Parish Fair and Orange Festival, held the first weekend in December. To the south of St. Philip lies Bayou Mardi Gras, so called by Iberville when he camped there in 1699. This was the first non-Indian designation for a place in the Lower Mississippi Valley apart from the name of the region itself, which La Salle called Louisiana in honor of King Louis XIV. Near the river, just outside of Fort Jackson, stands a fluted, cross-topped, sixty foot high monument dedicated (in 1967) to La Salle, the first European to travel the lower river. A metal relief shows the explorer holding a paper and a map of the Louisiana Territory, while a Latin inscription recalls his claim of the vast region for the French monarch on April 9, 1682. Homer once wrote that rivers were "heaven sent"—literally true, as they originate in rain—but, oddly enough, Louis XIV did not deem La Salle's claim of the Mississippi Valley a heaven-sent opportunity for France. The king wrote the Marquis de Seignelay, son and successor of Colbert, Louis XIV's famous financial and diplomatic advisor: "I am convinced, like you, that the discovery of the Sieur de la Salle is very useless." Undeterred, the explorer managed to convince Louis that colonization of the Mississippi Valley would prove quite useful to France, and so—near the very end of the great river—began the French dominion over the Louisiana Territory.

It is somehow poignant to pause here by the La Salle Monument, which commemorates the beginning of the river's evolution, where the Mississippi begins to end and, in effect, "stand amid time beginningless and endless," in Walt Whitman's words. All rivers flow through time as well as place, and although the waterway soon loses itself in the depths of the sea, its course through the years winds on, as it has since time immemorial. "No thinking mind can contemplate this mighty and restless wave, sweeping its proud course from point to point, curving round its bend through the dark forests, without a feeling of sublimity," wrote Timothy Flint in his 1828 *A Condensed Geography and History of the Western States, or The Mississippi Valley*. And here, near where La Salle asserted his claim over the indomitable waterway, a river traveler's thoughts play over the sublime stream's long flow through time and place, from the rivulet in the remote Minnesota north woods and de Soto's discovery in 1541 to the Mississippi's here and now.

Now the numbers on the little green and white mile markers alongside the River Road begin to dwindle, and a certain sense of drama builds as the end of the road draws near. North of Venice, helicopter bases to serve the off-shore oil rigs line the highway. Then, just past the Marathon Oil Venice Terminal, the "Mile 1" sign appears, and one slows the car to savor the last mile. The road finally reaches Venice at the town's ship-cluttered port. Front Road runs to the left, while off to the right Jump-Tidewater Road branches, both leading out to oil industry facilities. Around 1840, fishermen dug a small canal through a tiny spit of land which the river eventually "jumped," thus giving an early settlement the designation "The Jump." Locals renamed it Venice in 1892, supposedly because boatmen stood up to pole their vessels here like Venetian gondoliers. The new channel became known as Grand Pass, one of the web of channels the Mississippi follows as it flows into the Gulf beyond Venice. Colorful fish establishments at the picturesque port—"Sharkco: Cash for tuna, shrimp," "Kong's Seafood: We buy crabs"—recall the old Cannery Row in Monterey, California. The many oil-related installations in Venice's outskirts remind the river traveler of the petrochemical facilities which line the waterway between Baton Rouge and New Orleans.

Both the River Road and the world's longest continuous levee end at Venice; the latter stretches along the Mississippi and Arkansas Rivers for 650 miles. The Missisippi, however, flows on beyond Venice for another ten miles, to Head of Passes, 964 miles below the Ohio River. It is from that point where distances on the Lower Mississippi are measured. There, the waterway branches off into Southwest, South, Main, Pass a Loutre, and other Passes which vein the seascape. The early French seamen favored Southeast Pass, a branch of Pass a Loutre, where they built a fortification called Balize, a name derived from the French word for beacon. Over the years, five Balizes—or settlements at the Mississippi's mouth—served guarding and guiding functions. The first two lasted for a total of 130 years, until the passes they served grew too shallow for ships. The third occupied a sliver of ground by Southeast Pass during the Civil War era. In 1876 James B. Eads, the famous river engineer (see the St. Louis section in the Missouri chapter) constructed jetties to enable the currents to keep South Pass deep and free-flowing. Jetties installed at wider Southwest Pass in 1909 made it the main channel for ocean-going vessels. In his *The History of Louisiana*, published (in translation at London) in 1774, Antoine Le Page Du Pratz described early-day installations at the Southwest Pass: "Balize is a fort built on an island of sand, secured by a great number of piles bound with good timberwork. There are lodgings in it for the officers and the garrison; and a sufficient number of guns for defending the entrance of the Mississippi. It is there they take the bar-pilot on board, in order to bring the ships into the river."

To this day, more than two centuries later, the bar pilots and the river pilots trade off duties at the current version of Balize, the hamlet of Pilottown, the last inhabited settlement on the Mississippi. It is necessary to charter a boat at Venice, twelve miles upstream, to reach the watery domain where Pilottown perches on stilts above the river's final currents. In its heyday the village boasted, apart from the transient pilots, some 350 inhabitants, including trappers, fishermen, and their families, but now only seventeen permanent residents live at the remote town.

A green carpeted boardwalk elevated above the water leads from the marina to an attractive white wood building fronted by an entrance arch labeled "Riverboat Pilots." The Mississippi River pilots stay here. They take over inbound, ocean-going vessels for the 106 river miles up to New Orleans, while the outward bound ships take on the bar pilots at Pilottown. They sail the boats to a landmark buoy twenty-two miles out in the Gulf, where the regular captain resumes control for the voyage on the high seas. The bar pilots stay in a comfortable, two-story clapboard house next door to the river pilots. In the lounge of the dwelling, built in 1918 and later remodeled, an antique Seth Thomas clock stands, which ticks off the seconds until each boatman's ship comes in. Near the clock hangs a wooden board, embossed with a pilot wheel emblem, dating from the 1930's. Headed "Pilots on Turn," the device contains fifteen slots for personalized plaques bearing the boatmen's names. A large notice board contains "Outbound" and "Inbound" lists of ships underway and also a section for noting the river stages, tides, obstructions, and other data pertinent to navigation.

Now the oceans begin to leak into the Mississippi's story, for soon the river will meet the sea. Pilottown's only street, an elevated concrete walkway, leads past a scattering of other houses—1969 Hurricane Camille wiped out the village's few commercial establishments—to the trailer which serves to house the post office, the hamlet's social center during the morning mail sort after the 10 a.m. delivery from the mainland.

Farther south, the Mississippi fragments, dissolves, disperses. "The River itself has no beginning or end," wrote T.S. Eliot. "In its beginning it is not yet the River; in its end, it is no longer the River." Such is the case here at the end, where beyond Pilottown the Mississippi becomes a muddy maze of islands and bayous, channels and passes, where the water and silt from thirty-one states and part of Canada arrive after the long journey down the watery artery through the heart of the continent. "All the rivers run into the sea," says Ecclesiasties, and even the great Mississippi finally finds its way to the sea, at last meeting its end in the Gulf of Mexico. But what a trip through the long years and over the long miles the timeless Mississippi has made—a journey across history-filled lands where mens' dreams and dramas have played out over the centuries.

"The beginnings of a river are insignificant," Pliny wrote, "and its infancy is frivolous." But, "Gathering strength in its growth, it becomes wild and impetuous...It passes through populous cities, and all the busy haunts of men." And then, "Increased by numerous alliances, and advanced in its course," the river "in majestic silence, rolls on its mighty waters, till it is laid to rest in the vast abyss." The waterway spills away from its last link with land and flows into the Gulf. For a distance the Mississippi's brown currents streak the blue sea, and then those vague evidences of the Father of Waters lose themselves in the ocean's vast depths and, finally, all traces of the great river cease to exist.

LOUISIANA PRACTICAL INFORMATION

Phone numbers of tourist offices in Louisiana's principal Mississippi River cities and parishes: Baton Rouge: 504-383-1825, outside Louisiana 800-LA ROUGE; Donaldsonville: 504-473-4814; Gretna: 504-363-1505; Kenner: 504-468-7228; Lake Providence: 318-559-3995; New Orleans: 504-566-5031; New Roads: 504-638-9858; Plaquemine, and Iberville Parish: 504-687-0641; Plaquemines Parish: 504-392-6690; Pointe Coupee Parish: 504-638-7171; St. Charles Parish: 504-764-1248; St. Francisville:

504-635-6330; St. John the Baptist Parish: 504-652-9569; West Baton Rouge: 504-344-2920.

Other useful numbers for travel along the Mississippi include: Louisiana Office of Tourism: 504-342-8119; outside Louisiana, 800-33-GUMBO. For information on the arts, archeology, folklore and historic preservation: Department of Culture, Recreation and Tourism: 504-348-8200. Office of State Parks: 504-342-8111. Department of Wildlife and Fisheries: 504-765-2918. Center for Wetland Resources at Louisiana State University: 504-388-1558.

Louisiana operates tourist information centers on U.S. 61 north of St. Francisville; at the state Capitol in Baton Rouge, 504-342-7317; and in New Orleans at 529 Saint Ann Street on Jackson Square, 504-568-5661.

Bed and breakfast reservation services in Louisiana include: Southern Comfort, 800-749-1928, and Bed and Breakfast, Inc., 800-749-4640.

BIBLIOGRAPHY

Since the first accounts of the Mississippi by members of Hernando de Soto's 1541 expedition appeared, books on the river have literally flooded from the presses. Of the many works pertaining to the waterway and its valley, the ones listed below I found among the most useful or interesting. Omitted are books I consulted on individual states, on specific sections of the Mississippi, and other such more narrowly focused materials dealing only with certain aspects or areas of the river.

Alvord, Clarence Walworth. *The Mississippi Valley in British Politics*. Cleveland: The Arthur H. Clark Company, 1917.

Anthony, Irvin. *Paddle Wheels and Pistols*. New York: Grosset & Dunlap, 1929.

Ayars, James. *The Illinois River*. New York: Holt, Rinehart and Winston, 1968.

Baldwin, Leland D. *The Keelboat Age on Western Waters*. Pittsburgh: University of Pittsburgh Press, 1941.

Bissell, Richard. *My Life on the Mississippi or Why I Am Not Mark Twain*. Boston: Little, Brown and Company, 1973.

Blair, Walter and Franklin J. Meine, ed. *Half Horse Half Alligator: The Growth of the Mike Fink Legend*. Chicago: The University of Chicago Press, 1956.

———. *Mike Fink: King of Mississippi Keelboatmen*. New York: Henry Holt and Company, 1933.

Brackenridge, Henry Marie. *Views of Louisiana*. Pittsburgh, 1814.

Bradbury, John. *Travels in the Interior of America 1809-11*. London, 1819.

Bragg, Marion. *Historic Names and Places on the Lower Mississippi River*. Vicksburg: Mississippi River Commission, 1977 (reprinted 1990).

Burman, Ben Lucien. *Big River To Cross.* New York: The John Day Company, 1940.

Carter, Hodding. *Man and the River: The Mississippi.* Chicago: Rand McNally & Company, 1970.

Carter, William. *Middle West Country.* Boston: Houghton Mifflin, 1975.

Caruso, John Anthony. *The Mississippi Valley Frontier: The Age of French Exploration and Settlement.* Indianapolis: The Bobbs-Merrill Company, Inc., 1966.

Childs, Marquis. *Mighty Mississippi: Biography of a River.* New Haven and New York: Ticknor & Fields, 1982.

The Culture of the Middle West. Appleton, WI: The Lawrence College Press, 1944.

Daniel, Pete. *Deep'n As It Come: The 1927 Mississippi River Flood.* New York: Oxford University Press, 1977.

Devol, George H. *Forty Years a Gambler on the Mississippi.* Cincinnati: Devol & Haines, 1887.

Dondore, Dorothy Anne. *The Prairie and the Making of Middle America: Four Centuries of Desperation.* Cedar Rapids, Iowa: The Torch Press, 1926.

Dorrance, Ward. *Where the Rivers Meet.* New York: Charles Scribner's Sons, 1939.

Dorsey, Florence L. *Master of the Mississippi: Henry Shreve and the Conquest of the Mississippi.* Boston: Houghton Mifflin, 1941.

———. *Road to the Sea: The Story of James B. Eads and the Mississippi River.* New York: Rinehart & Company, Inc., 1947.

Drury, John. *Midwest Heritage.* New York: A.A. Wyn, Inc., 1948.

Early Voyagers Up and Down the Mississippi. Introduction by John Gilmary Shea. Albany: Joel Munsell, 1861.

Elberg, Carl J. and William E. Foley, ed. *An Account of Upper Louisiana, Nicholas de Finiels.* Columbia: University of Missouri Press, 1989.

Falconer, Thomas, ed. *Discovery of the Mississippi, Robert Cavelier De La Salle and Chevalier Henry De Tonty*. London: Samuel Clarke, 1844 (facsimile edition).

Feldman, Stephen and Van Gordon Sauter. *Fabled Land, Timeless River: Life Along the Mississippi*. Chicago: Quadrangle Books, 1970.

Ferris, Jacob. *The States and Territories of The Great West*. New York: Miller, Orton, and Mulligan, 1856.

Finley, John. *The French in the Heart of America*. New York: Charles Scribner's Sons, 1915.

Flint, Timothy. *A Condensed Geography and History of the Western States, or The Mississippi Valley*. Cincinnati: E.H. Flint, 1828.

———. *Recollections of the Last Ten Years in the Valley of the Mississippi*, edited by George R. Brooks. Carbondale: Southern Illinois University Press, 1968.

Forman, Samuel S. *Narrative of a Journey Down the Ohio and the Mississippi in 1789-90*. Cincinnati: Robert Clark & Co., 1888.

Foster, J.W. *The Mississippi Valley: Its Physical Geography*. Chicago: S.C. Griggs and Company, 1869.

Galloway, Patricia K., ed. *La Salle and His Legacy: Frenchmen and Indians in the Lower Mississippi Valley*. Jackson: University Press of Mississippi, 1982.

Graham, Philip. *Showboats: The History of an American Institution*. Austin: University of Texas Press, 1951.

Hall, James. *Notes on the Western States*. Philadelphia: Harrison Hall, 1838.

———. *The Romance of Western History*. Cincinnati: Applegate & Company, 1857.

Hall, Steve. *Itasca: Source of America's Greatest River*. St. Paul: Minnesota Historical Society, 1982.

Hart, Adolphus M. *History of the Valley of the Mississippi*. Cincinnati: Moore, Anderson, Wilstach & Keys, 1853.

Havighurst, Walter. *Voices On the River: The Story of the Mississippi Waterways*. New York: The Macmillan Company, 1946.

Hennepin, Father Louis. *Description of Louisiana*, translated by Marion E. Cross. Minnesota Society of the Colonial Dames of America, 1938.

Hereford, Robert A. *Old Man River: The Memories of Captain Louis Rosché, Pioneer Steamboatman*. Caldwell, Idaho: The Caxton Printers, Ltd., 1942.

Hosmer, James K. *A Short History of the Mississippi Valley*. Boston and New York: Houghton, Mifflin and Company, 1901.

Howard, James Q. *History of the Louisiana Purchase*. Chicago: Callaghan & Company, 1902.

James, Leonard F. *Following the Frontier: American Transportation in the Nineteenth Century*. New York: Harcourt, Brace & World, Inc., 1968.

Johnson, Clifton. *Highways and Byways of the Mississippi Valley*. New York: The Macmillan Company, 1906.

Kirkpatrick, John Ervin. *Timothy Flint: Pioneer, Missionary, Author, Editor 1780-1840*. Cleveland: The Arthur H. Clark Company, 1911.

Lane, Ferdinand C. *Earth's Grandest Rivers*. Garden City, NY: Doubleday & Company, Inc., 1949.

Lewis, Henry. *The Valley of the Mississippi Illustrated*, translated by A. Hermina Poatgieterl and edited by Bertha L. Heilbron. St. Paul: Minnesota Historical Society, 1967.

Lloyd, W. Alvin. *A Southern Book of Great Interest: W. Alvin Lloyd's Steamboat and Railroad Guide*. New Orleans: W. Alvin Lloyd, 1857.

Madson, John. *Up On the River: An Upper Mississippi Chronicle*. New York: Penguin Books, 1986.

Markham, Chris. *Mississippi Odyssey*. Stafford, VA: Northwoods Press, 1980.

McDermott, John Francis. *The Lost Panoramas of the Mississippi*. Chicago: The University of Chicago Press, 1958.

McDermott, John Francis, ed. *Before Mark Twain: A Sampler of Old, Old Times on the Mississippi*. Carbondale and Edwardsville: Southern Illinois University Press, 1968.

———. *The French in the Mississippi Valley*. Urbana: University of Illinois Press, 1965.

———. *Frenchmen and French Ways in the Mississippi Valley*. Urbana: University of Illinois Press, 1969.

———. *The Spanish in the Mississippi Valley 1762-1804*. Urbana: University of Illinois Press, 1974.

Mississippi Panorama. Catalogue of an exhibition "of the Life and Landscape of the Father of Waters and its great tributary, the Missouri." City Art Museum of St. Louis, 1949.

Monette, John W. *History of the Discovery and Settlement of the Valley of the Mississippi*. New York; Harper & Brothers, 1846.

Murphy, Edmund Robert. *Henry de Tonty: Fur Trader of the Mississippi*. Baltimore: The Johns Hopkins Press, 1941.

Nasatir, Abraham P. *Spanish War Vessels on the Mississippi 1792-1796*. New Haven: Yale University Press, 1968.

Ogg, Frederic Austin. *The Opening of the Mississippi*. New York; The Macmillan Company, 1904.

Parkman, Francis. *La Salle and the Discovery of the Great West*. Boston: Little, Brown and Company, rev. ed. 1879.

Petersen, William J. *Midwest River Panorama: Henry Lewis Great National Work*. Iowa City: Clio Press, 1979.

———. *Steamboating on the Upper Mississippi*. Iowa City: The State Historical Society of Iowa, 1968.

Pittman, Captain Philip. *The Present State of the European Settlements on the Mississippi*. London, 1770.

Price, Willard. *The Amazing Mississippi*. New York: The John Day Company, 1963.

Raven-Hart, Major R. *Down the Mississippi*. Boston: Houghton Mifflin, 1938.

The River: Images of the Mississippi. Minneapolis: Walker Art Center, 1976.

Roosevelt, Theodore. *The Winning of the West.* New York: G.P. Putnam's Sons, 1894.

Rozier, Firmin A. *History of the Early Settlement of the Mississippi Valley.* St. Louis: G.A. Pierrot & Sons, 1890.

Seatsfield, Charles. *The Americans as They Are; Described in A Tour Through the Valley of the Mississippi.* London: Hurst, Chance, and Co., 1828.

Seifert, Shirley. *Those Who Go Against the Current.* Philadelphia: J.P. Lippincott Company, 1943.

Severin, Timothy. *Explorers of the Mississippi.* New York: Alfred A. Knopf, 1968.

Shea, John Gilmary. *Discovery and Exploration of the Mississippi Valley.* Albany: Joseph McDonough, 1903.

Spears, John R. *A History of the Mississippi Valley.* Philadelphia: A.S. Clark, 1903.

Sprague, Marshall. *So Vast So Beautiful A Land: Louisiana and the Purchase.* Boston: Little, Brown and Company, 1974.

Tousley, Albert S. *Where Goes the River.* Iowa City: The Tepee Press, 1928.

Watkins, T.H. *Mark Twain's Mississippi.* Palo Alto: American West Publishing Company, 1974.

Weddle, Robert S., ed. *La Salle, the Mississippi, and the Gulf.* College Station: Texas A & M University Press, 1987.

Wendt, Herbert. *The Romance of Water,* translated by J.B.C. Grundy. New York: Hill and Wang, 1969.

Whitaker, Arthur Preston. *The Mississippi Question 1795-1803.* New York: D. Appleton-Century Company, 1934.

Wilhelm, Paul, Duke of Wurttemberg. *Travels in North America 1822-1825,* translated by W. Robert Nitske. Norman: University of Oklahoma Press, 1973.

Winsor, Justin. *The Westward Movement.* Boston: Houghton, Mifflin and Company, 1897.

INDEX